KT-593-232

ALL HE'LL EVER BE

Copyright © 2019 by Willow Winters All Rights Reserved.

No part of this publication may be reproduced, stored in a retrieval system, or transmitted in any form or by any means, electronic, mechanical, photocopying, recording, scanning, or otherwise, without the prior written permission of the publisher, except in the case of brief quotations within critical reviews and otherwise as permitted by copyright law.

NOTE: This is a work of fiction.

Names, characters, places, and incidents are a product of the author's imagination.

Any resemblance to real life is purely coincidental. All characters in this story are 18 or older.

Copyright © 2019, Willow Winters Publishing.
All rights reserved. willowwinterswrites.com

Commissioned art from both Haley Powers, paperbirdartshop.com and Wovoka Trudell, www.instagram.com/wovoka_trudell_art.

DEDICATION

My grandmother used to write. Her dream was for her stories to be published one day, but unfortunately that never happened.

Times were different back then.

Although she's gone, she's always with me in my heart and even in my writing. Pieces of what I remember of my grandmother have been sewn into these stories and I hope that you've fallen in love with her, even if you've never had the pleasure to meet her. I hope she would be proud of me if she were to see me now.

The ones we love never leave us.
Mommom, this book is for you. I love you.

MERCILESS

BOOK 1

From *USA Today* bestselling author Willow Winters comes a heart pounding, edge-of-your-seat gripping, romantic suspense.

I should've known she would ruin me the moment I saw her.
Women like her are made to destroy men like me.
Given to me to start a war; I was too eager to accept.

I didn't know what she'd do to me.
She sees through me in a way no one else ever has.
Her innocence and vulnerability make me weak for her and I hate it.
I know better than to give in to temptation. I should have known that she would change everything.

A ruthless man doesn't let a soul close to him.
A cold-hearted man doesn't risk anything for anyone.
A powerful man with a beautiful woman at his mercy … he doesn't fall for her.

PREFACE

Carter

"I SHOULD HAVE FUCKED YOU SO MUCH SOONER."

I remember that first day, how she screamed and cried for me to let her go, back when I hated her and she hated me.

Even with my tight grip on her throat, with my touch sending sparks through her body, she forces her head to shake, not taking her eyes off of mine.

"No," she whispers and my dick hardens even more, begging me to punish her for daring to defy me. But then she adds, "This is how it was supposed to be."

Her breathing is heavy as she closes her eyes, her body bowed on my lap. She's completely at my mercy and her pouty lips are there for the taking.

All of her. Every piece of her is mine and she knows it.

Mine.

CHAPTER 1

Carter

WAR IS COMING.

It's something I've known for over two years.

Tick-tock. Tick-tock.

A tic in my jaw clenches in time with the rhythm of the clock, while the skin over my knuckles turns white as my fist squeezes tighter. Tension rises in my stiff shoulders and I have to remind myself to breathe in deeply and let the strain of it all go away.

Tick-tock. It's the only sound echoing off the walls of my office and with each pass of the pendulum, the anger grows.

It's always like this before I go to a meet. This one, in particular, sends a thrill through my blood, the adrenaline pumping harder with each passing minute.

My gaze drifts from the grandfather clock in my office to the shelves next to it, then beneath them to the box made of mahogany and steel. It's only three feet deep and three feet tall by six feet long. It blends into the wall of my office, surrounded by old books.

I paid more than I should have simply to put on a display. All any of this is merely a façade. People's perceptions are their reality. And so I paint the picture they need to see so I can use them as I see fit. The expensive books and artworks, polished furniture carved from rare wood… All of it is bullshit.

Except for the box. The story that came with it will stay with me forever. In all the years, it's one of the few memories I can pinpoint as a defining moment. The box never leaves me.

The words from the man who gave it to me are still so fresh, as is the image of his pale green eyes, glossed over as he told me his story.

About how it kept him safe when he was a child. He told me how his mother had shoved him in it to protect him.

I swallow thickly, feeling my throat tighten and the cords in my neck strain at the recollection. He set the scene so well.

He told me how he clung to his mother, seeing how panicked she was. But he did as he was told. He stayed quiet in the safe box and could only listen while the men murdered his mother.

He offered to barter for his life with the box. And the story he gave me reminded me of my own mother telling me goodbye before she passed.

Yes, his story was touching, but I put a gun to his head and pulled the trigger regardless.

He tried to steal from me and then pay me with a box as if the money he embezzled was a debt or a loan. William was good at thieving, at telling stories, but the fucker was a dumb prick.

I didn't get to where I am by playing nicely and being weak. On that day, I took the box that saved him as a reminder of who I was. Who I needed to be.

I made sure that box has been within my sight for every meeting I've had in this office. It's a powerful reminder I can stare at as I make deal after deal with criminal after criminal and collect wealth and power in this godforsaken room.

It cost me a fortune to get this office exactly how I wanted it. But if it were to burn down, I could easily afford to replace everything.

Everything except for that box.

"You really think they're going through with it?" I hear my brother, Daniel, before I see him. The remembrance fades in an instant.

It takes a second for me to be conscious of my facial expression, to relax my jaw and let go of the anger before I can raise my gaze to his.

"With the war and the deal? You think he'll go through with it and take her tonight?" he clarifies.

A small huff leaves me, accompanied by a smirk as I answer, "He wants this more than anything else. He said they set her up and it's already happening. Only hours until they're done."

Daniel stalks into the room slowly, the heavy door to my office closing with a soft kick of his heel before he comes to stand across from me.

"And you're sure you want to be right in the middle of it?"

I lick my lower lip and stand, stretching as I do and turning my gaze to the window in my office. I can hear Daniel walking around the desk as I lean against it and cross my arms.

I tell him, "We won't be in the middle of it. It'll be the two of them, and our territory is close, but we can stay back."

"Bullshit. He wants you to fight with him. He's going to start this war tonight and you know it."

I nod slowly, the memory of the smell of Romano's cigars filling my lungs at the thought of him.

"There's still time to call it off," Daniel says, and it makes my brow pinch and forehead crease. He can't be that naïve.

It's the first time I've really looked at him since he's been back. He spent years away. And every fucking day I fought for what we have. He's gone soft. Or maybe it's Addison who's turned him into the man standing here now.

"This war has to happen." My words are final, and the tone is one not to be questioned. I may have grown this business on fear and anger, each step forward followed by the hollow sound of a body dropping behind me, but that's not how it started. You can't build an empire with bloodstained hands and not expect death to follow you.

His dark eyes narrow as he moves closer to the window, his gaze flickering between me and the meticulously maintained garden several stories below us.

"Are you sure you want to do this?" His voice is low, and I barely hear it. He doesn't look back at me and a chill flows across the back of my neck and down my arms as I take in his solemn expression.

It takes me back to years ago. Back to when we had a choice and chose wrong.

When whether or not we wanted to go through with any of this still meant something.

"There are men to the left of us," I tell him as I step forward and close the distance between us. "There are men to the right. There is no possible outcome where we don't pick a side."

He nods once and slides his thumb across the stubble on his chin before looking back at me. "And the girl?" he asks, his piercing eyes reminding me that both of us fought, both of us survived, and we each had a tragic path that led us to where we are today.

"Aria?" I dare to speak her name and the sound of my smooth voice seems to linger in the space between us. I don't wait for him to acknowledge me—or her, rather.

"She has no choice." My voice tightens as I say the words.

Clearing my throat, I brace my palms against the window, feeling the frigid fall beneath my hands and lean forward to see Addison beneath us. "What do you think they would have done to Addison if they'd succeeded in taking her?"

His jaw clenches, but he doesn't answer my question. Instead he replies, "We don't know who tried to take her from me."

I shrug as if it's semantics and not at all relevant. "Still. Women aren't meant to be touched, but they went for Addison first."

"That doesn't make it right," Daniel says with indignation in his tone.

"Isn't it better she come to us?" My head tilts as I pose the question and this time he takes a moment to respond.

"She's not one of us. Not like Addison, and you know what Romano expects you to do with her."

"Yes, the daughter of the enemy..." My heart beats hard in my chest, and the steady rhythm reminds me of the ticking of the clock. "I know exactly what he wants me to do with her."

CHAPTER 2

Aria

T HERE ARE A FEW THINGS YOU SHOULD KNOW ABOUT ME.
I like to wake up with a hot cup of coffee every morning.
Preferably with enough creamer and sugar to drown out the
taste of the bitter caffeine addiction.

I love red wine at night. I can't have white; it gives me a headache
and a hangover that will leave me miserable when I wake up.

Well, those aren't things that really matter. They're the superficial
details you give people when you don't want to tell them the truth.

What do you really need to know?

My name is Aria Talvery and I'm the daughter of the most violent
crime family in Fallbrook.

The reason I like to have wine at night is because I desperately
need it so I can get a few hours of sleep.

My mother was murdered in front of me when I was only eight
years old and I've never been okay since then, although I've learned to
be good at pretending I am.

My father's a crook, but he kept me safe and tolerated me even
though every day he reminded me how much it hurt him to look at my
face and see nothing but my mother.

It's because of my eyes. I know it is.

They're a hazel-green concoction, just like hers were. Like the soft
mix of colors you'd see in a deep neck of the woods when looking up at
the canopy of leaves in late summer, early fall. That's how my mother
used to describe it. She was poetic that way. And maybe some of that
rubbed off on me.

Fact number… whatever we're on: I love to draw. I hate the life
I live and hide away in the sketches and smeared ink. Away from the
madness and danger my existence inherently brings.

And that love of art, the one thing I have that still connects me to my mother, is why I ended up at this bar, tracking down the asshole who stole my sketchbook from me. The prick who thinks he's funny and that I'm some stupid joke or a toy he can play with because I'm a woman living in a man's world, a dangerous one at that.

But I inherited my temper from my father. And that's why I ended up at the Iron Heart Brewery on Church Street. Yes, a bar on a street called "church." What's more ironic is how much sin has seeped into these walls.

And so I went willingly, after my precious notebook that was stolen and walked right into the enemy's arms.

It was a setup, but my mother would have called it kismet. You should know I'm smiling now, but it's a sarcastic smile as a huff of feigned laughter leaves me. Maybe all of this is her fault to begin with. After all, that notebook was irreplaceable to me because the only picture I had of her was tucked into the spine.

The last thing you should know, and the most important of them all, is that I refuse to break. I don't give in and I don't back down. Not for anyone, and especially not for Carter Cross. The bastard who took me from my family. Locked me in a room and told me in simple words that my life was over, and I belonged to him.

It won't be his cutting words from his sharp tongue. Or his broad shoulders and muscular arms that pin me down and trap me. It won't be his charming smile that utters filthy words that makes me cave. And it won't be that spark in his eyes, the flames licking and flickering brighter and hotter every time he looks at me.

No, I refuse to give in. Even if that same heat echoes in my chest and travels lower.

But there's this thing about breaking; the more you harden yourself and try to fight it, the easier and sharper the snap is when you inevitably break.

And I know this all too well.

The day my life changed forever...

There's a constant ringing in my ears. My fists are clenched so tight that my knuckles have turned white. Every time I have to face these assholes my father works with, this is how it feels.

Like I'm on edge.

My heart thuds, thuds, thuds as I pass the all-glass front door to Iron Heart Brewery and keep walking like I'm not going in. The front exterior is all windows, so they can easily see who's coming and going; bulletproof, too. Because of the clientele. Word is my father fronted that bill, but that seems overly generous for a man like him.

Cold. Selfish. Greedy. That's how I'd describe my father, and I hate myself for it.

I should be grateful; I should love him. But I'm loyal at least, and loyalty is all that matters. When you grow up in this life, you learn that little tidbit quickly.

Resting my shoulder against the dark red brick just past the windows, I take a look at the parking lot across the street. They aren't here yet.

A frustrated breath leaves a trail of fog in the tense fall air as I cross my arms.

This is where my father's men go on a night off and I know Mika is going to be here.

I hate being here alone, but I can't wait for someone to save me. I hope Nikolai will come with them too. He's a childhood friend, although now a soldier of my father's, and my saving grace. Really, he's my only friend and he's put that bastard Mika in his place more than once when my father wasn't there for me.

Even knowing that to be true, that if Nikolai comes there won't be any problems in the least, I hate that I have to be here at all. My thumb runs along the tips of my cold fingers, remembering how I held the notebook only moments before Mika came into the room. The photograph was tucked safely inside. Waiting for me to be inspired by it.

A notebook is only a notebook, but that photograph is the only one I have of my mother and me the year she died.

My father didn't have time for my "meaningless shit," as he called it, and the vise around my heart tightened at his response.

A shiver runs down my shoulders and I let out another heavy breath. I can feel the chill on my nose and cheeks. My thin jacket isn't doing a damn thing to help me. I hadn't realized fall had come with intentions of revenge on the smoldering summer.

Peeking up through my lashes, I read the chalkboard sign above the bar through the windows. They're all locals, all drafts. I guess I could have one drink while I wait.

The smooth music hits my ears as I walk into the bar, my heart beating faster as I take in a few of the men seated on the stools. It's funny how a bar being mostly empty sends greater fear through me than one that's packed. One where I can blend in.

Right here, right now? I don't belong, and every soul here knows it.

Maybe this is why Mika thought he could get away with it, I think bitterly as I try to ignore the scared little girl inside of me. He thinks he can steal from me because my father won't stop him and I'm too spineless to even come out of my room unless called upon.

I force myself to straighten my back as I move closer to the bar and set down my clutch. I have a plan and I go over it as I try to swallow, form a smile, and order a drink.

"Vodka and Sprite," I order easily as I slip onto the barstool and meet the bartender's eyes. With a nod he moves seamlessly to the glasses, making them clink and then filling one with ice.

I'll wait for the guys. Even if they scare me because I know what they're capable of. I'll look Mika in the eyes and tell him to give my sketchbook back to me by tomorrow. And then I'll walk away. No threats. It's a simple request. He wants to play around and tease me and I won't give him the time to do so. That's the only reason he took it.

He gets a thrill from goading me.

The wind batters against the glass windows to my right and it startles me. None of the men lining the room seem to have noticed it.

I'm too busy watching the hanging sign for the brewery banging against the window that I don't see the bartender come up to me.

The sound of the glass hitting the hard maple bar top sends a spike of fear through me and I jump in surprise.

The sudden stillness and immediate silence that accompanies all of their eyes on me force me to tense. I can barely form a smile as I stare straight ahead and thank the bartender.

First, I feel a rush of embarrassment, followed by fear that they know I'm weak. Then that all-consuming anxiety that everything is going to go wrong washes over me. Very wrong.

It makes me want to throw up, but instead, I lift the cold glass to my lips. One sip of the sweet cocktail does nothing. Two, and my throat still feels dry.

I'm a foolish girl. I lick a bit of soda from my bottom lip and set the glass down on the counter as I stare at all the colorful labels of liquor bottles lining the shelves.

There's no one who will stand up for me and I can't even bring myself to think about confrontation without getting jumpy. Trying to swallow proves useless and so I push myself off the stool with both hands clinging to the cold bar.

My palms are clammy, and I nearly tell the bartender I'm just going to the restroom as if he'd care. As if anyone cares.

That feeling of complete insignificance follows me with each step to the left of the bar as I head down a skinny hallway. It's the only way to go, so the restrooms must be there. I only make it a few steps before I think I hear a shot. My body tenses and my heart goes still. It knows that if it were to beat, I wouldn't be able to hear a single thing else.

There's no scream. There's nothing but the sound of the music. I must have only thought I heard one. It's all in my head.

My eyes close as I will myself to breathe. But then they bolt open at a familiar noise.

It's not the harsh sound of a gun going off. It's the whiz of a gun with a silencer, followed by the thud of a body hitting the floor.

Bang, bang! Two of them back to back, and this time everything sounds closer. Another shot. My body clings to the wall as if it can hide me.

I force myself to move, to head to the back and find a way out or place to hide. I might be a scared little girl, barely surviving in my father's world, but I'm not a fucking idiot.

I quicken my pace as I round the corner, motivated by the sheer will to live. But every bit of strength I have, even if it is minuscule, is for nothing.

The scream that's torn from my throat is barely heard as a thick bag covers my head.

My clutch falls to the floor, hitting my thigh as I kick out and miss the man in front of me. My heels go with it, each kick accompanied by the rough laughter of several men.

I try to fight, but it's no use.

It's more than one man, I know that. Their hands are strong and their bodies like bricks.

I don't stop and won't, but nothing I do is helping. I punch and yell and kick as terror flows through me, begging me to push them away and run. I can't see, and my arms scream in pain as they're pinned behind me.

I only know we're outside because of the wind slicing through my thin jacket. I only know I'm in a trunk because of the telltale sound of it opening before I'm tossed in, my small body crashing against the back of it as it's quickly shut.

Silence.

Darkness.

My breathing is ragged, and it makes me lightheaded.

When my screaming stops, my voice is hoarse, and my throat burns with harsh pain every time I try to swallow. When my banging ends, my wrists are rubbed raw and cut from the cuffs and my muscles are aching with the type of pain that's scorching hot and forces me to tremble.

Another feeling takes over. It's not quite panic. It's something else.

It's not a sense of hopelessness. Not that either.

When you're alone and you know nothing is okay and nothing's going to be okay, there's this feeling that's overwhelming and inescapable.

My heart keeps ticking along despite everything. But it's going too fast. Everything is going too fast and it hurts. And I can't stop it. I can't stop any of it.

When you've done everything you can, and you're left with nothing but fear of both the unknown and the known, there's only one way to describe it.

That feeling is true terror.

CHAPTER 3

Carter

"YOU'RE GOING TO KEEP HER HERE?" IT'S NOT MUCH OF A question from my brother; more of a statement as he looks around the cell. Jase was the middle child of five boys and never learned how to start a conversation without being direct and blunt. I suppose I can't blame him. The thought reminds me of Tyler. The fifth brother who died years ago. His memory numbs the reality of the present, but only for a moment.

Jase leans against the far wall with his arms loosely crossed and waits for me to answer.

We leave in only an hour. Each small tick of the Rolex on my wrist reminds me that I'm so close to having her. Only time separates us now.

Glancing from the thin mattress lying on the floor to the metal toilet on the other side of the cell, I tell him, "I think I'll add a chair."

His quizzical expression only changes slightly. He may not even realize it, but I see it on his face. The disappointment. The disgust. I can hear the unspoken question that lingers on the tip of his tongue as he shifts his gaze from me to the steel door behind us. *When did you become this fucked up?* He has no idea.

"I'll need a place to sit." I keep my voice even, almost playful as if this is a joke. It's Jase though, and he knows me better than anyone. Much better than either Daniel or Declan. The three of them and I make the four Cross brothers. But out of all of us, Jase and I are the closest.

As much as I can hide the anxiousness of getting my hands on Aria from everyone else, he can see it. I can tell by how careful he's been around me since I told him.

"How long?" he asks me.

"How long what?"

"Will you keep her here?"

"As long as it takes." *For what?* The question is there in his eyes, but he doesn't ask it and I have no intention of telling him regardless. I could lie and tell him as long as it takes for the war to end. As long as it takes to see if she'll be useful in negotiations if Talvery wins. The lies could pour from me, but the truth is simple. As long as it takes for me to decide what I want from her.

"There's no shower," he remarks.

"There's a faucet by the side of the toilet and a drain. She'll figure it out while she's in here."

Time passes and a chill settles in the already cold air. I know this is something I've never done, and it crosses more than one line. But in times of war, there is no right and wrong.

"I could give her other things. Little by little." Although I'm answering his question, I'm merely thinking out loud.

"Last time I was here, I was getting some very useful intel," Jase comments as he moves to the corner of the room. I know he's looking at the rim of the drain, inspecting it for any remnants of the blood.

The cell has only been used for one thing prior to this. It's what Jase excels at.

"Are you planning on getting information from her?" Jase asks with genuine curiosity and before I can answer he quickly adds, "I don't think Talvery is known for speaking business openly."

I would commend Jase for prying, but this isn't a matter I want him or anyone else involved in. She's mine and mine alone in this deal. And I'll do whatever I want with her. My brothers and everyone else can go fuck themselves where she's concerned.

"No, I don't think she knows anything."

Jase walks casually around the small room. Ten feet by ten feet. That's more than enough space. His boot brushes against the mattress and then he kicks it. There are no springs or coils in the thing. There's nothing in here she could use as a weapon.

I made sure of that.

"Just a mattress and a chair?" he asks, still skirting around the questions he wants answered. After years of me leading us and making the decisions, he knows better than to question me, but this is fucking killing him. It's eating him alive that he doesn't know what I want to do with her or why I want her. And the knowledge that it's killing him only thrills me.

"For now. I imagine she's going to want to fight and the fewer things in here, the better."

"And you think this is a sign that we can trust the Romanos? He gives you the girl, risking everything to get her, and you trust him to go to war? If he really has her and is willing to hand her over to you?" He's reaching, prying still.

"We can't trust anyone." I make sure he holds my gaze as I add, "That truth will never change." We only have each other. That's how we survived, and that's the only way we'll continue to live.

He's smarter than that. I imagine Jase will realize why all of this is happening before anyone else. That's his job, to gather any and all information necessary. By any means.

"Then this is a test?" he questions. His forehead is creased, a deep line evident. He's lucky he's my brother and that I still feel guilty for bringing him into this. For bringing all of them deeper and deeper into my hell I've created.

"The Romanos want the Talverys dead and vice versa. All over a decade-old feud for territory. The Romanos need allies and the upper hand. It was only a matter of time before I agreed to war; she just happened to be the first casualty. I wanted something, and Romano is going to give it to me, so we back him and not the Talverys."

"Casualty?" he asks to clarify if I really am going to kill her.

"You and I both know if she stays with her father, she'll die at his side… or worse," I say easily as I leave the cell. Jase's footsteps echo behind me.

"Why save her?" Jase's question echoes in my veins. Agreeing to take her is a risk I shouldn't have taken.

"It was an impulsive decision."

"It's unlike you," Jase pushes, and I have to steady my breathing to keep from telling him to fuck off. He has no idea that Aria once saved me. No one does, not even her. Whether I hate her for it, or something else, I have yet to decide.

"After this is over, what do we do with her?" Jase asks me.

Closing the steel door, I shut it tightly and pull the edge of the painting back over the barely visible slit of the frame. The door is designed to be concealed. If you didn't know how to maneuver the painting just so to unlock the hidden seal, you'd never see a door at all.

It's a soundproof cell no one would ever find. Impenetrable and fitted with an electronic cloak so any type of tracking is silenced. It's Aria's new home.

His question resonates with me as I turn my back to the cell. *What am I going to do with her afterward?*

"I haven't thought that far ahead," I reply, and the tone of my answer puts an end to his questioning.

CHAPTER 4

Aria

MY HEART WILL KILL ME BEFORE THESE MEN DO. THAT'S ALL I can think as it races in my chest. I've never felt fear like this.

Maybe it's a lie that I've never felt it before. But it's been so long, and I don't remember my heart pounding like it is now.

My hot breath makes me feel faint as I try to breathe steadily. My eyes open even though all I can see is darkness with the bag still wrapped around my head.

I have to be smart. As much as I'd love to fight, I have to be smart or I'll die.

It's impossible to be smart when you're terrified though.

The dry lump in my throat feels scratchy as I swallow, opening my eyes to see nothing but the scant light that seeps through the burlap. I can't make out anything but I can hear everything. My erratic heartbeat blasting in my ears, the sound of several men in the room, and the scraping of chairs across the floor. One of them is named Romano and I'm fully aware that he's a man who hates my father. *I'm in the hands of the enemy.* I know I'm on a plastic tarp. I can feel the slickness beneath my fingers. It almost feels like a trash bag beneath me.

That's what scares me the most. I've never seen my father kill anyone, but I know they line the floor before they go through with it. It makes it easier for cleaning up.

I try to swallow again, gently lifting my head because I feel like I'm going to suffocate if I don't breathe.

"Bitch is up." My breathing hitches at the gruff voice coming from somewhere in front of me.

I tried and failed, not to let them on to the fact that I'm awake. Even when the cigar smoke woke me, and I thought I was in a fire,

I was still. A few minutes have passed at most; I haven't learned shit that's going to help me though, other than that I'm lying on a floor and helpless.

Someone else responds, "Just in time." And then rough laughter erupts in the room.

My aching body stiffens, my hands clenching and making the cuffs dig deeper into my broken skin. I'm so terrified, I don't react to the pain shooting up my arms.

Every second that passes is agonizing. They speak calmly, softly, and in Italian. A language of which I know very few words.

I know *baldracca* though. It's the word for whore and hearing that makes my shoulders hunch in a useless and pathetic effort to hide myself as a new sense of fear overwhelms me.

There's no doubt in my mind that I'm being held captive by one of my father's enemies. Romano, and he's one of many. I would give them anything to be able to run back home and stay there forever.

"Please," I can't help the attempt to bargain that slips from me. "My father will pay you whatever you want." The tears come without notice and my voice cracks on every other word. The warmth of my breath makes my heated face feel even hotter.

I've never thought of myself as such a weak person. But tied up and knowing my fate includes death or being a whore, the desperation outweighs anything else.

"There is no saving you Talvery trash," a man sneers as he walks closer to me with deliberate steps. His heavy footfalls get louder and quicker. Instinctively I try to back away, despite being on my side with my ankles and wrists cuffed behind my back. The struggle is useless. With my back against a wall and nowhere to go, all I can do is hunch my body inward as the heavy boot kicks brutally into my gut.

The air leaves me in a harrowing instant. Pain bursts inside of me, radiating outward but coiling in my stomach. It sinks deep inside of me, making me want to throw up to get rid of the agonizing pain.

I sputter and heave, trying my best to remain quiet. Bastard tears leak from my eyes and I can't stop them. I can't do anything.

This is a hell I've been terrified of for so damn long. A nightmare that I knew could be a reality. Helpless takes on a new meaning.

My body trembles and the fear is overwhelming. But then I remind myself, be quiet. Be smart. There is always hope. Always. I'm smart enough to find a way. The idea is soothing for a moment until I hear the boot rise again and my instinct to cower is greeted with laughter in the room.

I pray that maybe I'll wake up. Although I know it's not a possibility I'm asleep, because pain doesn't follow you to your dreams. Not this kind.

But the thought gives me a heady comfort that allows me to stay quiet as the men talk and laugh, their banter mocking me and my helplessness.

My father will come for me. That last thought I nearly whisper to myself. My lips mouth the words and I stay in the fetal position with my eyes closed.

He will save me.

It's his pride at risk. If for no other reason, stealing me is a sign of weakness for him. He won't allow it. My breathing slows at the thought, the adrenaline in my blood seemingly ebbing away from me. He has to save me.

"Do you think we should torture her first? Get any information out of her?" The two questions are asked by another man farther away from me and on my left. One with a casual and lighthearted way about the fucked up questions which leads to the room being filled with Italian comments and some amused chuckle from my right.

Sweat covers my skin. Turning hot and cold as the air smothers me.

The laughter is silenced with the sound of the door opening and greetings are exchanged. Only three men speak, and I can't make out the words until the door is shut again.

Something's changed. The air in the room is different. I can feel it.

"Is that her?" a deep, rough voice asks. The velvet cadence of the man who interrupted the jovial laughter makes everything still. Goosebumps flow over every inch of my skin.

There's no answer for a moment, but I imagine someone may have nodded.

Again, my heart beats and I wish it would stop. I need to hear. All I can think is that I'm going to be slaughtered.

I can't be. Not like this. Please, God, not like this.

My adrenaline spikes and I can't help that my head turns to hear better. Everything in the room is still and so quiet that I can hear the puff of a cigar. It's so clear I can imagine his lips as he exhales, the deep breath overshadowing everything else.

"I didn't think you'd do it," the new man's voice says calmly and in control. The others had an accent to them, but this one is from here. American descent, born and raised. Still, his voice commands fear. There's something about it, the intonation that feels like power in and of itself. He says, "It's very rare that I'm proven wrong."

Fear and hope flow through me. The fear I expected, but hope doesn't make sense. It's alive in me though. Some part of me urges to beg the smooth-voiced man to save me as if it knows he's my savior.

"Aria Talvery." He says my name with reverence, but even so, as he steps closer to me, the tread of his shoes on the floor not nearly as heavy and foreboding as the man who kicked me, I instinctively move away.

I don't even notice how calm my heart is until he says the words that create utter chaos.

"The deal wasn't meant to be taken literally." A slew of Italian fills the room. Not everyone's yelling, I know that, but several are and their anger ricochets through the room.

"You said you'd do it; you'd side with me in the war in exchange for her. Are you going back on your word?" One voice is louder than the rest. Deeper and raspier. It sends a sickening chill through my bones.

"I didn't, actually. And terms need to be negotiated."

The man with the raspy voice responds quickly and doesn't hide his irritation as he retorts, "You've known about this for three days. Three fucking days!" He yells the last three words and they make me jump as much as I can in this position.

Speaking with nothing but control, the man who sent for me answers him, "Like I said, I didn't think you'd do it."

"*Bastardo*," a new voice spits and it's followed by the crunching sound of a punch.

"Fuck!" another man yell, but I don't recognize his voice, and the sound of guns being cocked fills the room.

"Jase, no need."

My eyes are wide open as I lie helpless on the ground. My finger-tips search for something, anything to help me but the only progress I'm making is pulling at the plastic beneath me.

Without any warning, three heavy steps come closer and the bur-lap bag is ripped off my head, taking a bit of my hair with it and forcing a scream from me. The bright light blinds me as I'm pulled up by the nape of my neck, clear off the ground and then hurled down to the floor.

I have no hands free to catch myself, they're still cuffed behind me and so my shoulder hits the ground first, then my face. The hint of blood fills my mouth, and pain shoots up my shoulder.

Fuck, it hurts. Everything hurts.

I rock onto my back as I cry out.

Please, make it stop. Please. I wish I could take myself away from here. I wish it were only a dream. But as my arm twists and scrapes on the cement in an effort to right myself, I know this is real. I can't escape this. I whimper and give into the pain. There is no nightmare to wake from. This is my reality.

"You said you'd back me if I gave her to you!" A violent scream tears through the small room. My neck cranes to see the man who spoke over a table. A rough and splintered, unfinished wood table. The man's dress shirt looks damp with sweat and his face glistens with it too. Dark, black eyes stare across the room toward me, but not looking at me. The anger on his face is undeniable and I can't look anywhere else as he screams words that make my body shudder with fear. "I won't let you go back on this!" My eyes close tight.

I've heard the whispers of war for years from man after man. It's been so long since I've actually feared the hint of it. Maybe that's where I made my first mistake. I forgot that I should be terrified and that the dangers are always lurking and waiting to strike.

Please take me far away from here. I can imagine this going wrong so quickly. I could be shot and never even given the chance to escape. My heart races wildly and the terror makes my body tremble.

"And now you've damaged her," the man, the one with control, says quietly and calmly but with an uncontained anger that's brimming with threats. The deadliness of his simple sentence silences the room once again. It's only then that I dare to open my eyes, slowly peeking up through my lashes.

Dark eyes stare deep into mine as a tall man crouches down in front of me. Not black like the other man's, not so darkened. But a mixture of browns and amber, like a piece of burned wood from a raging fire.

There's no heat there though. His eyes are so cold they make my blood freeze and instantly the air turns to ice. There's a hint of something in his gaze that speaks of inexplicable things. My body tenses, my lungs fear to move and I stay still like prey caught in the beautiful hunter's gaze.

Time passes slowly as he considers me. And I find myself hoping and praying that he'll save me. How ridiculous that I would, but there's something about his eyes. I can't refuse the pull, the electricity surrounding him that seems to bend the air between us, making me feel closer to him. So close that he could save me.

His intentions aren't any better than these men. But there's only one of him and he's a man of control. I prefer that to the chaos I'm currently in.

I know it. He can save me.

Even if it's only by killing me right now in this moment and ending the pain. And I'm acutely aware he could do it. There's not a thing about him that could hide the fact that he's a ruthless, cold-hearted killer.

His fingers brush along his stubble as he tilts his head, considering me. The sole light overhead, a bright light in the middle of the room casts a shadow down his face that somehow makes his chiseled and hard jaw look even sharper.

His presence alone speaks of a power that steals the air from me. I'm nothing beneath him as he towers over me. My eyes close slowly as he reaches out and gently brushes the hair from my face. His hot touch melts everything inside of me. It's tender but deliberate. The soothing caress makes me weaker as his fingers travel down my chin and to my throat.

His masculinity is undeniable, the fear of his power only adding to the forbidden desire that rages through me. The man is everything I've been taught to fear, although the sensation is mixed with something else entirely. Something I'd never admit.

And that's when he grips me, his fingers wrapping around my throat and forcing me to open my eyes, staring back into the dark abyss of his gaze.

CHAPTER 5

Carter

"I ASKED FOR HER, YES," I FINALLY ANSWER ROMANO ALTHOUGH I'm still staring at Aria's face, those lips of hers parted and swollen from the fall as I tighten my grip just slightly. Anger ripples through me at the sight of the fresh wounds. That fucker put his hands on her. They hurt her. They hurt what's mine. The tic in my jaw spasms again as the rage intensifies. They should know better than to touch what's mine.

I force the boiling rage down to a simmer; I'm not a fool. There are six men in this room and only one is on my side. I'm not just outnumbered. I'm not prepared to fight. And I don't intend to either.

I want to take my gift and leave this prick to his war. I want that feeling back, humming in my veins. The sheer power of having her at my mercy, feeling her breath cut short and her blood rushing beneath my grasp. She's mine. Finally.

"But not for a beaten and broken version of her," I grit the words through my teeth and they come out lower than I expected. I'm barely contained as I loosen my grip, allowing her to break eye contact and suck in a deep breath.

If I hear another plea or whimper from her in reaction to this fucker, I know I'll shoot Romano without a second thought. And that can't happen. Not yet. The second I get my hands on Aria, her father will be after me. I need Romano to distract him just as much as Romano needs me.

Romano doesn't answer, and I imagine it's because my back is to him as I look over Aria. But he'll have to fucking deal with that. So long as she's here, she'll be looking at me and no one else.

I scan every inch of her and each time I see an injury, my teeth clench, and my muscles coil. The cut on her swollen lip. The scratches and scrapes around her wrists. There's a bruise on her arm and I'm sure there are more I can't see.

"We just got her two hours ago. She's not broken. You better not fuck me over." Romano's words are rushed and desperate as I stand tall, leaving the girl where she is.

My heart races, but I don't let on. To them, she's only a girl I randomly chose. A girl who was harder to kidnap. Just a challenge for them and nothing more.

"This isn't a fight or debate," I tell Romano with my back still to him. I want him to know in his truest of hearts that I'm the one helping him, and it's only out of my desire to do so. He's fucked over more than one of his allies in the past. I'm going to make him think twice before he decides I can be used as a pawn.

Even knowing how much is at stake in this very moment, I can hardly think.

I can't pry my eyes from Aria. Her chest rises and falls steadily as she rolls onto her side. Her lips are a gorgeous hue of red. Her hair tousled and flowing over her bare shoulder. But what's better is how she keeps looking at me with a mixture of both fear and hope swirling in those striking hazel eyes. I didn't imagine she'd look like this. The sight is addictive.

"Plea—" she starts to say—to me—but Romano cuts her off. His sickening and desperate voice hushes the soft sounds of her speaking to me. My fists clench, nearly splitting the tight skin across my tense knuckles and instantly my suit feels like it's suffocating me. His ignorance will be the death of him.

"We had a deal and it will benefit both of us, Cross."

As I loosen my collar, walking closer to him in the filthy room, he continues, "You don't have to do anything but give me that territory, Carter." He raises his hands in defense when I stare daggers at him. "Only for a little while, just so we can strike first. You're closer to Talvery. You don't want your men to do the work, so what other choice do I have than to take it over?"

My gaze sweeps over a pile of crates in the corner of the room. There are three of them on top of empty pallets. The wooden table is etched and weathered. I can only imagine the blood and sweat and drugs that have seeped into the wood. Even over the smell of smoke, the stench is revolting.

Each man in the room is dressed similarly, except myself and Jase. I always wear a suit; it's better to overdress than under. Romano's attempt at an ill-fitting suit didn't last long. His wrinkled jacket is a puddle of cheap fabric laying across the back of his chair. The others wear nondescript hoodies and shirts with faded baggy jeans. Each of the thugs looks at me as I survey them, and each one of their questioning gazes falls without a word uttered from their insignificant lips.

And then I look back to her. Back to the soft curves of her waist, the messy halo of dark hair around her pale skin. Her slender throat that's so exposed as she writhes quietly and hopelessly on the ground. This beautiful, broken creature. She's all mine.

"Your men are positioned between Fourth and Weston, give that territory to me so I can take his men down." Romano starts to speak terms. "We'll take them all down at the same time on every edge of his territory. Any man who stands against us after that will die. It's simple. They back us, or they die like the rest of them."

"I've heard this all before," I mutter. He says he'll kill them all. Erase any trace of Talvery from our existence. It's related to unfinished business started a decade before me. All in the name of greed.

"Just give me access to that territory and the suppliers for the guns." He reeks of desperation as he adds, "That's what you agreed to!"

I expected a lot of things when I came here. But this amount of irritation is something I never accounted for. As the seconds pass, I imagine how I could kill each and every one of the men in this room. How long it would take. How many shots they'd get off. Jase is behind me and I know he could hold his own.

I have to will away the temptation and eagerness to get Aria alone. Leaving the image of her beautiful figure crumpled at my feet, I focus on the business at hand.

"You want me to back down, clear the path for your men?" I ask him.

"They'll never see it coming if we take them from both your side and mine. We take over on the edge of your territory—" I cut the fucker off before he can finish.

"He'll think it's me killing them off. When his men around the edge of my territory start dying, he'll come after me without a second thought." My words come out deadly. "This isn't me starting a war, it's you."

"I'm giving her to you for a reason." He rushes his words with sincere bewilderment.

"No deal," I say and turn to leave, but Aria's whimper pierces through the air. Even without a word spoken, I can hear her plea not to leave her at their mercy. It does things to me that it shouldn't. Just the knowledge that the threat of my absence can create a reaction from her is everything to me in this moment.

"Wait!" Romano's hands smack on the wooden table in the center of the room. "What if," he swallows visibly as he pushes off the table and then lets out a heavy breath. I peek at Jase for the first time since we've been in here. In a slim-fitting suit and his arms hanging loosely in front of him, he could be the usher at a fucking wedding right now. Well, if it weren't for the glare on his face that can only be read one way, for anyone looking at him to fuck off.

"What if..." he pauses and clears his throat before looking me in the eye. "Once I take over Talvery's territory, we could split it." He earns himself a small reaction from me, the tilt of my head for him to continue. "I want to start flooding the product at the top, closest to just outside of the tri-state area, to keep the cops away from our bases."

"And?" I question him. "None of this is relevant to splitting a damn thing."

"I only need his territory in the Upper West Side. I don't even have enough men to cover the rest," he says in a lighter, nearly comical tone as if the problem's already been solved.

"I'm not interested in more territory," I state, and my barely spoken words cause the hopeful expression on his face to fade. "But I'd happily take a percentage of the profits to cover my losses," I offer. "Fifteen percent every quarter until my losses are paid."

"Deal." Romano is so quick to oblige, even his own men stare at him rather than at me. They can't be that stupid. An even-numbered war is never a good thing. They need men and territory and backing. I'll give them the minimum, and pray they still kill each other off.

I nod my head once. "Deal," I say and while forcing a semblance of a smile to my lips, I offer him an outstretched hand.

I have to keep the grin from spreading as I turn my attention back to the wide-eyed girl, still tied up on the floor. "Jase." I speak to my brother although I keep my gaze on her, "Put her in the trunk."

CHAPTER 6

Aria

IT'S ODD, THE THINGS THAT YOU THINK WHEN YOU'RE ALONE FOR hours in a room filled with nothing but hopelessness and anger. Some thoughts make sense of course.

Thoughts of Mika and how he should have been there. He should have been at the bar, and I find myself wondering if he knew. If he took my notebook because he knew how much I loved my art and I'd know he had it and come after him. I find it hard to believe he wouldn't expect me to go after it. Or else why do it? I've spent hours trying to determine the intentions of a psychotic asshole.

But the truth is that I wouldn't have gone after him for any other reason. I wouldn't have left the safety of home… if that picture hadn't been tucked safely inside.

The thoughts of Mika and how bleak my reality is seem reasonable.

Other thoughts though… other thoughts don't make sense.

Like the flashbacks of my mother.

I've been haunted by so many images of what happened the day she died for years now. But none of those keep me company as I rock on the cement floor in the corner of the cell.

It's the sweeter things I remember that are driving me mad.

My thumb brushes against the cut on my lip, sending a sharp pain through me that reminds me this isn't a dream.

"Aria," I hear my mother call out for me in the memory. I was hiding in the closet, so proud that I'd hidden so well. "Ria?" Her voice changed to fear and desperation, and my smile vanished. "Ria, please!" she begged as her hushed cry from the hallway beckoned me to show myself. My fingers gripped the door of the closet just as she forced the guest room door open. I remember how her light blue dress swung around her knees. How her perfectly pinned hair didn't come undone. Yet her voice and her bearing were nothing but distraught.

I wish I could go back to that moment. Where she was running toward me and so close. Where she'd inevitably be in reach.

"Don't hide from me." Her words were ragged as she pulled me into her chest. She rocked me too fast, she held me too hard before gripping my arms and making me look her in the eyes. I'll never forget how hers watered over. "You can't hide like that." Her words were so pained, they came out as only a whisper.

"I'm sorry, Momma," I tried to speak the words, so she knew I meant them. "I was only playing."

Tears leaked from the corners of her eyes as she pulled me back into her arms and rocked me.

She whispered many things, but the one that's stayed with me is that we don't live in a world where we can play.

I should have known better than to run after Mika.

Every possible situation of a setup runs through my head as I bite my thumbnail and rock against the cement wall. I can't sit. My legs beg me to run, but with nowhere to go, I simply stand and lean on the far wall across from the door. Waiting for it to open.

I was only playing myself, thinking that I could prove myself to be anything when I went to hunt down Mika. I was childish and foolish. I can hear my mother saying it now. How foolish she was, she said it all the time before she died. And foolish is what I've become.

I keep whispering that I'm sorry, and I know the man is watching me. Carter. That's what the men called him.

Carter Cross. I know he can hear my whispers of despair.

I'm not saying it to him though; it's an apology to my mother. I should have known better than to chase after the memory of her in that picture. The words are spoken as I focus on the metal drain in the corner of the room.

Between the toilet, mattress, and drain, I know this room is meant for prisoners, but also for torture and murder. One and then the other.

I've searched every inch; the sides of my hands are bruised from pounding against the tall steel door. There's simply no escape. One way in, and one way out.

I should have fought harder when Jase Cross, Carter's brother from what I overheard, held the rag to my mouth.

Stolen, drugged, and reassigned to a prison: that's what my life has become.

The faint sounds of the camera moving drag my attention back to it. It's the one thing in the room I wish I could destroy. There's only one from what I can tell, and it's in the far right corner of the room.

But the camera is encased in cement and untouchable, if throwing the metal chair was any indication. As I stare at the mattress, I wrap my arms around myself. I won't sleep on it; there's no way my back will ever touch it.

I suck in a deep breath, reliving the feeling of those dark eyes pinning me in place.

I know what he wants from me, but he'll have to fight me to get it. I'll kick him, bite him, scratch him until my nails break and bleed.

I'll make him regret this if it's the last thing I do.

My fingers lift slowly up to my jaw and then trail down my throat. Remembering how his gentle comfort so easily became a threat.

My heart thumps hard, once then twice as I hear the fucking camera move again.

"What are you moving it for?" I scream out like a madwoman, as loud as I can. My throat is hoarse from the screaming before, my body screaming along with me in a shuddered breath.

"I'm not fucking going anywhere!" I scream again and then wrap my arms tighter around myself as I fall to the floor on my ass and then my side. Just the way I was when that monster first found me.

The cuts on the sides of my wrists touch the dirty cement floor. I should lie on the mattress. I know I should, even as my tearstained cheeks rest on the unforgiving floor.

If, for no other reason than to have the energy to fight another day. He's waiting me out, I think. And that's something I can't fight. Hours and hours have passed.

I don't know how much time has elapsed exactly, but I know I have to sleep. I can't stay awake forever, waiting for whatever's next.

I'm powerless and completely at Carter's mercy. And he's not even here. He had me stolen from my home, then nearly left me in the kidnapper's arms. And now that he has me, he's left me to go crazy on my own.

That's exactly how I feel as my heavy eyes stare at the steel door and sleep threatens to take over. When you don't know what's waiting for you, what you'll have to fight, it can do that to you. It can make you feel crazy.

Another hour passes, or more. So much time escapes and all my fight has gone. In its place, only fear and exhaustion remain.

"Why are you doing this to me?" I whisper as I stare at the camera, imagining all the answers it could give me. And not a single one of them offers me comfort.

I find it hard to believe that when I first heard his voice, I was so desperate for him to take me away. The blame lays on my survival instincts. The fear of what those men would have done to me made me desperate for Carter to steal me away. My mind drifts back to that moment, and I wish I'd looked harder for a different escape.

He's going to come back. And I need to be able to fight him. But how can I, when I don't know when he's coming, and I have to sleep? Eventually, I have to sleep.

I doze off once, at least once that I know of, and startle awake only to find myself aching on the floor. Forcing myself up, I try to open the door once again and then cry on the floor beneath it. I imagine him opening it in that moment, and that alone scares me to move to the farthest corner in the room.

How heartbreaking it is, that the only bit of comfort I have is knowing that when the monster comes back, I'll be as far away from him as I can possibly be. Even if it is only ten feet.

But it's what I needed to finally give in to sleep.

Of all the things to dream about, I dream of my mother.

And once again, I should have known better than to let my mind wander to the memory of her death.

CHAPTER 7

Carter

S HE FELL ASLEEP AFTER FOURTEEN HOURS OF LOOKING FOR AN
escape, slamming the chair into the door, screaming profanities,
rocking against the wall, and whispering all her regrets.

And I watched every minute of it well into the early morning.
Obsessed with what she'd do and watching the fight leave her as every
hour passed.

After she'd realized her efforts were hopeless, she hummed softly.
So low, that I thought it was only a buzz from the camera until I
turned up the volume. She hummed for hours. I don't even know if
she noticed.

She'd finally fallen asleep, the hum of a lullaby still soft on her
lips. The thrill of victory sang in my blood.

It was only then that I left my office and the monitors, reminding
myself to be patient. I wouldn't be surprised if the carpet beneath my
desk is worn from the pacing of my shoes against it.

My last thought as I left the office and checked the monitor on
my phone, was that as much as she was fighting now, she'd cave. She'd
give in and obey. She has no choice. And time is on my side. Not hers.

An hour into going through orders and updates on each of the
deliveries, I heard her screaming again. But instead of it bringing the
buzz of a challenge, her screams curdled my blood.

The sweat is still hot on my skin by the time I finally get to the
cell and kick the door open with the gun cocked in my hand. My
heart pounds in my chest. Aria's screams are violent and shrill.

I don't know what the fuck happened, who the hell got to her or
how they got in here. But someone has their hands on her.

My heart hammers and the anger of her defiance is dulled by
something primal, a raw fear that sends a prickle of unease through

my body in an instant. I can hear the terror in her voice as she cries out into the dark room for someone to help her.

Someone's in there. Someone's hurting her. It's undeniable in her screams. I can't fucking breathe. I finally have her in my grasp. *Mine.*

My breathing is barely controlled with the gun raised in the air above her place on the floor. Whoever it is will die a painful death for taking what's mine. "Please!" she cries out, her eyes shut tight as her body stiffens and her back arches on the mattress. She screams again, trembling, and helpless. Her small body is cradled into itself.

"Carter!" I hear Jase call out to me, the door to the cell still open. I can hear him running down the hall.

Now that the cell is open, anyone and everyone in here can hear her screams.

My gun lowers slowly as Jase enters the room behind me. His breathing is ragged as he closes the distance and stands next to me. Our shadows tower over her small frame, lying destitute in the bed. She doesn't stop crying out, and although she doesn't sob, the sounds are there.

She's captive to her dreams.

"Night terror," Jase says with a heavy breath. The metal of his gun rubs against his jeans as he slips it back into place and then looks at me. "I thought someone got in here." Tiredness is etched onto his face, but also the raw look of fear. He takes a moment to compose himself before starting to tell me, "I thought…"

As he starts to speak, she screams out again and the sharpness of the pain sends spikes over my skin that scrape their way down my body.

It's a desperate cry that sounds foreign to my ears, although I'm so used to hearing something similar. Pleas for mercy, which I never show.

"What do you want to do about it?" Jase asks me. He's still catching his breath, just like I am. I can feel him staring at me, wanting to know what to do next. I can't tear my eyes from her as she curls on her side.

Jase turns to the door as the sounds of someone else coming down the hall makes their presence known.

"I'll put her on the mattress," I tell him absently. "Take care of whoever that is and shut the door behind you," I order him, and my words come out flat. I try to keep the emotion away, but a sense of despair is evident. This wasn't a part of my plans. My fingers dip into my pocket, fingering the clicker that will open the door to the cell while I'm on the inside.

"You think they did something to her? Romano? Or maybe it's what she thinks is coming?" Jase asks and finally I turn to look at him.

"How the fuck would I know?" My words come out harsh. The anger at him suggesting her terror is caused by thoughts of what I'll do to her is unexpected and more than that, unwanted. Of all the things I expected from her, I didn't anticipate this.

It cuts me in a way I can't explain. I want to consume her every waking thought. I want her to live and breathe for me and my desires. And maybe this is the cost of it all. That I can have her during her days, but her nights will destroy her.

"Just a nightmare then," Jase says as if it's a casual observation. The whimpers still slipping through her parted lips are accompanied with a strangled sound of pain.

"You aren't supposed to wake them, you know?" Jase breathes out. "When they have night terrors, you're not supposed to wake them up."

The light from the door is blocked and the shadow of someone else covers Aria's slender neck and bared shoulders. I don't turn to look, but I don't have to. It's Declan, asking what's wrong. He knew she was here, but he doesn't want any part of this.

"It's fine," Jase tells him and then continues, "I don't think you can do anything really."

"Just go," I tell them both and stand as still as I can as they leave the room, taking with them the light from the hall as the door shuts. The creak of the steel is met with a thud and then the click of the lock. It takes a moment for my eyes to adjust. Another moment of her small cries and then a scream. A terrified scream.

"What did I do that earned me this?" I question her although I know she can't hear. I haven't touched her; we haven't even started. I almost touch the cuts on her wrists, but I pull back. I'll give her ointment and bandages in the morning. She'll have to do it herself until she earns my touch.

"Please don't," she begs in her sleep. Her words are whispered so softly, and I wonder if they came out that way in her dream. "Please," she begs.

"You don't know what you're asking, songbird," I tell her softly and consider my own sanity in this moment. "You never had a choice. The moment your father left me alive, your fate was sealed," I confess to her. Something I've never said aloud to anyone.

He should have killed me. It's Nicholas Talvery's fault I'm allowed to live another day.

His fault… and someone else's. The moment the thought comes to me, I see her tremble. Beautifully weak on the cold, unforgiving ground, the sleep taking more and more of her as her words become quieter.

She worries her bottom lip between her teeth, and it's the only part of her that moves. "*Please.*" Her lips mouth the word.

Kneeling before her, I'm slow and deliberate as I pick her up. Conscious of where my gun is tucked away in case she's playing me. She's light and fits easily into my arms. I thought she may fight me. That she'd react in fear to my touch. But instead, she molds her body to me and her slender fingers grip onto my shirt. Holding me tighter to her.

Her lips brush against the crook of my neck as I carry her the few feet to the mattress. Her pleas are still whispered, and the gentle warmth of her breath sends a tingle down my spine. I barely contain a groan of desire as I move her to the mattress. She clings to me still, holding tightly and begging me. This time she begs me not to leave her.

"Don't go. Stay with me… please," I barely hear her words. Her face is still pained, but there's gentleness in her cries as I shift her onto the mattress.

Her hand fits in mine as I pull her fingers from me and place them on her chest. Her chest rises and falls as she calms herself, slowly drifting to a different place.

Time passes quickly. Too quickly as I sit on the mattress, making it dip with my weight and staring down at her. Her heavy sighs emphasize her breasts, the bit of lace from her black bra peeking from her shirt. It almost tempts me as much as the dip of her waist.

My gaze caresses each curve of her body as I remember the first time I heard her name.

The day my life changed forever.

Her bed groans in protest as Aria turns in her sleep, settling into the mattress and my body stiffens. I shouldn't be here right now. That's not how I gain the control I want. I can't breathe until she's still and her own breathing evens out. But as I move to stand, shifting my weight ever so slightly, the mattress slumps and her hand falls, her soft fingers brushing mine, the tips touching.

My hand stays still beneath hers, but it begs me to explore. To thread my fingers between hers. Closing my eyes and inhaling deeply, I remind myself that there is time.

Time will change everything.

My eyes open at the reminder. Just like that day did years ago.

The day my father dropped me off at the corner of West and Eighth by the liquor store to sell that last bit of his pain pills. I was more approachable, according to him and we needed to pay the bills. It didn't matter what I said or how much I didn't want to do it. I was the oldest of five, my mother was dead, and I had nothing left in me. Nothing but pain.

My father dropped me off on Talvery's territory unknowingly. And it wasn't long before I learned what it meant to sell drugs on his ground.

I was only a child before that day.

But one day changes everything.

CHAPTER 8

Aria

WAKING UP WITH MY HEART BEATING OUT OF MY CHEST, the hope that it was all a nightmare crumbles into dust when all I can see is cement and cinder block walls.

I have to close my eyes and cover my face to keep from losing it. "This can't be happening." The trembling words leave my lips unbidden. Wrapping my arms around my knees, I try to tell myself that it's all a dream. I rock back and forth, and as I do, the sounds of the mattress creaking beneath me and the feel of my heels digging into the comforter makes my body freeze.

I try to remember last night, and I know full well I slept on the ground only a few feet away. I know I did.

My hands fly over my body. As if they could check to see if I was touched.

I feel the sharp edges of a scratchy throat but swallow thickly, trying to suppress the terror of what he could have done to me.

I must have crept into the bed and not remember it. I know I haven't been touched. I would know, wouldn't I? "I would," I say the words aloud as if I was speaking to someone else. Maybe I just needed the reassurance. I don't remember a thing after falling asleep. I wish I could have just stayed awake.

The whispered words echo in the hollow room as I glance up at the door. And then to the camera as it moves. Carter Cross, I almost speak his name aloud. I've heard his name before, always spoken with anger. I know he's one of a number of brothers and the head of a drug cartel. That's where the information ends. My father never liked me knowing anything and the only bits I learned were slivers of the truth from Nikolai. And he only told me what I needed to know. They said it was to protect me, but I would give anything to know what I'm up against.

I'd give anything to know what Cross is capable of.

Is he just going to leave me here to die? My throat pains in a way I didn't think was possible.

"Let me out," my raspy voice begs and the words themselves are like knives raking up my throat. I haven't eaten or had a drink of water since I've been here, and I don't even know how long that's been.

I stand a little too quickly, and nearly fall as I try to make my way to the door. I'm dizzy, lightheaded, and I think I may throw up.

Still, I head straight for the door, pulling at the doorknob and desperately trying to open it. My fist slams against it, over and over.

There's no use, stupid girl.

Again, I slam my fist and scream out, "Let me go!" but I'm only met with an unmovable door in an empty room, with no way out and no idea of what will happen to me.

The pain from the next slam of my fist makes me wince and cradle my hand to my chest. My back presses against the door as I fall down slowly onto my ass, resting my head against the door.

So many slow moments pass. Moments where I just try to breathe. Moments where my fingers brush along the cuts at my wrists. Moments where I stand and stretch and pretend like it's not odd to stretch when you're caged like an animal. What's the point if there's no escape?

It takes me longer than it should to see the foam tray with a grilled cheese sandwich and the cup of water next to it.

And a bucket of water with a sponge behind it. I spent so much time staring at the door, I didn't see it.

He came in here.

He was here.

My chest heaves and again my fingers travel to my thighs. He didn't. I would know. I can barely contain the fear of knowing he came in here while I slept. It's hard to swallow and I stay far away from the tray of food.

Time slips by again. And then more time. There is no change in my predicament, save my sanity.

Although my stomach grumbles and the delicious scents of butter and cheese are all I can smell, I leave the tray where it sits.

I don't eat, and I don't undress to bathe myself. Not with him watching. The anger boils and rises to such an extreme that I almost slam the bucket across the room, straight at the camera.

I'm not his pet or his test subject. He can take that foam tray and go fuck himself with it. At least that's what I think when I first move closer to see it; the thought even gives me joy. Hours pass and then more. How much time, I don't know. There's nothing in this room and loneliness and boredom are only two of the emotions I'm not sure I'll be able to handle if this is how my new life will proceed.

My mind starts playing tricks on me and I find myself etching small things into the cinder blocks with a button on my shirt. The shirt's already ripped so it doesn't matter. The top two buttons have been pulled off, the first one long lost and the second now a writing tool. A small and poor one, but there's nothing else to do but pace and let my mind wander.

And that leads me to awful places.

I'm busy carving a pattern, a useless, meaningless pattern of birds and vines into a block that's not even deep enough to be seen clearly when the door opens behind me.

My heart lurches and I swing my body around so violently that the back of my head collides with the wall, the button slips from my hand and the sound of it pinging to a stop on the ground fills the room.

The flood of light is lost quickly as Cross steps inside my cell and closes the door behind him. His figure is like a shadow of darkness as he walks toward me.

"What do you want?" I ask instinctually, barely able to breathe, let alone swallow the pathetic words before I can speak them. I'm glad I didn't eat because if I had I would have lost it all in this moment. Panic rages inside of me.

He's quiet as he takes one step forward and then another. He only takes his eyes from me once, and that's to look at the chair in the corner of the room.

"My father will come for me," I tell him as he walks toward the chair and positions it so he can sit and face me. "He's going to kill you," I add, and my words are strangled, but audible.

All I'm rewarded with is a soft smile on his lips. The stubble on his jaw is more noticeable and his eyes seem darker, but maybe it's just the light. Everything else about him is more foreboding than I remember. His height and broad shoulders, the lean build of his body with the rippled accents of his muscles. God made him to do deadly, sinful things. One look and that's obvious.

As if reading my mind, he grins at me, forcing me to take a step back, which only widens the grin to a charming and perfect smile. I feel like I'm caught in a cage. A little mouse to a lion. And he's only toying with me.

"You're sick," I spit at him, clenching my hands into fists.

"I'm well aware of that little fact, Aria. Tell me, what else do you know about me?" His voice is smooth velvet, and it echoes in a deep way from wall to wall in the room. The kind of echo you feel deep in your gut, one that haunts you so much later in the night.

"I know my father will gut you," I answer him with sickening contempt.

"He isn't going to do anything. He doesn't even know I'm the one who has you." His head tilts slightly as he examines my every reaction.

"Yes, he does," I breathe as if it will be true if only I say it is. His look turns to pity, but only for a moment. It passes so quickly I wonder if I even saw it, or maybe it was only the dim light in the room playing tricks on me.

"He doesn't and even if he did, he's useless." Menace lingers on the heels of his words, falling hard and crashing to the ground around me.

He adds, "He couldn't even defend your mother's honor."

"Fuck you," I dare to sneer at him. Anger rises quickly inside of me and my breathing quickens.

"You fight now, but you'll submit later," Cross says easily, completely unaffected by my words.

"Submit?" the fear is evident in my voice.

"You'll do as I say. Every command. Kneel at my feet, undress, lie in my bed… Spread your legs for me." The depth of conviction in his voice is frightening.

"I'll die before I submit to you." My throat dries and tightens. I can barely breathe as he stands.

He's not quick, not hurried in the least to stalk toward me. I can run. I know I can, but the room is small; there's nothing to hide behind and he's so tall, it wouldn't take much beyond a lunge for him to catch me.

My knees weaken, and I nearly fall to the ground, but I don't. I stay as tall as I can although I have to crane my neck to look Cross in the eyes. My heart pounds chaotically as if it's trying to escape. For every step he takes forward, I take one back until I've hit the wall.

"How did you sleep?" he asks me in an eerily calm voice.

"Like a baby," I say, and my answer is nothing but defiant. I surprise myself with the immediate answer. Fuck him. Fuck Carter Cross.

A crooked smile twitches onto his lips. "Do you always have nightmares?" he asks and the strength inside of me wavers. My gaze flickers from him to the floor.

"It seemed like a terrible dream," he adds, his eyes blazing with a threat.

I get the sense that he was here, that he knows I had a nightmare because he was here, not from the camera. As much as I'd like to hide the sickening sense of defeat from my expression, I can't. He sees my weakness, and I can't hide from him.

"Answer me." His command comes out tense and deep.

I almost tell him, no, but then decide on silence, pretending to ignore how the fear that's growing inside of me makes my limbs feel numb. I expect anger from him, but all I can see is the twinkle of humor in his eyes.

"You will give me everything that I want," Cross says and then reaches out to me. My eyes close tightly as his fingers brush the hair from my face. He tucks the lock behind my ear and I think about biting him, about fighting him when I remember the first time he touched me so comfortingly, only to then grip my throat and hold me like his prized possession.

With another step forward, he bathes me in darkness, blocking the light and forcing me to push myself against the wall and stare up at him with genuine fear I wish I could deny.

"You're going to love doing it too," he whispers in the small space, heating the air between us and my body betrays me at the thought.

It makes no sense at all. Save the scent of his presence. He smells like the woods. Inhaling the deep scent reminds me of the way my mother used to describe our eyes. Like the canopy of the forest after a long day of rain. Maybe I could blame it on instinct.

Or maybe I'm just meant to be the whore to a monster.

I don't admit my response to him. There's no way in hell I ever would.

"Let me go," I whimper the plea and hate myself for it. I can pretend to be strong. He can't see what's deep inside of me. I can pretend to be stronger than he knows.

His only response is to chuckle, a deep and rough masculine sound that rumbles his chest and the anger I feel from it overwhelms me.

I'm barely holding on to my composure. I know if I strike him, he'll respond, and I will lose. I'm not stupid. *This is what he wants.* The realization makes my eyes widen. He's playing with his shiny new toy.

"Just kill me." My muscles scream as I stiffen them, refusing to lash out. Although my body heats and adrenaline pumps faster at the thought of him doing it, I still tell him to just get it over with. I don't want to be played with. "I'll never give you anything."

"Now what would that accomplish for me, songbird?"

I don't want to cry and give him the satisfaction. I refuse to. My eyes are already burning from being so fucking weak. I won't be weak. I won't let him win.

Be smart. A million possibilities run through my head at what the smart choice would be in this moment, but the only situation I allow to rule my actions is to not give in. I'll wait. I'll survive day by day until my father comes. He will come. I know he will.

"I'll fight you until the day I die," I sneer at him with every ounce of conviction I can gather.

It only makes him smile. A wicked grin that sends a chill through my blood. "You'll find comfort in thinking that… for a little while." With a growing smile of triumph, he leaves me where I am. His shoes smack on the ground, and the sound grows quieter as he confidently strides to the door and turns the knob with ease.

How? He's simply walking away, and the door opens for him. I don't have time to consider anything. All I know at this moment is that the door is open. And whether or not he's there, I need to try to run. He opens the door just enough to get through. But I still run to it. I do my damnedest to make it to the door before it shuts and like the merciless prick he is, he leaves it open.

My bare heels bash against the cement as I sprint toward the light, but just as I make it, my hopes are so easily dashed. Just as the hope that I'll actually get out of here so easily burns into my chest, his tall broad frame fills the doorway, standing with a foreboding presence and taking a large step toward me.

A step so powerful and undeniably in control that I stagger backward, my foot scraping against the cement and throwing me off balance.

My ass hits the floor first and my head would have smacked against the concrete as well if Cross's hand wasn't wrapped firmly around my forearm. His fingers dig in and I let out a squeal of both surprise and pain.

"You're smarter than this," he hisses. The rage in his eyes swirls with darkness, but with it are golden flecks of intrigue and delight. "You won't leave this room until I say so."

I'm paralyzed by the certainty in his voice. The strength of his grip. The desire that drips from each of his words.

"You. Are. Mine. Aria." He says each word lower and lower until I can barely hear him over the pounding of my heart. The concept of being owned by this man is a deadly concoction that sends a ripple of both fear and desire straight to my core.

Without warning, he releases me, and I fall to the ground, still shaken but staring up at him. "I'm not an object to own. No one owns me!" I scream at him even though I don't believe my own words in this moment.

He merely smiles at me. As if it's all a joke to him.

"Let me go," I try to scream at him as if it's a demand, but the words are a pitiful plea even to my own ears.

Still, I try to stand, to get back up as he smiles and closes the door, leaving me right where he wants me.

I swear I hear him answer me before the steel door closes with finality. I would swear on my life I heard him say, "Never."

CHAPTER 9

Carter

D ANIEL IS MY ONLY BROTHER WHO DOESN'T KNOCK. HE NEVER
has.

I know he isn't going to this time either. His steps are
hurried, angered and I have to suppress a sigh of irritation. I'm fucking
tired and I don't have time for his bullshit.

"This war between Talvery and the Romanos doesn't have anything to do with us."

Daniel's always had a knack for speaking as he enters the room,
regardless of whether or not my gaze is down on my desk, focused on a
spreadsheet of product and how much is selling. Having high demand
is good, but some of this doesn't make sense. And it's only on the border of our territory that touches the Romanos' territory.

Pinching the bridge of my nose, I ignore him.

"Did you go to the club with Jase?" I ask Daniel as I continue down
the order of supplies.

"Did you hear me?" Daniel questions me, kicking the office door
shut and making his way across the office to sit in the chair opposite
me.

"I did. You didn't tell me anything I don't already know." Shutting
the laptop computer, I finally give him my attention and for a moment
I'm caught off guard.

"You look like shit," I say, and I don't hide the surprise in my voice.

My brother's eyes spark with a hint of humor as he smirks at me
and replies, "And you look like a fucking Ken doll. Drug dealer Barbie
style."

A huff of a laugh escapes me as he runs his hand along the scruff
on his jaw. "Addison isn't sleeping. She's having a hard time with this."

"With what?" I ask him, feeling a chill in my blood.

"With the shit that's going on. The war, not knowing who tried to take her or what they were planning."

"She doesn't need to know about a damn thing," I say beneath my breath with every bit of humor long gone. "You shouldn't have told her anything. We stay on lockdown. We wait for the Talverys and Romanos to trim their own numbers. If you have to tell her anything, that's all she should know."

Daniel's head tilts back slightly and he runs a hand down his face, his body slumped in the chair. "She's not allowed in the north wing and I don't want her leaving without me or someone else with her... and I'm not supposed to tell her anything?" he questions me, letting his chin drop and daring to look me in the eyes.

"The women should stay out of this." He fucking knows better.

"Says the man who started a war over a piece of ass."

"Careful." He cocks a brow at my response, but I stay firm.

Leaning forward, he puts both palms on the desk and asks quietly, like it's a secret, "What's going on with you?"

I steady my back against the leather chair, letting one hand fall to the armrest, my fingers tracing along the steel nail heads.

"I wish I knew," I tell him in a breath. "We have to move forward with this and there are some things that will benefit us, but it's a careful walk from here until the end."

Daniel nods his head, his eyes never leaving mine. "And when are we getting revenge on Marcus? The man who tried to take what's mine?"

"We don't know that it was Marcus who tried to take her."

"Who else would have done it?" Daniel asks but even as the last words slip out, his conviction wanes. Our enemies are surrounding us. The only saving grace is that they fear us, and they have other wars to fight.

"He has yet to answer any of our messages and no one's confirmed he had anything to do with it." Daniel's nostrils flare as he slams himself back into his seat, making the front legs of the chair nearly come off the floor while he looks past me and out the window.

"So, I'm supposed to do nothing and keep Addison in the dark?" Daniel asks with contempt. "I need to do *something*. I can't let him or whoever the fuck it was get away with it." His frustration is getting the better of him. And I understand. I do. But we have to be smart and know how best to move forward before we act.

"We don't know who did it. There will be nothing done until we do." My answer is absolute, with no room for negotiation, and the air tenses as Daniel considers me. A moment passes, and I can't breathe. My brothers are everything to me. All I have. And they've never questioned me. Not until this past week.

I'm losing my grip; I can feel it. And that's never a good thing.

Finally, he nods once and relaxes his posture, moving one ankle to rest on his knee.

"Can I ask you something else?" he asks, and I rest my elbow on the desk and then my chin in my hand, nodding as I do. He's going to ask me regardless.

"What are you doing with her?"

"It's personal." That short answer already reveals more than I've told anyone else, but Daniel shakes his head, a look of disappointment clearly written on his face.

"You aren't the brother I remember." He'll never know the pain that comment causes me.

"Tell me what you remember, Daniel? You never saw anything past Addison." I practically hiss her name.

"What the fuck does that mean?" His anger is evident, and his jaw tightens.

"You had her and I had no one." My voice cracks at the revelation. Time marches on as we stare at each other. He has no idea how she saved him. Having someone to love, even if it is from a distance can give you hope. And hope is everything.

"We had each other," he finally tells me. I know he's thinking about the same shit I am. All the shit we went through. There were five of us, five brothers, but Daniel and I were the oldest and the two our father paid more attention to. If you can call what he did *attention*.

I let the anger and every other emotion fade, opening up the laptop to cue that this meeting is over. The truth slips by me unintentionally as I point out, "It's not the same."

"I just want to know you're not hurting her." He won't let it go. My grip tightens on the laptop as I try to remain calm.

"You have to trust me. Everything is about to change and if that girl had stayed where she was, she would have died." He waits for more. Proof, maybe. I don't know what he wants, but the less he knows, the better. "There's so much you don't know."

"You could tell me." There's a hint of sadness in his voice, or maybe I imagined it.

"Soon," I promise him. "Soon."

He doesn't say goodbye as he walks away. But as he makes it to the door, gripping the handle and swinging it open, I remember what he said about Addison. "Daniel. Give her this," I call out to him as I open the drawer. I have a few vials of S2L inside the small safe and toss one to him. He nods once and says something about Jase, but I don't hear, and he's already gone before I can question him.

Staring at the closed door, I think about how my brothers are the only constant I've had. Only them and no one else.

But admitting the truth out loud… I can't trust myself to do it.

The last time I admitted something of this weight, my world changed. I sparked the depraved monster inside of me to life and it changed everything.

The day Talvery left me to rot where he found me. I'll never forget the feeling as I heard my father's truck come to a stop. The old thing sputtered, and the sound was so comforting until his door shut and the anger in his voice was clear.

"What the fuck are you doing out in the open? Do you want someone to call the cops?" he yelled at me and when he tugged on my arm, the burns and cuts shot a horrible pain through my arm that made me scream in the dark alley. Bloodied and bruised, my father still tossed me around like I was nothing.

Couldn't he see what they'd done to me? I could hardly open my eyes.

"We'll get whoever did this, but come the fuck on before someone sees," he hissed between his teeth.

"They wanted to know who I worked for," I barely spoke as I hobbled to the car. Every bit of me hurt just to breathe. I slumped into the seat as he rounded the truck. And I know they saw. They had to have been watching me. Waiting to see who would come.

Country music played out as my father shut his door and took off down the street toward the dirt roads. I wanted to roll down my window so badly. I remember thinking I was dying, so I wanted to feel the wind on my face one last time. I'd coughed up so much blood, there was no way I'd be okay. My father ignored me as I asked him to do it, and instead, he turned down the music so only the sounds of the rumbling truck and his questions could be heard.

"Who's 'they?'" my father asked as he raced over a speed bump and my body jolted forward. I cried out like a bitch and he screamed the question again at me. It was fear in his voice though, not anger.

I know it now. Fear is what dictated his actions. Not strength like the man who'd done this to me.

"Talvery," I answered in a single painful breath. As I said his name, I remembered the look of Nicholas Talvery's freshly cleaned face only an inch from mine. I would never forget the way he looked at me like I was nothing and how much joy it brought him to know he could do whatever he wanted with me.

"What did you tell him?" he asked, and I looked at my father. I made sure to really look at him as I told him he was safe.

"I said I was just selling my dead mother's cancer meds. I said I was no one. And they believed me."

My heart has never hurt as much as it did at that moment when my father nodded his head and seemed to calm down. He was good at taking care of himself. He was good at living in fear.

That was the last day he looked at me as if I was a pawn in his game. My wounds were still fresh when I started hitting him back. And I never stopped. I wouldn't do the stupid shit he wanted me to. I would make money, a fuckton of it. But I never set foot on Talvery's turf again. I wasn't a dumb fuck like my father. And the next time he pushed me into the truck and screamed in my face so loud it shook my veins and the spittle hit my skin, I let my anger come forward, slamming my fist into his jaw.

I let the fear rule me in that moment. But it's the fear I saw in my father's eyes that defined the change between us.

Each time I went out, leading a life I didn't choose, I thought it would be my last. I wanted to die, and it wasn't the first time in my life that I wished for sweet death to end it all.

But without fear of death, I learned what power really was.

And none of my brothers understand that.

Not a single fucking one of them.

CHAPTER 10

Aria

HIS EYES WON'T LEAVE MINE.
He won't leave the room.
He won't give me any space.

I don't know how many days I've been here, but I do know that today is different by the look in Cross's eyes.

It's hard to count the days. My eyes flicker to the carving of stripes on the wall just beyond Carter Cross's never-changing stern expression. Sitting on the metal chair a few feet from me puts him at the perfect height to block the etched stripes. One for each of the days I've been here. But I stopped a while ago.

My sleep is fucked and there aren't any windows in the room. I've noticed that when I lie down and curl up to sleep, the lights go off. Which means two things, as far as I can tell.

He wants me to sleep. And he doesn't want me to know how much time has passed. It could be midnight a week from when I was taken. Or it could be noon with even more days between now and my last day of freedom.

There are four stripes on the wall. One scrawled after each time I slept. But on the fifth day, I slept on and off with terrors of my childhood that woke me up constantly.

The first two days I got three meals, always delivered the same way. A small slot in the door opened, the food was shoved inside on a small foam tray and then the slot quickly shut with a deafening slam. I waited for hours by it on the third day, praying I could catch it, snatch the hand… I don't know what. All I knew was that on the other side was freedom. But I quickly found that the slot only opened when I was in the corner of the room farthest from the door. Otherwise, no food would come.

I can barely eat as it is, but hunger won a few times. And instantly, I slept afterward. I don't know if he drugged me or not, but the fear of sleeping is at war with the need to eat.

Either way, the food I'm given doesn't aid me in knowing what time of day it is. There doesn't seem to be a rhyme or reason as to what's on the tray.

There haven't been any breakfast foods at all. The last thing I ate was a biscuit and a chunk of ham. It was glazed with honey and my stomach was grateful. I devoured every scrap and then immediately regretted not eating whatever it was he'd given me before. If I don't eat what's given, he simply takes it away when I sleep. And somehow, he knows when I'm faking sleep. I tried that, too. I don't know how many times I laid in the darkness waiting for him to open the door, only to fool myself into sleeping and waking to the tray being gone.

So much wasted time.

Maybe losing the time is the first sign of victory for him.

But I want it back.

"What day is it?" I ask him and it's the first thing I've said in the time he's been in here.

He comes in every so often, merely watching me. Scooting his chair closer and waiting for something. I don't know what.

"It's Sunday."

Sunday… It was Thursday when I left to go to the bar. I know it was Thursday. "So, that means it's only been three days?" I ask him although inwardly my gut churns. It's not possible.

A devilish smile plays across his face.

"You slept a lot, songbird. It's been ten days."

His words steal the bit of courage from me and I turn to face the door rather than him, pulling my legs into my chest and sucking in a deep, calming breath. Ten days of screaming and crying in this room. Of not knowing when help is coming, or if it ever will. Of barely eating and only bathing from a bucket of water while hiding under my dirty clothes.

"If you would only kneel for me when I come in, I would give you so much more than this."

"Why are you doing this to me?" My question is a whispered

breath. No tears come from my dry eyes and the pain in my chest is dull. There's only so much a person can take before they break. I don't need sleep or food even. I need answers.

"You ask that often," is his only response, as he straightens himself in the chair. Squaring his shoulders toward me and making the pressed dress shirt stretch tight across his shoulders.

His handsome features look like nothing but sin as he stares at me. I have to rip my eyes away from him. I can't look at him. He's a monster and that's the only thing I need to know about Carter Cross. A beautiful monster who enjoys depriving me and watching me fade into nothing.

"How about we play a game?" he asks me, and a chaotic laugh erupts from my lips.

"Come now, I promise you'll enjoy it," he says, and his voice is a promising caress.

"And what's the game, Cross?" I say his name out loud, staring defiantly into his eyes. I imagined his aggravation, maybe even anger at my response, but instead, he only grins at me. A crooked grin on a charming face. I wish I could smack it off.

"An answer for an answer," he says and that's when it hits me.

"You think I know a thing about my father's business? You're wasting your time," I say but my voice betrays me as I speak. It cracks on my last words.

So, this is his plan? Steal me, lock me in a room with nothing for days until I'm desperate for change so he can get information from me? I know it's merely because I'm a woman. That's why they haven't tortured me. But it will come eventually, and I have nothing to give them.

My eyes burn with the need to cry, but I don't let it happen. "I swear to you," I barely get out and then stare into Cross's dark eyes, willing him to believe me, "I don't know anything."

"I know you don't." It takes a moment for me to register what he's said.

"Is this a trick?" I ask him, feeling as if I must be going crazy. The hope in my chest is fluttering so strongly. "I don't want to die," I whisper the confession.

"I'm not going to kill you." He answers simply, devoid of emotion, giving me nothing to hold on to other than the matter-of-fact words. "The Romanos would have killed you. You would have died or been captured and given a much crueler fate if I hadn't taken you first." I'm silent as I listen to him talk about me as if I'm merely a pawn to sacrifice. "Your best chance at surviving what's to come is with me."

Tears threaten to leak down my cheeks at the thought of men infiltrating my father's estate. At Nikolai being shot as he sits at the kitchen table where he always sits on the early weekend mornings. At my father being killed in the same room where my mother's life ended.

"Do you want to play the game?"

"I've never done well with games," I answer breathily, watching every inch of his expression for a hint at what's to come.

"The blanket is yours for playing," he says and nods toward a pile of fabric he'd tossed at my feet when he came in. And inwardly, I'm grateful. "Why don't you eat?" he asks me, and I know the game has started. An answer for an answer and he holds the first question.

Staring down at myself, I answer him with half honesty. "I'm not hungry." Ten days... I try to remember how many times I've eaten. Maybe six meals. At the realization, my stomach roils.

A moment passes before he shifts in the chair, leaning back but keeping his hands on his thighs. "If you lie, then I can lie," he says and the way he says the word "lie" forces me to stare into his eyes. It's like the devil himself discussing deceit. "That's the way this game works."

"I don't trust that you aren't going to drug me or poison me. Or something." The truth so easily pours from my lips.

My eyes drop to the ground at the reminder of all the horrific ideas that have flitted through my head since I've been here.

"It's only food and you need to eat." Again, there's no emotion, only a statement of fact. I watch him intently as he leans forward, resting his elbows on his knees and clasping his hands in front of him. "Your turn."

"What are you going to do with me?" I ask him without thinking twice.

"Feed you and keep you in here with nothing but what you have until you submit to me." He readjusts in the chair and adds, "You're a social creature and lonely. I can see how lonely you are." As he speaks to me, my gaze wanders and the hollow ache in my chest rises.

"I'm used to being lonely."

"I hear your prayers in the dark, songbird. I hear your wishes for someone to save you. Your father. Nikolai... Who is Nikolai?"

"A friend," I answer him, feeling the pain and agony sweep over my body. And feeling like a liar. The word friend sounds false even to my own ears, but it's been so long since Nikolai was anything else. And a friend is what he needed to be. Nothing more. Or else my father would have found out.

"Wrong answer. He is no one anymore. They're all gone, and no one is coming to save you."

"Gone?" The word comes out like a question, but the monster in front of me doesn't answer. My eyes close as I inhale deeply, thinking he's lying. They're coming. They'll come for me.

"You're bored, alone, and starving yourself into nothing. You will submit to me, or you will stay like this forever."

My lips kick up into a small smile I can't contain, and I don't know why. I must be going crazy.

"You think that's funny?" A hint of anger greets his words and it only makes my smile grow, but it's accompanied with tears leaking from the corner of my eyes. And I don't even know when I started crying.

Shaking my head, I brush away the tears from just under my eyes. "It's not funny, no. And now it's your turn." He's going to keep me here like this? He could keep me here forever.

Even as I think the statement, the overwhelming loneliness consumes me. I have nothing and this prison is eating my sanity alive. Hours pass where I simply stare at the wall, praying it will offer me something different than the day before.

He watches me as I sway from side to side slightly.

"What does submit mean?" I talk over him just as he starts to speak. My words are harsher than I thought they'd be and he cocks his brow, not answering me and then asks his question.

Rules of the game, I suppose.

"What is your favorite food?"

Dizziness overwhelms me for a moment and I rest my head against the wall. He's going to win this game. And all the others. He's cheating and I'm deteriorating.

"Bacon, I guess. Everyone loves bacon," I answer halfheartedly, partly because I'm tired of this game already and partly because I need a little humor in this situation. "There's this sandwich from the corner store by my house. My mother used to take me there." I stare at the ceiling while I talk, not really to him, but just to talk and think about something other than this. Although it's nice to have someone around. I feel an empty hollowness inside of me. I'd rather that than the sickening feeling of defeat.

Licking my lower lip, I continue. "She took me there every weekend. Coffee and pastries for her, but they had this sandwich I loved, and they still have it. It's turkey and bacon with ranch dressing on a pretzel roll." My head lolls to the side and I glance at Cross, whose usual stern expression has been replaced by a look of curiosity. "I think that may be my favorite."

The memory of my mother makes me smile and I almost tell him more. I almost tell him about the day she died and how we went there first. But she didn't get her usual pastries or coffee, and we didn't stay long. I was so upset that she didn't get me my sandwich, but she promised we'd get it tomorrow.

If I hadn't been so young and foolish, I would have known what was happening. How my mother was running from someone she'd spotted. How she ran home for protection, only to find the monster was already there.

God, I miss her. I miss anyone and everyone. I hadn't realized how lonely I'd become.

"Would you like to go home when this is over?" Cross's question distracts me from the thoughts of the past.

"When it's over?" I ask for clarification and I only receive a nod from him.

A deal with the devil. It's all I can think. The war doesn't matter, even if that's what he's hinting at. He'll keep me however long he wants, regardless of what he tells me now.

"You already know the answer to that." They're the only words I give him. It's my turn once more, so I ask him again, "What do I have to do to leave?"

"There is no leaving unless I want you to leave."

"Then why I am here?" The desperation is evident.

"I've already told you. I want you to submit to me. To desire my touch and earn it by kneeling and waiting to obey me. To be mine, in every way."

"You know that would never happen," I say absently. "I'll stay in this room forever or wait for something else to happen. I have nothing but time."

"I'm going to make a change to your routine," Cross says as if it's a threat.

Again, my head falls to the side to look at him, my energy waning. "Is that so?" I ask him, and he quirks a devious grin.

"You'll only eat when I feed you. Bite by bite." His eyes flicker with a heat that should scare me, but it does other things to me that I choose to ignore. "You should have eaten before, songbird. Your defiance is only hurting you."

The thought of him feeding me is something that will haunt me for hours once he's gone, I already know it. It's not just the loneliness that attracts me to Cross. I felt it the moment I saw him.

"I wasn't going to eat anyway," I tell him in a single breath rather than allowing my imagination to get the best of me. I've heard death by starvation is a horrible way to die and I know I'll have to figure out another way. I know I'll cave, just like I already have. As if reading my mind or maybe knowing better, Cross smirks at me, but it's different from the previous ones. There's something almost melancholy about this one.

"You'll eat," he tells me and then stands up without another word. As he turns the doorknob, I close my eyes knowing the bright light is coming. Even with my eyes closed, I can see it. And then it's gone, and once again I'm alone and trapped in the room.

I should feel a touch of ease, knowing he's given me some information I can hold on to. But all I can think about is my mother and the last day I saw her.

She wanted to leave and run away. She begged me to understand. And I cried when she told me, "*Ria, please.*"

I'll never forget the wretched way my name fell from her lips that day. The fatal flaw of any mother is how much her love for her children will blind her. It's my fault. Fresh tears leak down my face and I don't even bother wiping them away as I crawl to the mattress.

It takes a bit longer than usual for him to do it, but with the blanket wrapped tightly around me, the lights in the room go off. Loneliness is my only companion unless I give in to the memories. And I hadn't realized how harmful they can be. My own past is becoming my enemy.

I find myself filled with nothing but regret as sleep takes over.

If only I could go back and not fight her.

If only I could go back and tell her, we can't go home.

CHAPTER 11

Carter

IT's DIFFERENT WHEN I'M IN THE CELL WITH HER. WHEN THERE'S nothing but an isolated war between the two of us. I know she'll break, and she'll love it when she does.

When I'm in there with her, staring her down and watching every small, calculated movement from her, all I feel is the need to bring her to that edge and watch her fall.

I can picture her beautiful hair a tangled mess as I fist it in my hand, taking my pleasure from her even if she'd give it freely. She'll be on her knees, desiring the same things that I do.

It consumes me when the four walls of the cell surround me, but the moment the steel door closes behind me with a finality that another day has passed where I don't have control of her, the desire changes to desperation.

She *has* to submit. To kneel when I walk into her cell and to wait eagerly for my command.

And soon.

I have other plans and I want her to be a part of them. She needs to give in. It starts with a simple kneel.

I'm still reeling from seeing her sweet defiance when the door shuts tight. Slipping the painting back into place, I get a glimpse of my brother as he walks toward me in the hall.

"You're waiting for me?" I ask him, and he matches my pace as we head toward my office.

"I think I know why it's hitting heavier on the edge of the south side, closer to the Romanos." He doesn't waste a second to start talking business.

"The supply?" I ask him for clarification. The drug market is predictable. That's the best part about an addiction. It's steady, rampant, and easily maintained. When demand increases in only one area, there's a reason for it. And I need to know why this shift is so unexpected.

"Romanos have their hands on it. They have to be producing it by the amount they're selling." My blood chills in response to Jase's revelation. My jaw tenses as we make our way down the stairs. Each step only emphasizes the hollow pounding in my ears.

He wanted an ally.

He wanted to do business together.

He's nothing but a liar, a thief, and a spineless prick.

But none of that is news to me.

"He's selling S2L?" I ask him. "Are you sure?" The drug is ours. Ours alone. It was only a matter of time before everyone else wanted it, but instead of getting the details, Romano stole it. The stupid fuck.

"I'm positive," Jase answers me and I imagine Romano's ugly snarl of a smile as I punch his teeth in. I can practically feel the way the tight skin of my knuckles would split as his teeth broke under them. "I got a sample from their streets, took it back and it's definitely our mix. A heavier version than what we got off Malcolm."

"Do you think Romano knows why the pharmacy pulled it and the side effects?" I ask Jase as I push my office door open.

We acquired a banned drug, manipulated it, and just started selling S2L, street name Sweet Lullaby. It was designed to help with anxiety and insomnia. It can aid in weaning off an addiction to harder drugs. But S2L is the most addictive because of the way it calms you, assures you and your entire being that everything is just as it should be and lull you into a deep sleep. Thus, the name, Sweet Lullaby. The undesired side effects were too great to risk… for them. Not for us.

"I think they know exactly what it is," he says with a touch of anger, "seeing as how they fucked with the formula." The door practically slams shut from the weight of his push. He doesn't look me in the eyes until he's seated in the chair opposite mine. It's only when he says the next sentence that I finally fall into mine. "They made it more potent. It's practically lethal with the way it numbs the senses, slowing the heart and forcing the body into a deep sleep."

My thumb brushes against my jawline as I consider what Romano is up to. "He stole our drug; he's selling a version that's deadly on his territory…" I think out loud, not bothering to hide my string of thoughts from Jase.

Jase is the one who got a hold of the drug from an asshole who owed us a debt but had secrets within the industry. Malcolm was useful enough that we let him live. For a little while.

"He's selling on his territory. Sweet Lullaby but the lethal version is going by ST, Sweet Tragedy. He must not have enough, or else we wouldn't see the increase in demand."

"The thing about demand is that those who are addicted are still living."

"Unless it's being used on someone else."

"So, he's selling it as a weapon? Not as a drug?" I have to admit the thought occurred to us as well, but until we have a preventative drug that renders the deadly version useless, I wouldn't dare to even hint at the possibility.

His fingers tap, tap, tap with a nervousness on the armrest. "The thing that doesn't fit though… What doesn't add up… is that there isn't a rise in the death toll. There's no sudden spike in murders or people dying in their sleep."

"They're either buying and not using, or they're selling it elsewhere. Maybe overseas?"

"I think the Romanos aren't keeping up with the production of S2L, they have a small demand, but word got out that we're the suppliers. So, Romano decided to up the ante, make the potent version which got someone's attention. Someone who wants control of the market. Whoever it is, he's buying every drop he can of the potent version, and every bit of ours so he can make the change himself, concentrating it and making an untraceable weapon."

"How could Romano be so fucking stupid?" The words are pushed through my clenched teeth. We sold the drug as a relaxer, a way to ease pain and keep people from ODing on the deadlier shit. It's the perfect way to make an addiction last. And Romano's greed had to fuck it up.

I'm silent as I consider Jase's theory.

"Whoever's gathering it is on his side, not ours. Someone who wants his territory, maybe?" he suggests, and I can only nod in response. Whoever it is isn't doing a good job of hiding their whereabouts and intentions. Unless of course, they wanted it to be known. My thumb brushes along my chin again as I consider every asshole I know who could want Romano's place. Maybe they wanted us to know.

"I want Mick's crew on the south side, tracking the information of every buyer and to find a connection. I want to know who's fucking with it and if they're selling anywhere else."

"It's expensive shit, this potent version. And whoever is buying in bulk has to be waiting to resell."

"Maybe they think Romano will lose the war, and they'll come in to a territory with a built-in high demand, already supplied with the drug?"

Jase nods at my prediction, clucking his tongue and still tapping his finger on the chair. "That's not a problem for us," he adds.

"You think they'd stop at the Romanos?" I question him and like the intelligent fucker he is, he shakes his head, the small grin ticking up his lips. Jase loves a challenge. He lives to snuff out those who think they can threaten what we've worked so fucking hard to build.

"So, we don't tell Romano?" he asks me.

"Not a word. He stole from us." I look him dead in the eye as I come to the conclusion with my brother.

"You still want to do the dinner next week?" he questions me.

Romano thinks it's a celebratory dinner.

Talvery is weak. It's almost a letdown at how easily everything is crumbling around him. There's already a crack within his own factions, or so says the word on the street. Half his crew is taking bribes from Romano. I'm reluctant to let my guard down. Looks from the outside can be deceiving. I know that all too well.

Nonetheless, Romano will come here to this celebratory dinner. And I'll have the utmost enthusiasm as his host and partner in celebrating the fall of his longtime rival. Long enough to lure him in at least.

"Yes." I can't stress my words enough as I stare at the box under the bookshelf on the right side of the room. "Next week he'll be here, at our table, in our home."

"It's not about the war or the drug though, is it?" Jase's question brings my gaze back to him. "It's about her?"

His intuition freezes my blood. I have to remind myself that he's my brother, that he would know because he's been so close for so long. I have to remind myself that there isn't a way another soul could even begin to guess the truth.

"Yes," I reply cautiously as our eyes lock and I wait for his reaction. Once again, I fall prey to the ticking of the clock as he carefully chooses his words. "She's part of it."

"We could give her money and let her run," he offers. And he assumes wrong.

"She'll run right back to her father, and you know it."

"Then let her," Jase says and shrugs as if it's no concern to us if she were to retreat back to her father.

"And have the Romanos and everyone else think we're so weak that we just let a girl walk away?"

"Since when did you start caring what they think?" he asks me, still feigning that this conversation is a casual discussion that means nothing.

"They need to *think* that I don't care what they think. But how they see us matters more than anything. For us to control what they do, we have to know what they think. We have to be able to manipulate it for us to know what they'll do next."

"You can say you grew tired of her." Jase continues to make suggestions and this time it spikes my anger. I've grown tired of him pushing me to let her go, to eliminate her from the equation. She's too valuable to me.

"Never," I answer in a single breath without thinking.

"Never?" Jase asks questioningly, only now dropping his guard, his grip tightening on the leather armrest and letting an inkling of anger show.

"I wanted her... before."

"Before Romano offered her?" Jase's interest is piqued.

I only nod in response, feeling the confession so close to coming to life.

"Why?" he asks me, and I don't answer him. I can't. Instead, I offer him a small truth. "He didn't offer her. I told him it would be her or no one," I say softly, to ensure the words will vanish by the time he can hear them.

"What are you going to do to her?" he asks me again. My brothers keep asking me that and it only pisses me off.

"She has to fear me… for a while." My thumb nervously runs along my bottom lip. "It won't always be like this."

"You need to give me more," he demands, and I quickly spit back, "I don't need to give you shit."

A beat passes and the rage slips into my blood. The memories and everything I've worked for, everything we've become turns to hate and ruin.

"This conversation is over," I tell him. He only smiles. A coy knowing smile, and nods. The tension evaporates and without another word, he leaves the office. Although I know he's left with far more than he gave.

As I watch him leave, the ticking of the clock won't stop. Tick tock. Tick tock. Tick tock. My gaze moves from the box to the laptop with a black screen staring back at me.

Deep breaths. In and out. Deep breaths bring me back to her.

When I flick the monitors back to life, to see what my little songbird is doing, she's already asleep.

It's been so long since these memories have haunted me, but they come back slowly as I turn off the lights in her cell.

Memories that made me. Memories she's a part of, even if she doesn't know.

The memory of the day I learned who Talvery was and what fear could really do to a person.

There comes a point when it doesn't matter what the last punch broke or how much blood you've lost. It's a point where you can't feel anything anymore.

Your vision is blurry, and you know death is so close that you pray for it. It's the only thing that will take it all away.

Nothing makes sense. Even as my head snaps back and more warmth bubbles from my mouth, the pain is nothing. And knowing the end is near, it provides a comfort. The chains holding me to the chair fade away and I can hardly feel them digging into my skin.

But even in all of that, she meant something. I knew it instantly. She had the strength to destroy the hope that it would all end soon.

Her small fists banged on the door that was so close but so far away.

Her voice called out and broke through the fog of reality.

I couldn't hear what she screamed, but it was something so urgent, her father put down the wrench. I remember the heavy metallic sound of it falling onto the floor mixing with her sweet feminine pleas for him to help her through the closed door.

I was so close to everything being over, and she saved me. Even if she doesn't remember it. She never even saw me.

It took years before I let myself think of her again. And of that day.

I almost had an out. I was so close to leaving this life a good soul. Maybe not pure, not perfect, but a better man than I am now and an innocent soul.

She's the reason I lived and turned into this.

I don't just want her at my mercy.

I want everything she has.

I'm not going to stop until I have her and her everything.

CHAPTER 12

Aria

I THINK IT'S BEEN TWO DAYS SINCE CROSS CHANGED THE RULES. IF I'm right, it's been almost two weeks since I've been here. And two full days of not eating anything.

I refuse to eat from his fingers like a dog. I'm not his pet. The way he looks at me like he'd wish for nothing more than for me to kneel between his legs and accept each morsel is riddled with both desire for me and desire for power over me. The combination is heady, and it plays tricks with my mind. I'm addicted to the hunger in his eyes but I'm afraid of what's to come if I give in.

I don't want to submit and kneel in front of him. At least, that's what I keep telling myself. Each ache I have reminds myself of this. As the loneliness stretches and the boredom makes me wonder if I'm going crazy, I have to remind myself. It's always a reminder.

The thoughts make my breathing heavy and my stomach rumble. The sickening part of all of this is that I'm looking forward to him opening the door. I want him to come in tonight like he did last night and the night before. With a silver platter of temptation.

I'm starving and I know I have to give in. I know I will at some point. He's right. I will eat. I'm already praying for him to open the door, even as I curse him and clench my hands into fists, swearing I'll be strong enough to refuse him.

He's going to win. I can feel it.

I'm praying for him to come, so I can have something to eat. Whatever he brings, if he were to come right now, I'd accept. No matter how much I wish it weren't true. I would do anything to eat right now. To eat anything at all.

My eyes lift from the ground to the door as it creaks open. I don't lift my head and I stay on the dirty ground, stiff and unmoving.

I can feel his eyes on me, but I can't look at him. The only thing that holds my attention is the tray balanced in his right hand and held at his chest. I can't see what's on it yet, but I can smell it.

My eyes close slowly and I nearly groan from the sugary scents that flood my lungs. When I finally open my eyes, cued by the sound of him moving the chair across the floor and closer to me, I see it all. I see the tasty treats that will be responsible for my pathetic undoing.

The tray is full of the sweetest things. Berries and chunks of mango and fresh pineapple.

It's all brightly colored and arranged beautifully. Like I said, a silver platter of temptation.

"How's your hand?" Cross asks me and it's only then that I even acknowledge him.

"Fine." My short answer is rewarded with him pulling the tray closer into his lap. "I think it's bruised," I offer him in an attempt to give him what he wants.

"You were banging your fist on that door for over forty minutes." My teeth grit at his response.

"Well, you heard me at least," I say, although I can't deny that it hurts. I'm so fucking alone. And tired and sore and aching with pains. But so alone more than anything else.

"I did," is all he says.

There's a routine that comes with Carter Cross. He likes things to be done a certain way, maybe so that it can appear that he's predictable but I'd much sooner think it's so he can force my own behavior to be predictable for him.

In these sessions, the ones where food is offered, he attempts the semblance of a conversation before offering food. And today, I know I'll talk back. I know I'll do what he wants. I'm that desperate.

"You're dirty," he tells me with what seems like sincere sympathy. "You don't wash yourself like I'd hoped you would."

I bite my tongue at the perverted comments, but I can't hold it all in. "I'm not a dog to be bathed." I can't hide the anger. I should fake my tone like he does, but I choose not to. He'll feed me regardless. I hope. He only smiles at me in response and it nearly makes me back away from him. Not because of the way he's looking at me, but because of how my body reacts to the smile. How he seems to enjoy it when I don't hold back. It's dangerous. *He's* dangerous.

"You're tired."

"It's difficult to sleep on the floor." Even as I answer him, I can feel how heavy the bags are under my eyes.

"There's a mattress at least," he quips, and those piercing eyes stare deeper into me like he can see through the wall of defense. Just the way he looks at me makes me question everything.

Time evades me as I stare back at him, feeling those same walls crumble deep inside of me. I try to suppress the hate I have for him in this moment, just so I can get this over with and eat.

"You look weak, songbird."

"You keep calling me that," I bite back.

"I've never called you weak," he says, and his answer is just as stern as mine.

"I meant 'songbird.' You keep calling me songbird." My voice cracks. I don't want him to call me anything. Not my name, not a sweet nickname. It doesn't reflect how he truly sees me. It's meant to weaken me, make me soften. "Stop calling me that."

"No," he says in a hardened voice. "Now come here, songbird Come kneel in front of me and let me feed you."

This is the second part of his routine and the one where I've told him to go fuck himself over and over again. But today, I slowly move my body and get on my hands and knees. I swallow my pride and it hurts. It physically hurts. I didn't know pride was a spiked ball until I move one knee in front of the other. My body is hot with embarrassment and shame as I stop at his feet.

I can't open my eyes until his rough hand brushes against my jaw. I wish I didn't feel the need to lean into him. Loneliness consumes me every day. If I could pause this moment and pretend I'm somewhere else, with someone else, I'd lean into his strong touch. I'd allow myself to enjoy his warmth and comfort.

But as it is, I'm staring into the dark eyes of a man who's held me like this before. And then so quickly shown how easily he could hurt me.

Swallowing thickly, I wait for the third part. Only seconds until he tells me to open my mouth.

As if reading my mind, Cross lets his thumb brush along the seam of my lips. It's a gentle caress that ignites something primitive in me, heating my core and making my heart beat furiously inside my chest. My knees inch forward, obeying the command from my body to move closer to him.

Closer to the man who controls my freedom. Closer to the gentle touch.

"Open," he commands me, and I feel my lips part of their own accord.

My eyes stay closed until his hand moves away, and his warmth is replaced with the chill of the air in the cell.

My heart flickers with fear until I watch him pick up a chunk of strawberry and lift it to my lips. I'd be ashamed at how greedily I eat the small piece of fruit if only consuming it didn't make me feel as though I'm starved. The sweetness falls into a pit of hollow hunger pains. And again, my body moves closer to him.

He doesn't say anything or hint at anything other than his desire to keep feeding me. And I accept every piece with a hunger that only seems to intensify. My hands find their way to his knees, gripping him as I swallow the next piece he's offering me.

It takes me far too long to realize I'm touching him. His groan of approval is what cues my awareness, but as I try to pull away, he does the same to the fruit in his grasp.

"Stay." He gives me the simple command, and so I do. I cling to him for more.

The part that's truly shameful though is how much hearing him tell me to stay made me crave more of him. His hand on mine, watching him watch me.

A moment passes where I realize he knows my forbidden thoughts.

My greatest fear is that he'll voice them and bring them to life. I force my fingers to dig deeper into his leg and I open my lips wider, silently begging for more, so I can hide the temptation that grows hotter between us.

I think he's doing it slowly on purpose. Picking up the bits of sweet fruit and taking his time before he slips them between my lips.

"Open wider," he commands me and it's only because my stomach pains with the need to eat that I obey him, that's what I tell myself. I close my eyes, holding back every other thought.

"Look at me," he commands as I swallow the small morsel and his strong hand cups my chin, forcing my head up. The juice from his fingers wets the underside of my chin in his grasp. He's so close, his dark eyes swirling with an intensity that holds my gaze captive. "You're so strong," he tells me, and I hate him for it. "You don't believe me, but you are."

The rough pad of his thumb brushes against my bottom lip and I almost bite him, just to spite him. To prove to him that whatever he assumes I'm thinking is all in his head. I catch the broad smile growing on his face as I look back up at him.

He offers me another piece and I take it in my mouth. I have to wait for him to pull his fingers away, but he doesn't.

My gaze moves back to his and he lowers his lips to my neck, his fingers still in my mouth and the juice of the fruit tasting even sweeter. His short stubble brushes my collarbone and then he whispers in my ear, "See how strong? You'd love to bite me, but you know how to survive."

His hot breath tickles my neck and sends goosebumps down my body. Shamefully, my nipples harden and my back bows slightly. "Such a good girl, Aria," Cross says, and I pull away from him, leaving the fruit between his fingers and brushing my ass against the cement as I scoot backward, putting distance between us.

The fear is alive within me, but it's changed. I fear what I'm capable of and how much I'd enjoy it.

The vision of him pinning me down on the ground flashes before my eyes and cruelly, it only makes me hotter. I swallow thickly, feeling my cheeks heat with a blush.

Cross doesn't move from his chair. "You're all done?" he asks me. I can't look him in the eye. I don't even trust myself to speak. Maybe this is what it's truly like to be broken.

"Is it because you've finished, or because you're wet for me?" he asks me in a husky voice that only adds to my desire for him.

"Fuck you," I say beneath my breath, narrowing my eyes and letting my blunt nails dig into the cement.

Cross lets the trace of a smile play on his lips, but it doesn't reach his eyes as he stands up, towering over me. "I told you I wanted you, Aria. And I get everything I want. Just remember that."

CHAPTER 13

Carter

SHE HASN'T EATEN, SHE'S BARELY MOVED SINCE SHE GAVE IN LAST night. I've come in twice since then and both times she's denied me even though in three days all she's eaten is a handful of fruit.

I can feel the tension between us. I know she's at war with it as much as I am. But she spends her nights screaming and barely sleeping. The little bit of progress during the day is erased and there's nothing I can do about it.

She's going to cave again and I can feel it on the horizon. I've never been so eager to come into this cell as I am today.

I have to hide my smile as she slinks from the mattress to the floor. She never stays on the mattress when I come in. At least, she hasn't yet.

My heart beats hard as I watch her expression fall.

There's no tray tonight. No offering for her.

It's easy to see her breathing pick up as she registers I'm here for something else.

I intentionally let the chair drag along the floor as I make my way to her.

"I don't have anything to say," she tells me as I sit down only a few feet away from her. Far enough so that she can crawl to me and kneel. The crawling part I'm not interested in. She decided to do that on her own, but I don't care how I get her on her knees in front of me. So long as she submits.

"That's interesting that you would start the conversation then, isn't it?" She doesn't respond. Her collarbone looks more prominent today than it ever has. I couldn't see it on the monitors, but three days of barely eating is starting to show and I don't like it. Starved is not how I want her.

I should feel remorse, not anger at the observation.

"Why make it harder on yourself?" I question her with a deep tone of disapproval.

And once again, she doesn't answer.

"You'll cave again. You can't help yourself. You realize that, don't you?" She's a smart girl. Anyone with any bit of intelligence knows that starvation is painful, and the instinct to survive will kick in over pride.

"Just let me go," she says weakly, brushing under her eyes and hiding the tears. So close to breaking. So, fucking close.

"I'm getting tired of hearing you make that request."

"Then both of us are tired," she says softly, picking at her dirty clothes. I would give her everything if only she'd obey me.

"You wanted me," I remind her, and she huffs a pathetic sound of disgust.

Her eyes narrow as she looks me in the eyes and tells me, "You aren't what I want."

"What did you want then?" I ask her, leaning forward in my seat so quickly that I startle her. I'm only inches away and so close I can feel the heat from her body. She turns away from me, looking toward nothingness on the blank wall.

"Answer me," I say and there's little patience in my voice. My body tenses as I move forward in my seat so I'm as close to her as I can be. I don't like what she does to me, but even more, I don't like that I don't know what to do with her. I don't want her like this. I need her to break now, her mind before her body.

She looks at me with a stare of contempt before barely speaking the words, "I don't know what I wanted."

"You wanted me to fuck you," I tell her in a voice intended to be seductive. I practically whisper. "I'd feed you, care for you, fuck you and put you to bed used and sated." She's silent as I move back to a relaxed position in the uncomfortable chair. "That's what you wanted."

"I just wanted my fucking notebook back!" she screams at me with a bite of anger I know must've hurt. Swallowing thickly, she looks away from me as her eyes turn glossy.

My heart pounds hard, just once, then stops for a moment as she wipes her eyes.

"You want a notebook?" I ask her, although I don't know what the fuck she's talking about.

Her chest rises and falls steadily as she looks at me. Each breath deepening the dip in her collarbone. "Tell me," I command her.

"My drawing pad," she murmurs softly, anger and contempt forgotten. "That's what led me to the bar where those assholes got me," she whispers with defeat. "I just wanted my drawing pad back."

"A specific one?" I ask as my brow raises slightly. It's not going to happen. I can get her a new one, but I'm not risking what's already been set in motion to find something she's left behind.

"Yes," she whispers and parts her lips to tell me something else, but I can't and won't hunt down any of her possessions.

"It's gone," I say flatly, cutting off her words.

I watch as she swallows and note the way the sadness returns to her eyes. "Any would do." Her eyes search my face warily as she sits back against the bed, making it dip with her weight. She's frail with a look of submission brimming close to the surface.

"A drawing pad. What else do you want?" My fingers itch to trace along her jaw and force her to look at me. To force her to make this easier on herself and both of us.

She peeks up at me through only slits, her dark lashes barely letting me see any of her eyes. But in the small bit she offers me, I see nothing but rage.

"You have something to say?"

"Fuck you," she spits.

I've never felt the urge to kiss her until now. In filthy clothes and all. It's quiet between us as I imagine gripping the nape of her neck and taking her lips with mine. She'd bite me. I know she would because she thinks she should, and that only makes me harder.

"That mouth of yours. That's what's going to get you into trouble."

"As if I'm not in trouble already," she answers me through clenched teeth, lifting her chin at me.

"You will be if you don't obey me." Each word comes out heavy, making my chest clench with a tightness of what's to come. My breathing is shallow, and my blood burns a little hotter.

I can see her lips twitch with the need to speak, but she bites her tongue.

This is the version of Aria that I want. The raw anger of knowing and accepting that she's at my mercy.

"Tell me what you really think, Aria," I say softly although the words ring out loudly in my ears. My gaze is locked on hers. My blood rushing in my ears. All I can do is wait for her.

One beat. Two beats of my heart before she whispers in a cracked voice, "You're a monster."

"And why is that?"

"Because of what you want from me," she says quiety, but she doesn't break eye contact.

"What is it that I want from you?" I ask her as I grip the edge of the chair tighter.

"You want to fuck me." She doesn't hesitate to answer but the anger in her expression morphs to pain as she rips her gaze away from mine.

"Of course, I want to fuck you," I tell her in as calm a voice as I can manage. My gaze slips down to her curves and I have to force them back up to see her doe eyes back on mine as she scoots farther back on the bed. She's searching for comfort and safety, but all she's doing is making me want to pursue her.

I lean forward, resting my elbows on my knees. "The second I saw you, I wanted you." My confession comes out a whisper and the memory of her weeks after that night happened years ago flashes through my mind. I had to know the face of the angel who'd saved me. If only she had known then what she was doing, if only she'd known I wasn't worth saving. The hate and love I've had for her has warred for years within me.

Silence separates us for a moment. And then another.

"Just get it over with," she breathes the words but doesn't look up. The tone of defeat rings false.

"Is that because you want me too, but you don't have the courage to admit it?" I dare to challenge her and again that anger comes back full force.

"Fuck. You." She leans forward as she says each word, practically spitting them. And the rage and defiance only make my cock more eager to thrust deep inside of her.

"You will, little songbird." Lust pumps through my blood as she inches back on the bed yet again, her gaze fixed next to me as if she's watching my every move but doesn't want me to know it.

That only makes the hint of a smirk on my lips grow.

The chair scoots back as I stand and the sound of it scratching the floor frightens Aria. She sits up a little straighter, a little stiffer and watches me with wide eyes as I take two steps closer to her.

"You want to get it over with?" I ask her as I reach for my belt. I want her to see how hard I am for her. And teach her a lesson.

My belt slips through the loops of my pants, leaving the sound of leather brushing against the fabric to sing in the air. My blood is laced with adrenaline and lust as I watch her breathe heavier and faster.

The metal of the buckle clinks on the ground as it lands and then I unzip my pants. A flush travels up Aria's chest and into her cheeks.

"Come here," I give her the small command with the bit of breath left in my lungs as I grip my thick erection through my pants and she watches. I swear her lips part and her thighs clench as she watches.

Her wide eyes dart from my cock to my eyes.

"Come here," I tell her again when she doesn't move. I know she wants me. Maybe not like this, but I have to show her what power she has. Until she submits, all she has is power over me. "Get down on your knees in front of me," I add and palm myself again. "Aria." Her name comes out hard on my lips, but dripping with sin and desire as I add, "I fucking want you."

I don't miss the small gasp from her lips as she hesitates another second.

I watch every small change in her expression. From how her nails dig into the mattress, to how her body tenses and makes the bed creak as she inches forward as if she's going to listen to me. She swallows so loudly I can hear it as she slowly climbs off the bed. She stands on weak legs before dropping slowly in front of me, down onto her knees.

My pulse quickens but I don't know how. All the blood in my body feels like it's in my dick.

"If I leaned down and shoved my hand between your thighs," I ask her, holding back a groan from the thought, "how wet and hot would your cunt feel right now?"

Her eyes widen, and she leans back, but with the way she's seated, with her knees under her, she can't lean back far without being off balance.

"Do you know what it will feel like when I finally shove myself deep inside your tight little cunt?" I ask as my dick pulses with need and I have to stroke it once more.

She breathes out heavily, nearly violently and avoids my gaze.

"You're going to scream my name like your life depends on my mercy." I stroke myself again and again. Fuck, I'm so eager for her touch my dick is throbbing so hard it hurts. "I won't show you mercy, Aria, I'm going to fuck you like you're mine to ruin."

She whimpers and struggles to remain still in front of me. Her thighs clench as I kick the chair behind me, so I can crouch down in front of her.

Her hazel eyes are wide and filled with desire.

"I want to give you everything," I whisper as I lean forward, letting my lips trail along her jaw. A ripple of unease runs through me as I realize the truth in those words.

She shivers, and I watch her nails dig into her thighs. "You have to tell me what you want, and when I ask you how badly you want my cock, you better tell me the truth."

I pull away, letting my fingers trace down the right side of her face, and then lower, to her neck and collarbone. Then lower to her chest. "I want to see how you react when I pinch and bite these," I tell her as my fingers travel to the peaks of her breasts.

"Do you think you'll enjoy it?" I ask her. And for the first time, she admits a small truth, nodding her head once and then ripping her eyes from me.

Her breathing is chaotic, and I know she's ashamed.

"I desperately want to feel you cum on my cock," I admit to her, whispering in her ear since she still has her head turned. "Tell me what you want."

All I can hear is our tense breathing mix in the hot air between us.

"Tell me, songbird," I say, willing her to give in.

Time seems to stretch on forever.

"A drawing pad." Blinking away the haze in her eyes and still denying what she truly wants, she utters useless words.

And I leave her just like that, wanting and panting and flushed with need.

She'll learn to ask for what she wants. Or she'll stay here forever.

CHAPTER 14

Aria

I'VE NEVER FELT LIKE THIS BEFORE.

Like there's nothing left of me but a shell of a weak and pathetic person. I'm on the edge of loathing myself and the way my body begs me to give in to Cross.

But most of all, I pity myself and that's what's driving the hate.

My father isn't coming. Nikolai isn't coming.

I was worried that they were dead, but Carter told me yesterday that they're still alive and the war is only getting started. I don't know if he's lying to me or not. If he wanted to offer me hope so he could crush it. I don't know anything anymore and nothing gives me hope of getting out of here.

Even as the thought hits me, I crumple forward and bury my face in my grimy hands. They smell of dirt but as I struggle to breathe and maintain any sense of composure, I don't give a damn. No matter how many times I bathe myself with the warm water that waits for me when I wake up, I feel dirty. The kind of dirty that doesn't wash away.

I'm alone. A prisoner. And I don't see any way out of here. There's no white knight planning on barging in here. I'm not worth it. If I was, they would find me, they would come for me. They would save me and make Cross pay for keeping me here to starve and torment with thoughts of being his fuck toy.

Fate sent a dark knight after me instead. With dinged and scratched armor and a taste for something that I shouldn't crave. My face is too hot when I pull my hands away, calming my breath and leaning my head against the wall behind me.

Exhaustion has taken over and I know it's because I don't eat.

But I could, a little voice whispers in the crevices of my mind.

The same dark corners where the memories of yesterday send a warmth through my body.

My teeth dig into my lip as I remember how his skin felt against mine. How everything felt. It was… everything.

Like electricity sparking through every nerve ending all at once, with a heat and fluidity that made me want to rock my body.

Yes, the dark knight is good at what he does. He's damn good at making me want to cave and give in to both his desires and mine. I lick my lower lip, wincing at the cracked skin as my back stiffens and I glare at the steel door that refuses to budge.

As if knowing I was thinking about him and what he could do to me, the door to this prison opens and my hardened expression shifts to one of worry, curiosity, and eagerness.

I hadn't realized how dark it was in the room until the bright light from just beyond the cracked door makes me wince. My tired eyes sting with the need to sleep.

I suck in a small breath, but I don't cover my eyes or leave them closed for long. Pressed against the wall, I wait with bated breath until my eyes adjust.

I expect to hear the door close, but it stays open.

And the man I thought was coming in? It's not him. It's not Carter.

Thump, thump. My heart slams hard in my chest as Jase takes a step inside. Still the door stays open and my eyes have to glance at what's beyond it.

A hallway and nothing discernable, but I know it's freedom. That barely ajar door leads to freedom.

"Now don't make me regret this." The deep voice seems to echo in the small room and I swallow thickly. It's only when my throat stings and I feel as if I could choke that I realize how dry my throat is.

"Jase?" I chance a word and it makes the man smile. I remember him from the night I was taken. That's what Carter called him. He put the rag to my mouth. He's one of them.

He gives me a sexy lopsided grin that should frighten me. But instead, his charming looks put me at ease. He must be younger than Carter. His eyes are softer. But I remember them all too well, for the wrong reasons.

"You remember me?" he asks me and takes a step forward, grabbing the chair that Carter uses. He's just as tall as Carter, but leaner and in only a white t-shirt and faded jeans, he looks less threatening.

But looks are deceiving.

My lips part to speak, but I can't get out a word. A million questions are running through my head.

Why are you here? Where's Carter?

Are you going to let me go?

I can only nod.

"You're looking a little on the rough side," he says and then his voice drifts off as he looks behind him. I follow his gaze to the open door, but quickly my sights are back on his and the chair in his hand that scratches along the concrete. Turning it backward, he sits on it. As if he's deliberately acting casual.

He is. This is a setup for something. In my head, my words are strong and demanding, but when forced out they sound weak and desperate.

"What do you want?" I swallow, and this time the scratchy sensation in my throat is almost soothed. But the pain in my chest grows with every thump in my heart.

Jase breathes in deep and turns to look back over his shoulder, toward my freedom, and then points to it with his thumb. "He doesn't seem to be taking care of you, is he?"

Thump. Another thump.

"Is this a trick?" My question is meager at best.

Jase's chuckle comes from deep in his chest and his smile widens, showing his perfect teeth.

He shakes his head. "No tricks. I just know he can be stubborn and sometimes he gets in his own way." He's being far too kind. There isn't an ounce of me that trusts him.

My gaze falls to my feet. My dirty feet and scraped knees. And then to my nails, the dirt beneath my fingers that doesn't seem to leave.

My teeth dig into my lower lip to keep me from spilling all the desperate pleas begging me to come up, but it hurts. "What does he want?"

"You." Jase's voice is soft and at ease. As if the answer was simple.

"What about me?" For the first time, my voice is as strong as I imagine it would be.

Resting an elbow on the back of the chair, Jase places his chin in his hand and considers me. He parts his lips but then closes his mouth.

"Just tell me," I beg him.

"I don't know. This…" Jase trails off, then clears his throat and looks away from me for a moment before looking me back in the eyes to continue, "isn't something he does."

"This?" I ask sarcastically, and like a madwoman, a grin forms on my face and I swear I could laugh. "Which part of this?" I dare to spit back at him. And for the first time since Jase has walked in here, pure fear pricks down my spine at the sight of his expression.

That cold, heartless look in his eyes is there and gone just as quickly as it came.

He stares ahead of him, at the cinder block wall and ignores me for a moment. I almost speak but I don't know what to say. And even if I asked the questions that keep me up at night, Jase wouldn't know the answers.

Mindlessly, I pick under my nails. Maybe if I begged him, he'd let me go. The huff of a genuine, but sarcastic laugh gets Jase's attention. I can feel his eyes on me, but I don't look up until he speaks.

"Carter said to buy you a drawing pad. But I thought maybe you'd want something else as well?"

"Sleeping pills," I answer him without thinking twice. I'm hungry, but more than that, I need to sleep. "It's hard to sleep in here."

When I peek up at him, Jase is looking at me like I'm trying to fool him and that thumping in my chest beats harder and faster. "I need to sleep," I beg him. "I take them at home. That or wine some nights. Please, I'm not trying to drug anyone or OD or anything. I just need to sleep, please." My voice cracks and that pathetic feeling that plagued me only moments before he walked through the door comes rushing back to me, hard. It nearly makes me bury my head between my knees with shame.

"I just want to sleep," I plead.

"Sleeping pills… any particular brand?" Jase's question eases the anxiety slightly.

Composing myself as best as I can, I brush my hair behind my ear and answer him, "I've tried a lot of them. There's a pink box at the drugstore. I forget the name," I say then close my eyes tight, trying to remember it. Trying to picture the box that sits on my nightstand.

They open quickly at the sound of the chair scratching on the floor.

But Jase is just leaning back, grabbing his cell phone and typing into it.

"Do you want anything else?"

"Tarot cards," I blurt out without really thinking and the expression on Jase's face tells me that I'm being stupid or naïve or weird. I don't know. I mean, even if I am losing my mind I do realize it's an odd thing to ask for. "I've been bored out of my mind and I like to think with them. It's just something I like." With each sentence, my words come out softer.

Every day I read my cards. The damn things didn't tell me this was coming though.

"Maybe clothes?" Jase asks me, giving me a pointed look and my cheeks flame with embarrassment.

"Clothes would be nice." I haven't thought much about my actual clothes; I know I'm dirty and covered in filth. The only place I've sat or slept is on this tiny mattress and I know I smell.

"I could use a lot of things-"

Jase cuts me off. "I'll get you some toiletries and you know… those things."

I nod my head, swallowing down every bit of humiliation that threatens to consume me.

"You're very nice for a prison guard," I tell him although I stare straight ahead at the empty corner of the room.

He huffs a short, humorless laugh and asks, "Food?"

"Carter said he has to be the one to feed me," I answer Jase immediately and then close my eyes as my empty stomach tightens with pain. I should have eaten before. I have to be smart. But how many times have I told myself that, only to end up in the same place with no change?

"That sounds like something he would say."

Everything hurts at this moment. My body from exhaustion, my heart from hopelessness. Starvation is only third on my list.

"What else would Carter say?" I ask him, just to continue talking. To get to know him. To make him feel like I want him to stay. My heart flickers with the hope that he may hold the key to me leaving.

"Carter would say he's sorry it had to be this way." I'd laugh at Jase's words if they didn't hurt me the way they do.

"I don't think I believe that," I nearly whisper.

"He never wanted any of this," Jase tells me. "He was only a kid when everything escalated, and it was kill or be killed." The silence stretches as I imagine a younger version of Carter, one who hadn't been hardened by hate and death.

"You always have a choice," I manage to speak, although I find it ironic as I sit in this cell, without a single choice of my own.

"It's a nice thought, isn't it?" Jase offers. There's no sarcasm, no sense of anger or sadness. Only matter-of-fact words.

"I'd like to leave this room," I tell him although it comes out a question. As Jase nods, hope rises inside of me.

"It will happen," Jase says. "I know it will."

"Would you let me go outside at least? Or by a window for some fresh air?" Jase tilts his head and narrows his eyes as if to ask me if I think he's stupid.

"I promise I wouldn't run or anything like that. I swear." My throat tightens as he considers me.

"I'll see what I can do," is all he says to my racing heart. But it's something. It's a tiny piece of hope.

"Why are you being nice to me?" I stare into his dark eyes, willing him to answer me but inside, I hope for a lie. I want him to tell me everything is going to be okay. That he's going to get me out of here. But it's all wishful thinking.

"I'm not a nice guy, Aria, so get that out of your head." He stands abruptly and then looks back at me as he opens the door wider, so he can leave.

My blood pounds in my ears at the sight of the wide open door, with Jase's figure blocking it. His shadow fades into the darkness of the room.

Smart. I repeat it over again. Be smart.

Now is not the time. *Be his friend.* The thought hisses and I listen. He could help me. He could have mercy on me where Carter doesn't.

"I'm just following Carter's orders."

I only nod once and force myself to look elsewhere. Anywhere but toward the false sense of freedom beyond the door. He'll be back. Next time I'll be more prepared.

And with that, I'm left alone again.

CHAPTER 15

Carter

THREE HOURS HAVE PASSED, AND EACH HOUR SHE'S MORE AND more comfortable.

She hasn't stopped drawing since Jase left the cell. And I haven't taken my eyes off of her. There's only one camera in the room and without being able to zoom in, it's hard to see her features.

A pile of clothes and her blanket are neatly stacked and folded on the bed. But she stays on the floor, scribbling away. One page after another as if she's obsessed and unable to stop.

I need to know what she's writing down. Especially if it's some sort of account of what's happened in the last few days. A message, maybe? Maybe it has something to do with why she screams in her sleep nearly every night.

Unease creeps up my spine at the memories. I'm not surprised the first thing she asked for were sleeping pills. I can't fucking sleep anymore either. Every other night, she cries out in terror and it's only getting worse.

I thought things would change after the other day.

Another paper flies across the floor, but before its fluttering has even stopped, she's already sketching on the page that was beneath it.

Change is necessary. Even if I have to force it.

The walk from my office to the cell takes too fucking long. My fists clench tighter and my heart beats faster as I get closer.

I keep the door open and leave the chair where it is this time.

As she scoots back onto her ass and away from the piles of paper to get away from me as I approach, I lower myself to them, crouching down and picking up the closest one.

There are still a few feet between us, but the expression on Aria's face is of complete fear. Not the defiance I've grown to expect.

"Caught you off guard?" I ask her, cocking a brow. Maybe she thinks I've come to steal her gifts, or maybe the lack of food reminds her of what happened the other night. I know she ate every bit of that tray Jase gave her with her new possessions earlier today.

I wonder if she thinks it's a secret he kept from me.

"You look scared," I add when she doesn't answer my initial question. Her doe eyes are wide, and the colors stir with so much thought and curiosity.

She doesn't answer me. She looks like she isn't even breathing as her eyes glance from the paper in my hand to the open door.

"Don't think about running, Aria. I don't want to have to take these away the second you got them."

Slowly, her chest rises and falls. Her stiff body loosens although she stays back. With her head lowered, she only peeks up at me. It's an interesting difference, the way she looks at me compared to my brother. I fucking hate it. But fear and control are everything. One day Jase will see that.

With my jaw hardened at the thought, I look down at the paper before turning it over in my hand to see what she's drawn. It's upside down at first and it takes me a moment to realize that.

It's drawn with pen, but it's beautiful. Fine little lines and sketches that depict a bleeding heart with three knives stabbed through it. The background is a storm and the ink smears only add to the emotion clearly evident on the paper. Although the knives seem to pierce through the heart easily, the rain behind it is so violent, it detracts from the knives a little.

"What is this?" I ask her without looking at her. I know she's looking at me; I can feel her careful gaze. She doesn't like to look at me when I'm looking at her. Although it's a habit I need to break, I'm more concerned with getting answers than obedience.

"The three of swords," she answers in a small voice and it beckons me to look back at her. For a moment we share a gaze, but then she drops it, focusing on the paper in my hands.

"One of your tarot cards?" I ask her and then straighten the paper in my hand, noticing how it resembles a card.

"Yes. Jase said he bought me a deck online but until they arrive I thought I would draw them myself."

I consider her for a moment. Of everything she could ask for, of everything she could be doing at this moment, this is what she chose. "Why?"

"I like to think about things and it helps me." She nervously picks at the edge of her dirty shirt where a thread has come undone. "It's been lonely, and I haven't been able to think of anything new. It was just something…" her voice trails off and she takes in a shuddering breath. Weeks of doing absolutely nothing but living with your demons would haunt and break the strongest of minds. But she's survived.

"Do your clothes not fit?"

"They do, I just get dirty doing this. So, I thought…" she pauses to take in a short breath and then another. "I just wanted to take care of this, and then I'd planned to change and try to clean myself up."

Nodding, I hand the paper back to her asking, "What does it mean?"

She's hesitant to reach out and take it, but when she does, her fingers trace the edges of the knives. "The three of swords represents rejection, loneliness, heartbreak…" Her words aren't saddened by the information, merely matter-of-fact.

I wonder if she's lying. If the one card that she's drawn I happened to pick up, would really mean those things or if she's toying with me. She could be trying to weaken my resolve by gaining sympathy. It will never happen.

"But yours was reversed," she says, and it cuts through my thoughts of her intention.

"And what does that mean?" I ask her, expecting her to spit back that I'm the one causing it all. For her to blame all of this on me. And in so many ways it is my fault, but she's to blame as well and she doesn't even know it.

"Forgiveness," she whispers the word and then slowly inches closer to pick up each of the fallen papers, dozens of them, gathering them together and avoiding me at all costs.

The word resonates for a moment, lingering in the space between us and striking something deep inside of me.

My blood pressure rises as my eyes search her face for an indication as to what she's getting at. But she doesn't look at me and her body seems to cower more with each passing second.

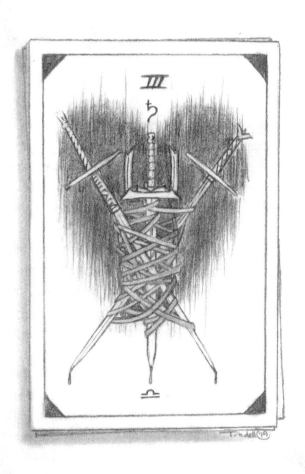

The moment passes, and she neatly arranges the stack in front of her and still doesn't look up at me.

Stubborn girl. The familiar tic in my jaw begins to contract as I wait another moment. And then another before she looks up at me through her thick lashes. Instead of seeing disinterest, resentment, or whatever I was expecting, all I see is the unspoken plea for me to let her have this small bit of happiness.

But nothing in this life is free. And she should know better than that.

"When I come in here, I want you to kneel for me."

She flinches as she realizes what I've said and as her head lowers, the dip in her collarbone seems to deepen to a level that sickens me.

She's resistant to obeying, but she needs to understand. There is an expectation both of us need to meet. And what's been done can't be taken back. That's not an option. "I admire your strength. I do." I talk with her eyes on my back as I stalk to the metal chair at the far wall. I debate on leaving it there and giving her space. But that intention is quickly forgotten.

Picking up the chair, I take it back to where she's still seated, shaking her head as her shoulders hunch in.

"You keep saying I'm strong and I have to admit I don't get your humor." I'm taken aback by the severity of her tone and the venom that veils each syllable as she speaks. She offers me a smile that wavers and then adds, "Did you let him give it all to me so you could simply take it away?" Maybe the small taste of what used to be and what she could so easily have is what she needed to remember her defiance and ignite the spark between us again.

I'd love for her to fight me, but I'll only allow it after she submits.

"I'll do as I see fit," I answer simply, and she refuses to look back at me, her fingers tracing each of the papers. "All you have to do is obey me and I'll give you everything you need."

"I'd rather die." Her hazel eyes simmer with indignation as she waits for my answer. "You can have it back."

I take my time, sitting on the chair in front of her. Towering over her small frame, I lean forward and speak calmly. "My songbird, it's one thing to have the balls to say that. I respect it. But it's another to go through with it. You've already obeyed twice. And I didn't ask much, did I?"

She huffs in a tone that's both weak and strong. A manner that reflects her tortured state. So close to having what she wants and needs, and yet so close to losing everything.

"It was a cruel joke, wasn't it?" Her eyes narrow as she gazes at the door like it beckons her.

"I don't joke, Aria. Your life belongs to me. Everything you will ever get for the rest of your existence will come from me." My words come out harsh and irritated. I'm sick and fucking tired of her denying both of us. "Get. On. Your. Knees."

"Fuck you," she spits out, and instantly my fingers nearly wrap around her throat as the rough pad of my thumb rests against her lips. I can feel the rush of her blood in her neck as I grip her tightly, her gasp filling the air along with the sound of the chair scraping from the rapid movement forward.

She stiffens with my touch but she doesn't protest, staring back at me with that burning expression as I tighten my grasp. Her breath comes out with a shudder, but she stares back at me expectantly, waiting for what I'll do next.

My heart hammers and my dick stiffens with each passing second that she holds my heated gaze. I see the moment she realizes that her hands are on my waist. Pulling herself toward me, not pushing me away.

Her eyes spark and I nearly crash my lips against hers, urging for more. Instead, I leave her there, letting a low hum of approval fall from my lips so she knows I know exactly what she's thinking.

A fire ignites between us as she grips me tighter, so tight the sound of her nails scratching against my pants is all I can hear.

"You think you shouldn't do it, simply because you've been taught it's wrong. But is that what you really want?"

"I don't want you," she says breathily, not even attempting to hide her desire.

"I won't let you ride my cock until you tell me how badly you want to cum on it." I hold her fiery gaze as I ask, "Do you understand me?"

Her body sways slightly as she holds back a strangled groan of lust.

"Humor me, Aria. I already know you're strong."

"You make me weak." Her voice breaks and the tension from the other day returns in full force. She steadies her trembling lip between her teeth.

"Is that what you're afraid of? Being weak?"

She nods her head slightly, ever so slightly. And I can see the last bit of her walls crumble for me. Crashing down to the ground in small, insignificant piles of rubble.

"I don't want you weak." I lean forward, whispering against her lips, "I want you mine."

Her eyes close and her body bends forward; she rests nearly her entire weight on me. "I will never submit to you," she says, and her words are a weak confession. As if she hates their existence.

She's close. So close. I need to offer her something.

Hope. The offer of hope is something a desperate person can never afford to pass up.

"I made a deal I shouldn't have. But I need to go through with it for as long as I have to. And it has to appear that I've done what would be expected. You're going to help me and then I'll give you whatever you want."

"What do you need me to—"

"Obey me," I say, cutting her off. "Kneel when I enter and do as I wish." My hands tingle with the sensation of feeling her so close to caving. They clench and unclench at my side.

Time passes in slow ticks as she pulls herself away from me. She can try to pretend she has somewhere else to go. But I'm her only way out of this. And eventually, she'll beg me for something. She. Will. Beg.

"Anything?" she asks, and she already knows the answer. "Like my freedom?"

"Almost anything." I don't lie to her.

"There's nothing else—" she starts, but I cut her off. "There's always something else." My words are sharp at first but I correct myself.

"There's always something else," I repeat and then add as I stand up to leave, "It's something you so desperately need, but you don't even see it."

CHAPTER 16

Aria

PART OF WHAT KEEPS ME FROM GIVING IN TO CARTER AND THE feelings that have been taking over my every waking moment is obvious.

The fear of the past returning. The truth in the terrors that devour my nights.

And the nightmares I remember of a past monster erase everything I've felt for Carter. There is nothing that will change that.

Sometimes it's the feeling of Stephan's hands on me that wake me up screaming. It's been so long since I've felt it. Or at least since I've been aware of it.

It used to be every single night. I couldn't sleep at all without seeing his face. Without feeling him rip me away from my mother as I begged her to stay with me. She was already gone though. Even as a child I knew she was dead.

He'd killed her.

The sleeping pills the doctor gave me at my father's request worked for a little while. Then I stopped and even though everyone else would say I was screaming, I didn't remember. I couldn't remember a single dream. Nothing but darkness as I slept.

It's come back to me though in the last few months. Even the pills can't dull the nightmares anymore. They don't stop them from lingering once my eyes have opened.

It's like I've gone back fourteen years, and my nights and days are both haunted by the memories.

"Please, Stephan," I begged him. I looked up into the eyes of the man dragging me away from her. My nails scratched and bent on the wooden floors as I kicked him, falling hard to the ground.

And he snarled, "You little bitch."

My heart races and the tears stream down my face. My fingers dig into the mattress and the sweat turns to ice along my skin. I don't know if I'm asleep or awake, but I know what's coming. I can't move; I can't breathe.

I can see myself rocking, but I'm still. I'm aware of that. It's a different time, in a different place.

I'm safe, I whisper and try to will the images away. I'm safe.

But when I open my eyes and try hard to keep from crying any more tears, I remember where I am.

It's been years since the nightmares have tortured me like this. It makes sense that they'd come back now. But without a place to hide, not in my sleep and not while I'm awake, I don't know how much longer I can go on.

I can't live like this.

I can't and I won't.

I want to call out for Carter of all things. He could hold me and take it away.

The bed beneath me groans as I roll over, and for the first time since I've been here, my back is to the door. I'm conscious of it. As conscious of it as I am the feeling of Carter's hand on my jaw. The strength, the power, the heat, and fire that lick their way up my body when he holds me like that.

Like I'm his.

I remember his words, *"I made a deal I shouldn't have. But I need to go through with it."* How he said I have to help him. I've spent weeks in this cell with no hope, until now. My imagination is wild with thoughts of what could come. But each and every one of them leads back to one scene. One that makes my thighs clench tighter.

Slowly, I lift my fingers to where his were and close my eyes as the tips of my fingers tickle my skin. The memory calms me and yet, it makes my heart beat faster.

It's his hands on me that I think of as I try to drift back to sleep. And I almost do.

But the realization of how much power he has over me with something so simple as a touch meant to control me, easing my pain steals any chance I have of falling back to sleep.

CHAPTER 17

Carter

STEPHAN. ALEXANDER STEPHAN.

It's his name screamed. He's who terrorizes her in her sleep. I know it is.

I've listened to it over and over again, each time the anger intensifying.

Last night she screamed his name.

All these nights I thought it was me causing the terrors. I thought she hated me and that she truly dreaded what I could do to her.

I've never been so fucking wrong in my life.

The door to her cell opens with a small creak, but it cries out loud in my ears as Aria's bloodshot eyes stare back at me.

"Can't sleep?" I ask her, leaving the door open and walking with evenly paced and deliberate steps to the side of her bed.

She looks so frail beneath me. Barely eating and not sleeping for more than a few hours for over a week will take its toll on anyone. She doesn't answer me. Her eyes follow me though.

"I won't kneel," she says weakly.

"I didn't come for that."

Her brow scrunches and she nearly questions me. She knows she's disobeying, still fighting a losing battle, but my guard is down. It almost makes me smile.

"I asked for pills to sleep," she says, and her pleas are desperate. But I had to know more. There would be no pills to take it away when she wouldn't share it with me. How else would I have found out? It's her stubbornness that will make her suffer.

"I want to know how you know Alexander Stephan." Even though my words come out softly, meant to be gentle, she pales in front of me and I can see the chill spread over her body as she backs away from me.

There's only so far she can run in here and I'm tempted to grab her and force her to answer me, but I already know everything I need.

I was stupid to think I knew everything there was to know about Aria. I didn't consider anything other than who she was five years ago. I didn't consider the past that made her into that girl.

I knew her mother was murdered by a now-associate of the Romanos years before our family existed in this reality. At the time, he was the right-hand man to Talvery. Betrayal is thick in this business. Her mother's murder is what started the feud years ago, but it's been quiet for over a decade. No one's made a move since the unsuccessful retaliation on Talvery's part. Each side was simply maneuvering pieces and has been waiting for the other to strike since then.

My blunt fingernails dig into my palm as I resist touching Aria. Her back is pressed against the wall and she gathers the covers closer to her chest as if she has hope that they could save her.

But there's nothing that can save you from your past.

When she finally speaks, it's anger that threatens to come out in her voice. "Don't give me to him, please."

Anger sparks through me. This girl has a way of igniting it within me like no one else.

"You belong to me." The simple words gritted between my clenched teeth make her stiffen, but her eyes show a different response. Hope, maybe.

"Any man who thinks they can lay a hand on you will die at mine. Is that clear?"

Her eyes search mine for sincerity, even as she nods her head. "I told you, you belong to me."

The shift in her demeanor is slight. The heavier breaths, the gentle relaxation in her shoulders, and the defiance that begs to come out in the gorgeous blend of greens in her stare.

"Who is he to you?" I ask her again and watch as the cords in her slender neck tighten when she swallows.

"He killed my mother." She doesn't show much emotion; she tries to hide it, to appear devoid of it. But sadness and fear emanate from her voice.

I consider what to ask her next, but I don't want her to know what I know. If she doesn't already, she wouldn't believe me.

"Tell me more," I decide to command her, rather than asking for specifics.

She brushes the hair from her face and as she does, the blanket falls from her chest. It's only then I notice she's finally changed clothes. The thin, pale blush cotton shirt complements her complexion. Her fingers wrap around the cuffs of her sleeves as she pulls her knees to her chest.

"It's not something I like to talk about," she says simply, and then rests her cheek on her knees and looks up at me. The air is different between us. The tension of the game we've been playing isn't here and so I scoot closer to her, wondering how she'll react.

And she does. My little songbird.

She keeps the space between us, shifting to the other side of the bed and straightening her shoulders to keep her eyes on me.

The corners of my lips kick up into a half grin.

"Even now?" I ask her and the defensiveness fades, but she doesn't answer.

A moment passes, and then another. Finally, she looks toward the open door. It's the first time she's done it this morning; usually her gaze flickers to it constantly.

"You screamed his name last night," I tell her and when she looks back at me, I know she's not breathing.

"I'd like to know why," I say to finish my thought.

She swallows visibly and again pulls her knees to her chest. As she does, I inch closer. Only one. Although she stares at my hand, lying flat on the mattress and closer to her, she doesn't move away.

"I was there when he did it."

"You saw her die?"

She nods. "I was hiding. I was only playing." She shakes her head and I inch forward again, beckoning her for more. But nothing comes.

"What aren't you telling me?" My question comes out as a demand and that's when the defiance returns and the girl I'm used to seeing returns.

Her dry lips part but after several moments, she never says a word.

I stand up, pushing off the thin bed and making her sway with the dip in the mattress.

"I don't like hearing you scream," I confide in her and I'm met with silence.

I turn to look over my shoulder and see her soft eyes staring at me, brimming with unshed tears.

"I'm sorry," she apologizes to me and I find it hard to swallow as she turns her gaze from me to the blanket.

This is moving too slowly. Far too slowly. She's close to breaking and for both our sakes, I have to push her. I will not let her move backward. We're so close, and time never stops its ticking.

With that in mind, I reach down and take her blanket from her. She stares up at me like a scared child and I have to push out my words, although they come out with the control and power I always have. "You need to bathe. I don't trust you. So you'll have to trust me."

CHAPTER 18

Aria

I'VE NEVER WONDERED WHAT A PRISONER WOULD FEEL LIKE WHEN led from chains to a feigned freedom. Like a courtyard or elsewhere. I wonder if they feel the same initial instinct to stay close to their warden, the way I do with Carter.

Or, maybe it's because I'm tired. I'm so fucking tired. Of fighting, of starving myself, of not sleeping. I'm not broken, but I am so fucking tired.

The rich mahogany furniture, high ceilings and carved molding accents move around me in a blur. Without shoes, my bare feet pad softly on the polished floors, and it's all I can hear.

I'm not sure if I should peek up and take in my surroundings, but every time I do, Carter gently brushes my shoulder and I instinctively pick up my pace, focused on what's to come. Still, I try to track everything, to pay attention to every doorway and window, every possible chance of escape.

My heart beats fiercely as he leads me to the right and I see a thin stream of light in the darkened hall from a room in the distance. The sounds of chatter and even laughter echo around me, although Carter pulls me in the opposite direction.

Adrenaline courses in my veins and my throat tightens.

There are other people here.

"Don't be stupid, Aria," Carter whispers in the shell of my ear, making my heart lurch and forcing me to jump back. I hadn't realized my thoughts were so obvious.

"Come," he orders me, offering me his hand. My own is small in his as he wraps his strong fingers around mine and leads me deeper down the darkened hall. All I can think about as he takes me closer to where he wants me, is that there were people here, all this time, and I have no idea if they heard my screams or what they would have done had I screamed just moments ago.

Carter unlocks a door, the clinking of metal keys accompanied by his rough voice as he says, "My brothers stay up late. They always have."

His brothers. Jase. Who else? There isn't enough curiosity in the world that could lead me to ask him. But deep in my soul, I'm crying for answers although I can already hear the hiss of the truth in the back of my skull.

There is no mercy here. Not from anyone.

The door opens with a muted creak and I only nod as he gestures for me to head inside. The small bit of hope fluttering in my chest is strangled. I can barely swallow, barely do anything but place one foot in front of the other through a large bedroom, until I hear the flick of a light switch.

The dim light flows across the black and white marble tile. Carter doesn't wait for me to enter before turning on the bath at the far side of the room. I'm struck by the sheer size of the bathroom. Even coming from wealth myself, I'm taken aback.

"It's beautiful," I speak softly. Although how I'm able to speak, I don't know.

The feel of the cold tile under my feet has never been so welcome.

The sight of the plush towel folded neatly on the counter makes me itch to touch like nothing else ever has.

The sound of a running bath has never felt so soothing. And yet, I'm so aware that I'm only a prisoner in a gilded cage, and this moment outside of the cell may be my only chance of escape.

My body is tired from not eating much and having terrors wake me every time I sleep. But I still feel the need to fight.

Carter doesn't respond to a thing I say, or to the next step I take into the bathroom, letting my fingers trail along the pale paisley pattern on the silver wallpaper. My gaze flows through the room easily but stops when I see the tub.

I can't take my eyes away from the steam that billows around the edge of the clawfoot tub.

Leaning over the spotless porcelain, Carter's back is to me with his muscular shoulders pulling his shirt tight, and I imagine how I could push him and run. I could shove him with every ounce of strength I have and run out of the room. I doubt I'd get far though, and I don't know where I'd go.

Now I know his brothers stay here. They're here somewhere.

No, I'm sure I wouldn't get far.

"I want to feed you before I bathe you." Carter's statement cuts through the visions of me running until he adds, "Strip down and get into the tub while I get your dinner."

The dead hope is resurrected; he's leaving me. The thought makes me more anxious than anything.

As he leaves, Carter grips the door and adds, "I won't be long."

Left with only the heat and comfort of the running water, my heart beats once, then twice.

My eyes close and I whisper, "Don't be stupid." The aching inside, the desperate need to run, it's all outweighed by the knowledge of what would come if I disobeyed.

Would I really deny myself a reckless chance of freedom for a warm bath? For food and his touch? Have I been so deprived that such small comforts would rate so highly?

My nails dig into my palms as I war with myself, and when my eyes open, all I see is myself in the mirror. My hair is tangled, although I've run my fingers through it daily. It's oily and dirty, which is to be expected.

My face is thin. Much thinner than I remember. Lifting the thin cotton shirt above my head, I inspect my body, running my fingers over my sides and down to my waist. The cell is so dim; I didn't see the bruises from when I was taken. The cuts around my wrists have left thin white scars, and the bruise on my ribs is an ugly shade of dark brown that's faded to nearly nothing.

I hadn't felt defeat until I was led from my cell, giving up the possibility to run only to see how damaged I've become.

The sound of the water striking against the surface harder brings my attention to the tub.

It's nearly full. The steaming hot water and relaxing fragrance of lavender bath oils Carter poured in it, beg me to cave. To let go and stop fighting. To be good and do as I'm told. If only so I can rid myself of the sense of failure and remember who I am again.

And I still remember those words he spoke days ago. He made a deal and I'm to help him. There is more to this than I know. "Be smart," I whisper to myself. I'm playing a game without knowing the rules. Without knowing the next phase. The little bit of hope and wonder push me forward toward temptation.

Turning the iron faucet, I realize it's the first thing I've touched in weeks beyond the few items in the cell. Something as simple as turning a knob feels both foreign and nostalgic. I never want to go back to the cell. My chest feels hollow as I think, *never*, but I know that the choice isn't mine.

It is, a small voice murmurs in the back of my head. The voice that takes advantage of my pain and promises so much hope in whispers of deceit.

Jasmine and lavender fill my lungs as I inhale the calming scents and quickly remove my shirt and shove my cotton pants down my legs. Although the clothes are new, they're still dirty. Everything in that cell is dirty.

The fabric clings to my toes and I have to kick it off and toward the puddle of clothes. Just as I do, I hear the heavy footsteps of Carter coming back.

Fear keeps me from moving for only a moment, but then I quickly place a foot into the steaming water, hissing at the onslaught of heat and causing the water to splash around the tub. Water hits the floor as I move to step with my other foot into the hot bath, the heat becoming more and more welcoming as my body adjusts to it. With my back to the door, I hear Carter enter, but I ignore him, lowering myself into the tub filled with a warmth I so desperately needed. And hide myself from him.

"How does it feel?" Carter's voice carries through the room with a powerful resonance.

Like heaven, I think as I turn slowly, careful not to splash the water, but also careful to stay under and somewhat hidden beyond the white bubbles on the surface.

I try to tell him that it feels wonderful and thank him when I finally meet his gaze, but I'm silenced by the intensity within. His eyes swirl with the danger of a man close to getting what he wants. An animalistic heat passes between us and I can only nod for fear of what my voice would sound like if I dared utter a word to him.

Thankfully, he tears his gaze from me and picks up a ceramic plate from the counter.

"You need to eat." Carter's command sounds more like a reminder to himself. And again, I merely nod.

I've had delicious food before. I've gorged myself on delicacies without thinking twice. It's one of the only benefits of my upbringing. But the food Carter brought me makes my mouth water and my grip tighten on the tub to keep me from ripping the plate from his hands.

He must see my eagerness; he always smiles that devilish grin when he knows I'm eager. Bastard.

"Open," he commands me and like a good girl, my lips part and I nearly moan when he slips me the small chunk of filet dipped in au jus with a dab of herbed butter smeared across the top. The meat melts in my mouth, the tastes singing on my lips. My eyes are still closed as I relish the food, thinking it's the most delicious thing I've ever eaten when Carter brushes another piece against my lips.

Instantly I open my lips for him, and his finger brushes against my tongue as he gives me a second piece and then another. My teeth scrape against his fingers and my eyes widen with worry that he thinks I did it on purpose, but he only feeds me more.

The fear and worry slip away, just as the time does with each slice of tender meat.

Blistered tomatoes and peppers along with roasted potatoes find themselves in the mix as Carter feeds me until my stomach is full and I can't take another bite. It's been so long since I haven't felt hunger pains. It feels like forever since I've sunk into a deep tub, covered in hot water. I rest my head against the side of the tub and pretend like everything is alright. It's only a small moment until the clinking of the ceramic plate on the tile floor disturbs me and brings me back to the present.

My body stiffens slightly, sloshing the water toward the edge of the tub away from Carter as he dips a washcloth into the tub.

His fingers brush against my skin and sinfully, I welcome the touch. It's been so long, and I've been so lonely. I want more. I need more. I find myself wishing for him to take me like I know he wants to.

Has he really broken me so easily? Or is this something I should want the way I do? The questions bring a haze to my mind and a thrumming in my blood. The washcloth travels over my body, starting at my feet and working its way upward. My calves, my thighs and so close to between them.

I know he can hear my heavy breathing; he can see how I grip the edge of the tub. But he doesn't touch me there. Instead, he tells me to wet my hair and takes his time massaging my scalp and lathering my hair. The scent of the chamomile shampoo overwhelms me, and I hum ever so slightly until I hear it and stop myself.

Everything feels so good.

"Back under, songbird," he tells me in that velvety voice. The voice I don't want to disobey, and so I don't. I do as he says. With every command he gives me, I do exactly what he says.

He massages the washcloth over my shoulders and I whimper as he kneads the pain away. I hadn't realized how much my body ached until he showed me so. A low groan of approval forces me to open my eyes and stare into his. But he's not looking at my gaze. His eyes are focused on my hardened nipples, peeking up from the water.

The washcloth makes a splash as it hits the water and slowly sinks to the depths of the tub. Carter lets his fingers trail down my chest, plucking one of my nipples and then the other. It happens slowly, his fingers determined but also giving me a warning. His rough thumb circles them first before tugging on them and causing my head to fall back and my thighs to clench. Each tweak sends a sharp spike of need between my legs, and I nearly spread them for him. My clit pulses with need. I feel it so strongly I don't think it would take much at all for me to cum for him. And I can't find it in me at all to find any shame at that fact.

The dull desire that hasn't faded, shoots through me and I welcome it.

Carter's dark eyes find mine, but instead of reaching lower, his arm dips into the water next to me and he gathers the washcloth once again.

I'm reminded of his patience. How slowly he does everything. I don't know if he finds pleasure in teasing me or if it's simply that he doesn't want this moment to end, but either way, I lean my head back as he continues bathing me, and I don't object until his hand is right where I've secretly been wishing for it to be.

He brushes the washcloth against my throbbing clit and I gasp, moving away from the intense pleasure and making waves in the tub that splash over the edge. Fear and desire mix into a confusing potion that I drank long ago. And at this moment, I'd drink the bottle again, I'd suck it dry and lick the edge of the neck where the last beads of liquid would gather. That's how badly I wish for him to do it again.

"Don't let go, Aria. If you do, I'll stop," he warns me and my lungs still. My body's on fire with need. I slowly lower myself back under the warm water, until my breasts are hidden again, and I hold Carter's eyes as I slowly reach back up and grip on to the edge. My body's still, so still as Carter's gaze flickers between my pussy and my stare. I bite down on my bottom lip as he reaches between my legs again.

His movements have been steady and slow. Careful and considerate even. But as the washcloth falls into the water, brushing against my thigh and ass, and his fingers replace the cloth, his movements are nothing but savage.

He shoves his fingers inside of me. My back bows as the sudden spike in pleasure crashes through every inch of my body.

"Carter," I whimper his name as he pushes his palm against my clit. I've never been touched like this. Air is torn from me and I can't breathe or move or do anything but grip tighter and try to stay still as he finger fucks me harder and harder.

"Carter," I cry out his name louder into the hot air and grip the edge of the tub as hard as I can. I can't let go but my body is begging for me to run, to move, to both get closer to the intense pleasure and to leave it quickly.

I know when I do cum, it will split me into pieces and he'll love how I shatter under his touch. It both terrifies me and thrills me.

I should be ashamed as I writhe in the water. I should be embarrassed as he hisses when my pussy clamps around his fingers and my orgasm tears through me, coming faster and harder than it ever has before.

My heart shouldn't pound for more. My body shouldn't ache for more. I shouldn't sit up so quickly with the intention of gripping his wrist and pleading with him for more. The waves are still crashing through me as he turns around, grabbing the towel and ignoring how I've just come apart for him.

My fears cloud the desire; they dim the sensation of lust that ricochets through my blood, my breathing steadying.

But when he turns to face me, I know it's alright. I know I did well to let him touch me. From the way he looks at me, it's like he's never wanted anything more in his life.

CHAPTER 19

Carter

SHE'S TOO GOOD. TOO FUCKING PERFECT.

And that's how I'll keep her so that each and every time I can ruin her. It's a delicate balance, knowing what to offer her and when to take from her.

Tonight, I've given more than enough, and I'll feel her break beneath me. I'll feel her shatter under me as I take every bit of her that I want. And she'll fucking love me for it.

The water falls around her in a patter onto the tile floor. She lets it drip down her back and sides. Even the thick towel I'm wrapping around her waist can't hide her from me. I've felt every inch. Every curve is burned into my memory.

Her skin trembles beneath my fingertips as I brush them against her shoulders.

I take my time, letting each small touch catch her off guard. The gasps and sharp breaths only add to the thrill. My cock is harder than it's ever been as I lead her to the bedroom and she clings to that towel as if she'll be able to keep it.

Her small frame casts a shadow on the thick carpet, the moonlight shining through the drapes. I can practically hear her heart beating as she stares at the bed. My fingers slip over her silky skin and I let my lips fall to her shoulder, so I can whisper, "You don't need this anymore." My fingers slip between the plush towel and her soft skin. I half expect my songbird to object. To continue to pretend like she doesn't want this.

But to my surprise and delight, she lets the towel fall and gently steadies her back against my chest when I take that small step forward, discarding the distance between us.

My fingers dip into her cunt, her hair tickling my fingers as I pet her still-swollen clit. I'm rewarded with her ass pushing against my cock, her back bowing, and a small moan that's barely muffled.

"It's my turn, Aria," I say, and my voice nearly trembles at her name when I feel her thighs tighten around my fingers. "Are you ready again so soon?" I turn her around, her small breasts a beautiful flushed color and her bottom lip drops in surprise like she's been caught.

"You're eager to cum again and feel that sweet, sinful torture paralyze your body?" I take a half step forward, forcing her ass to bump against the bed.

"I bet I could make you cum just from sucking these," I tell her and pull her pale petal pink nipples between my middle and pointer fingers. I tug on both at once. Her head lolls slightly, but those beautiful hazel eyes stay on mine as she moans.

"Sit." I give her a simple command. And she obeys. I can't describe the pride, the satisfaction from watching her so eagerly waiting for another command. "Good girl," I add, the words slipping out easily, and my hand rests gently on her thigh. I move it upward until I grip her ass and toss her higher onto the bed.

"Show me your cunt." Her cheeks blaze a bright red, even in the darkness, but letting her head fall back and staring at the ceiling, she parts her legs and then bends her knees, digging her heels into the comforter beneath her so I can see my prize.

"Look at me," I tell her, surprised by my own irritation. Her eyes instantly find mine, widened slightly. "Watch me. I want you to know how I look at you. What I think of you. Do you understand me?" She doesn't hesitate to nod. And glancing between her face and her spread pussy lips, I make sure she's watching me intently.

My fingers trace along her lips, soft and wet with arousal. Goosebumps travel over her thighs and she shivers when I gently push on her swollen nub. Her back arches off the bed as my fingers slip over her entrance and then back up.

"Beautiful," I say the one word, and that gorgeous blush in her chest creeps to her cheeks. I'm careless as I rip my shirt off on my way to the nightstand.

I have two sets of cuffs, but I'll only use one pair tonight. Pulling the door open, I grab the set and grip her wrist to move it where I want it. Her inhalation of surprise is met with the sound of the cuffs tightening, one on her wrist and one on the bedpost. Outstretched, she struggles not to object.

I can tell by the way she readjusts herself that she knows what's coming. I unbuckle my pants and she stills; they fall to the floor and my stiff cock juts out. I've never known how badly my cock could ache to be inside of a woman. Until now.

Gripping it and stroking once, precum already beads at the head.

My gorgeous Aria whimpers with need.

"Spread your legs for me." Before I'm finished speaking the words, she's already obeyed.

"I've waited so long for this," I admit to her as I crawl up the bed and over her small frame. My hips fit between her thighs and my cock nestles in her pussy as I lower my lips to the crook of her neck.

I've agonized over how I'd fuck her the first time. Whether I'd make her ride me so she couldn't deny how badly she wanted me. I wasn't sure if I'd be slow and steady, making her scream for me to fuck her harder as she got closer to the edge of her orgasm.

But now that the time has come, I realize how selfish I am. How truly and deeply to the core selfish I am.

All I want to do is take what's mine. To slam myself inside her to the hilt and fuck her like she's my whore. Mine and mine alone.

And that's exactly what I do. In one swift stroke, I ravage her. Her tight pussy is already hot and wet and eager for my cock. She takes all of me and screams out a sweet sound of utter rapture. With her free hand, her nails rake down my chest as her heel digs into my ass.

The need to keep still inside of her while she cums violently on my cock is overridden by the desire to piston my hips and rut between her legs. The sweet smell of her arousal and the sounds of our flesh smacking together repeatedly are everything I'll need to justify what I've done.

She struggles under me, her shoulders digging into the mattress with each hard thrust. Every time I pound into her, she responds like she was made just for me. The tightening of her pussy, the strangled cries, and sweet tortured moans are better than I ever could have imagined.

Her nails dig into my shoulder as I keep a relentless pace. My balls draw up and my spine tingles with the desire to cum deep inside of her.

But I need more. Gritting my teeth, I fuck her harder and faster until a cold sweat breaks out on my skin.

She screams out again, but the scream is different this time. It's pain. It's reflected in her face too. My heart sinks in my chest until I see her wrist, being pulled against the metal cuff.

Fucking hell. I'm agitated and reckless as I climb over her, her arousal covering my dick as I dig in the nightstand for the key to unlock the fucking cuff.

It takes longer than I'd like and when it's finally free, I don't waste a second to grip her hips, then flip her over so she's on her knees with her ass in the air. She yells out in surprise, but it's silenced when I slam all of me back into her welcoming heat.

The sweet sounds filling the air are heaven. With every thrust, she cries out in pleasure.

I grip her ass with both of my hands, nearly cumming with her as she spasms on my cock. Her nails dig into the sheets and her thighs tremble with the ripple of her release.

I wanted her to beg for it. In the tub, in my bed. I wasn't going to let her cum until she was begging for me to fuck her.

But the best-laid plans never do work out.

And as I thrust into her with an unrelenting pace, feeling her struggle to stay on her knees until she finally falls beneath me while I rut into her savagely and she screams out incoherently with pleasure, I realize I'd rather have her beg me to stop. I'd rather take every ounce of pleasure from her until she can't take any more.

Until she's limp and spent and can do nothing but hold on to the comforter beneath her as if it can save her from me.

CHAPTER 20

Aria

I'VE NEVER FELT SO DELICIOUSLY USED AND BARED BY SOMEONE so savagely.

My body aches as it has for weeks, but in a different way. In a way that makes me feel like my body will give in and collapse if I try to move. As I roll over in the bed, I can still feel him inside of me. Taking everything and pushing me over the edge, time and time again. The reminder sends a wanting desire through my blood.

He fucked me like he owned me.

Because he did.

He does still.

The thought makes my eyes pop wide open. My gaze travels slowly over the brightly lit room with gray walls and a tray ceiling painted even darker. The room has a sense of power to it. It's bold and dangerous even. Sharp and modern furniture and not a thing out of place.

Except for me.

My body is still, knowing I'm in Carter's room.

Not in the cell; a breath leaves me slowly, as quietly as I can allow it. I never want to go back there.

I don't hear anything. Not a sound. Another moment passes, and slowly I will myself to reach behind me, searching for Carter's presence, any sign that he's sleeping next to me.

I find nothing but the chill of empty sheets.

It takes me longer than I'd like to admit to have the strength and will to turn over, still pretending that I'm sleeping. But after moments of sensing no one else in the room, I take a chance to look around and find the room empty and the bedroom door open.

I take in his bedroom as slowly as I did the other side and wait for a sign that Carter's here. But there's no trace of him.

A pile of vibrant clothes, at odds with the bright white comforter, catches my attention.

Daring to sit up and wincing from the dull ache between my legs, I cautiously pick them up and find a silk robe and negligee that I would never wear.

It's scandalous and for the body of a model. It makes no sense that my initial thought is that he's going to be disappointed with me. That I could never do this delicate combination of lace and silk justice. Other than to justify it with the thought that if I disappoint him, he'll send me back. And I never want to go in that cell again. Never.

I don't even realize I'm clutching the fabric to my chest until Carter's voice pierces through the threatening thoughts.

"What's wrong?" he asks as he enters the room.

My head shakes of its own accord, making my hair tickle my bare shoulders as I do and reminding me that I'm naked.

I should have searched through his things. I should have tried to escape. A bulleted list of all the ways I've disappointed myself weighs heavily on my chest as I watch him pull one drawer open and then the next until he sets a pair of metal handcuffs down on the dresser.

His casual stance is a façade; power still radiates around him. Carter stalks toward me.

I'm only moving from the cell where I could deny him, to his bed where I'll be his whore.

"If you don't like it, there are more." Carter's tone is dismissive at best and I don't know what he's referring to until he nods at the ball of clothes in my hand.

I let the fine fabrics fall onto the comforter, not knowing how to answer. I'm on pins and needles as I sit here trying to decide what I need to do to keep myself safe and in the best possible position to gain my freedom back.

"I like you nervous." Carter's voice draws my eyes back to him. He looks more casual today than I've ever seen him. It's not the clothes he wears, but his posture and the way he stalks toward me. Stopping at the edge of the bed, I get a strong whiff of his scent and

I hate how much I love it. Even more so I hate how my thighs clench and the twinkle of a grin threatens to pull at his lips when I whimper.

"I enjoyed you last night," Carter's voice rumbles in a way that ignites my nerve endings on fire. Reaching out to cup my chin in his hand, he stares at my lips, running his thumb along the bottom one.

And something shifts inside of me. This is a man with so much power and control, someone who could destroy me and in many ways has already. Yet all I want in this moment is for him to kiss me. He hasn't yet, and deep inside a part of me needs it.

But his thumb stops the soothing motions and his expression falls as he speaks, although it's worded as a question. "You haven't eaten?"

"I only just woke up." The words come out like an excuse with a plea coating them. The weak sound on my lips disgusts me. I was stronger in the cell. I breathe in harsher, knowing I'd bite back a quip if only my ass was on the thin mattress in the dark cell in this moment.

But I don't want to go back. I'm ashamed to know it so clearly and to hold onto that truth like I'll die if it slips from me. In an effort to diminish my hate of that pathetic fact, I remind myself that are far more chances of escape out here.

And there is nothing but agony in that cell. The ache of loneliness and starvation and sleepless nights filled with past pains.

I refuse to go back.

Carter's touch falls as he turns away from me, back to the dresser. "There's breakfast in the kitchen. If you see anyone, ignore them and they'll ignore you. Understood?" He tosses the cuffs inside a drawer and searches for something else.

I nod once when he glances over his shoulder, although inside I'm reeling. All I can think is that there may be someone here to save me. Someone to show mercy. Maybe Jase? Or else I can run.

"Verbal responses, little songbird," he says casually as if he's telling me what the weather is. The drawer shuts tight with finality and I find myself nodding my head again as I answer him, "Yes," with my eyes fixated on the metal peeking through his clenched hand.

"And you'll wear this," he tells me as he holds up a thin chain. Every inch or so there's a small pearl, alternated with diamonds. It's long, so long it would fall to nearly my belly button and as I take it in I see the diamonds grow larger as you near the end. There, in the center, is a large tear-shaped diamond.

But all that sparkles is only sin disguised in beauty.

"A collar?" My heart beats like a war drum inside my chest. He must hear the defeat on my tongue.

"You can't collar a songbird, Aria, but you can tether one or cage it. The choice is yours."

"Either the cell or the necklace?" I ask him to clarify, and just the idea that I can save myself from going back there has my hand reaching for the necklace.

Carter nods once, and my eyes are brought back to his.

"Turn around," he orders me, the fire flickering in his eyes. Steadying my breathing, I turn my back to him and feel the sweet sensation of a shiver run down both my front and back as he moves my hair to the side. My nipples harden as the cool diamonds and pearls fall down my chest and over the crook of my shoulders and neck. Carter lets his hands trail to my breasts once he's done, his hot breath tickling the shell of my ear as he whispers, "Beautiful."

But just as quickly as he's shown me gentleness, he leaves me, his absence intensifying the coldness of the air. And I'm left naked on my knees in his bed. Wearing a collar and making decisions based on fear.

Thoughts of my father and Nikolai return. Shame accompanies the image of their disapproval and disgust. As much as I'd like to lie, I loved what Carter did to me last night and I'd let him do it again.

"Why are you doing this to me?" The words are torn from the other side of me. The side I want to hide and tell to be quiet.

Walking back to the dresser, I think Carter's ignored me until he answers, "Because I can," he answers in a tone not to be questioned or defied. "A man asked me what I wanted, and I could buy anything I want, yet I saw your picture and knew I could never have you." He turns to face me, leaning against the dresser and waiting for my response.

I remember the words I've held so dearly that he spoke days ago. The words that gave me hope. How I would help him and he would give me everything. I wonder if it's a lie, or if what he's telling me now has anything to do with that deal he shouldn't have made.

"And now that you've…" I trail off, then swallow my words.

"I don't have you, Aria. Not yet. But when I do, you'll be begging me to stay." What strikes the most fear in my heart is how utterly and completely I believe him.

Walking toward me, I can see something begging to escape from his lips. Something that's maybe a secret, maybe not. But he merely runs his fingers along my lips again and tells me he'll find me when he's ready for me again before leaving me and keeping the bedroom door open.

When something is hard to the touch and so sharp it would draw blood, you have to always be careful. It's the gentleness of it that will break you. You can't ever let your guard down.

If you're smart, you avoid it and if you have to be around it, you stay away from the parts that hurt. But those aren't the parts that destroy. It's the parts that you begin to crave, the parts you don't want to resist that bring you to your knees. They make you forget or maybe they make you think the sharpness won't cut you, as if you're somehow immune or no longer prey to it.

Even knowing so, I fall helpless to the way he cups my chin like that. And I sit there for far too long with my fingertips lingering where I can still feel him.

I can't breathe as I wake up. The cold sweat that covers my skin makes me shake, as does my racing heart. The room is dark, and I can't see for a moment, but the hands gripping my shoulders and holding me down aren't the ones in my nightmare.

It's not Stephan, I try to think logically as I hear Carter's voice yelling at me to wake up.

My chest heaves as the light filters into my vision and I see him. The anger in his tone is absent from his pained expression.

My shoulders hunch forward as I try to calm down. It was just a night terror. I can't control them. I can't stop them.

"Please don't send me back," I barely push out and it causes Carter's fingers to dig deeper into my shoulders before he releases me. Stalking to a chair on the far side of the bedroom, he sits with his body leaning forward, his dark eyes staring at me through the dark room.

My skin tingles with a numbing fear. I can't go back to the cell. Tears leak from my eyes at the thought that one fear of mine, a man who destroyed my world and threatened to do more, would keep me from being safe from yet another, the cell.

"Please," I plead weakly and before the word is completely spoken, Carter commands me, "Come here."

Although my body feels weak, I force my limbs to move quickly as they fight with his sheets. I practically fall to the ground and quickly crawl to him, the rug brushing against my knees.

In nothing but a pair of silk pajama pants, his abs ripple in the faint moonlight. His body looks like it was carved in marble. Even with the fear still strongly present, I can feel the itch of my fingers to run down the carved lines of his muscles. If nothing else, he's a beautiful distraction. He can use me, fuck me into a deep sleep. And I would beg for it in this moment.

I'd beg him to use me and take away everything else.

I slow my pace as I get closer to him, the necklace nearly dragging on the ground. Its presence makes my nakedness very much at the forefront of my mind. His knees are parted, and I settle in between them. In the darkness and with that look in his eye, he radiates power as I kneel at his feet.

Slowly, I reach my hands up to his thighs in the silence. He hasn't said a word, but I'm sure I have to please him. I can't go back to the cell. Not over this.

My fingers slip between the silk fabric and his hot skin at the deep V on his hips.

My actions are cut short and my heart lurches when Carter's strong fingers grab my wrist and yank my hand away. I can barely breathe as the intensity in his gaze ignites.

The silence stretches as he stares at me and I feel helpless, not knowing what he wants.

"Get on all fours," he commands me, barely loosening his grip so I can quickly obey him. My heart thumps so hard it's all I can hear.

"Face on the floor," he tells me, and I do as he says, keeping my ass in the air. "Palms up and at your knees," Carter tells me and again I do as he says, but he repositions them. All the weight of my body is on my shoulders and neck as I lay my head on the floor and my arms stay behind me, not useful in balancing or aiding me in any way. I'm completely bared to him and at his mercy.

A moment passes and then another as Carter paces around me. I try to swallow, but I can't. The fear of him finding me less than pleasing makes my knees tremble, and he only responds by moving my legs farther apart. The moment I close my eyes, his deep and rough voice commands me to open them and look at him. Towering over me, I have no idea what my dark knight thinks of me or what he plans to do to me.

"Tell me what you were dreaming of," he finally says, and I answer him, the rug rubbing against my cheek and my breath feels hot against my face.

"I don't remember," I tell him and although it's true, I know what the terrors consist of.

"It wasn't important to you? Not important enough to remember?" he asks as he crouches behind me. I can't see him, but I can feel him. I can always feel Carter's unyielding presence.

"No," I shake my head against the ground and answer him how I think he wants me to. "It's not important and I'm sorry," I tell him, and the silence stretches.

My body jolts forward as his hand brushes against my ass. The rough pad of his thumb follows down to my pussy, gently trailing along my clit and then back up. He grips my ass cheek in a bruising manner and my eyes shut tight as I prepare for more.

Whack! His hand slaps against my ass and forces a cry from my lips. I sink my teeth into my lip and take another. The sharp stinging pain is accompanied by his hand sliding up my front, so he can roll my left nipple between his fingers. The combination of pain and pleasure is directly linked to my clit. My body rocks to the side, unable to stay still as he pulls my now hardened peak.

He instantly releases me to push down on my upper back between my shoulder blades, and he spanks the same spot on my ass again. Biting down on my lip, changes the cry to a muffled whimper and the pain that shoots up my body ignites every nerve ending in my body, heating my core and stealing my breath.

Panting against the rug, I wait for more. I can feel my pussy clench around nothing, praying for pleasure to take the pain away. His splayed hand on my back travels along my spine, leaving a trail of goosebumps. I can feel his breath against my ass before he bites down, making my mouth form an O with both surprise and something else. The pain is nothing like what I expect and my body trembles with delight at the thought of more.

Quickly, he pulls away and another sharp smack meets my heated skin, this one sending tears to my eyes. The pain and intensity have gathered into a ball in the pit of my stomach and I don't know that I can take anymore.

"Please," I whisper, but I don't know what I'm asking for.

"Why am I punishing you, Aria?" His deep voice is a soothing balm to my broken cries.

"Because I woke you," I answer him as I feel his hips brush against the backs of my thighs. He settles behind me and lowers his lips to my shoulder. He plants a small kiss on my shoulder as the head of his cock gently presses into my entrance. It's only a tease and I find myself rocking backward, praying he'll fuck me and take the pain away.

His hot breath tickles the crook of my neck as he whispers, "Because you lied to me."

I can't respond because he immediately slams inside of me and fucks me exactly how I wanted him to.

CHAPTER 21

Carter

"THERE ARE FIVE WINGS IN THE ESTATE. AND EACH HAS their own lock." I glance down at Aria, listening to her bare feet pad on the marble tile as we enter the foyer. The double-doored entrance is only feet away and I know she's resisting the urge to look at it.

"There are locks everywhere, inside and out." She chances a peek at me and stills when she meets my gaze. "I often invite those who I don't consider friends here and sometimes I don't want them to leave."

She's silent as she considers what I've said. Nervousness trickles down her body. It's in the way she swallows, the way she holds her hands in front of her. The way she almost trips over her own feet. And I love her nervousness.

"The front door, for instance." I motion toward it and she turns stiffly as if she wasn't dying to look at it. "That box there, to the right of it. You need a code to open it, from either inside or out."

"I thought you said it was one or the other." Her soft voice is questioning. Her hazel eyes peer up at me as if I've wronged her. As if I've hurt her. "You said a bird can be tethered or caged, not both."

A smile tickles my lips as I reply, "Haven't you learned that all you need to do is ask?"

Her lips turn down into a frown, but she stays quiet. She knows she's caged. Wherever she goes, she will go with me, caged and protected just the same.

"I'm a prisoner," she says as her voice cracks, and she looks longingly at the front doors. The architecture foreboding in a way that seems to forbid a guest from leaving.

"You were before in your father's home." My voice is deep and echoes in the foyer. Her eyes reach up to mine in shock as I continue, "Afraid to leave. Afraid to do anything without permission."

"I wasn't afraid," she whispers, and I know she's well aware of the lie she's spoken.

"You let fear rule you. Don't lie to me." Unease trickles through me. The realization of what she truly fears could change everything.

"How do you know what I did and didn't do?" she asks weakly, denying the truth and deflecting her attention to something else.

Since she lied to me, I present a lie to her in return. "When you were offered to me, I did my research. I have friends in your father's army of men. Eyes and ears who offer information for a certain price. I know you spent almost all of your time alone in your room. Maybe that's why it took so long for you to obey me. You're used to cells."

Her mouth parts, no doubt with a rebuttal, but wisely she slams it shut before a word is spoken.

Time passes as we move on. Both of us quiet. Both of us in our own world of denial.

"Your things can be moved to my office, den, or the bedroom. The drawing pad and whatever else you want," I offer her but still, she's quiet. Her fingers fidget with one another throughout the tour of the two wings she's allowed to enter. She doesn't seem to look at anything or notice anything at all unless we pass a window, which, as I pointed out, have locks on them as well.

"Why are there five wings?" she asks me as I lead her to the grand kitchen. She still hasn't eaten and she needs to. There's no reason for her not to and the threat of sending her back to the cell if she doesn't, is so close to being spoken to life. I'd rather save it for something else, something more meaningful. But my little bird needs to eat.

"I had four brothers and decided they should each have their own wing," I tell her and step into the kitchen. The garden is just beyond the back wall, lined with black glass from floor to ceiling. The floors are a dark walnut and polished so smoothly I can see our reflection in them.

Her eyes move across the sleek, modern kitchen, from the high-end cabinets to the white granite countertops. Everything is done in white. It's clean and modern and balances the black glass perfectly.

I anticipate her saying many things, but not the next words that spill from her lips.

"I'm sorry."

My forehead pinches with a deep crease. "For what?" I question.

"You said you had four brothers. I take it that one or more have passed?" She turns to face me and her hip brushes one of the stools to the island. I can tell she's not sure if she should sit or not, and I leave her wondering. Just like I leave the pangs of regret and sadness to settle in my gut. Instead, I focus on how discerning Aria is. She's a deadly combination of beautiful and perceptive. I need to remember that.

"Carter," Jase calls out from behind me and when I turn his steps slow. His eyes drift from where I am, almost blocking Aria from view, and then to her.

"I didn't realize you were busy," he says to me although his eyes travel down Aria's body. Even with her robe tied tightly with the sash and covering her décolletage, she looks like she was made to tempt.

"What is it?" I ask him and again he looks at her. From my periphery, I watch her glance at the floor and those fingers of hers continue making tight knots around one another.

Gripping the back of her neck, just slightly, she stops her fidgeting.

They both want to know what she is to me. I can see it written on their faces as much as I can feel the tension in the air.

It doesn't matter what she is, so long as they all know she's mine.

Even more, I know Jase is questioning the way I hold her at this moment and why she's out of the cell. Maybe he's wondering how long I'll keep her out here. Or how long I'll keep her period.

I make soothing strokes with my thumb along the back of her neck as Jase tells me something about a car. I don't know what the fuck he's talking about. I don't give a damn either. I assume it's some update about the supply, but he doesn't want to speak openly in front of Aria.

My little songbird relaxes under my touch, peeking up at me every so often. I know she's wondering what he thinks of her.

"Aria," I say her name in the middle of whatever Jase was saying and he falls silent. "I'd like you to step outside, so I can talk to Jase." All I can hear is her breathing in this moment. The fear, the hope, the surprise of her surroundings. My poor Aria knows so little. But she'll learn.

She quickly nods but she doesn't move until my hand slips down her back, leaving a trail along the silk. Jase stays by the island, his hands in his pockets as I lead her to the door. It's black glass as well and blends into the wall, only opening when a verified print is pressed against the biometric security panel. Aria watches intently, but she wouldn't be able to open it if she tried and with fifteen-foot walls around the garden and a guarded fence around the estate, she won't be able to run.

I can see it on her face when the realization registers with her.

"And when I'm done with this conversation, it's back to the bedroom." I lean in closer to her and whisper in her ear, "I'm going to fuck you until I've had my fill."

The sound of Jase's footsteps lets me know he's coming as I watch Aria walk into the garden, letting the sun hit her face as if it's the first time she's ever experienced it.

"I have Jared on the lookout at the club. We'll have a list of the heavy buyers of S2L by the end of the week."

"Perfect," I answer him although I watch Aria walking deeper into the garden to lie on a patch of grass. "Anything else?"

"Talvery knows we have her."

A smile pulls my lips up. "It took him long enough. One of Romano's men leaked it?"

I turn to Jase, who's watching Aria as he nods. "It couldn't stay secret forever." He turns to look at me before adding, "He'll come for her."

"He'll want to," I correct him. "But which of his men would be willing to come here and die for her?"

"She speaks highly of Nikolai," Jase offers, and I can see the hint of a smile on his face. Aria's first week in the cell gave me plenty of information as she talked out loud to nothing but brick walls, begging for help and companionship. Nikolai's name slipped from her lips nearly every single fucking day.

"Let him come. He can be the first of them to die."

CHAPTER 22

Aria

T HE SMELL OF COFFEE IS WHAT WAKES ME, AND WITHOUT
thinking I roll over in the large bed, stretching before I'm even
fully awake. The soothing ache of my muscles is comforting, as
is the gentle fragrance of clean linens and the hint of a masculine scent
that makes my core both ache and heat.

And then I remember.

It's always like this.

I've been out of the cell for three days, and yet when I wake up in
Carter's bed, it takes me a moment to remember. Maybe I don't want to
admit that it's real. Maybe a part of my subconscious is far away from
here. But each morning I have to remember.

Slowly, I calm my beating heart and wait for a noise, any sign that
he's here. He's a sinful addiction, creeping into my blood and fueling
the lust and fire for the forbidden. I crave him, his acceptance, his
dominance, and yet I'm so aware that's all wrong. That small voice that
whispers there must be a way out of here is getting quieter by the day.
That's what scares me the most.

Three mornings I've woken up in Carter's bed, and just like the
last two, he's not here.

Not physically, but he's watching. I learned the hard way yesterday,
only the second day of being out of the cell. I thought I couldn't waste
another day, listening and obeying. I had to try to find a way out of
here. The memory forces my gaze to the dresser.

I was snooping. How could I not? He wasn't here, and I still have
no way out of his grasp. No one comes in and no one goes out. The
place is a fortress and I its prisoner.

And so, drawer after drawer, I slipped them open, hoping to find
something. I'm not sure what. A gun or a weapon.

I'm not sure he'd listen to me if I made demands and held him at gunpoint, or that I'd be successful in rushing him or forcing him to let me go. Somehow, I find it hard to believe, but still, I had to try.

My eyes close and my body tenses, remembering his deep voice and how it shook me to the core. The drawer slammed shut as I screamed out and dared to look over my shoulder at Carter leaning against the doorframe.

"Kneel." The one word I've refused over and over from Carter brought me to my knees. My words tripped over one another as I tried to apologize or hide what I was doing.

But I've always been a terrible liar and he knew better.

"Open your mouth." Hearing him give me the command made my pussy hot and clench with desire. He throat fucked me. A punishment, I suppose, but it's not what it was for me.

With my fingers digging into my thighs, my eyes burning, and my breath cut from me, he shoved himself down my throat. And I was nothing but wet for him.

The fear was still present. It's always present. The knowledge that when he was done using me, he could send me back to the cell kept that fear very much alive.

He wasn't done with me when he pulled away and allowed me to breathe again. As I heaved for air, he forced me to all fours. Shamefully, my face turned hot as it hit the rug and he slammed inside of me. My back tried to arch as I moaned a ragged, strangled sound of pleasure.

I came nearly instantly, and Carter stilled deep inside of me. Gripping the hair at the base of my skull, he forced me to arch my back and whispered in my ear, "You fucking love what I do to you." And I couldn't deny it.

I fucking loved it. But it was a punishment and I was reminded of that and what I'd done before he left me panting and sated on the floor.

"Next time it will be the cell." His words ring clear in my head as I glance at all the drawers I have yet to open.

I may love the way he fucks me, but that doesn't change much. I don't fight the urges anymore. I want them, and they help me to survive, but it doesn't make me any less ashamed, because I know very well I'm a prisoner here and Carter can do with me as he wishes.

Although I crave my freedom, that doesn't mean I don't have desires in my captivity.

The one thing I always notice is what Carter doesn't do.

He never kisses me. Never once. And he doesn't talk to me the same way when there are people around. I've met two of his brothers and each time I anticipated being tossed aside or demeaned. But each time, Carter's talked to me as if I'm a friend, maybe. Or a business acquaintance. As do his brothers, although their words are few.

When we're alone, it's different. There's a comfort in his voice I didn't expect that's only replaced by a heavy cadence of desire when he gives me a command.

The combination of all of this is a whirlwind of chaos in my mind.

But one fact remains the same: Another day survived is another day I'm Carter's whore.

My bare feet sink into the rug beneath the bed as I slink off of it and walk toward the cup of coffee on the dresser. It's still hot to the touch.

A million thoughts bombard me every waking moment. Why is he doing this is the one that's a constant. Carter's a man of intentions. Calculated and manipulative.

Lifting the hot cup of coffee to my lips, I blow across the top and feel the heat caress my face.

He could have slipped something into the cup. He could have left it on the dresser intentionally to remind me of yesterday. My feet are planted right where I was when he punished me.

I go over every possible reason he could have had for putting a cup of a coffee within sight and leaving it for me. It's flavored with enough cream and sugar that the bitter coffee flavor is less evident. Yesterday I made a cup for myself, my first cup of coffee since I've been here. And he must have watched.

Maybe that was the reason he left this here; he wanted me to know he was watching. Maybe he just wanted me to wake up.

Swallowing the sweetened drug, I decide it doesn't matter. I could wonder all I want, but I'll never know.

The only thing that matters is that if I didn't drink it, he would know, and I imagine he would be disappointed. Which is something I don't want to risk happening after yesterday.

I'm determined to be cautious and smart with every decision.

To not go back to the cell, but also to help Carter. I haven't forgotten his deal. He said I would help him and then he'd give me everything. I'm waiting, staying in his good graces. But something is going to change. I can feel it in my bones. All I have to do is obey and wait for the time to strike. Either for his plan to come to fruition or for another opportunity to make its presence known so I can escape and go back to the safety of my father's home.

Before I even realize it, the ceramic mug is empty in my hands and I leave it on the dresser to change into the clothes he left for me on the end of the bed.

Another routine of his. It's the routines that give me comfort. Knowing what to expect, and how to react. That's something that doesn't frighten me, if nothing else.

The fabric is thicker today. Nothing sheer or delicate. I have to grip the shoulders of it and hold it at arm's length to discover it's a black cotton wraparound dress. It's beautiful and as I slip it on, the soft fabric tickling just above my knee where it stops, I start to feel beautiful myself.

The necklace, the dress. They're classically elegant and hug my curves. I'm tempted to brush my hair and use some of the toiletries Jase bought for me.

More than anything, I want to draw the image of the woman I used to be onto the new canvases I was given last night. A blank page begs to be covered in ink, and I feel and look so different now. Maybe not so much on the surface, but everything I think and feel is no longer a semblance of what once was.

But first, I dress how he wants me to, I'll seek him out, and then I'll bide my time hiding in the art where I can remember what used to be and hold on to the last piece of the girl I used to know.

I know I'm only playing into Carter's hand as I thread my fingers through my locks and make a braid, placing it over my shoulder and then reach for the cosmetic bag. I don't recognize myself.

But the woman in the mirror is lovely. The kind of lovely that fills other women with envy, but as I drop the mascara onto the counter, I know that no one would envy me and all I am is a pretty fuck doll for Carter.

For now. It's what I have to be. Or at least that's what I tell myself. I try to dignify it by convincing myself that I have to in order to survive. But I can't deny the thought of him commanding me to spread my legs for him sends a wave of heat and want to my core.

Stepping out of the bedroom makes me nervous. It doesn't make much sense to feel safe at all here, but there is a hint of safety in knowing that only Carter will come into his bedroom. I know what to expect. Outside of the confines of those walls are things I have yet to explore.

I know where the den is, and I spent a good bit of time there yesterday. Photographs upon photographs and beautiful art lined every inch of wall in the den. It was easy to lose myself, and take in each one, imagining I had somehow slipped away and fallen into the art, away from here.

Someone in here has a fondness for old trucks. Nearly ten photographs had trucks in them, rusted and worn down, the hoods covered in snow or blue flowers peeking out from under the tires. I've never felt so strongly that old trucks are beautiful until I felt the emotion from the photographs. Maybe I'll draw that instead. Or both. I have plenty of time for both.

I know where the kitchen is from Carter's bedroom too.

And I've ventured there on my own once, but the other times Carter's brought me there.

Yesterday he made me kneel in the kitchen. The way he said it reminded me of the punishment in his bedroom, and I quickly fell to the ground to obey.

The cold floors were smooth and unforgiving against my legs, but I stayed still and at his feet as he fed me bits of his meals. I think he truly enjoys doing it. Having me on my knees beside him and at his mercy. And I have to admit, I didn't hate it, at least not until someone came into the kitchen.

I could hear whoever it was walking in, but they didn't say a word. I remember how I stilled, how I didn't know what to do.

Carter continued to place the chunks of salmon between my lips. And within seconds, whoever had entered, left.

From what I know, there are four men living here. The only other one who's talked to me outside of Carter is Jase. But I imagine it's only when Carter permits it. And I have a mental note in the back of my head to befriend him. The more ammunition I have, the better.

But I'll be careful. I'll be smart. And for now, that means obeying.

I'm nearly to the right threshold of the grand kitchen when I see Carter leaning against the counter, an iPad in his hand and his attention focused on it.

I can't help the way I freeze. As if I could somehow blend into the rich hall and vanish before he could see me.

Even if his touch lights every nerve ending of mine on fire, I still fear Carter. That will never change. Letting out a shaky breath is my downfall; Carter peeks up from his task and sees me. His gaze is lethal as he takes in my appearance.

Slowly. Ever so slowly.

Every inch of skin where his gaze lingers is instantly set ablaze.

"Come." It's the only word I'm given. A command not to be denied, and that rapid hammering in my chest intensifies. One step after another.

My life has become a series of careful steps.

Before I've even come fully into the kitchen, he commands me to kneel and I hesitate. His voice is different. The reverence and desire are absent. Something's wrong and immediately I feel defensive. My hands feel clammy as I wonder what's changed. I nearly swear to him that I haven't done anything wrong.

I've only ever kneeled at his feet, but the power in his voice makes my knees weak and I drop to the floor where I am, feet away from him in the hall, although I'm afraid he wanted me next to him. Fear. Fear commands these so carefully taken steps.

A moment passes and then another before he glances my way, through the doorway to the kitchen. "Here, songbird. Come kneel here." There's an edge of annoyance in his voice and I nearly cry. It's ridiculous. Utterly ridiculous that his reprimand would upset me to that extent, but as I crawl the last few feet to sit beside him in a kneeling position, my body nearly buckles, and I realize why this morning Carter seems different. Harder and less interested.

"You have her trained well." The man's voice sparks anger in my blood. It mixes with the fear, confusing me and I have a difficult time managing my expression, my movements. Everything in me is screaming to look at Romano, to stare into his cold dark eyes and tell him to go fuck himself.

"There's still plenty for her to learn," Carter speaks absently, swiping the screen of the iPad and focusing his attention on it. He doesn't touch me. Not like he does around his brothers.

My head hangs low, so low it nearly hurts my neck, but I don't want Romano to see my face. I have to bite the inside of my cheek so hard that it bleeds to keep from speaking up.

Be smart, I remind myself although it doesn't soothe a damn thing I'm feeling.

"How's—"

Carter cuts Romano off and states, "I'm happy with it. Let's move forward."

With his simple words, Carter leaves my side to walk the few feet across the kitchen, passing the iPad back to Romano and I chance a peek up. In his crisp dress shirt and dark gray slacks, Carter's expensive, dominating appearance is at odds with Romano's mien. His shirt hangs baggy in the front, not tailored to be fitted, I'd suspect because of his weight.

"When does it begin?" Carter asks with his back to Romano as he stalks toward me. He catches my stare and holds it until he reaches me, forcing me to pull my chin up so I don't break his gaze.

He only looks away when his hand reaches my hair and he cups the back of my head. The satisfaction and thrill of having him hold me so gently and possessively are undeniably fucked up. But still, I nearly smile.

The more comfortable I get, the more I grow to crave his small touches and the warmth of his body.

It's not supposed to be this way, but I can feel myself slipping into this new reality.

"Next week," Romano answers him and I can practically hear his grin. "We'll start taking them out all at once. As many as we can."

Adrenaline pumps in my veins, remembering the conversation from weeks ago. He's going to kill my father's men and all I can think about is Nikolai, my first kiss and only true friend in this world. My family and everyone I grew up with.

I know, and yet I can do nothing. The air around me is suffocating as I sit there silently, remembering how easily some of them have killed before, how I've wished that those men would die so many times. But not all of them. Not my family. Not Nikolai.

Inside I scream at myself to beg for answers, to beg for mercy. But on the surface I stay calm and wait for Romano to leave. There has to be a way for me to spare some of the people I love. The only people I love. The only family I have.

Please, show mercy. I nearly whisper the words as Carter leaves me yet again, walking Romano to the door and leaving me lonely and pathetic on the floor of the kitchen.

I don't make a sound. I stay silent.

But I will beg. I will fight. I will do anything. I won't let them kill my family.

There has to be a way.

If he cares anything for me, he'll show mercy. My gaze drops to the shadows of the two of them in the hall. The saddest part of the last thought is that I already know he won't show mercy. I'm only his whore.

CHAPTER 23

Carter

T HE FIRE CRACKLES. I'VE ALWAYS FOUND COMFORT IN THE soothing sound. My songbird's humming is the only thing that's come close and whether or not she knows it, she's been humming every so often since I left her in the den.

Gripping the back of the tufted sofa, I watch the glow of the fire play across her face. The shadows only make her look more beautiful. Even though she's drawing near the hearth, she hasn't turned on the lights. The sun set hours ago, taking the daylight that filled this room with it. But she's stayed by the fire, consumed with her art.

"Aria." I attempt to keep my voice calm and gentle, so I don't startle her. But I achieve the opposite and the black charcoal in her hand leaves a mar across the center of the piece she's drawing. Surprise and fear are evident from her parted lips but she shifts her expression quickly, leaving her pad and the charcoal on the hearth to kneel for me.

She doesn't address me any other way, simply waiting for a command. Her submission is beautiful, but there's a twisting in my gut. She's faking it. It's only because of yesterday. She's only being good because I caught her searching through my room. She doesn't fool me.

"You did well this morning," I compliment her as I round the large sofa. Her eyes watch me; they watch every movement I make.

As much as I see her, I know she sees me. It's one of the things that's pulling me to her every second of every day.

I don't want to miss the little hints of honesty that she can't hide from me.

"I don't like that man," she says under her breath, daring to raise her eyes to me. "Romano." A grin pulls at my lips. "I couldn't tell," I say, toying with her.

She did perfectly. Submitting to me and showing him how I have her under my thumb. That I've gained control of her, even when she couldn't contain her contempt for him.

She's helping me set him up for his own demise, and she doesn't even know it.

"Can I tell you a secret?" I ask her as I sink into the sofa, relaxing against it as she nods once and then whispers, "Yes."

"Come here." I pat the seat next to me and watch her debate on whether she should crawl or stand to get here. Glancing at her right hand, covered in charcoal, she chooses to stand and reach for the towel on the coffee table. She's deliberate in her motions as she quickly cleans her hands and then walks quietly to sit beside me. Only the crackling of the fire occupies the silence.

As she sits, I slip my arm around her waist, pulling her closer, lowering my lips to her ear then nipping her lobe before moving to her neck.

When I'm touching her, she knows exactly how to behave. She loses that constant inner questioning and gives herself to me completely. Letting her breathing quicken and her head fall to the side. She can't hide from me when my hands are on her.

It's a heady feeling I've grown addicted to.

I imagine she doesn't realize how often she touches me. Like now, how she reaches out to my shoulder as I rake my teeth up and down her neck.

Nipping her ear once more and feeling the thrill of her ragged moans deep in my chest, I whisper to her, "I want the man dead."

Her lashes flutter open and as they do, Jase enters the doorway. He hesitates and nearly turns around, but I gesture for him to enter. Time and time again, she seizes up when another person is added to the equation. She forgets how to react and becomes a lost little bird with a broken wing. Stiff in my embrace, she struggles to know where to look as Jase enters.

Slowly she pulls her legs up onto the sofa and bows her head. I know Jase is watching me, but I can't take my eyes away from her.

"You're mine," I tell her in a voice that commands her to look back at me. "You will hold your head up high." Her eyes widen slightly and then follow my fingers as I trace them from her collar down the center of her chest. "How else will they see this?" My pointer intertwines with the necklace and she nods in understanding.

I can feel her heart racing just beyond my touch, but I let the necklace fall into place and turn back to my brother. The judgment and disgust that lingered in his eyes only days ago are gone, replaced now only by curiosity. It's all going better than I'd hoped, even if it has taken longer than I'd planned.

"It's set for next week." As the words register with Jase and he tells me the shipments are coming in early for Romano, I notice how Aria's demeanor changes again.

She already knows too much. As much as I enjoy her presence, she shouldn't be privy to the knowledge of how her father's empire will fall.

"You look lovely tonight," Jase speaks directly to her. Surprise lights up her face as the fire continues to cast shadows over her.

"Thank you," she says, but her voice is soft, too soft and she clears her throat to repeat herself. "Thank you."

"I admire your art," he adds, and I glance down at the scattering of papers on the floor. Three new ones today, and each more stunning than the last. She's not rushed anymore. She takes her time, and the beauty she creates is captivating. I never expected to feel proud of what I thought was only a distraction.

The thrill rings in my blood. She craves acceptance, protection, and a tenderness that I can't always give her. But my brothers can. Even now as she worries and struggles, his kindness makes her weaker toward me. Each small gesture of acceptance makes her more willing to obey me.

"She's talented." I compliment her as well, although I speak to Jase.

"Thank you," she says again, and the fidgeting stops momentarily, replaced by a calmer demeanor.

"We'll go over the rest tonight," I tell Jase and he takes the cue to leave easily enough. No more of this in front of her. She needs to be perfect for the dinner.

And then everything will change.

"Tonight then," Jase says and nods a goodnight to Aria. A gentle smile flickers on her lips, but she struggles to speak to him in return.

"You're doing so well," I speak to her gently as Jase leaves us. Her hair is soft under my fingers as I push the locks from her face. "Apart from yesterday morning, I mean."

The reminder makes her stiffen, but only until I trail my fingers back to the necklace, the mix of pearls and diamonds strung together on a thin platinum chain. So delicate and breakable, just like her.

"I'm sorry," she apologizes again.

"No, you're not." The words come out with a sternness that's irrefutable. "I expected as much, but you aren't sorry."

"I'm sorry I disappointed you," she says, and the statement sounds genuine, even as she closes her eyes and swallows noticeably. I take in every hint of her features, seeing nothing but sincerity.

"Aria," I tell her as I slip my hand to the nape of her neck, "you haven't disappointed me." My voice is deeper than I intended, laced with the lust I still have for her.

I thought I would grow tired of her but having Aria and playing with her has become my favorite game.

She only sighs at my statement, a soft sound that's a mix of want and need and something else.

I whisper at the shell of her ear, "I can spoil you; this doesn't have to be something you hate."

"I will give you anything," she whispers and those beautiful eyes peer into mine, searching for mercy, "Please don't kill my family."

"I had to pick a side, but they'll both die, Aria. There's no changing that." If I could steal the pain from her, I would.

"You said you wanted him dead. Romano. Why not side with my father?"

"Do you think your father would spare me, Aria? Do you think he'd allow me to live?" My voice comes out harder with each word, remembering how my life was almost snuffed out by his hands. Her gorgeous eyes turn to dark wells of sadness. She knows the truth about her father, but still, she continues.

"He would," she whispers with hopefulness.

"He wouldn't," I tell her, expecting to be angered by her naivety, but it's only pity for her that I feel. "You need to stay out of this, Aria," I command her, and she nods once, but I can see the pleas written on her face.

"I can't just do nothing," she whispers.

"You must, or you'll leave me with no choice." It's not a threat, but it's full of truth and I pray she behaves. "You're smarter than this. You know how to survive."

"I'll always be a prisoner," she murmurs, and her voice is soft but desperate. Her eyes open and she almost says something. She almost begs or pleads or questions. But she doesn't.

"I want to steal the fight from you," I say the words without thinking, without realizing how honest they are. "I will have all of you, Aria."

It takes a moment for her to respond, and when she does, it's with her eyes closed and her words are laced with pain. "I know you will."

She holds on to that pain so well. Gripping it chaotically, just to hold on to something. In a way, that enrages the very core of my being. But soon all she'll hold on to is me. So soon. I have to be patient with her. If nothing else, time will dull her pain and then all she'll have is me.

"Lie back," I give her the command and she obeys instantly, falling onto the sofa and resting her head on the decorative pillow. Brushing my hand against her inner thigh, she parts her legs for me. The cotton slips up higher, but I have to lift her ass up and push the dress up to her waist to see all of her.

"You're always wet for me," I utter the words beneath my breath as my cock hardens. My fingers trail up and down her shaved pussy. Her lips glisten with arousal and her breathing hitches.

I unbutton my collar and pull my shirt off first, dropping it carelessly to the floor. Every second that passes, Aria's breathing gets heavier. The sofa groans under me as I shift my weight to move my shoulders between her thighs.

Gripping her ass to hold her in place, I start with a single languid lick of her tempting cunt. When I look up and find her lips parted, her eyes wide and her cheeks that beautiful hue of pink, I decide I won't stop licking, sucking and tongue fucking her cunt until she can't fight me any longer.

And then I'll have her writhing under me, cumming on my cock like she was made to do.

CHAPTER 24

Aria

THIS ISN'T WHAT LIFE IS SUPPOSED TO BE LIKE. NOT FOR someone like me. Surrounded by luxury and chained to a gilded cage, I shouldn't wake up feeling at ease.

But that's how I feel. I know that so long as I obey Carter, I'll be all right. I'll be safe and pampered even.

While my family is murdered, and I do nothing.

I can't allow it. I won't.

I have to remind myself with each kindness he offers me.

Like last night. I was holding onto a deadly combination of hate and hope. Desperate for a way out of here so I could warn my family, or a way to convince Carter to be on my father's side to present itself.

And I slipped into sleep knowing I needed to do something. That today I would act and find a way. But each kindness makes me weaker.

I'll never forget the way he held me. Gripping me to him as I lay on my side. My heart raced, and fear was real in my veins. As real as anything else. Sleep still held my eyes tightly shut until I heard his voice, recognized the deep measure of his determined words. "Come back to me." His breath was hot on my neck, his hand strong as it splayed across my belly. He held me so close and so tightly, I couldn't move when I woke up.

I could still feel the drum of my racing heart as he flipped me onto my back and buried his head in the crook of my neck, kissing me ravenously, as if he'd been deprived of it. And I pined for his lips on mine, but he didn't give them to me. I was still blinking away sleep when he whispered, "If you're going to scream a name in your sleep, it'll be my name."

I woke up wondering if it was a dream if he hadn't really taken me from a nightmare and fucked me into a deep sleep of desire. But he was still holding me the way he had when I woke up and there was no denying it was real.

"You stopped humming." Carter's deep voice pierces through my thoughts and I look up at him from the ground beneath his feet. Rolling the black charcoal between my fingers I lie to him, something I know I shouldn't do.

"I'm just thinking about what I'd like to draw next."

He knows my response is a lie. His eyes narrow, but he allows it. I don't think he wants me to go back to the cell any more than I do. Although part of me wonders if one day he'll start fucking me on that mattress and I'll be confined there.

The only thing that relieves that thought is the knowledge that Carter enjoys others seeing how I've become his. How I obey him while he gives me this freedom. If you can call it that.

My gaze wanders across Carter's office and lands yet again on a bench that doesn't belong. It peeks out from under the bookshelf across from me and it simply isn't supposed to be there.

The wood is old and unfinished, at odds with the dark polished shelves housing beautifully covered books.

The hinges have a hint of rust. I tap the charcoal in my hand against the paper and stare at it. Wondering why Carter would allow it to stay.

"Where did the bench come from?" I ask him on a whim. I haven't asked him anything. Not for a single thing. Nor have I initiated conversation. But if I have any hope of changing his mind about my father, I have to be able to speak up. And it starts right now, with that bench. Craning my neck to look at him over the desk, from where I'm seated on the floor in front of him, I wait for his reaction.

"Bench?" he questions, although I already know that he knows what I'm referring to.

Pointing straight in front of me, I answer him, "It doesn't look like it belongs."

I can hear his chair creak as he leans back, and I know he's debating on telling me something, although I don't know what. It's only an old, beat-up bench.

"Do you want to see what it can do?" he asks me, and the tone of his words catches me off guard. He must sense the hesitation because as he rises and makes his way to the bench, he adds, "It's a safe box."

The charcoal in my hand makes a small thud as it hits the paper and I watch Carter open the lid to what I thought was just an old bench.

"It's bulletproof, and it can only be locked from the inside."

"Someone could just pick it up…" I state my thought absently and he gives me a small, sad smile.

"If they knew you were in there, they could try, although it's heavy. So heavy I couldn't lift it with Daniel the day I got it."

I let my eyes graze over Carter's shoulders then back to what I thought was only a bench. I take a quick breath, ready to ask him if it was from his childhood. It's obviously far too small for him. Although I know I could easily fit. But I don't question him.

"The lock is here," he tells me and fiddles with something inside of it that clinks. I have to stand up to see and since I'm standing, I walk closer to him and to the contraption.

"Is it really safe?" I ask him and he's quiet until I look up at him. His eyes question mine. "As safe as a box can be."

Now that I'm closer to it, I'm certain I could fit inside. It would be tight. As if reading my mind, Carter tells me, "You'd fit. You'd be safe."

My eyes drift to the brass locks on the inside. There are only two, but they travel along the entire top edge. A long rod of steel falls down and slips into place when locked. I imagine you could open it with a welding torch, but with all this metal, the person inside would be burned, scarred, maybe killed before the box would actually open.

"Can you breathe in there?" I whisper my question.

Carter nods and runs his finger along small slits in the box, designed so they can't be seen from the outside, but light filters through them.

I swallow thickly as Carter places a hand on my lower back and asks, "Do you want to get inside?"

I should say no, the fear inside of me is there at the forefront, screaming that the small space is dangerous. It may look like safe, but the cell was much larger, and it was instrumental in my downfall.

But the fear is so minuscule. So quiet. It's hard to be scared of something so… insignificant when my life is in the hands of a man like Carter. And I think he'd like it if I got inside.

I nod once and as I do, I'm already lifting my right leg. With Carter's hand to balance me, I slip inside easily.

"The locks are here, but you'll have to feel for them when the lid is shut, it'll be dark."

"Are you going to close it?" I ask him and my heart pounds. I don't want him to leave me here. He towers over me and answers, "You'd be the one to close and lock it, Aria."

"Right. Of course," I say then shake my head and reach for the lid. As if it's the obvious thing to do. It strikes me then as odd that he would grant me this, a safe place to be away from him. But I could only stay in here so long.

This box is meant for hiding. The thought occurs to me as I lower the lid. It's meant to hide, to stay quiet and not be seen.

My heart thumps once as the lid shuts tightly and a tiny ray of light shines through. It's filtering in through a small slit. One that can't be seen from the outside, but I can see it clearly.

My fingers trace the locks as they slip into place, a heavy thump from the steel rod falling causing my body to react by bucking back.

Thump, thump. My heart hammers.

It reminds me of the door being kicked in when I was hiding in the closet.

My throat closes and my eyes water as I clearly see my mother through the slit. Just like I did when I hid in the closet. The memory is vivid. It's too real.

"Stop!" I scream and struggle against the lid. Panic consumes me. *I can't stay here, I can't be quiet and let him murder her.*

Screams rip through my throat. "Stop it!" I scream and it's only then that I hear Carter.

His fists pound above me.

The tears that stream down my face seem to burn my skin as I fumble for the locks.

"Carter, please!" I beg him.

"Lift the locks!" he yells at me, but I can't. I can't see them. All I can see is him holding my mother down, stabbing her over and over. The blood was everywhere. He was too fast. I couldn't save her.

"Please," I beg him and feel the entire box lift from the ground only to fall hard on the floor beneath me. Jostling me and reminding me where I am.

"Open it, Aria!" he yells at me and I try to find the locks. It takes me a long moment. Each second, images of my mother pass before my eyes. The way she tried to fight him. The way she tried not to scream. I know she didn't want me to hear or to see.

But you can only hide so much.

Finally, the locks slip back into place in my shaking hand and the mechanism opens with a loud thunk. Carter practically rips the top open. His strong arms pull me up and I'm safe in the light of the office. The images fade and I find myself huddled in his arms, feeling foolish and unable to explain what happened. My body won't stop shaking.

I hate the box. I hate it. I hate it more than the cell.

"Shhh," he shushes me and brings me to his chair. I think he's going to set me down in it, but he doesn't. He keeps holding me tight in his arms. My body shudders and I wish I could calm myself down and take it all back.

I can't stop crying.

I haven't had a panic attack in so long. It's only been night terrors for years.

"I'm sorry," I mumble the words and brush my tears away furiously. They're hot and I can already feel my eyes becoming puffy. I can hardly breathe.

"I hate the box," I push the words out as if I could blame it.

"It's okay." Carter's answer is soothing. He doesn't ask what happened. He doesn't push me for anything.

He only holds me and comforts me, running his hand up and down my back. His warmth and strength and scent surround me. And I want more of it.

I would die for more of it.

A knock at the office door startles me. "Hush, songbird," Carter whispers against my hair before calling to the door, "Come in."

It's Jase. It's almost always Jase.

He stands in the doorway, gripping the knob and not letting it go. I get the sense that he doesn't like to stay when I'm around. Like if I wasn't here, he'd have taken a seat. A shudder runs through my body, and I bury myself deeper into Carter's arms, wishing I could go back to just a minute ago.

"I just wanted to let you know, the dinner is set to go as planned."

Seeing Jase, reminds me of everything once again. Like being woken from a deep sleep. Back to realizing all of this is wrong and there isn't a piece of it that should feel right.

Back to the fact that I'm nestled in the arms of the man who's set to destroy everything I am.

The thought of dying for more of Carter's touch is still vibrant in my mind. And it withers like the petals of a broken flower in the scorching heat as the sane side of me remembers what I really am and who he really is.

"He's coming?" Carter asks and there's a deep rumble of anger hidden beneath his words. It's enough of an edge that my body stills in his embrace.

Jase nods, his gaze moving from me to Carter. "He's coming."

"And are we still on for tonight?" Carter asks Jase in a tone quite different. A tone that makes me curious. Curious enough to peek at Jase.

Jase's gaze flickers to me again before he answers, "Yeah, we're on for tonight." Patting the doorframe, he nods toward Carter and leaves us alone.

The tears, the flashback, and panic, they seem foolish now. It was only a glimpse at the past. Carter loosens his hold on me as my body stiffens and I hold my arms to my chest.

Why does he hold me and comfort me, when I'm nothing to him but a play toy? It's so he can make me weak. I know that's why. I'll fall powerless to him so easily. And he'll use me up and throw me out.

I can already see it happening.

"I'll be gone tonight." Carter's voice seems deeper, rougher even. The sound forces me to look at him as he speaks. It's odd to be at nearly eye level as I sit on his lap.

His gaze is so sharp, I can barely look him in the eye.

"You can get yourself dinner. And wait for me in either the kitchen, den, or bedroom." I stare at the knob on one of the drawers of his desk, nodding my head in obedience and feeling awkward and too afraid to speak.

My body shudders as he lays a hand on my upper back, between my shoulder blades and working his way down to the small of my back.

"Maybe you need a drink?"

When I turn to him this time, I want to yell at him. I want to hide. I want to cry.

The question is on the tip of my tongue, *why are you doing this to me?*

But I already know the answer. It's why Carter does everything.

Because he can. Because he wants to.

CHAPTER 25

Carter

THE RED ROOM WASN'T MY IDEA. IT WAS JASE'S, OF ALL PEOPLE. He's quiet, keeps to himself, but he created a club that's the perfect cover-up and a successful business at that. He always stays in the back, where other business is conducted, but nonetheless, Jase's creation is something he's proud of. And every time I come here, I'm reminded of that fact.

The music thrums in my veins before the large red glass doors even open. In a gray tailored suit, I don't exactly blend in with the nightlife. Not like Jase does in his faded jeans and crisp, button-down, open at the collar.

I prefer a suit. Jase prefers to blend in. Each method has its advantages.

"Welcome back, sirs," Jared greets us as we step into the club, the music at full volume and the smells of alcohol and sex appeal hit me instantly. With the dark red paisley wallpaper that lines the walls and black chandeliers hanging from the sixteen-foot-high black ceiling, The Red Room looks like a nightclub of sin at first glance.

As the alcohol pours throughout the night and the bodies grind against one another, sin is an accurate description. The money flows as easily as the liquor.

Walking past the grinding bodies and kitten eyes from several women holding drinks in one hand and their clutches in another, I ignore it all, listening intently to what Jared has to say.

I stopped everything to come down here with my brother. All because Jared, the club manager, and head of business while we're away, said he had a girl who would talk.

"You sure it's her?" Jase asks him.

"Yeah," Jared nods as we pass the second bar and make our way around the edge of the dance floor to get to the backroom. "She comes in every week asking for it."

"What'd you tell her?"

"Nothing. Just that the delivery is on a delay." The DJ starts a new set and the dance floor roars so loudly the ground shakes as the steel doors to the backroom push open and then close softly, finally silencing the distractions of the club.

"Thanks for waiting for us," Jase tells the two men in the back of the room. Mick is one of them; I don't know the name of the other, but Jase does. This is Jase's place to run. Everyone knows him, and he knows everyone, so I let him lead and stay quiet.

Quiet is dangerous, and that's exactly how I want them to see me.

"Of course, Mr. Cross," Mick says and nods his head at Jase then quirks a smile at me as he adds, "and Mr. Cross."

The small girl seated at the lone table in the room grips the plastic cup of a pink drink that's probably got just as much sugar in it as alcohol. Her lips part open with a hint of disbelief and then she licks them, smiling although it's thin and withered. Just like the state of her body under the too-tight tube top.

"You're waiting for the delivery?" Jase asks, looking to the left and right as if he doesn't want to say it out loud and get caught by someone. I'd laugh at him and his display, but he's damn good at what he does, and I do enjoy a good show.

The girl imitates him, looking over her shoulders at the two hired men of ours in The Red Room t-shirts and black jeans before she nods. "You guys have the best sweets."

"Sweets?" I ask, and she grins at me like she knows a secret she can't wait to tell me.

"It's what the streets are calling it now," she says and bites down on her lower lip, letting her body sway. Jase and I pull out our chairs across from her, the legs scraping across the floor. Sweets. Plural. Because that fucker Romano has his version out. I keep the small hint of friendliness firmly in place. But I'm nothing but pissed at the reminder

"Sweet Lullaby, you mean?" Jase asks, lifting an eyebrow. And again, she nods.

"You're buying a lot of this stuff," Jase tells her although it comes out a question. Her nails scratch down her arms as she glances all around us. She's jittery and the chair legs beneath her keep rasping on the floor.

"I just need it, okay?" Her words are rushed. The air changes around her instantly.

Noting her hollow cheeks, dead eyes, and pale lips, the humor, and vibe that she's down to have a good time have vanished.

"Is it really what you need?" Jase asks and leans forward to stare into her eyes. "'Cause we've got some other stuff you might want?"

She's in need of a hit. That's for damn sure and if I had to guess her drug of choice is heroin. Maybe coke.

"I just need to grab it and get back," she answers, but her voice is breathy and uncertain. I wait a moment, glancing at Jase as we both hear her swallow over the muted sound of the music playing in the club.

"I think we have some coming, sorry about the wait, miss...?"

"Jenny. Jenny Parks," she answers him and then reaches into her purse for her phone. The two men behind us make a move for their guns, and the little blonde doesn't even notice.

"Fuck, it's already past nine," she says and her face crumples with a mix of anxiety and fear.

As she slips her thumb into her mouth to chew on her nail, Jase asks her, "Hey, is there anything I can get you while you wait?"

"Anything to calm you down a little? Another drink or something stronger?" I add.

Her breath comes out harder. "Yeah, maybe," she replies as her eyes dart from me to Jase. "I just wanted to come in and get the stuff. It'll be here soon?" she asks again, looking down at the phone to check the time. "Like, how soon."

"It could be a bit," Jase says and shrugs, looking at Mick and she watches him shrug too. "We've got other stuff while you wait," he offers but she's already shaking her head, still biting that thumbnail.

She speaks over the finger in her mouth. "I need the sweets first."

The problem with a junkie is that they have a one-track mind. They want the drug. And it's obvious that she gets hers when she delivers our drug to the real buyer.

Jase shrugs again. "An hour, maybe?" He glances at me and I nod my head.

"Fuck," she mutters and cradles her face in her hands.

"You want us to drop it off somewhere else?" Jase asks, and she peeks up through her lashes. We're getting the address of where this product is going. Either from her telling us or from us following her. Whatever the fuck we have to do.

"I have to get back. I'm sorry," she rushes her words as she slides her phone off the table and into her purse.

"We can get you something to take the edge off while it comes in and we can talk a little?" Jared suggests to her from where he's standing guard by the steel doors. She seems to get it then. The reality of what's going on hits her like a ton of bricks and she's shit at hiding it.

"It's just... it's my brother. You know? He needs it, and he doesn't like me to be late."

"Your brother?" Jase questions and I glance at Mick, standing behind the seated blonde, who shakes his head once. Little Jenny doesn't have a brother.

"Yeah, and he doesn't like people to come around, you know?" Again, her words are rushed and she looks at the men behind her then at us.

"I can just come back another time," she mumbles. Her breathing is sporadic as she pulls her purse to her chest.

She takes a second to stand up, but Mick's hand on her shoulder makes her pause.

A second drops between us all, heavy with the consequences of what's to come.

She's buying for someone else and lying to cover it up. Someone who keeps her doped up and someone who scares her enough to give her the strength to resist her next hit from us.

Her head turns slowly so she can see Mick's large hand gripping tighter onto her shoulder. The fear that drifts from her is palpable and sickening.

"You tell your brother we're sorry we couldn't get it to him tonight, Jenny," Jase speaks up and instantly Mick's grip on the girl loosens.

I can practically hear her heart beating as she looks at Jase wide-eyed. She's frozen still until he leans back in his seat and tells her with a wink, "We'll have it for you next time."

"You let us know if you want to talk anytime now, you hear me?" Jared says as he opens the door to the club and the music flows into the small back room.

Jenny nods her head furiously, stumbling into the empty chair next to her before taking off out of the room without another look back.

"Follow her," I tell Mick and with a single nod he's gone. Jase's blunt nails tap against the table as the door closes and the sound of the nightlife beyond it is muted once again.

"You let her off easy," I say quietly under my breath.

"Girls don't need to be dragged into this shit." That's his only answer and he doesn't bother to lower his voice like I did.

The same table he's tapping, I've covered with blood in the past. It wouldn't have come to that with the blonde, but a little lie to get her talking wouldn't have hurt her. Showing our cards that we know she's buying for someone else, well that might have gotten a word or two from her. Maybe a name.

"Maybe he's sending girls because he knows you're weak for them," I suggest. All of us have our limits. And women happen to be the common thread between us.

"Fuck you, I'm not weak," he tells me although I can see him considering it. It's in his eyes.

The corners of my lips tip up into a smirk as Jared lights up a cigarette. But with a puff and the words that come out of his mouth, the smile vanishes. "With the Talvery girl shit, they should know we aren't pussies when it comes to women."

The silence stretches in the room for a moment with neither of us commenting.

"The Talvery girl," I say beneath my breath and it gets a comment from Jared, but I don't bother to listen to him. "She's mine," I tell him, cutting off his joke or whatever the fuck was coming out of his mouth.

I stand abruptly, letting an anger I haven't felt in a long time dictate my words. Staring into Jared's eyes, the words rip from my mouth, "The next time someone refers to her as that, *the Talvery girl*," I practically spit out the name, "you tell them, she's all mine."

My teeth grind against each other so hard, I swear they'll crack.

Jared doesn't speak, doesn't move. I don't think he's breathing, although the cigarette in his mouth stays oddly still with the glow of amber making his expression look even paler.

My muscles coil, waiting for him to call her that again. She's not *the Talvery girl*. She doesn't belong to them.

"What's her name?" I ask him, tilting my head and that cigarette wavers in his mouth. "Take out the fucking cigarette and tell me what the fuck her name is." My eyes pierce into his as he drops the cigarette from his mouth, barely catching it between his fingers and swallowing thickly. The cords of his neck are tight, and I can hear him swallow.

"I—I—" he stutters, and I lean in closer to scream in his face, the words of my question scratching and ripping their way up my throat, "What's her name?"

"I don't know," he says in a quavering admission.

"It's Aria," I say then pat his shoulders with both of my hands as he struggles to look me in the eyes. The anger wanes as I feel his sweat beneath my hands.

"It's Aria, and she doesn't belong to the Talverys anymore." My words are calm, eerily so.

"Of course, she doesn't," Jared shakes his head slightly, his lips turning into a hesitant smile. "She's yours. Aria is yours and she's called Aria."

He won't shut the fuck up, the poor prick.

"You let anyone who calls her otherwise know," I tell him, nodding my head once toward a spot on the brick wall. The bricks are redder, newer and don't blend in.

"I'd hate to lose it and have to blow some fucker's poor skull open because he pissed me off."

"Yeah," Jared's answer is a whisper of fear. "Aria, and she's yours."

Jase's hand hitting the back of my shoulder is the only thing that rips my gaze away from Jared's.

"Keep up the good work, Jared." Jase adds, "Good job tonight," and pushes the door open to go back out into the bar.

He holds it open for me and I move around Jared, still very much stuck in his place and only nodding his response as if he's scared to speak. As I take a step to leave, I glance down at him, the disgusting smell of piss overriding the scent of cigarettes. The fucker pissed himself.

I wish I could smile or feel any sense of pleasure from knowing how deeply rooted the fear goes. But all I can think is that these assholes are calling my Aria, *the Talvery girl*.

She's so much more than that.

"You've got to back down with that," Jase tells me as we walk side by side through the club. There's no one around us that could hear, but still, I want to tell him to fuck off.

"I don't have to do shit," I respond in a grunt, the rage still looming, but even as the words are spoken, I know he's right. They could use her against me. She could so easily become known as my weakness.

"What's the point of doing that?" he asks me, cutting off my train of thought.

But I don't have an answer ready. There's always a reason. Everything I do has a purpose. It takes the entire walk through the club for me to respond, and not until we're out of the front doors where the cool air greets us, and the moonlight lingers over the parking lot.

The wind whips against my face, and Jase slips his hands into his pockets as the valet pulls our car up to the curb. "The point is that they've forgotten she's mine when they call her a Talvery. I won't have anyone forget she belongs to me."

CHAPTER 26

Aria

CARTER HAD ME DRINK A GLASS OF WHISKEY WITH ORANGE bitters but somehow it tasted like chocolate. I don't know what it was exactly, but it's still humming through me. He left me with a second drink in his office and it's the second one that did this to me.

Even as I stand in the kitchen, busying myself with something to take my mind off everything that's going on around me, I can feel the alcohol numbing the pain. As if I'm spared from what's going to happen, and it's everything else that's moving. I'm just standing here.

But I hate it. I don't want to be helpless and beg for mercy from a man who won't show it. I don't want to seem helpless, but I have no choice.

The refrigerator is full of nearly anything I could want. Fresh eggs, deli meat, fruits, and vegetables. Most of the meats for dinner are frozen, but there's plenty to satisfy me.

I'm not hungry in the least, but Carter told me to eat and so here I am.

It took me a while to get started, long after Carter had left.

Instead of doing anything at all, I stared at the door. And then each of the windows I passed. And the windows to the garden. I wish I could leave and tell my father they're coming, but I'm sure he knows. That's the only comfort I have in this powerless state. My father must know they're coming for him.

The knife slices through a tomato. It's so sharp the skin splits instantly without any pressure at all. I suck the taste of the whiskey from my teeth. I can't do anything, but I need to do something.

The thunk of the knife on the cutting board is the only thing I hear over and over again.

"What are you making?" A deep voice from behind me makes me jump. The knife slips from my hand and I'm too scared to jump away from it as it crashes to the floor. I stand there breathless with anxiety shooting through my veins.

"Shit," the voice says as my heart races and pounds in my chest.

It's Daniel. I've seen him before and I know that's his name. But he hasn't said a word to me. He never even looks at me. Yet, now I'm alone with him, and Carter's nowhere to be seen. In dark jeans and a black t-shirt, he runs his hand through his hair with a shameful look on his face. "I should've come from the other direction, huh?" There's a sweetness about him, but I don't trust him. I don't trust any of the Cross brothers.

"I'm just keeping an eye on you," Daniel says easily, and his lips quirk up into a half smile. "A salad?" he asks.

"Yeah," I say, but my answer is a whisper. It's odd to be a prisoner yet remain free to move about. Even odder to have a conversation with someone as if there's nothing at all wrong with my position.

I force myself to swallow and bend down slowly, keeping him in my periphery, to pick up the knife. My body trembles as I turn my back to him just enough to walk to the sink and rinse it off. "Avocado, tomato and Italian dressing. I was craving something like it," I tell him as the water pours down onto the sharp edge of the knife. The light reflects in the water and my heart thumps again.

"Salt tooth?" he asks me, and I nod, eyeing him but trying to just have a conversation. I wonder what he thinks of me. What he thinks of Carter for keeping me here.

All I can look at is the knife in my hand, the alcohol is thrumming, my nerves are high, and I don't know how to survive anymore.

The idea of an escape plan is forming, but the anxiety is so much higher.

His footsteps give him away as he walks to the other side of the counter, closer to where the chunks of avocado and freshly cut tomato wait for me. My mind is highly aware of where he is. And who he is.

He knows how to get out of here. He could be my ticket to freedom.

"Did you find the bowls?" he asks me as I turn around to face him, the knife feeling heavier in my hand.

With the water off, the room is silent. Eerily so. Or maybe it's just because of the thoughts running through my mind. The counter is hard against my lower back as I lean against it to keep me steady as I watch him open a cabinet and pull out a bowl.

He smiles at me like he's my friend or my companion, and not a guard to keep me here. And he lets me hold the knife. He doesn't even look at it. I have a weapon and I'm a prisoner here, yet he doesn't care in the least. *Why would he, you weak girl?* the voice in the back of my head taunts me and laughs.

"Thank you," I say, and my voice sounds small and weak. Gripping the countertop behind me, it feels so cold, so unforgiving in comparison to how hot my body is right now.

The ceramic bowl clinks as it hits the countertop and Daniel smiles at me. A handsome, charming smile with his hands up in the air as he says, "I'm not going to hurt you; I promise."

I'm the one with the knife.

I keep thinking it as I take each small step toward the counter.

My bare feet pad on the cold floor.

I offer him a small smile, but I don't say anything and neither does he.

Until that knife slices so easily through the tomato again. I imagine the way it would go down, but it's hard to focus. I couldn't kill him. He'd have to push in the code and then I'd run.

"Is he treating you alright?" he asks me, and my grip tightens on the knife. He could so easily push in a code and grant me freedom. And then I could tell my father they're coming.

Raising my eyes to his for the first time, I ask him, "What do you think?" I'm surprised by the strength, but I crave more of it.

His gaze flickers to the door behind me and then back to me.

Silence descends upon the kitchen.

"He's in a difficult position," Daniel offers me when I start to cut the slices into chunks, trying not to think of what would happen if I failed. What Carter would do to me if I tried to escape and failed. My chest hollows and my stomach drops at the thought. The cell. Or worse, the box. He knows what that box would do to me if he put a lock on the outside of it.

My blood runs cold.

"He's not a bad man," Daniel says, and I watch as the knife in my hand trembles as it hovers over the remaining slices.

Bad man? He's not a bad man? If only Daniel knew what I was thinking.

"Good men don't do what he's done," I tell Daniel without looking at him. "I begged him last night to spare my father. My family," I say and my voice cracks.

"I'm sorry, but you know he can't do that." It's his only response and I crumble inside. My heart twists in a painful way. It's a horrible ache that I can't explain when I hear Daniel turn to walk away.

He's leaving me. Because he can. Because it doesn't matter if he leaves me to wallow all alone. All I'll ever be is alone and pathetic if I don't even try.

My fingers wrap around the knife until my knuckles are white and I cry out for him. "Daniel!" His tall, lean body stiffens, the muscles in his shoulders rippling as he turns around.

He's maybe five feet from me. But the kitchen island separates the two of us.

Be smart, I remind myself. But at this point, nothing I'm about to do is smart. Lowering the knife to my side, the blade nearly caresses my skin when I clear my throat.

"I'm sorry," I offer him although I can hardly hear myself over the furious pounding of my heart in my chest. "Could you show me where the seasonings are?" I have to swallow before I can add, "Please."

Daniel's mouth is set in a grim straight line; his eyes pierce deeply into me like he knows exactly what I'm about to do. But he walks toward me. He walks to my side of the island. Inside I'm screaming that it's a trap, that he knows. My blood rushes in my ears and the sweat from my hand nearly makes the knife slip.

Five feet becomes four, becomes three, becomes two.

And he turns his back to me, reaching at eye level to open a cabinet before turning around and finding that knife pointed at his throat.

The sweat that crawls along my skin is sickening. It covers every inch of me as I try to speak, but my dry throat won't allow it.

Stupid girl! I hear the voice yell at me. Regret and fear are instant, but the knife is in the air and I can't take it back. My hand feels as if it's shaking, but the knife is steady.

I can't go back. "Get me out of here," I breathe as he stares at me with disdain.

"You don't want to do this, Aria." Daniel's words are so genuine, so sincere, that I almost regret taking the step forward and nearly pressing the blade to his throat.

"I want to leave." I somehow push the words out. How strong they sound, although I'm panicked.

Daniel's eyes turn sympathetic, or maybe they just look back at me as if I'm the pathetic one. I can't tell. He deceives me so.

"I can't help you with that." My heart plummets and races at the same time. This is my only chance, my only hope.

"Open the front door." As I give the command, I step forward and my trembling hand pushes the knife closer to him, slicing the skin of his upper neck, just slightly. A small nick, but it cuts him. *I cut him.*

The horror of seeing the bright red blood distracts me for a moment, a moment long enough for Daniel to shove his hand in front of me and try to grip the knife.

He may be fast, but my fear is faster. The knife pierces through his shirt and bicep, easily cutting into him, slicing his arm as I stumble back.

My heart beats so hard I swear I'll die from terror alone.

The hot grip of his hand burns into my forearm even after he's let go. My back hits the counter and I jump slightly, but I keep the knife up and sidestep slowly around him. The adrenaline is higher than I've ever felt before.

This is bad, my heart screams in terror, *this is fucking bad.* And I've lost the advantage of surprise, the threat of the knife minuscule compared to what it was a moment ago.

"Let me go!" I yell at him as he seethes at me. His grimace grows to something else. Something that looks hurt for me once again. And I want to sneer at him and his pity, but I feel sorry for me too. And there's nothing lower than that.

"I said let me go!" I'm too afraid to get closer to him and every step feels like my knees may give out from the pure adrenaline pumping through me.

"Even if I opened the door, there are two guards at the gates and I'm not leaving anytime soon. They know that." His voice is stern, and he takes his eyes from me to look at the cut. "Damn, you got me good," he says, still not even bothering to look at me. As if I'm not a threat.

"You could hide me in your car." My voice skips over my words as I struggle to think about the next step.

"And be scared of your knife that's with you in my trunk?" he asks and my head sways. My body threatens to sway with it. I failed. I already know I've failed.

Stupid girl, the voice says, but even she pities me and the earlier anger from her is absent.

My heart sinks and it doesn't stop like it's in a never-ending free fall even though I can already feel it in the pit of my stomach. "Get me out of here, please. You can get me out of here," I say although my voice cracks and I take a step forward with the knife. "Please," I beg him.

He finally glances up at me and says, "Put the knife down." That's all he says, in that disinterested tone that all of the Cross brothers seem to have. A tone that's utterly dismissive.

"Fuck you," I almost cry as I tell him off. I have to step closer to him, I have to go through with this. He nearly got the knife from me last time and if he does this time, I'm going back to the cell. Fuck. My throat closes in on itself.

As if hearing my thoughts, Daniel tells me, "I could grab my gun, Aria, don't make me."

His words kill the last bit of hope. What would I do? Throw the knife at him if he ran to get his gun? "Put the knife down."

"Please don't," I plead with him. Tears prick my eyes at how stupid I am. At what's to come.

The cell. I'll be in the cell tonight. And for however long it takes for Carter to let me out after.

The heavy knife feels heavier and I want to point it at myself. A very big part of me thinks I could get farther if I would threaten to hurt myself. But I don't want to be in pain. "Please help me," I barely get the weak words out.

Daniel's response is immediate, his steps deliberate and powerful. My body shakes as he comes close enough to grip the knife, but this time when he wraps his hand around my forearm, I loosen my grip and the knife falls from my hand to his other hand and only then does he let me go.

I cower like a disobedient child or worse, a dog who knows he's about to be beaten.

Silent tears fall, and I wipe them as I listen to the knife drop into the sink before Daniel turns on the faucet to clean his cut. The cut I gave him.

"I'm sorry." My words are choked, and I try to repeat them again but fail. My breathing comes in shallow pants. "I can't go back. Please, I can't."

"Hey, it's okay." Daniel's voice is soft as he approaches me, but fear is the only thing I have to give him until he says, "We don't have to tell Carter."

His words make me stare into his dark eyes. They're so like Carter's. But the heat and desire aren't there. Just sincerity.

"I won't tell him, okay?" His comforting voice soothes the fear in me. "This will stay between us." The relief that replaces the anxiety nearly makes me throw up.

"Why would you do that?" I question him. "I hurt you."

"Because I would have done the same." His simple answer is comforting, but it doesn't give me any hope.

"I'm sorry," I mumble my apology and have to clear my throat. I'm choking on my words. "I didn't want to... to hurt you."

"Why'd you have to do that?" I shake my head, wiping under my eyes. He adds, "I would have done it, but I thought you were smarter than that."

"I'm sorry." It's all I can say. "I need to get out of here," I insist, and my words bleed with despair.

"It's better that you're here," he tells me. "You're not safe at your father's and I know Carter may not seem like the best person to you right now, but I know there's a reason for all of this."

"My father." The words tumble from my lips. *I'm failing him.*

"You need to eat," Daniel says, backing away from me and not acknowledging me. It's the same thing Carter told me. I just need to eat. And obey.

"You're going to kill him," I say and it's a statement, not a question. I can't even think about eating. The thought is repulsive.

Daniel opens the fridge and ignores me, although he angles his body so he can see me in his periphery.

He closes the door to the fridge with his elbow as he twists off the top to a beer and takes a quick swig, making the dampened shirt of blood glisten in the light and that bit of red on his throat stare back at me.

I almost tell him I'm sorry, yet again. Even with knowing his plans for my father. It's a sickening feeling to not know what's right and wrong, but regardless, you have no choice.

The bottle smacks down on the counter and he finally answers me. "It was going to happen whether or not we stepped in."

"What was?" I ask him in a hushed voice, cautiously, barely raising my eyes to meet his gaze. The only thing I keep thinking is that I need to be nice to him, so he doesn't tell Carter.

"War."

The one-word answer forces my gaze to the polished tile floor. It's quiet while he drinks, and I clean up the mess of the cubed vegetables I won't eat.

"You won't tell Carter?" I feel selfish for daring to bring it back up, but I need to know he won't. If Carter were here for that… I can't even begin to think of what he would do.

"Look at me," Daniel's voice beckons and I do as he tells me. "I am not going to say a word to Carter. Not one word." His voice is soothing, but I find it hard to be anything close to being okay.

"Thank you," I tell him and press my hand to my face to cool it down.

He finishes the beer, all the while I stare at the spot on the floor until I turn instinctively at the sound of his name being called out by a feminine voice.

"Shit," he says under his breath. He's quick to grab me by the arm. His grip is tight, demanding and catches me off guard with that fear returning and spiking through me.

"Go to the den," he demands beneath his hushed breath and attempts to push me out of the kitchen from the other threshold. My feet slip across the floor as he pushes me toward the den.

"Daniel?" the voice calls out again, this time closer and he urges through clenched teeth, "Go."

My shoulders hunch forward and I feel like nothing. Like absolutely nothing. Worthless, pathetic and a weak thing to be pushed around at anyone's whim.

"Don't do it again, Aria. You're smarter than that," he tells me before turning his back to me and walking briskly to the other side of the kitchen.

His words numb me for a moment, even though my feet move of their own free will.

I'm supposed to be smarter than that. Maybe I used to be, but a mix of desperation and the feeling of falling into a dark abyss is all I can see anymore... that mix is deadly to any semblance of intelligence that I have.

My hands tremble and I struggle to breathe, but I try to remember Carter's words from what seems like so long ago. I try to remember what he said that made me feel like I had hope. I try, and I fail.

It doesn't matter what they were. Everything is insignificant when there's nothing you can do to change your fate.

And now that I've been so fucking stupid, he's going to put me back in the cell.

I shouldn't have done that. A heavy breath nearly suffocates me. I need to listen.

With my eyes closed, I whisper, "Daniel won't tell him." But the words have little mercy on my pain, because I know I won't be able to hide it from Carter. He sees me. He sees all of me. And he watches everything.

"What the hell did you do?" A woman's voice carries through the kitchen with shock and worry, startling me and cutting through my thoughts. As quietly as I can, I slink to the side of the doorway, so I can listen but won't be seen.

I didn't know another girl was here. But the way she's talking to Daniel make it obvious that she's with him. Not a prisoner of him. Jealousy and fear mix inside of me and I don't know why I'm so scared of being seen by her. Maybe the trickle of shame as I grip the doorway is indication enough.

"I was drinking and cutting up shit and I thought it would be cool to toss the knife." I hear Daniel give an excuse that's not at all believable. But the girl believes him.

"You could have killed yourself," she reprimands him, although her voice carries a tinge of disbelief. Guilt seeps into my blood. And a part of me knows it's ridiculous to feel sorry for trying to save myself. But so is all of this.

Daniel chuckles. "Of all the ways to die, I don't think it's going to be this, Addison." I can hear him take a drink before telling her, "I got you a beer." I almost walk away, but Addison's next words keep me planted where I am.

"We need to talk." The severity of her tone is sharp.

"Not right now." Daniel talks to her differently than the way he talks to me. Differently than the way Carter talks to me. There's an edge of comfort in his voice and I don't expect it.

"It's always not right now," she responds. "Something's going on." Her tone softens, pleading with him. "Why can't I leave?" she asks him with desperation clinging to every word.

"It's just better to be safe," he replies so lowly I hardly hear him. The thrumming of curiosity flows through me. She can't leave either?

A moment passes and another, I can't see what's going on and I inch forward, hoping to get a peek before the conversation continues. Hoping to see this woman.

"You don't need to know," Daniel says firmly and with that I creep around the corner to see Daniel leaning against the stove. I see him and a beautiful girl around my age shaking her head so hard that her dark wavy hair falls around her shoulders. She covers her face as she gasps, "You keep lying to me." Pain is etched into her ragged voice.

Daniel makes a weak attempt to wrap his arms around her before she pushes him away, his ass hitting the stove and she leaves the kitchen, heading back the way she came. Small sounds of her crying linger behind her. Daniel opens a large drawer that blends into the cabinet and he drops the empty beer bottle and cap into the trash, with a wretched pain in his expression that tears at my own heart.

As he turns to leave, I creep further back into the kitchen, but he hears me and peeks over his shoulder.

Not hiding his pain and then leaving me to mine.

CHAPTER 27

Carter

I CHECKED THE BEDROOM FIRST. THE DEPRAVED SIDE OF ME hoped she would be waiting for me, already warming my bed.

But it was empty.

The den was next, after assuming I'd see her drawing on the floor of the hearth like she enjoys doing.

But the fire wasn't burning, and the room was silent.

Then the kitchen. The empty fucking kitchen. My teeth grit as I pull up the security monitor and cycle through the cameras.

My pulse races and I can hardly see straight as the monitor flickers from one to the next, each proving to be useless in showing me where my Aria is.

I told her to wait for me in the kitchen, den, or bedroom. Those were the only rooms she was permitted to be in, yet my obedient Aria isn't in a single one of them.

My heart pounds and my temperature rises.

She didn't get away.

I only left for three hours. Just enough time to drive to the club for the meet and then back. Daniel was watching her. I have to remind myself that she's still here somewhere as the cameras loop back around to the beginning.

"Fuck!" My anger gets the best of me, but as I spit out the word and feel the tension in my shoulders and chest rise, I both see and hear her at the same time.

The wine cellar in the corner of the kitchen passed in a blur on the screen the first time, but there she is, in the corner, cross-legged with a bottle in her lap. And the sweet sound of her humming travels through the kitchen.

I walk quietly to the cracked door, only a sliver of light shining into the kitchen.

Listening to the cadence of her soft voice, her humming rises and a word slips out, but I don't recognize the song. The melody is somber, somewhat melancholy.

I inch closer, careful to be quiet and slip the door open as a bottle clinks against the tile floor, notably empty judging from the hollow sound.

Aria's dark locks fall back away from her face and chest as she lays her head back against the wall, her nose pointed toward the ceiling as she hums a little louder.

It's addictive, listening to those sweet sounds. Her voice has always captivated me and I suppose it always will. What saves you from the darkness is something extraordinary.

"This isn't the kitchen," I say and break up her melody. The green and amber colors swirl into a deadly concoction of fear in her gaze as she takes in my words. I watch her throat as she swallows; I can practically hear her tense breathing as she seats herself in a kneeling position to tell me, "I didn't know."

She still doesn't look at me when she speaks. Sometimes in the evenings, she'll peek at me. But she doesn't like to look me in the eye.

Her cotton blouse is loose and baggy, offering me a glance down her shirt, although her hair lays in the way as it hangs in front of her. Even still, I catch a glimpse of her breasts and the pale pink of her nipples. My dick hardens, and I stifle a groan.

"I thought this was a part of the kitchen," she says and I hear the drunkenness on her words. Her thick lashes flutter as I stay standing in the doorway to the wine cellar, silently.

I wait for her to peek up at me, and when she does I hold her captive with my stare. It's never made sense to me before why the expression of 'doe eyes' exists. But right here, right now, I understand. It's a glance you can't break. One that pauses time and holds you still. That's what she does to me in this moment with that gorgeous gaze.

"I swear I didn't realize," she breathes the words and licks her wine-stained lips.

"From one cell to another," I tell her and my little songbird bites down on her bottom lip to stifle a smile. "You find that funny?" I ask her as my own lips threaten to tip up.

"I would prefer this one," she tells me as a flirtatious blush creeps into her cheeks. "If you saw fit to put me in a cell again, the wine cellar would be a bit more my style."

A genuine grin pulls at my lips and I find myself walking toward her and crouching in front of her small, delicate frame. Although she seems sweet, engaging even, the nervousness is still present.

I almost ask her what's gotten her into such a pleasant mood, but the empty bottle of wine to her side and the mostly empty glass sitting next to it answer my question. Her pupils are dark and large, but the beauty and desire behind them are enticing.

"You've enjoyed yourself while I've been gone?" I ask her while cupping her cheek, but instead of leaning into me, she pulls away and moves to sit on her ass. She pulls her legs to her chest.

She shakes her head once, and the happiness leaves instantly, chilling the room and my blood.

"I have something I should tell you," she speaks to her knees with her head buried in them, "but Daniel said he wouldn't." Some of her words are slurred. And even with the cuteness of her tipsy demeanor, knowing Daniel was housing a secret with her steals any sense of humor from me. "But I should."

"Yes," I tell her as I sit on the floor in front of her, "you should." A vise grips my heart as I creep closer to her. Secrets can't be tolerated. Secrets destroy all they touch. And Daniel would keep a secret from me?

She scratches behind her ear and glances at the door before looking back at me. Her lips part, but then she simply licks them, still trying to find her words. I can hear the steady beat of her heart in rhythm with mine.

"Tell me, songbird. It will be much worse for you if you don't." A crease of sadness mars her forehead and her eyes darken with worry, but the threat was needed. And with it comes her confession.

"I cut him," she says quickly and then clears her throat. "Daniel. I held up the knife and threatened him to let me go but I didn't mean to cut him, I swear."

"You want to leave me?" I ask contemptuously. The anger has come so easily tonight, my emotions getting the best of me. And it's because of her. It's all because of Aria.

"No, I just," she swallows thickly and pushes the hair from her face. "I don't know why, but when you left me… it's different when you aren't with me." She struggles with her words and I wait a moment in silence for her to go on.

"I was angry. I wanted to leave to tell my father." She doesn't see how my body tenses and rage creeps into my expression at her confession. She will never leave me. Never. And her father can burn in hell for all I care.

Gritting my teeth, I let her continue.

"He came to talk to me, and I had a knife. I was drunk and it was stupid. Or maybe just tipsy? I'm so sorry. I didn't mean it. I'm just a mess and I don't know what's right or what I should do and I…" She trails off, her breathing and words chaotic at best.

Has Daniel really gone so soft that he would let her threaten him? The sense of disappointment in both of them is mixed, but so much stronger with Aria. She wanted to leave. I have to resist every urge to throw her back into the cell and keep her there where she doesn't have an ounce of escape.

It's only the genuine sadness in her eyes that dulls the anger and brings out the curiosity I felt when I first watched her from the monitors.

It takes a moment of heavy breathing and silence between us for me to realize that it's my fault. She wasn't ready to be left in someone else's hands. I should have known better. But things will change quickly. I nod at the thought, although my gaze stays on Aria. Soon.

"He let you cut him with a knife?" I ask her, wondering how reckless Daniel must've been.

It's because she doesn't fear him. Fear changes everything.

"Only a little," she answers in a meek voice while lifting those gorgeous eyes up to mine and I find it humorous. With a gentle smile tracing my lips, I clarify, "You cut him… but only a little?"

She dares to let the peek of a smile show, but it's quickly gone. "I feel awful for doing it."

"You would have killed my brother?" I ask absently, making a mental note to watch the tapes of her while I was gone.

"No, but I know you'd kill mine." Her words are a well of sadness, but also of acceptance.

"You have no brother," I tell her as if her statement is irrelevant, but she's right. There are no limits to what I've done and what I'm about to do. There is mercy for her, but not for anyone else.

"You really tried to leave me?" A spike punctures through my chest as I voice it out loud. Earlier, I was more concerned that she shared a secret with Daniel. But the fact remains that she tried to run away. That she wanted to leave me and was willing to kill to do it.

"It was an awful attempt," she tells me as if it makes it better. And a part of me softens at her response. "I'm sorry. I'm sorry about it all. I think I'm going crazy," her words come out breathily as she drops her head back to lean against the wall. "You've made me crazy, Carter. All I am is sorry. It's all I know how to be anymore."

With my hand cupping her jaw, I wait for her to look at me with glassy eyes on the verge of tears. "No, my songbird. All you are... is mine."

"Yes," she says simply. The acknowledgement giving me a headier rush than I've ever felt.

My head nods on its own. "I didn't think you'd dare to be so bold while I was gone."

"I'm sorry." Fear traces her whisper.

"I didn't want to punish you tonight of all nights," I tell her, letting my fingers run along the necklace she wears, "I had different plans in mind." My dick is already hard as I consider what to do with her. "But you tried to leave me and there's no greater sin than that."

"Please," she whimpers as I shush her. "I don't want to go back." She doesn't cower from my touch; she welcomes it as I rest a hand on her bare shoulder, my fingers skimming under the fabric of her shirt. Her mesmerizing hazel eyes stare into mine and beg me for mercy.

"Didn't I tell you your next offense would lead to the cell?" I remind her with a question and her face crumples. She inches toward me, both of her hands on my thighs as she begs me, "Please." Her fingers slip across the expensive fabric of my pants as she crawls between my legs, begging me for forgiveness. How I've dreamed of her like this. Just like this.

"What would you do to stay with me?" I ask her, wanting to give her the mercy she begs for. I've never felt it so strongly before.

Her chest rises and falls heavily. "Anything," she answers me quickly with desperation.

"Not to stay out of the cell, but to stay in my bed. There is a difference, Aria."

Her expression falls and she struggles to voice what she's thinking. Dread seeps into my gut as she fails to answer me, but with that soft voice of hers, it leaves me at once.

Her fingers lace through the necklace as she says, "It's only when you're gone that I remember."

"What do you mean?"

Her voice wavers as she tries to explain. "I don't want you to leave me. It's harder for me when you do."

"I asked you what you would do—"

"And I said anything," she cuts me off and I can feel my brow pinch together as I look over every inch of her expression to gauge her sincerity. "When you're with me, I know that I can't leave, and I don't want to even try. But when you're gone… it's harder. So, I don't want to leave you. I don't want you to leave me."

She's a siren. I see it so clearly. It's her beauty, her broken strength, her denial, and her acceptance. It all calls to me and I will do anything I can to wrap my grip tighter around my songbird while she sings beautiful lullabies.

"Tomorrow night, you'll come to dinner with me. Kneeling beside me. You will obey. You will sit beside me, proud to be mine." She nods her head as if she's accepting a punishment, but this is so much more than that. "You'll do as I say. Every fucking thing I tell you to do." I emphasize each word, my finger running up and down her throat. "In front of my family and guests, you will show them how willing you are to obey me."

"Yes, Carter."

The way her breathing catches and she swallows the eagerness of accepting the punishment, almost makes me feel guilty for what I say next. Almost. "And tonight, you will sleep in the cell for daring to take advantage of the freedom I've given you."

"Yes, Carter," she replies although her words crack and her eyes close in agony. Her thick lashes flutter, as she opens her eyes again and she stares deeply into my own, waiting for more. The deep well of lone-liness is already settling into her gaze. The look of sadness is something I've seen before, but in her eyes, it looks so beautiful.

"You'll stay there until I feel you've learned your lesson."

She nods and wipes the tear from under her right eye, but dutifully answers, "Yes, Carter."

My own breathing quickens at the thought of having her to myself before sending her away. "As for right now, you'll lie across my lap, feeling my hard cock dig into your belly as I punish you, spanking your bare ass and playing with your cunt until I feel you've paid enough for the offense of trying to leave me."

"I will," she says softly and raises her head to meet my gaze. When her eyes meet mine, she nods in agreement. "I will," she repeats breathlessly.

The command falls instantly from me. "Tell me that your cunt is mine to play with."

"My cunt is yours to play with." And her obedience falls from her lips just the same.

"And your ass?" I prompt.

"It's yours." There's no hesitation in her voice.

"And what about these lips of yours?" I question her in a deep voice ragged with desire as my thumb traces her pouty lips.

"Whatever you'd like to do with them," she whispers against my touch.

"Lift up your dress and lie here," I tell her as I sit on the ground of the wine cellar, too eager to have my hands on her to move us to the cell.

Her movements are rushed and reckless as she pulls the cotton dress up and moves to my lap. Her hips are balanced on my right thigh, but I move her ass to the center, forcing her to yelp as she tries to brace herself with her hands.

"Behind your back," I command her, and it takes a moment. Her hair is everywhere, but I slip it over one shoulder, taking my time to gather it together before grabbing both of her wrists in one of my hands. My fingers easily slip down her panties, the lace fabric almost tearing, but I'm careful with it, letting my touch send goosebumps flowing over every inch of her skin.

She moans slightly, already enjoying her punishment. But I'll enjoy it more.

With my hand rubbing a circle on her ass cheek, I tell her, "I think you misbehave just so I can punish you."

She shakes her head, writhing over my lap and making her hair toss slightly. "I don't want to upset you." Her words are soft and saddened, but her whimpers speak of nothing but pleasure.

The first smack is light and followed by my grabbing her ass and then smacking the other cheek harder. Her body bucks, but I don't even get a gasp.

Leaning to my left, I see her eyes shut tightly and her teeth digging into her bottom lip. I let my fingers slip to her cunt, and my cock aches with the pain to be inside of her.

"So tight," I tell her with reverence in my tone and then rock her, so she can feel my cock.

She only moans and waits for more, but her teeth let up slightly while I take my time with her.

"How many do you think, my Aria?" I ask her and just as her lips part, my hand pulls back and I whip her ass with an open hand that leaves my skin stinging with pain. She cries out, throwing her head back as the pain and pleasure mix and my fingers dip back to her cunt.

"I asked how many?" My voice is calm but deadly. Inside I'm burning hot with a desperate need.

"How many—" she starts to answer me, and I spank her other cheek even harder than the last, forcing tears to her eyes. The sharp, sweet pain travels from my palm up my arm. Gripping her reddened skin, I wait for her to answer but with her eyes watering and her breath taken from her, all she does is part her lips to breathe.

"Answer me, Aria." Before my words are finished she says as quickly as she can, "However many you'd like."

A beat passes where she hangs her head to suck in a breath. Another beat passes where I pull my hand away from her skin and watch as she tenses on my lap.

The rapid succession of my hand hitting her tender skin over and over again until my arm is screaming with pain and my hand feels nearly numb passes in a whirlwind.

Her cries get louder as she fights me in my lap, naturally wanting to pull away from me. I nearly lose my grip on her wrists, but I manage to keep her steady and where I need her to be, so I can fulfill her punishment.

Her ass is bright red and my skin humming with a delightful sting by the time I slip my fingers back to her soaking wet cunt. Her body shudders and her yelp of pain turns to a sinful moan.

Over and over I spank her viciously, the underside of her ass, the right cheek, the left one… and then her pussy. My hand's wet with her arousal as she trembles beneath me.

My fingers dip into her pussy with each smack, giving her only the tiniest bit of penetration. The intensity of the teasing bends her back even farther and her lust-filled gaze stares back at me with her strangled moans of pleasure and pain echoing off the walls of the cellar.

"Good girl." I praise her and watch as she peers up at me with a wondering look in her eyes and her cheeks tearstained.

"Tonight, I'm going to fuck you into that mattress on the floor like I should have the moment I got my hands on you."

Her pussy clenches around my fingertips and I reward her by pushing them in deeper and stroking her front wall.

Her back arches and I have to push her shoulder down to keep her right where I want her as I pull my touch away from her in order to leave her wanting. Her small moan of frustration is met with another slap of my hand on her bright red skin. Smack!

Her head flies back and those gorgeous lips of hers part with a deep gasp of longing. It's no longer pain. She's too close to the edge of pleasure to feel anything but.

Soothing the pain of the smack with my hand, I rub her right cheek and then pull back for one more strike.

"You would have learned sooner if I'd been rougher with you, wouldn't you?"

She moans her answer with her eyes closed and her body still, knowing another punishing blow is coming, "Yes, Carter."

Her answer is absent of sincerity. She'd tell me whatever I wanted to hear right now as she sits on the edge of pleasure and pain.

The days come back to me. Each of them and what I'd planned to do with her is in such stark contrast to what I've done. I let the fingers of my right hand trail over her ass, my blunt nails gently scraping along her tender skin and making her squirm on my lap. My left hand grips her throat, finally releasing her wrists, and I pull back, forcing her to look at me.

Her hazel eyes are filled with longing and lust. The haze is a fog in the forest. Unable to see, but so tempted to go forward.

"I should have fucked you so much sooner."

I remember that first day, how she screamed and cried for me to let her go, back when I hated her and she hated me.

Even with my tight grip on her throat, with my touch sending sparks through her body, she forces her head to shake, not taking her eyes from mine.

"No," she whispers, and my dick hardens, even more, begging me to punish her for daring to defy me. But then she adds, "This is how it was supposed to be."

Her breathing is heavy as she closes her eyes, her body bowed on my lap. She's completely at my mercy and her pouty lips are there for the taking.

All of her. Every piece of her is mine and she knows it.

Mine.

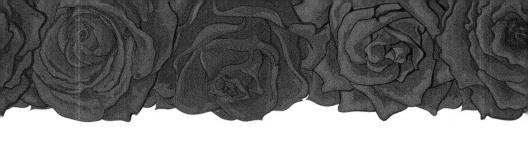

CHAPTER 28

Aria

YESTERDAY WAS FULL OF REGRET.

The moment I saw Carter again, I wish I'd taken back those hours he was gone.

He always keeps his word. And true to form, he took me back to the cell and fucked me on the mattress. Maybe it was the drunkenness, maybe it was something else, but the fear of the cell was absent and instead, I did everything I could to please him. My body begged me to.

Not because I felt the need to obey.

I wanted him to kiss me.

I needed him to. And every time his lips trailed down my neck, I tried to capture them. Tried and failed. He knows I want him though. A shudder runs through my body at the thought and it's met with the dull ache between my thighs.

He fucked me until I couldn't move anymore and even as I laid on my belly on the mattress, unable to grip onto it, unable to keep my back arched as he commanded me to. Even then he rutted behind me, pistoning into me and giving me a punishing fuck.

Last night I was his whore. He balled my hair into his fist and pulled back so he could rake his teeth along my neck and force my body however he wanted it.

And I wanted nothing more.

The realization should startle me more, but instead, all I can think about is that he knows I want him to kiss me, and yet he didn't let me.

It's different when he's with me. The security I have with him is everything.

The sane part of me knows it's not healthy and that I should keep fighting, but the sane part of me is the only part of me that's held captive in this reality. If only I let it go, I feel free.

Free enough to feel safe for another day.

Free enough to know that what happens in the war will happen regardless of whether I'm here or not.

Free enough to slip on the dress that Carter's laid out for me and stare at the image of a beautiful woman in the mirror. One who I envy. One I can't believe is me.

With my hair smoothed and clipped at the side, the bit of makeup adding a definition of beauty to my porcelain skin, I feel so much like a songbird who sings soft melodies of hope, with her wings clipped in a gilded cage.

My fingers graze over the delicate lace and my eyes close, remembering last night.

The bruise on my ass sends a reminder of the pain through me as I smooth the soft lace down my curves. The sensation is directly linked to my clit and instantly my body begs for more. For me to put an ounce of pressure against the bruise.

A soft breath leaves me, a wanting one at that, and when I open my eyes, Carter is standing in front of me.

My heart slams and then does a soft trot. As if it's galloping toward him, even though he's the one walking toward me.

Each step is deliberate, but with a softness I've never seen from him and it captures every bit of my thoughts.

"You look beautiful, songbird," he says, and his voice is like velvet as he rounds me. His steps echo in the bedroom as he walks in a half circle and stops at my back.

I can hear his breathing hitch as he pulls at the lace, sliding it up my backside and sending a thrilling shiver up my body. His fingertips trail ever so gently along the marks. "Beautiful," he remarks before hiding them under the lace once again.

"Thank you," I dare to whisper, meeting his gaze as he walks to stand in front of me. My fingers slip to the hem of the dress, toying with it to hide the anxiousness of wanting to touch him as he's just touched me. I'm not allowed to today. When he opened the door to the cell, he told me if I obeyed every wish of his today, I would never see the cell again.

One day, and the rules of the game change forever.

I feel so much like a songbird who sings soft melodies of hope,

with her wings clipped in a gilded cage.

A million thoughts are scattered through my mind, but only one of them matters.

"I'll be good tonight," I tell him in a voice I don't recognize. One of obedience, but also strength. "I won't disappoint you." A past version of me would slit my throat before letting herself hear those words. There's only a faint blip of pain in my heart at the realization.

The earlier version of me was foolish.

This version of me will survive. And this version has the audacity to admit that I enjoy it. Every fucking bit of it. To be wanted by a man so powerful who wants for nothing is a heady feeling.

"Aria," Carter says my name in a way that makes fear blossom deep in my gut. "You're going to want to defy me," he tells me, and the worry shows on my face. I can feel it tugging my lips down as it dries out my throat. He stalks in a circle around me, occasionally picking at the lace of the dress. They're cages. Each of the pieces of lace is a birdcage. And there's never been a dress that's adorned my body as beautifully as this one does.

"You may even hate me," he says in a purely seductive cadence. His hot breath tickles the bare skin of my neck as he whispers at the shell of my ear, "But you will obey me."

I nod my head and then croak out, "Yes, Carter." It's so silent in the room with neither of us speaking, moving or even daring to breathe. It's so silent I swear the darkness itself could whisper and I would hear its threatening tongue.

"Your necklace suits this dress perfectly," Carter says out loud although I don't think the words were meant for me.

Absently, I roll one of the pearls between my fingers and then feel the thin chain slide under my thumb as it moves to the diamond teardrop. It feels heavier tonight. Everything feels heavier when Carter looks at me like he is now.

With dark eyes that pin me in place and keep me still, right where he wants me. It's a silly thing, how the same gaze that once caused fear to ripple through my body now only heats my core and begs me to bend at the knees for him.

"Thank—"

Carter places a finger against my lips, silencing me. The small touch is addictive and the tension of the dinner tonight amplifies.

"Remember what I told you last night." He speaks as he toys with the necklace, holding the large diamond and lifting the weight from me. "You will kneel beside me, and you will obey every command."

Instantly my body heats. I worry my bottom lip between my teeth, wanting to ask him so many questions, but I already know he won't answer. There's only one thing to say. "Yes, Carter."

A moment passes, his eyes searching my gaze for something and I can hardly breathe.

"After tonight, no one will question that you're mine." His eyes darken and the flecks of gold that are buried beneath the coal there turn to fire. A fire that ignites my own and soothes the worries.

"Come with me," he commands me as he reaches for my hand.

CHAPTER 29

Carter

M Y WALK IS CALM AND STEADY, EVEN AS ARIA FREEZES.
The cocky smirk stays plastered on my lips, even as
sickness stirs in my gut.

Every bit of my body is screaming to act, but this is for her. It's all
for her.

"Come," I command Aria as she stares straight ahead at the entrance to the dining hall. Her chest rises in slow motion as her lips part
with the hint of a shaky breath. "Aria," I say, and her name slips from me
like an admonishment, "I said come." The demand is there, but the look
she gives me in return is one of defiance and betrayal. There's so much
hate in the dark greens and ambers of her eyes that I almost regret this.

But she needs this. That hate for me won't be there for long.

Stephan and Romano's shared rumble of deep laughter is the only
sound in the large room as they see her. With the blood-red velvet
curtains shut tightly, the only light in the room shines down from the
scattered crystals on the chandelier.

The smell of beef wellington, seated beautifully at the center of the
table, greets us as we enter the room. The light shines off the butcher's
knife beside it.

Aria's walk is hesitant but she obeys me, even if there are tears in
her eyes.

"I was beginning to think I'd have to come up and get you," Jase
says as I take Aria's hand in mine and motion for her to kneel beside
my chair across from Stephan. Her palm is clammy, and her grip tight
as she lowers herself to the floor. The pain I feel for her is nothing compared to what she'll have in only moments.

As quickly as she can, she tears her hand from mine. And again,
laughter from the two guests echoes off the walls.

"Still so defiant." Romano's eyes sparkle, but I ignore him, taking my seat.

I hate that for the moment I can't keep my hand on hers, but soon I'll have her again.

"No need," I tell Jase, meeting his gaze and forcing a smile on my lips that grows as I turn my attention to Stephan, nodding a greeting and then turn to Romano. "Thank you for coming, gentlemen."

"The pleasure is all mine," Stephan says at the same time as Romano nods his head, the thin smile growing on his lips and turning wicked.

"It's a delight to see you've taken a liking to our gift."

Anger burns deep in my chest at the memory of him having his hands on her only weeks ago, but it stays where it is as I return his smile, placing my hand on the back of Aria's head. She remains stiff, not leaning into my touch, which only intensifies the fire inside of me. But I will have patience, even if she tests me.

"I wish I could see her better," Stephan says, sitting up from his seat for a moment and making a comical face. Jase gives him a bit of laughter, I'm sure because he knows what's coming. He'll enjoy this, but not nearly as much as I will.

"No sense of humor?" Stephan speaks to Daniel and then glances at Declan, both of them quiet. It's only the seven of us in the room, although the kitchen is abuzz with the sound of dishes being plated. And the men waiting for my order.

"I know a few jokes," Daniel says wryly, but then he picks up his drink and leaves the unspoken words hanging in the air. Romano's shoulders stiffen and a hard gaze meets his eyes.

"Come up here, Aria," I say and pat my lap and then glance at Stephan. "I'd like for our guests to see you better."

From the corner of my eye, I see Romano's tension ease. The room is silent, so silent I can hear my songbird swallow as she stands up on weak legs. I'm quick to pull her into my lap, pressing my hand against her ass and reminding her of last night. Her eyes widen, and she gasps, thrilling the men she doesn't dare look at.

"Excuse her," I speak to no one in particular. "She's not used to company."

With all eyes on her, I place her exactly how I'd like her, nestling her ass into my crotch and wrapping my arm around her waist. "Relax," I whisper into her ear, knowing full well the other men can hear me. Her hair tickles against my jaw and shoulder as I move it from one side of her back to the other so I can expose her neck.

"You can't say hello to an old friend?" Stephan asks.

"If I recall, she's more fond of begging." Romano's comment doesn't go unnoticed.

"She's a little frightened," I say before kissing the crook of her neck and feeling her body relax for the first time, although I know the moment will be gone before I'd like.

"One of the many Talverys who will fall to their knees," Stephan gloats and raises his glass to toast, but I don't reciprocate.

"I thought she would, but she betrayed me last night," I tell them and reach for a goblet of water.

"Betrayed?" Romano's voice is low.

I nod and look to see how my brothers react to my words.

"I thought she was doing well?" Jase comments and leans forward in his seat to look at Aria, his stare commanding her to look at him, which she does, but only for a moment. Her head is held high, but her glassy gaze stares at nothing.

"She tried to kill Daniel," I tell Jase and he gives me a look of shock but then turns to Daniel, who's smiling.

"Kill you?" he questions Daniel.

"As if she could," he says, leaning back in his seat. Aria struggles to breathe as we talk about her in front of her like her presence is a meaningless joke. But everything has a purpose.

"It was only a knife." Daniel looks at me as he answers, and I reach for the one in front of me.

"This one?" I ask him, and Aria rocks forward a moment, her ability to stay strong being questioned. When I peer up at her, her eyes are shut tightly. "Look at me, Aria." My words are lethal on my tongue.

Instantly, her eyes open and a scattering of tears lines her lashes. Instead of wiping them away, I hold up the knife and ask, "This one?"

She shakes her head gently. "No," she says, the word a mere whisper. I can feel the pounding of her heart.

"Take it," I demand as I grab her hand and put it over the handle of the knife. "Would you like to use it on him now?" I ask her.

"No," she says and her voice trembles, but again she shakes her head and answers me. "How about on me?" I offer her. "Would you like to slit my throat, Aria?"

"No." Her answer is a barely spoken breath and her grip on the knife loosens.

"I told Daniel this morning," I begin, addressing Romano to my right and giving him my full attention, "that it was his fault. There was no fear of him and what he'd do to her."

Romano considers me, his brow raising and his lips turning down into a frown before he nods in agreement. "Fear is powerful."

"I choose other tactics," Daniel speaks up and then looks at Aria as he adds, "I let her do what she thought she needed to, so she could at least feel that she'd tried." His voice is neutral, devoid of the empathy I know he has for her. It's all a show. That's the real difference between us; Daniel likes to hide behind an image.

I am the image of what's to be feared. It exists in my being and there's no hiding it.

"Do you remember me, Aria?" Stephan dares to ask her, leaning across the table to be every bit closer to her that he can.

"Oh, she does," I answer for her as she struggles to respond. "My poor Aria, I know this is hard for you," I say and hold her tighter, although she's stiff doing her best to stay seated on my lap.

"I imagine it is," Stephan says and then adds, "She's grown to be just as beautiful as her mother."

My blood sings with both rage and vengeance, and it's a feeling I adore. A smile creeps across my lips as I confide in him, "She sings for me, but the memory of you is strong enough to stop it." I turn to Aria, letting my finger trail over her shoulder to slip a lock of hair to her back and then turn to Stephan. "I can't have that."

Confusion mars his face for a moment and I let time pass for a moment in deadly silence.

"I could give her a different memory to hold onto," Stephan suggests and the laugh that creeps from Romano's gut is tight with tension.

"I don't believe Carter enjoys sharing," Romano comments, but I hold up my hand to stop him, speaking only to Stephan.

"I do believe she needs a different memory. I'm tired of hearing her cry out in her sleep." As I speak, Aria's expression crumples and I pull her closer to me, forcing her back to my chest and whisper in her ear, "Should I let Stephan fuck you?" I don't let them see the anger, the hate, the deep-seated pain of watching my songbird relive the memories in front of her tormentor. They can't see yet, but they will suffer. I swear they will pay.

Deep in my core, I have the fear of breaking Aria, of pushing her too hard, but she needs this.

"Carter," Jase warns, and I only shoot him a gaze of contempt. If this is to go as planned, Romano is the witness whose testimony matters. His perception is the only one that matters.

Aria breaks down at the mere question, her reality again failing her. Each bit of her shatters with hope fading from her very existence. It's then I know I've truly broken her and the beautiful shards of what used to be Aria Talvery can fill the crevice of my soul she broke long ago. And I can use those pieces how I'd like. Creating perfection in her from what's been broken.

As she gasps an answer, a plea from her lips that only I can hear, I pull her tighter to me, feeling her warmth and her small body pressed securely against mine. The knife is still in her hand, although weakly held.

"You still have the knife, Aria," I remind her. "Would you like to cut me now?" As I ask her the question, her hazel-green eyes strike me with every ounce of pain she feels at this moment. "Why are you doing this to me?" she asks, her small voice revealing her agony.

I let my fingers slip up her dress as Romano says something I don't care to listen to.

Letting my lips trail along the back of her neck, I whisper just for her. "Do you think I'd let him fuck you?" I ask her and press my fingers to her clit, forcing her to push back and feel my cock on her bruised ass, hard at the very thought of what's coming. "That I would let him even imagine taking what's mine?" The hiss of my voice travels throughout the dining room, but I'm certain no one could know for sure what I've asked her.

Her eyes, still shining with unshed tears, finally meet mine and stare back at me as she whispers, "No."

A smile threatens to pull at my lips and I let it as Romano and Stephan cluck their tongues in disapproval, as if they have any control at all over her. As if they know what's coming.

I rock her into my lap again and the sweet gasp that parts her lips brings a light to her eyes. A light that I've given her. Only me.

Bringing my lips to the shell of her ear, I whisper, "Do you think I'd *ever*," I stress the word, "let him touch you?" As I prompt her, the demeanor of my guests change.

"No," she says with the strength of realization. My sweet girl. I watch as her breathing calms and she glances at Stephan and then Romano before looking back at me and answering me again, her head shaking and letting those locks play around her bare shoulders. "No," she repeats softly.

"She's rather bold, don't you think?" Romano asks Jase, who doesn't respond to him.

"I love how strong she is," I say aloud, ignoring the comments from Stephan at the end of the table for a moment before adding, "Her will was difficult to break, but it was worth it."

Declan speaks up, tired of the show I imagine. He has no patience and he states pointedly, "The dinner is getting cold."

"Of course." I lean back in my seat and splay my hand against Aria's stomach to push her small body against mine. "Would you like to carve the meat, Aria?" I ask her and glance behind me toward the kitchen. "Bring out the plates in just a moment," I call out and catch Romano's gaze. "This chef is to die for."

"I can hardly wait," he says beneath his breath.

"Aria," I tell them, "will cut the wellington and serve us, I think." A half grin ticks up the corners of my lips as Romano smiles.

"I didn't expect this from you," he tells me, and I cock a brow at him. "I didn't think you enjoyed this as much as you seem to."

My grin widens. "You have no idea how much I enjoy this." Tonight, my songbird will be changed forever. And I'm the one who will give it to her. She will never fear anyone but me ever again.

"You have her sit at the table?" Stephan questions me with a glint of humor in his eyes. His thin lips twitch into a smile and I manage a smile back, remembering that this is for her. She's the one to do it. My grip on her waist tightens, to keep me from ruining everything.

"You do as you'd like in your home, but do not question me in mine." My words are sharp and not to be taken lightly. They force the smile off his pale face while Romano coughs at the head of the table.

"I think he only means that we were expecting to see her on the floor... where slaves belong."

Picking up the large butcher knife on the table, I put the knife firmly in Aria's hand and command her to carve the beef wellington. She can barely reach, and I do my best to balance her as she reaches over the table, the sharp blade piercing the puff pastry shell with a slight crack that's audible in the silent room.

My breathing comes in harder and harder, knowing what's next. I can taste the sweetness of it already as the meat falls onto the platter.

"Carter has a soft spot for her, I think," Jase offers, and he and Daniel share a look. One of my brothers on each side of me. Both of them ready for when I cue the kitchen.

"I want a nice meal, for fuck's sake," I say with a touch of humor to break the tension and put both Stephan and Romano at ease. "We start a war tomorrow. And technically, shots have already been fired," I say, and shrug then place a small bit of meat onto the platter as Aria's movements become strained.

"Yes. Here's to victory," Romano says, raising the glass of champagne in front of him. The bubbly liquid rises in the air, and with it, both of his hands. It's like I'm watching in slow motion as I turn my attention to Stephan and see him do the same. An empty hand palm up on the table and his other raised in the air, holding a glass.

"Cheers, bring out the dinner," I call out as I raise my glass, not bothering to reach for my gun.

My voice rings out and our men from the kitchen bring out the serving dishes. My closest men, disguised as servers, quickly make their way around the room with their trays.

They unveil each of the covered platters at once to reveal their guns, aimed at both Romano and Stephan. All while Aria's carving the meat with shaky hands.

Stephan and Romano both suck in a breath but keep their hands raised even as curses fill the air, as do the sound of pistols being cocked.

Aria drops the knife on the table, her shoulders hunched and a squeal of both terror and surprise forcing her backward and into my arms. I wish I could have warned her, but Romano is going to live to tell the tale.

Her shoulders are cold in my embrace as I pull her close and whisper, "You're all right."

All three of my brothers raise their loaded guns, but I keep my hands on Aria, still trembling. Declan, seated at the opposite head, keeps his gun pointed at Romano and my other two brothers keep theirs pointed at Stephan as they face him.

"What the fuck is this?" Romano is quick to speak with indignation and attempts to lower his arm. My eyes pierce into Stephan's, who's staring straight at me with a bitter hate that I'm used to seeing from men I've fucked over. It's always followed by the milky gaze of dead eyes. He doesn't dare lower his arm. Because he knows the truth better than Romano does.

I hear the distinctive sound of a gun with a silencer going off, but I don't bother to look and verify that the bullet landed just behind Romano as a warning shot. My eyes stay fixed on Stephan's. Just as his are on me.

"This is a show for you, Romano," I finally speak when he stands abruptly. "Help him sit, Jase."

Without a word, my brother rises and I can just barely see Aria in my periphery. My sweet, haunted girl. She grips the table and watches intently as Jase pulls out the chair for Romano, waiting for him to sit a few feet away from the table where his hands can easily be seen.

Jase stays behind him, his gun still trained on Romano although now he could easily shoot Stephan as well. But his death is for Aria, and Aria alone.

"The knife, Aria." I address only her. She's so small on my lap as she looks at me and then slowly around the room. She's hesitant to pick the knife back up and the cursing yell from Stephan nearly startles her into dropping it again.

The rage in my blood turns from a simmer to a boil. "Even now he holds a fear over you, my Aria," I tell her in a low voice of reprimand. "I won't allow it."

I can feel her skin turn cold as she waits for my command. She's barely breathing, still scared and confused. With the knife in her hand, I pull her back into my lap, taking my time to calm her so she can see clearly.

Fear can cloud everything, turning reality into falsehoods.

"Are you mad at me, songbird?" I ask her gently, cupping her jaw in my hand. I can feel her swallow tightly and peek back at Stephan before looking at me. "Why?" she asks me with such sadness.

"You needed this," I whisper against her lips, nearly pressing mine to hers in an effort for her to understand how crucial this moment is, both for her and for us.

Her bottom lip quivers as tears prick the back of her eyes. "I thought you were giving me to him," she confesses as her voice cracks and her shoulders shudder.

Gripping her tighter I speak clearly, loud enough for everyone in this room to hear. "You are mine and Romano lied to me when he gave me to you," I hiss.

"Bullshit!" Romano dares to interrupt me and my hackles rise, the anger brimming. But I'll deal with him once I'm through with Aria. She will always come first.

"You were damaged." Her expression crumples at my words, shame filling her hazel eyes as I add, "You were so fucking broken I couldn't have my hand in it." I turn my head to sneer at Stephan. "Not when someone else has such control over you."

"I'm sorry," she whispers, and the tip of the knife hits the table as her grip loosens.

"Did I tell you to drop the knife?" I ask her and instead of taking the hint and holding it tighter, she drops it to the table, covering her face with her hands and leaning into my chest.

"I really thought…" she pauses as her chest heaves and I give her this moment. I comfort her and make the men wait. They will wait for her. And so will I.

For this I've waited so long already, another minute can be spared for her pain.

"I thought," she continues to stammer, and I kiss her hair, rubbing her back as she tells me, "I thought you were done with me."

Pulling at her shoulders, I force her to arm's length in my lap. "Never," I tell her with all sincerity, feeling the truth down to my core, coursing through my blood and in every thought I could ever have.

Aria's breathing calms as she stares into my eyes, while a softness I've never felt drifts over me. "You scared me," she whispers.

Running the tip of my nose against hers, I whisper against her lips, "It's a gift for you."

When I pull away, her eyes are still closed, but slowly they open and I nod toward the knife.

"Kill him, Aria."

Romano curses, but one of my men presses the barrel of his gun to his head.

"Pick up the knife and end him."

I watch Aria's shaky fingers pick up the knife, and then she stares at her prey. He scowls at her, but she doesn't back down. Her chest heaves again and the way she holds her chin up lets me know she's scared but doing her damnedest not to be.

Fear can never hide though.

"I won't be with you if you don't," I tell her and instantly regret the words. Her eyes widen, and she sucks in a breath. "I can't let you continue like this," I tell her, wishing I could take back the first words I gave her.

Her eyes flicker from me to Stephan and she nods her head slightly, but still, she doesn't move.

Even knowing she has the knife in her hand, I lean forward and rest my head against her chest. "This is for you, Aria," I whisper in the hot space between us. "It's all for you."

Inhaling her scent and feeling her body against mine, I kiss her throat and move to the crook of her slender neck. Her nails dig into my shoulder as she gasps.

It's an apology for the threat I just made that never should have left me.

My lips slip down her shoulder and she moans softly, relaxing into me as my hands travel up her waist.

"Kill him, Aria," I command her and continue kissing her neck, my touch turning ravenous.

Raking my teeth down her jaw, I worship her.

My brothers are witnesses to what I'd do to have her be completely mine. Romano and the dead fuck Stephan watch with a series of slurs and profanity.

Let them all see. Let the entire fucking world see.

My cock is hard when I pull away, seeing her breathless and in need.

"First, you take care of him." I nod toward Stephan and then tell her, "And then you will be truly mine."

Aria's nod is swift and she's quick this time to leave my lap, although her touch lingers on my shoulder as she steadies herself.

Three guns are pointed at Stephan, but he's only looking at her as she rounds the table. I follow her at a distance, giving her this.

Stephan's smile is grim and unnerving as he sneers, "She'll never do it. Just shoot—"

Before he can get the last word out, Aria whips her hand through the air, slicing his neck open and forcing blood to pour from his neck. As his hands reach up to his throat, she screams a bloodcurdling sound, slicing again in the same pattern. Only this time, it cuts through his hands, nearly severing one of his fingers.

She doesn't stop. She stabs frantically into his chest, hitting his arm, his shoulder, his throat again. Her aim is reckless, and my men take a step back, blood drenching his shirt and spraying from his cuts.

She's savage in the stabs. Chaotic even. For a moment, I want to tear the knife from her for fear of her cutting herself.

She screams out as the knife pierces through the expensive fabric and into his soft flesh, the blood seeping through his clothes. The cry from her is sickening. Not because of the piercing scream, but because of the overt sadness. She kills him with her pain.

"Let it out," I say without conscious consent. I can see Daniel turn his attention from her to me, but I ignore him. None of them matter right now.

She needs this more than anything.

Romano stands from his seat, backing away and it's only then that I break my focus on Aria.

"Sit," I practically snarl. The anger is mostly because he dared distract me from this.

He grits his teeth and feigns irritation as he slowly obeys me, but he can't deny the utter fear I can see in his gaze.

With both hands on the armrests, he slowly takes his seat and I can focus on Aria again.

Her energy has waned and she's silent as tears stream down her face. Her small body looks weaker and weaker, but she doesn't stop stabbing into Stephan's lifeless body. She's obviously exhausted, but she doesn't stop.

Not until I give her the command, my low voice foreboding and dominating in the silent room. "Aria. Give me the knife."

Her wild eyes glance at me, only for a moment as the knife trembles in her hand and she shakes her head, no.

"Aria," I raise my voice, forcing it to echo in the room. The only sounds I can hear are the blood rushing in my ears and Aria's ragged breathing as I grit my teeth and tell her one last time. "Give. Me. The knife."

HEARTLESS

BOOK 2

At first, his words were harsh and his touch cold.
I knew he was a dangerous man and he could destroy me if only he wanted to.

That's not what he wanted though. It's not what he needed.
It's not what I desired either.

It's so easy to get lost in the touch of a man who's powerful and unattainable.
A man who wants for nothing… except me.
Soft touches and stolen glances made my blood heat and my heart beat in a way I never knew it could.

Yes, it's easy to fall into a haze of lust and desire.
But there's a reason his reputation is one of a heartless man.
And I should have known better.

PROLOGUE

Carter

RAIN IS COMING. THE KIND OF RAIN THAT MAKES YOUR BONES ache. The dark gray sky is streaked with dry lightning that splinters the crack of pain even deeper.

There's only so much a man can take. Only so far he can be pushed to the brink and still want to survive.

First, my mother lost her fight with cancer.

Then Tyler, my youngest brother, was struck and killed by a car.

And now, my father has been murdered in cold blood.

The blame for my father's death is easy to place. A group of thugs who wanted the highest high, and they were willing to do whatever it took to chase it.

They didn't fear my father. Not like they fear me.

I know that's why they waited for him to be the one on the street corner, instead of me dealing from the back of the truck. When my mother died, selling drugs was what we needed to do to pay the bills. But months have passed, and it's more than an income stream now. Dealing, and the fighting that comes with, it is now my obsession.

I'm not just peddling dope or selling off stolen prescriptions. The drug trade is lucrative beyond anything I could have ever dreamed.

But Talvery taught me more than anyone else could.

He taught me where the boundaries were. Taught me what fear is capable of.

He showed me what it takes to make the pain go away and replace it with something more addictive than heroin. Power is everything.

And I feel it flowing through my veins.

Crack! Lightning strikes again, followed by a boom and shaking of the ground.

Rain is coming, but I'll stand here for as long as it takes.

The priest's voice is a dull monotone and the cries from distant family members, who I've only ever seen a handful of times in my life, numb me.

The casket in which my father's body lies reflects the first droplets of water. The sprinkling is just the beginning of the downpour threatening to fall any minute now.

He would still be alive if they'd had the same fear of him that they have of me. If he'd learned the hard lesson Talvery had taught me months ago.

Revenge will come for the pricks who killed my father. Not because I love him. Or *loved*, rather. I think I hated him in the last few years. Truly and deeply despised the piece of shit he became when my mother got sick. The realization is freeing.

That's not why I'll hunt down each and every one of those assholes and take a baseball bat to them in their sleep, or a gun to the side of their heads as they creep through dark back alleys, or a knife along their throats in the restrooms of their favorite bars. One by one, I'll kill them all.

It's not because I want revenge or because I don't want my father's death to go unanswered.

No. I'll murder them because they thought they could take from me. They decided it was worth the risk to take from me. Anger rises in my chest, heating my blood and forcing my hands into white-knuckled fists. I have to clench my teeth in an effort to hide the rage.

No one will ever take from me again. They won't take more of my family. They won't take a goddamn thing from me. Never again.

The day my father was laid to rest, the demon who had long slept inside of me awakened and destroyed whatever bit of goodness that had lingered in my heart. From that day forward, I decided that everyone would fear me. Simply because it was easier to survive that way, obsessing over the power that fear would bring me.

I craved their fear the way I used to pray for the pain to go away.

It was all-consuming and only the tiniest slivers of this new armor ever broke off. Only when painful memories forced me to confront who and what I used to be. But even the smallest shards of my armor were so easily replaced by the blood of those who dared to threaten what I'd become.

So long as everyone feared me and those closest to me, I would not only survive, I would thrive.

They needed to fear my brothers.

And now they need to fear her. *My songbird.*

They will. I refuse to let anyone take her.

No one will take her away from me. No one.

CHAPTER 1

Aria

I CAN'T STOP SHAKING. MY ENTIRE BODY IS CONSUMED BY FEAR AND I'm trembling all over. My hands are shaking chaotically, and I can't make them stop.

The heavy knife is gripped tighter than I've ever gripped anything in my life. I don't even feel like it's my hand holding the weapon. Another person's hand, on top of mine, is forcing it to stay in my grip. To hold it tighter and tighter until it hurts so much that my body begs me to fall to my knees in agony.

I won't allow my body to betray me. I can't drop the knife. I can't stop myself. The fear and rage are mingling into a concoction that's far too powerful to deny.

The blood on the blade drips down onto my hand and feels like fire on my skin. The tension, the anger, the pure rage, and terror all boil in my blood as I stare at the dead, milky white eyes of the monster in front of me.

I can't look at Carter. I can't rip my gaze from the motionless stare of Alexander Stephan.

I'm waiting for him to blink. To jump up and grab me. The fear I feel is paralyzing, but the adrenaline coursing through me is going to burst my veins. He's limp in the chair, his throat split wide open although the blood isn't gushing anymore. It's only a slow trickle at this point.

It reminds me of the way my mother's throat was slit. *The way he did it.*

I remember it so clearly. That scene has haunted my dreams for as long as I can remember. How he stood behind her after he'd abused her. How he didn't do it slowly; instead it was vicious and violent. It was all I could think to do to him here in this chair and at my mercy when Carter handed me the knife.

"Aria," Carter's voice breaks through my terror and the memory as he commands, "Give. Me. The. Knife." His words mix with the sound of my heavy breathing.

Carter's voice is demanding and on the edge of anger. I barely peek at him, the fear of Stephan waking and taking the knife from me is all too real. Blood seeps into his shirt, and his mangled body is unmoving. But I know he's going to take the knife back. Stephan will take it and do to me what he did to my mother.

I squeeze the steel handle harder. I won't let him.

Tears prick my eyes as Carter yells at me, his voice booming in the silent room and sending a violent vibration through my chest. It hurts. It all hurts.

My head shakes in defiance. I shouldn't disobey him. Bad things happen when I do. *The cell.* At the thought, my shoulders hunch and my knees go weak, ready to surrender and kneel to the man who's held me captive yet given me this revenge.

Given me the means to avenge my mother's death.

But I can't move. "I can't," I say, and my words are weak and fall from my lips like a pathetic whimper. "I won't." Those two words come out harder and I reach out, swinging my arm violently in the air and slicing into Stephan's throat again. In my periphery, I see a man back away, and then another.

A small cry slips through my lips unbidden as Carter wraps his hand around mine, his other hand on my shoulder and keeping me steady as he pries my fingers back. The murmurs of the other men in the room barely register. All I can hear is Carter shushing me, and all I can focus on are Stephan's eyes. The depths of his irises never seemed as dark as they do now.

The steady shaking of my shoulders turns violent as I try to move backward, away from the monster, away from his grasp. To run and hide like I did all those years ago.

But I can't. Carter won't let me.

It's Carter, I tell myself. Carter is holding me. Focusing on regulating my shaky breathing helps steady me back to reality.

My left knee falls to the ground first and it makes my right knee slam against the ground.

"Shh," Carter shows me mercy. Stealing the knife from me but guarding me against my fears.

"It's over," he whispers as he finally pries the knife from my grasp. And I let him. I let him take it, but I won't move until I know Stephan is dead.

"He'll come for me," the scared child inside of me speaks. He can't be dead, because then it would be over. And with Stephan, it's never over. He's haunted me for as long as I can remember.

"She's fucking insane." The sharp and disgusted voice of Romano cuts through my thoughts. *Thump, thump.* My heart beats harder as I remember where I am. "This is insane," Romano says with anger.

"Shut up." Carter's voice once again tears through my body, thrumming through my blood and for the first time, I close my eyes. But then I remember Stephan is only feet from me, and they fly open again.

The room falls silent, just as Carter commanded. His fingertips are gentle on my shoulders, one hand on each as he lowers his lips to my ear and tells me, "Go upstairs and wash yourself off."

My head shakes on its own, my eyes not moving from the body in the chair in front of me.

"He's not dead," I speak softly as if it's my excuse. Logically, I know he's dead. He must be. But the fear that he's not is so real, so visceral that I can't contain it. I can't shut it down.

Carter's grip on me tightens as I hear him breathe heavier before huffing a low sound mixed with a grunt of anger. The second he moves away from me, all I feel is the chill of loneliness.

With one heavy step, Carter kicks over the chair, sending Stephan's heavy body to the floor with a thud, and again the men back up while Romano says something I can't hear. It all turns to white noise as Carter kicks the limp body. Stephan's head falls to the side and I have to move to my right, my knees rubbing against the unforgiving floor as I look into his eyes. Still open, still staring aimlessly.

"He's dead, Aria. He's fucking dead!"

My head shakes as my pulse quickens, the palms of my hands sweaty. "He can't be," I say but my words are weak.

Carter leans over the dead body, gripping my chin in both of his hands and pulling me closer to him, but I react quickly, terrified that

Stephan could reach up. That he would get me if I dared to take my eyes from his.

"Un-fucking-believable." Carter's mutter sends hatred through me. Hatred toward myself and my cowardice. How many years have I woken in sheer horror at the vision of the man lying dead at my feet? Enough that logic betrays me, making me think there's no way that he's dead.

"I'll give you his head," Carter says and not understanding, my eyes lift to his for only a moment, but he's already crouching down, the knife in his hand. He lifts it high in the air and strikes it against the open wound in Stephan's throat. His muscles tense in his neck as he hardens his jaw. Anger is evident in his strained expression as he strikes again and again, taking his frustration out on Stephan's neck.

He holds the knife in place, sweating and panting with both anger and exertion. Carter's shoe slams against the slick side of the knife. Over and over each thrust of his leg is accompanied with more power, more anger—no, outrage, that Stephan's neck doesn't split beneath the blade. My body jolts with each impact, and the awe of watching Carter destroy Stephan by tearing his head from his body slowly helps restore my sanity.

A crunch that makes my gut twist and turn echoes through the room, as does the deep growl of irritation that rumbles from Carter in a snarl. As Carter lifts his bloodstained shoe, Stephan's head rolls backward, parted from his body.

My erratic heartbeat settles as Carter stands tall in front of me. His usually impeccable suit is a wrinkled mess against his tanned skin. He drops the jacket to the floor and rolls up his sleeves one by one, taking his time as he steadies his breathing. I watch every bit of him morph back into the controlled man I know him to be. With blood splattered on his shirt, his hard jawline seeming even harder in the light from the chandeliers above us, Carter has never looked more dominating as he towers over me.

Men talk around us, but they don't exist in this moment. Not when Carter's dark eyes pierce through mine and the shards of silver in them hold me hostage.

"Upstairs." The word slips from my lips before he opens his mouth.

I watch as his tongue wets his lower lip and he considers me. His eyes leave mine to trail down my body and then back up, and it's only then I remind myself to breathe. "Upstairs to wash myself," I repeat Carter's command from a moment ago, letting my gaze move to Stephan's be-headed body.

When I raise my eyes back to Carter's, I know he was waiting for me to look back up at him.

I've left him waiting.

I've disobeyed him.

Everything moves around me slowly as I regain what little com-posure I have left.

Carter steps over Stephan's dead body and grips my chin force-fully in his hand. I can't breathe as he lowers his lips to mine, his eyes never leaving mine and tells me calmly with a voice loud enough for everyone to hear, "He'll never have power over you again. The only thing you have to fear, is me."

CHAPTER 2

Carter

"WHAT THE FUCK IS THIS, CROSS?" ROMANO FEIGNS anger in his voice, but the terror is unmistakable.

Picking up Stephan's untouched and still neatly folded cloth napkin from the table, I wipe the blood from my hands and arms.

My shoulders rise and fall as I go over the last ten minutes. So little time for so much to happen. Romano isn't meant to die tonight, but I lost my composure. If he doesn't pull his shit together over Stephan dying, I'll have no choice but to kill him.

Or, if I think he'll speak a word that could ruin everything I've built and everything I have planned.

I can't hide what she does to me. I can't disguise the power Aria has over me when she doesn't listen.

Romano knows too much.

The thought forces my neck to tilt to the side and crack. And then to the other side as Romano asks again, "You set me up?"

The indignation in his voice is sickening. As if I owe him any loyalty. Dropping the napkin to the floor, I walk toward Romano, my shoes crushing fallen glass underfoot as I near him.

"He's a traitor," I say simply. "He *was* a traitor." Romano swallows and his hands ball into fists and then loosen. His gaze shifts to each person in the room. All of them with me, and none of them with him.

I could so easily destroy him. Take him out and be done with him. And then I wouldn't have to worry about the impression I've left him with. I wouldn't have to worry about him telling anyone else what Aria means to me.

But at that very thought, I know I'll let him live and walk out of my home unscathed. *I want them all to know.*

My eyes close at the realization. As I take a deep breath and fall into the calmness of my decision, I hear Jase's voice cut through the fog.

"We received some information from our leak at the Talvery headquarters," Jase says and then adds, "Stephan couldn't be trusted." His voice is calm. Calmer than Romano's as he replies with some sort of defense. I can't focus on what he says; all I can do is replay each moment in my mind, trying to decipher how Romano viewed it. How my brothers saw me. How the men who work for me watched me lose control.

They'll all know what she means to me. What she can do to me. I want every one of those pricks to know.

As my eyes slowly open, I see Romano and I grin at him, a slow methodical grin.

"Relax, Romano," I tell him as I reach out and grip his right shoulder. I give his shoulder a firm squeeze.

I listen to his breathing hitch and watch as his pupils dilate. I've seen this look so many times before. The look of fear and hope mixing in the eyes of my enemies is undeniably familiar to me.

"He had to be dealt with, and I know you had a soft spot for him," I tell him evenly, giving his shoulder another slight squeeze as I force a faint, but kind smile to my lips. "I didn't want anyone to think you had a hand in this." I release him and add, "I know you two were close."

With my back to him, I survey the room, and a few of my men are cleaning up the evidence already. This isn't the first time blood has been shed in this room and they're more than capable of making it go away. The glass clinks as it's swept up.

"I don't have any room for traitors in my alliances," I speak to Romano, although I still have my back to him.

"I could have been informed," he responds, and I finally turn to him again.

"I thought you would enjoy the show. I was told you have a fondness for theatrics." A flash of fear sparks in his eyes and I have to school my expression to keep the sheer delight from showing. The only thing that makes this moment better is knowing that Aria is upstairs, and she'll be waiting for me.

"Next time, I'll be sure to tell you in advance." With my final words, I nod to Jase.

"I'll show you out," Jase says to Romano with a smirk and heads to the door, not waiting for his response. I merely stare at the old man and his ill-fitting suit that's rumpled and marred by a small splatter of red up his arm. His eyes narrow and his chest rises once with a heavy breath. I can only imagine the taste of blood in his mouth as he bites his tongue.

"Next time," are his parting words and they're followed by the hollow sound of his footsteps as he leaves the room.

"You want to keep any of him, boss?" Sammy asks. He's a young kid, but smart and eager to learn. Crouched near Stephan's body, he gestures to the head. "Or trash it all?" He looks up at me without any fear, but in its place is respect. I think that's why I like the kid. A very large part of me envies him. He never went through the shit I did. He didn't have to learn the way I did.

"Burn all of him. No trace. I don't want a single piece of that prick left in here."

Sammy nods once and immediately gets to work.

"How long until he turns on us?" I hear Jase's question from behind me and I turn to face my brother.

"He'd already turned on us, remember?" I remind him and Jase only smirks at me.

"He was still willing to deal with us while ripping us off. But I imagine that's going to change now." He leans against the wall and slips his hands in his pockets as he watches the men clean up the room.

"Both Talvery and Romano will come for us. You know that, right?" Daniel asks as he moves to join us. Declan follows and the four of us form a circle in the corner of the room.

"As long as they don't join forces, it doesn't matter," I respond without thinking. My thoughts immediately go back to Aria. Consequences be damned; this was for her.

"What's to stop them from doing that?" Declan asks. He wasn't concerned before tonight. Of all four of us, he's the least interested and the least informed. Because of that, I imagine he was the most shocked as well.

"A decade-long feud, greed, arrogance?" Jase answers.

"All of this, and for what?" Daniel's question comes out harder. "It was for her, wasn't it?"

Silence engulfs us for a moment as I watch my brother.

"There was no reason to go about it like this. To make a scene and piss off Romano like that."

"It had to be done." Jase is quick to answer and firm with his response.

"But we didn't have to make Romano an enemy. Not now, not when Talvery is coming for us." Daniel's anger is evident, but more so, he's scared. Scared because Addison is here with us.

"She's safe," I tell him, moving to the heart of his concern.

My brothers are quiet as I take in Daniel's stance. He's tired and anxious. "I want this shit to end, but now we've added gasoline to the fucking fire."

Jase answers before I can. I'm struck by the fact that I never considered Addison. I didn't care what the cost was for giving Aria the revenge she so desperately needed. "The guns are in, we just have to spread them and hit them hard."

"Who are we hitting? Talvery? Or Romano?" Daniel asks Jase, but then all three of my brothers look at me. All of them wanting to know.

Daniel doesn't hold back his concern as he says, "I know you've been lying to us. And now you brought war to *our* doorstep for her."

"I never lied," I mutter, and my words are a harsh whisper. Anger seeps into my blood as I watch the chaos in Daniel's eyes heat.

"What does she mean to you?" he asks as if my answer will assuage all of his fears.

Only if I answer truthfully.

Jase's gaze moves to the men behind us and then back to me with a subtle unasked question and I nod my head.

"Leave us," I call out and wait to speak until the sounds of men shuffling out of the room subside. My brothers are patient. Not speaking and holding back until we're left alone.

"She's getting to you," Daniel speaks softly. "You're making calls for all of us, but she's clouding your judgment."

His words feel like a knife in my back.

"You're questioning me?" I ask him, not holding back the bite of anger, but deep inside I know it's for me. I'm angry because he's right. My brow pinches and I force in a deep breath and then another, staring behind my brother at the soft gray wall where bright red blood is smeared.

"She saved my life," I tell them while turning to look away. Guilt washes through me. I know I was thinking of her, not of us. But this was meant to happen. I can feel it ringing inside of me like a singular truth never has. "And I hated her for it." The confession comes out with a gentleness and careful touch.

The silence from my brothers begs me to look at them. To know for certain their reaction to my confession. Although there's a hint of shock in Daniel's eyes, there's something else there too. Something I can't place.

"Why didn't you tell us?" Jase asks. "She saved you?" he adds for clarification.

"It was years ago, the night Dad had to call his friend in." I know they know what I mean by the reference. There was only one night Dad called in a favor for me. One night where I almost met death.

"Shit," Declan bites out and runs his hand down his face. He was only a child. It was so long ago.

"As long as I'm living and breathing—she will be mine." My response is brutal and unmoving. "Whether she likes it or not."

"You took her because you hated her for saving you?" Daniel asks although there's no confrontation in his tone, nothing but genuine curiosity and concern.

"I wanted her to know what it was like to wish you could just die and not have to live another day with the person you've become." I almost tell him I didn't know that I loved her. But I change the words as I add, "I didn't know that I cared for her. Not until she came here."

She gave me a new reason to live. Not only all those years ago when she saved me, but also this past month when I finally got her beneath me.

The silence stretches between us and it feels suffocating. I've never felt shame for what I've become, because everything I am and everything I've done is for the three men who stand in front of me, judging what I've told them.

"And Stephan?" Declan asks. He's the only one of the three who didn't know why I was letting Aria kill him. He didn't care to know, like so many other things he'd rather not be aware of.

"He raped and murdered her mother. She cries at night in her sleep because of him."

The dark pit of sadness that narrowly exists within me expands at the memory of the first night I realized the power he had over her. "I had to give her this," I explain and my last word hisses from my lips.

Jase is the first to nod in agreement, followed by Declan and then, finally, Daniel.

"They're all going to be coming for us now," Daniel says, but this time his voice welcomes the challenge. The moment of wondering what my brothers think of me, what they think of *her*, ends as quickly as it came.

I answer Daniel the only way I know how. With the only acceptable answer there is.

"Let them come."

CHAPTER 3

Aria

I DON'T KNOW HOW LONG I'VE BEEN SHAKING. MY HAND TREMBLES as I reach for the faucet and turn the scalding water even hotter. My skin is bright red, but I can't feel anything. Everything is numb and out of my control as I lean against the tiled wall. My knees quiver and my body begs me to heave. The heavy diamond on the necklace ever present around my neck hits the tile of the stall and I hold on to it as if it can save me or take me away.

Is this what it feels like to kill someone? I've only seen two people die in front of me before.

My mother was the first. And the second ruled my life until the fateful day Carter changed my life forever.

I remember thinking about that second time when I watched someone's life being taken in front of me, right as I stood at the side of the bar. Completely unaware that when I entered, my entire life would change forever. I just wanted my notebook back.

I suck in a deep breath of the hot steam as I lean my head back against the tile and close my eyes. The memory takes me back to only weeks ago, but that memory is far better than the reality of my bloodstained skin.

Shoving my hands in my pockets to keep them warm, I let my fingers trace over the keys to my car. It's the only weapon I have.

And keys are a weapon. I've seen someone slice a hole in a guy's throat with a key. I stood there numbly as the man's hands tried to reach his neck, but my father's men gripped his wrists and pulled them behind his back. Blow after blow, each one puncturing his skin as he was restrained and unable to defend himself.

A chill flows over my skin at the memory and it takes me a minute to realize I'm not breathing.

I remember the sound of sneakers kicking small rocks across the pavement. The sound of the busy street at the other end of the alley.

Three men my father employs were supposed to be escorting me back home from the studio I wanted to rent, but they decided to take a detour.

And I stood there in shock; it all happened so quickly.

Mika was with me then. His thin lips tipped up into the evilest smile I'd ever seen. That smile held pure joy. Joy at my shock? Or my horror? Maybe my pain, because I knew the man they'd killed.

Mika's dark black hair was slicked back. His beard was shaved off and it was only stubble that caressed his skin that night. Conventionally speaking, Mika's a good-looking man with a deep, rough voice that can bring any woman to her knees.

But I've seen who he really is. And knowing he's the man I've come to see and make demands of, sends a spike of fear through me.

But I won't let anyone steal from me. I can't let them push me around and let them think I'm weak. And like my father says, it's time for me to demand respect. It's what the Talverys do.

My eyes slowly open to the sound of the water hitting the bare tile. Every movement, every noise, makes my body tense.

I try to steady my breathing, ragged from the memories. The one of the night I was taken, and the other of that night two years ago when I saw a man murdered. I didn't leave home for a long time after that, and I never moved out. My father wanted it that way anyway.

I thought I knew what fear was before I walked into that bar. I was wrong.

Staring at the lifeless corpse of a man whose existence has tormented you for years is true fear. It wasn't until his head rolled away from his body on the carpet, that I could even consider the possibility that he would never hurt me again.

My gaze drifts to the pool of water at my feet. The water contains dark red splotches until it swirls and morphs to pink as it flows to the drain.

First, I watched my mother's death.

Then the death of a man who betrayed my father.

And now I've killed the man who betrayed both of my parents.

I wait for a sense of relief, or victory—righteousness, maybe. But nothing comes. There's only a hollow emptiness in my chest and a flood of unwanted memories.

The sound of the glass door to the shower sliding open nearly tears a scream from my throat.

Mika, my father, Stephan... of all the men responsible for me leading a life riddled with fear, none of them compare to the man standing in front of me. The steam billows around him as it exits the shower stall, allowing the chill of the cooler air to leave goosebumps along my skin.

Carter's gaze narrows as he assesses me, glued to the wall and still shaking, still struggling to do anything. I've never felt so weak in my life as I do right now.

Killing Stephan may have felt freeing during the moments the knife sliced into him, but I've never been so chained to memories as I am in this instant.

"What are you doing?" His deep voice comes out a question, but I don't think he expects me to answer.

"I can't stop shaking," I tell him in a staccato cadence that reflects my inability to do anything clearly. Each word is forced out as I grip my wrist with my other hand and will it to stop, finally letting go of the gem.

Carter doesn't answer me. Instead, he steps into the stall, still clothed. He hisses through his teeth as the hot water batters his arm and splashes along his bloodstained shirt, now sticking to his skin. He turns the faucet, cooling the water until it's only warm and no longer scalding hot.

The cool air feels refreshing as it caresses my skin more and more the longer he stands in front of me with the door open. My head feels light and the panic that was all-consuming only a moment ago, wanes.

In one breath, Carter strips from his shirt. In another, he closes the door behind him and pulls me into his arms. The warm water gently splashes along my back in time with Carter's soothing strokes. It takes a moment for me to return the embrace, to wrap my arms around him and press my cheek to his bare chest.

His heartbeat is steady as he holds me and it's calming. *So calming.* The trembling subsides quicker than I could imagine.

My eyes close and I welcome the darkness of exhaustion until Carter clears his throat, startling me from the comfortable silence.

"I'm sorry for telling you that I wouldn't be with you," he says and his voice rumbles up his chest. I stay tense against him, caught off guard. I barely remember his words from earlier. Everything happened so quickly; of everything that happened tonight, the last thing on my mind is the threat he gave me before I knew his intentions and every piece of the puzzle fell into place.

An apology is something I would never expect from him.

Carter is never sorry. Carter is unapologetic in everything he does.

Without an answer from me, he continues, "I shouldn't have said that. And I'm sorry for it." Another moment passes, and the cloudy haze slowly dissipates until I can peel myself away from him. My nakedness and the reality of what I am to him are slowly coming back to me.

Today has been a whirlwind of emotions. The most prevalent being pain.

I swallow thickly before stepping away from him and out of the flowing streams of water to tell him it's okay.

I don't know what else to say.

Pushing the wet hair from my face, I look him in the eyes and the intensity in his gaze sets my body on fire.

"It's not okay. And it won't happen again," Carter replies as his eyes darken and he moves in the suddenly small shower, stalking toward me to place both of his palms against the tile wall on either side of my head.

His broad shoulders eclipse everything else as he towers over me, and the sheer power that radiates from him forces a deep urge of need down to my core. The pulse is uncontrollable and threatens to overcome my senses.

It would be so easy to fall into his arms. To get lost in the lusty haze that is Carter Cross.

"I forgive you," I tell him in a single breath and try to swallow down the desire. Suddenly, I'm hotter than I was before. All over, and all at once.

My nipples pebble and my fingers itch to reach out to him, to spear my fingers through his hair and pull his lips down to mine.

But Carter doesn't kiss me. He never has. My gaze stays pinned to his lips as he lowers them, oh, so slowly, but they pass my own and travel to my shoulder. His rough stubble grazes my neck and makes my pussy throb. His tongue sweeps along my skin and a heat flows through me that I can't deny.

If I could hold on to this moment and hide from the pain of my reality forever, I would.

Just as I dare to reach up, to let my fingers travel along his shoulders and then higher, a sudden knock at the door cuts sharply through the moment.

The white noise of the shower dims as Jase's voice carries through the door, calling out to take Carter away from me.

Don't go, my heart begs me to plead with him. I can't be alone right now. *I'm not okay.*

Carter nudges the tip of his nose against mine, letting a soft hum of approval vibrate up his chest before telling Jase that he's coming. He lowers his voice and looks me in the eyes as he tells me, "Finish here and wait in bed for me."

The command and heat in his eyes is something I could never refute. "Yes, Carter," I answer obediently, and it only makes the heat between my thighs grow hotter.

It's not until he's gone that I realize how much I want him.

How much I need Carter Cross right now. I have no one else.

And how much that very fact scares me.

CHAPTER 4

Carter

"HE SAID HE'S COOLED OFF, BUT THE FUCKER'S ALREADY talking." Jase updates me the second I step into the den. The adrenaline from tonight had subsided. The ringing in my blood had dulled.

Until I saw Aria still shaking.

One look at her delicate form trembling from the aftershocks changed everything. The normal rush of triumph was replaced instantly by something else. Something I don't care to look farther into right now.

I need a drink. A strong one, at that.

"We knew we couldn't trust him," I answer my brother as the ice clinks in the glass. I fill it with three fingers of whiskey and let it sit on the ice to chill. The amber liquid swirls as I consider every aspect of what we could face from Romano.

I know his friends. I know his enemies. And most owe far more to me than they do him.

"Do we need to send anyone a reminder?" I ask my brother as I lift my eyes to his and throw back the whiskey. If anyone wants to prove themselves to Romano, I need to shut down that train of thought before it turns into anything tangible. A small reminder of what we're capable of could silence any ideas anyone has of turning on us. It's best not to entertain any delusions of grandeur they might have.

Jase shakes his head but doesn't return my gaze. Instead, he taps his finger against the back of the chair he's standing behind before continuing. "He messaged Talvery," Jase tells me as the whiskey burns its way down to my gut.

I cock a brow at his statement. "Is that intel from our informant?"

"From one of them," Jase answers with a confidence I respect.

"So, he told Talvery that I allowed his daughter to kill her enemy. That's interesting, isn't it?" I can't hide the amusement that plays along my lips.

"Not exactly. He only confirmed that we have Talvery's daughter."

A sneer of cynicism comes out as a grunt. "Of course, he did," I say absently as I fill the glass once more.

"And then he left a message for us." I don't breathe or move until Jase tells me, "He says he understands and that he enjoyed the show."

"Fucking prick." I let the words slip out before downing the alcohol in a single gulp. He's a coward. Pitting Talvery and me against one another while pretending to stay by my side. Revenge will be sweet when it comes time for that.

The whiskey is still burning down my chest as my brother asks, "Are we still with him? The guns have shipped. We have the upper hand. We can still pull back from our deal."

"Or side with Talvery?" I ask him and Jase tenses. "We could drop Romano and give the guns to Talvery."

"Why would we do that?" Jase asks with a glimmer of distrust in his voice as he walks closer to me and then settles against the side table, leaning against it and waiting for me to answer. The adrenaline returns full force as if knowing it would be a fatal mistake to put any trust in Talvery. His greed knows no bounds and to aid him could backfire immediately.

I watch the ice in the glass, seeing nothing but Aria. Hearing her pleas to spare her father.

The way she molded her body to mine in the shower was intoxicating. But she's still holding back. I would do anything to have her completely. This could be it.

But the risk is considerable.

Give it time, I hear a voice urge in the back of my head, but it can't be mine. Patience can go fuck itself.

"Of course... Aria." My brother answers his own question given my silence and then runs a hand down the back of his head. It takes him a moment before he reaches for a glass and then takes the bottle of whiskey from my hand.

I let him. I already know she's making me think differently than I should. Making my actions unpredictable. She has a control over me that's undeniable and more and more apparent each day.

"You've never let anyone come between you and business before." He downs the first shot, not waiting for a reply. Sucking the whiskey from his teeth, he asks, "Why her?"

Silence descends upon us. I've never told anyone the complete truth. About how I wanted to die all those years ago. I was so close, and she stopped it.

Before tonight, I hadn't told them that I'd hated her for it. I didn't tell anyone that I'd prayed for it all to end. That at my greatest moment of weakness, I'd given up.

Until she stopped it all.

Jase considers me for a moment. He's my second-in-command. My partner in all of this. And I never told him. I didn't want to speak the truth to life. "I need to know what she means to you at least."

"Everything." I don't hesitate to answer him, although my voice comes out lowly and full of possessiveness.

"And she wants you to side with Talvery. The man who tried to have us all murdered in our sleep? The man who set our house on fire?"

"She doesn't know." I'm quick to defend her and even I feel the irritation of it. As if it seeps from the tone of Jase's voice straight to my head.

"She doesn't know shit," he responds with slight agitation, but one look at him and he looks away, staring at the liquid swirling in his glass.

"She's loyal."

"She doesn't owe him her loyalty." He finally looks at me. He's not telling me anything I don't know already. "Does she know about her mother?" he asks.

"It's a rumor. We can't prove it." Even as I answer him, I know I'm merely playing devil's advocate. I'd do anything in my power to give her hope for the one thing she wants. Mercy toward her father.

"I'd planned to torture it out of Stephan," I tell my brother, reminding myself. I'd intended to give her truth tonight, along with the vengeance she so desperately needed. "I lost sight of that goal."

Jase only huffs, although when I glance at him there's a shimmer of delight in his eyes and a smirk on his lips before he sips the expensive whiskey.

"She'll never believe me." As I give Jase yet another excuse, I feel a vise around my heart. Squeezing it tight. "She would never side with me over her father." The truth is damning.

"I don't mind telling her." The ease with which he speaks catches me off guard. He must see it in my face though because he shrugs and adds, "I'll be gentle, but I'll make her understand."

"I don't want you getting between us." The rise of anger is something I didn't expect. Clearing my throat, I return to the whiskey. One more and then I go back to my Aria.

"She's fucking with your head," Jase says with a hard edge before adding, "I've never seen you like this."

"Like what?" I ask him, daring him with my tone to question me. Although, I already know the answer.

"Indecisive and emotional. We should have already annihilated them. You're taking your time and stockpiling more weapons and men than necessary."

"I don't want her to hate me." I expect to see shock in Jase's expression. Maybe even disgust. She's a weakness I never intended, but one I refuse to give up.

Although he's taken aback, he doesn't argue, and a tiredness sets in his dark eyes. The weight of everything I've been feeling is settling down on his shoulders now.

I propose to my brother, "We have to choose. Talvery or Romano."

"I'll die before siding with Talvery," my brother confesses without a hint of emotion. It's merely a fact. And one I can support and respect, given everything Talvery has done. "I'd rather take them both out."

Feeling the heat and buzz of the liquor slinking its way into my thoughts, I merely nod and then roll my tense shoulders. I'm tired. Not just of tonight. But tired of fighting.

There's no way to make it end though. The moment a man stops fighting in this business, is the moment he's executed.

"We've pissed them both off, so it's better to choose a side and make sure they don't put their past behind them to take us on together. Just because Romano slipped him intel doesn't mean anything more than he's fueling the flames between them... but he knows what he's doing. He's redirecting Talvery's hate."

Jase's head falls back as he downs the whiskey and sets the glass down heavily on the tabletop. He breathes out long and low as he nods his head in agreement.

"We can't let that happen. But between the two, Romano is the best choice." He stares at me, making sure I listen to his final words. "You already know that. Siding with Talvery will be the end of us."

He's not wrong. And dropping my gaze, I give in to what I'd already decided. To what I knew had to happen. Romano can't be trusted, but he can be manipulated and used. Talvery would slit our throats the second he got a chance. He's already tried to wipe us out before and failed. And for that reason alone, allowing him any mercy would be a sign of weakness.

Instead of answering my brother, I give him a short nod and turn to leave him, to head back to Aria.

"How is she?" he asks me, changing the subject before I can depart.

"Handling it well, all things considered." The image of her trembling form in the shower reminds me that she's not well. "Today was hard on her. I should go back."

"You should," he says beneath his breath, although he speaks so quietly I'm not sure if the words were meant for me or for himself.

"It had to be done," I remind him, and he nods his head in agreement.

Feeling the conversation is over, I start to leave, but he calls out for me one more time.

"Carter..."

Looking over my shoulder, I see the sincerity in my brother's expression when he tells me, "Be gentle with her."

The moonlight filters through the slits in the curtain and washes over Aria's curves, hidden beneath the covers. Her hair is a messy halo, still damp on the pillow as she lies on her side.

My cock instantly hardens, remembering how I left her. Naked and wanting.

She's a good girl, my little songbird, so I know she'll be naked with the exception of my necklace around her throat. She'll be ready for me to take her.

The words from Jase still ring clear in my head. *Be gentle with her.*

Jase doesn't know her like I do, but he knows women far better than I ever have.

The images of me slamming into her and rubbing her clit until she's screaming my name push me to forget Jase's advice. To continue fucking Aria into obedience… until the moment I come closer to her.

She's still trembling. Her hands clutch one another in front of her and her eyes are closed tightly. As if she's praying in the bed.

Her breathing is a mess of stutters.

Not all of us are made to be killers. I knew that when I gave her the knife and set Stephan up to be her victim.

"It's the adrenaline," I tell her quietly, cutting through the hushed night with my tense words. Her body jolts under the sheets and she stiffens, but her hands and shoulders still tremble.

I watch as she swallows and then her lips part. The look in her hazel-green eyes is a mix of utter sadness and fear.

"I can't stop," she says, and her words are a whisper.

The need to make it all go away rides me hard as I quickly crawl into bed with her, pulling back the sheets and letting her fall into my arms. "Please, help me," she begs me.

"Shh," I hush her, petting her hair and pulling her closer to me. Her small body clutches at mine as if she can't get close enough. "I shouldn't have left you," I whisper out loud and into her hair, feeling the wisps tickle my jaw.

She only responds by moving her hands to my chest and burying her head beneath my chin. She's so frail in my embrace.

Which is anything but the Aria I know.

Maybe I've finally broken her. I already knew I was a monster, but the smile that begs to creep onto my lips at the thought is a validation of that fact. I'm not worthy of a single breath, let alone the woman in my arms.

She's not broken; a woman like Aria can't be broken. A voice whispers deep in the back of my mind, where it hides in the crevices. And the smile that begged to come out before forces its way to my face. I can only hide it by kissing her hair as I rub soothing strokes up and down her bare back.

"You're fine, songbird," I tell her, and I know she can feel the hum of my deep words with her face pressed so firmly against my chest. "It's only the adrenaline."

She doesn't move from her spot, but her lashes tickle my chest as she opens her eyes and then blinks. Her breath is hot and her nails scratch lightly against my skin, but she doesn't ask the question on the tip of her tongue. *How do I know?*

Her hands continue to shake as she attempts to inch even closer to me. With her refusing to let go of me, I reach down and pull the covers tighter around her before telling her my story.

Not all people are made to be killers, but sometimes even the sweetest of creatures have to murder. I may not have ever been innocent, but there was a time when I wasn't the callous and brutal man I am today.

"The first man I killed was a bartender named Dave," I speak quietly without pausing my strokes along her back. Kissing her hair again, I stare at a sliver of light that flits across the bedroom floor. I only know Aria is listening because of the flutter of her lashes again. "I was sixteen," I confess to her as I'm taken back to that night.

"My father didn't deal with my mother's impending death all that well." A huff of ludicrous laughter makes my shoulders shake and her body moves with mine. "He was a coward, I know that now, but to face the deaths of the ones you love... well, I can't blame him for being a coward, but I can blame him for bringing me down with him."

"What happened to your mother?" Aria asks gently, and her soft breathing is steady. It's only then that I see her shaking has turned into a slight tremble.

"She had cancer. It took two years to kill her." The memory makes my chest feel tight, but I continue with the story, the one that makes me angry, not the one that I don't have the strength to face. "My father couldn't stand to see how she deteriorated. So, he drank himself into the man he was without her."

My gaze drops to the comforter. "I swear he was a good man with her, but knowing he was going to lose her changed him." My voice lowers, and I force aside the emotions that come with her memory. To vanish into the back of my mind where they belong.

"One night, my father got himself into trouble and my mother was barely breathing." The image of her on the hospital bed they'd sent to our home for her hospice care causes my voice to crack, but I don't think Aria can hear it.

"He hadn't been home in nearly twelve hours and I knew she wasn't going to make it much longer." He knew too. He had to have known. We were only boys and even we knew she was going to die. "She died while I was away looking for him."

Aria's grip on me loosens, her nails trailing on my chest as her head lifts to look at me. I can feel her gaze on me, but I don't return it.

I can still hear the way the fall leaves crunched under my sneakers and feel the way the water from the earlier rainstorm seeped into a hole on the bottom of my sole as I trawled through the alleys looking for him.

"He used to go to a few bars I knew." I was young, but the bartenders knew me by name at that point. Aria doesn't stop looking at me, and I feel vulnerable and exposed under her eyes.

She makes me weak.

"I found him in the bathroom, beat up pretty bad. He said it was the bartender. I forget what excuse my father had, but then he cried and said he couldn't move. He cried and that's something he never did. He always drank away his pain. They beat him up and then cuffed him to the radiator, so they could come back and do it again. And again. All the while my mother waited for him."

Aria sniffles against my chest and whispers an apology.

As the memories come back to me I tell her, "My father was a poor excuse for a husband. And even a man. But what they'd done…"

I can't explain to her how the anger spurred me on. In the moment that I thought I was going to lose both of them in one night, the anger is what kept me from breaking down.

Licking my lower lip and trying to play off the hoarseness in my voice as anything but emotion, I continue. "The bartender knew my mother was dying. He knew we were on our own. He could have done a lot of things. He could have called the cops to remove my father. He could have locked the doors. But he wanted to humiliate him. He wanted to have a punching bag as payment for the debt my father owed him."

I remember the way Dave looked at me that night when I left my father where he was and walked behind the bar to demand the key. He had a smile on his smarmy face. I knew he was a dick the moment I saw him, from his slicked back hair and the glint in his eyes. I'd heard around town that he liked to get the young women who came to his bar drunk and take advantage of them. I didn't want to believe it though, not when I saw my father laughing with him other nights I'd come to get my drunkard of a father back home.

"I went to get the key and Dave tried to punch me. He was piss drunk. I was only a kid."

"You never should have had to—"

"In the streets where I grew up, it wasn't uncommon, Aria." I cut her off before she can show me sympathy or even begin to suggest that I was too young for what I saw and what I was involved in. I'm not the only one who's gone through this shit and I won't be the last. Everyone leads different lives and there are no pretty promises or mercy for some of us.

"I grabbed the chair and I didn't stop hitting him with it. The other guys there never got up when Dave went after me, but they did come for me. Not at first. Not the first time I struck him with the metal legs. The ring of the metal bashing into his head was louder than the basketball game playing on the one TV in the corner of the bar." Aria remains silent, and I continue.

"They didn't even get up when he fell to the floor. I didn't stop cracking his head in with the chair. I couldn't." A lot like Aria tonight. I hadn't made the connection until the thought hit me.

I remember how I didn't even think I was breathing. I didn't think it was real. I didn't want it to be.

"I didn't kill him that night," I tell her and then kiss her hair. My grip on her shoulder tightens and I pull her back into my chest. "The other assholes there dragged me away from him, but the minute I was free, they let me go. I got my father after leaving Dave on the floor bloodied up and moaning."

I can see each of their faces now, full of fear and disbelief that a scrawny boy had nearly killed the man on the floor. My chest heaved but the adrenaline took over.

I killed him a week later after my mother had died and we'd buried her. He came to get money to cover the hospital bills for his broken nose. Money we didn't have, but he expected we would from the life insurance that didn't exist.

No one else was home and I wasn't supposed to be home either, but the guilt of leaving my mom that night kept me from going anywhere for days.

My mother died while I was gone, and I know if I had to put the blame somewhere, it should be on my father.

I know that Dave wasn't the reason that my mother died. But as he stood in the doorway of our home, telling me that the life insurance money from my mother's death was going to him, I lost it. I already knew there was no life insurance. There was no money. There was no helping my father, a man who didn't want to be helped. There was no bringing my mother back.

I knew all of that. I also knew that the man in front of me didn't care.

He didn't care about any of that. And so, I let him into our home, grabbing the pistol my father kept by the door as I closed it. I walked Dave into the kitchen where my mother died on the hospital bed under the pretense of retrieving the check sitting on the counter. I shot him in the back. Just once, with shaking hands. But once was enough.

I didn't stop shaking, not even hours after Sebastian had helped me throw Dave's body into the river. He was the only friend I had and the only person I could turn to. He was older than me, stronger than me and he was there for me when I had no one. He didn't stay for long though. He had his own demons to run from, and plenty of them.

I couldn't stop shaking. If it wasn't for my brothers, I don't think I could have continued living. In a way, it was our first act together that led to this empire. Nothing can bring you closer to someone than death can.

I remember how I didn't want to bury Dave like Sebastian suggested because I couldn't stand to see upturned dirt after watching my mother being lowered into the ground only days before. I threw up as Sebastian dug a hole. I couldn't take it. I couldn't deal with what I'd done and what I was capable of.

And so, we tossed the body in the bed of the truck instead after covering the partially dug shallow grave, and Sebastian disposed of the body in the river. All while I uselessly rocked myself in the passenger seat of the truck, loathing myself and what I'd done.

"When did you kill him?" Aria asks me, breaking up my thoughts and bringing me back to her. I blink away the memories and the heavy sadness in the pit of my chest.

It takes me a minute to realize I hadn't voiced the last bit of my story. She thinks I just lost it at the bar. She doesn't know that I did it days later and that I led him into the house knowing I wanted to see the man die.

"Does it matter when he died?" I ask her, wanting to keep the truth from her and thinking that it makes it better if it was just heat of the moment. But nothing makes being a murderer better.

She doesn't answer me, she only lowers her cheek to my chest and I continue holding her, remembering how I shook that night after ditching Dave's dead body into the river. "The shaking will stop," I whisper.

Time passes slowly, neither of us speaking until I finally feel the weight of the day and tell Aria to sleep.

"I don't want to sleep," she tells me wearily and then forces herself to swallow. "I'm afraid I'll see him. He'll be there waiting for me."

"Shh," I hush her again, cupping her chin in both of my hands and gently placing a kiss on her forehead. I notice then how calm her body is.

It's amazing what a distraction can do to a person. It can make you forget about everything.

"He's gone," I remind her, although her prolonged fear worries me. Killing him was supposed to set her free.

It will, the voice hisses and calms the worry creeping up on me. Nodding as if in agreement with the voice, I kiss her once more, pressing my lips to her smooth skin and then pull back, waiting for her to look at me.

"I told you. All you have to fear is me."

Aria's hazel eyes are deep with emotion, swirling with an intensity that pulls me in and pins me down until her lips part and my gaze drifts to them.

The yearning to press my lips to hers nearly wins, but instead, I remember yet another aspect of tonight that I'd planned and forgotten about.

"Wait here," I command her, and disappointment causes her gaze to lower, but she releases me for the first time since I'd crawled into bed to be beside her.

As I walk to the dresser, I strip off my shirt and pants before grabbing the case with a syringe in it and a bottle of oil from the drawer. I haven't needed it for so long, but she needs it tonight. It will let her sleep if nothing else.

Standing next to the bed, I motion for her to come to me before telling her to turn around and get on all fours. I've come to expect a lot of things from Aria. Her sass and her mouth, her questions, and defiance.

But tonight, all she does is obey, and that stirs up something inside of me. Both the pure and the depraved desires. She doesn't even ask why.

My hand gentles on the curve of her ass then moves up to her waist and back down before I give her the shot, making her jump slightly before she steadies herself and then I can push down the plunger of the syringe.

"Birth control," I tell her and then smirk at the thought as I add, "it's better late than never."

Aria only murmurs a response, placing both her hands flat on the sheets and her cheek follows as she turns her head.

"I have this for you too," I tell her after setting the empty syringe down on the nightstand and pushing on her hip. "Sit up," I command her, and she obeys easily, wincing slightly as her ass presses against the comforter.

"It should help you sleep," I explain as I pull the liquid into the bulb syringe. The oil is clear, a pure drug that will hit her hard the first night. "Have you ever heard of Sweet Lullabies?" I ask her, and she tilts her head with a crease in her forehead indicating her confusion.

"Lullabies? I know a few-"

"No, the drug."

I don't expect her to. We've only just started selling the adapted version that's marketable. She shakes her head, proving me right although the confusion in her expression stays in place.

I lift the syringe to her lips and she obediently opens her mouth, tilting her head back slightly for me. I admire how the moonlight reflects off her slender neck and plays with the shadows down her body as the liquid hits her tongue.

"Suck it down." The command I give her makes my dick stir, but she'll be out soon. Within minutes, I would bet.

"What is it?" she asks me, and I debate on telling her how it came to be and how it's responsible for so many of the reasons I am who I am, but she yawns, cutting me off before I begin.

"Just lie down," I tell her gently, and pull back the covers for her to nestle in beside me. I've had her in my bed a number of nights now, but she's never readily slept this close to me.

With the rustling of the sheets silenced, I let my hand rest on her hip and rub soothing circles there. I breathe in the scent of her hair and leave a small kiss there as I listen to her steady breathing and know that sleep has taken her before I could even begin to admit what this drug really is.

CHAPTER 5

Aria

I USED TO DREAM OF THINGS I'D BET ALL GIRLS DREAM ABOUT.
I would dance so beautifully, my hair swinging in the air as I
landed a perfect pirouette. In my dreams, I could be and do anything. I'd dance in a ballet center stage, and amidst a crowd of thou-
sands, I'd perform beautifully.

I'd climb the mountains and find a magical field of flowers where
they came to life like the story of *Alice in Wonderland*. I could talk
to the animals and drink tiny cups of tea that would make me small
enough to follow the rabbits down the rabbit holes.

I could be anyone I wanted to in my dreams. But those visions
were from long ago. It's funny how they come back tonight.

Each of the scenes flashes through my head as if on fast forward.
I see myself as a young girl performing the arts I wanted to before I
realized my insecurities would keep me from even trying. I watch as I
remember a dream I had of kissing a boy in my class. I imagined my
leg would kick up behind me as he deepened it.

But even as the memory of my dreams from long ago comes to life
before me, I'm aware that they're only dreams. I never kissed Paulie.
I never had the courage to and if I had, I know it wouldn't have happened the way I pictured it.

For a moment, I question if I'm dreaming or awake. Everything is
so vivid. So real.

But the scenes keep going. They don't stop for me.

The hairs at the back of my neck prick as I know what's coming.
They're all in order, like a timeline of my hopes as I watch the scenes
play out. I know I'm getting older. I know what's to come, and I want
it to stop.

My head shakes. Make it stop.

But they don't.

I watch as I dream about my mother and me in the park. She's there with her friend like she always is. And I'm there drawing instead of playing with the other girls. I dreamed of drawing something that day, but when I look down at the paper it's blank. I can't remember what it was. But it doesn't matter. All I can focus on is her face. This is the dream that turned into a nightmare. The first dream of so many I had over and over again.

Make them stop. My throat closes, and I want to scream. It's too real, too vivid. And I can't stop it.

I can feel my nails digging into the sheets. I'm awake, but I can't open my eyes. I can barely move, and I can't stop the images.

My heart races as I see myself in the closet.

Please stop, I whisper in my dreams, but my throat doesn't feel the words. Not like my chest feels the pounding of my blood.

There she is standing with her back to me, facing the door. My mother's standing there and I'm terrified. Why did she tell me not to leave? Not to scream. Not to move except to hide.

Terror races through my veins.

I wish I could move and go to her. To help her.

Please make it stop. I don't want to see it again.

I don't want to see him push the door open and force her down on the ground. She barely fought him and now I know why.

I can feel the tears leaking down my cheeks and I try to scream, but my words are voiceless.

Stephan looks so young. So much younger than he did when I stabbed him. When I murdered him and put an end to the sick smile on his face.

I can't watch, but I can't close my eyes. I can't turn it off. There's nowhere to run in your dreams.

Please, I don't want to see this. I don't want to remember.

The pain grows in my chest and it paralyzes me. The shaking overwhelms me as he pulls out the knife. It's only a small knife, one like Daddy has for fishing.

Run! I try to scream to myself. *Save her!* I will my limbs to move, but I'm victim to my dreams.

She's still on the ground with her back to him. She's crying so hard but trying not to. She's pinned beneath him as I cover my screams with my hands over my mouth in the closet.

Please, Mom, run, I want to say, but my plea is only a whimper. I know she won't. I have no control here and I've seen this nightmare so many times. The memory haunts me in my waking hours just as much as it does in my sleep.

I didn't know what he was doing to her. Not when he held her down and pushed himself inside of her and not when he pulled out the knife. I didn't know it was over until he sliced her neck open. I knew what death meant and when I saw the bright red blood leaking from her and the way she covered it with her hands as she tried to keep it from flowing, I knew what was happening.

But what he did to her before, I didn't know. It wasn't until a month later when I told my cousin Brett that he explained it to me with a pained expression I'll never forget. I told him everything, but he didn't want to hear. He said Talverys don't cry, we get revenge. He was wrong about both of those things.

Nikolai would listen to me though. He let me cry and didn't make me feel ashamed of that fact.

Even the thoughts of Nikolai don't stop the visions before me. Of my mother with her hair pulled back by Stephan as he slit her throat, of her looking toward the closet where I hid when the life left her.

Her lips are moving.

I can't hear what she's saying.

She's saying something. A chill flows down my arms. This isn't what happens. This isn't what I've dreamed before.

Is this real?

The hairs on my body stand on end. My breath is caught in my throat. I don't watch Stephan like I have before. I know the look of triumph on his face as he wipes off the knife on her bare back. I know what he does next. But my mother is still alive as her face falls to the floor. The blood pools around her cheek like it always does. But this time she blinks slowly and looks at me.

"Mom," I whisper, wanting to move but not able to. *Move*, I will myself hopelessly.

My mom blinks again and she speaks. I know she does. *"I can't hear you, Mom. Please. Please don't die,"* I beg her.

Is this real?

Am I breathing? I can't tell anymore.

I watch her lips, the right side of them covered in her own blood.

But the movement from the man standing behind her steals the attention from her.

Stephan stole what used to be and I can never have it back. Him dying doesn't mean anything.

No, I whisper and shake my head as my small fingers of the child I was, reach out and grab the closet door. I can feel it. I can feel exactly what the edge of the closet door felt like.

My shoulders shake violently; this isn't what happens in my dream. The chill leaves and I feel hot, too hot. "Wake up!" I hear Carter's voice and it begs me to open my eyes, but before they obey, I hear my mother's voice say, "You can't forget me."

I suck in air as my eyes shoot open and I stare at the ceiling of Carter's bedroom through a haze of tears. The lights are bright, so bright it hurts, and I close them just as quickly.

With both of my hands covering my eyes, I feel the wetness and try to rub it all away.

My chaotic breaths are matched with Carter's as I slowly come back to reality. Back to Carter's bed. Back to the safety of this moment and not the nightmare of the past.

It was so real. Again, those goosebumps flood every inch of me as I reach Carter's gaze. His eyes are dark as he stares back at me.

His lips part, but he doesn't say anything for a long moment.

"I was screaming?" I ask him, although I know it's true. My throat feels raw and my words are hoarse.

"For almost half an hour," he tells me with nothing but concern and then visibly swallows as my blood chills. "You wouldn't wake up."

It's been years since I've slept through the entire nightmare. Or even since each second played out as if it were an eternity.

Years have passed, but I know the terror was never like that before.

"I don't know what you need," Carter intimates to me, sealing me from my thoughts like he's confessing a sin. I watch his throat as he swallows again. Pulling his arms around my chest I try to lie back down as if this is normal. As if this is okay.

"Hold me," I tell him although I stare at the ceiling, seeing the vision of my mother looking at me in the haunted memory. Her still alive on the floor even though I know she was dead.

"Please, just hold me," I plead with him and turn my head, so I can look at him.

Confusion mars his face, but he doesn't say anything. He only climbs closer to me on the bed and pulls me tighter to him.

I need him to hold me more than I've ever needed anything. Other than my mother to come back to me.

CHAPTER 6

Carter

TODAY IS THE FIRST DAY I SEE ARIA AS STRONGER WHEN SHE'S with me. And I can't shake that thought as I enter the den.

I've only left her for a few minutes here and there. Staying quiet behind her and watching her every move. But she knows I'm there and each time she's started to break down, she comes to me.

Of her own free will, she comes to me, asking me to hold her as if my touch could take her pain away.

My poor songbird hasn't realized my touch only brings pain, and I hope she never does.

The drawing pad shows a clean page. Not a mark lays against the stark white.

With a pen in her hand, she lies on her belly on the rug in front of the fire and stares at the blank sheet as if it'll speak to her.

I would stay there longer, standing behind the sofa, listening to the crackling of the burning wood, and waiting for her fingers to move across the page, but with a shift in my stance, the floor creaks beneath me and breaks her focus.

With lack of sleep, she's slow to move, but she does. Sitting up on her knees she faces me, waiting for whatever it is that I have to say.

It's funny to me how she says when she's with me she forgets, and life is easier.

When I'm with her it's the same until she asks questions, and then I remember everything.

"It's time for the question game again," I tell her, and she drops the pen, letting it roll off her thigh and onto the floor. The frown that's marred her tired expression all day stays in place.

"It feels like forever since we've played this game," she says absently.

Her tone, her body language, everything about it is off today. It feels dampened, depressed even. More so than I've seen her before.

Clearing the tension in my throat and letting my hands clench and unclench I remind her, "It hasn't been that long since you've been out of your cell."

A smirk tips her beautiful lips up and she stares at me as if defying the fact. "I said it *feels* like it's been forever… there's a difference."

Her soft gaze trails across the sofa and then back to me. "Am I staying here?"

"You can move wherever you'd like."

"You haven't come near me today like you usually do," she comments and my gaze narrows at her. I recount the day and each and every time she's come to me. The thrill of her choosing to approach me is dulled by the fact that she realizes things have changed between us.

I search her expression for what she's thinking. For a hint as to how this will modify her behavior. But I can't predict her. Not when it comes to what's between us. And thus, it's time for me to question her, to try to gauge what she's thinking based on her own questions.

"That's not a question," is my only reply to her.

She shrugs as if it doesn't matter, and tension spreads through my jaw. "It wasn't my turn to ask," she says simply with a calmness in her voice that only increases the strain.

Be gentle with her. I remind myself again.

Jase offers me a lot of advice though, and my typical response is for him to fuck off. Aria watches me as I walk to the sofa and take a seat on the right side. She decides not to move from her place, but she adjusts to sit cross-legged.

There's a sudden crackle from the fire and she barely acknowledges it. Just like the tension between us.

"How are you feeling today?" I ask her and tell myself it's because I want to get into her head, not because the last twenty-four hours have changed everything.

"Tired," she tells me and the small bit of strength she's shown since I've walked in wanes. She picks at the fuzz on the rug beneath her and answers with a catch in her throat, "I don't know how to feel right now. There's so much…" her voice trails off and I ask her, "So much what?"

The smirk on her face is nothing but fragile as she asks back, "Isn't it my turn?" The walls around her are toppling down. I can see it. I can *feel* it. She's too weak to hold them up any longer, but the girl beneath them isn't what I imagined. She's a girl who's been left alone far too long. A girl who should never have been left alone at all.

And the realization tugs at me like nothing else ever has.

I force my lips into a straight line and give her a small nod.

"Why did you do it?" she asks me in a whisper. Still picking at the imaginary fuzz and only glancing at me occasionally. As if she's afraid to catch my gaze and see something there that could ruin her.

"Do what?" I ask her, although I already know what she's referring to.

Why did I bring her to the dinner? Give her a knife. And let her kill the man who's hurt her so cruelly.

"Why did you... give me the knife?" she finally asks, and her words are twisted and tortured. As tortured as she's been all of today and last night.

"Why did I let you kill him?" I clarify for her, making her come to terms with the truth. She sucks in a heavy breath and pushes the hair from her face as I speak. "Why did I give you a knife so you could kill Alexander Stephan?"

The sofa groans and the fire hisses as I sit back and release what sounds like an easy breath. "Because I wanted you to do it," I tell her and almost elaborate, but the sarcastic huff that spills from her lips as she looks away from me and toward the door stops me from giving her more.

"What did you dream of last night?" I ask her, and I can't help that my body leans forward, eager for her reply. She hasn't been forthcoming, but she always answers me when I give her the opportunity to ask whatever she'd like.

She licks her lower lip, still shaking her head from my non-answer.

"Dreams," she answers with a hint of indignation in her retort. The words I wanted to speak moments before nearly come to life, but then she adds, "I dreamed lots of dreams," shaking her head with the smallest of movements. Her voice is small, and she speaks as if she's not even talking to me.

Like she's validating what she saw with herself.

"It was like my life sped forward in the form of the dreams I had growing up."

My brow furrows as I listen to her. I expected it to be only nightmares with the way she screamed. The memory of her shrill screams and the terror of her cries sends a bite of cold down my back that slowly rolls through every limb.

I couldn't do anything but listen to her and I've never regretted a damn thing in my life as much as I regretted giving her that knife like I did last night while she screamed.

Licking her lips, she continues and then that crease in her forehead returns as she looks at me. "And then I dreamed of the night he killed her."

My head nods on its own. I knew to expect it, that seeing him would elicit those fears for her, but I expected her to be different after she killed him. For the realization that he's dead, to free her in a way she could never be while he was allowed to live.

Give it time, the voice hisses again and the irritation I have for it shows on my face, silencing Aria.

"You can keep going," I tell her, fixing myself and then adding, "if you'd like."

But the moment has passed and instead she takes her turn.

"Are things still the same?" she asks me.

No. The answer is instant and obvious in my head. Strong enough that I feel the word echo through my veins. "Do they feel different?"

"That's not how this game is played," Aria answers with the trace of a smirk on her face although the tiredness has never been so evident in her eyes as it is now. "I asked you first," she tells me and waits for a reply.

"Kneel," I command her, wanting to prove that the power I held over her before is ever present. Even if the fear she held for me has vanished.

The realization that is what's different sends a spike of regret through me, but it's fleeting. I harden my voice as I tell her again, "Kneel and then ask me if things have changed."

The heat ignites in me as Aria narrows her gaze, the hazel reflecting the flickers of the flames that linger behind her in the fire.

Her lips part and she squirms in her place, but as her eyes close, she only smiles at me while shaking her head.

"I don't want to," she dares to defy me.

My dick hardens instantly, but my knuckles turn white as I grip the arm of the sofa.

Everything inside of me is at war. It seems fitting, since my little songbird seems to be in the same predicament. Her body begging to bend to my command, yet her strong will preventing her from giving in.

"I don't want to punish you today. Not when you need comfort. Don't mistake my gift to you for anything other than what it was." I push the words through clenched teeth, not wanting this tension between us to end. I love her fight. I love it, even more, when I can take it from her.

"And what was it?" she asks me, her eyes sparking with the desire for the truth.

The grin on my face grows as I realize she's set me up, seeking the answer I wouldn't give her when she asked her first question. *Why did I do it?* The tension in my body eases slightly, although the thrill of punishing her is still ringing through me.

"Taking away the fear you had, so I could end it and be the only thing you have left to fear."

"I think you're lying," she bites back although her voice is teasing, sensual even. Not believing me for a moment. Her gaze doesn't waver as she challenges me. I love that she knows better, but if she knew the power she had over me, I could lose everything. She's still loyal to the enemy. There's no denying that.

The thought makes my gaze drop to the fire behind her and it only returns to her when she adds, "But I don't know why you're lying to me."

"Because you don't need to know," I tell her simply and at first her lips part, ready to tell me off, but then she questions herself.

"You're biting your tongue so hard that I imagine you can taste blood," I point out and try to force a smirk to my lips.

"I've asked you two questions and you haven't answered either truthfully," she tells me and then glances at the fire behind her. "What's the point?" she asks no one in particular with a faint whisper.

"Maybe you're asking the wrong questions," I offer her although my entire body is alive with fire. Yesterday was hard on her and she performed exactly as I wanted, but her defiance today is uncontained, and I have no idea how to handle her. Not when she needs me to give her comfort. I wish I'd had her when I was in this same position years ago.

Even knowing that I've had enough of her insolence.

Those hazel eyes pierce through me at that moment, as if she heard my thoughts. The turmoil inside me twists into a knot until she asks the one question that solidifies my decision to leave her on her own for a few hours, so she can feel the need for me once again.

"Are you still going to let him kill my father?" she asks me. Her voice is steady, with maybe even a hint of provocation there.

Let him.

Let Romano.

She doesn't know that if I could do it myself, I would. If I could be the man to pull the trigger, I'd do it without a second thought.

The silence is only broken by the burning wood, now cracking and hissing. As our conversation continued, the sun has set and with the dimming light from the windows, shadows play along Aria's small form.

"I have to go out tonight."

"That doesn't answer my question," she's quick to reply, not taking her gaze from me.

"The game is over." My voice hardens, the anger pushing through.

She is mine. She will obey. Or I will risk everything to reign over her. There is no question in my mind what will happen if she doesn't take her place beside me.

"How convenient," she responds and that's when I meet my limit. There's only so much she can push.

It only takes three large steps until I'm towering over her. One swift motion and my hand is around her throat. My fingers press against the pulse in her veins as her fingers wrap around my hand. Her eyes widen but not with fear, not even with shock. They widen with hate, with anger… They widen with a spark of fight that rivals the roaring fire behind her.

She's never looked more beautiful to me than she does now.

Her nails dig into my skin, but she doesn't pry them away. She just wants to hurt me. She wants to show me what she's capable of.

Oh, songbird, I already know. She's the one who's only just now realizing what she's capable of.

I lower my lips to hers, deliberately placing a knee between her thighs. Invading every inch of space that separates us.

With the heat of the fire igniting the tension, I whisper against her cheek, "You've forgotten your manners, Aria."

"Manners," she bites out as if the word disgusts her and with the small bit of movement, I squeeze a little tighter. She can breathe, she can speak, but my grip on her is unyielding.

My other hand roams her body, drifting down her waist as I nip along her shoulder and then the fleshy bit of her earlobe. My fingers trace down her thigh and then back up, pulling up her skirt as I move back toward her waist until I let my fingers slide to her inner thigh.

And she moans.

She fucking moans, closing her eyes and letting her head fall back slightly. Even with the fight in her, she craves pleasure more than anything.

"What should your punishment be, songbird?" I whisper against the shell of her ear. The shiver that it ignites in her makes my dick harden to the point that it's painful not to thrust inside of her.

Her answer is a muted moan followed by an attempt to swallow. I don't loosen my grip to aid her; instead, I force her to look at me, to open her eyes and answer me.

"How should I punish this mouth of yours?" I ask her in a low and deep voice, not bothering to contain my desire for her.

"Fuck you," she barely pushes out and then licks her lower lip. Ever the defiant one.

"You would love that, wouldn't you?" I whisper against her lips, letting the words mingle with the heat from the fire and the lust between us.

Her hazel-green eyes swirl with a concoction of everything I know she's feeling. The anger and fear, but more than anything, the longing to be pleasured and cared for.

"Get on your back so I can play with your cunt," I command her the moment my fingers loosen on her throat, nearly making her fall backward. But she catches herself, then lies down as I told her to, one elbow at a time, her eyes never leaving mine.

"You obey so easily when you know you're going to get off, don't you?" I toy with her and the hint of a smirk pulls at the corner of her lips. Her intuition will be our downfall. She thinks she knows who she's playing with. But she doesn't realize what's at stake.

A gentle push on the inside of her thighs has her pulling them apart for me. My pointer trails up the thin black lace of her panties, dampened at her core with her arousal, and then to her swollen clit. Her head falls back, and her nails dig into the threads of the rug as she attempts to hold back the moan that threatens to spill from her lips. I can already hear it though. She's so fucking close. So in need.

"You need to get off. I should have done it last night."

The lace tears easily as I hook my thumb through it, ripping it from her sweet cunt to give me full access to her. With a quick intake of air, she lifts her head to watch me.

All that anger means nothing when I can give her this.

I shove two fingers inside her ruthlessly. Her hips buck and her lower back comes off the floor with the sensation it elicits.

I splay my other hand across her belly and push her back down, not stopping the brutal strokes against the ridges of her front wall.

Her head thrashes and she bites her lip. "Fuck," she says but her plea is only a whimper. Her fingers move to my hand on her belly and then up my forearm. Never stopping, pulling, and searching for something to hold on to.

"Let go," I tell her and for a moment she lets go of my arm, but that's not what I meant. "Give me your pleasure. Let go of everything holding you back from falling," I whisper in the air above her as I watch the light dance across her face. Her lips are parted and make a perfect O although her forehead is scrunched with the strain of holding back her strangled cries of pleasure.

The scent of her arousal permeates the air and precum leaks from my dick, begging me to slam inside of her.

With my cock pressed against my zipper, I finger fuck her furiously, pushing a third finger inside of her and my thumb against her clit. "I'm not going to stop until you cum on my hand, Aria. I'll fuck you like this until you can't think straight if you don't give me what I want."

Her head thrashes from side to side and then her back bows. I have to push harder with my hand on her hip to keep her down and strum her faster.

"You want another finger?" I ask her and then kiss the inside of her knee. She's so fucking tight I don't think I could though. It's an idle threat, but the idea of stretching her to the point where I could fist her cunt and give her undeniable pleasures she's never felt, has my hand moving harder and faster in unrelenting strokes and I don't stop.

Even as she cries out my name.

Even as her pussy spasms.

Her body rocks with the force of her orgasm and I don't stop, drawing it out and taking every bit of pleasure from her that I can.

It's not until her breath comes back to her and her eyes find mine that I pull away, sucking each of my fingers while she watches.

"Your cunt is so fucking sweet," I tell her and watch her reddened cheeks blush even more violently.

"I'm growing to love your punishments," she says breathily with her eyes closed and the power I feel vanishes. My dick, still pulsing with need, begs me to push her onto her stomach and rut between her legs. She'd cum again. And again.

The worst thing a man of power can do is to issue a false threat. Yet, I've done it with Aria. More than once.

My goal isn't to punish her though; I only want her to obey.

Just as I begin to unbutton my pants, my phone vibrates in my pocket, the timer going off.

Time is up.

With her eyes closed and an angelic look of content on her face, I question leaving her, but I have to.

"Clean up and make yourself dinner." I stifle a groan as I stand, hating that I won't be able to get lost in her touch for hours.

"I'll be back later." I give her the parting words and start to leave. Each movement makes my hard cock ache even worse, but I'll have her tonight.

"Carter?" Aria's soft voice cuts through the air and stops me just as I've started to leave.

"How long will you be gone?" Traces of fear and loneliness linger on her question. This is the new side of her I'm not used to.

The side I've only seen since last night. Back to being the girl behind the broken wall instead of the woman who's angry at being left alone for so long.

"A few hours, maybe."

Her expression falls as she slowly picks herself back up. She only nods in understanding as she covers herself again.

"Do you want anything while I'm out?" I ask her out of instinct, wanting to see her eyes on me again. Wanting her to show me more of this vulnerability. I can offer her so much more than she ever dreamed.

The very thought spikes awareness through me.

She's the one with control. Topping from the bottom. Sly girl. I need to take it back, for her own good. She needs me to have control, even if she doesn't want to give it to me. Even if she has no idea how much she needs to give it to me.

"No," she answers me with a small shake of the head. "Thank you, though."

"Manners and all," I say to play with her as I leave the room.

Her sweetness numbs the thoughts of demanding more from her, but only so much.

CHAPTER 7

Aria

H OURS HAVE PASSED SINCE CARTER LEFT. THE SMELL OF garlic is still fresh on my fingers as I head into the dimly lit wine cellar. With a flick and a click, the cellar lights up and a beautiful array of wine bottles shines in the light.

An easy breath leaves me at the thought of getting lost at the bottom of a bottle. One glass or two, and I'll still have my wits with me.

But the wits can go fuck themselves tonight. I don't know what to think or feel. I don't know anything anymore. The memories of what once was and what I am today are playing tricks on my sanity.

I'm acutely aware of it but helpless to do anything about it. That's the worst part.

That, and how I feel about Carter.

It's an ever-changing relationship, but I'm fully aware of the cracked wall between us. He's pretending it's not there, and maybe I'm a fool to think something has changed, but I see the pain and sadness behind his eyes. He can't hide it any longer.

He's broken. It takes a broken soul to know one.

Even what I've been through in only the last twenty-four hours, pales in comparison to how broken and shattered Carter's been for years. And I desperately want to heal him. I want to take his pain away more than I've ever wanted to heal myself.

Deep inside, there's the inkling of some other part of him. If only I could show him.

The pain that claws at my heart only grows at the thought, but with a deep breath I let it all go. I don't know what I am to him anymore. But I care for him regardless, especially after last night.

And until I know what haunts him for sure, there's not a damn thing I can do to change anything. And so, wine it is.

I crouch down at the first row, gripping onto the steel bar of the rack and glancing at each of the labels. Pinot noir. Burgundy. Each of them. I love a good glass of red with spaghetti and Bolognese, and right now, I prefer Cabernet. The next row makes my lips curl up, for the first time in God knows how long.

I can pretend that there's nothing wrong. I can pretend for a short moment. I'm good at doing that. At continuing to go through the motions even though deep inside, I know nothing is okay and there's no way to right the wrongs.

The heavy bottle of dark red wine means I can have a moment. A small, seemingly insignificant moment, to simply breathe.

Well, only while I stay in the kitchen. The thought steals the happiness from my lips and as I stand, I feel my muscles tense once again. At least, until Carter comes back.

When Carter leaves, I'm scared to go anywhere other than the four rooms I'm familiar with. The den, his office, the kitchen, or his bedroom. This place is huge and I'm curious to see more of it. But his brothers are here. Somewhere. *And they're the enemy.*

It's easy to forget when I'm with Carter. He has a compelling power over me. Just being in his presence sets my body on fire and I move with him. Every step, every breath.

But the moment he's gone, I'm so very aware of everything.

"I just need to eat, to drink…" I whisper as I flick off the light and head back with the bottle in my hand to retrieve my dinner from the kitchen island, the aroma wafting to greet me as I shut the door.

But the second I hear the door close, my heart drops at the sound of another person in the kitchen.

"Damn, this smells good," Jase says as he walks closer to the large pot sitting next to the stove. I've already mixed the pasta and meat sauce. He towers over it, picking up the serving spoon and smiling down at my dinner.

My grip nearly slips on the bottle; my palms are so sweaty.

"You make enough for all of us?" he asks me with a charismatic smile.

A truly charming expression graces his face. With his stubble growing out longer than I've seen before, he looks different, but the similarities between him and Carter are still striking.

I can feel myself swallow before I attempt to answer him, but just the sight of him reminds me of last night. I can see him sitting in the chair to my left, smiling while my gaze drifts back to Stephan.

My heart pounds in my chest like it did last night in the shower. I can feel the anxiety and adrenaline mix and it takes everything in me to stand up straight.

"Whoa," Jase says as the spoon hits the steel pot and he practically jogs around the island to come closer to me. As soon as I register that's what he's doing, I instinctively take a step back, my shoulder hitting the closed cellar door. Every time I blink, I see Stephan. Sitting at the table, glancing between Carter and me. Waiting for me to kill. Waiting for me to become a murderer.

He knew. They all knew. And they let Romano walk away.

With both hands raised, Jase widens his eyes and slows his steps, even dropping his stance a few inches and crouching down. "You look a little dizzy," he says softly. "You already have a bottle?" he asks me and to my disbelief, a short huff of a genuine laugh leaves me.

Of course, he would think that I'm drunk and that's why seeing him would cause me to react with significant panic.

It's not that I saw him only last night, a few rooms away as I murdered a man who'd haunted me for years and continues to do so. It's not that I'm still forced to stay here even though I so badly wish I could run home and hide in my room from all the terrors that plague me. My body heats with anxiety, but the knowledge that I have a grasp on the present gives me much needed strength.

He takes another step closer and I shake my head, pushing off of the door and going around Jase. One of my hands grips the neck of the bottle, the other runs through my hair. "I'm just having a moment," I finally answer him weakly although my back is to him as I walk back to the counter where my wine glass is.

My heart races again. It won't fucking stop. Off and on all day, it's been like this. *I need Carter.* The bottle hits the counter hard and it's only then that I risk a look over my shoulder at Jase.

Jase's eyes are narrowed and he's still standing where I left him. I can't take my eyes away from his as he pins me in place with his gaze.

Much like Carter does, but Jase is assessing me.

I have to give him something, but all I can think of is to answer his earlier question. Whether or not I made enough food for everyone else.

"I made the entire package, so there's definitely enough." With the answer coming out easily, I turn back to the wine and opener. Easily uncorking it as I talk to him although I can feel my hands start to tremble again, and my heart threatens to trot out of my chest.

"I wasn't sure if anyone would want a plate, but I was going to save it for leftovers if not." I can hear Jase walk back toward the pot slowly, even though he's still assessing me. The second the wine glass is full, I lift it to my lips.

"So, wine is your therapy?" Jase asks as he stalks over to stand only a few feet from me but leans his lower back against the counter.

"We all have our vices," I offer him and lick my lips. The sweet taste offers little aid to the chaos coursing through my blood. But his soft expression does something to me. It loosens something hard and sharp that was lodged deep inside of my chest, suffocating me.

"I get it," he tells me, his forehead smoothing as he turns and reaches for another glass in the cabinet. "Mind if I have one?"

The shake of my head is weak, but not because I don't want to share. I don't mind at all, especially, if it will give me a chance to win over Jase. I remember a thought I had that feels like forever ago, a thought about using Jase to gain my freedom. Or maybe to ask for mercy for my family.

No, the shake of my head is weak because Declan joins us, striding in as if I called a meeting.

Jase stands beside me, glass in hand as Declan takes Jase's former spot, repeating the motion Jase did when he first walked into the kitchen. "Oh, damn," he says over the pot with a reverence in his voice. "You made us dinner?" Declan asks with a boyish grin.

That's not exactly the truth, but I don't deny it. "I wasn't sure if you'd like it, but there's plenty."

Declan grabs the plates, the clinking ceramic filling the room as Jase gives me space, walking to the other side of the U-shaped island and leaning against it, opposite me. The thought of being in the room with Carter's brothers scared me literally only minutes ago. But an ease washes over me as I watch Declan make a plate and then point the spoon to Jase, who answers the unspoken question.

"Yeah, I want one, I haven't eaten yet."

I lean forward a little off the counter, ready to ask him to make me a plate too, but Declan speaks first.

"You didn't poison it, right?" Declan asks with a shit-eating grin. "You know I've got to check," he jokes and then makes Jase's plate.

And there goes the sense of ease and the smile that graced my lips. It washes away like a lone shell on the shore before the tide.

I'm still the enemy. I will always be the enemy. And that's what they'll always be to me.

I offer him a tight smile and force down the well of sadness and pity. "Not yet, you got here too soon." A tight knot forms in my throat, but I drown it with the wine as Declan chuckles, still piling spaghetti onto the plate. Bastard tears prick at my eyes and all I can think is that I wish either Carter were here or that I was back at home, under the comfort of my blanket.

"I don't think she's eaten yet," Jase tells Declan in a tone that has no trace of the humor I forced into my response. He grabs the two plates Declan's made and motions for me to follow him to the small table to eat in the kitchen. Declan looks shocked at Jase's reaction and the seriousness in his tone and objects to him taking both plates, one of which was his. His forehead creases with confusion… until he sees me.

I've always been shit at hiding what I'm feeling. My father used to tell me I'd fare better in this world if I could learn to lie.

My body moves unwillingly to follow Jase, but at least I grabbed the bottle. I can't look at Declan as he watches me. I know he sees through the faint humor I veiled my emotions with in my response.

"Are you okay eating here?" Jase asks. The legs of the chair make a scratching noise on the floor as he pulls it out for me. I stare at the chair for a moment, marveling at the kindness while questioning his intentions.

He feels bad for me. That's all I can think. He's being nice because I'm wounded. That's all this is.

"I'd rather be alone," I finally answer him, finding my voice and feeling the cords in my neck tensing as I look back at him. I have to force my words out of my dry throat and they hurt as I do. "I just need to be alone for a moment." My breath shudders and the back of my eyes prick as I see the visions of last night again. Only three rooms down. The grand dining room is only three doors down from here.

"Please," I say quickly in a whisper and place the wine down on the table with as much grace as I can.

With both hands on the table, he looks over his shoulder and says something to Declan, but I don't hear what.

"You going to be okay?" he asks me as I hear Declan's footsteps leaving the kitchen.

"How long does it take to be okay after murdering someone? Even if you feel it was justified in every way?" I ask Jase and he merely looks past me at Declan's exit before bringing his eyes to mine.

Jase doesn't answer me; he simply looks back at me as if I hadn't spoken at all.

I start to think he'll leave me like that, taking his plate with him, but instead, he asks me his own question, "You want me to grab another bottle?" to which I can only nod in response.

He's kind enough to grant me both the loneliness and the second bottle I desire.

CHAPTER 8

Carter

YOU WERE SUPPOSED TO BE GENTLE WITH HER.

Agitation leaves me in a singular deep groan. I don't respond to Jase's text and I don't intend to. He doesn't recognize the severity of the situation. He doesn't know shit about her.

He doesn't know what she needs.

The bitter thought stays with me as I shut down my phone and quietly enter the kitchen. I know she's still sitting where she was an hour ago and just as I expect, she doesn't see me come in.

She never does. She always gives me the opportunity to watch her, to see what she's like when she doesn't know I'm looking.

I'm hardly ever disappointed, but watching as she fills her glass again, the pleasure of being in her presence again is dulled.

It's becoming a crutch. If she knows I'll be gone, she drinks. It's only happened twice, but still, I notice. Part of me recognizes her condition. Her situation. I realize it may be easy for her to give in to a vice and let herself slip somewhere where the pain is absent, and the choices are meaningless. But I don't want it to become a habit.

With a twist of her finger, she pulls my necklace she wears up closer to her lips, letting the diamonds and pearls play there in between sips of wine and absentminded hums.

Her lips part slightly as she sways in her seat and stares at a black and white photograph that's in the hall. She hums against the gemstones and I wish I knew what she was thinking. The sadness and tortured stare tell me she's still there, my little songbird with clipped wings.

I don't recognize the song that she hums. I never do. Sometimes it sounds more like a conversation than a song.

I follow her gaze as I walk closer to her; the black and white photograph is a picture of the side of our old house. The one that burned down. The one that *her father* had burned down, expecting the four of us to be inside and sleeping.

I feel a sudden pinch along the edge of my heart, reminding me the damn thing is there.

"What are you thinking?" I ask Aria, ignoring the pain in my chest and causing her to jump from the tone of my deep voice.

Her expression is soft, as are her eyes when she turns in her seat. There's even the hint of happiness on her lips.

"You're back," she says and there's a lightness in her statement. She can't hide the relief that slurs with her words. And that bit of disappointment I have at her drunkenness returns.

"I said I'd be back tonight." It's all I offer her as I pull out the chair next to her, letting the feet drag across the floor noisily.

"What were you doing?" she asks me with a pleasantness that seems genuine.

She's naïve to think I do anything pleasant this late at night.

I was ending the life of a thief. A drug addict who bought more and more of SL and wouldn't answer a simple question.

What was he doing with it?

It's a rare day that Jase can't get a response from someone. He's good at what he does. He left the junkie to bleed out and waited for me to come. It's my name they fear the most.

If pain and the threat of death can't get an answer, true fear is quick to provide one.

And it did. The only word the prick spoke before life slipped from him was a name. *Marcus.* All I got was a name. But it was all I needed.

It's a name I'm growing to despise more and more as the days go by. Daniel used to have a good reputation with Marcus, a man who lives in the shadows and never shows himself. But that was before he found Addison again. Since then Marcus has yet to be found, but apparently, he's been busy.

"Work," I answer, and my short response tugs her smile down.

"There are leftovers," she offers me even though the smile's vanished. I can feel how the sweetness inside of her has hollowed out.

As she reaches across the table to play with the stem of her glass I ask her, "You made me dinner?"

"If you didn't all look so alike, I'd know you are brothers by the way you react to a damn meal," she offers with a somewhat playful nature.

I can't pin down what she's thinking. Or what she thinks of me as I stare at her.

"It's been a long time."

"Since you've had Bolognese?" she asks as if my words are nonsense.

"Since someone's made us dinner," I tell her and think of my mother. Once again, Aria looks at me as if she's read my mind. The pretending to be happy and acting like things are normal slips away.

"I'm sorry," she whispers, and I choose not to respond. Sorry doesn't take anything back.

"I like to cook," she offers after a moment, breaking up the silence and tension. "If you'd like... I don't mind cooking more?"

I used to avoid the kitchen and dining room when my mother got sick. It's where she died. None of us liked to go to the kitchen. It was better to be in and out of that room as fast as we could. In a way, I should be thankful Talvery burned that house down. It was nothing but a dark memory.

Her slender fingers move up and down the glass and I expect her to drink it, but instead, she pushes it toward me. "Would you like some?"

I shake my head without speaking, wondering if she knows what I think about her habit.

"I don't like it when you're gone," she says before pulling the glass toward her again.

"Why's that?" I ask her, grateful to talk about anything other than the shit going on outside of this house. Enemies are growing in number each day.

"I start thinking things," she says quietly, her gaze flickering between the pool of dark liquid in the glass and my own gaze.

"Is that right?" I ask her, pushing for more.

"It's better when I don't have a choice," she admits solemnly. "At least, for the way I feel about myself."

"What's better?" The question slips from me as a crease deepens in my forehead.

"My thoughts are better," she states but doesn't elaborate.

"How's that?"

"If I'm with you, I don't worry about my family, the fighting..." her voice cracks and her face scrunches. "That's awful, isn't it?" She shakes her head, her flushed skin turning brighter. "It's horrible. I'm horrible." And with her last word she picks up the glass, but I press my hand to her forearm, forcing the glass back down to the table.

"You're many things," I tell her evenly as I scoot the seat closer to her, "but horrible isn't one of them."

"Weak. I'm weak," she answers with disgust on her tongue. Her gaze leaves mine, although I will her not to break it. Instead, she stares at the stem of the wine glass. There's still a good bit in her glass, but from what I can tell, this is her second bottle. "I'm so weak that I want to have no choice," she says disbelievingly. "How fucked up is that?"

"You're in a difficult position, with few options and severe consequences." I've never been good with comfort, but I can offer reason. "And deep down inside, you know whatever you do, it won't change anything." The truth that flows easily from me is brutal and it causes Aria to visibly cower from me.

"Thank you oh so much," she says with a deadpan voice as she lifts the glass and then downs all the remaining alcohol. "I was beginning to feel pathetic and like my life had no meaning whatsoever." She raises her hand in the air and then slaps her palm down firmly on the table. There's a bite of anger to her words that pisses me off. The glass hits the table before she looks me in the eye and tells me with an expression devoid of any emotion but hate, "Thank you so much for clearing that up for me."

"I do enjoy your fight, Aria. But you'd be wise not to speak to me like that." My own voice is hard and deadly, but it does nothing to Aria.

"Would I now?" A simper graces her wine-stained lips. "I'm not sure there's a single wise thing I could do, is there, Mr. Cross? Other than obey your *every* command."

Her defiance is fucking beautiful and only makes me hard for her. My cock stiffens and strains against my zipper as I lean back to take her in. It feels as if we're picking right back up where we left off and I couldn't be more agreeable with that situation.

My breathing quickens as she stares at me, daring me to disagree with her.

"You love being angry, don't you?" I ask her, although it's not a question. "There's so much more power in anger than there is in sadness." The statement makes her lips purse.

"You have no idea what you're capable of," I tell her a truth that could destroy me. "Women like you were made to ruin men like me."

"Oh?" she asks. "Us women who aren't capable of changing anything?" She seems to remember her fight as she adds, "You'll have to clear that up for me. I'm either too drunk or stupid to understand."

"Or too blinded by your past?" I offer her. "So consumed with changing something that's meant to happen. That *will* happen, so much so that you can't see what lies ahead."

"What's meant to happen? As in?" she questions as she noticeably swallows. Her hands grip the edge of the table as if she needs to hold it in order to sit upright.

"You know exactly what I mean, Aria."

"If it happens, if what I think you're referring to right now happens, there will be no future for me. The willing whore of the enemy who could do nothing to save the people she loves. What kind of life is that to lead?"

My blood runs cold at her words. Numbly I watch her reach for the remains of the bottle closest to her, only to find it empty.

Would she kill herself? Is that what she's saying? My blood pounds in my veins at the thought of her leaving me, let alone leaving me in such a manner. I can barely look at her as she sags back into her seat and turns to give me her attention again. "If you were me, what would you do?" she asks with genuine curiosity.

I'm still reeling from her earlier confession to answer quickly, but I finally find words that have a ring of truth to them. "I'd take care of myself and my own survival."

"My own survival?" she asks with a sarcastic huff of disbelief. "If they're dead, then who am I?"

My breathing becomes ragged, tense, and deep at her question. "You are mine." My answer is immediate, stern, and undeniable. Each word is given with conviction.

But all they do is turn her eyes glossy. "And that's all I'll ever be. A possession."

The sadness is what destroys my composure. She unravels me like no one else ever has. She'll devastate everything I worked for, everything I am, but so long as I have her, it will all be worth it.

"I was meant to have you. I only fucking lived to have you." I've never spoken truer words.

Her breathing is shallow as her chest rises and falls. "Carter?" She says my name as if I'll save her from what she's feeling, from the truth breaking down every bit of her own beliefs.

"You were made for me to have. To fight. To fuck. To care for," I say as I lean closer to her, my grip tightening on the back of her chair as I lower my lips until they're just an inch from hers. My eyes pierce into hers as she stares back at me with a wildness I crave to tame. "Do you understand that, Aria?"

"You're a very intense man, Carter Cross." She speaks her words softly with tears in her eyes that I don't understand.

All I can do at this moment is crash my lips to hers, to silence the pain, the agony, all of the questions she has. The kiss isn't gentle; it isn't soft and sweet. It's a brutal taking of what's mine. What's been owed to me for years.

The instant I capture her lips, she gasps, and I shove my tongue inside of her mouth, pushing myself out of the chair and hearing it bang on the floor as I take her face with both of my hands. My tongue strokes hers swiftly and she meets my intensity with her own. Her fingers spear through my hair and her nails scratch at my scalp, pulling me to get impossibly closer.

She moans in my mouth as I pull away, desperate to breathe. In one movement, I pull her down to the floor while shoving her skirt up her thighs, maneuvering her beneath me. Her belly presses to the floor and my erection digs into her exposed ass.

"You're such a dirty girl, not bothering to cover this." I cup her already wet pussy as I ask her, "Aren't you?"

My other hand grips the hair at the base of her skull and pulls back hard enough to make her back bow. Her lips part with a sweet gasp of both pleasure and pain as I ruthlessly rub her clit.

"You're mine, and nothing else. You'll let go of everything but what I command you to do and be." My words are whispered against the shell of her ear. They mingle with her moans as I stare at those gorgeous lips. Desperate to take them again, I give in to what I want. Removing my hand from her cunt, I grab her throat from behind and crash my lips against hers.

"Carter," she heaves my name the moment I break the kiss and without thinking twice, I release my cock and slam inside of her.

Feeling her hot, wet walls spasm the moment I enter her drives me insane. She's so fucking tight, but she takes all of me to the hilt with a strangled cry.

My hips piston with a relentless pace to claim her and everything she is. Everything she'll ever be.

"Mine," I grunt out and release her throat and hair to grip her hips with a bruising force.

Her arms barely bracing her as she cries out her pleasure.

Over and over I fuck her as hard as I can. And each one of her strangled moans, combined with her hopeless scratching at the floor beneath her, only fuels me to fuck her harder.

"Mine." I push the word through my teeth as she cums violently beneath me. My own release follows, my balls drawing up and my toes curling as thick streams of cum fill her pussy.

She lies there panting, her small body sagging as she desperately tries to support herself and breathe at the same time. Both efforts seemingly in vain.

My cum leaks out of her as she whispers my name again and again. Bracing one forearm on each side of her, I rake my teeth up her neck and nip her chin before kissing her again.

And she kisses me back, reverently and sweetly. Her hands find my chin and her fingers brush along my scruff to keep my lips pinned to her own.

My chest heaves in air as I fall to the floor next to her.

The cool air relieving my heated skin.

The only effort Aria makes is to inch closer to me, to have both her bare and clothed skin touching mine.

"I've been waiting for that," she says softly as she nuzzles next to me, content with being held.

"For what?" I ask her, still catching my breath.

"For you to kiss me like that."

To kiss her. The memory of her lips hot on mine begs me to kiss her again, but her words stop me.

"It was worth the wait." The words fall easily from her lips, the same lips that look swollen and reddened from our kiss.

The reality comes back to me in this moment.

This isn't what this was supposed to become.

I don't know what the fuck she's doing to me, but it can't continue like this.

I'm ruining everything.

CHAPTER 9

Aria

I'M SURPRISED I SLEPT AS WELL AS I DID.

No terrors, just a much-needed deep sleep. From whenever Carter brought me to bed, until nearly 2 p.m. this afternoon.

There isn't enough sleep to mend the exhaustion I feel, but I'm grateful I've gotten through one night undisturbed.

As I shift on the wooden floor in Carter's office, the ache in my muscles intensifies and I wince. I'm so fucking sore from last night. From this whole past week, maybe. I don't know if this is normal or not, but I hurt. Every moment of the day, I feel him inside of me still and it takes me to the edge of both pleasure and pain.

Both physically and emotionally.

There's no denying Carter is a broken and lost soul. And there's no denying that I want to make all the wrongs in his past right.

My mind is a whirlwind of what I wish could be undone, but there are no answers that take pity on me and provide me with clarity. All I can think to do is offer him kindness. To obey, to be good for him. And maybe he'll feel something other than the anger and hate that cloud his judgment.

I can only imagine the world he grew up in. The small pieces I've been given are jagged and harsh.

I shouldn't pity the monster he became.

I shouldn't love what he does to me.

But I do.

The short piece of chalk rolls back and forth between my fingers as I study the paper lying on the floor. I can't remember what I drew at the park. The questions I had in my dream from not last night but the night before, are still alive and vibrant in my mind.

I can't help but to think there are answers in my subconscious. Answers in my dreams.

But I can't remember what I drew that day.

Instead, I keep drawing the same thing, the house from the photograph in the hall. It's quaint and small, with rustic features. It's definitely a backroad setting but there are other houses beside it. Close to each other.

The brick was old, and the mortar seemed even older. The weeds that grew up the side of it felt as if they belonged there like nature was intent on reclaiming the structure.

Whoever took the photograph captured the beauty of the home perfectly, but why does it call to me? Why do I keep drawing it and only changing the flowers that grow around it?

"There are four steps." Carter's voice breaks into my thoughts and I glance up at him, not registering his words. He takes his time rolling up the crisp, white sleeves of his dress shirt. I can't help but admire the corded muscles under his tanned skin and remember how his hands gripped me last night, leaving bruises on my hips that still ache to the touch.

He gestures to the drawing. "The front porch had four steps."

It takes me a moment to comprehend and I offer him a small smile before asking him, "This was your house, wasn't it?"

He nods and adds, "You make it seem more alluring than it was."

My heart tugs and a small knot forms in my throat as he returns to his laptop. Maybe if he grows to care for me, everything can be okay. It can be made right.

What a naïve thought.

"What are you thinking?" Carter's question brings me back to the present again.

"I keep drifting into thoughts I shouldn't," I answer him without much conscious consent. Maybe I've rested so much that the sleep refuses to leave me, making me drowsy and my thoughts hazy.

"Like?" he prompts.

"Like, wondering why I love this house so much," I answer him cautiously although my gaze stays on the paper.

"I hate that house," Carter says after a moment and I move my eyes to his. The coldness in his eyes is ever present and it sends a chill down my spine.

"You hate everything," I tell him absently.

"I don't hate you," he says pointedly, and his rebuttal sends a warmth flowing through me.

"How do you feel about me then?" I ask him and busy my fingers with the piece of chalk.

His words are softly spoken and it's the first admission from him of any kind. "The very idea that you're mine makes me feel as if there isn't a thing I can't conquer. But actually having you is… everything."

I don't know if he realizes how powerful his words are. How intense he is. Just being around him is suffocating. Nothing else can exist when he's with me.

"What do you remember about last night?" he asks me, and I blink away the trance he held over me.

"Everything," I answer him as if it's obvious. "You came home. We had a conversation and then more on the kitchen floor…" I trail off and my teeth sink into my bottom lip at the memory. "And then you took me to bed."

Carter nods slowly as if gauging my response. "You don't remember what you told me when we got to bed? Do you?" My heart flickers once, then twice as I try to remember.

But I don't.

"I fell asleep," I tell him as if it's an excuse.

It's quiet for a long moment and an uneasiness washes through me. Like I've said something that I should regret but I don't know what it was. Swallowing thickly, I steel myself to ask, "What did I say?"

But he doesn't answer me, he only tsks in response.

A pounding in my chest and blood makes me feel on edge until Carter rises and stalks toward me. He looms over me, owning me with his presence as he likes to do. My eyes close as he lowers his hand to the crown of my head gently and then twirls a lock of hair between his fingers.

My heart races with his touch and I don't know if it's from fear or lust.

"All I want to do is fuck you until there's no question in your mind who you belong to." His admission forces my thighs to clench and that tender ache returns.

The tension and fear dissipate with each small touch he gives me.

"If you gave yourself to me, everything else would fall into place."

His fingers trail lightly along my collarbone and up my chin then move to my lips, tracing them with a tender touch that I would have once found difficult to believe belongs to Carter.

"Is that all? Just give myself entirely to you to use as a fucktoy? That would solve everything?" My comeback is weakened by the gentle way the words flow, the flirtation that I can't deny in their cadence.

His cock is right in front of my face, obviously hard and pressing against his pants. My mouth parts and my fingers itch to reach out and take him.

The throbbing between my thighs intensifies and I struggle to remind myself that I'm his captive, his fucktoy, his whore, and nothing more. All I can think is how much I want to pleasure him like he did me last night.

I want to bring him to his knees and make him weak for my touch like I am his.

"I want to…" I have to stop myself and swallow my words, feeling dirty.

He crouches in front of me, his gaze penetrating mine with an intensity that begs me to lean away from him, to run from the beast of a man who isn't hiding anything from me.

His darkly said words are whispered from his lips. "Tell me what you want, Aria."

"I—I—" I stutter. Like an insignificant unequal.

It takes every ounce of courage in me to raise my gaze to his, to inhale a breath, and on the exhale confess, "I want to suck you."

"You want to wrap these pretty little lips around my cock until I cum in the back of your throat?" he asks easily with a huskiness that comes from deep in his chest, moving his pointer to my lips and tracing them once again.

I nod, forcing his finger to alter its path and graze against my cheek instead. I'm breathless, full of desire and want, numb to everything but him.

What has he done to me?

The thought hits me as he leaves me panting on the floor to grab one of the chairs in front of his desk and move it directly in front of me. He wastes no time, performing the task quickly.

He doesn't speak as he sits down, both of his hands resting easily on his thighs.

My hand is shaky as I lift it to his zipper, but he catches me before I touch him. His grip is hot and demanding and steals my attention and breath just the same.

I'm pinned by the lust in his eyes as he asks me, "Have you done this before?" He tilts his head to ask, "Have you done anything before me?"

"Yes," I answer him although it feels like a half-truth and just thinking that I'm partially lying to him makes my pulse quicken and body heat. It's not the same. What I did with Nikolai wasn't anywhere close to this. We were young, and I needed someone to offer me comfort. Nikolai was the only one there for me. I kissed him first, and I begged him to touch me.

I loved him, and I knew he loved me. Even if he would only ever be a friend.

But my father could never know about us and when Nik moved up in the ranks and I grew bolder, my father grew suspicious. I don't think Nikolai ever wanted to risk his position for me.

And I didn't want to risk our friendship.

What I had with him was nothing like this.

"Who was it?" Carter asks me. "More than one?" His head tilts as he releases my hand and my heart beats like a war drum.

"None of your business," I tell him playfully and grab both of his wrists to move his hands to the armrests of the chair. "Let me play," I tell him as if it's a command, but the words come out as if I'm begging.

He doesn't answer me, but his fingers wrap around the armrests and he doesn't say anything to stop me.

I fumble with the button, my nerves getting the better of me as I move to my knees in between his legs. The sound of his pants rustling and the deep hum of desire from Carter's chest fuel me to ignore my nerves.

He lifts his hips to help me after I unzip his pants and his cock juts out in front of my face. Shock catches me off guard. It's larger than I thought. Veiny and thick. Instantly, I wonder how he fit inside of me. Squirming in front of him, I know he knows what I'm thinking. The rough and masculine chuckle gives it away.

I glance up at him as I wrap his dick with both my hands. I can't possibly close my fingers around him, but the part that worries me is how I'll fit him in my mouth.

I imagined taking all of him and pleasuring him to the point where he couldn't control himself, but now I question if I can take a fraction of him without gagging.

Slowly, Carter lifts his hand as if asking for permission and moves it to the back of my head. "You can lick it first," he offers low and deep, not hiding how his breathing has hitched.

The bead of precum at his slit entices me to lick it, and so I do. A blush and pride rise to heat my cheeks as the man seated in front of me shudders at my touch.

His large hand splays and brings me closer to him, urging me on for more. But I tsk him, grabbing his hand and placing it back where it belongs on the armrest.

He readjusts in his seat, but his eyes never leave mine. They're darker than before, which only makes the silver specks stand out even more. The heat there leaves me wanting and I lean forward, finding my pleasure by covering the head of his cock with my lips.

The salty taste of precum and the feel of Carter's thighs tightening under my forearms as I brace myself, make me moan with my mouth full of him.

"Fuck," he groans, and his hips buck slightly, pushing him further into my mouth, moving against the roof and down my throat. And I take him easily, although my teeth scrape along his dick.

Using my lips to shield my teeth, I put pressure on his cock, taking every inch of him that I can.

My eyes burn as I lower myself more and more, and each time I get hotter and hotter for him. The thought of getting on top of him and taking my pleasure from him crosses my mind, but I resist. I want to show him I can give him pleasure like he gives me.

My nails dig into my thighs as I feel the head of his dick hit the back of my throat. It takes everything I have not to react. To not pull away and gasp for air as he suffocates me when his hips tip up and he shoves himself just a bit past my breaking point.

I sputter slightly, forcing him out of my mouth so I can breathe. I lean back but I don't stop. Even knowing there's saliva around my mouth, I keep working his cock with my hand and quickly take him back in and try to deep throat him again. The deep, gruff groan that Carter unleashes as I hollow my cheeks makes me feel like a queen. Like a powerful queen able to bring this man to his knees.

Through my lashes, I peek at him. At his stiff position and his blunt nails digging into the leather of his chair as he holds onto it instead of reaching out for me. My eyes drift upward as I take him deeper, trying to swallow. And at that moment Carter breaks.

"Enough," he bites out and stands up, pulling his cock from my mouth and leaving me on my ass in front of him. My palms hit the floor hard, but I don't care. The only feeling in my body I care about is the throbbing pulse between my thighs.

I can barely control my breathing as I look up at him. Carter Cross. Unhinged and unable to give up control. "I want you," I plead with him from beneath him.

It's true. I want him, and I'm unwilling to hide that fact any longer.

He turns his back to me, his pants sagging around his waist until he shoves them down, showing me his tight ass and muscular thighs.

His forearm braces against his desk and in one swift motion he clears it all to the floor. The phone, pens, his laptop, the papers. They flutter and crash to the ground all at once, but none of those things matter. The only thing I can do is stay victim to the intensity of Carter's needs.

"I want you to ride my face. I need to feel you cum on my tongue." His words make the ache between my thighs even greater. My need to feel him come undone even stronger.

My legs feel weak and ready to buckle as I stand, but it doesn't matter. Carter grips my hips and forces a yelp from me as he lies across his desk, his still-hard cock jutting out as he lets me sit on his chest.

Before a single word is spoken in between my gasps for breath, Carter shoves my skirt up and shreds my panties.

As I watch the tattered lingerie fall to the floor, Carter reaches for my blouse, ripping it from the top and exposing my breasts. He tears at my clothes like they're nothing. And they may as well be, judging by how quickly and easily they fall to his whim.

He said he wanted me to ride him. But Carter's a fucking liar. His fingers grip the flesh of my hips and ass and he keeps me right where he wants me. He drags his tongue from my opening up to my clit, where he sucks to the point of me falling forward with a blinding pleasure that lights every nerve ending on fire.

My breasts hit the desk above his head and as I scream out, the door to the office opens.

I cover myself and try to hide, but Carter's still ravaging my pussy when I catch Daniel's shocked expression.

"Fuck," is all he says, and he turns as quickly as he can to leave, reaching behind him for the doorknob but failing to grab it. I'd laugh if I wasn't petrified, knowing I'm about to cum. The pleasure swirls into a storm in my belly and threatens to ride through every limb, moving to the tips of my fingers in waves.

"I'm going to cum," I cry out to the ceiling as Carter lifts me off him, shoving me down against his hard cock where it brushes against my ass, so he can see who the hell opened the door.

The door slams shut finally, and Carter sits up, making me fall back against the desk while his thick cock runs along the length of my pussy and I cum. The feel of his cock just barely brushing up against my entrance is what does it.

I cum violently, with my face and every inch of my body heated. I can hear Carter grabbing his pants and pulling them up his legs even as the pleasure rolls through me, paralyzing me and heating my body all at once.

Daniel Cross, brother to the most powerful man I've ever met, just witnessed me riding Carter's face and taking my pleasure from him.

I shudder as my hand reaches up to cover my breasts. I can barely breathe as I hear Carter pull up his zipper.

I should feel shame of some sort. But I can't bring myself to do it. I feel nothing but sated, breathless and fulfilled.

"I have to see what Daniel needs. Leave one heel on each side of the desk," Carter commands me while grabbing each of my ankles and spreading my legs apart on his desk. "Wait for me."

He grips my hips, pulling me closer to the edge of the desk as I nod. My skirt is rumpled around me and my hands instantly move to my pussy.

"If you want to touch yourself, do it." His command comes in between his ragged breaths. "Cum as much as you want while I'm gone."

I lie there, my back on his desk, my ass directed to the seat he rules in and my chest heaving as he leaves me.

I'm still catching my breath when I hear the door close.

Touch yourself, I hear his words again and moan just from the command. From the deep voice and cadence that can only come from a man's voice filled with desire.

My fingers trail over my clit, but I can't do it.

I'm so sensitive to even the slightest touch that I have to stop my movements before pushing myself over. I can't do it. It's so intense, I simply can't bring myself to the edge.

I clench around nothing, I picture Carter between my legs, on top of me, smothering me with his weight as he pounds into me and I have to scissor my legs. My hands fly to my hair, pushing it from my face and trying to get a grip.

When I open my eyes, I stare at the blank ceiling, accompanied only by my heavy breathing and the ticking of the clock.

It doesn't stop ticking, but with each stroke, my needs diminish, and my sanity comes back to me.

I lie there for what feels like hours, and when I check the clock, it's accurate. Over an hour has passed, my back is stiff and the desire I had is all but gone, subdued by concern, replaced with a feeling of rejection. As I sit up, everything hurts. My back, especially. I stare at the door, willing Carter to come to get me. But he doesn't come back.

Not this hour and not the next.

Any bit of power I felt, fades to nothing, which is exactly what I feel like when I slink out of the room, covering myself with the torn shirt.

I haven't stopped staring at the clock in the bedroom and wondering if I should go back to the office. I can't possibly lie there waiting for him for hours. I'm almost certain he didn't expect that when he left me.

But every minute that passes warns me to go back. To stop defying Carter and show him that I can be what he wants, and maybe that would convince him to do what I want. To spare my family.

The pride and thrill are long gone and in their place only uncertainty.

All I'm doing is worrying as I restlessly wait in Carter's bed.

The moment I hear the click of the door opening, I sit up straight in bed, getting on my knees, clutching the sheets to my chest.

Carter walks in slowly, his gaze on the floor. He looks exhausted and beat down like I've never seen him. I can't get a word out, shocked by the sight of him in this state, but the excuses I've drummed up and rehearsed in the last few hours don't matter anyway.

He apologizes. Carter apologizes to me for the second time in only a matter of two days.

"I'm sorry I kept you waiting this long. I didn't realize..." his voice trails off as he heads to the dresser, carelessly dropping his Rolex into a drawer and then taking his time to strip down.

The muscles in his shoulders ripple as he undresses with his back to me.

"Is everything okay?" I ask him, daring to pry.

His five o'clock shadow is thick, and his eyes look heavy. It's only then that I wonder if he slept at all last night.

I barely sleep as it is, and Carter's always awake when I drift off and always out of bed when I wake up.

"Daniel isn't in a good place at the moment," he tells me in a single drawn-out breath before climbing into bed.

"Problems with Addison?" I can only guess.

Carter's gaze turns curious, but also guarded as he watches me scoot closer to him. I wonder how much of this is an act, and how much of this is really my desire to get closer to Carter as I let my hand fall to his chest. It's awkward at first for me to lay my cheek on his bare chest while my fingers play with the smattering of chest hair that leads lower and lower. But the more he allows it, the more he wraps his arm around me like I belong there, the more comfortable I feel taking what I want from him.

"What do you know about her?" he asks me, and I feel the words rumble from his chest.

"Just that she's with Daniel," I tell him and then remember the first time I saw her. How upset both of them were over something I wasn't privy to. I add quietly, "I think they love each other."

I don't have to look up to know that Carter's smiling, but I do. But the small smile is weak; the bleakness can't be hidden even by Carter's handsome lips.

"She's not handling lockdown well," he confides in me. Lockdown. I've heard the term more than once. I know what it means, and it reminds me of the reality. My father would often leave me in the safe house for days at a time if he had to leave during lockdown. It was better when he would only be gone for hours and I could hide in my room, which I did regardless of whether we were on lockdown or not.

The words are barely spoken as my chest tightens. "I can imagine."

"You stayed in your cell for longer than I thought you would without submitting to me. You have a mental strength that most don't." I don't know how to take Carter's statement. It's not a compliment, although it feels like it.

"Still, I can see her wanting to leave. To not be..." I try to think of the right word, a word that won't upset Carter and ruin the conversation. My fingers weave around the thin chain ever present around my neck. The expensive necklace that's truly a collar.

"Tethered?" Carter questions and I can only nod, my cheek brushing against his chest as I stare straight ahead.

The silence lasts longer than I'd like it to, but all I can do is listen to the steady rhythm of Carter's heart until he speaks.

"She's safe here. She's cared for." The way he says his words is careful, yet tense. That, combined with the way his heart picks up its pace, makes me think we're not talking about Addison anymore.

"What would you tell her then?" I ask him, wanting an insight into Carter's thoughts. "The moment she's alone and the thoughts of leaving race back to her?" I have to know what he would say. "What would you tell her?"

Carter moves for the first time since I've settled next to him. He lifts the arm wrapped around me and lets his fingers slowly trail along my skin as if he's carefully considering his answer. He kisses my hair once, then twice before using his other hand to lift up my chin and force me to look at him. His touch is gentle. So gentle it could break me.

"I'd tell her she has someone here who loved her before she even knew the darkest levels to where love can take you. And that there's no better protection from the shit life we lead than that."

My heart stops. I feel it cease to beat as he continues to stare at me, and I can't will it to move again. There's nothing but sincerity in his gaze and the last bit of guard I have crumbles.

Love. The word love breaks something deep inside of me.

"I need this one for me," Carter says before I can respond. He rolls over, pinning me beneath him and fucks me roughly, kisses me ravenously and then holds me to him, my back to his chest. All the while I break more and more. So much so, that I know I'll never be the same again.

CHAPTER 10

Carter

"**W**HAT'S THE UPDATE?" I ASK JASE, LEANING AGAINST the wall in the hall. My eyes stay pinned on the carved glass doorknob with my thoughts on what's behind it.

"Same as before." Jase's answer comes out low as we both see Aria and Daniel making their way toward us. They're far enough away that she won't be able to hear. Her fingers twist around one another as she walks quickly to keep up with Daniel's pace.

I don't know what Daniel tells her with a wide grin, but it cracks the solemn look on her face and she smiles back at him.

"Romano's ready to strike when we are. As far as everyone knows, it's the two of us taking out Talvery."

"And the drug? What about the buyers hoarding it?"

"They're all saying Marcus. But it's only a name." I know what he's getting at. When a man is close to death, he'll tell you anything you want to know, either to make his ending quick or to try to save himself. Four men now, each hoarding the drug we know to be lethal and each only giving up a single name in their last breath. Those are the only four buying in bulk, except for the girl I saw a week ago. I'd rather not seek her out, but our options are dwindling.

"Why not give more information?"

Jase's palm presses against the wall and I can feel his gaze on me as he leans closer. "What does he have on them that they keep his secrets even as they die?"

"Maybe they don't know anything else," I offer, but Jase shakes his head. I only glance up at him because of Aria. She sees his expression and the bit of happiness Daniel provided her instantly vanishes.

Jase looks worried, angry even with a scowl plastered across his face.

"We'll talk about it later," I tell him lowly, but he doesn't stop.

"They didn't give me anything. Not a drop-off point, not a procedure or any details at all." He leans in closer to me to emphasize, "Only a name."

Our gazes are locked for a moment longer than they should be.

Daniel clears his throat at the same time that I hear his and Aria's footsteps come to a stop behind me.

"Then we have a name," I tell Jase and a small twitch gathers on the corner of his lips.

"Later," I remind him. "We'll talk later." He nods, pushing off the wall and finally nodding a hello to Aria.

"I hope you like it," Jase tells her, and she glances between the two of us, not knowing what the hell he's talking about.

As Daniel and Jase walk away, heading back the way Daniel and Aria came, she tells him, *thank you*, to which she's given a smile from both of my brothers.

Her nervousness is still visible as she barely glances toward me and continues to run her fingers along the seam of her blouse. Anything out of the normal routine causes this reaction in her.

I wonder how long that will last.

The drunken comment she made the other night hasn't left me. That night, as soon as she was asleep, I made arrangements.

She said she's going to leave me one day. That she's going to run away and hide in her room until the war is done with. She was drunk, but she said it as if it was a fact.

She doesn't remember saying it, but that doesn't change anything.

I won't let her leave me. She's never allowed to leave me.

I asked her why she'd leave me, and she said so simply, that sometimes she just wants to breathe but can't even do that without overthinking everything.

I won't give her a bedroom, but she can have a room to run to.

I can hide what's going on from her until her questions fade and all she has left is me.

"What is this?" Aria asks as the door opens.

"It was a storage room," I answer her with one hand splayed on her lower back and one hand on the door to push it open as far as it'll go.

"And now?" she asks aimlessly as she takes a step into the brightly lit room. Her face is filled with awe as she steps further into the lushly decorated room.

Other than a gray paisley wallpapered wall to the left, where one would presume a bed to sit, the remainder of the walls are a soft blush, nearly white.

The chair at the vanity is lined with a matching gray striped fabric and beyond it are glass vases and a matching glass standing light.

Gray and blush are the only two colors. The decorator referred to the color scheme as mineral tones, but it looks feminine as fuck to me. I wanted Aria to know this room was designed for her, so every piece of furniture and item contained in this room was meant to ensure she knew it belonged to her.

Everything else, from the plush white rug in the center of the room to the sheer curtains, is white. A glass table and mirrored nightstands allow the light to shine through with no obstructions.

It didn't take long for the company to put it together. Her room is at the other end of my wing, farthest away from my bedroom. It was Jase's suggestion and the only reason I agreed was due to my impatience. I needed it done quickly considering we're only days away from all-out war.

"What do you want in return?" Aria asks me hesitantly.

My expression turns hard for a moment while I consider her. "This isn't a negotiation or a game, Aria. It's a gift." Her beautiful hazel eyes widen slightly and her lips part to apologize, but I interrupt her to ask, "Do you like it?"

"It's beautiful," she says reverently as she admires the details of each of the pieces, only taking small glances at me to keep track of how I'm assessing her as she reacts to the room.

"There's no bed?" she asks quietly with a touch of confusion as she stares toward the wall where one should obviously sit.

"You can sleep in my room…" I almost add, "or the cell," but I choose not to. She seems to hear the words regardless, her eyes drifting to the floor as she swallows thickly.

"This isn't a room I'd like you to consider your bedroom." My words bring her gaze back to me. Choosing my words carefully, I tell her, "You belong with me, but this is a place for you to go if you need... space."

She only nods, and I think that's all the reaction I'll get until she peeks up at me, her fingers trailing along the patterned wallpaper, and says softly, "Thank you." The gratitude melts the tension between us, and it soothes a deep need inside of me for her to want what I can give her.

I watch Aria walk hesitantly to the vanity, intricately carved and an antique, but stunning. She barely touches the cut glass knobs before pulling out the drawers and finding her things there.

Not the ones she had at her home, but new ones to replace each item she had.

Her hand hovers above them for a moment, almost as if she's afraid she'll be bitten by something inside if she moves too quickly.

Her pace is quicker as she moves to the closet, filled with all kinds of clothing. From expensive dresses and lingerie to nightshirts I was told she prefers.

"I enjoy picking out what you wear," I tell her and catch her attention as she turns to look at me, although her hand is still caressing the silk of a deep red blouse.

"And you choose red," she says beneath her breath before turning back to the closet. "There's certainly a theme."

"Red complements you well," I answer her although she doesn't respond. I take a single step toward her, but she continues to examine the room, taking in each bit with care.

"If you'd like something changed," I tell her as she opens a night-stand drawer, "it can be arranged."

She stares at me as she shuts the drawer. There's an edge to her movements.

"How did you know?" she asks, and her question is laced with tension.

"Know what, exactly?" I ask her, my muscles coiling from the tone of her voice.

Her gaze shifts to the open door before her eyes land on me. Her fingers play with the edge of her blouse in a nervous fidget.

"You have a lot of things here." She licks her lip and debates on continuing, but she doesn't need to.

"I asked for a list," I answer her before she can ask how I knew what she'd want.

"There's a rat," she whispers, and her posture turns stiff.

"How did you think Romano knew when and where to acquire you?"

"Acquire… is that what you call it?" Her voice rises as she stalks toward me. Slow, deliberate steps and I can feel the tension rolling off of her shoulders. "The rat told you where to acquire your whore and what to fill her room with?" she asks me with shaky breaths and tears in her eyes.

"I wanted this to be nice for you." The hard words linger between us as my throat tightens. Anger is written on my face; I can feel it like stone, but I can't change my expression.

Of every smart comment and tiny bit of anger she's shown me, this is the worst.

Distrust is clearly evident. I didn't earn her distrust. I'm not the fucking rat.

"How did you expect me to react to being told someone was spying on me?" she asks with genuine distress as her lower lip wobbles and she catches it between her teeth before turning her back to me. I thought she already knew. She's a smart woman, but I forget how trusting she is. How loyal.

Her arms cross and uncross as she debates on how to handle the revelation. She paces from the dresser to the vanity. Already pacing in this room. I have to fight the urge to smirk as I watch her pace back and forth over the white rug, which is exactly how I pictured her in here.

But not so soon, and not like this. This room is better than the cell if nothing else.

"I thought you would have assumed," I tell her honestly and nervousness prickles my skin as she glares back at me. It's unsettling and I debate on leaving her here, but I refuse. She's not going to take her anger out on me. Not when it belongs to someone else. "It wasn't supposed to upset you. I wanted you to have everything you could have possibly wanted," I admit to her and try to keep my voice even and calm, but the anger toward her response still lingers.

The nervousness grows inside of me, and I'm sickened by it. I thought she would appreciate this. I thought she would be excited to have everything she had before. Or at least grateful. I thought wrong.

I should feel irritated or pissed, but that's not what I feel at all. I've done this to her. She can't accept a gift without being cautious of my intentions.

With a growing pit in my stomach, I speak without meeting her eyes. I stare straight ahead at the hanging curtains that are only meant to add beauty to the locked windows that will never open for her.

"I wanted to make you happy," I tell her and clear my throat of the spiked knot. "I thought this would make you happy," I pause to run my hand over the back of my head, feeling the ever-present crease that reminds me how shitty I am at knowing what she needs beyond a good fuck and finally look into her thoughtful gaze that's already softening, "or at least provide you comfort."

My heart beats faster as she stares back at me with a kindness she hasn't before given me. "I'm trying to be gentle," I confess to her.

"I'm sorry," she whispers in a choked voice. The second I feel myself wavering and losing the man I am to this woman, she wanders toward me and wraps her arms around my waist, her hands splaying on my shoulders as she hugs me.

It takes me a moment to hold her to me and when I do, I kiss her hair and bury my face in it before she pulls away.

Her eyes are glassy but she doesn't cry; she sounds strong, although a few of her words crack as she says, "It's just a reminder… of everything that I'll never have again." She gestures to the room and exhales deeply before adding, "It's beautiful and it does give me comfort. You have no idea how much I love this. I do." She swallows with her eyes closed and then runs her fingers through her hair. I wait patiently for her to continue.

"I'm sorry, it's just… there's always something that happens that proves I know nothing and I'm lost."

"You're not lost." My response is immediate, and my tone is one I expect from myself. It's not to be questioned. "You belong here, with me."

Her shoulders steady as her breathing calms and her formerly emotionally-distraught features calm once again, but it's an act. She's brimming inside with a mixture of fear, betrayal, anger, and confusion.

"You're only lost because you want to be," I tell her low and deep, reaching out and pulling her small body closer to me.

Her hands land on my chest and she gasps slightly before looking up at me.

"I can give you everything. I can give you what you never even dreamed of before." I mean every word. I can and will.

Her long hair shines in the light as she nods, making it swish along her collarbone. She's compliant, but her wide eyes are full of questions. Questions she doesn't ask me. Some of them I'm grateful I won't have to answer.

"If you want to run, you run here."

"Carter, there are things you can't replace." She looks straight ahead at my chest as she speaks and her shoulders shudder. "Money can't replace—"

"I'm fully aware of what money can't replace. Nothing can erase the past. Nothing can bring it back." The sharp edge of my words and the pain and anger I refuse to hide in them erase her desperation to beg me for what I will never give her.

"I'll give you what I can. Everything that I'm able. But sometimes what we want most is impossible to achieve." My throat tightens with emotion and just as it does, Aria props herself up on her tiptoes, gently caresses my face and kisses me.

It's short and only a peck. Only a small kiss. Nothing like what we've shared before.

It feels different than it has before. Her touch is hesitant. A different kind of fear is in control of her and shows in her eyes. The kiss is meant to put an end to the conversation. She's hiding in that act.

"Tell me what you're thinking," I command her although the edge of desperation is evident to me. I don't think she can hear it. I pray she can't.

Her answer doesn't come quickly. She tries to leave me, and I cling to her, but she grabs my wrists and pulls my touch away as she tells me, "I'm scared."

"You don't have anything to fear if you obey me," I tell her, pinning her gaze to mine.

"You don't understand," she whispers.

The unspoken words between us are causing a crack in the delicate balance of what we have.

The reality that she's still my prisoner.

The truth that I won't rest until her father is dead.

The fact that she won't forgive me for killing everyone she's ever known and loved.

And the fact I never want to be without her and I think she feels the same about me. If only she could accept what's to come.

The Talverys will be massacred. And she, the sole survivor of her name, belongs to me.

CHAPTER 11

Aria

I   T'S TOO MUCH, I THINK WITH MY THUMBNAIL IN BETWEEN MY
teeth as I lie in the soaking tub.

Every day, something changes, and I never know how to react or what it means for us. What it means about me.

How could I not have known someone was watching me?

It must have been Mika.

He was always watching and taunting and teasing, but I thought it was just because he was an asshole on a power trip.

I lower my hand back into the steaming water and try to settle against the edge of the tub. My foot slips up to the faucet, feeling the hot water splash against it.

I can feel my fight leaving. The urge to keep fighting and keep holding on to the girl I was before Carter *acquired* me is trickling out of me day by day.

He's going to kill my family. My father. Nikolai. I know Carter will, no matter how much he cares for me.

That's the most painful part. I think he does care for me, but Carter is ruthless and there's nothing I can do to stop him. There's no point in trying.

The hopelessness presses against my shoulders, threatening to push me under and drown away my sorrows.

I wish I was numb to it all. There's nothing worse than being fully aware yet having no way to change any of it. Without fighting, I feel like a traitor. I'm not just surviving anymore. I'm living, and I don't know how I can forgive myself for having feelings for the man who's responsible for so many horrible sins.

Just as I feel tears pricking at my eyes, Carter's voice startles me. "You're tense."

I try to hide my sniffling and feel pathetic that I'm crying at all. Carter ignores it though, offering me that small bit of mercy as he strips down and slowly sinks into the tub, scooting me forward so he can lie in the bath behind me. The water sloshes and rises higher up my body as he sinks into the tub.

His touch is gentle, and I don't fail to notice that he's hard already. Just the thought of his cock makes my thighs clench and the dull ache that never leaves sends a wave of want through me.

Maybe that's why I don't want to fight him. The only thing that takes away the pain and anger is the one thing he gives me constantly. And that makes me a whore of the worst kind.

The water sways and a shiver runs down my spine as Carter's large hands press against my shoulders, pulling me into his chest. His fingers drift down my body, over the pearls and diamonds of his necklace that I always wear because he told me to, and the faint touch hardens my nipples and leaves goosebumps in his path to the hot water.

"What are you thinking?" Carter's deep voice rumbles just as I close my eyes and I open them to stare at the tiled wall and answer bluntly.

"I was thinking I don't want to kill you anymore because you fuck me so often." The truth spills out easily, not even questioning my answer to him.

His rough chuckle almost makes me smile as he reaches for the sponge and then dips it into the steaming water.

"I'm so tired," I say absently as Carter runs the sponge along my shoulder and down my forearm.

"It's late. Later than you usually stay awake." I spent hours in the gilded room. That's what I'm calling it now. That's all it is. Even if it is beautiful, and I do love that he had it built for me and I'm grateful to have my things back… or replicas of them.

"When do you even sleep?" I ask him. "You're always awake when I go to sleep, and awake when I wake up."

"I don't like to sleep," he answers me. "I can sleep when I'm dead."

His even tone and lack of humor make my heart tense. Like it doesn't want to beat when he talks like that.

Readjusting, I watch the film of bath oils move on the surface of the water and nestle my foot under Carter's calf.

"You know we could have started this way," I say weakly, not sure if I should broach the subject, but what do I have to lose?

"What way?"

"With you giving me a room and being less of a monster." The words slip out easily and Carter's ministrations pause at the last word. But then he keeps going, continuing to wash me.

"And what would you have done? Destroyed the room and used the shards of glass to kill me?"

He's not wrong. I could easily see that happening and the reality makes the small hairs on the back of my neck stand up.

What happened to that fight? To that edge I'm fully aware would have come out had the situation been different.

Nothing has changed. Carter stole me, keeps me prisoner and he's going to kill my family.

None of that has changed. Yet here I lie against him, loving his touch and finding my heart being ripped into two.

"We should talk about something else," Carter suggests.

The sound of the water falling from my shoulder to the tub is calming. Which is anything but what I should be feeling. The sponge is still hot, and it soothes my tired muscles.

"I could fall asleep in here," I murmur absently. All I want to do anymore is sleep. I don't know if I'm depressed, worn out, or if that's what happens when you lose your fight.

"Can I wash you?" I ask him, wondering if he'd let me.

A moment passes and then he dips the sponge back under; I expect him to give it to me, but that's not what happens.

"I like washing you," he whispers against my ear, his warm breath creating a wave of want that flows through me. But my eyes stay open.

Of course, he wouldn't want me to wash him. He couldn't even let me suck his dick. A small huff of feigned humor leaves me, and I readjust in the water so that the sound of it splashing will drown out the huff, but he hears it anyway.

"What?" he asks and leans forward to look at my expression, pulling my shoulder against his to keep me from avoiding him.

I meet his dark gaze, the grays and silvers seeming to take over in the bathroom light. "Nothing, it just feels good. It's nice to feel cared for."

Without speaking he leans back, kisses the crook of my neck, and moves the sponge to my neck and chest.

"Did you think it would be this way from the beginning?" I ask him. Truly wanting to know what he thought back then, only weeks ago. The reminder of the cell, of me starving and dying of both boredom and fear should make me angry, but all it does is make me pity Carter.

"I didn't know what to expect from you. I only knew I wanted to have you."

"To have me," I echo and settle my head in the crook of his neck. The movement makes my breasts rise above the surface of the water for a moment and the chill is unwelcome until I settle back into the water.

"Your choice of words always seems to amaze me." My voice is flat, and I wish I could take it back. Silence stretches, and I wonder how long I've been in the water.

You can't wash everything away, but I wish I could.

"How did you think this would end?"

"You're asking a lot of questions tonight," he says instead of giving me an answer and places the sponge back on its shelf rather than answering me.

"Oh, and I see I've found the question that crosses the line," I tell him with a smile although a deep pain courses through my heart as I shut my eyes. Each beat feeling harder and taking more of me just to keep going. I can only imagine what Carter wanted to do with me.

"It all changed when I saw how much you wanted me. When I saw how much you craved my touch… how much you needed me." I open my eyes as Carter's fingers reach for my chin, the water dripping into the tub as he forces me to look into his eyes.

"I need you to want me still when this is over." Carter's words hold an edge of sincerity that's too much to handle.

I almost ask why, but I'm afraid of the answer I'll get. I'm afraid what I feel for him isn't reciprocated. I've been foolish before, and I'm almost certain I am now.

"I'm not afraid of you," I confess to him, wanting to at least hint at the depths of what I feel for him.

"You should be." He doesn't try to make his words gentle in the least. "You need to be."

In his presence, my body turns to fire. He ignites something inside of me like no one else ever has. I doubt anyone else could ever affect me the way he does. Some moments, I hate him and who he is, and what he's done and will do. But unless those thoughts are on the forefront of my mind, the hate fades and it's replaced with a lust that clouds my judgment and demands my body bow to his. To show him love like he's never seen and the power of what it can do to heal him.

What's more? I crave it more every day. I'm addicted to Carter Cross. And the shame of that fact, although present, has quieted.

But the voice is still there and picks away at me. It's relentless, but so is Carter.

CHAPTER 12

Carter

S OME MOMENTS, I FEEL CLOSER TO HER.
Others, more distant.
I wish I knew what to make of her tonight. Nothing went as I thought it would and that puts me on edge.

She fell asleep in the tub, and as I carry her small form wrapped in a towel to bed, I can't help but notice how peaceful she looks.

Tonight, was like knowing you're in the eye of a storm. She's calm and placated but beneath the surface, everything she's truly feeling rage inside of her. She needs to let it go.

I have to set her down and pull the comforter from underneath her before she can bury herself into the mattress.

As she nestles into the sheets, she wakes calmly.

Rubbing her eyes, she comes to and asks, "Is it morning?" She practically hums the words.

With her damp hair a mess and sleep lingering in her expression, she's fucking gorgeous.

I cup her cheek and plant a soft kiss on her lips, to which she lifts hers up and deepens it. I'm growing addicted to the way she kisses me. How she doesn't hide her passion in her touch.

Unlike in her gifted room today. I want them all to be like this one.

I've never kissed a woman before her. Never let myself fall for anyone or given them that part of me. So, every peck, every time she deepens it, it means so much more than I thought it would. I need more of *this* from her.

"Not yet, songbird." Whispering against her lips I tell her, "You fell asleep in the bath."

She slowly sits up as I climb into bed next to her.

"Well, I don't feel tired now," she tells me and sits cross-legged.

Exhaustion sweeps over me as I lie down and pull her close to me. "Good, I can have you then," I tell her, letting my lips drag against her neck to leave a trail of open-mouth kisses. I rock my erection into her hip and then pin her under me. "I wanted you in the bath."

I'd planned on putting one heel on each side of the tub, just as I'd told her to do in the office, but her questions were more important. More insightful, even though I didn't like where they were going.

It feels like she's slipping from me, slowly. I'm losing her, and I don't know how or why.

But I'll get her back. She has nowhere else to run and no one else. She only needs to accept that.

Her hand sweeps behind my neck and she pulls my lips to hers, taking and demanding. "Make me forget," she whispers against my lips and my chest aches at her words.

I need to forget, just as she does. It's so easy to get lost in her.

My fingers trail down the dip in her waist slowly until I find her cunt. Already hot and wet and needy, she rocks herself into my palm and I smile against her lips.

Nipping her lower lip and guiding my cock to her entrance, I tease her, "You're always ready for me."

"Always," she mewls just before I slam into her to the hilt.

"Fuck!" she yells out as I pull out and then thrust into her slowly, taken aback at the tone of her strangled cry.

Her palms press against my chest, pushing me away as I kiss the crook of her neck and she moans a painful sound. "Carter," she whispers my name with agony. Her brow is etched with a look of pain.

"It hurts," she gasps, arching her neck as I pull out of her completely. "It hurts," she repeats, trying to close her legs. Shit. My body tenses concerned that I hurt her. Fuck. Not like this.

"Shh," I whisper against her neck and kiss her lightly as my fingers find her clit. She needs to feel good under me. I can't have her any other way.

Instantly, she moans that sweet sound of pleasure I love hearing. "I was wondering how much I could fuck you before you'd be too sore." She only replies with a quick inhale and the buck of her hips which does nothing but give me slight relief.

"Look at me," I command her, and her head turns instantly to face me. Her gorgeous hazel-green eyes burn into mine. My thumb rubs ruthless circles around her clit and Aria bites into her lower lip, desperate to keep her eyes on me but knowing the pleasure will rock through her soon.

Her back bows slightly and her breaths turns to pants, but instead of letting her get off, I lower my fingers, trailing them through her lips and gathering the wetness to bring it lower.

"I could always take you here," I say lowly, pressing my fingers against her forbidden entrance.

Aria's answer is to open her mouth wider with a look of shock, but more than that, sinful curiosity.

A smile stretches across my lips as I say, "Not tonight though. I have to play with you first." Her eyes light again with curiosity and the guilt I felt a moment ago diminishes. I bring my fingers back to her clit then down to her entrance, pressing them inside her gently, but even that makes her wince.

I have to pull the covers back to look at her slick folds; she's red and swollen, well used.

That doesn't mean I can't give her pleasure and that I can't have mine in return. If I've learned anything about Aria, it's that the more I give her pleasure, the more compliant she is.

Her eyes stay pinned on me as she looks down her body and waits for what I'll do to her.

I run my tongue up and down her pussy and then suck on her clit. She's so fucking sweet. The taste of her on my lips makes my cock twitch with need. With her hands in my hair and her heels digging into the bed she finds her release, screaming out my name.

She curls on her side as I move back up the bed and lie next to her, not waiting to position her just as I want her. With one hand on her breast and the other pushing the hair away from her flushed face, she's still reeling from her orgasm when I move my cock between her thighs.

"Arch your back," I tell her, and she obeys instantly, jutting her ass out. And it tempts me. The curve of her waist and the round flesh of her ass are so seductive. I can just imagine gripping on to her and rocking into her as she screams in ecstasy.

She's not ready for my dick to take her ass though… not yet.

I settle on pushing the head of my cock inside her, only the head and wait for her reaction. A small moan escapes her lips as she rocks gently, finding the aftershocks pleasurable. I know there will be a bite of pain, but there's nothing better than when pain and pleasure mix.

"Grab my cock," I give her the command, and she reaches around to take my cock and stroke it. "Harder," I say then put my hand over hers and show her how to jerk me off. She only has a grip on the base of my dick, but her unsure hold and the lust in her eyes are enough to get me off. Even without her pussy clenching around the head of my cock.

"Fuck," I groan as she rubs me and slowly pushes more of me inside of her. With my hand on her hip, I stop her from pushing more of me inside of her. Even with her getting off, it'll only make her worse off and all I need is this.

"I want you every night, however I can have you." My words are tense as I sit on the edge of my release.

The air between us is different now. There's a raw quality neither of us can hide, although I'll never admit it.

Her pressure is firm, her strokes even and deliberate, and then her pussy spasms around the tip of my dick as she cums again from me rubbing her clit.

But it's the way she's looking at me that gets me off. Like I'm hers to play with. I'm hers to fuck, to use.

Like she owns me, as she strokes my dick and I cum inside her.

My eyes beg me to close them as I revel in the sweet burst of satisfaction and I mark her again. But her gaze stays on mine, our breath mingling, and I'm forced to get lost in her hazel eyes. I'm still cumming when she releases me, turning and kissing me hard, crashing her lips to mine and devouring me.

My cum leaks from her and onto the sheets, but she doesn't care and neither do I.

Her heart races as she presses her breasts to my chest and belly to mine. Once again wanting to get closer to me, and I feel for the first time today I have her back. She's mine again.

The day I stop fucking her will be the day I lose her. She needs my touch like I need the air she breathes.

"I think I might be able to sleep now," she whispers and then smiles against my lips.

"Sleep well." I keep my voice calm and soothing, rubbing my arm up and down her bare back as she settles her head on my chest, a new habit of hers. One I approve of.

Looking up at me with her head resting on my arm she tells me, "Sweet dreams."

I kiss her gently as she drifts off to sleep in my arms with the faint taste of lust still on her lips.

Addicts will get high on anything. My father's words ring in my ears. The white lights are too bright. I wince.

Where am I? My head lolls to the side; it's so heavy I can't lift it. *Everything hurts.*

Slowly, I feel each of my limbs. My wrists won't move, pinned against a metal chair. The same with my ankles and every inch of me is in pain, but the worst is radiating from my stomach.

I heave up a breath that squeezes my chest, coughing up blood.

Fuck.

My right eye is swollen, and I try to open it, remembering how my mother's pills fell into the gutter. No, we needed that money.

My father said the addicts would buy them, but hardly any of them did. I stayed out all day, and only two buyers paid me anything. And then the men showed up. Talvery's men.

"How long was he there?"

I hear someone from across the room ask the question and open my eyes to see a swinging light and a man in a crisp suit with long black hair slicked back tossing my wallet across a metal table littered with tools.

A groan tears from me as I try to move. Try to get away. I know he's going to kill me. I know it.

But it's hopeless.

"I'm sorry," I spew and more blood spits up. "I didn't know," I try to say but my throat is so dry and feels bruised. I don't think they heard me, so I repeat myself, pleading for mercy. "I didn't know."

"You didn't know what, kid?" a man hisses in front of me. Pain spikes at the back of my scalp as he grips my hair and shakes my head to look at him. "You didn't know you were dealing on my turf?" His eyes are a pale blue and ice cold. "The whole east side knows it now. So, you're fucked." He spits out the words then leaves me, picking up something from the metal table.

Every crunch of bone, every rip of my skin, every deep gouge pushes me closer and closer until I'm holding on to life by a thread.

I even cry out for my mother.

They all laugh in the room. But still, I cry out for her. Praying she can't see this and what's happened only weeks after her death. Shame and regret and pain make my head feel light and slowly I feel weightless. So close to death.

Please, just end it. I don't want to live anymore. I can't.

Bang. Bang. Bang.

At first, I think they're guns that wake me, stopping me from drifting to lifelessness.

Bang. Another bang at the door so close to me, yet impossible to reach.

"Please, I need you," someone says, and her voice sends a chill through my body, but at the same time, warmth. "I need you." The words are feminine and soft, but with a plea that begs me to listen.

She needs me.

The pain is still vivid with every move of my limbs, but I can hear her if I listen.

The voice turns harder, colder and the air goes frigid.

"I need you, Carter," she says again but this time there's no negotiation in her tone. "I need you!" she yells at me.

The anger rising and a storm brewing around me, she screams at me, her voice reverberating in the room, "I still need you!"

CHAPTER 13

Aria

H IS ARM FEELS SO HEAVY. I CAN BARELY HEAR MY GROAN AS I wake up and try to push away Carter's arm.

I struggle, but he only squeezes tighter.

My shoulders twist and I push against his arm, but the muscles are coiled, and his grip is too much. I can't breathe.

My eyes shoot open, realizing this isn't a dream.

"Carter!" I cry out in a strangled breath, fighting his hold and letting the anxiety rush through my blood to make me kick backward, shoving and heaving to get him off of me. "Wake up!" My heart pounds harder.

I struggle to breathe. My voice croaks and my lungs burn as I yell, "Carter!"

My chest flies forward as he jolts awake, instantly releasing me and leaving me breathless and crumpled on the bed. The mattress dips and groans as Carter gets up. I push the hair from my face and then try to steady my ragged breathing.

It was only a moment—a small moment—maybe a minute in time, but I thought he was going to kill me, he held me so tight.

"You scared the shit out of me." I barely get the words out, my eyes still burning.

Without an answer, I turn to him and it's then I see he's breathing just as heavily as I am. With both palms against the wall, he leans over and tries to calm himself down.

My blood runs cold at the sight of him. "Carter?" My voice carries across the room to him, ignoring how my muscles are screaming still from fighting against his grip.

Getting onto my knees, I crawl to the edge of the mattress. His shoulders are tense, and he won't look at me.

Cautiously, I climb off the bed and go to him. "It's okay." I try to keep my voice soothing, but my body hasn't caught up to the fact that he needs me. "I'm okay," I say, trying to reassure him.

With my heart hammering, I gently place a hand on his arm but he's quick to rip it away and stalk to the bathroom, leaving me with a pounding fear racing through my blood.

"Carter," I say hesitantly, but he doesn't respond to me at all.

The question is clear in my mind, go to him or let him be? I'm still catching my breath and waking up as I push my hair from my hot face, registering what just happened.

If I've ever seen a man who shouldn't be left alone, it's Carter. He's too broken, and there's no telling what he'll do.

"Was it just a nightmare?" I ask him innocently, wanting him to give me anything. I can feel the rug end and the wood begin as I walk toward him in the dark.

He flicks on the light in the bathroom and runs the water. And I walk toward the sound and strip of light from the bathroom that guides me.

"Carter?" I ask him softly as I push the bathroom door open and see his back to me again. His muscles ripple as he washes his face.

"Please, talk to me," I whisper weakly when he still doesn't answer me. Even after he's dried off his face. "Are you okay?"

I can see him swallow in the mirror. I can see the weary expression of a man who's led a horrible life. The fatigue in his eyes. The pain etched in the faint scars on his back.

He presses his palms to his eyes and breathes in and out. "Go to bed," he commands in a harsh tone I don't expect, although, I don't leave as asked.

My heart squeezes with pain. I won't leave him like this. "I don't want to," I tell him with barely any courage, the words coming out shaky.

"What happened?" I ask him in a comforting whisper. "It was just a dream," I tell him, hoping they'll have more comfort for him than those words do for me.

For the first time, he looks at me in the mirror, and the sight of him sends a chill down my spine. The power, the anger, the man who rules and gives no mercy expecting none in return, pierces me with his gaze.

"Don't tell anyone." His words are soft and they hang in the air with a threat. An unneeded and ridiculous threat.

"Tell anyone what?" I question his sanity at this moment, only to realize he doesn't want me to tell anyone that he had a nightmare. "I wouldn't. I would never." My words come out quickly as tears prick my eyes. "That's not why I'm here, Carter."

"Go to bed," he tells me again, although this time his words are softer.

"Are you okay?" I ask him, taking another small step toward him, but still not sure if I should touch him. All I want to do is hold him, pull him close to me and tell him it's all right. Just like the way he's held me over the past few weeks. But I don't even know what happened.

With his grip on the edge of the sink and his head lowered, his voice comes out quietly and nearly menacing but more than that, heart-wrenching.

"Look at me, Aria." He speaks to me in the mirror, his eyes bloodshot as they stare back at me. "Look at who I am. Nothing about me is okay."

I stand there shaking, my words and breath caught by the intensity of the man in front of me. Even as he turns off the light, leaving me in darkness as he walks around me, his skin barely grazing mine, I tremble. His pace is ruthless as he leaves me, slamming the door and I'm left stunned and shaken. More than anything, I'm saddened by everything that just happened and so aware of how alone I am as I cry myself to sleep.

CHAPTER 14

Carter

S OMEHOW, I FUCKED UP.
  She's the one who was supposed to change when I gave her the knife.

She's the one who should need me.

Not the other way around.

I can't shake last night or the knowledge that every day Aria seeps deeper into my blood and every thought that I have.

I'm consumed by her. I can't deny it. She brings out a side of me that should have stayed dead.

"Are you listening?" Daniel asks me, tearing my eyes away from the drawing Aria made yesterday.

He looks as worn out as I feel. It's because of Addison. She's not okay being back here. She didn't realize what this family became after she left. Time changes everything, but she didn't know. She couldn't have. And this lockdown leaves us nowhere to hide.

"She needs more than this. She's not handling the transition well. She needs… she needs to not feel trapped." Daniel hunches over in his chair, both hands on the back of his head, his elbows on his knees. When he looks up at me, I feel like I truly am the monster Aria calls me for putting him through this. For putting both of them through this. With tears in his eyes, he tells me, "I'm losing her. I don't want this for her."

"You're protecting her," I remind him. She's the one they went after and tried to kidnap, to kill, to do whatever they wanted with. She may have been safe if he'd never chased her. If they hadn't realized he loved her. But you can't change the past.

"She doesn't care," he tells me as he swipes his eyes with the heel of his palm, hiding his pain with a look of anger and annoyance I know is just a ruse. "She thought at first I was overreacting. That it was all in my head and over the incident at her place." He shakes his head silently before looking me in the eyes. "She said I was being ridiculous. She had no idea. So, I had to tell her."

"You told her what?" I ask him, just now realizing he's told her more than she needs to know.

"That men are going to die, and those men want us dead first. I told her we're at war. She still wants out. She doesn't like this. And I don't like keeping her here against her will."

My voice feels tense and catches in my throat watching him in pain over this.

"She didn't agree to this. This wasn't what it was like when we were kids. She had no idea, and I brought her back blindly. I was selfish." His words are laced with regret. The last sentence comes out in a harsh whisper. "So fucking selfish." The pain radiates off of him. "I can't lose her again."

"You can't risk her safety either," I reply and I'm firmer with him than I usually am. We're at war, and Talvery and his men will attack us the moment they can. "If I were them," I tell Daniel, "I'd be waiting and any chance I could take to strike first, I'd take it."

"I know," he murmurs and hangs his head. "They know they're dead men; they have nothing to lose. And they'd kill her just because I love her."

"It'll all be over soon," I say to try to offer him comfort as he rests his elbows back on his knees and steeples his fingers, keeping them against his lips.

"I don't know if she'll still love me then," he whispers his pain.

"I know what you mean." The words slip out and I can't stop them. Daniel's eyes hold a question, but he takes a moment to ask it. Waiting and stretching the silence.

"Have you thought for a moment, that maybe keeping her locked up is putting her more at risk? There's only so much you can control for someone until it turns on you."

"What choice do I have?" I retort, and his gaze moves to the floor again. "We're all prisoners of war," I remind him. "But it will be over soon."

"When it's done with… she'll stay? Aria will stay with you?" he questions me.

I search his face for the intention, why he would even consider her leaving.

"She won't hold it against you?" he asks me as if knowing what I needed to hear him say in order to answer.

"I don't know. She's mine. And she'll stay with me. Forgiveness will come."

He starts to say something, readjusting his footing but then he shakes his head.

"I came in to tell you something else, although I'm not sure you want to hear it," he tells me and straightens in his chair.

I gesture for him to go on. Although, I don't know why I'm in a rush. I've barely spoken to Aria this morning and I'm not sure I'm ready to, not after last night.

I expect him to tell me the same shit Jase has been saying, that Marcus is up to something. Marcus is going to strike. That we have three enemies now, not just one.

Without any proof other than the word of dead men. A single word. The enemies will fall in order: Talvery, Romano, and then Marcus. When we have more proof. I'm not in the habit of starting a war over a single word from the lips of a soon-to-be-dead addict.

"Nikolai is asking around for her," Daniel tells me and that catches me by surprise.

"Is that right?" I ask as my thumb taps against my lip. Resentment stirs inside of me. He brings out a side of jealousy in me that I've never felt before. *He had her first.*

Daniel nods with the hint of amusement at his lips. "Ever since Romano confirmed it."

"And what's he asking?"

"How he can get her back." He doesn't hide the thrill in his eyes from delivering this news to me.

"You're a prick for loving this as much as you do."

"It certainly adds an interesting dynamic, doesn't it?" he asks and a mix of curiosity, hate, and jealousy mingle in my blood.

"He has nothing to bargain with and even if he did, there's nothing I'd want in her place."

"He's already been told that and that it would be pointless to even ask you, but he *demanded* you be told."

"Did he?"

I can't blame Daniel for being so amused. "He seems to really care for her."

"Is this the first or second time I've told you I want him to die first?" I ask Daniel and he only snorts a laugh. Every night in the cell that Aria spoke his name, my hate for Nikolai grew. And she did it often. I'm fully aware of how *close* they were. Too fucking close for him to keep breathing when all of this is over.

"You really think she'll forgive you?" he asks with a cocked brow. I don't think he realized what his question would do to me.

She'll have to forgive me. There's no other way.

I don't like leaving Aria or being away from the estate right now, especially knowing that every moment I'm away is a moment that threatens to make her question what she should do. That's a dangerous thought to leave her with; all she should do is what I tell her, but I have to be present for this.

There are times when it's required to be seen. This particular instance is one of those times. With slicked-back hair and a sharp suit, Oliver looks younger than I remember him. Maybe it's the wide grin on his face that adds to his youthful appearance. Maybe it's the shot of what looks like whiskey that he clinks against Frank's beer and then throws back as he takes his seat. Neither of them sees me, but the security and Jared notice the moment I enter. They tense as I let the back doors close easily behind me, listening to Frank's hard slap on Oliver's back in congratulations.

Frank's all right I guess. He's a little older than me, only by a few years, but he's perpetually twenty-one. A punk kid with no goals in life other than making a buck on the streets and letting everyone know he's proud of it. I don't give a fuck what his motivation is, so long as he listens. I catch his light blue gaze and he slides back in his chair with a broad smile. "The boss is here," he utters but his jovial words are slurred.

"Your mom waiting up for you, Frank?" I ask him, hiding my grin as I walk toward the table they're sitting at in the right corner of the room.

Glancing over my shoulder, I take notice of who's counting the money down the hall. All the drugs come in and out of the Red Room, Jase's nightclub. As does the money.

"Ma can wait up all she wants." He blows off my comment, not taking the hint that he should make his way out.

"I think there's some business," Jared points out and gestures between myself and Oliver, his head tilted as he tries to convey to Frank that he should get the fuck out of here.

The shot glass sounds heavy as it hits the table and Frank pushes out his chair. "All right, all right, the big guys gotta talk." He mutters without looking at me, "You don't got to tell me twice." As he's putting on his jacket, I lay a hand down on his shoulder and wait for him to look at me. I stand close to him, catching him off guard and creating a thick tension that's undeniable. Fear looms in the depths of his eyes as I tell him earnestly, not breaking eye contact, "Thanks for understanding."

"Can we get another?" Oliver asks, the happiness not at all dampened. He doesn't see how Frank stumbles backward; he doesn't notice the change in the air. Frank does, and all he says on his way out is, "Of course, boss."

Yeah, Frank's an all right guy.

As I pull out the chair across from Oliver, letting it drag across the floor, Frank leaves, entering back into the club, bringing in the pounding music. It's quick to fade as the door closes with a resounding click.

"Thank you, thank you," Oliver thanks Jared, who's pouring out another shot of whiskey in front of Oliver and then filling the empty glass Frank just had.

"To finally snuffing out the fucking Talverys." Oliver's age finally shows as he raises the glass in the air and doesn't hide the hate on his face. He's new to the crew. Not at all like Frank, who started with me only five years ago. I picked up men as I took over street by street. Giving the men who ran them the option to come with me or die.

Oliver came to me though. Pissed that Talvery didn't want him, he offered up his services as muscle on the street. If it wasn't for Jared's word, I never would have hired him. Too old. Too cocky. More than that, he's too eager to make a name for himself.

With a nod of my head, the old man throws the drink back, clicking his tongue against the roof of his mouth as he sets down the glass and shakes off the burn of the shot.

"I heard everyone's ready to get it over with," I tell him, resting both of my arms on the table. A sly grin kicks up his lips. "Couldn't be more ready, boss."

My own grin shows itself. An asymmetric smirk as he calls me boss.

The dumb fuck should have remembered that earlier today.

"So, what happened," I ask him easily, motioning with my hand palm up for more, "give me all the details."

He's grinning from ear to ear as he tells me what I already heard, what *everyone* heard.

"There were four of them right across the street from Dale's bar, on Sixth Street. I saw them walking in and knew they'd be there for a few."

In my periphery, I see Jared stiffen; he knows me well enough to realize that this isn't going to end well for the man he stuck his neck out for to get on the crew. I bet he's wondering what that means for him. If I was him, I'd be wondering too.

Oliver still hasn't caught on. He's nothing but proud as he tells me how he walked in and shot all four of them before they ever grabbed their guns.

"All on Talvery's turf? That takes balls." I compliment him although inside my heart is pounding, adrenaline raging inside of me and the tension building. I've been needing a release for all of this pent-up anger. Wiping the smirk off old Oliver's face might be exactly what I need. That, or falling back into bed with Aria.

Just the thought of having her makes me want to speed this shit up and get back to her.

I've already been gone long enough.

"No one's making a move, but they were right there," he says and emphasizes his words, shaking his hands in the air. No one's crossing lines, and no one's made a move, not even Nikolai. But this dumb fuck thought he could do it and get away with it.

"How many shots have you had so far?" I ask him, my foot tapping against the ground as my impatience grows with every thought of getting Aria under me tonight.

"This is my fifth since Jared brought me in." He sways slightly in his chair as he tells me, but the smile only widens.

"Two for each of the four," I say loud enough for everyone to hear me and stand up. I have to walk around the table to pat him on the shoulder as I tell him, "Three more, all on me."

The smell of whiskey hits me hard as he reaches up to return the pat on my arm. His touch is firm with the first pat, but I don't stay in place, making the second one turn to a tap. My gaze is on Jared as Oliver says something behind me. A thanks and another cheers to killing the Talverys. I don't fucking care what the dead prick has to say.

Pausing in front of Jared, I keep my voice low as I tell him.

"It's on you to slit his throat when he's done those three shots."

On cue, Oliver calls out for another. The blood drains from Jared's face, but he nods and with a low voice he answers, "Of course."

There's not a hint of anything but remorse on Jared's face. He's tense, but he had to know it was coming. "No one does a damn thing until I say so." My shoulders stiffen, and the anger threatens to show itself, so I reach out, straightening Jared's tie and then add, "If there are any other dumb fucks who want to show off and not wait for my orders," I look Jared in the eye to tell him, "don't bother me and make me come in here. Kill the pricks where they stand."

CHAPTER 15

Aria

T HE FRONT DOOR IS OPEN; IT'S NEVER OPEN.

The soft pads of my feet patter against the marble floor as I make my way to the entrance, following the bright light of day.

I can already smell the fresh air and the warmth before I step outside. The grass in the front yard is lush and although it's fall, the weather is lovely.

I haven't stepped on the porch at all. Not once since I've been here, and the thought seems too odd to be a reality, but it is. I was carried inside, and I've only ever looked through the etched glass of the windows but I don't try to do that often as it is. It just seems cruel to tease myself like that.

I glance behind me, down the foyer, and then peek outside, but I don't see anyone. Not at first. Not until I take a step onto the smooth slate porch and then another.

I hear him first, Jase. With a phone to his ear, he walks around the side of the house and then back up. There's a hitch in my breath and a slam in my chest; I freeze, but only for a split second.

I'm walking outside.

I'm not trying to run away. Although I have to force my limbs to move, I do just that. Staring Jase in the eyes, I walk to the stairs. They're grand and massive, just as you'd expect for an estate like this. Not to mention beautiful. Everything about this place looks expensive and each detail intricate, from the trimmed bushes and groomed flower beds to the arched driveway paved with cobblestone, reflects an elegance from whoever lives here.

I nearly snort just thinking about Carter choosing all these details. Carter is anything but elegant.

I hold Jase's gaze as I slowly sit on the steps. A large column blocks me from his view and I can imagine he'll come running.

So sorry to interrupt his phone call. The captive is fleeing; call the guards, call the guards!

A genuine laugh makes my shoulders shake at the sarcastic thoughts. As I lean against the column, enjoying the sun that dances across my skin and the fresh breeze, Jase comes running up the yard, just as I anticipated.

Rolling my eyes, I give him a face. A face that says, *are you fucking kidding me?*

"I'm on break from being the prisoner. I called in a temporary replacement," I mutter.

His lips twitch like he wants to smile, but he doesn't. He doesn't say anything, not to me and not for a few minutes. I can hear the sound of someone speaking from his phone although I can't make out the words. He doesn't seem to pay attention to them at all.

My heart beats a little harder and anxiety trickles slowly into my veins. My foot nervously taps on the stone steps, but I hold my ground. Even as I start to get emotional, knowing that I can't even step outside without someone losing their shit, I stay right the hell where I am and enjoy the fucking porch.

"I'll call you back," Jase finally speaks, although it's still not to me. My muscles get rigid and my teeth clench together. *If he thinks he's taking me inside...* I swallow thickly at the thought. What am I really going to do? I can at least kick him. One good hard kick, maybe in the shin. I nod my head faintly at the idea, keeping my eyes on a few leaves that have turned a beautiful shade of auburn as they sway in the gentle wind. If he puts a hand on me to force me back inside, I swear I'm going to kick his ass.

A soft grin tugs at my lips. It's nice to feel like a tough girl at least. And like I have a choice.

"You picked a good day," Jase says, and I lift my gaze to see him slipping the phone into his pocket before he climbs the first few steps to sit by me but on a stair lower than mine.

I'm quiet for a moment, gauging how he looks so comfortable and acts like this is normal. Just like he did in the kitchen.

"It is nice." I nip at my lower lip before adding, "I used to have a balcony off of my bedroom. I liked sitting out there."

He glances back at me for a moment but ends it with a short, almost sad smile and then he leans back, bracing his forearms on the step behind him.

I guess my guard has decided to pretend to be my friend and just sit by me.

"Who designed this place?" I ask him, wanting a distraction and to think of anything but last night.

I woke up alone and that's exactly how I've felt all day. Miserable and alone.

I could sit peacefully in silence on my own, but Jase interrupted that. If he's going to babysit me, then he's going to have to talk to me. A punishment for a punishment. I smile at the snide remark in my head and think about raking up all the good lines I've had since I walked out here. I guess I'm in a bitchy mood. *Good luck to my adversaries.*

"We did," he answers with a smirk that doesn't hide his pride.

"No, you didn't." I don't even hesitate to call him out on his bullshit.

"Why would you think we didn't?" he asks me, a quizzical look on his face.

"You're telling me that you chose lilacs and peonies for the front yard?" I question him, challenging him to tell me that any of the Cross brothers wanted those plants.

Jase's expression turns guarded and he clears his throat as he looks toward the very bushes that give me my argument.

"Our mother wanted lilacs and peonies." His admission is spoken simply, flatly. "She asked for them for Mother's Day, but she died just before," he tells me, and his voice dims toward the end.

"I'm sorry," I say and keep my tone gentle. "I didn't mean-"

"It's fine," he says and waves me off. "I get what you mean, but yeah, we designed it. A few years back." A gust of wind blows by, sweeping some of my hair in front of my face and some behind my back, leaving a chill in its wake and reminding me that it is, in fact, fall.

"Well, it's beautiful," I tell him genuinely. I ignore the chill in the air and wrap my arms around myself. Goosebumps threaten, but I'm not ready to go back inside and the sun feels warm. I could lie in the sun all day, but it looks like I barely have an hour before the trees on the edge of the estate will hide it from me.

"You aren't planning on running, right?" Jase asks me and turns around to look at me with a stern look on his face. "I'd like to keep my balls, and I'm sure Carter would take them if I let you leave."

Laughter erupts from me just because of how serious he looks. His expression changes to one of humor and I find myself surprised by him yet again. Shaking my head, my hair tickling my shoulders I tell him, "Daniel told me it's useless with the guards." I shrug as if it's all a joke.

That's what my captivity is apparently, a fucking joke. Yet, there's only a modest pang of despair from that thought.

Jase huffs and looks over to the right side of the yard. And the way he does it makes me think Daniel's lying. Like Jase is hiding something from me.

"There are guards?" I question him. "Aren't there?"

He looks me up and down for a moment like he's considering telling me something.

"Yeah," he nods and tells me, "we have a few posted along the fences."

I acknowledge what he said with a small nod, but don't respond. Instead, I think about taking a walk to clear my head, but I'm sure Jase would follow me like a lost puppy and I wouldn't be able to think anyway.

"We told them to just taze the pretty brunettes, though."

I give Jase's joke a small laugh and lean forward to run my hand down my legs before considering if he was being truthful. "You're joking?" I ask him, and he shrugs like an asshole with a shit-eating grin on his face.

"You're in a good mood today," I mutter sarcastically.

"Right back atcha."

Time passes easily for a moment, but much to my dismay the clouds come in and capture the sun before I'm ready for the warmth to leave me.

"You want a blanket?" Jase asks me, and I glance at him, watching as he stands up, stretching his back and wincing as he holds his ass.

"You might want to bring a chair out too if you're staying longer," he tells me, and I can't help but smile.

"I may go in; I don't know," I tell him and that's when my dumb heart reminds me that I'll have to see Carter and that he's being weird and distant… and stupid and guarded and a fucking dick. My throat goes dry and I let out a distressed breath. I can't look at Jase when I do. I know he saw, though.

"You know he has it bad for you, right?" he asks me and that dryness in my throat travels higher, making me feel like I'll choke if I speak, so I don't.

"Don't hurt him," Jase tells me, and I whip my eyes to his, craning my neck since he's standing up now.

"Me?" I ask him incredulously. "First of all, I don't hurt people. Secondly, he won't let me close enough to even think of hurting him. Whatever we have is very one-sided and," I try to keep going, but my words crack, and I hate it. I hate that I'm emotional over this. I hate that I'm close to admitting how much I feel for him and that whatever he feels for me isn't even close to being the same. I get why Beauty fell in love with the Beast, but it doesn't change who Carter is. There's no magical rose or kiss that will turn him into a prince. All Carter will ever be is a beast.

That ragged breathing comes back, and I stand up, ready to make a cup of tea and go hide in the den, or maybe the new room, the white room, the pretty room with the replicas of what I used to be in it. Whatever the hell that gilded room is. My hideaway room.

"Hey, hey," Jase's voice is comforting, and he takes a step closer to me, but doesn't touch me as he says, "He's had a hard time."

"Yeah, well, so have I." I bite out the words and surprisingly keep the bitterness in my voice to a minimum.

"He's had a decade of hard times, of people he loved dying, his only friend and brother leaving him, and then other fucked up shit. It was a never-ending cycle until he became the person he is now."

I glance up at Jase, but only for a second because I don't want to cry. He looks sympathetic at least, and genuine, but right now I need to know something will change. I don't need excuses; they're never good for anything.

"What are you doing out here?" Carter's sharp voice makes me jump and I nearly fall backward on the stairs but catch myself. My heart pounds and for the first time, I feel real fear since coming outside.

"Are you crying?" Carter asks me with disbelief and then turns to Jase with a look that could kill.

"She was just talking about you, actually," Jase answers Carter slowly, and the two stare at each other for a long, hard moment.

"I wanted some fresh air for a minute," I say to break up their *moment*, not holding back my anger as I continue. "I got lucky enough that my cage door was open." With those parting words, I step past both of them, brushing against Carter as I do and hating that I breathe in his scent, feel his warmth, and love them both.

I need a cup of tea, a good book if I can find one in my new room, my hideaway room, and some time to ignore the world.

But Carter doesn't give me that. I make it two steps inside the door before he snatches my elbow. I rip my arm away and he looks at me like he doesn't understand. Like I'm the one who's acting out of the ordinary.

"What's wrong?" he asks me, concern lacing the demand to answer him.

"Are you fucking serious?" I don't contain my outrage even though I should have. Carter's eyes narrow and darken, but I don't let it stop me. My heart races and it hurts harder with each thump.

"You're being an asshole. An even bigger one than usual."

"Be gentle," I hear Jase say quietly as he shuts the front door, hiding the last bit of light from the day and leaving us with the sound of his trailing footsteps. Part of me wonders if he's talking to me or to Carter.

"I'm sorry," Carter says through clenched teeth, almost like those words weren't meant to come from him in this moment. He shifts his weight from his left to his right and looks down at me with a look that elicits both fear and that dark desire I can't deny.

A rumble of low irritation settles in his chest as he tells me, "Mind the way you speak to me."

"You should do the same," I bite back without thinking. But it's true. His eyes flash with anger, but he doesn't speak. His jaw is held firm and I bet if he were to clench his teeth any tighter, they'd break. "You treat me like a child," I tell him and then swallow thickly, feeling the knotted ball grow tighter in my throat. "You don't want me near you, you don't talk to me. And last night…" I can't finish because again I feel like I'm going to cry, and I swear I'm not going to. Not here.

He doesn't let me love him. But it's because I'm his whore. I already know that's the answer. It's why he didn't kiss me for as long as he did. I'm meant to be his whore and nothing more.

A moment passes where I'm just breathing. Staring into the eyes of a man who can make me feel so much, but right now it all hurts. I want him to hold me and let me hold him back. I want to slap him and tell him he's an asshole and that I hate him. I want him to tell me that he loves me, and he doesn't think of me like I think he does.

In a matter of seconds, I go through a fantasy where everything will be okay.

"Give me your hand," Carter commands me. I jut out my chin, hellbent on telling him to fuck off, but he has a pull over me. The depth of pain in the hollows of his dark eyes makes me bend to his will. Slowly, I bring my hand up for him to take it. Even if I am just his whore, obeying his command.

I watch as he presses my hand to his phone, flattening it and then turns his back on me, walking to a panel by the front door.

I can feel my eyebrows pinch together.

Carter already said he's sorry once. I doubt he'll say it again. At this point, I don't even know what I want him to say. His words aren't the problem, it's his actions.

"If you're going back outside, grab a coat." His words are stern but there's a trace of melancholy there. *Press your hand here*, he demonstrates. He gave me access. My heart flickers to life, and I hate that it does. It's the things like this that make me question what I am to him.

"I wasn't going back out tonight," I tell him weakly. Wanting more from him, but not knowing how much to push him. My eyes dart from his to the door. Carter's a hard man and maybe he's had a hard life, but I need more than what he gave me last night and today.

I don't know if I'm in a position to ask for it, to demand it, or if

Carter is even capable of giving me more than this. And if he goes through with his plans, all of this is for naught.

"Well, whenever you do," Carter tells me but when my eyes reach his, he moves his attention back to his phone.

I glance down at what he's doing only to find him exit whatever it was and that's when I see today's date.

And that's when this little truce no longer matters.

Nothing matters.

CHAPTER 16

Carter

THE MORE I GIVE HER, THE LESS I HAVE HER.

The moment I let her have access to outside, she stormed away from me. Not with the anger I expected given her outburst, but with a heartache that's inexplicable.

The color drained from her face and she ran from me. Literally ran away from me and straight to the white room. She ignored me when I called out to her and tried to muffle her cries.

Everything shattered in front of me. There was no sign, no warning.

It's my fault; she wasn't ready. I can't push her to move faster when the final deed has yet to be done.

That's the only thing I can think of that would make her run from me like she did.

Her door is locked, a feature I considered excluding, but I know I could knock it down if I needed to.

I haven't moved my eyes from the monitor on my phone but watching her cry hysterically on the floor was brutal. It was fucking torture.

It's been nearly an hour since she's stopped, but she hasn't moved from the floor. Sitting cross-legged and picking at her nails, she's just sitting there, rocking on and off, humming and crying. The only saving grace I have is that my necklace is still around her neck. She hasn't taken it off since I put it on her.

I told you to be gentle, Jase's text message interrupts the feed and I click over to it. He's the only reason I haven't lost my shit. Although I'm on the verge of ripping the door off the hinges of that room and demanding she tell me what set her off.

I fucking was. I quickly text him my reply and then add, *How much time has to pass before I can go in there?*

You can't. He answers immediately and even though a part of me knows he's right, a bigger part of me knows she needs me. She needs someone, and I want to be that someone.

What if we side with Talvery? Over Romano? I'm grasping at straws just to keep her.

It will be a sign of weakness. Jase's response is swift, and the next question is quick to come to my mind. I know no one will understand or respect why I'd allow Talvery to live. Not unless it's clear why. And undeniable.

What if I married her? I type the words, but I can't send them. The thought of her as mine truly, in every way, sends a thread of hope passing before my reach. So close, and so delicate, just like the necklace around her neck. And I think maybe she'd do it. She'd agree if I agreed to spare her family.

But being a wife to a monster only makes her vulnerable. The hope dies as quickly as the flame of a fire only meant to have an ember.

She's not feared, not respected. My enemies would kill her the first chance they got, just to hurt me. I know they would. Just as they tried to take Addison from Daniel.

Jase sends me another text. *She needs to tell you what happened.*

He's right. I need something to fix. Some way to control what went wrong.

If it's her family, you're fucked. Jase texts me again before I can text him back and I almost fling the phone at the wall when it shows on my screen. Instead, I flick to her monitor, but she's not there.

She's gone.

Just as I abruptly stand up, ready to hunt her down wherever she's gone off to, I hear her walking down the hall and slowly she comes into view.

Adrenaline spikes through me and I try to stay still. Because if I move, she might change her mind. She might go back to that fucking room, but I can't let her. I swear to God, I can't let her.

She enters the bedroom with bloodshot eyes, the hair on the side of her face damp from her tears and her face reddened. Fuck, I've never felt pain like this. Even in the cell, she didn't cry like this. She's never cried like this.

It's as if she's mourning.

I can barely breathe, but I swallow the pain down as she steps into the room, refusing to look at me and then glancing at the bathroom.

"There's no bathroom in the other room. The hideaway room," she says, and her words are roughly spoken, but she doesn't cry.

"Come here." The command is soft, an attempt to comfort her. I know she likes being held and I can do that.

I can hold her better than anyone else can.

She walks numbly and when I wrap my arms around her, she doesn't react. She doesn't hold me or lean in. She doesn't stiffen either. She's just there. Her entire body feels frozen under my touch and I instantly pick her up, cradling her in my arms to put her into bed, to force her to rest and lie down with me. Everything will be all right in the morning.

But the second I take a step toward the bed, Aria jolts and slams her palms into my chest, kicking at the same time and deliberately falling out of my arms and crashing onto the floor.

"Fuck," I grunt out and reach down to help her up, but she scampers backward, crawling away from me before standing up again and facing me like a caged animal intent on running.

A thousand shards slice into every bit of me. Into my numb skin, making their way inside my blood and up my throat.

"Aria, tell me what's wrong," I demand but she only shakes her head, pushing her hair away and then rubbing her hand against her tearstained cheek.

"You already know what's wrong," she says woefully, and I know I've failed her.

"You'll forgive me," I speak lowly, my hands clenching into fists.

Her eyes reach mine and they gloss over as she whimpers, "I know." She sniffles once and turns to go to the bathroom, but I can't let her.

"Tell me something," I say, raising my voice but she stops and then slowly turns. "Ask me anything," I add.

A moment passes where she only sways in the knee-length sleep-shirt she's changed into. She almost says something twice, but in the end, she only shakes her head.

Finally, she asks me something I hate, but I know I deserve.

"Will I ever be allowed to leave?" Her question reflects her hopelessness.

"Yes." I want to tell her more, that I'll take her wherever she wants to go, but I'm afraid if I speak too much, she'll break down again. Every word has to be spoken carefully.

"When?" she asks.

"After the war is over," I tell her firmly. "There's no exception to that."

"And when will that happen?" Her words are small, nearly insignificant, reflecting exactly how she must feel.

"Soon." I try to be short, not wanting to hurt her any more than she already is, but also not wanting to lie.

"I would like to at least say goodbye," she whimpers and her voice cracks.

"He knows where you are. If he wanted to say goodbye, he could."

"He knows I'm here?" The shock in her voice is unexpected and I feel like a prick. She's going to have the same reaction she did yesterday when she learned I had someone spying on her.

"Yes." I swallow thickly, but at least she's talking to me.

"And he hasn't come for me?" she asks with such sadness, but it only enrages me. Doesn't she know the man her father really is? He wouldn't risk his life for anyone. Not a damn soul. "How long?" She visibly swallows and hardens her voice as she asks, "How long has he known?"

"Since the dinner," I tell her and then count the days. "Four days."

Aria's face crumples and she covers her mouth with her hand, looking impossibly more dejected somehow.

"When you're at war, you eviscerate them first. I'm sure he has plans…" I want to lie to her, to tell her he has plans to get her after he's killed me. But I don't believe it. Talvery would bomb our estate, killing her with me, if he thought he could get away with it.

"Where does that leave me?" Aria asks in a weak whisper.

"What do you mean?"

"You're going to *eviscerate* the Talverys… where does that leave me?" she asks with surprising strength and tenacity.

"You belong to me." It's the only answer to that question. And the truth she already knows. She's already accepted it. I know she has.

"What would you do if I told you no? That I don't want you?" She steadies her breathing as best as she can and straightens her back. "That I don't want to be your whore anymore?"

"I would know you were lying. And you're not my *whore*." My heart pounds accompanied by a prickling along my skin.

I expect her to come back with some quip asking what she is to me then. But she doesn't. Instead, she tries to destroy what little goodness she's given me.

"What if things changed, and I didn't want you at all?" she asks me with each word clear and just as sharp as the knife it feels like.

"Why would you? Why would you *lie*?" I dare her to tell me it's the truth. That she doesn't want me anymore.

"You would have sent me back after the bath if I'd said 'no,' wouldn't you?" she asks me and I have to take a minute to realize what she's even referring to.

"Our first night? You didn't sleep with me because you wanted to stay out of the cell," I practically spit the words out of my mouth, brimming with outrage. "You didn't even know you weren't going back." My voice rises and I feel it scrape up my throat. "Your heels dug into my ass that night, spurring me on. You fucked me because you *wanted* me." I emphasize each word, taking a steady and dominating step closer to her with each one until I'm so close to her, I can feel the tension radiating from her. "You wanted to know what it would feel like to have my cock inside of you." Lowering my lips to hers I whisper, "Or am I wrong?"

She stares into my eyes and I stare into hers. The mix of greens and blues and golds are vibrant and alive amongst the shards of blotchy red and white.

"Did you want it or not?" I harden my question just as my gut twists with disgust and I start to question if she never wanted me at all. If I was so fucking obsessed with her that I was wrong all this time.

"Yes, I wanted you!" she screams at me although her last word crumbles before it leaves her lips. "And I shouldn't still want you." She doesn't hide the pain when she tells me, "I should hate you."

Relief, sweet relief, is short and minuscule, but there's so much relief in her admission.

"Why's that?" I ask her softly, wanting her to keep going. To work through this because, in weeks, this fight will be meaningless. She'll forgive me. She already knows she will.

"Because you're going to kill my family and everyone I love. That's why." The fight leaves her with the last sentence.

"Yes." I keep my voice strong, although I don't know how. "I am."

"Please don't," she whispers her plea and I wish I'd already done it. I wish I'd already shot the bastard, so she would stop this.

"Is your father a good man?" I ask her, knowing this is going to hurt her, but she's already so low, there's not much lower a little more truth can take her. "Do you think the men who protect him deserve to live long enough so they can try to kill me?"

"They won't," she tries to tell me, shaking her head vigorously and reaching out to take my hand with both of hers but I rip it away. I won't let her beg for his life.

"They've already tried," I say, and my nostrils flare as I tell her. "Right after his drug addicts killed my father. They murdered him for forty dollars and a bag of pills." I remember how my father looked on the metal table in the morgue. How his knuckles were bruised from fighting back.

"And your father was pissed that I dared step onto his turf to kill them. To get revenge. He protected them!" I scream at her and wish I hadn't. Tears flood from her again and she gasps for air. "Your father sent four men to our house. Our rundown, piece of shit house. The house my mother died in. The house you love so much." I can't help but sneer at the thought. "We weren't there. Thank fuck we weren't there."

She's barely breathing through her hands that are covering her face as if they can shield her from the hard truth as I tell her, "He had them burn it down with incendiaries. I should have killed him then, but I couldn't get to him. I sure as fuck can get to him now."

"I'm so sorry," she whimpers, and tries to calm herself down. And I almost reach for her, to hold her, because I want to. Right now I need to hold her too. But then she speaks.

"Things have changed," she offers weakly, wiping the tears from her eyes although they don't stop flowing.

"How can you still defend him? After all this?" The pain won't fucking stop. I'm bleeding out the pain.

"The odds of me allowing your father to live are slim to none. Even if I want you to be happy, you know why he has to die. I bet you even think he deserves it," I tell her. "A small part of you has to think he deserves it."

"You said you'll kill them all, but all of them don't deserve it," she continues to plead with me, not offering me any comfort as I try not to break down remembering the soot and ash that stood in place of the home I'd grown up in. "It's not just my father who will die. Nikolai was my only friend. And my family will stand with my father. You can't kill everyone I've ever loved."

"If they stand against me, they deserve to die."

"Not all of them-"

"Like who? *Nikolai*," I sneer his name with disdain and she flinches.

"Please?" she begs me, but the loss is already clear in her eyes.

I turn my back on her, feeling lonelier than I've felt since she came into this house as I say, "You can make new friends."

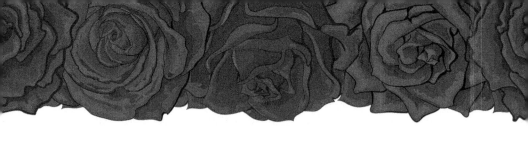

CHAPTER 17

Aria

I T'S MY BIRTHDAY, BUT IT WASN'T UNTIL I SAW CARTER'S PHONE that I knew what the date was.

No one here knows it's my birthday; why would they? They also don't know that yesterday was the anniversary of my mother's death. The day before my birthday.

And for the first time, I didn't go to her grave.

I start to cry again, and I don't know if I'm crying for my mother, for my family, or for Carter and the boy he used to be. I could cry forever, and it wouldn't be enough for the tragedy our families combined have suffered.

My back leans against the wall of the bathroom. To my left, the door is shut and in front of me, the shower is running to drown out the sounds of me crying. I wanted a shower to wash it all away. A hot, scalding shower.

Instead, I'm crouched on the floor by the door. I can barely stand, I'm so lightheaded and exhausted. I don't trust myself in the shower. I don't trust myself or anyone else anymore.

I know my father is a horrible man. A godawful man condemned to hell. I didn't know what he did to Carter. I had no idea. "I didn't know," I whisper to no one. I was so blind for so long and I wish I could go back. I hate all of this. I hate all the pain. I hate that there's no way to go backward.

I can already accept my father's death, as cruel as it sounds. For what he's done, there's no mercy in his death. More than that, he lived when my mother died. And he knows I'm here, yet he's done nothing. Nothing was ever done for my mother's murder. I'm sure my father would do nothing to honor my death.

Flames along the side of the house I've drawn flash before my eyes. I can't forgive him. I can't forgive my father, and I don't even want to know when he's gone. I don't want to give him the honor of mourning him.

But it's not just him.

It's Nikolai too. Why hasn't he come for me? Please, he can't be the same man my father is. A staggering breath leaves me. I know he's not, and I can't accept it.

I won't.

I've never felt so torn—no, so ripped apart.

But I'm sick of crying. I'm sick of dealing with death, time and time again. I'm my father's daughter. I live in a world where attachments are limited and mourning only fuels hatred. I've stayed hidden and quiet, attempting to go unnoticed for years and stay out of the way, and therefore, out of the sights of men who would see me as a bargaining chip. Yet, here I am, in the hands of a man hellbent on murder and vengeance.

But as I thought about how every anniversary of my mother's death, Nikolai brought me to her grave, I started to despair. How every birthday, I woke up finding a text from him and a note that he would take me wherever I wanted to go.

And how that didn't happen this time.

And how it never will again, and there was no way I could stop it. There's no way I can save him.

I mourned the death of a man who still breathes. Not being able to hear him today or talk to him and let him know how I miss him and wish I could do something to stop it all, is a death in and of itself. And in its place is what I've been taught to hold my entire life. Hate.

It's as if Carter's already killed him; he's taken my only companion in this world away from me. And the anger in that realization grows by the second. Hardening my heart.

Maybe next year, when I visit my mother's grave, Nikolai's will be near.

The thought and visions of an old gravestone next to a newly carved one bring a new flood of tears.

That's all I can do. To mourn them.

To mourn us all. And to cling to my hate for a man I'm growing to love.

A soft click causes my eyes to lift to the doorknob and I watch it slowly turn. Haphazardly wiping my eyes, I slowly rise to my feet, leaning against the wall as Carter opens the door. Steam that fills the room drifts to the open space and the hot air makes my heated face feel that much hotter.

Carter stops after one step in the room, staring at the empty shower for a moment before turning to me when I let out a heavy and broken breath. The look in his eyes showed true fear until it settled on me.

I saw fear in the eyes of a man who does nothing but revel in it.

Still, I feel like nothing beneath him as he stares down at me. "I thought you were in the shower." His eyes roam my face, searching for something.

I try to swallow, but I can't. Instead, I shake my head softly and pray for him to leave. I should have stayed in the hideaway room.

"I don't like to see you like this." Carter's statement sounds genuine, but all I can give him in return is a sick and sarcastic huff of a laugh. It croaks from me and I can barely breathe in after. Reaching for the tissues by the sink, I turn my back to him. My shoulders are still shuddering with the mess of sorrow that weighs down on me.

His large hand settles down on my shoulder, carefully, gently, and he tries to pull me close to him. To hold me like he's done before. With half a step forward, he attempts to hug me from behind, he even closes his eyes and lowers his lips to kiss my bare shoulder.

But I'm quick to turn, push him away and step out of his embrace. He can't hold me and think it makes it all go away. Not anymore.

The tissue is balled in my fist as I push him again, shoving him away.

He doesn't let me comfort him, so I won't let him do the same to me. To use my pain against me. So, he can do as he pleases, regardless of the consequences they hold for me.

"No, you don't get to touch me." My words come out sharply with a fierceness I didn't know I still had in me. Rage heats in his dark eyes as his expression hardens and he stills where he is, his jaw tense and his shoulders rigid.

"Tell me now that you don't want to throw me back in my cell."

Again, emotion cracks my words. I stare back at him, waiting for a response. It's difficult not to see the sorrow and fear in his gaze that he's showed me before.

"The only place I want to throw you is on my bed to remind you of what I can give you." He speaks quietly, in a deep tenor that sounds raw to my ears. "You still belong to me," he reminds me.

My lips twitch up into a sad smile. Sad for him that he thinks he could possibly ever have me the way he wishes. It will never happen.

A flicker of anger, the cluck of his tongue, one step toward me, and Carter morphs back into the man I recognize from weeks ago. Cold and calculated.

But you can't go back. He, of all people, should know better.

"Kneel," he commands but I can hear the desperation in his voice. He may want to pretend but he knows can't control me when I'm like this. I can barely control myself.

"Send me back to the cell." My demand comes out strong and with defiance, no one could deny.

I'll be better in the cell. Better there than the hideaway where I'm simply avoiding him. The cell leaves me no options. I need it. I need to get away from the man standing in front of me.

If Carter touches me, I'll cave. I know I will. I'll forget the pain and the anger. I'll forget to mourn. There will be nothing of me left but what he wants there to be.

I'm weak for him. "I need to be away from you," I whisper with harsh anger on my tongue.

"No." His denial of my request should only strengthen my resolve to disobey. But my limbs feel weak, and I so desperately need to be held. I want him to be the man to do it.

"Do I need to try to run?" I ask him in an obstinate breath, not daring to look him in the eyes.

"As if you could get away from me." His answer comes out softer than it should. And with more comfort than I can resist.

"Fuck you," I spit out at him in a last-ditch effort.

"You really want to go back to your cell, don't you? I could always keep the door open if you prefer. So you can pretend I'm the monster you want me to be."

I could always keep the door open. The words force tears to my eyes. He would take it away. Take away the pretense that I have absolutely no choice. Instantly, I hate him for doing this to me.

"I hate you," I spit at him, every bit of anger and sadness mixing into a deadly concoction.

Carter's eyes blaze with heat in the mix of all of this as he steps closer to me. With each step forward he takes, I take one in reverse until the back of my knees hit the edge of the tub.

"Admit it," he whispers so closely to me I can feel how hot he is. The hot water sprays down behind me, filling the room with white noise and heat. I can't take my eyes from Carter's as he leans in closer. His shoulders cage me in and his angular jaw holds nothing but dominance as he tells me, "Admit that you understand, and you know this has to happen. Admit it," he asserts.

"There's always a choice." I barely get the words out as he touches me. As he lays a finger, a single finger on my collarbone and lets it travel lower. His touch is fire to my skin. And I'll be damned if I don't want more of it. When my eyes reach his again, my heart twists with unbearable pain. The sadness conveyed in his expression reflects his low tone as he utters, "It's comforting to think we have choices."

When his eyes lift from my throat, where his finger travels up and down in a soothing stroke, the pain in his expression vanishes and once again the hardened man commands me, "Admit it. And admit you're mine."

Slap! I can't explain why I did it, even as my hand stings with severe pain, my lungs refuse to move, and fear overwhelms my body. A bright red handprint marks Carter's face and slowly he tilts his head back up to face me.

I slapped him. I struck Carter Cross.

One breath and he grabs both my wrists and shoves them above my head.

"Carter." The way I say his name is like a plea although I don't know what I'm begging for. I'm in over my head, feeling lightheaded and full of nothing but fear. Fear of him, of what's to come. Of everything.

"Aria," Carter's voice is strangled and reflects exactly how I feel.

I open my eyes to beg him for forgiveness, to apologize, but his eyes close and he crashes his lips to mine.

Pressing them deeply to mine with a savagery I need to feel, nipping my bottom lip, devouring me until my own lips part and my tongue seeks his.

Fuck. I need this. I need him.

His fingers tighten around my wrists and he stretches them higher as his other hand roams down my body.

I don't know at what point the mourning and defiance changed to this. To the absolute need to be fucked by him, worshipped by his body. The feel of his powerful hold and brutal touch that turns soft the instant I need it to be, is addictive.

It's worse than any drug.

His left hand nearly releases my wrists, but the second I try to move, he tightens them again. "Carter," I say, and his name is a strangled moan as I squirm against the hard wall while his right hand finds my panties and shreds the lace. The thin fabric falls down my leg, tickling me in its wake and during all this, every nerve ending in my body is on edge.

"Aria," Carter moans my name, his scruff scratching my shoulder as he breathes against my neck. I'm so hot. Everything is hot and ready to be lit aflame.

His thick fingers drag along my pussy, the moisture there aiding in how easily they travel up to my clit then back down to my entrance. Pausing each time to tease me and bring me closer to the edge.

"Tell me you don't want me, that you're really done with me and I'll stop," Carter whispers and then drops his head to the crook of my neck. All I can hear is the mix of our heavy breathing and the white noise of the shower behind us.

My eyes open as I shudder and try to breathe, to make sense of any of this, and that's when I see us in the mirror. A sad, ragged girl with red eyes and nothing but pain reflected in them. Pinned to the wall by a man built to consume and bred by this world to hate.

And my heart breaks.

It breaks for both of us.

I don't want to cry anymore. "Please," is the only whimper I can manage, and I don't know what I'm pleading for.

Maybe just to take the pain away, if only for a little while.

Carter's strong chest presses hard against mine, trapping me and overwhelming me as he shoves his fingers deep inside of me while ravaging every inch of exposed skin with his lips.

I heave in a breath; my neck bows and my body rocks with the immediate pressure building deep in my belly. It rocks through me like waves. So close and threatening.

My nipples harden and my toes curl, my hips threaten to buck, to move away knowing the heavy hit is coming. But with Carter, there's nowhere to run. And the pleasure is an onslaught, an unforgiving bliss I'm submerged in.

My body is paralyzed by the blinding pleasure, and it's only then that Carter releases me. He doesn't let me sag against the wall, he immediately grabs my body, hugging me to him until he can lower me to the floor and shove his pants down.

He fucks me like it's the only thing he's ever wanted.

He takes his time, although each thrust is punishing.

I claw at his back and he bites my shoulder.

I scream out his name and he screams out mine.

Neither of us breathing, save the air from each other's lungs.

The heat, the passion, the need... it's all undeniable. I can admit that. Of everything Carter wants me to admit, I can admit that he has a part of me I didn't know existed and a part of me no one else will ever have.

"How can I hate you and love you at the same time?" I ask him in staggered words as I struggle to breathe. My eyes open wide, realizing what I said, but Carter either doesn't hear or doesn't care as he climbs off of me, his cum leaking from me as I lie on the cold floor, panting.

A part of me cracks as he stands and runs his hand over his face and then down the back of his head. Standing with his back to me, a part of me shatters. I'm such a fool. A foolish girl at the whim of a monster. Lost in my pain until he can overpower it with pleasure.

He carried me to his bed. Wordlessly.

He wiped between my legs with a warm, damp cloth and then carried me to his bed. I can't look at him; I can't do anything but lie here. And every tick of the clock makes me wonder if I should climb out and go sleep on the floor of the hideaway.

My heart hurts too much.

At least he's not touching me. Every time the bed groans and the covers shift over my naked body I tense, thinking he's going to hold me, but he doesn't.

I replay the last twenty-four hours over and over again.

"Why did you look scared when I wasn't in the shower?" I finally ask him, breaking the silence and the pretense that I could even try to sleep. "I don't understand." I give him the reasoning for the question as it came seemingly from nowhere. They're the only words that have been spoken between us since the slap, apart from the confession that went unheard.

"Jase had a lover once," Carter answers me, softly spoken, but rough and deep. I can hear him breathe heavily, feel it even with the dip of the bed and then he adds, "She killed herself in the shower."

My lips part, although I stay lying on my side, my back to him. More pain. More tragedy. I wonder what Jase did to her that made her kill herself. I didn't think he was capable of such a thing. The question is on my tongue, but I don't ask it.

Carter had fear in his eyes when I wasn't standing in the shower because for a moment, for one brief moment, he thought I was lying dead in the tub.

CHAPTER 18

Carter

I WONDER IF SHE REALLY LOVES ME.

I'll never forget the way she said it. It gutted me. She may grow to love me, but she'll always hate me.

I can't blame her for that, but I want to hear the words apart from the hatred. So, I can pretend it comes without a caveat.

I want her to say it again, and this time to mean it. Those words shouldn't have fallen so recklessly as I pushed her to the edge of pleasure. They're addictive and they did something to me I can't describe.

She's drawing so slowly today. Lying in front of the fire in the den, she's only been working on one picture. One single piece of art for the last three hours. I'm still not sure what it is, all I can make out is a field of flowers, but there's something beyond the black smudges of petals.

I don't have time to question her about it though. Other questions are too precious to be wasted by another moment of silence.

"What do you want more than anything in the world?" The fire crackles once my deep voice has broken the void of silence between us. The tension is still there, but it can't exist forever. I won't let it.

Aria's hazel eyes lift, and she peeks at me through her dark lashes, not bothering to move from lying on her elbows. She glances back at the drawing and visibly swallows before shrugging slightly and looking back up at me as if she doesn't have to answer.

At this point, she doesn't. I don't care what she does or how she treats me with the door closed, so long as she doesn't run or hurt herself.

"I want my family to be untouchable," I confess to her.

"That's quite an ambition," she answers, crossing her ankles and still staring at the drawing pad in front of her. She's still cold.

"Isn't that what you want, too?" I ask her. "That would seem to be especially desirable given the current environment." I can't keep the smug tone from my voice to cover up the pain from her reaction. If she would talk to me, she'd see. She has to see that there's only one way for this to end. And once it's over, it will all be better. I'll make it better for her.

"I want everyone to fuck off and leave me alone," she answers with a bite that tips the corner of my lips up into a half smile. I love the fight in her. She'll live, she'll survive. A girl like her knows how to survive if nothing else.

"Anger is something I didn't expect. And someone like you shouldn't be left alone," I tell her.

"I don't want to cry today. So, I'll settle for anger." Her answer comes with muted irritation. She throws down the stick of charcoal onto the paper and then meets my gaze to ask, "Why shouldn't I be alone?"

"It's one thing to say you want to be alone. It's another to truly be it. You pretend like you don't exist in the same world as I do. Locking yourself away and acting like that's what you want. But you belong here. You were born to this life. You need to accept that. And loneliness in this world leaves you vulnerable and that's a life neither of us can afford."

"I was alone in the cell," she says solemnly. I don't think she slept at all last night; I know I didn't. "I survived."

A melancholy huff leaves me. "You weren't alone. The first night you slept, I'd drugged your dinner to make sure you would. So, I could tend to your wounds and the cuts on your wrists."

"You did?" Her eyes are filled with shock. "Why?"

"You were mine to take care of." My shoulders stiffen, as does my gaze and she drops hers, falling back to the smudges of charcoal. "I knew you would live. And you would break quickly. Everything needed to happen quickly."

"Why?" she asks me, and I don't know how she can't know at this point.

"I'd intended to show how willing you were to be mine to everyone who was watching. So, there would be no question where you stood in the war."

Her eyes close and she chews the inside of her cheek at my admission, trying to keep her emotions in check. I know the truth of the situation is raw for her. An open wound. But she needs to see it all. She has to accept everything for what it is.

"Instead, there's no question where I stand when it comes to you. I never liked Stephan. Once a traitor, always a traitor. But giving his death to you, allowing you to have vengeance? It spoke more words than I realized it would."

Her face scrunches with the painful memory and then she hangs her head, avoiding my gaze and rubbing her cheek against her shoulder. She pushes the hair out of her face and when she speaks, she doesn't look up.

"But you're still going to…" She doesn't bother finishing her question. I know she already knows. She'll come to accept it.

"Your father doesn't deserve what he has. He's not half the man Romano is. And Romano is a pathetic excuse for his title. They'll both die. Along with everyone who fights for them."

"Please. Not everyone. I'll do anything." Her words are spoken with conviction and she lifts her hazels up to meet my dark gaze. "You want me to kneel at your feet? I'll kneel."

She still doesn't get it. And my heart aches for hers.

"What if I wanted you to stand at my side?" I ask her, my heart racing in my chest. It's a risk to give her more. Every time I do, she fails to cope with it. But I need her to know what I really want from her. What I desire more than anything.

"You would tower over me," she answers.

"That's not how it works, songbird. And it's not what I want. You've only ever had broken wings, but I can show you what true freedom is."

"You're still going to kill my family?" she asks me as if that answer is the end all, be all.

"I'm going to do a number of things you're going to disapprove of. You need to accept that." My answer is hard, leaving no room for any intolerance. "I'm not a good man."

"Is this what it would be like to stand by your side? To have no control and to simply accept what you do?" I'm surprised by her answer but eager to discuss terms.

That's not how it works,
songbird.
And it's not what I want.

You've only ever had
broken wings, but I can
show you what
true freedom is.

"On some matters, you'll never have control, and you'll have to accept what I choose. Whether or not you want to know about them is your decision." I know part of her despair is because she knows everything, yet she's a casualty with little recourse.

"I'm sorry you know as much as you do," I tell her and then almost take it back, thinking she'll take it offensively and that's not what I intended.

She doesn't though. Instead, she cracks, showing me the side of her I love. The raw vulnerability.

"I don't want this life," she whispers, slowly pushing the art away so she can rest her head against the rug. The light from the fire licks along her skin.

"We don't get to choose," I remind her. I've told myself so many times that I wish things were different, but you live the life you're given.

"You're wrong," she tells me as if she has another option.

"Do you love what I do to you? How I fuck that pretty little cunt and force you to scream out my name?" I'm crude and harsh with my question.

She doesn't answer me, but she doesn't have to.

"Then no, you don't have a choice. I had a choice once. I chose wrong."

"You'll get tired of me," she whispers, her eyes seemingly vacant but the depths of them harboring pain. "One day I won't be a shiny new toy. One day, you'll want someone to fight you and I'll have none left in me." Tears pool in her eyes. "One day, the idea of shoving your dick inside of me won't interest you in the least."

She has no idea how wrong she is. I'm only growing more obsessed with her. Breaking every rule to satisfy her.

Risking everything to heal the broken pieces of her she refuses to acknowledge.

I'll never let her go because she isn't a toy. She isn't a challenge. She isn't the fuckdoll she thinks she is and secretly loves being.

"Will you let me go then?"

"Never."

She turns to face the fire and I whisper to her, "You're so wrong, Aria. If you weren't so set on hating me, you'd see."

"You give me every reason to hate you," she tells me. In the reflection from the mirror above the mantel, I see the fire dancing in her eyes.

She'll never know how much her words hurt me. Or maybe she does, and that's what she was after.

"Why are you doing this to me? Why me?" she asks me in a single breath and I offer her a singular truth in return.

"Your father set a series of events in motion," I reply, remembering the night his men took me from the street.

I remember how the pills spilled into the gutter even as they slammed their fists against my jaw and I fell to the cold cement. With her, I only see what lies ahead. But she's caught in the past. And that's what will destroy us.

"So, it's my father's fault?" she asks me with a sadness in her eyes, as if I've robbed her of some fantasy.

"No, it's mine." My confession confuses her for a moment, but before she can say anything else, I continue.

"I thought I loved you," I tell her with a bitter hardness that forces the words to sound violent on my tongue. Her eyes widen as she turns back and stares at me. Her stance changes to one of prey, realizing it's stumbled into its worst enemy. The shock in her eyes fuels me to push her farther. For her to realize the man I truly am.

"For a long time after I left your home, when they kicked me back out onto the street after brutalizing me, I thought I loved whoever belonged to the sweet voice that stopped them from killing me." Aria's expression changes to one of fear and knowing.

I tell her to break whatever thoughts she has of love. And whatever thoughts I have of it. Weakness crushes down on me as I tell her what I used to think. What I expected this to be when I stabbed the knife into her picture and told Romano to bring her to me.

"I knew I hated your father, and eventually I hated everything. I hated you for letting me live." Aria is silent, waiting with bated breath to see what else I'll say.

"I'm condemned to hell. Of everyone on this Earth, God knows I deserve to burn. And it's because I was allowed to live. It's because of you."

"It has nothing to do with me. My father—"

"It has *everything* to do with you," I tell her, feeling the rage from the memory take over. "You're the one who banged on the door and pleaded with your father. I was so foolish. For a long time, I thought when you were crying out, 'I need you,' that in some fucked up way, you were calling out for me."

As I take another step closer to her, the wildness returns to Aria's eyes, the fear I know and love swirls within them. Her cunt is still feeling the pleasure I give her, while her heart beats with the knowing fear of me.

"I didn't—" she starts to protest, and I stop her.

"You're the bird in the forest who lured the child out of safety until he fell into a black hole he could never get out of. And still, the bird sings so beautifully, taunting the child as he becomes a man of hardness and hate, stuck in a hell he didn't know was coming. Do you know what that man dreams of more than anything?" I ask her, remembering the moment my gratitude changed to hate for the very girl who sits in front of me.

She barely shakes her head, not taking her gaze from me.

"First to get out, for the longest time, just a way to get out. But when he realizes he can't, that there's no changing who he is and where he's damned to, he searches for the songbird. Eager to capture it. Just to silence the song forever. That's why I wanted you."

I lean forward, pinning her with my gaze as I tell her, "Aria, that was before I held you. No matter how much you choose to hate me, I swear I'll never let you go. You mean so much more to me than I would dare to admit to anyone."

CHAPTER 19

Aria

BANGED ON THE DOOR.

The stove ticks with the flame licking up from the burner and I turn it to medium before setting the pot of water on it.

I can't get over Carter's confession.

I would never go to the half of the estate where my father does his business. My mother died on the second floor in that half of the house and I swear I can still feel her there.

Whatever he thinks happened, didn't.

I never interrupted my father's work or even attempted to be anywhere near his business. I never banged on the door. I never called out that I needed anyone for anything.

I wouldn't dare.

Carter chose wrong. The woman who called out to him and saved him… she wasn't me.

I'm not his songbird luring him into the forest. I'm not the girl he thought he loved yet grew to hate.

It was never supposed to be me.

The hollow emptiness I've felt since he left me there in the den all alone, is unexplainable. I should be happy; I should tell him how wrong he was to take me. I should confess that voice he heard didn't belong to me. Instead, I swallow the dark secret down and let it choke me as I watch the pot of water boil.

"What are you making?" Daniel asks me and disrupts my thoughts. "Damn, you look like hell," he says, scratching the back of his head. In bare feet, faded jeans, and a plain white t-shirt, he looks relaxed, but he can't hide the exhaustion in his expression.

"Ditto," I tell him and spoon the potatoes into the pot. I've already cut everything else I need to make potato salad. Now I just wait. My mother used to make the best potato salad. I swear it's better the day after though, once it sits in the fridge for a full night.

I'm not hungry at all. I'm simply going through the motions, pretending the truth of my situation doesn't destroy every fiber inside of me.

Daniel opens the fridge as I spoon in the last few chunks. With the door open and his face hidden from me as he reaches for something, he asks me, "Want to talk about it?"

A genuine, yet sad smile tugs at my lips.

"You want to talk about *your* problems?" I ask him back.

"I asked you first," he says with a hint of humor, shutting the door and revealing a jug of orange juice.

"You sound like your brother," I tell him absently.

"Well shit," he tells me, pulling out a glass. It clinks on the counter as he smiles at me. "Don't go offending me left and right there, Aria," he jokes, and I let the small laugh bubble up although it sounds subdued and futile.

I stir the hard potatoes even though I know I don't need to. But I completely forgot the timer, and the realization makes me lean forward to start it.

With the beep of it being set, and the numbers counting down, I take a step back and lean against the counter.

"What'd he do this time?" Daniel asks me, mirroring my position as he leans on the other side.

"Nothing new," I tell him and the honesty in those words is what hurts the most.

The soft smile that lingered on his lips vanishes at my reply, and so I focus on the numbers, watching them as if I could speed them up if only I stare hard enough.

"Why won't he let me leave?" I ask him in a whisper.

Because he thinks you're someone else. Someone who saved him.

My throat dries, and my words crack as I tell him, "This isn't right."

It's silent for a long while, with only the sound being the water beginning to boil again.

"Because he cares for you," Daniel finally says, and I look him in the eyes, letting him see the real effect Carter Cross has on me.

"What a way to show it. Killing my family is just the cherry on top." My sarcastic response makes Daniel's expression harden.

"I have opinions of your father as well," he tells me softly, in a tone I haven't heard from him yet. My heart slams once and I'm forced to look him in the eyes. "I'll keep them to myself though," he tells me and then opens the fridge to put the orange juice back.

No doubt so he can leave me. So he doesn't have to tolerate my self-pity.

"And what about everyone else? Everyone I've ever known and loved?" I can barely breathe as I push him for justification.

"If you knew the truth," he tells me, facing me after shutting the fridge doors, "you wouldn't blame him." There's so much sincerity from him, I almost question my resolve.

"It's not just my father. So, I can, and I will blame him," I respond despondently, although I'm undecided on whether or not I believe my own words. When I look up at Daniel, my heart races chaotically and my body freezes.

Addison walks into the kitchen slowly, glancing from Daniel to me before offering me a small smile.

I can't breathe, and I don't know what to do. Anxiety pricks at my skin as she takes me in. My hair is still damp from the shower and I'm wearing a sleep shirt. I know my eyes show the lack of sleep and I look like a fucking mess.

More than that, I know Addison doesn't know who I am. She's normal. She's not forced to stay here like I am. Not the same way, at least.

Daniel plays it off far better than I do, wrapping his arm around Addison and giving her a soft kiss that forces her eyes back to him.

Shifting my weight, I glance at the timer and consider just leaving. I don't know what I'd say to her if I could even look her in the eyes right now.

Hi Addison, I know all about you and I know you don't know anything about me. I'm Carter's whore and he's going to kill my entire family soon, so I'm not allowed to leave. Nice to meet you.

Although that's not quite true. He admitted I mean more to him. *But it's because he thinks I'm someone else.* I've never felt more shame than I do right now. Every time I remember his words, I want to cry. Because he never wanted me and the moment he finds out the truth, he'll throw me away.

"Addison," Daniel's voice breaks up my spiteful thoughts as he says, "This is Aria. She's with Carter."

She's with Carter.

His words echo in my head as Addison smiles sweetly, pushing a lock of hair behind her ear and giving me a small, but friendly wave while staying where she is. "It's nice to meet you," she says kindly although she glances back at Daniel, no doubt wondering what's wrong with me.

"Hi," I offer up a single word and it croaks. I'm not *with* Carter; I'm against him. Except of course when I'm writhing underneath him.

"She's having a hard day," he tells her softly. My heart thumps in the way that hurts. The way that makes it feel like it's a tight ball that needs air and without it, it only gets tighter.

"Sorry." I swallow and tell her, "I'm not usually this weird." I roll my eyes and force a huff of a laugh up to ease the tension.

"You're not weird," she says and shakes her head at my words. "Just looks like you're having a hard day. That's totally reasonable," she adds with her hands waving out in front of her. "No judgment here."

I get the feeling that Addison is lonely from her tone, from her awkwardness. Or maybe I'm just projecting what I feel myself.

"Let's get back," Daniel says and the tightness in my throat grows. At least I got to meet her, and he said I'm with Carter. It's respectable. Well... to some. I'm sure to her it is.

"Sure," she tells him softly, with an answer spoken so low it's just for him, but then she raises her voice and speaks to me.

"Do you want to come with me to the gym tomorrow?"

I blink at her question. I'm surprised by it and not sure what to say.

"I just took a shower, so..." she starts to say and then rocks on her heels, wrapping her long hair around her wrist nervously.

I don't know if I'm even allowed to talk to her alone. Anger rises inside of me. I don't need permission. And one day, she'll know what I am and why I'm here. I can't hide it forever. Then what will she think of me?

"I don't know," I offer her. My gaze flickers to Daniel, but he stands easily beside Addison as if nothing's wrong. Like none of this is abnormal. The way the Cross boys do.

"Come on, we can drink wine while we do the back thing. It feels good," she says playfully. "I don't even like working out," she says and then looks at Daniel as if looking for permission, but not waiting for any. "But being locked up here is killing me and it's at least something different to do."

I watch the happiness drain from her and the smile only staying where it is because she's forcing it. "If you want company, I could really use some girl time," she says softly and then rolls her eyes as the emotion plays on her face. "Sorry," she huffs, shaking her head and leaning into Daniel as he holds her close. "I'm having a bad day too."

"I can work out," I tell her immediately, saying what she wants to hear just to take away her pain. I bite my lip as my heart sputters, wondering if Carter will stop me from going.

"I'm not a runner though," I warn her, trying to lighten the mood and force a small smile to my lips.

A genuine happiness lights up her face and she nods enthusiastically. "Oh, yeah, for sure." She laughs a little and breathes out easily, "If you ever see me running, you should start running too because there's someone behind me trying to get me," she jokes and doesn't see how Daniel responds. How his lips turn down and then press into a thin line. She's oblivious to it, but when she glances at him, he's quick to hide it. To offer her a peck of a kiss and then tell me although he's still looking at her, "I'm surprised she's using the gym at all."

She shrugs and points out, "There's not much else to do."

"We could just drink in the den?" I offer, grasping at a way to make it more acceptable. Carter knows I go to the den, so if Addison happened to come in there, he couldn't blame me for that. Well, he could. He'll probably find some way to stop it from happening as it is.

"That sounds perfect," she tells me with a broad smile. Daniel drags her away just as the timer goes off on the stove.

With a genuine smile and a short wave, she says sweetly, "I'll see you tomorrow."

It's kind of her, but I have no idea if I will.

Seeing how blind she is to everything, I'm reminded of how little I knew in my father's house. Even being oblivious to everything else, she still has a sad smile. I guess there's not much difference between knowing the truth and being blind to it. The effect is still the same.

CHAPTER 20

Carter

S HE'S SO LOST, MY ARIA. I CAN'T TAKE MY EYES FROM HER AS
she stares at the comforter, her fingertips barely grazing it
before she pulls the sheets back. Her expression is a mix of
emotions. Sadness, confusion, the barest hint of anger. As the seconds
pass, her chest flushes, and the lust of knowing what's to come takes
over. But her brow stays furrowed as the bed groans with her small
weight and the sheets rustle.

I don't think for a second that she's gotten over her anger, but it's
not as raw as it was hours ago, let alone where she was yesterday. I
still don't know what set her off at the front door, but I'm going to
find out. She can't hide from me forever and I don't buy that bullshit that there was nothing in particular. I watched the surveillance
cameras over and over again. Something happened. I just don't know
what.

I loosen my watchband, feeling the slick metal brush against my
wrist before placing it back in its spot in the drawer. My gaze is still
pinned on Aria, who's looking anywhere but back at me, her fingers
fiddling with her necklace. Another second, another heavy breath.

The internal war is waning, but war leaves casualties, and I
know she's taking record of everything she's lost and what's left of the
woman she once was. I watch as she swallows, her chest rising higher
and her breathing quickening.

She's so close to submitting everything to me. So, fucking close.

She doesn't even see it.

"You can't stay mad at me forever," I tell her as I pull my shirt
over my head, grabbing it by the back of the collar.

I kick off my pants and ready myself to join her in bed, wondering if she'll tense when I wrap my arms around her. It's only fair that

it guts me every night when she does it. I'm more than certain I deserve a harsher punishment.

"Do you know Addison spoke to me today?" she asks me with an edge of anxiousness rather than acknowledging what I've said. She doesn't seem to have taken my confession in the den earlier to heart, but she's more guarded now than she was before. Maybe she doesn't remember, but I thought it would change something between us. For the better.

My lips twitch with the hint of a feigned smile. "I do," I tell her, and she finally looks at me with a pleading expression.

"And?" she asks with clear curiosity but the desperation weighing heavier.

"And what?" I ask her as if I can't comprehend her line of questioning. Addison knows who I am, and I agree this situation is less than moral, but if she were to learn the truth, she would still love my brother. She'd still be family. She'll forgive me. Daniel's sins have been substantial, and she's forgiven him, mostly.

"Are you going to let me go?"

Her bottom lip wavers, but she waits patiently as I drop my hand to hers, thinking carefully about my next words.

"You'll like Addison," I tell her genuinely. "I won't stop you, and I won't be there to control you; I don't have any interest in it either."

"So, you don't care?" she questions.

"I care, but not in the way you think. Why would I want to stop you two from getting to know one another?" I ask her and then add, "My brother won't either. You two should get to know each other." I don't let on how anxious I am to hear what she tells Addison and whether or not she confides in her.

"I could tell her you're holding me hostage, that you trapped me in a cell for weeks..." she answers me with a cocked brow although she can't hide the sadness that still lingers in her expression. I can see so clearly that the very idea of how we became what we are now, tortures her.

"Would you really want to bring her into this?" I ask her pointedly. "She's having a hard time, and you and I both know she wouldn't react well to that."

"What if I say something I shouldn't?" she whispers quietly with genuine concern. I watch as she picks at the blanket, clearly on edge with the prospect of saying something that would cause more problems for our already delicate situation.

"Don't," is the only answer I have for her. "Be careful with what you say."

The silence stretches for a moment and I consider her.

"Maybe it's best you forget all this for a moment, and just talk to her as you would have anyone else a month ago."

I have to be so delicate with her. Ever so delicate. She doesn't answer, although the careful tiptoeing around her words slips away as she adjusts under the covers.

"We have other matters to discuss," I tell her as my thumb runs along the stubble of my jaw.

Although she nods, a heavy sigh leaves her in a staggering way, the sleep showing in her expression. She's overwhelmed and exhausted. Neither of us slept last night. Even after crying half the night, she woke every hour.

"What happened yesterday can't happen again. You have a choice. You can take your punishment now, or you can have it after your date with Addison."

Her body tenses and she struggles to form words, her lips parting and strangled breaths taking the place of whatever her question is.

"You won't be sending me back to the cell then?" she finally asks, her voice as strained as her body is stiff.

"That wouldn't do you any good." I wrap my arm around her, comforting her and leave a small kiss on the crown of her head. I whisper, "I told you, you shouldn't be left alone. This punishment is to benefit us. I promise you that," I tell her and feel the weight of everything looming in my thoughts.

I can see her swallowing her words. Practically reading her mind, I can see how she wants to tell me that we would be better if I would let this war go or let her go, but she doesn't dare speak it.

"What is it?" she asks me.

"I haven't decided yet," I tell her honestly.

"Tomorrow then," she tells me softly with defeat in her expression and it shreds me, but tomorrow she'll see.

"Is this what it will always be like?" she asks. "I do something you don't like, and I'm punished for it and then fucked until I forget I hate you?"

I don't think she meant her question to be humorous, but a short chuckle makes my chest shake. Running my fingers down her arm, I decide to tell her more, to set boundaries. But with them comes new rules.

"In the bedroom, I want you to obey. Anywhere else," my blood pumps harder and hotter as I finish, "I want you as mine."

"There's a difference?" she asks with feigned sarcasm. That mouth of hers is going to get her in trouble. Her disobedience shouldn't make me as hard as it does. As much as I love it, tomorrow night she'll be punished. There's no mistaking that.

"You already know there is," I say and although my voice comes out deep and foreboding, I try to lighten it. "It's time for a new game, Aria."

"No games." Her voice rises, and she has to lower it before adding, "I'm done playing games with you, Carter."

"You'll never be done with me." My words whisper against her skin. "You already know that."

Her fingernails dig into the sheets, pulling them tighter as she continues to avoid looking at me. I know why she doesn't want to meet my heated gaze. It will make hers fill with desire, too. She can't deny what she feels for me and how much power is in the tension between us. The push and pull that drives me wild does the same for her. The difference is that I can admit it; even if it will destroy me, I can fucking admit what she does to me.

"What do you want?" she asks me although she stares straight ahead, her expression flat and indifferent. "Tell me what you want from me," she says, and a spike of anger plays in her tone. "Tell me what it means to be yours," she asks through clenched teeth and I merely stare back at her. She already knows. We both know that she knows exactly what it means.

"Here you fuck me... you punish me like you did before." I don't miss how her eyes darken as she gazes around the room, looking to where I've spanked her, throat fucked her, made her cum harder than she ever had before.

"Yes," I tell her and watch as her pupils dilate and her legs scissor to ease some of the heat growing between her legs.

"And what do you expect outside of this room?" she asks and when she does, her voice wavers. She knows how much is at stake.

"For them to fear you." Her eyes flash to mine and suddenly my songbird is very much interested. I continue, "The way they fear me."

She laughs a sad and pathetic sound, ripping her gaze from me as she shakes her head. Her soft lips part, but no words come out and instead, she continues to shake her head and stares at the knob of the bathroom door across the room. Looking anywhere but at me.

"Fear is easy to attain," I tell her the simple fact. And it truly is. Keeping it is the curse that never fades. But I can bear the weight of that burden. She only needs to play the part. They have to believe it.

She shakes her head gently as if I don't understand. She tells me, "I want to draw. Maybe own a studio one day. That's my ambition. Or sell some of my pieces to people who would love them the way I do. I want them to feel what I feel when they look at them." I can see the light of hope in her eyes as she tells me a dream of hers I would never have known otherwise. I can give her that, so easily. All she had to do was tell me. "That's the only thing I've ever wanted beyond being happy. Having a family and making them happy."

A family.

I can give her that too, and the thought of her swollen with my child makes me force back a groan of want in my throat. Closing my eyes, I remind myself she needs time. All in good time. Once the war is over, everything will change.

Opening my eyes, I ask her, "And what does any of that have to do with what I've asked of you?" My question catches her off guard. "You forget the world you live in." A family, a gallery. It's all so easily attainable. But only when we have control. And that requires fear. They *must* fear her.

I ask her, "You want that studio? A gallery? Children, Aria? Do you think your name alone is one that wouldn't put a target on your back?" She flinches at the question and I can see the doubt and worry play across her face. Her lips turn down as her breathing picks up. It doesn't matter if Aria stands beside me or not; the minute she was given the name Talvery, her entire life was at risk.

"Anything that gives you pride or happiness is a weakness waiting to be exploited. But only if anyone would dare to cross you. And Aria, if you haven't noticed, the stunt I pulled the other night will lead to whispers of what you mean to me. And that makes you a far greater weakness to exploit than you ever were to your father."

"So, that's what I am? A weakness?"

The tension grows between us as her expression softens but stays riddled with curiosity. She whispers a question I know has been torturing her. I watch her soft lips as she asks, "What do I mean to you? *Me*. Not the girl you thought I was."

I replay her words that one of her greatest ambitions was to make her family happy, feeling my heartbeat slow as if time is forced to pause for me to consider how to answer her.

The mere idea of ensuring her happiness is becoming a greater ambition to me than anything else has ever been. If I spoke those words to her now, she'd laugh in my face. She doesn't see what I see. She doesn't know what I know. I could never tell her. I don't have the words even if she was ready for them.

She doesn't have the forgiveness to offer me for what I've put her through and what I'm going to put her through.

She wouldn't believe me if I told her this is for her. That it's all for her. And if she did, she'd still use it against me. She doesn't even realize the woman she can be. The defiance and stubbornness that makes her perfection in my eyes.

"I'll show you what you mean to me, Aria." My voice is rough and deep but holds nothing but sincerity. "Until then, the new game has started. This room is for fucking you, punishing you and giving you pleasure beyond imagine. And outside of this room, you will be mine, and you will demand respect and earn the fear that's owed to you."

Her hazel-green eyes brim with something I've yet to see.

"Carter Cross," she whispers my name. "I don't know that I'm the woman you think I am." Her words are etched with sorrow as if she really believes what she says.

I lean in closer to her, resting my lips against her shoulder and running the tip of my nose along her skin. My lips caress her jaw where I kiss her gently and then nip the lobe of her ear.

I whisper along the shell of her ear, watching goosebumps form down her shoulder and across her chest, pebbling her nipples. "You have so much to learn and so much to accept, but Aria," I open my eyes to stare into hers before I continue, "I know you won't disappoint me."

My gaze focused on her lips, I speak more to myself than to her, "It's all been leading to this."

CHAPTER 21

Aria

I HAVE THREE HOURS AND A SINGLE BOTTLE OF WINE. I SHOULD'VE grabbed a second bottle, knowing Carter will be waiting for me in his bedroom when this rendezvous is over.

There's a tension in my chest, a faint flicker of life in my heart with the nerves of what's waiting for me.

The idea of running back to the hideaway room flutters into my mind every so often. Carter held up his word that he wouldn't come for me the first time I fled there, but what are the odds he'll do that again? If I try to avoid the punishment and him, I have a feeling everything will only get worse. There's a single distraction I'm grateful for though. Someone to talk to and someone who doesn't know what I'm going through. I'm indebted to Addison, even if she has no idea. In fact, I'm grateful she has no idea.

Popping the cork out of the bottle, I stop pretending as if hiding will do anything at all. I may fear Carter at times, along with the thoughts of punishment, but there's a darker piece of my soul that craves it.

I can't deny the idea of being throat fucked or tied up by the most powerful man I've ever met has every nerve ending in my body lit like a fuse waiting to go off.

Even as I pour the wine, listening to the sound of it, I think of every way Carter's punished me before. How hot and eager he made me for more as he played my body against my emotions. Even still, I'm numb with grief.

It makes no sense. Save the fact that my heart is truly torn and in disarray.

The dark liquid swirls as I set the bottle down and lift my glass to my lips, breathing in the dark blend to fill my lungs. Maybe I've truly lost it all. Maybe I'm crazy at this point.

I need something to give. Everything is about to fall apart in front of my eyes and just out of reach. But how do I change any of it? What I truly need is mercy from a heartless man dead set on revenge.

"There you are," I hear Addison before I see her and my heart attempts to leap up my throat, beating chaotically as if caught in an unspeakable act.

"Hey," I breathe out and my voice wavers. The wine in my glass swishes from being jostled and to steady it, I hold the stem with both hands.

"This kind of feels like a blind date, doesn't it?" Addison jokes with a genuine smile. Her mood is greatly improved from yesterday. She almost seems like a different person from what I've seen before.

Carefree and excited. There's a sweetness about her and the air around her as she walks into the room. Without hesitation, she picks up a glass and fills it.

"It kind of does," I agree with a dry laugh and a half-smile and the awkwardness wanes. My hands are clammy as she lifts up her glass for a cheers and I do the same.

"To new friends." She tilts her head with the same smile on her lips, but it's softer as the glass clinks.

Sighing, she settles into the sofa, making herself comfortable. "I've only been in this room the one time," Addison starts talking although she's not looking at me at all. She tucks her legs up under her as she sets the glass down on the end table and stares at a black and white photograph framed just to the right of the mantel. "Carter wanted to show me he'd hung my pictures," she says softly and then glances at me. "I think he just wanted to make me smile and feel welcomed, you know?"

My brow raises in surprise. "These are yours?" I ask her, finding the conversation a wonderful distraction for the well of emotion that constantly pulls me into the tide of depression I've been feeling. The idea of Carter doing anything for her just to make her happy has questions drifting in the forefront of my mind, but I swat them away. No thoughts of Carter or anything else. I've proven to myself I'm incapable of processing it all.

Every few minutes, my mood has changed today. Whether I think of Nikolai and his impending execution, my father and what he did to Carter and the Cross brothers, the fact that he hasn't come for me, or Carter himself and the cruel things he says and the murders he has planned.

Yet the prospect of falling into his arms for him to soothe all the painful twists and turns this week has given me, somehow clouds my judgment and that's where I want to stay. Accepting a comfort and turning my back on reality.

Maybe that's why I'm growing to hate myself. Yes, I truly think I'm going insane. And I'd blame Carter if only I could remember what he's done and what he plans to do when he kisses me and takes all the pain away.

"All of them but those two," she says and points out two abstract watercolor paintings behind us that straddle the entrance to the den. Tugging my skirt down, I clear my throat and smile. The kind of smile I've given others before when I know that's what they expect to see.

Sometimes that smile turns into a genuine one, and that's what I hope this turns into. I pray that's what it will be.

"You're very talented." I have to admire her work yet again. It's not the first time I've noticed them. "They're stunning."

Her fair features blush and her shoulders dip a little as she waves me away and jokingly says, "Aw shucks," causing me to let out a gentle laugh. "That's kind of you."

"I love art," I tell her and for some reason the generic statement makes me scrunch up my nose. "I love the ones that make you feel." My hands gesture in the air toward my chest to make my point. "Like with yours." My words fail me, and I have to close my eyes, shaking my head for a moment, so I can put the right words in order to get out exactly what I mean. "It seems so simple, even with the black and white taking away even more of what we'd see normally. But in the simplicity, there's so much more there that speaks to a raw side of your soul like you can feel what the photographer feels, or any artist by focusing on an object that would have such little meaning if you saw it in passing. In the art, it begs to tell you a story and you can already feel what the story is about."

"I knew you were a girl of my own heart," Addison says and

offers me a kind smile. "I have to admit," she leans forward, hushing her voice, "I've seen your drawings and I could say the same right back to you."

"Thank you," I tell her, feeling the happiness of a shared interest, but also realizing the ice has been broken and the questions she has for me are probably similar to the ones I have for her. The questions beg to slip through and bring me back to the train of thought I was on moments ago.

It's too easy to just be friendly, to sit on the surface of the world we live in and pretend that everything is just fine.

"So where are you from?" Addison asks me, taking another sip, her lips already staining from the wine, and then she reaches for the throw blanket. I finally take a seat on the armchair I've been leaning against. The leather groans as I sink down in it and sit cross-legged to be comfortable.

"Close to here," I tell her and ignore how my heart beats harder, my fingers tracing along my ankle to keep them busy while I carefully avoid details. I can't look her in the eyes as I wonder if she knows where I come from and who my family is. My throat dries but before it can cause my words to crack, I quickly ask her, "What about you?"

Glancing at her, I can feel the anxiety course harder in my veins, but her expression stays casual and easy. I get the impression that Addison is more laidback than I am. Harder to shake. Stronger in a lot of ways. And for some reason, that thought weighs against my chest heavily as she answers.

"I grew up around here, but left and traveled for the past, like five years, almost six years now?" Her voice is light as she continues. "I've lived all over."

"That's amazing," I say with wonder. I've never left home. I've never ventured outside of the parameters I was given.

"Did you live on your own?"

Addison nods with a sly grin and then clucks her tongue. "I was kind of running away at first," she says, and her voice is lower as she shrugs and then takes a heavy gulp of wine. She licks her lower lip and stares at the glass as she says, "It was too hard to stay." She peeks up at me and her piercing green eyes stay with mine as she says, "It was far too easy to just keep going, you know? Rather than staying still and having to deal with it all."

The jealousy I felt only moments ago instantly turns to compassion. Her tone is too raw, too open, and honest not to feel the pain of her confession.

"Yeah, I get that," I tell her and settle deeper into the seat. "I really do."

Time passes quietly as I slowly pick through the questions, one that won't open up a raw wound unless she cares to go there herself. "What brought you back?" I ask.

"Daniel." She rolls her eyes as she says his name, but she can't hide how her smile grows, how her cheeks flush and she pulls her legs into herself as if his name's only home is on her lips. "We bumped into each other a few towns over and he brought me back."

My smile matches hers as she continues her story. "We grew up together—kind of. I kind of grew up with him and his brothers I guess. It's a complicated story," she says then waves me off, wine glass in her hand, although she takes a long minute before sipping it again, staring past me at the mantel.

"This one is delicious," she says before finishing it off.

"I love the dark reds." My statement is spoken as absently as she spoke hers.

"They're the best," she says wide-eyed and then reaches for the bottle for another glass.

"You two getting along all right?" Daniel's voice carries through the den before he's even taken a step into the room.

My skin pricks with unease, being brought back to reality when I'd been slipping into a hiding place of Addison's story. I keep my smile plastered on my face as he glances between the two of us.

I wonder if he thinks I'd tell her why I'm here and what happened. That I'd warn her away from Daniel and expose that he knew. That I'd beg her to help me and frighten her.

My heart feels like it collapses in on itself as the two of them go back and forth in lighthearted banter although a touch of tension is obvious.

"Always hovering," Addison says although there's a quiet reverence there that Daniel doesn't seem to grasp. He sighs and runs his hand down the back of his head before saying, "I just came to see if you two needed anything."

Addison playfully slaps his arm as he stops behind the sofa where she's sitting. "Liar. You came to eavesdrop."

"You got me," he says and lets her shoo him away with a simple, "Get out," but not without a kiss.

Addison lifts from her seat, making the blanket around her waist fall as her ass lifts up. "Love you," she whispers and then gives him a peck. Then another and another. Three in quick succession.

With the tip of his nose brushing against hers he says with his eyes closed, "Love you too."

And there isn't an ounce of me that doesn't believe them both. My smile falls and there's no way I could fake one in this moment. Love exists in their exchange; it breathes in the air between them.

It's undeniable and nothing like what binds me to Carter. It's not lust, it's a meeting of souls, the two of them needing one another and recognizing that truth.

"You need anything?" Daniel asks again as my gaze drifts to the side table. The edge of the carved wood grants me a small escape from their display.

"Aria," Daniel's voice is raised as he addresses me directly. "You need anything?" he asks me, and his eyes carry his real question, *Are you okay?*

"I'm fine," I tell him as evenly as I can and then clear my throat before reaching for my glass again.

It takes a long moment after he's left for the tense air to change.

"So, you and Carter?" Addison asks me, cocking a brow to be comical. She sips the wine but keeps her eyes on me and the expression on her face makes me laugh.

"Yeah, me and Carter," I tell her tightly, but with humor.

"He's keeping you trapped here too, huh?" she asks and the easy interaction that existed before turns sharp.

"You could say that," I reply but my voice is flat. Chewing on the inside of my cheek, I consider telling her the truth for a split second, but there's no way I ever would. Not because I don't trust her, but because I'm truly ashamed in this moment.

I've given up. I'm lying in bed with the devil. And as much as Addison appears to like me, there's no way she'd ever respect me if she knew the truth. I don't even respect myself.

"I'm guessing he chased you?" she asks speculatively. "The Cross boys tend to chase."

"Again, you could say that."

"When I first I met Carter," Addison starts to tell me a story, realizing I'm not open to sharing my own Carter tale, while her thin finger drifts over the edge of the wine glass, running circles around the rim of it. "He was different from the other brothers."

"How so?" I ask, watching her finger as my shame eases.

She glances at me for a moment with a pinched expression. "He wasn't around as often, and he was always quiet when he was around, but you knew the moment he was in the house. He *was* the authority."

"What do you mean?"

"Like their father wasn't the best, you know? After their mother died, he took it really hard." She swallows as if a painful memory threatened to choke her if she continued, but she goes on. "So, if anyone needed anything, it was Carter who was asked. Carter who made the rules. Carter who got whatever was needed."

I watch her expression as she tells me their story.

"This one time, it was so stupid." Her eyes get glassy but she shakes her head and brushes her hair back. "These kids stole our bikes," she tells me, forcing strength to her voice.

"Tyler took me to the corner store and we left our bikes outside, and these assholes stole them." She laughs the kind of laugh that you force out when you want a release from the need to cry.

"You knew Tyler?" I ask her, feeling a chill run down my skin, leaving goosebumps along their path. Nikolai told me once that when you have that feeling run through you, it means someone's walked over your grave.

She only nods, her eyes reflecting a sad secret, and then continues. "It had to be these guys, they were older and there were like six of them. Grown ass men who had nothing better to do than steal bikes from high school kids." She breathes in deeply before smoothing the blanket down across her lap and telling me, "We walked home and the last ten minutes it rained the whole way. We were soaked when we got back."

"Daniel wasn't there; Tyler went to him first because he didn't like to bother Carter. None of the boys ever liked to bother him with petty stuff, you know?" she asks me, and I don't know how to respond but she doesn't give me time to regardless.

"So, Carter was there and asked what happened. He was quick to anger back then, so much different from now," she tells me, and I look at her as if she's crazy, but she doesn't see. She picks at the blanket and continues. "He and Tyler left together in the truck, Carter told me to stay back and within hours, both bikes were in the back of the truck safe at home. Tyler was never one to fight. He was a lover and a kind old soul, but he said those guys wouldn't mess with us anymore. I kind of wish I'd seen what Carter had done." She says the last words like a spoken thought that had just come to her. All I can think is that she's probably better off not having witnessed what Carter did to those men.

"I guess that's not the best story," she says and shrugs. "Sorry, I kind of suck at telling stories."

I offer her a soft smile and say, "I liked it."

"Anyway, that's what Carter does. He takes what he wants and doesn't take any prisoners or put up with any bullshit."

Her words strike me in a way I can't explain and the same tears that she'd wiped away haphazardly at the start of her story, threaten to fall from mine.

"Are you okay?" she asks me, although judging by the way her smile wavers, I could ask her the same.

My lips part ready to do what I've always done, to tell everyone that I'm fine. To pretend like nothing's wrong.

"Only if you want to talk," she quickly adds, practically tripping over her words. Even her hands come up in protest. "I'm not usually this weird, I've just been on edge lately and it's so nice to be able to talk to someone else. Someone who's not…," she stops and holds her breath, searching for the right words but none come. I can see it in her eyes that she's suffering like I am. Something's wrong and I can only guess that it's because she's trapped here. Trapped like I am, but for such different reasons.

"I'm okay, and I get it… I do." My attempt to reassure her falls flat. She offers me a weak half smile that doesn't reach her eyes.

"I wish I could tell you something," she whispers and then shakes her head as if she's losing her mind. Maybe I'm not the only crazy one in this room. Wiping under her eyes she looks to the door and exhales a harsh breath. "I should go." Maybe she had a curfew time too. Or maybe she just doesn't want to break down in front of a stranger.

Glancing at the clock, I see nearly three hours has already passed. I feel like we've only just sat down.

"Yeah, I should too." I clear my throat and try to think of something to say that's comforting for her even though I hardly know her. A piece of her though, her heart and soul, I know well. "I'm here if you ever want a drinking buddy," I offer.

"Or to binge-watch something good on Netflix?" she offers, and the genuine happiness lights up her expression.

"Sure," I offer her a smile with my upturned voice and imagine the loss I can already feel doesn't exist.

"This might sound weird," Addison tells me as she picks up her wine glass and downs the last remaining bit before looking me in the eyes, "but you look like you could use 'a somebody.'" She sets the glass down, the clinking of the glass breaking up the white noise that drowns me when Addison stares down at me, standing up on her way to leave. She pushes the hair off of her shoulder and tells me solemnly, "I didn't have 'a somebody' for a long time. And I know how it feels."

It's hard to describe the pain and hollowness of having a stranger seem to see through you and when they look there, they want to help you, to be there for you with a genuine kindness. When you look back at them, you see it too. It's so obvious but speaking the truth would make it real, and it's so much more comforting to run and hide or pretend like everything is okay for at least a little while.

I have to clear my dry, scratchy throat before I tell her, "I might take you up on that."

CHAPTER 22

Carter

THE FLOOR CREAKING ALERTS ME TO HER COMING. THE bathroom light is still on and the soft yellow light filters into the room, casting a shadow where she stands. Aria's never looked so tempting and radiant. Licking her lips in defiance even though there's fear and defeat in her gorgeous hazel eyes. Naked, with her skin flushed from the prospect of what's coming, she stands there caught in my gaze.

I've never been so hard in my fucking life. I know she needs this. We both need it. The last few days have been large steps back with only meager steps forward.

She stands before me as my equal, daring, and relentless, although on the opposite side from where I stand.

"Come," I command her as I sit on the chair and run my hand down my right thigh.

She walks in from the bathroom hesitantly, her body stiff but still she comes to me, stopping in front of me and waiting.

"Sit," I tell her, and she instinctively reaches for my hand as I pull her ass down to nestle in my crotch. She stiffens her back and continues to pretend she doesn't need this. She knows better if only she'd open her eyes.

"I've thought a lot about what's causing tension between us." The statement comes out deep and husky, unable to deny my desire for her. I let my middle finger slip along her shoulder and watch as it makes her nipples pebble. Her beautiful skin both flushes and at the same time pricks with goosebumps.

"The first thing I'm going to do is punish you." Her lips part with a quick breath, but she nods her head in understanding. "The second is to give you something you want, and something you need..." I pause my movement and wait for her beautiful hazel-green gaze to meet mine before adding, "If you take the punishment well."

Her breathing quickens, and I can see how her blood pumps harder in the veins of her neck but still, she nods in obedience. Her eyes continue to flicker to mine with questions, but she doesn't ask them.

"Lie across my lap," I tell her gently. There's no need to be firm, knowing what's to come. Nervously, she obeys but tries to hold on to the chair as her balance is off and her legs dangle aimlessly.

I adjust her, so she's positioned perfectly, her hip on my right thigh and she gasps in protest, but it's short-lived.

"Hands behind your back," I command her, and she obeys, although she's awkward in my lap, trying to balance herself. It doesn't matter though, the second I grip both her wrists in my left hand and press them to the small of her back, she's steady. And that's how she'll stay until I decide this punishment is over. Her pussy is already glistening; the mix of fear and desire is a powerful thing.

My blunt fingernails trail over her pale, supple ass as I give her a simple command. "Tell me why you ran from me when I gave you access to the front door." My chest feels tight with worry that she'll never see. I won't allow her to question my control. Not again. Never again. She needs to know in every fiber of her being, that I can take control from her but that more than that, she needs it.

"I need to know what set you off, Aria," I say clearly enough to be sure she understands how much this means to me when she doesn't answer.

"I don't know," she tells me with a tense voice before blowing a strand of hair out of her face.

The lying will come to an end shortly.

Slap! My hand stings all the way down to my wrist as the bright mark lands on her right cheek and Aria cries out, her hips bucking uselessly as I hold her down with a firm grip and do the same to her other cheek. Moving to her center, I slap her there and then again on the right cheek. All the while, she writhes in my lap and cries out with muffled screams of protest.

My heart hammers and my dick hardens when my fingers drift

lower to her cunt. Her breathing hitches, and her entrance clenches around my fingertips but she gets no reward for lying to me.

I speak softly as I gently lay my hand on her hot cheek, rubbing soothing strokes over the sensitized marks. "Tell me the truth." My command falls into the silence that mixes with her strangled moans as the pain and pleasure combine. I dip my fingers to her cunt, letting them run through her slick folds. My middle finger trails down to her clit and I circle it once, tempting her and rewarding her obedience as she stays where she is, where she belongs on my lap. "Tell me, Aria."

With a shaky breath, Aria's back attempts to bow and her thighs clench. She visibly swallows, and I know she's going to cum, so I stop. My finger is still pressed against her, but without the movement, she lifts her eyes to mine, breathing heavily with her lips parted.

"I don't know," she answers, her mesmerizing hazel eyes begging me to believe her. I don't wait for her to prepare. I spank her other cheek and then move back to the right before returning to the left repeatedly, feeling a burn that runs up my arm as my hand goes numb.

Aria's scream echoes in the room as her body stiffens across my lap. She seethes, sucking in air through clenched teeth as tears prick her eyes. My own breathing rages from me as I land the last blow and keep her steady where she is.

Gulping for breath and hanging her head low while attempting to fight the need to struggle against the hold I have on her, she turns her head away from me. But I see the tears.

Instantly, I place my hand over her heated skin, ignoring how she jumps and applying enough pressure to soothe the pain. My heart skips once, then twice as she struggles to maintain her composure, the tears falling freely as her face reddens.

"I've got you," I whisper to her and she turns to glance up at me, a look of pure hate on her expression. "Tell me what happened, and it stops," I offer her again, and watch as her bottom lip wavers. "I won't let you go until you tell me."

Her face crumples and she sobs out, "It's stupid," before letting the tears fall again.

I continue rubbing soothing circles, occasionally squeezing her ass to keep the blood flowing and the nerve endings on edge. The endorphins flowing in her blood will make her pleasure that much greater. Both the body and mind always prefer pleasure to pain.

And I'll give her both. Although she hates me now, she'll love me when this is over.

My fingers drift to her core this time, pressing inside of her and I'm instantly rewarded with her arching her neck, her eyes closed as a small moan of pleasure drifts from her reddened lips. Her cheeks are tearstained, and a few droplets still linger on her lashes.

Her cunt clamps around my fingertips, begging me for more.

A strangled moan fills the hot air as my cock hardens even more and presses against her belly. Fuck, I want her. I *need* to have her to-night and claim her again. To remind her of how much she belongs with me.

"Tell me now, Aria," I demand, my voice deep and rumbling with the need I feel alive in every cell of my body.

She only whimpers, and then defiantly shakes her head. "I don't know, I swear I—"

Before she can even finish, I slap her ass as hard as I can. The pain that had numbed brightens back to life. Under her ass cheeks, on her ass, on her pussy. I spank her in a new spot each time, rotating between them but the pace is ruthless, the slaps unforgiving. My jaw clenches and the pain rips up my arm as she screams out.

"Stop lying to me," I barely get the command out through clenched teeth as I stop the punishment, forcing myself to breathe and instantly soothe her reddened skin.

She heaves in a breath and then another. A shudder runs down her body that morphs her sobs to moans. She's close to this being so much more. But what I want are answers and she won't cum until I get them. I'll make damn sure of that.

The hair on the side of her face, wet from her tears, is stuck to her skin as she says, "I saw the date."

Her upper body rocks and she tries to move away from me, groan-ing with a pained expression before telling me, "I saw the date on your phone." Her words are spastic at best, but I know I heard her right.

My breathing is still erratic, my hand stinging with pain and my lungs refusing to move as I take in what she's telling me.

My fingers loosen on her wrists slowly as I wrap my arm around her waist, careful not to touch her ass until I'm ready to set her on my lap.

She winces and seethes, not moving her arms even though she freely could.

Bringing her into my chest, I let her collapse in my arms. Her hands lift to my shoulders as the tears soak into my shirt. The feel of her cheek on my shoulder as she buries her head in the crook of my neck is already a soothing balm to me.

"You saw the date?" I prompt her to tell me more. To explain it to me as I comfort her.

"The day before was my mother's—" she gasps, not finishing and I run my hand up and down her back, letting her cling to me.

I shush her, letting my warm breath whisper along her hair and I wait for her to settle.

"You missed the anniversary of your mother's death?" I ask her, feeling a pain inside me crumple every bit of strength I have.

"Yes," she croaks and tries to climb closer to me as if she wasn't already pressed against me. "It was the first time," she says in between breaths, "that I didn't go to her grave."

Holding her while she cries, knowing the pain she's feeling could have been avoided so easily. I could have done something to help her, even if it meant gathering dozens of men to protect her while she saw to her mother's grave. I could have done something if only I'd known.

"I'm sorry." I try to put every ounce of compassion into my apology. "Please believe how sorry I am," I say and kiss her hair, her shoulder and then pull her away to kiss her swollen red lips.

She buries herself back into the crook of my neck and then cries out as her ass brushes against my pants.

"Thank you for telling me," I say as I maneuver her on my lap, so I have access to her cunt. "Hold on to me," I command her, and she does instantly. She needs someone to hold and someone to hold her, I've never been more sure of it.

"This will make the pain go away," I tell her, although my words are hollow. Pleasure can hide only one specific kind of pain. I rub her clit first, letting the intensity from the unique pleasure that comes after both pain and mourning flow through her.

She bites down on my shoulder, her fingernails digging into my skin through my shirt. She writhes on my lap, so close to the edge already, although each time her ass brushes against the fabric of my pants, her voice hitches, and her grip on me tightens.

Pressing my fingers inside her, I stroke her ruthlessly and butt my palm against her clit. Her back bows and I have to hold her closer to me, laying my hand against her shoulder.

"Cum for me," I whisper in her ear. My cock is hard and desperate to be wrapped in her hot cunt, but I can't take my pleasure from her like this.

It's all for her.

"Carter," she gasps my name as her body rocks with pleasure and her head falls back. I don't stop until she's trembling, and her cries have stopped completely.

My heart races against hers, sweat covering my skin and every muscle in my body coiled.

Time passes slowly as I wait until she's calm and coherent. And each second, I carefully select the words she needs to hear.

With weak balance, she finally lifts her head to look me in the eyes. Her expression pinches as she leans back, feeling her raw ass brush against my pants once again, but this time her lips part and another orgasm threatens from the faint touch.

"I need more from you," I tell her, breaking her moment and forcing her hazel eyes to stare into mine.

"I have you here," I say as I let my fingers fall to her pussy and then cup it, watching as she gasps, throwing her head back and rocking herself into my hand. My lips drop to her throat, whispering against her skin, "So needy."

Before she can get off again, I stop and wait for her eyes to reach mine, dark with desire and lit with lust. "I'm getting to you here," I tell her and smooth her hair back on the crown of her head.

A moment passes with a tense beating in my chest before I drop my fingers to her chest, between her bare breasts and ask her, "What about here?"

My eyes flicker between where I'm touching her and her own gaze, now swirling with a hopelessness and sadness I wish I could take away.

The ever-present vise tightens on my heart as she asks me in a whisper, "If I gave you that, what would I have left?"

It tightens further, and my heart refuses to beat. The answer is so obvious. "You'd have me." I watch her expression remain unchanged and I have to look away.

Breathing in deeply, I ignore whatever I'm feeling, every last bit of it, knowing logically, she's close. I know she is.

She comes and goes, and that's because of her father. If he wasn't in the picture, she would be mine completely. And Nikolai…

"You know what I need, Carter," Aria finally speaks and when she does her voice cracks. Tears linger in her eyes. "For you to have my heart, you can't destroy it. You can't kill them."

I cave. Knowing what this could be, I offer her something, just to have a chance to break through the wall that guards her heart. "I'll call him, but you'll be silent."

With a look of shock and gratitude, she leans in closer to me and starts to speak but I press my finger against her lips, silencing her and halting her movements.

Fear is power. And every day, I fear her never loving me more than the day before. I've given her the power and I don't know how I let that happen.

"I will call your father and you'll listen only. Is that clear?"

Although she nods, she doesn't speak until I move my finger away. "Yes, Carter."

It occurs to me how little she obeys unless she has hope. I instantly regret telling her I would call her prick of a father.

I need to give her hope in something else. Because when this war is over, her father will be dead, and she'll have to find forgiveness or be miserable and hate me forever.

CHAPTER 23

Aria

I DON'T KNOW HOW I SLEPT AT ALL.

I keep wondering if he's really going to do it. If Carter is going to call my father and if he does, what would he say? I almost ask Carter if I can call Nikolai, just to tell him I'm safe but I don't know how Carter would react, and I don't want to push him when he's given me this hope.

If my father knew Carter gave me Stephan to kill, literally forced to stay put with a knife placed in my hand, wouldn't that offer some sort of truce between them?

My hands are shaking so much from the anticipation and anxiety of what they'll say that the picture in front of me is blank, not from lack of inspiration, but from the inability to create even a simple line.

An hour has passed with me sitting on the floor of Carter's office, listening to the tapping of keys and the steady tick-tock of the clock. All the while, I can't focus on anything. Not a damn thing except for when Carter's going to call him like he said he would.

Glancing up at Carter, I catch his gaze and I know the look in my eyes is pleading and expectant.

"You need more." Carter's voice is deep and low, and it booms through the office. Or, maybe it's just that I'm on high alert and everything is thrumming to life as I wait for what's to come.

My throat tightens, feeling the dejection once again for the one thing that could change everything, but I stand on shaking legs and go to him.

It doesn't escape me that he has me under control again. That my only desire is to obey him, so he'll give me what he claimed he would. He may have given me false hope.

My heart flickers like a candle so close to its flame going out. He wouldn't do that to me. I refuse to believe it. I know he feels something for me. He must. I can feel it in the very marrow of my bones.

Carter pushes the phone farther away from him, an old desk phone, and I stare at it as I hear him push the laptop and stacks of papers out of the way.

It's right there. *Just call him.*

Pat, pat, he pats the top of the desk and I take the hint, lying on my belly, knowing he's going to lift the dark red chiffon dress up my thighs and bare my backside to him.

My cheek presses against the hard desk and I can feel my heart hammer against it. Gripping on to the edge of the desk, I wait for the cool gel to hit my sore ass. There aren't any bruises this time, but somehow it hurts more. This morning I nearly cried waking up to the pain until Carter used the ointment.

Sucking in a deep breath, my eyes close and I feel Carter rub the soothing balm into my hot skin. It's tender still, but even more so, it makes me crave more of his touch.

A soft hum of gratitude and want leaves my lips, and it's met with a rough chuckle from Carter. Opening my eyes, I glance up at him, although I have to push the lock of hair out of my face.

My heart does that flickering again.

"It looks much better than how it was last night and this morning."

"It feels better now too," I tell him easily, watching his expression as he pays close attention to where he's rubbing the balm.

"You didn't tell me the entire truth last night," Carter says before opening a drawer and then closing it. My heart thumps once, thinking of what I left out but having nothing come to mind.

I don't know if he just put the gel back or if he's taken something else out.

Before I can answer, Carter tells me, "You forgot to mention your birthday."

He finally meets my gaze and there's a softness there that I hardly ever see from him, but it's the side I pine for most.

"I didn't think it was important," I try to speak, but my words are whispered. Of every reason I'm breaking apart, that fact is meaningless and even speaking it as if it could contribute to this pain is disrespectful to the tragedies that surround us.

He's gentle as he repositions me on the desk but doesn't pull my dress back down. It's bunched at my hips and that's what I'm thinking about when I hear the first cuff open and look up at the feel of metal grazing the skin on my wrists.

"Your other hand," Carter commands and I give it to him although I'm riddled with a slight fear.

"Carter?" His name comes out as a question as he handcuffs me to two metal loops on the side of his desk. Again, he repositions me, sliding my body down so I'm stretched on my belly across his desk.

"I don't have a gift for you at the moment," he says absently as he steps away from me, leaving the cool air to hit my ass which is still very much exposed to him. "But I'll have to find something nice for you."

The flicker instantly morphs into a thrumming with a slight fear of the unknown.

I try to turn around and look at him as he fiddles with something on the shelf. I don't see what he has but whatever it is, he has it in his hand.

"Carter, I'm sorry." My first instinct is to beg my way out of another punishment. My ass is still so sore. But even as the adrenaline spikes through me, I can't imagine he'd do it. That he'd punish me for not telling him it was my birthday. "Please," I whimper.

"Hush," he says, and his voice is calming as he lays a hand down on my lower back. His touch is an instant salve to my nerves. The rough pads of his thumbs rub soothing circles and that alone calms me. "This is for pleasure, songbird."

A slick oil drizzling between my ass crack makes me jump, but I'm held down by his hand and the cuffs. Again, he chuckles, deep and low at me, ever amused but I love it.

I love that sound.

"I need to spread you, and then you need to push back," he commands, and I force myself to swallow, feeling the pressure of a cool metal object press against my forbidden hole. I'm instantly hot and tense. The nerve endings come alive and the heat spreads like wildfire through my body and along my skin.

The thrumming intensifies, my heart slamming and lust consuming the ounce of fear that lingers.

A shudder of pleasure and a hint of stinging pain make me clench everything, but the second the tension is gone, Carter pushes the plug deeper inside of me. Oh. My. God.

I can barely breathe as the new sensation takes over. My nipples pebble and rub against the desk as I squirm beneath his ministrations. He fucks me with the butt plug, pushing it in and out, over and over.

"Carter," I moan and then whimper, feeling close to cumming so soon. I feel so full. So hot. The little hairs on the back of my neck rise as my head thrashes.

"Your cunt is clenching around nothing," Carter observes, and his deep voice forces my eyes open. Just as I feel the need to raise my ass higher, Carter pushes the plug in deeper and stops everything, leaving me feeling full and hot and on the edge of desire.

"Arch your back," Carter demands as he presses his fingers against my inner thigh, spreading my legs for him even though they tremble with the threat of an orgasm so close.

I swear I can feel it in my pussy. The arousal is there even though I'm so aware that nothing's inside of me… not there.

The metal of the cuffs digs into my skin, my ass is in the air, and each wrist bound to the desk. A soft moan escapes and the heated blushes rise up my face to my crown as Carter brushes his fingers across my clit and then up and down my pussy. "Should I tell your father the truth?" he asks me.

"Should I tell him I wanted you so badly that I was willing to start a war to keep you?"

While his words force a moan from me, they push my emotions over the edge.

It wasn't me he wanted.

The little voice in the back of my head reminds me, and I have to close my eyes tightly, pushing away the immediate sadness and dejection.

I feel tense and on edge in more ways than one. The swell of both emotion and lust beg me to tell him, but Carter's silent and his touch absent. I force my eyes open to see him watching me. His dark eyes staring deep into mine, searching for something.

I know I should tell him, but if he knew the girl who banged on the door calling out that she was in need wasn't me, would he want me still? I can't bear for that answer to be no.

"Do I need to gag you?" Carter asks. My heart hammers and my pulse quickens.

"For what?" I ask in return, but then immediately assure him, "I can be quiet," for whatever he's thinking. I'll do anything he asks.

"It's time to call your father," he tells me, and a mask slips over his face. An expression of indifference that makes the angular lines of his jaw look that much sharper. I can see the moment he changes into the Carter I first knew and hated. It happens right before my eyes; I see the darkness take over.

"You can stay on edge for it." His voice is a hum of both desire and amusement. "Think about how good it's going to feel when I fuck you and finally let you cum."

CHAPTER 24

Carter

ALL I CAN THINK ABOUT AS THE PHONE RINGS, IS HOW MUCH control I'm going to need not to fuck Aria senseless until she's screaming my name while her father is on the line.

I press the numbers slowly, one at a time, remembering the look of absolute agony on her face when I mentioned starting a war for her. I didn't mean for it to break her.

It's only the truth.

Putting the phone on speaker, the tension boils inside of me as the phone rings and Aria struggles on the desk.

Ring.

I trail my finger down her backside all the way to her knee, and she whimpers. "Hush," I tell her, watching goosebumps form along her smooth skin.

Ring.

"You don't want your father to hear you," I say and don't bother to whisper. The sound of her breathing hitching begs me to look into her eyes. They're pleading with me, and I swear I'll try to give her something from this call.

Something that will help her.

I'll show her what kind of a man her father is.

Ring.

The third ring is only partial, followed by a low click and a pause before I hear the voice of my enemy. "Cross," he answers the phone.

Anger erupts up my throat at the sound of his voice. I can only concentrate on Aria's tempting body sprawled on my desk to calm me. Oh, and she does. Letting my fingers delight in her soft touch, I drag them up her wet lips and slowly push against the plug in her ass.

The suppressed moan tugs a sick smile onto my face as I answer, "Talvery."

Continuing to fuck her ass with the plug and reveling in the faint sounds of the metal clinking as Aria tries her damnedest to both hold still and quiet the sounds of pleasure gathering inside of her and threatening to go off at any moment, I speak clearly, "I thought you may want to have a conversation?"

There's silence on the other end as Aria's lips form a perfect O and her lower back and thighs tremble. She's so fucking close. Slipping a finger inside of her cunt, I use enough pressure to get her off.

"Maybe about my arrangements with your daughter?"

Her leg raises and slams down on the desk, twice. Two loud slams that jostle the phone as her face scrunches and she bites into her lip.

That's once.

"You son of a bitch," Talvery sneers at me, oblivious to what I've just done to his daughter.

Aria's eyes pop open, although her face is still flushed and she's struggling to breathe quietly.

"Don't you know you should have more respect for women than that?" I tell Talvery and drag my fingers back down to Aria's clit. The shiver that runs through her makes it all the more thrilling.

"How did you get her?" Talvery's question makes me pause, taking my fingers away from her to consider his question. His *first* question. Not whether or not she's well or safe, but *how* did I get her.

Two options exist. He knows of the informant and wants it verified, or he truly has no idea.

"She was a gift," I explain to him evenly, my eyes narrowing on the phone and waiting for his response to give me more insight.

The sound of Aria's sharp inhale reminds me of my songbird, and that she's listening. Leaning forward, I plant a kiss on her thigh, one meant to soothe whatever pained thoughts are running through her head.

"From Romano?" he asks me, breathing heavier into the phone. "Is that what you expect me to believe?" he sneers, and Aria raises her head on the desk, ready to object and speak up, but I silence her, gripping her chin and shaking my head once. I know my expression is hard as fucking stone, which is what makes her flinch, but she cannot be allowed to speak to him.

I won't let her be any more involved in this war than she already is.

"You can believe what you want. You asked a question. I answered."

She's tense on the desk and she's facing away from me, trying to look at the phone, as if there's anything there to see.

She scissors her legs, to turn her body so she can see the phone, and again my lips tug into a smile when she moans softly.

He can't hear her as he tells me, "I've been informed."

I don't give him much thought. I know what he's been told, and he can go fuck himself with that misinformation, while I fuck his daughter.

I move back to her ass, teasing her and fucking her with the plug. Her nails scratch against the table as she tries to fight the desire to moan out loud.

I hit mute for just a moment, ready to hear that sweet sound I love. Her father continues although he can't hear us in return.

"What'd you do to her?"

I whisper to Aria, grabbing her ass with my other hand and forcing that beautiful sound to spill from her lips. The mix of intense pleasure and sting of pain too much for her to control. "Look at me while I fuck your ass, Aria." Her eyes widen with fear and I smirk as I explain, "He can't hear you, but I'm unmuting now, so be quiet, songbird."

Those beautiful lips part with both a sigh of relief and then a quiet whimper of pleasure as I go back to teasing her pretty little cunt. Her eyes nearly close, but she whips them open, obeying my last command to look at me.

"I'll kill you if you touched her." Talvery issues a false threat as I unmute the conversation.

"How could I not touch her?" I ask him.

I hear a small whimper of protest from Aria and feel like a prick that I'm goading her father in front of her.

With apprehension coiling in the pit of my stomach, I speak. "I've given her everything she needs. She's having hard days." Although her father is listening, these words are just for her as I add, "She seems to be fitting in well, and at times she even seems happy."

Her hazel eyes soften and nearly gloss over, her eyes never faltering from my gaze.

"What do you want, Cross?" Talvery's harsh and bitter voice forces my jaw to clench.

I think about telling him how she told me she loves me. But repeating those words to him and using them like that would be a travesty.

She's calmer, wide-eyed and waiting with bated breath for my answer.

"Just to talk. I have someone here who wanted to hear your voice."

I push my fingers into her tight cunt and my thumb presses against the butt plug. The clinking of the handcuffs is loud enough for Talvery to hear and knowing that, a conceited grin stretches across my face.

"Let me speak to her," he says but his demand is pathetic. I'd never do anything because he ordered it. I'd go through hell just to spite him.

"She's a little tied up at the moment," I tell him, feeling the arrogance surge inside of me, but wanting to contain it enough to keep it from hurting my Aria. I circle her clit ruthlessly, knowing she gets off so easily with this touch. I'd rather she be in such blinding pleasure that she can't hear or even comprehend the conversation.

"I'll fucking kill you," he says, and he doesn't hide the anger in his voice.

"You keep trying to do that," I retort and the anger seeps into my voice with every passing moment. And although concern is clearly written on Aria's expression, her thighs tremble with the upcoming release and her teeth sink into her bottom lip so hard she'll be tasting blood if she bites any harder.

I mute the conversation again for only a second to command her, "Cum for me, Aria." And then finger fuck her harder.

Her back bows and a soft, strangled cry slips by her lips just as I tell Talvery, "I promise I'm being good to her. I know how to treat a woman."

At my words, she cums, hard and violently. Her entire body showing the tremors of pleasure that race through her.

"Did Romano tell you what she did?" I ask Talvery, more to remind myself. This strong woman is mine. I'm fucking proud to have her as mine.

"Stephan?" Talvery asks as Aria's eyes meet mine and I whisper harshly in response, irritated by his interruption, "Yes."

Breathing heavily, Aria tries to look up; she tries to will the phone to give her more of a response from her father.

But nothing comes.

There's nothing but silence on the other line.

And I hate him for it. Truly hate him for the tears he brings to her eyes.

"You didn't come for her." I have to swallow the spiked ball growing in my throat. "How long have you known?"

When he doesn't reply, the edge of hate comes on thicker and I say, "I know Romano spilling a little secret wasn't what tipped you off."

Her face crumples and I lean forward, kissing every inch of the curve of her waist.

"Give her a message for me," Talvery says, but I ignore him in preference for the sweet sounds of gratitude I can barely hear from Aria.

"I couldn't tell her before this, but I'm telling her right now."

"I'm listening," I tell him, only to mute the phone again as I kiss Aria's reddened skin on her ass and gently move the butt plug in and out once again. She's so close already.

"Tell her I said, 'Stay quiet while I'm gone and stay in her room.'"

Unmuting the phone, I answer him quickly, "I'll be sure to let her know," and then hang up the phone, done with him and this conversation. And ready to hear her scream my name.

Moving her legs off the desk and fueled by her gasp and the sounds of her nails scratching along the desk, I unleash my cock and shove myself all the way in her to the hilt.

"Fuck, yes," I groan as my limbs tingle. "Fuck, I need you," I whisper along her back as I lower my lips to kiss along her skin. I stay still inside of her, letting her adjust and waiting to make sure she feels nothing but pleasure.

"You have no idea how much I want him to know you scream my name every night."

"Is he—" Aria asks before throwing her head back with a strangled cry of pleasure as I slam inside of her again.

Still, she turns to look at the phone, with her face scrunched and struggling to stay quiet, and I know she's wondering if he can hear.

Even as my cock is inside of her heat, she worries.

I won't fucking allow it.

I bang the phone down over and over, so she can hear. One hand on the phone, the other with a bruising grip on her hip. I fuck her in time with the violent banging until she can register the dead tone.

Shoving the phone off the desk, I tell her, "He doesn't matter. Nothing else matters." My words come out with a hard grunt as her pussy spasms around my thick length. "There's only us," I push the words out, pistoning my hips and feeling my balls draw up once again.

As I pound into her, I ask her, "How does it feel to have your ass and pussy filled at the same time?"

"Carter," she whimpers my name as she cums again. And then again. As I ride through her pleasure, each one harder and stronger than the last, I beg my body not to give in.

I want to stay in this moment forever. Her chained to my desk, feeling nothing but the heat of my desire and the thrill of me fucking her until her legs are weak and shaking.

But I have to. And on the third time her cunt grips my dick with her orgasm, I thrust myself as deep inside of her as I can, and cum harder than I ever have in my life.

I'm breathless when I pull the plug from her, giving her yet another wave of pleasure. I'm panting when I uncuff her and pull her into my lap to feel her heated skin tremble against mine.

The sound of our mingled breathing doesn't last long. Aria's hair tickles along my shoulder as she pulls away from me, reaching for the phone.

Her shoulders shake with her ragged breath and her eyes look lost in the distance.

"It's fine," I tell her, the swell of rage and worse, disappointment, brewing inside of me.

"Can I call him back?" Her question is immediate and laced with a mix of fear and worry. "Just me, please?" she begs me in a broken whisper.

Watching her swallow, I gauge her desperation that seemingly came from nowhere.

"I don't trust your father," I tell her honestly.

"You can trust me," she suggests weakly, the pleading tone still present.

I give her silence as I search her gaze and the desperation transforms to anger when she adds, "You didn't have to taunt him like that," but her voice cracks.

She's worried. Something's wrong

"Please let me call him back," she begs again. "I promise it's okay. I just want to tell him I'm all right." She worries her bottom lip between her teeth as she looks me in the eyes, both of her hands gripping on to me.

"No, what's wrong?" She won't look me in the eye at my response, so I grab her chin, forcing her eyes up and searching for the truth inside of them.

"Why does it have to be like this?" Her words crack, and tears leak from the corners of her eyes.

"What the hell happened?" My eyes narrow as I watch her lose it. Losing every ounce of composure. "What's wrong?"

"I love you," she answers with pain. "I'm sorry," she whimpers, wiping her eyes and trying to get away from me and out of my hold.

"I would never hurt you," I tell her as my heart races, knowing I can't give her the same words back. "You know that?" Going over everything that happened, all I can think is that it's the way I spoke about how she came to me. The way we started and the arrogance I showed. "The way I was talking-"

She stops me, pressing her fingers to my lips, "I would never hurt you either."

My phone going off distracts me; the message is from Jase. *You need to see this, now.*

Pressing a kiss to her soft lips, I try to end her worries. She attempts to deepen it, but I pull away, pressing my forehead to hers and wishing I didn't have to leave her right now.

I whisper against her lips, "Wait for me in the bedroom." I open my eyes to see the longing in hers and a well of emotion that knows no depths.

She only nods, loosening her grip as I set her down on the ground and stand up with her.

"I have something to take care of and then I'll come to you," I tell her, but her expression is absent of accepting a thing I'm telling her. One day she'll understand that I'll take care of everything so long as she trusts me to.

But she goes just the same and I watch her walk away from me as I stand outside the office door, wondering if she holds the same opinion of her father now that she did hours ago.

She glances behind her one last time, giving me a sad smile before disappearing around the corner to the stairwell.

I don't make it down the hall before Jase is up the stairs, full steam in his gait until he lifts his head and sees me.

"We need to talk." Jase's voice carries down the hall with an edge of urgency. "Now."

"What's going on?" I ask him, feeling my forehead crease and the adrenaline pumping harder.

"There's been a breach. Looks like we're going to have company." His eyes reflect the welcome of a challenge and my lips curl up in agreement.

"Talvery?" I ask him, wondering if her father was already in motion before the call, or if he stupidly acted off impulse.

Jase nods, but worry lines his expression. "There are only six."

"Six men?" I question. "Talvery isn't that fucking stupid."

"One's an informant and probably how they got past the first gate. Two are her blood."

"You think someone helped him?" I question Jase, thinking the informant was aided by someone he's spoken to, but he shakes his head quickly.

"We were alerted the second they were spotted. Where's Aria?" Jase questions and I'm quick to answer, "She's safe in my bedroom. She won't leave."

My throat dries and tightens, thinking about them stealing her, but worry and fear will only bring my downfall.

"There's no way he thought he could succeed in doing anything but sending his own men to be killed with only six."

"There's definitely something off," he adds and pulls up the feed on his phone. Six men along the inner tower, fully armored. I watch with him as he asks me, "We could question them?"

My chest tightens as I recognize the face of one man. "Nikolai."

He dared to come here. To try to take what's mine? Anger fills my blood and a seething mix of jealousy and vengeance turns my vision red.

"I was thinking we eliminate the three that don't matter but bring the cousins and Nikolai in for questioning." His statement is spoken in a low voice as he looks behind us, back to where Aria waits for me.

I lick my lips, knowing that Talvery is fully aware all six would die in an attempt to infiltrate and kill us, to rescue Aria.

"Nikolai is foolish and desperate. If he came because he knew she was here, I could see him only being followed by a few men."

"They're all high ranking," I say quickly, knowing each one of them. Recognizing a few who have killed on my streets.

"There's no way they came without Talvery knowing."

"Did they come to kill? Or to take her?" I ask Jase but had I waited for a second longer, I wouldn't have had to ask at all. I watch as one of them drops a grenade on the edge of the garage, followed by another a few feet farther down. *They came to kill.*

"They left explosives lining the gate. A scan shows they have enough on the bags strapped to their backs for the entire estate if they could get through it." My lips twitch with menace. "The same as before?" I ask Jase, remembering the site of the ash and rubble my former home was made to be. "You think it's the same men?"

Jase and I share a look, but he doesn't answer me verbally.

A call to Jase's phone replaces the surveillance on his phone. The moment he answers, my own phone rings to life in my pocket.

"It's Aria," Jase tells me before I answer my phone. He doesn't hide the nervousness as he tells me, "She's not staying in the bedroom."

"Where is she going?" I ask him, but then realize it doesn't matter. If she sees, she'll have to choose.

"Let her be, let her come if she chooses." My heart races as Jase tells them my orders and my phone dies in my hand. She'll see what they're capable of and what I need to stop, what I need to protect.

Let her see, let her choose.

"Have them kill the three, now." My voice is hard although inside tremors of rage grow. The three bodies will drop the second the command is given, leaving the other three scrambling but trapped on our estate. "Bring the other three to me."

CHAPTER 25

Aria

I F ONLY CARTER WOULD LET ME CALL MY FATHER OR GO TO HIM. My skin pricks with goosebumps that won't leave and the constant chill I feel is at odds with the heat boiling my blood.

I can convince my father that there's another way.

I heard what he said. The message for me. He was speaking in code. He's coming. In only hours, my father is coming for me.

Stay quiet while I'm gone and stay in your room.

My father would tell me that before leaving for the night when we were on lockdown, but only when he would be gone for a few hours. If it was any longer than that, he'd have me go to the safe house.

There's no way those words were a coincidence. I'm sure of it. He wouldn't have said it if he wasn't coming for me. He wouldn't have said *those words* if something wasn't happening by tonight.

My heart hasn't stopped racing. My throat is tight with guilt and fear. It can't happen like this. I don't know exactly what he's planning, but those are words said in times of war. Something bad is going to happen. I know it. I can feel it in the pit of my stomach. It's going to change everything.

I can do something. But I need time that I don't have.

Pacing up and down the corridor to Carter's wing in the estate, I try to formulate an excuse for my father or a reason that would justify Carter not reacting to my father's threats. I can't go into the bedroom and just wait. I refuse to simply stand by.

The conversation that was just had on the phone repeats itself over and over again in my head and I start to debate if I heard my father right.

Tension squeezes my chest so tightly I can't breathe.

After days, my father decides to come. After weeks of me being missing, he's finally coming for me. And there's nothing I can do to stop him.

My hands are shaking horribly, and it does nothing but piss me off. Forming a fist, I slam it into the wall. How could he do this to me?

Both of them.

Carter's not innocent. He knew that conversation would piss my father off. He was goading him, practically laughing in my father's face.

And I took pleasure in it.

Every bit of that pleasure I wanted. There's something sick and twisted about how I craved Carter pushing me to the edge while my father spat hate at him.

Carter has proven there's a side to me that desires depravity and a sense of justice that's sinful and warped.

I should have known better. We were playing with fire but after weeks of being with Carter, of being his, of growing to love him made me feel invincible beside him.

I've always been foolish like that.

Brushing the hair away from my face, I rid myself of the regret and focus on the now and the present.

I have to tell Carter, but I don't know how I can save my father if I do. And I know it won't be my father coming. He won't storm Carter's castle. It'll be hired men, or worse, Nikolai. Telling Carter will only ensure that his guns will be ready and whoever is coming will be killed before they even come close.

"Fuck." The word slips from my lips in a strangled breath.

I was so full of hope, so eager to have this call happen, and instead, my worst nightmare has come to life. I've brought the war to me and to Carter's doorstep.

A moment of clarity comes over me, and my eyes whip open.

I start moving before the thought is even clear.

He's not in the office. Carter is not in the office where the phone is. *And I don't remember him locking the door.*

I'm well aware that Carter has cameras everywhere, and that's why I walk as if nothing's wrong. My shoulders are square, and I try to keep my expression impassive even though tears prick at my eyes and my chest hiccups with the need to break down.

These men will kill me before they get a chance to kill each other.

The doorknob rattles under my grip, but it turns, and the door pushes open easily. I don't waste any time, knowing Carter will come if he sees me, and I fall to my knees, gathering the phone still carelessly tossed on the floor from earlier.

My finger shakes as I press the buttons, but I do it. I grip the phone with both hands as I hold it to my ear and watch the door. If he doesn't know already, he'll know soon enough.

Ring, ring.

Every pause of the ring grips my heart harder.

My throat feels as if it's closed up, clogged by something unseen when the call goes dead. Not unanswered, but dead.

Clank! I slam the phone down over and over again, just as Carter did before, feeling the heat of anxiety roll over my skin. My teeth are clenched as I slam it down again before bracing myself over the desk.

Deep breaths. I need to stay calm and find a way.

Not another second passes. Not another tense breath heaves from me before I pick up the phone and hit redial again.

To no avail.

Tick-tock, tick-tock, the clock on Carter's office wall taunts me. Showing nearly fifty minutes have passed since Carter left me.

The only other number I know by heart is Nikolai's. I don't know if he would listen. Or if my father would listen to Nikolai. I don't know anything for certain, but still, I dial in his number.

One number at a time.

And he doesn't answer.

The phone goes to voicemail, but the inbox is full. A ball of barbed wire seems to unwind in my throat as hopelessness steals the breath from me. With every breath, I swallow more of it and it pains my chest. My fingers dig into my shirt right over my heart, gripping and trying to pull the spiked pain away. But it only grows.

Tick-tock. Tick-tock.

I try my father's number again, putting it on speaker this time, giving up any pretense I had before. If Carter walks in, I'll tell him everything. There's not any other light of hope left in the dark clouds that settle around me.

With the sound of the dead tone coming from the phone, I set the phone down, politely resting it in its cradle, and collapse into Carter's seat.

I try Carter's computer. It's password protected.

I type in Tyler. Rejected.

Cross. Rejected. I would try birthdays and old exes if I knew any. But I don't have a damn thing to work with.

My mind wars with itself, the stakes growing higher and higher as the seconds pass. Pulling open his drawer and flipping through files I try to find anything that could hint at his password, but I come up with nothing.

Tick-tock. Tick-tock.

The clock plays tricks on me. An hour and a half has passed.

My pulse is so fast; I can't hear anything else. I feel dizzy and light-headed as I stand up and I have to brace myself to keep from falling over. The desk feels so cold and hard and the edges of it sharper than they did before.

I squeeze them so tightly that I think I may have cut myself but when I look down, there's been no blood shed.

"I have to tell him," I whisper to no one.

I can't balance myself as I walk. I have to rest my head against the wall for only a moment to catch my breath and think of the right words to say, the only words to say.

My father is coming. Men are coming to kill you.

I fight back the rush of oncoming tears and force myself to move. *Or maybe only to rescue me.*

I shut the door behind me and take in a shuddering breath.

I walk down the hall toward the stairwell, feeling cold and numb.

Deep breaths, one foot in front of the other. That's how I'll end my father's life and all those who stand with him. My cousins, my uncles. *Nikolai.*

God help me, please.

I pray as I grip the railing tightly and take each step carefully as my knees feel weaker.

Show me what to do. Please.

I'm halfway down the second set of stairs, toward the back half of the estate I never venture to, when I hear a gun cock. I freeze.

The sounds of a slap and a grunt mix with a cry of agony. My knees nearly buckle. *They're here.*

I'm too late. *No, please no.*

"Fuck you." I hear a voice I think belongs to one of my cousins and another hard smack as my knuckles go white from gripping the railing.

I can't breathe as my bare feet pad on the cold floor and I sneak closer to where the voices are coming from. My heart is beating so loud, I think they'll hear me.

How could I have let this happen?

How could Carter? The thought goes unfinished, but either way, my heart breaks.

"We'll take it from here," I hear Carter's voice as I see the backs of two men leaving, walking out from an open doorway, and heading to the rear exit. Both dressed in black and carrying guns. Not handguns or pistols, but automatic weapons. I nearly fall backward on my ass trying to take cover in the closest doorway, so I go unseen.

The sound of metal scraping against the floor can only be guns being kicked away.

Guns and questioning. It's an interrogation. My heart races and I struggle with what I can do to stop this.

"Where is she?"

Nikolai. I grip the wall, just around the corner from the front room where the voices carry from. The mix of adrenaline, fear, and betrayal riding through my veins in waves and overwhelming my ability to even think.

"I'll ask again, nicely. What were your direct orders?" Jase's voice is cold. Colder and harsher than I ever could have imagined. "Or did you not have any?"

I can barely breathe and when I do, it sounds so loud. My heart's beating out of my chest when I peek around the corner, getting low to the ground and praying no one will see me.

"Did your boss really send you to your death on a whim? Six men against an army?"

I cover my mouth with both of my hands and nearly fall forward at the sight in front of me as I round the corner, the rushing of my blood drowns out the voices of the interrogation, but the sound of a gun smacking against skin and crashing into bone rings clearly.

With my eyes shut tightly and a sickness stirring in my stomach, I force my eyes open. I force myself to see everything.

Nikolai makes up one of the three. The other two are my cousins, Brett and Henry. They're brothers and years older than me. We've shared every holiday. I was a bridesmaid in Brett's wedding. Every event we've been to together for years flashes before my eyes as I see Brett spit blood onto the floor. The left side of his face is already bruised and the black chestplate of his armor is covered in blood.

My heart squeezes. I don't want to see this. I can't. I can't watch, but I have to do something.

"We're not telling you shit," Brett sneers and Henry struggles next to him. With their wrists bound behind their backs, Henry sways. His right eye is swollen and that's all I can see, but he's not well.

What did they do to you? My heart bleeds at the question.

Jase and Declan have guns pointed at the back of their heads, with all three of them kneeling in a row in front of them.

"You want to join your friends sooner, rather than later?" Jase questions them.

I've never felt so betrayed. So sickened. Bile rises in my throat as my gaze drifts across the three men I've known all my life so close to their lives being over if only a trigger is pulled.

"Fuck you," Nikolai grunts out, pulling my focus to him. Although he stares at Carter with nothing but hate, his eyes show his pain. And it's my undoing.

The war has never felt so alive as it does now.

That's when I see a light shine, directing my eyes to what matters.

Carter's gun is tucked in the back of his pants. It's staring right at me, the light from the room reflecting on it. And the guns on the floor behind him. Three guns and one I recognize as Nikolai's.

He took their guns, he kicked them away from my family. And now they kneel in front of Jase and Declan, waiting for execution. The sound of a gun being cocked pushes me forward and leaves me no choice.

My hands shake as I crawl toward the guns. One scratches across the floor as I try to pick it up and I know at that point they see me. So, I do the only thing I can.

I point the gun at the enemy who doesn't have a gun.

I stand on weak legs and grip the gun as tightly as I can. Aiming it at the back of Carter's head. Knowing I've made a choice and hating myself for it but fueled by the need to protect my only friend and family.

"Carter," I call out his name and feel the eyes of everyone else in the room on me as Carter turns slowly around to face me.

His eyes flash as he lets out a breath, but he doesn't retreat, he doesn't even seem to take me seriously. He looks at me the way you'd look at a child playing dress-up. Non-threatening and as if they're simply being cute. It cuts me in a way I didn't think was possible.

He really cares so little for me. He's really going to kill them all and expects me to fall in line, obeying and submitting to his every whim.

As he steps toward me and I pull the trigger back even though my hands tremble, his expression morphs, and the damage I've done is so clear to me in this moment. His firm expression of disapproval and irritation changes to one I've never seen. A mask of hardness and sharpness that makes his chiseled features look even more dominating and villainous.

I can hear him breathe as he stops in his tracks. Everything about him is terrifying, save the look in his eyes. Those dark eyes with bright specks of silver still shine with something else. Hope, maybe? But it vanishes when I call out to him, feeling the tightness in my throat and chest squeezing the courage from me. "Let them go," I force the words out and they come out strong. I don't know how because at the moment I feel nothing but weak.

I feel like I failed the boy still hurting inside of Carter. I've lost the trust. I can see it as Carter's eyes glaze over and the darkness overwhelms them. I've never hurt so much in my life as I do now, but what else was there for me to do? I'm in a hopeless situation and there's no possible way for me to win.

My palms are so hot and tingling with the rush of adrenaline and mix of fear that controls my every move, and I nearly drop the gun but somehow, I hold it steady and keep it pointed on Carter.

"The girl we've all been waiting for," Carter says without a change in his expression. No arrogant smile. Nothing but a menacing look of hatred and disgust.

His head tilts and he says a word low and deep in his throat that sends a sickening chill down my spine. "Talvery."

BREATHLESS

BOOK 3

Her lips tasted like Cabernet and her touch was like fire.
I was blinded by what she did to me. I so easily fell for something I thought I'd never have.

I was weak for her and should have known better. I should have known she could never love a man like me.

She brought out a side of me that I wish had stayed dead.

I won't make the same mistake twice.
I don't care how much she begs me.
I don't care that I crave her more than anything else…

This is book 3 in the Merciless series. It picks up right where book 2, *Heartless*, left off. They must be read in order.

CHAPTER 1

Carter

I T'S BEEN A LONG TIME SINCE SOMEONE HAS DARED TRY TO KILL ME in my own home.

Even longer since someone has pointed a gun at me and lived to tell the tale.

I can barely hear a damn thing due to the ringing in my ears. I've waited for this moment, but this isn't how I thought it would go.

She loves me, I remind myself. She fucking loves me. I know she does.

Aria's face is flushed, and her hand trembles as she fights to hold the gun steady.

I take one step toward her and she cocks it. The click fills the room. Whatever remaining semblance of a heart I had shatters in my chest, the small shards shooting waves of pain through my body.

The sick grin on my face wanes even as I struggle to hold it in place, focusing on those gorgeous hazel eyes. Eyes that drew me to her, that begged me for mercy, that made me feel more than I've felt in years.

Eyes that fooled me.

"Drop your guns," Aria demands, her voice shaky but clear and loud regardless. It's fucking insane that in this moment she strikes me as utterly gorgeous. In her strength, she's at her most beautiful.

"Drop them!" she calls out more strongly and the gun wavers. It's obvious she's never held one before, or at the very least, never fired one.

Yet, she's pointing it at me. It could go off accidentally, killing me. *Would she regret it?* I question and feel a strong tug in my chest. A well of emotion threatens to break my composure. Every inch of skin is numb as I stare at the barrel, feeling everything crumble around me.

In front of the enemy.

In front of my brothers.

In front of her.

"Carter?" I hear Jase without seeing him, asking if they're to listen to her or not.

Two of my brothers, Jase and Declan, are behind me with guns pointed at three men kneeling on the floor. Two of them are her cousins, and the third man is her former lover and friend. The name she prayed to while in the cell, the one name I'm tired of hearing her speak, belongs to him.

All three are men who wanted to kill us only moments ago. Men that Aria is protecting, and willing to kill me to save.

Those fucking shards dig deeper into whatever wound they've gouged in my chest.

Swallowing the knot in my throat along with the distress I'm feeling, I answer Jase although I don't take my gaze from Aria. "Drop them." Instantly, relief shows on Aria's face, and she even relaxes her grip on the gun until I add, "But don't let those fuckers have them. No one holds a gun," I swallow thickly and add, forcing a smirk to my face, "but Aria."

The control is still in my demand. They'll listen to me, everyone who's worth a damn in this room will... but as time passes, I can feel it slipping away. I can only imagine what her family thinks, but it's what my brothers are seeing that fucking shreds me. They know I love her.

And now they're watching her betray all of us.

"Let them go," Aria commands in a weaker tone, one filled with a plea. Visibly swallowing, she finally breaks my gaze to look at them. Her startled, sharp intake of breath at what she sees destroys me. Her mercy and compassion for them are sickening.

They came to kill me. She fucking knows that.

She might kill me yet.

I loved her. I know I loved her, and that was my first mistake.

Anger rises and rings in my blood. My sanity finally comes back to me, hardening me and reminding me of who I am and everything I've worked for.

It's all going to crumble. All because of her.

I would have done *anything* for her.

"Let's go." I hear Nikolai's voice, low and riddled with pain. The blood is still bright red from the split on his lip and a bruise has already formed on his face. My knuckles turn white as my fist tightens. All I need is one moment to take out every bit of my aggression on him. I want to break his jaw for daring to speak those words to my Aria.

I've never felt rage like I do now as he reaches for her like he can take her away from me.

Because he can.

Because she's willing.

"Go," she says, and Aria's voice is strong as she glances at him. Again, the gun is slack in her grip. She doesn't seem to notice how loose the gun is in her hands. I could take it; I could chance it. But it would risk putting her in danger, and my gaze falls at the thought.

"Now," one of her cousins hiss, tugging on Nikolai's arm. The shirt tightens around his neck as the fabric is pulled. Peeking at him from my periphery, I'm disgusted, as is Nikolai, judging by his expression.

"Come with us," Nikolai urges, raising his voice to command her, but also beg her, and I take my focus from Aria, staring at the man Nikolai is.

He reminds me of the boy I once was.

Foolish and reckless. But he never went through the shit I did. He was bred into this life, he wasn't thrown into it and forced to fight to survive every fucking day.

Yet he thinks he can take her.

"I'm staying," Aria says with authority before I can say anything. Her declaration makes Nikolai flinch. A small bit of hope flutters in my chest. My throat tightens, and my chest aches, feeling as if it's on the verge of ripping wide open. *She's staying.*

"We don't have time for this!" one of her cousins yells out, glancing around the room as if any minute now, I'll change my mind and kill them all.

He'd be right if it wasn't for Aria.

She wanted them. She chose them.

"I'm not leaving without you," Nikolai growls and stalks to Aria, ready to take her. That's my cue to reach for my gun.

Their reunion has lasted long enough, and I refuse to let him take her. No one will take her from me. No one.

Adrenaline races through my blood, my breathing coming in heavier as my jaw clenches. The gun is hot in my hand. Hotter than it's ever felt before. It's pointed at Nikolai; Aria's is pointed at me.

My voice is deep and rough as I tell the three of them, "You have two minutes to run."

"Carter," she says, and Aria's voice is a desperate plea, but she has no room to bargain and I have no mercy remaining, not even for her. I ignore her, feeling the rage from what she's done seep into the marrow of my bones as I finish stating, "and then we'll open fire."

My brothers move slowly, reaching for their guns as Aria's expression crumples with pain and she rocks backward toward the wall, with her nervousness evident.

Nikolai's jaw is tense, his light blue eyes sparking with hate. "Come with me," he says beneath his breath. "Take her!" he commands his allies.

But they run, leaving him alone and leaving her behind. "She had her chance!" one of the men yells behind him. Their sneakers squeak as their footsteps pound on the freshly polished floor. Cowards. Talvery men are cowards.

"Aria, please," Nikolai begs her as if it breaks his fucking heart. Fuck him.

"One minute," I grit between my teeth and he finally looks at me. My grip tightens on the gun. One squeeze of the trigger and I'd be rid of him forever. I'm so close to pulling it, just to end it all. He looks me in the eyes and I wish the look I give him back was enough to kill him.

"Go," she whimpers, her eyes flickering from my gun to him. "Get out of here!" she screams at him.

"I'll come back for you," he tells her as if she's his long-lost love.

I hope he does come back for her. My nostrils flare and my chest aches as she gasps for breath watching him leave. *Come back for her, Nikolai. Come back, so I can break your fucking neck.* I bite my tongue, tasting the metallic tang of blood in my mouth.

I will kill him if it's the last thing I do.

He's still running away from her. My blunt nails dig into my palms as my fists tighten and the anger and jealousy mix into a deadly concoction. Red bleeds into my vision and it's all I can do not to pull the trigger as it follows his movements.

"I wanted to tell you," Aria sobs as the sound of Nikolai running away fades in the hallway. "I didn't think—"

"Tell me what?" I ask her.

"That they were coming," she says with a pain in her voice that matches the one swirling in her eyes. She's breaking apart, barely breathing and I can see the regret, the remorse. But only one thing resonates with me.

"You knew?" I question her and feel a chill rush through my body that sinks all the way to my bones.

She never loved me. She never did. You protect the ones you love. Always. And she didn't protect me.

I was a fucking fool and she isn't the woman I thought she is. She's a fucking liar.

"Are we really letting them go?" Declan's question slices through the haze of disbelief and treachery.

"You knew?" I ask her again, my temper coming back anew.

"I, I..." she stutters over her words, her gaze darting over my face, fear and pain causing her hazel eyes to glass over with tears. She lowers her gun all the way down, not daring to point it at me anymore and I drop mine as I move closer to her, each heavy step sounding more foreboding than the last.

"Carter?" Declan yells my name, demanding an answer.

With each step closer to her, she takes one in reverse until her shoulders hit the wall.

I holster my gun before ripping hers out of her hands, although she doesn't put up a fight. "Carter," Declan calls out again, not caring at all that the woman I loved set me up. She knew they were coming to kill me, to kill all of us, and she did *nothing*. "Are we letting them go or not?" Declan asks.

With one hand braced on the wall above Aria's head and the other pinning her hip to it, I look her dead in the eyes, ignoring everything about her gaze that draws me in. She can't have that anymore. I'm taking that power away.

Feeling the dominance of hatred flow through me and wanting to hurt her as she's hurt me, I answer Declan in a deep voice that's barely audible. "Kill them all."

Jase

I'm quick to follow Declan out of the room, even though I know it's a mistake to leave Carter alone with Aria.

I'll be fast. I have to do something to stop this.

"Declan." Raising my voice, I call out to my brother and the sound of his footsteps echoing in the hallway stops instantly. He turns to me, anger and tension still rolling off of his shoulders.

He can barely look me in the eyes.

"Yeah?" His voice is tight as I make my way to him, closing the distance as quickly as I can.

I keep my voice as low as possible and ignore the banging of my heart against my ribcage as I look over my shoulder to make sure no one followed, to make sure no one can hear me defy my brother's orders.

"Don't tell them to shoot to kill." I start to talk before I've even fully faced him. My words are mixed with my tense breath from the adrenaline flowing through my blood. "If they shoot, tell them to make sure they miss."

Declan hears me; I know he does by the shock on his face. The roar of anger coming from the foyer behind me reminds me of how unhinged Carter has become. He's going to do something stupid. Something he'll never be able to take back.

"I'm going back to them," I tell Declan and turn away only to have him grip my arm and pull me back to him. He doesn't say anything at first, but I can see the question in his eyes, the feel of betrayal from him.

And it shreds me.

"You know he loves her," I tell him, feeling the ache of sadness rising inside me. It hurt Carter, but it's more than that. She betrayed us all.

"Not after that," Declan nearly whispers. Shaking his head slightly with a defeated expression on his face, he continues, "Not after she—"

"It's not her fault she had to choose," I push the words through my clenched teeth, knowing in my gut that she's fighting with what's right versus where her loyalties should lie. "She never should have known."

The tension in Declan's gaze wavers, and he looks behind me before reaching my eyes again.

"She made a choice to stay. Let Talvery know that. She chose to stay. It'll fucking kill Nikolai and make the crack in their factions that much deeper. Nikolai has to live."

I know Carter will be pissed at me, but he'll get over it. He'll thank me when it's all said and done. It has to go down like this. I can't let him ruin everything.

With a tight nod, Declan runs his thumb over his chin but doesn't say a word.

"Tell the guards to let them go back to Talvery. But make sure they all know she chose to stay. She chose Carter."

CHAPTER 2

Aria

I've always known Carter to be a beast of a man. Barely contained and waiting for an outlet to release his rage. As his chest rises and falls with each heavy intake of breath and his muscles coil, his shoulders get more and more tense. With each ragged second of anxiousness passing between us, I know there's nothing holding him back.

"You chose them." His words are calculated, spoken with control although he looks anything but in control. The tension winds tighter and my body grows hotter with every hard thud in my chest.

"No," I try to tell him although my throat constricts to the point where I think I can't breathe. I start to shake my head, but he lets out a snarl, flipping the front table over in one swift movement. The carved wood antique crashes into the wall with a loud bang that forces my body to tremble as he screams, "Get out!"

The rough cadence of his voice carries through the room and I back away from him, my shoulders hunching as fear consumes me.

Tears prick my eyes and I try to speak, to tell him I didn't have a choice. I just did what I thought I needed to. "I'd never have—"

He turns to me, taking three large strides forward, the cords in his neck taut and bulging as his dark eyes pierce into me.

"Shot me?" he questions me with nothing but disbelief and rage burning in his eyes.

The intensity of his stare alone makes me cower.

"Carter," Jase speaks up from behind us, but Carter doesn't turn away from me. He stares at me like I've betrayed him. As if what I did was the ultimate sin.

Has he forgotten that they're my family? That I've begged him to spare them and yet he was going to execute them? Did he forget that he stole me from them and locked me in a cell for weeks?

He stares down at me as though he hates me.

I feel it. It's raw and palpable.

At this moment, I feel he truly hates me. And that's what breaks me.

Because no matter what he did to me, I never hated him. *I love him.*

Tears flow from me easily as Carter informs Jase in the most unfeeling manner that I'm to be removed from the premises.

My heart hollows and collapses, but my feet move, my body shoves me forward. And Carter follows, blocking me from running down the hall to the bedroom.

"I thought you loved me," he sneers at me and I cover my mouth with my hand to hold back the agony.

I do love him. I do.

I swear I love this man.

Even if he hurt me and even if I hurt him just now.

I can't voice a single word as his warm breath covers my face and my body wracks with a sob.

"Carter!" Jase yells, grabbing his shoulder and forcing him to look at anything other than me.

The moment he does, I bolt. I turn to run past Jase. I don't dare try to run past Carter. He could block me, catch me, and throw me away. He could see to it himself to banish me from his home.

The hideaway room is past the bedroom, so that space isn't an option either. And given the state Carter's in, I don't trust him to keep his word and let me recover from what's happened, so I can try to explain.

Instead, I run as fast as I can, on shaky legs and with adrenaline coursing through me, in the opposite direction. The muscles in my thighs scream with pain as I take the stairs two at a time. The pounding of my heart and footsteps are overwhelming. I'm hot and sweating and not okay in any sense of the word. I have to make him understand somehow.

He starts chasing me, although at his own slow and teasing pace. The second I hear Carter behind me, I slip. My elbow and hand crash on the hard, wooden stairs as does my knee, sending shooting pains through my body. I could cry, and I hate myself for it. I did this. This is my fault. I look behind me and see Carter start to climb the stairs. A mask of anger and dominance appears set in stone on his handsome features.

The cell.

The thought hits me at that moment. I force myself to get up and run to the cell. I know it's behind a painting. He wouldn't be able to get in if I ran to the cell and locked myself in. It'll take him time to get a key; time I desperately need. He needs to calm down and I need time. Time so I can figure out how to explain things to him in a way he'll understand.

Running up the stairs and using that momentum to push off the wall at the top, I careen down the hall.

Which one is it? My breathing is unsteady and a cold sweat breaks out along every inch of my skin. My heart won't stop racing; pounding chaotically. I can barely see straight.

There are six large paintings in the hall and my fingers fumble around the first, trying to heave it to the side, but it's not the right one. I tremble as my gaze is whipped toward the sound of him coming.

The second painting I push so hard that it falls, nearly toppling over on me. It's at least five feet long and four feet high. And it's not the right one either. The frame splits and cracks and I have to high-step over it, scraping my shin as I go, but I don't care. *Where is it? I need to find it, please.*

"You can't run from me." Carter's deep voice reverberates through the hall, and glancing behind me, I see his shadow as he climbs the stairs.

Thump, thump, my heart pounds harder and harder. I can barely breathe.

I don't know which one is the cell. I don't know.

The box.

The very thought has me sprinting down the hall to the last set of stairs. Up one more floor and on the left. I run as fast as I can, gasping for breath. Just the idea of Carter not giving me a chance to even speak to him, to explain, to ask for forgiveness, is crushing me with every step.

He just needs time. He has to understand. I can make him understand.

Visions of his face when I pointed the gun at him flash through my mind as I run.

Carter, seemingly over the desire to move slowly and let me run from him, picks up his pace as I get to the hall. I can hear his footsteps pound up the stairs, so I run as hard as I can, nearly slamming into the closed door of his office. Tears prick as the hurt and betrayal of what I've done set in.

I scrabble with the knob so clumsily in my own chaos that I think it's locked, but it's not.

It's open and a wave of relief runs through me although it's short-lived. Nothing is okay at this moment. Not a damn thing is all right.

I don't waste any time; I don't bother to close the office door either. Sprinting to the box, I rip the top open and practically fall into it, scraping my thighs and back. A scream is ripped from me, but it's merely instinctual. I don't care about the pain; I don't care about anything other than shutting the lid and locking myself in.

I have to reach up to get the top of it lowered and when I do, I see Carter in the doorway. Fear paralyzes me when I see his face, contorted with a look of outrage and red from running. My skin is ice cold as I reach for the lid. My fingertips feel numb as I slam it down.

There's a snap, I hear it, but I don't know what it is. It comes with a tug at the back of my neck that's accompanied by a sharp pinch I try to ignore as my fingers slip along the edge of the lid searching for the lock.

Shrouded in darkness, I struggle to find the lock, hearing Carter's footsteps getting closer and closer, but my trembling fingers find it and the multiple clicks assure me I'm bolted in.

All I can hear is my staggered breathing for a moment and then another.

With a deafening roar of anger, the box lifts off the ground only an inch, if that. Through my tears still streaking down my hot face, I can see Carter lifting it with all his strength, but it's meant to outlast such acts and so it does.

Crouched in the box and gripping on to myself, I hold my breath knowing he can't do a damn thing about it.

It's only then that I hear the rolling of the beads. It's only then that I feel the pearls rolling around me. I shriek in terror at first, thinking that something is alive and in the dark place with me. But it's only my necklace. The beads that have fallen off the broken chain.

Tears leak freely at the realization.

My chest hollows as I cover my mouth to keep from crying harder.

The box moves a little more and I close my eyes until he drops it, making my body sway and tumble in the small amount of space I have. A small yelp escapes me, but I focus on calming down. I'm on the verge of a panic attack or worse.

My eyes are closed tighter than they've ever been. Shock and horror still threaten to suffocate me as I struggle to inhale.

A few minutes pass and all I can hear is Carter's chaotic breathing. For a moment someone comes in, I think Jase, speaking quietly and trying to tell Carter to calm down, but the door closes shut with a loud click and then there's silence again.

Nothing but silence and the slamming of my own heartbeat and the rushing of blood in my ears.

It's going to be okay, I try to reassure myself. *He has to understand.* Even the thought is fleeting in my mind. All Carter knows is that I chose them, my family and his enemies. I pointed a gun at him and cocked it.

Oh, my God. My head spins as the memory comes back to me.

I threatened the life of the only man I've ever loved.

When I finally open my eyes, Carter's are fixed directly on mine. As if he can see me, even though I know it's impossible. His dark eyes pierce through me, pinning me where I am and eliciting a new kind of fear.

His deep voice sends a jagged spike of despair through me as he says low beneath his breath, "You can't stay in there forever."

broken

CHAPTER 3

Carter

I'VE NEVER IN MY LIFE FELT LIKE THIS BEFORE.

The clock ticks as time passes. I can count on one hand every time I've been betrayed, but it's never felt like this because none of them were close to me. I've never let anyone in.

Not the guards I've depended on, not the boys I took in to help. I didn't feel betrayed by them when they only stole from me or tried to bargain with someone else who wanted me dead.

I've never let a soul close to me other than my brothers. So, no one can hurt me.

No outsider has ever been close to me… except for her, the only woman I ever loved.

A chill rolls through my body like the unrelenting tides of the ocean. The adrenaline has waned as I sit here in the chair, staring at that fucking box. My knuckles are bruised and cut, but I keep putting pressure on them, to keep me from thinking of a different pain, the aching in my chest.

Every time I blink, the barrel of her gun is there, staring back at me.

"Carter." Daniel's voice breaks me from my thoughts and brings me back to this reality. It fucking hurts; every piece of me hurts. Sitting up slightly in the chair, I finally take my eyes away from the box, away from Aria. I tilt my head as I take in my brother and the man standing next to him. Eli's one of our guards and head of security.

"Eli's finished the walk-through." He's struggling to keep his eyes on me; I can see it in the way he swallows visibly and clenches his hands. Even his voice is strained.

She did this. I know Daniel cared about her. And she betrayed him like she did me.

Eli steps forward to speak, telling me about each of the bombs they found and disposed of and where exactly the Talvery men ran. No surprises and nothing I give a fuck about at this point. Not when the woman who caused all of this is still right in front of me, but safely hiding in plain sight.

"All of them?" I ask just to pretend to be present, pressing my sore back into the chair and still staring at the fucking box. I can barely see Eli nod in my periphery as he answers, "Yes, sir." With his shoulders squared and his hands behind his back, he looks like the soldier he used to be.

But he defied me.

"You let them live," I say flatly, turning my attention directly to him for just a second, so he can see how pissed I am, hardening my gaze and my scowl. Then I look back to the box. The box I took from a man I refused to show mercy to. Aria's breathing picks up and she moves within its small confinements.

"I ordered Eli and the guards to let them live." Jase's voice sends a cold trickle down my neck. It's hard to swallow as my blood heats with anger.

One by one, they're all turning their backs on me.

Aria moves inside of the box again; I can faintly hear her crying. It's then that Eli catches on to the fact that she's in the box. Glancing at him, I can see his expression fall, the puzzle in his head forming as each of the pieces fall into place.

It takes a moment for him to fix his fucking face and wipe the look of disgust off of it.

She did this. She will suffer the consequences.

I gave her a chance; I would have given her anything had she simply chosen me. I was stupid for ever loving her. Or for thinking she loved me.

"Leave," I bite out the command, feeling the raw word scratch against the back of my throat. Eli's the first to turn around sharply and leave at once. Daniel and Jase step forward rather than retreating and my muscles tense, my teeth gritting as I lean forward in the seat I haven't left for nearly an hour now.

"Carter," my brother says, and Jase's voice is strong and

demanding. Not like the way Aria's been saying it as she whimpers in the box, begging me to understand. I won't hear it. There's no excuse.

"Fuck off." It's all I can say back to him. The rage blisters inside of me, eating me alive that they all defied me.

"Carter." Daniel's tone is softer, more placating. "Just relax for a minute. Calm down," he tells me.

I can barely inhale, refusing to believe everything that's happened.

"Did you hear that, songbird?" I ask her rather than facing my brothers. The legs of the chair scratch against the floor as I lean forward, searching for a seam in the box where I think she can see me. I stare at it with an unforgiving bitterness as I tell her, "I just need to calm down."

I can feel the depth of emotion roaring inside of me as Jase speaks, "It was an unfortunate event, but we can use this to our favor."

"Unfortunate?" I can't hide the disbelief and venom in my voice as I stare back at him, finally rising from my seat. The force of the abrupt movement shoves the chair back. All I can hear is my heart beat in time with my heavy footsteps as I move closer to my brother.

Same height as me, the same determination in his voice.

"Knock it off," Daniel says and walks between us, separating us with a hard hand on both of our chests. "What about Aria?" he says quickly as he pushes me back. His glare pleads with me to think about something other than her apparent betrayal. "She's not okay." He lowers his voice to tell me the obvious and then lets his gaze move to her before looking back at me.

"What about her?" I ask him in a hardened tone. My hands form fists so tightly, I can feel the skin across my knuckles nearly crack and the cuts that are there split even wider.

A whimper from the box catches the attention of my brothers, both of them looking toward her as I stare at them.

"What the fuck do you even care for?" I sneer at Daniel. I raise my voice to remind them of the hard truth, "She chose them."

The sobs return from the box behind me and it enrages me. "Now she cries," I say, talking to her more than to them as I walk closer to where she is. The box is off-center now, crooked and making the end of the rug uneven from my useless attempts to open it even though I know it can't be done.

"She wasn't crying when she held a gun to my head!" Everything turns to white noise. Whatever my brothers say, the relentless crying from the woman I loved as she hides from me for fear of her own life, all of it.

I hate everything at this moment. I hate everyone. But I hate myself the most.

"She wasn't crying when she found out her family was coming to kill us. To kill all of us!" The last bit comes out louder and harsher than I can control, and I reach above the box to the bookshelves, shoving aside a row of them. The hardcovers and pages fly into a flutter before slamming down on the floor.

"I was!" Again, I hear her cry out, "I was!"

But all it does is fuel me to continue wrecking every shelf above her. All of the books falling around her, some of them slamming against the box, only make her cry out louder.

I hate her.

I hate them all.

I hate everything.

It takes both of my brothers to pull me back against the office window and away from the shelves. As I catch my breath, I think about destroying all of it. Wrecking every piece of this rich interior. It mocks me. It's a façade of control and I have none anymore. Not a damn shred of control.

"You never loved me!" I scream at her. "I should have kept you in that fucking cell until you knew better than to defy me!"

"Please, Carter, let me explain," she weeps.

"I was too fucking good to you," I sneer at her as loud as I can, feeling my composure deteriorate just as any ounce of mercy has. I scream at the top of my lungs, wanting to shred something apart. Every last bit of my humanity will do.

"Stop," Daniel says, his head close to mine. As he uses all of his strength to push me against the cold glass window, he's so close that I can feel the burn of his body heat.

"It's okay," he tells me as Jase grunts, his expression strained and his face red with exertion. Every inch of my skin is numb with a pain I've never felt before.

I want to tell them all nothing is okay and that I'll never stop. Never. There's nothing left of me but this shell of a man. But before I can tell them that I'll find the men they let get away and I'll rip out their fucking throats before they can breathe a word of how Aria betrayed me, a small voice comes from the doorway.

"Fuck." Daniel barely breathes the word before releasing me to run to her, to Addison, but he's too late.

I don't know how much Addison saw, or what she saw, but her face is pale.

Aria's still crying uncontrollably, and it's going to be obvious. It's obvious I'm hurting her and that she's scared. She's scared of me because I've fucking lost it. Nothing else matters.

There's no hiding now. Not from my brothers, not from the Talverys. Not from Addison, the one connection I still have to my brother Tyler.

Shame and disgust are a painful cocktail to swallow, but I choke it down.

"What the fuck are you doing?" Addison's voice vacillates between strength and panic as she stands in the doorway to my office. Her eyes dart from me to Daniel.

"How long have you been standing there?" Daniel asks Addison.

"Long enough… to…" Addison struggles to even look at Daniel. "You're hurting her," Addison barely glances my way.

Aria's sobs are punctuated with hiccups as she breathes in heavily, like she's desperate to stop, desperate to quiet her cries.

"Aria?" Addison's tone reflects a despair I've never heard from her before and inside I shatter. Whatever bit of anger that lingered, fragments and scatters in the pit of my stomach. Sucking in a deep, shuddering breath, her eyes go wide with fear and she takes a half step back.

"Daniel," she says hesitantly, her eyes wide with shame and disbelief as her body shakes so strongly I can see it from across the room. "You can't be okay with this?"

Fuck. Fuck. It's all fucked!

I straighten my stance as Jase lets go of me, moving out of the way and taking a few strides closer to Aria, away from me and out of sight from Addison. But the movement makes him that much more obvious to her.

"Get her out," she says, and her demand is strained by the veil of fear. She's pointing to the box but doesn't dare to let it steal her gaze from Daniel.

"Addison, stay out of it," Daniel tells her as he takes another step closer to her, his hands held in the air.

"Are you fucking serious?" As each word cracks with disdain, pain grows on her face. "Daniel, help her." The last word comes out in a croak as she backs away from him, further into the office and closer to the shelves. She nearly trips on the fallen books but manages to keep herself upright. She only takes her eyes off of him to see where Jase and I are. Neither of us is moving as she struggles to get closer to the box, closer to Aria who's quiet, and for a moment, I worry if she's all right.

"Why did he say cell?" Addison asks, and I can't even begin to think of when I said that word or how I used it. All I can see is red and my memory is a white fog.

"Addison, please," Daniel begs her.

"He's hurting her, putting her in a cell?" she shrieks and then turns any bit of remorse or disgust into anger. "You're allowing it! You knew!"

"She put herself in there," I say, cutting off the interrogation directed at Daniel and feeling the need to defend us against Addison's unspoken, yet all too clear thoughts. "Tell her, Aria." I raise my voice, feeling my cold blood fill my veins and praying to hear her voice.

"What did you do to her?" Addison's breathy words are filled with accusations.

"Nothing." Aria's voice is finally heard, although it trembles and is minuscule compared to ours.

With a hardened jaw, I dare to stare back at her, narrowing my gaze and not allowing her to blame this on me.

"She ran up here and hid because she held a gun to my head." Each word comes out harder, but I stay where I am as Addison inches closer to Aria.

"Addison," Daniel says as he tries to reason with her, keeping his voice low, but not to be denied, "get out."

"Fuck you," she spits at him and then finally lays a hand on the box.

"Aria," she calls out to her, banging the palm of her hand on the box behind her, although she still faces Daniel with a defiant expression on her face.

Aria whimpers for Addison to go, to leave her alone and stay out of it.

"I'm not going anywhere," Addison's quick to reply, tears leaking down her face.

"Don't cry," Daniel pleads with her, stepping forward and trying to reach out for Addison. The resulting slap is so hard, so vicious, I practically feel it against my own skin. Daniel's cheek instantly turns bright red, his head rotating back slowly to face her as Addison screeches at him, "Don't touch me!"

"Addison, you need to." Daniel barely gets another word out before Addison loses her shit entirely. Her voice three octaves higher than it should be, her entire body shaking with a new kind of vengeance, she's only getting more agitated.

"What did he do to her?" She sways in anger as Aria's sobs are echoed in Addison's voice.

What did I do to her? To Aria?

I loved her the only way I knew how. My head feels light and everything I think I know means nothing.

I should have known it would never be okay. I'm too fucked up to keep a woman like her. To keep anyone at all. What did I do to her? I drove her to betray me, to threaten to kill me.

"What happens between them—" Daniel starts to try and defend himself, not me. Not the relationship I had with Aria. Because there is no defending that. I know it deep in my gut.

I try to take a step forward, toward the door to get out, but stop when Addison shrieks at Daniel, shoving him away as he tries yet again to go to her.

"Please, just go!" Aria begs her and that only makes Addison more adamant at getting her out of the box.

As Addison screams at Daniel, I force my heavy and numb legs to move forward. "You knew! You knew what he was doing to her!"

The ice in my veins freezes my blood, and my heart refuses to beat without the warmth. "How could you?" she wails.

In a single day, everything has fallen.

Even as I walk out of the office, shutting the door behind me and hearing the faint screams leak into the barren hall, I know everything is ruined and nothing will be the same.

Everything is broken, and I have no way to fix a single piece of it.

It's all dashed beyond repair.

CHAPTER 4

Aria

*T*HEY WEREN'T GOING TO KILL THEM. I WANT TO THINK CARTER and his brothers would never do that. *They wouldn't execute my family in front of me.* It's all I keep thinking as my eyes burn in the darkness of the box.

Nikolai would do it, though.

He would kill the Cross brothers, all of them, to set me free. But he doesn't know them and everything that happened. I haven't had a chance to convince him otherwise; all he knows is that I was taken. With every second that passes, I calm my panic, knowing I have to talk to Nikolai and stop this. I need it all to stop and for them to listen to me. For one of these thick-skulled men to just listen to me.

None of this would be happening if they listened to me.

A shuddering breath forces my body to tremble against the rough wood and my neck arches with a sudden deep breath.

I don't know if it's a panic attack or a sharp break from reality that's making me shake like I am.

Or the fear. The raw and paralyzing fear of what I know Carter is capable of and what I think he's going to do to me when I step out of this box.

"I love you," I whimper again, closing my eyes tightly and forcing the words out. I wish I could take it all back, but the alternative was watching my family die right in front of me. Watching Nikolai get shot in the back of the head. I cover my hot face with my hands, shaking my head like a lunatic at the thought.

"I don't want anyone to die." My strangled words are barely heard as the box shakes and then a hand bangs against the top.

"Aria, please." Addison's tone is desperate and I'm so ashamed. I don't want to leave this box. I feel like a child again, hiding in the closet and telling myself it's not real if I don't come out. If I stay here, none of this is real.

"He hurt you?" she asks, but her question is more of a statement. The question comes from a friend to a friend. Directed at a woman hiding from someone, someone she loves and crying hysterically. A grown ass adult, hiding in a box. I know exactly how this looks, but I don't know how to explain it to her, so she'd understand. She's not from this world. And she doesn't know Carter like I do either. Although, none of that makes this right. None of it. "How long has he been doing this?" Her voice breaks at the question and I hear her cry for me.

I wish I could die right here.

"Come out!" she screams to me, her voice sounding ragged as she thumps on the box.

I know we're alone; Jase made Daniel leave and I heard the door shut what feels like hours ago but is probably only minutes. It's only Addison in the room now, crying as she holds the box and apologizes to me as if she's done anything wrong at all.

"He wouldn't listen to me," I whisper to no one in the darkness of the box. Every time I tried to explain, he wouldn't hear me out. He'd cut me off and tell me to get out. Just like she is. At this point, I don't think there's a defense I could possibly have that would make what I did forgivable in Carter's eyes.

"Get out!" she yells even louder. Her voice sounds hoarse at this point, and I hear her lay her body over the box heavily, falling onto it and crying. "How could he do this?" she whispers and then sniffles. I don't know if she's talking about what Carter did to me, or how Daniel allowed it and defended it. I know to see him in this light… it changed how Addison sees him, and that fucking kills me.

"I never meant for this to happen," I tell her weakly, closing my eyes and feeling them burn from hours of straining to see in the darkness and shedding hot tears.

I can hear her move again, but I don't know what she's doing, and her voice doesn't travel far. "I'm so sorry. I didn't know… I didn't know."

Reaching up slowly, I force my numb fingers to unlock the box with a loud click that makes my heart pump hard, so hard it feels like it'll stop beating altogether.

As I lift open the top, the light filters in and I squint. It fucking hurts. My eyes feel like they're burning, but I force the top open further as Addison stands up in front of me on shaky legs and wraps her arms around me. I hold her back tighter, gripping on to her and bunching the thin cotton of her shirt in my hand as she pulls me hard into her chest. "It's not your fault," is all I can say, and the words are so flat, so lacking to my ears, that I harden them, pulling her back and staring into her forest green eyes.

"You did nothing wrong," I tell her.

She stands there with a troubled expression, wiping away her tears and shaking her head. "What did he do to you?" she asks me softly, still holding on to me as I climb out of the box on shaky legs, staring at the closed door. I feel cold; it's so cold.

There's not a piece of me that doesn't think Carter's watching. I know he must be. My first instinct when thinking he knows I'm out of the box is to hold myself. To wrap my arms around my shoulders and wait for him to punish me. I can barely stand looking at the closed door.

Addison grips me with a bruising force, shaking me until I stare into her eyes. "What did he do to you?"

I just want to cry. I don't know where to start, but the shame clogs my throat and keeps me from speaking at all.

"It's okay to tell me," she whispers although the words barely come out. Fresh tears leak from the corners of her eyes as she speaks so calmly to me. "Whatever he did, you can tell me. It's okay."

"It's my fault," I start, and an awful gasp leaves her as she covers her mouth. It hurts, everything hurts, but the way she looks at me like I'm wounded, and I don't know any better, I can't explain the pain it causes.

She shakes her head violently, staring back at me.

"You don't understand," I try to reason with her but my voice cracks and all I can think is to keep repeating that it's my fault. It is, truly.

"I knew he'd hate me. I knew..." I can't finish the sentence as the door to the office opens. Fear spikes through me and I jump back, hitting the back of my legs against the box and nearly tumbling in. Addison guards me against whoever enters as if she's my protector.

"Get out!" she sneers at whoever's entered and with equal amounts of curiosity and terror, I peek over her shoulder. Even though I'm feeling weak and pathetic, my fingers numb and my chest heaving in air.

It's only Daniel.

"Addison, please." Daniel's eyes are red-rimmed, and I'm shocked. "Let's get out of here, okay?" He talks softly with his hands held up, approaching us like the two wounded animals that we are. "We can leave," he offers her.

"I'm sorry," I say and can barely get the words out, seeking Daniel's gaze so he knows I mean it. "I'm so sorry." My voice is wretched.

"Look at her." Addison's voice ricochets in the office as she steps toward Daniel. "Look at her!" she screams in his face and he lowers his head, shaking it and trying to speak. Addison doesn't understand; all she sees is the pain. And there's so much of it.

"It wasn't my place," Daniel tells her sternly, but his expression is begging her to understand. How can she, when she knows nothing?

"She's not okay and your brother did this to her." She takes another step forward and points to me, still standing behind her. Her bottom lip trembles as she shouts, "You did nothing!" I grip on to my shoulders tighter and feel so small. It's hard to know what to think anymore, but I know what she sees, and it breaks my heart.

"He didn't have a choice—"

"Bullshit!" she cuts him off, screaming louder and louder, "You let him hurt her!"

Silence compresses the time, forcing the clock to tick faster. The moment passes quickly as my head feels woozy and I can't stop my breathing from coming in just as fast.

I hold onto myself tighter, struggling to remain upright.

"I'm leaving and I'm taking her with me." The anger is gone; there's only resolve in Addison's voice. "So help me God, if you stand in my way, I'll never come back to you. Never, Daniel."

"You're leaving me?" he asks, the look in his eyes hardening, the silvers sparking even as the tremors of intense emotion run along his hard jaw. His determination is still there, still unyielding.

"How could I stay with you?" she asks, trying to disguise the misery in her tone as she hurriedly wipes away the tears. "How could I stay here, knowing this?"

Any semblance of anger vanishes from Addison, the realization of what she's doing breaking through her rage and disgust. She's leaving him.

"Don't do this," I finally speak, pushing forward and grabbing Addison's arm. I plead with her, "You don't need to get in between; you don't need—"

"It's not about what I need to do," Addison speaks so softly, but with an evenness that's at odds with her disheartened expression. "It's about what I want to do." Her voice doesn't waver as she turns to Daniel, grabbing my hand in hers and telling him once again, "I'm leaving and I'm taking her with me." With a quick intake of air and tears brimming in her deep green eyes, she hesitates but then adds, "Don't follow me, Daniel."

"You know I will," he tells her with no remorse, but also with no objection to her leaving either.

My hand feels so cold in Addison's and I try to speak again, but she shushes me. "Please, don't make this harder on me," she speaks to me although it sounds like a desperate prayer.

It's quiet for so long, the agony lingering in the air. My gaze darts between the two of them; he's staring at her, but she's staring at the open door.

"I need to leave," she tells him again, squeezing my hand and I squeeze back, for her. I keep praying to hear Carter's footsteps or his voice. Any part of him to come to me and fix this. To fix the mess I caused.

"I don't want this to happen," I say, and the words are rough beneath my breath as I tug at Addison's hand for her to look at me. And she does. I can feel Daniel's eyes on me, but I don't look at him; instead, I beseech Addison, willing her to believe me. "He didn't know," I lie. I'd tell a thousand lies to keep it from tearing the two of them apart.

I can see Daniel shift uncomfortably out of the corner of my eye, but I don't react. Addison's expression turns soft and sympathetic as she squeezes my hand again. "You don't have to lie for them." Her voice is coated with a sadness that claws at my insides. She gives me a soft smile that's false and it falters when she tells me, "They're big boys and they knew what they were doing." Turning to Daniel she adds, "He knew I would never be okay with something like this." The emotion wrecks each of her words and in turn, the hardness of Daniel's gaze. I can't bear to look at him, watching as her words destroy them and whatever love was left between them.

"It's over. And I want out," she says in two breaths that linger between them. "Let me go, Daniel. Please. You need to let me go this time." Even as the tears fall down her cheeks, she stands strong. I look past Daniel, refusing to look at either of them as my vision blurs with tears. The pain I feel for them magnifies as I realize she's taking me with her, and Carter isn't here at all.

He's not fighting for me.

He doesn't want me anymore.

I cover my face, pulling my hand away from hers and letting out the tortured sorrow of leaving him, but in the back of my mind I hear the voices hiss, he won't let it happen. She won't be able to leave so easily.

They're silenced with Daniel's only parting words. "I'll have Eli take you."

He doesn't touch her; he doesn't wait for a second longer. Instead, he simply turns and leaves us without another word, which only makes the pain grow stronger.

Carter, please, come take me. Please.

Addison struggles to control her composure, watching Daniel leave without even a single goodbye.

"I'm so sorry," I tell her again, hugging her back as she hugs me tight.

"You keep apologizing when this isn't your fault." Her words are soft and interrupted by the sound of footsteps.

I barely peek at the man named Eli, dressed in a fitted gray suit, no tie or cufflinks which makes it seem more casual, and with worn black dress shoes that are scuffed but somehow suit him.

It's his gaze that forces me to look away. Sharp pale blue eyes that have nothing but sympathy in them.

I don't want it. I'm ashamed as Addison leads me behind Eli and another man called Cason.

He's shorter than Eli, but not by much, and with bulging muscles that make him seem larger. He's the one who carries two bags he says are for us, but I don't know what's in them. Addison cries harder although she nods her head. Her strength at this moment is something I admire. I wish I could move forward, to make the decision to leave even knowing what the Cross brothers are capable of.

With Cason behind and Eli in front, our footsteps echo in the quiet hall. At every corner, I both hope that Carter is there to stop me and pray that he's not, so I can escape and hide away from him.

Every second closer to the door feels like it pulls on my torn heart.

Carter never comes, and that makes the chill from outside that much colder.

The peonies have died from the season's passing, they never last long, and the pale moon is full, illuminating every bit of the path to the sleek black sedan waiting for us even though the night is still early.

As I stare up at the house, searching for Carter in any of the windows, Addison waits for me to get in the car with silent tears still falling. He's not there. He's not watching.

"We don't have to leave," I tell her softly once more, desperately wanting Carter to come out and say he understands and that he forgives me. As I do him. In every way.

For what happened in the cell. For what happened today. It's all fucked up and there isn't an ounce of good in any of it, but I swear I love him. And love is forgiveness, isn't it?

I forgive him for anything he's done. I just want him back. I want him to love me again.

Please, Carter.

But not seeing him here... Him knowing that I'm leaving, and not bothering to say goodbye or try to fight for me in the least, I know he doesn't want me. It crushes me.

That thought is what forces me into the car, my back hitting the leather with a forceful blow. The sound of the trunk opening and the murmurs from Addison and Eli speaking mean nothing.

I don't know where I'll go or what I'll do.

My skin is numb, and I can barely breathe.

How many times have I tried to run? Yet here I am, and I would give anything for Carter to stomp toward us and rip me from my savior to throw me back into the cell.

The leather seats protest as Addison gets in and buckles her seatbelt. I talk over the click. "I love him," I say, swallowing thickly. "I love Carter."

She barely glances at me, her eyes red and blotchy and her cheeks still flushed from crying.

"I love Daniel too." Her voice is hoarse as she leans her head back, resting it and staring at the ceiling of the car. "But love isn't enough sometimes. They can't do that to you."

I'm ashamed at her reply. I'm ashamed that I need saving.

I'm ashamed that I allowed it and with a single moment, she's seemingly put an end to it.

I wish I could rip my heart out and never feel love again. How easy life would be if you could truly be heartless.

Hours ago, I was in love with a man I know I should never have let near me.

And now he's watching me leave with zero objections, and it destroys me. I've never felt pain and regret like this. It doesn't matter what happened between us today; I would be feeling this tear in my soul regardless of what I'd done.

I should have known the concept of a happily ever after would never come to fruition when my last name is Talvery.

CHAPTER 5

Carter

S HE'S REALLY LEAVING.

She walked away. Straight through the front door. Never would I have seen it happen that way. She was always running and hiding in the shadows. I knew she'd leave one day, deep down in the pit of my stomach, but I never imagined it'd be like this. I never imagined it would fucking hurt like this either.

Swallowing thickly and ignoring the pain, I pick up another book from the floor, a hardback of *Lord of the Flies*. It's a collector's edition and I watch as I trace the spine of it with my fingers while asking Daniel, "Did you call Sebastian?"

He's leaning against the windowsill, but I can't fucking watch them leave like he is.

I won't watch her walk away from me.

"He knows already." His voice is low, not filled with the resentment I keep waiting for him to throw at me.

For being the hard man he is, Daniel always has forgiveness for his family. I wish I felt the same.

"How is that even possible?" I ask him while placing the book on the shelf and reach down for another. Someone else could take care of this and clean up my mess, but I don't want them to. I need to do something mindless before I deal with the consequences. Every time I bend down is another deep breath. Every book on the shelf is a piece put back into place.

I need to do this before I can deal with Jase going behind my back and everything that's happened over the last few hours. No one will come out unscathed. No. One.

Grinding my teeth together, I keep my back to Daniel as he answers me.

"Addison was ready to run; I could see it." He looks full of guilt and remorse as he stares out of the window, watching the car lights die in the thick of the forest as they move farther along the road.

Taking them away from us.

Taking her away from me.

Even glancing at the lights, so small and faint in the distance, shoves the knife deeper into my chest.

"So, I called him and asked if he would mind." He shrugs, attempting to refute the devastation of what's happened. It's clearly written in his expression, but he continues, "He's never used it and it's close, it's contained, and easily defended."

"Do they really think we'd let them go?" I ask him, feeling a surge of control again. She's never leaving me. Never.

"I'm sure Addison knows better." The urgency in Daniel's voice compels me to look back at him. He's leaning against the window now, facing the door to my office and staring at it aimlessly. "She'll try to leave, so we need to watch for that too."

"Always watching..." I mutter and then add, "For enemies coming and for our women leaving."

"Look at you, even now you care about her," he points out and Daniel's remark catches me off guard. "More than you admit to her."

"I just don't want them to have her."

A withering, sad smirk tugs at Daniel's lips, making him look even more miserable. "Our women." He repeats my words and the tension tightens around my chest. "Is there a difference with what's between Addison and me, and Aria and you?" he asks me in a voice laced with accusations.

"I love Addison," he tells me before I can answer, his breathing quickening as he struggles to hide the pain of watching her leave him.

He looks at the floor for only a moment, shoving his hands into his pockets before looking up at me and asking me outright, "Do you still love her?"

A beat passes, but only one. A single beat inside my chest and I know the answer. I breathe the word at the same time as the door opens and one of my men enters.

"Boss," Jett calls out my title while knocking on the open door.

"Do you have an update?" I ask him with an eyebrow cocked, looking at his knuckles on the door and wondering why he fucking bothered to knock.

Nodding his head and straightening his shoulders, Jett answers me without hesitation. Daniel's restless, leaning against the window then kicking off of it as he listens to the soldier. Jett's one of Eli's men. Eli's a lieutenant, the rank given to the men we trust implicitly to lead other men in our crime family. And Jett's the soldier he left behind to see that everything fell into place with him gone.

The four of us, my brothers and I, we each have two lieutenants and the area we claim is split four ways. It keeps things clean and or-ganized. All of the men who work for us call me boss though. I'm the one and only boss.

Yet this motherfucker listened to Jase. Jase gave an order that di-rectly countered mine, which should have been absolute, and this ass-hole listened to him.

A tic in my jaw starts to spasm as I remember, feeling the heat and anger of what happened only hours ago stir hate into my blood once again.

I can see the moment Jett realizes I'm not over that little stunt. His pupils dilate, and he stutters over a word before talking faster. That's what happens when you're fucking scared.

I have to remind myself that they didn't know. Jase is the one and the only person responsible.

"Eli and Cason are in the first car, and there are three decoy cars even though there's no trace of anyone watching or following." He swallows, and I can hear the dry gulp of his throat as I imagine tearing it out.

Jase defied me.

They followed his orders and didn't know of mine.

I remind myself of that fact, bending down to snatch another book off the floor and rein in the rage. Someone needs to have the piss beat out of them for what happened.

Slamming the book on the shelf, I see Jase's face. He let them go. Everyone will know that she put a gun to my head because of him.

"Would you like me to help—"

"No," I cut him off in a single, low breath, devoid of any emotion.

"Does 'anyone' include Romano's men?" Daniel questions and I watch for Jett's reaction, setting another book on the shelf. "Or better yet, who knows where Aria and Addison are going and that they've left the premises? Name every single man."

"Eli and Cason's men, the ten of us," Jett's quick to answer him and then stands silently at attention again. His gaze darts between the two of us, waiting for any other question or orders. The way he stands is firm and upright, same as Eli. But there's a nervousness about him that I don't like.

"I want thirty men spread out on the blocks surrounding Sebastian's place on Fifth," Daniel tells Jett, although I know he's talking to me. "The Red Room is on the northern side, so that street is already handled, but the other three sides of our territory are lighter on men and closer to Talvery than I like."

"We need fifty," I correct him. The east and south sides need to have a second row. If Talvery's going to come for them, if my enemies find out where Addison and Aria are, I want more men.

"We can do fifty easy," Cason answers as if it was a question and not a demand. He continues, "We just need to pull back on the lower east side, closest to Crescent Hills." Jett licks his bottom lip as he looks past me, using his fingers to tally up men absently.

I take a moment to really consider him as he tells me that "place" is always causing problems, but if we back off the problems take care of themselves anyway. As in the people we tend to have to control in Crescent Hills, simply kill the people that cause them issues if we don't step in.

I know that he's right because it's where I'm from and that's how it was when I grew up, but it pisses me off. The idea that we can move out of areas we've only just begun to take over and let them kill each other off because it's not worth it… it hits me in a way that it shouldn't.

Only because it's a place I used to call home. I know that's why, but it doesn't help control the rage that boils inside of me.

"Fifty then," Daniel answers and crosses his arms. From here I can feel him looking at me, but I'm still focused on Jett as he rambles on about which men can go where. I'm going to start calling him Mr.

Calculus if he doesn't shut the fuck up soon. My jaw is clenched so tightly I think my molars will crack from the pressure.

I could see me taking out my displeasure on Jett. I can already feel how his jaw would crack under my fist. It would take more than one punch without my brass knuckles.

"Carter," Daniel says, and it breaks the vision of me beating the piss out of this entitled fuck. An asshole who didn't grow up the way I did and doesn't give a fuck about anyone in that city.

"What?" I don't hide the irritation as the word comes deep from my chest.

"Put the poor book down," he tells me, glancing at the book I'm practically ripping apart in my hand. Slamming it into its place on the shelf, I run my hand down my face and then brace my hands against the carved wood details of the bookshelf. I stare at the empty place still waiting for the books to be replaced.

"Ever the fucking comedian," I mutter under my breath, trying to relax and shrug off the need to let all my rage out.

"Keep a watch on the two of them and tell us if they want to leave," Daniel gives Jett his orders, but what the dumb fuck says next pushes me over the edge.

"What if Aria wants to go home?" Jett asks, concern evident in his gaze.

"What's that?" I can feel my own gaze narrow in on him as I push off of the bookshelf. The room feels hotter, smaller, and adrenaline races through my blood.

The soldier doesn't pick up on my anger. He doesn't get that what he's suggesting is going to get his head bashed against the fucking wall.

"Get out," Daniel speaks up as I take two steps toward my prey.

Jett goes still at Daniel's command, looking back at him as if wondering if he heard right. "She's not going anywhere," Daniel tells him as he stalks forward, pushing his hand against my chest for the second time tonight. The harder, darker side of his soul shows as he grabs Jett by his throat and pushes him against the wall. So hard I hear a crack, although I'm not sure what it was that made the sickening sound.

Jett's body sags in Daniel's grasp.

"Both women will be there temporarily." Although they're of similar height, it feels as if Daniel's towering over Jett as he nods and quickly agrees with Daniel, staring him in the eyes and making sure his voice is clear.

"Of course. They're there temporarily. I know that."

"Make sure you don't forget that." Daniel's parting words are sneered as he releases Jett and the man struggles to steady his feet. "Get out of here." Watching him yell in Jett's face eases some of the tension. Only some of it.

Jett doesn't pause or wait for anything else from either of us. He must have some sense in him after all.

"I wanted to bash his head in," I tell Daniel as the sound of that fucker racing down the hall to get away dims.

"I know," Daniel says with his back still to me as he rolls up his sleeves. "That's why I had to do it."

The ticking of the clock marches steadily between his last words and his next. "With the war coming, we need all the men we can get."

CHAPTER 6

Aria

W HEN I HEARD ELI SAY WE WERE GOING TO A SAFE HOUSE, this wasn't what I was expecting.

It's on the far end of the city, away from the hustle and bustle, in a quieter area and close to Main Street with a few shops within walking distance. There are a few quaint houses that line the street, but nearly a quarter mile separates each of them on this street.

This isn't like the safe house my father has. This house is in plain sight, but it's built for war if only you look closely enough at the exterior.

The three-story building is made of stone, with a concrete fence around the property, covered in beautiful ivy. The front door is all steel but beautifully etched with what looks like a Celtic pattern. I only got a brief glimpse before I was led here to the second floor, and each floor seems to be self-contained, so multiple families could live here and never even see each other. I'm in absolute awe, although it doesn't take the pain away in the least.

The kitchen is open to the living room. The center of the room is focused around a stone fireplace with a darkly stained, reclaimed wood mantel. Its ruggedness matches the iron and spicewood chandelier. But it's at odds with the clean sleekness of the all-white kitchen, just behind us.

We're stuck here, with a large L-shaped chenille sofa and matching armchairs that hug the fireplace until the guards say otherwise.

"Only a few minutes," is what Cason said. But more than a few have already passed as we linger in the beautiful gilded cage.

I'm biting my tongue though; I don't dare say a word to Addison as I pace behind the sofa. Addison's still pissed, but it seems fake to me. Like she's just trying to be angry at being locked up here rather than being brokenhearted over what happened.

She's been staring for the last ten minutes at the clothes she dumped on the sofa, trying not to cry. I can't stand seeing her on edge like this.

I'm an asshole, but I'll admit I'm grateful to be distracted by her. If I was alone, I'd be huddled in a ball crying on the floor.

"This is bullshit," she grits out the words, still staring at the clothes. "This isn't what I meant when I said I was leaving!" she screams to no one.

"He said it would only be a week or so, right?" I ask her carefully, trying to calm her down just the slightest.

She nods and visibly swallows before rolling her eyes, seemingly remembering that she's annoyed with being held here rather than given free will to leave.

"For our protection." Addison picks up a dress and balls it in her hands before throwing it back down on the sofa. Pushing her hair out of her face, she leans her head back and takes a deep breath. She does that a lot, the leaning her head back and deep breaths. I've seen her do it a few times when she gets worked up.

"Is that like a meditation practice or something?" I ask her, wanting to change the topic if I can, to something… less devastating. I'm exhausted from crying, but tired of being exhausted from crying. I don't want to hurt right now; I need a distraction for just a moment. Just a moment to breathe before I face my reality again.

She nods her head, barely moving from the position and takes a moment before telling me, "It's a yoga thing, really, I don't know that I can meditate." She reaches for the duffle bag on the floor and picks up the clothes on the sofa, one piece at a time, to toss them back in. "My mind is always wandering, and I have to get up and do something."

I nearly smile, happy that she's talking to me about something else. It was silent in the car ride here and the tension has been suffocating me.

"Yeah, I get that," I answer her. "I tried meditation a while ago and it was not my cuppa."

"Cuppa?" she questions with her brow furrowed, and I stifle a small smile at her curious expression.

"Cup of tea." I shrug and add, "It wasn't my cup of tea." Staring at my own duffle bag on the armchair, I add casually, even as I feel the weight of my heart seem to grow and sink into my stomach, "I like tarot cards better."

"Oh!" The excitement in Addison's voice is not at all what I was expecting. Maybe she's better at pretending life is all right when it's in shambles than I am. "And like palm readings?"

I have to smile at her enthusiasm.

She keeps talking as she finishes gathering the clothes. "I went to see a gypsy in New Orleans once." She peeks over at me as I walk closer, taking a seat on the far end of the sofa. I have to, so I can hear her over the sound of the guards still walking through the safe house to make sure everything is in place. As in, cameras. I know those fuckers are putting up cameras.

I have to keep my mouth closed, my teeth grinding against one another at the thought, and keep the anger from showing as she tells me her story of the woman she met by Café du Monde. I swallow thickly as she tells me about New Orleans, a place I've never been.

She's still feigning an upbeat attitude and I'm trying to keep up. I wonder if she can pretend like this when she lies down. When there are no distractions and sleep evades her. Just the thought of what my mind will do to me tonight, makes me grab the throw blanket on the sofa and wrap it around me as if it could protect me.

"I wanted to get my coffee grounds read and all that too, but I didn't have time."

"Seven kids?" My brows haven't moved from their raised position since she casually mentioned that little fact the palm reader told her. "She said you're going to have seven kids?"

I didn't hear the rest of what she said about the reading as I stared off absently, pretending to listen but really thinking about tonight and how I know I'll cry again. I feel helpless, hopeless, and pathetic.

Addison's expression pales and she purses her lips before she carefully says, "Pregnancies." She doesn't hide the pain in her eyes when she clarifies. "She said seven pregnancies. She also said they wouldn't keep."

Fuck. I can't even look her in the eyes as I struggle to tell her I'm sorry. She only shrugs it off before pulling up on her bag to close it.

The sound of her zipping up the bag is accompanied by the sound of Eli walking back into the room. With his dress shirt sleeves rolled up, the tattoos on his arm are on full display. They're all in black and white with lots of detail. A compass that fades up his left arm catches my attention, but the tone of his voice brings my gaze up to his.

"The rooms are ready. We'll be downstairs at all times." Eli's blunt and has a hint of some accent. Irish or British maybe, I can't tell. It's subtle, but it's there.

"I don't want to stay here," Addison tells him again. Her shoulders rise and fall quickly as her breathing quickens. "I'm not with Daniel anymore." Her voice cracks, but she continues, "And I don't need a safe house. I need to leave."

Eli's expression is unmoving. I almost question if he's heard her as the silence stretches between them. The only sounds are from the other men behind Eli in the hall as they walk downstairs to their section of the safe house. "I understand." Eli's initial response takes Addison by surprise. She even flinches slightly, but then he adds, "There are some precautions that need to be taken first. But in one week, give or take, we will take you to wherever you want to go, and leave you alone."

Alone.

I hate that word.

"So, we're supposed to stay locked up in this fucking house?" Addison's anger rises as she asks the question, each word getting louder than the last. I watch as her blunt nails dig into her palms as she fails to rein in her anger.

"Main Street has several shops and a few restaurants. We have no objections to you walking the block… however, someone will be with you at all times."

My mind has been reeling all night with everything that's happened. I've been here for nearly two hours, and I'm only just now realizing why we have to stay here under house arrest with guards for one week. *And then we can go free.*

One week.

"He's going to kill them." With my gaze fixed on the sheer curtain, draped in the moonlight from outside the window, the crushing feeling in my chest returns. "One week until the war is over."

Addison turns slowly to face me, and I sink back further into the sofa.

"I'm being held hostage until my family is dead." My throat closes slowly like it's suffocating me, and my eyes burn hotter as the pain diffuses through me.

I've lost Carter. I've lost the chance to influence him because I failed.

And now I'm trapped in this beautiful place while everyone I love is murdered. My vision is blurred as I picture the house I grew up in, the blood on the walls, bullet holes in the doors. Licking my lips, I taste my salty tears. "Eli, can you answer me a question?" I ask him with a short breath I'm barely able to hold on to.

The lightheadedness floods my mind as he nods his head, yes.

"Is there someone to clean up everything you leave behind?" I struggle to breathe as I look him in the eyes and continue, "Or when I ask to go home in a week, will I be the one who has to clean up the bodies of my family?" My voice shakes on the last word, but he hears me. I know he does.

I picture my cousin, Brett, and his wife and their baby. In a moment, they're right where I last saw them during the holidays. And in a blink, they're lying dead on the floor, their eyes staring back at me as if seeing me for who I really am.

And I hate what they see.

Some of my family may be cruel like Carter, but not all of them are and so many people will die. I know what to expect. I've seen it before. I can't sit here and do nothing.

I refuse.

Eli stares back at me, assessing me and judging me, but I don't care. As long as I can hold on to the strength of my mentality, I don't care what he thinks. Knowing I can't and won't sit by and do nothing is all that matters.

"I know it's war, but I would rather be with them right now," I tell Eli, brushing the tears away as I realize that's where my place is. "I think it would be best if you sent me back to my home."

"Maybe when the week is over, you'll want to go somewhere else," is all Eli gives me.

It's not until he's gone that I realize Addison is silently crying. She can't even look at me, but I don't care.

I don't care about anything anymore.

"It's what this life is like," I tell her solemnly, remembering all the nights the men would fill the kitchen downstairs, clinking their beers and patting each other on the back. "I had an uncle named Pierce." I haven't thought about it in forever, but now I'm reliving a certain night when I was fifteen years old. The night that marks the first time I fully grasped what my family did for a living and began to really see the consequences that came with it. I can feel how raw my throat is when I pause to swallow. From screaming, from crying.

"I came downstairs while he was holding something up in the air and everyone else in the room was cheering." Their voices echo in my head. "I remember smiling, so happy that my father was in a good mood." I don't know if she's listening, but I keep talking.

"My uncle was so happy to see me." I remember the way his grin widened before putting down whatever it was he'd been holding and hugging me like he hadn't seen me in years. "I felt like a part of the family that night. My father even gave me a small glass of wine despite the fact I was only sixteen." I remember the way it tasted, and how I felt when he poured from his bottle and gave me the glass in front of everyone. "He said, tonight we drink. Tonight, we celebrate Talvery. And everyone cheered again when I took a sip."

I peek over at Addison, who's listening intently and waiting for the punch line.

"It wasn't until a few days later that Nikolai told me it was a human tongue. The tongue of a rat who was murdered, and they were celebrating because the charges were dropped with no witness living to testify." I had to beg Nik to tell me; he told me I wouldn't want to know, but I pressed him. After he told me, I knew I could trust his opinion if I ever wanted to know something again.

I stare at the fireplace, wishing it would crackle with a soothing flame, but it's empty and there's no wood here to start a fire.

"Talverys and the Cross brothers are the same. And they'll both kill each other or die trying." It's a truth I've wanted to avoid for so long, but now it seems as if I can only try to limit the damage they'll cause.

"That's not the way they grew up," Addison tells me with tears in her eyes. "They were good people."

"My family is full of good people too." My gut churns from trying to defend this life to her. To someone who didn't grow up in it. "They just do bad things. Like my uncle. He loved his wife, he loved his kids, and he would have done anything for me if he were still alive."

It's quiet for a moment as Addison slowly sits down next to me, holding onto herself like she'll fall to pieces if she doesn't.

She doesn't speak for a long time; neither of us does. But neither of us gets up either. "I don't understand how Daniel got into this. This isn't what they were like before. I swear to you. They were good and… and… I don't know how this happened." She looks lost like she had no idea. I've seen women before who are in denial, who turn a blind eye. But she's truly shocked. Maybe she didn't realize how real this life can be. How close to death it is.

"I do."

My response grabs her attention and she waits for more, but I don't know how much she really wants to know, or what she needs to know.

"For the longest time, there wasn't anyone south of Fallbrook. That's where I'm from and basically the territory my father keeps. My father talked about taking it a lot." I remember back when I was little, how I'd sit in his office coloring and he'd have hushed conversations about the developments in Back Ridge. "There wasn't anyone living there, no businesses, but then," I clear my throat and tell her, "then developments grew and there were more people. More opportunities, as my father called it."

"He and Romano had two territories side by side, and both wanted it. But the areas are like a cross, sort of." Four quarters, I draw it out on the blanket on my lap, the way Nikolai explained it to me. "Carter's area is the bottom left, but his portion is bigger now. The bottom right is Crescent Hills and it's not claimed, just a shit town with no one policing it, no one protecting it. Carter and his crew keep moving closer and closer, but they only take it little by little. My father has the upper left and Romano the upper right. They both wanted the territory where

Carter is now, but while they waged a cold war against each other because of my mother…" I swallow a dry lump not knowing if she knows but not in a state to explain. "Carter took over. One by one, killing the men who worked for my father who tried to stop him, or, sometimes, Carter took on my father's soldiers, proving he would be ruthless and that the area was his, but he had mercy for those who stayed with him."

"So, it was Carter?" she asks, and I can see in her eyes she doesn't want to believe Daniel was involved.

"I've heard Jase and Carter's names a lot." I almost say more, but I hold it back, swallowing my words. "But Carter is the one name that everyone knows. It's either Carter or the Cross brothers."

Addison's brow is pinched but her expression is riddled with anguish as she says, "I don't know why Carter would do that. I don't know why he'd want to live this way."

Again, I almost say, "I do," but I don't. It's because my father knew what Carter was capable of. He knew they would take over. My father tried to kill them before they could become the powerful family they are now, but he failed. His failed attempt is what made Carter who he is.

The truth, and facing the truth, causes a coldness to flow across my skin and I pull the blanket more tightly around me.

"I understand if you could never be friends with someone like me. Someone whose family makes a living through death and sin. Someone who…" I trail off, pausing for a moment before what I'm about to say next. I have to close my eyes to say, "Someone who broke you and Daniel up."

"Stop it," Addison breathes the command with a seriousness I wasn't expecting. "You didn't break us up and you're still my friend." She grips my hand in both of hers as I stare back at her, hoping she still feels this way in the morning. Because I have no one right now and, in a week, I may have even less than no one.

"It's going to be okay and we're going to look out for each other. You have to look out for the ones you care about. You know?" Her gaze begs me to agree with her, to stay strong. But I'm not like Addison.

Tears beg to run down my face, but I bite them back, refusing to cry any more tonight. Instead, I nod my head and force out my reply, although the words are strangled. "I'm trying to. But what can I do when the ones I care about want each other dead?"

The silence comes again, but she's quick to end it this time.

"Let's have a drink." She's off the sofa before I can even tell her how badly I need one.

I can only nod my head in agreement, still wrapping my head around the spiral of horrific events that led me here.

I can't think about anything but Carter as I hear her open a bottle of wine and the glasses clink on the counter. Instead, all I can do is picture Carter's face the exact moment I lost his trust and he lost his fucking mind.

It's going to haunt me forever.

If not that, then the sight of my family in coffins.

There was no way for me to win.

I don't want to do this anymore. I can't deal with this anymore.

I need to stop this.

CHAPTER 7

Carter

I T'S QUIETER HERE THAN I THOUGHT IT WOULD BE. SEBASTIAN PICKED a nice area. He had the place built two years ago but never came back. I don't know if it's the memory of him or everything that happened tonight that makes my heart twist like someone's wringing it out from inside my chest.

The whiskey didn't make the pain better. Not the first glass, not the second. Not when I threw the bottle at the window, shattering it and filling the room with the smell of liquor. Earlier, I spent too long sagging against the wall while sitting on the floor of the office staring at the box. The box that's still open, empty, and pushed up against the rug. I can't move it back. I can't bring myself to move it back as if she was never in there.

Everything is telling me to let her go.

Logic and reason. She will never love me because of the way we started. She will never love me after I kill her family. She will never love me, because of the man I am.

I know it all to be true.

But the idea of letting her leave fucking hurts.

"Do you want me to go in with you?" Daniel asks me from the driver's seat, ripping my gaze from the front of the house and cutting through my thoughts.

"Are you sure you're okay to see her?" he asks me the real question.

"I'm not going to hurt her," I tell him as I stare back at the house, praying I'm telling the truth. I want her to feel this pain. I want her to know how much it hurts.

"What are you going to do?" he asks me, his hands sliding down the leather steering wheel.

"I'm going to give her what she wants," I lie. I'll never let her leave me.

My brother's voice is stern and loud in the cabin of the car as he says, "You're making a mistake."

I'm taken aback by his criticism, staring at him as the dark night sky gets darker. "You can do what you'd like with Addison; I won't judge you. But stay out of it when it comes to me and Aria." It's all I can tell him because I don't know what to do with Aria. I don't know what I can do with a woman who would betray me like she did.

"Are you really going to let her walk away?" When I don't answer his question, he pushes me by saying, "She'll have no one when this is done with. No one."

I raise my voice to reply and end this conversation. "I said I'm going to give her what she wants. I didn't say I'd let her go." My blood rushes in my ears as Daniel's eyes narrow in the darkness.

"Are you coming in?" I ask him, refusing to let him continue.

"No, she's not inside. She walked down to the liquor store for more wine when Aria went to bed." He settles back in the seat and looks straight down the road to add, "I'm going to drive up there and keep an eye on her from a distance."

Pausing, he looks at me before adding, "Cason's with her and there are eyes are on her, but still…"

"She must know you'll be watching her," I say absently, remembering everything that happened months ago.

His nod is solemn. "I know she does. I'm sure she hates it too."

Giving him a tilt of my head to part ways, I grab the handle to open the door, but Daniel's words stop me. "I wonder if she'll know when I get to her."

With my fingers wrapped around the handle, I still, then ask, "What do you mean?"

"She used to know somehow. Years ago, when Tyler died. Every time I came close to her, she'd turn around as if she knew I was there. It didn't matter how far away I was or how many other people were around us. She always knew, back then."

He finally looks over at me, the sorrowful smirk still on his face. "I wonder if it'll be the same even now."

I don't know what advice to give my brother. I can feel his pain and there are no words to help him.

"Just make sure she's safe," I tell him, remembering all those years ago and everything that happened between them… between all of us.

"Always," he tells me and smacks the back of his hand against my arm. "Don't fuck it up." He forces a weak smile to his face, although it doesn't reach his eyes. I can't give the same back to him.

The sounds of the night greet me as the car door opens and then shuts easily. The crickets and the wind are all I can hear. The men posted on the side of the building see me and I acknowledge them with a simple nod. I button my suit jacket and walk up the sidewalk and onto the porch. With every step, the anxiety over my fears grows. The fear that I've lost her forever. That she never loved me, and I never really had her. The fear that tonight has destroyed anything and everything that's between us.

There's no turning back from what's happened. There's no denying that she's clouding my judgment and keeping her means losing the confidence and respect from my men.

Helplessness is something I haven't felt in so long, but it's with me now as I stalk toward the safe house.

Eli's been at the front door all day with his earpiece in and the phone displaying the monitors. He stands up straighter with the smack of my boots on the stone steps as I make my way toward him.

"Aria's in the north bedroom on the second floor. Addison's at—"

"The liquor store," I finish the sentence for him.

"Boss," he says and rewards me with the barest flicker of a smile. "Of course, you'd know." He opens the massive front door; it's solid steel eight feet high and three feet wide. The bright light from the foyer reflects off the freshly polished wood floors. It's been a while since I've been here and the memory of standing on this threshold with Sebastian makes me pause.

Chloe, Sebastian's wife, is the one who chose everything for this house. She wanted to come back. I really thought they were coming home years ago when this house was built, but they didn't.

Standing there, I remember my childhood like it was yesterday, back when I was a different person. Back before all that shit happened with Aria's father; before my best friend left and my mother passed away, leaving me on my own to take care of my drunkard of a father and my four brothers. I've never thought back on it and felt ashamed. But as I stand here, I think back to who I used to be and know I would hate the man I've become. I would hate who I've turned into and what I've done.

You can't go back though. You can never go back.

"Is there anything I can do for you?" Eli asks quietly, carefully.

"How is she?" I ask him. I've known Eli for four years now. He helped me take over the majority of this territory and he's the only reason I've moved deeper into Crescent Hills, where I'm from. There's no law in Crescent Hills, so moving my empire there is a task harder than most, and the income doesn't justify it. It's a hellhole no one wants, but I thought Sebastian would eventually come back and help me take it. I thought wrong.

"She's been crying on and off since Addison left." Eli's gaze doesn't stay on mine as he reports on Aria to me. He looks down at his shoes and swallows before looking me back in the eyes. "She saw some of the news. I'm not sure what she's most upset about. Leaving you or losing her family."

Anger is a slow simmer. I shouldn't have waited to pull the trigger. "If they were already dead, I wouldn't have this problem."

Eli nods in agreement. "We're ready when you are, Boss."

"Romano's already taking down the streets in the upper east."

Eli nods again and says, "It's been all over the news today. I imagine Romano will hit them from the south side this week."

"Talvery will be expecting it though."

"That's good for us here. Chances are good he'll take his men on the northernmost streets up there and hit him harder."

"They both react predictably."

"And they'll both fall... predictably." The grin on his face would be reflected on mine, but all I can think about is how Aria will truly hate me then. She was willing to threaten me to save them. Deep in my gut, I know the idea of vengeance is something that will cross her mind. And it fucking kills me.

"I don't know that I can ever trust her again," I speak the revelation out loud and regret it immediately. What the fuck is wrong with me?

"She'll get over it. I overheard her explaining things to Addison; she understands why this has to happen."

The night air clings to me, holding me here at the threshold instead of moving forward to face Aria.

"Where did you find that dumb fuck, Jett?" I ask him to get off the topic and remind him who I am. His fucking boss.

"He's a good shot, just a little shit when it comes to his mouth. I think he has Asperger's or something." He looks past me and into the night for a moment before continuing. "He's not too good at reading social clues, but in the war, he waited three days to get a shot on the insurgents in Afghanistan. Three days he stayed in the same bunker, barely bigger than a shack. He didn't fucking move until the three on his hit list were in his sights." He huffs a short laugh although it lacks genuine humor. "They came out for a smoke, thinking they were in the clear since it'd been quiet for three days. It only took him twenty seconds to get all three of them in the skull."

"I still want to rip his fucking throat out," I tell him absently, although my respect for Jett grows as I picture what he's been through.

Eli shrugs. "I've told him before that he could still shoot his gun if I cut out his tongue." He chuckles and adds, "Jokingly, of course. I owe him my life."

"I'll keep that in mind the next time I want to punch his face in." My words come out dull, lacking the conviction I had before.

"What'd he say?" he asks me.

"Nothing," I answer him, knowing I don't want to have this conversation with him. I respect Eli, but he's not my friend. This is business.

He nods once, opening the door just a hair more and the soft sound of it creaking is loud in my ears.

"Tell the men not to go in and to stall Addison until I'm done in here," I say, staring at the spiral staircase that leads to the second floor where my little songbird is now caged. "I don't want her to hear this."

"Yes, Boss."

I pat him on the shoulder as I walk in, but I don't look him in the eyes. Even though I'm staring at the staircase, all I can see is everything that happened hours ago. The gun she pointed at me, the box she ran to and hid in. The sight of the car as it pulled away and how she didn't object.

My throat's tight and the hammering of my heart gets faster and more painful as I climb the stairs. The railing is slick under my hot palm.

She's mine.

She's going to know I fucking own her when I leave her tonight.

Even if she still leaves me, she will always belong to me.

Always.

The thought makes the rushing of blood in my ears that much louder. Each step closer to the door my cock gets harder, thinking of every reaction she'll have to me.

Anger, hate even.

Or maybe she'll beg me to forgive her.

I close my eyes, resting the flat side of my fist against the wall to the right of her bedroom door at the thought of her begging me for mercy. Something she refused to do in the cell.

My eyes open slowly at the sound of the bed creaking from just beyond the door.

Aria

I heard his footsteps before the door opened.

I can't explain why I prayed for it to be Carter. The last time I saw him, all I had was fear of him.

With the window open, the wind drifts in, shifting the curtains out of place and letting the moonlight drape over Carter's dominant form.

My heart flickers in a weird uneven beat and I'm reminded of the first time I ever saw him. The same fear races through me, but so does the feeling that he could save me.

If only he wanted to, but from the sharp look in his eyes, that's not what he has planned for me at all.

At this point, I'm okay with that. He can do what he'd like to me because I already know I'll submit to him. I already know I still love him. No matter how fucked up it is.

"Carter," I whisper his name as I sit up in bed, letting the sheets fall into a puddle around me. A shiver graces my skin as the wind tickles my shoulder.

The floor creaks with his heavy step and the shadow across his face moves, hugging the sharp lines of his jaw as he stalks toward me.

"Get on your knees," he commands me in a rough voice. That's the only greeting he gives me and it reminds me of what life was like in the cell with him.

Defiance runs deep in my blood and it spikes anger high in my chest as my jaw clenches.

"That's what you have to say to me?" I question him with my voice wavering. Anxiety and heartbreak are equally present, making my toes curl and my fists bunch the silk sheets. I can barely breathe as I bite back the words, "You didn't come for me."

He pauses at the end of the bed, but only for a moment, a single beat of my wretched heart. He speaks softly, yet forcefully as he slips off his jacket and lays it carefully at the end of the bed.

"I have many things to say to you, Aria Talvery," he practically spits my name and I snarl back, "Fuck you," feeling the hate for him intensify.

I've always known he was my enemy, but I never felt as if he saw me that way. The tides have changed.

His deft fingers unbutton his shirt and my eyes leave his to watch as he strips.

"I told you to get on your knees," he reminds me in a voice that drips of dominance and sex. He tosses his shirt on top of his jacket, losing the control he had a moment ago.

My eyes are drawn to the leather of his belt as he unbuckles it and then quickly pulls it from its place, letting the leather hiss through the air.

My pussy clenches as he bends the leather into a loop and waits for me to obey him. "You've already questioned me, defied me, and lied to me today. Are you really going to disobey me again?"

I swallow thickly, knowing I want his punishment, and I want this. But I didn't lie to him.

"I've never lied to you and I never will," I tell him quickly, feeling my pulse quicken.

"You didn't tell me the truth. That's lying," he says, his voice louder and he doesn't hide his anger in the least.

"I won't..." I pause and trail off. Biting down on my lower lip, I hate that the one conflict we have that will tear us apart, again and again, is one we will never agree on. "I won't sit back and let you kill them. I won't."

Carter's movements are faster than I thought possible, sending a spike of fear through me. The belt hits the bed as he grips my chin and lowers his lips to mine. My heart races and lust mixes with terror. "You don't have a choice," he whispers against my lips.

I question myself even as the words leave my lips, "You're wrong."

I can feel his heat; I can hear his heart hammer in his chest as I stare into his dark eyes. I could get lost in them forever and at this moment, I wish I could. "I wish things were different," I tell him as his silence grows.

"They will be soon," he says. The darkly spoken words come with a threat. "On your knees, songbird."

It's his nickname for me, his grip on my chin, his lips so close to mine and the rapid pace of his heart, that all make me move.

I keep my eyes on his for as long as I can as I get onto all fours and let him slowly strip my pants from me. He pulls them down slowly, teasingly even as his fingers brush down my sensitive skin.

The cool air is all I can feel for a moment and I know the belt is coming. I brace for it, but there's nothing for what feels like forever.

"Do you think you deserve this?" he asks me with his voice low and not an ounce of resentment that I expect.

I breathe the word easily, truthfully, "Yes."

The belt bites the flesh of my right thigh from behind and I scream out in agony. He didn't waste a second.

My thighs tremble as I try to stay on all fours.

Smack! The edges of the belt scrape against my ass and send a wave of pain through my body while burning where they slice across my skin. I can't control the sob that claws its way up my throat. My toes curl as I grip the sheets tighter and fight back the tears.

I jump at the soft touch of Carter's hand against my heated flesh, wishing I'd said no, but then I would be the liar I claimed not to be.

"Do you know what happens to men who point a gun at me, Aria?" Carter's voice is laced with a deadly threat as he bends over me, his hard cock digging into my ass and just the feeling of it sends a deep-rooted desire to surface in my blood.

The lust nearly drowns out the pain. It's so close, and I wish it would, but Carter isn't finished punishing me yet.

His lips brush the shell of my ear as he tells me, "They don't live to pull the trigger."

I have to swallow before I can answer him. My skin alternates between pain and pleasure on the places where his hand still rubs soothing circles. "I never would have pulled it," I answer him in a soft voice while rocking my hips back against him. I've always been a whore for him. I bow to him and love it. Some sick side of me desires it. I imagine I always will.

"You don't care that everyone saw, do you?" he asks me and the weight of what I've done feels heavier.

"I'm sorry. I didn't want to do it." I swallow thickly, conflicted by my exhaustion, my pain, my greed for more of his touch. "You left me no choice."

He pulls away instantly, leaving my body feeling the chill of the air between us. I can hear the metal buckle of his belt clink and see him raise his arm in the shadows that play on the wall in front of me.

I close my eyes tightly but it doesn't help in the least.

Smack! The belt bites at my left ass cheek, and then immediately moves to the right.

I bite down as hard as I can on nothing and try to hold back my cries as the belt screams in the air and lands blow after blow against my tender flesh.

My arms buckle as the pain rips through me. Tears leak uncontrollably from the corners of my eyes.

Carter fists the hair at the base of my skull and forces me to look at him.

His eyes are dark and swirling with tortured emotion. "I need to see you, Aria. You can't hide from me."

My head shakes before I realize I've moved, the stinging pain making even the small movement of brushing my thigh against his absolute agony. "I can't," I whimper.

I've never felt a pain like this. I try to hold back the tears as my shoulders shake, but they come regardless.

"You can take this," Carter tells me, grabbing the reddened flesh of my thigh and squeezing it. The pressure forces the pain to shred every last piece of control I have.

With his right hand on my thigh, he cups my pussy with his left.

My back bows instantly and I'd collapse to my side if he wasn't holding me in place. The pleasure is unimaginable. Every inch of my body feels it. My nipples pebble, but my neck arches and my body begs for more.

"You can take this, Aria." Carter's voice is gentle, soothing, and deep as he rubs his fingers against my sensitive clit. From the way he sounds right now, I almost wonder if the lust he once had for me is now gone, but I know that can't be true. That can't be the case from the way he starts to touch me.

He pinches my clit and a lightning bolt of pleasure thrills every nerve ending in my body. I'm hot and cold at the same time. Quivering beneath the man who gives me pain I can't bear and pleasure that's as equally consuming.

And I crave more of him. I need his fingers inside of me.

He pulls away as the numbing pleasure races through me and I see him reach for the belt again.

"Carter," I whimper a plea. I love the pleasure, but the pain is terrifying. "Please," I beg him.

He hesitates. With my cheek on the pillow, staring up at the broken man who only knows how to break others, I beg him again. "Please, forgive me."

"I've already forgiven you," are the only words he gives me before gripping the belt tighter.

I close my eyes, waiting for more punishment, waiting for Carter to take me how he thinks he needs.

Instead, a soothing hand runs along the dip in my waist, and as much as I want to pull away, knowing his gentle touch is going to cause where he's struck me to flare with pain, I stay still for him. I let him caress where the belt met my skin, and bring the pain to the surface even more.

"I just want you," I whisper into the pillow. It feels damp beneath my cheek, soaked from my tears. "Please, Carter."

"This is me, Aria. This is who I am."

His words are a fire that licks along the wounds of my heart, split into two halves of who I am. The first half of me is a woman who's broken and in love with a man who's been hurt more times in this life than I could possibly bear. And the other half is a woman who wants to be strong and refuses to allow her will to be ignored any longer.

"You don't know who you are anymore, Carter. No more than I knew who I was when I held the gun," I tell him in a shuddering voice. "Take from me what you want," I concede. Closing my eyes, I bury my head in the pillow but then remember what he said. And so, I position myself on all fours again, even as my legs shake. "I'll give it all to you."

The belt drops to the bed with a thud and before I can turn my head to look over my shoulder at Carter, he plunges deep inside of me, his cock filling me and stretching me without mercy. One of his hands grips my hip to keep me upright as the force of his thrust nearly shoves my body into a prone position from the blow. Fuck! It's too much so quickly. The scream that's torn from me is silent.

With his other hand, he pinches my clit hard and the force of the pleasure tearing through me makes my back bow as I scream out his name.

His thumb rubs my clit relentlessly as he rides through my orgasm, fucking me like it's the last thing he'll ever be able to do.

And I take it all. Biting down on the pillow to mute the screams and writhing beneath him from the mix of pain and pleasure that confuses my body, I take all of him.

Over and over again.

I take it until I think he'll break me. Until my body begs me to flee, but even then, he doesn't stop. He's a brutal man, with brutal instincts and I don't know that he'll ever have mercy on me again.

I'm barely sane, barely coherent when I feel his thick cock pulse inside of me. The head of his dick is pressed deep inside of me, and I've never before wanted a moment to last forever like I do now. Feeling the most intense orgasm I've ever had while Carter groans my name and then lowers his lips to kiss my shoulder.

He breathes heavily as he lays his chest on my back, moving one hand to brace himself and the other to hold my belly, keeping my skin pressed to his.

The last kiss he gives me is a long one, his lips to my shoulder. Like he doesn't want it to end.

"I fell in love with the idea of you," he whispers after pulling his kiss away from me. "Then I fell in love with fucking you." There's an agony etched in his words. It sounds like he's telling me goodbye and I've only just now realized it.

"Carter," I say as I turn in his embrace, ignoring the pain from the belt which is still present, bringing my hands to either side of his hard jaw and try to kiss him back, but he pulls away.

"I thought I loved you." Every bit of the man who brings terror to all who defy him is gone. There's a softness in his eyes that begs me to accept it all, to bow down to him and bend to his will. No matter what it is.

But I can't. Not anymore. Not after what happened, and I saw the truth of what's to come. And if that means this is the end...

I gaze into his eyes as he stares into mine, and I can feel the unspoken words. Either I submit to him, or I'm his enemy.

"I love you, Carter. But I won't be your songbird anymore. Not when you chose to ignore the one thing I need from you."

"You want me to surrender and that's something I can't do." He swallows thickly, the hard edge to his tone growing rougher. "You're making it impossible for us to be together."

The tension between us is too real, so thick and so suffocating. "So are you," I tell him. "I love you, but I will go to war against you." My words are shaky as they leave my lips. "I still love you, Carter. And I still want you." The last words come out rushed and I beg him to believe me.

"I will kill every man of the army that backs you, Aria. I will destroy them all until there's no reason left to fight." He doesn't mention anything about love. Only war.

"I will die to protect them," I tell him the truth. They're my family. And they've protected me. "I have to," I plead with him to understand.

He doesn't conceal the pain my answer causes him. And that only makes my own suffering grow. "Where is that loyalty for me? For my brothers?"

"I will never hurt them or you." The thought of them dying at the hands of my own family clutches my heart in a vise. My voice cracks as I speak, "I only said I would protect my own."

"Little naïve songbird... I wish you could."

CHAPTER 8

Aria

EVERY TIME I MAKE EVEN THE TINIEST OF MOVEMENTS, THE ache between my legs consumes my body.

I both hate it and love it. I love the reminder that Carter came for me; I hate that I'm again faced with the reality I can't outrun.

I've been watching the news and listening to the guards. I know blood has already been spilled. Yesterday I got a glimpse of it, but I wasn't sure. Today Addison's kept the news on and I know for certain the war has begun.

I recognize the names of some of the men in my father's army. The soldiers. Men who have gathered in my kitchen late at night. Men who have shared dinner with my family from time to time.

Men who have been kind to me.

Men who have looked after me when my father wasn't there.

Men who have children and wives.

And the names I don't recognize from men who live on the east side of the state… I imagine they have families too. Or did. Before this happened.

My father made me go to the funerals whenever someone died. Always. I've never missed any of them. He said they were family and deserved that respect. As much as I've hated my father and as much as I think I'm nothing but a bother to him, or maybe a bad memory of my mother, I always respected the dead and their families.

This time I won't be able to, and for some reason that hurts me deeper than I think it should.

Two names that haven't come up are Nikolai and Mika.

The first, a man who I've loved in more way than one.

And the second, a man I've dreamed of killing myself.

In this world, there are men who are good, and there are men who are evil. I won't be convinced otherwise. In war, both types of men die. And both types of men populate every army.

"How are you doing this morning?" Addison's question pulls my gaze from the coffee maker to her. I meant to turn it on and never did. I can't concentrate on anything else but the war.

She looks like she didn't get any sleep at all. The dark circles under her eyes are a dead giveaway. "I came in to check on you last night, but you were already asleep."

My lungs seize thinking how grateful I am that she didn't come in while Carter was there. I've never felt so torn in my life as I did last night. It's an impossible situation.

"Yeah, I passed out." I offer the lame excuse and it feels fake on my tongue knowing I'm hiding the truth from her. I finally hit the button to start up the machine but then have to check to make sure I added water. I did.

All the while, Addison heads to the fridge as if it's any other kitchen, knowing Eli fully stocked it last night.

I almost tell her Carter came over purely out of guilt, but I swallow my words. She won't understand. She clears her throat and speaks before I can confess though.

"I saw Daniel... that's what took me so long."

Unshed tears shimmer in her eyes and she slams the fridge door shut before tossing the butter on the counter so she has both hands free to press her palms to her eyes. "I'm sorry."

"You have no reason to be. Out of everyone involved, you have no reason to be," I say and wish she could understand how empathetic I am to her. "I get it. Let it out," I tell her while putting my hand on her shoulder and running it back and forth to try to soothe her.

"I just can't believe he'd be okay with the way Carter treated you. That he would do nothing."

I let out a long breath, understanding why she's standing so strongly against Daniel, but hating that I'm a part of that reason.

"I've come to terms with two things," I tell her, hoping it will help her. "One, I love Carter even if he hates me." The first confession brings her eyes to mine. "Two, I'm not going to sit back and do nothing. I won't ever let him do something that will hurt me or my family without fighting him."

"How can you be with him, knowing...?" She doesn't finish, but she doesn't have to.

"I don't know how. I honestly don't. And I don't know if any of it really matters." I lean my back against the counter and grip on to it from behind. "I can't stop this war. I can't protect everyone. I can't stop the people I love from dying." As I say the last part, my mother comes to mind and I try to block her out. I'm already spent with emotion and trying to balance right and wrong, love and war, that any mention of her will be my undoing and it's not even ten o'clock in the morning.

"This life is brutal," I whisper and then clear my throat to face Addison again. "But it's my life. And I want to be in control of my own decisions."

"You know we're still locked up, right?" Judging by the hint of a smile on her lips, her words are meant to make me laugh and they do, a small breath of a laugh.

Reaching for the butter and content to let the conversation die, she adds, "Let's eat before we think of how we're going to escape."

"I can hear you," a voice says from behind us and scares the shit out of me. Eli's in the doorway, a smirk on his lips and if he was closer I'd be tempted to smack it off his face.

"I'm sure you all can," I answer him and look toward the ceiling. "I haven't found the cameras yet."

He doesn't respond to my jabs as I watch the coffee maker sputter the last bit of my caffeine addiction into a ceramic mug. Instead, he tells me, "You have a message."

He's so tall, it only takes four strides for him to close the gap between us and reach me, holding out a folded piece of paper.

"Did you read it?" I ask him before taking the small piece of parchment.

His stare is hard and unforgiving as he answers, "Yes." Pissed off from the lack of privacy, I easily toss the precious piece of paper onto the counter. I have no idea who it's from, but I continue moving around my warden to look for sugar in the cabinets.

"Does Carter know?" I ask him when I finally find it. I close the door slowly, holding the box of sugar tighter than I should.

"Yes."

I nod and then ask, "Is it from him?"

I would be surprised if it was, since he didn't have much else to say last night, and Eli proves my assumption correct with a single word.

"No."

I swallow down the sudden pang of anxiety, wondering who it's from and what it says, but I don't dare let on to Eli.

"You don't have to hate me," he says as I continue to walk around him and Addison as she fries something on the stove.

"You don't have to hover," I answer him immediately.

Without another word, he leaves, and I feel guilty although I know I shouldn't.

"What are you cooking?" I ask Addison after he's left, staring at the piece of paper without reaching for it.

"Eggs, do you want some?" she asks, peeking at me and then at the paper. I'm surprised she doesn't ask about it; I can see the question in her eyes.

"Sure," I answer just to be friendly. I don't think I could eat if I tried though. I'm already sick to my stomach.

"How do you like them?" she asks before flipping her own in the pan.

"Over easy, please, and thank you," I tell her, trying to keep my voice upbeat and waiting to open the note until I'm alone.

"Yolk?" Addison makes a face. "Eww. Really I don't know if we can be friends anymore." She's only joking though. I know she is, but the thought of losing her sends a wave of nausea through me.

"Fine," I tell her back in as playful of a voice I can manage, "I'll eat them however you're making them. I like eggs however they come," I lie. I've only ever had eggs over easy. I don't even eat hard-boiled eggs. I can't justify why I lie to her or why I'm so nervous and feeling so alone. But I do and am.

"I can make them how ever." Addison shrugs and then adds, "Over easy is the easiest way anyway. I just don't like the taste of yolks."

Her easygoing reply settles the nerves still racing through me, but I glance back at the note and notice when her gaze follows me there. Still, she doesn't ask questions and I get the feeling that's a learned habit of hers.

I watch as she cracks two eggs on the side of the pan, then takes a bite of hers from a plate on the right side of the stove.

"I can totally cook them if you want to eat," I offer, feeling guilty. I can't shake all these awful feelings running through me.

"I like it," Addison tells me and then takes another bite. The pan sizzles as the tension runs through my shoulders and the note stares back at me.

"Can I tell you something else?" Addison asks me, scraping her fork on the plate rather than looking at me. When I don't answer she peeks up at me and I'm quick to nod my head.

"I like that they're here in a way."

"Who?" I ask her, feeling my forehead wrinkle with confusion.

"Eli and Cason." She doesn't hide the guilt in her tone. "I know they're basically keeping us hostage but seeing all those people on the TV this morning," she pauses and visibly swallows. "Hearing the update on the death toll in this gang war?" She rolls her eyes as she repeats what the reporter called it. Looking over her shoulder at me and then reaching for another plate, she tells me, "At least I know we're safe."

I can only nod and accept the plate. I've been 'safe' all my life. There's no such thing as safe, only the illusion of it. Telling Addison that won't help her though.

My fork shuffles the eggs around on the plate while Addison watches, but she doesn't say anything about it. I try to take a bite and then another, but it's flavorless and it only makes the pit in my stomach feel heavier.

"Are you going to read it?" she asks me and then tilts her head toward the note.

I nod once and finally reach for it, but after I read it, I don't tell her who it's from. I don't tell her what it says either.

All I know is that Eli read it and I don't know what that means for me.

Aria,

Meet me tomorrow night. I just need to see you. I need to know you're all right.

Meet me at the candy shoppe on Main Street. You can walk there; I'll be there. I promise.

Tomorrow. Eight at night.

Yours,
Nikolai

"Are you all right?" she asks me as I feel the blood drain from my face.

The sound of my fork abruptly scraping against the plate drowns out my answer to her. I mutter, "I just need a second," as I walk past her with the note clenched tight in my hand. It feels like a betrayal of Carter to see Nikolai. But I need to. I have to see him. I have to know he's all right.

My steps are deliberate as I walk as quickly as I can toward the stairwell, intent on searching out Eli. I don't have to look far; he's waiting for me at the top of the stairs.

"Eli," I speak his name quickly like I can't get it out fast enough. The uncertainty I'm feeling makes my skin tingle as I hold up the note.

"Aria," he says my name back easily and as if nothing's wrong.

"You read this?" I ask him even though he already told me he did. He only nods.

"Are you going to stop me from seeing him?" I ask him, the strength in my voice threatening to vanish at any moment.

"It depends."

"On what?" I ask him with no patience at all.

"On what Carter tells me to do," he answers, and I stand here helplessly in front of him.

"Are you going to kill him?" It's the next logical thought.

He hesitates, and I plead with him, "I won't run from you if you let me go to him. I need to see him."

He only takes a moment to respond, "I'm waiting to hear Carter's decision," and I can't contain my frustration any longer.

"You go ahead and wait. My decision is made." I know my words mean nothing to the cadre of soldiers surrounding me. It's a false threat, but I'm done playing these games where I'm some damsel trapped in a tower.

"Before you storm off," Eli begins with a straight face before I can turn my back on him and do exactly as he thought I would, storm off.

He holds out a package and I stare at it cautiously rather than take it. "What is it?" I ask him.

"You don't trust me now?" he asks with a hint of an asymmetric grin.

I don't respond. This isn't a game to me, it's my life.

"It's from Carter." He holds it out to me and I finally accept it, reeling with emotions I can't even begin to describe.

"What is it?" I ask him, but he only shrugs. The box isn't particularly big or small, so I can't even begin to guess what it contains.

"Tell him I want to see Nikolai... please."

With a short nod, he puts his hands behind his back and takes his position as if guarding the stairwell was what he was told to do. And maybe he was. Maybe Carter thought I'd run down the stairs and out the door the moment I got a note from Nikolai.

I don't wait to get to the bedroom to open the package. I peel back the tape as I walk, and force open the box.

Inside is a phone, simple and black, and art supplies, a drawing pad, and colored pencils.

Such little things, but I stare at them on the bed for far too long in silence, wishing I hadn't grown up in this world.

CHAPTER 9

Carter

HOURS HAVE PASSED, BUT SHE HASN'T MOVED FROM THE BED. Occasionally she flips open the sketch pad, but she doesn't draw like she did before.

Mostly she looks at the phone, expecting it to ring.

She's waiting on me. She's waiting for my move, but I don't know what the best action to take is.

Every time my phone rings and I'm given intel on where the men are and where they're going, my orders are immediate, confident, and not to be questioned. All who stand in my way will fall.

But what Aria wants... I sit back in my seat, observing her as she stares at the pad in her lap. I don't know how much leeway to give her. Free of her cage, my songbird might very well never come back to me given what I'm planning to do. And I can't have that. Aria is mine.

"How many men did Romano send in there?" Daniel asks as he walks into the office unannounced. No knocking whatsoever. I guess some things don't change.

Taking a deep breath that stretches my back, I answer him, "Four."

"And he wants us to send a dozen?" His tone is incredulous, but I had the same exact reaction and I give him a look that says as much.

Turning my attention to Daniel, I take in his dark eyes and the rough stubble that's overgrown on his jaw. He's still in the same shirt he was wearing yesterday too.

"Did you sleep?" I ask him, and he shakes his head no, but he moves the conversation back to business matters. Back to busying himself and ending the bullshit that keeps him from having Addison back.

"Jett went down late last night to Carlisle. He said this morning that he counted at least twenty-two Talvery soldiers that come and go down the block."

"That's right inside the northern border between the two of us, not between Romano and him."

"Right," he answers me, but I didn't need him to say a damn thing, I just needed a moment to think.

"Are the rest of the areas high density like that?"

"High density?" he echoes, not understanding. He hasn't been back long and he's still catching up.

"Instead of spreading his men out, he's keeping them heavy and clustered in one area? Or is this the only street like that?" Crossing my right ankle over my left knee, I lean back in the chair and pick up a pen to tap it against the desk as I think.

"It's like that three blocks from the divide between Romano and Talvery on the upper east side. Bedford, I think it is."

"Where are the rest of them?" I ask him. "I want a count and whereabouts of his men at all times."

"We need more eyes out if we want that intel. Jett can't move if he wants to pick them off."

"Then get them."

"Most of our men are surrounding the safe house..." For the first time since beginning this conversation, he lowers his voice to confess, "I don't want to move them."

"So, we need to take on an army with only a handful of men."

"Skilled men hired for this express purpose. Men who have been waiting for this for how long?" Daniel reminds me. Most of the men we picked up came with us for a reason. Hate is a better motivator than fear is and Talvery's made more enemies in his decades of reign than I'd like to give him credit for. As he grew older, he grew harder.

I wasn't the first boy he nearly beat to death for dealing in his territory. The others had families though, families who knew exactly who was responsible. Families who came to me, knowing we shared a common enemy.

I glance at the monitor, at my songbird who's staring at nothing and consumed by her helplessness. For a split second, I wonder if she knows everything her father did. But I already know she doesn't.

Daniel continues the conversation, hellbent on coming up with a plan. "Jett thinks we could use eight men total, two on each corner of that street and the other four on the other side to clean up that area."

"Eight men, to take on their twenty?" My voice is flat, my gaze pinned to his, but all I can see is how this will go down. How we can take out each of them.

"Romano's supposed to be sending down four in the next two days to go in, since he wants clean kills to avoid the news and having to pay off more cops. But I think we should hit them tomorrow night with the automatic assault rifles we just got from the docks."

I nod my head in agreement. Clean kills take more time, time that they'll use to react. "Why wait until tomorrow?" I ask him.

"It's Sunday," Daniel reminds me. A huff leaves me, somewhat sarcastic, somewhat pathetic. There are rules in this industry if you can call it that. No women, no children. Give peace at funerals. And leave Sundays for families. They're signs of respect and boundaries. The only reason they're kept is that sometimes enemies become allies and it's easily justified by saying that the enemy always gave respect.

I know only one man who defied the laws and my little songbird stabbed that fucker to death. Not a soul defended him. And who would when his death was justified for breaking a sacred rule?

Well, that man… and then myself. I took Aria from Talvery.

"Tomorrow night then." Daniel's eyes shine brighter with the challenge of pulling this off.

"Jett can stay where he is and take out any of Talvery's men that survive the hit. We need the police to stay back for at least eight hours. Instead of going in to see who's still breathing, we let the men try to come out to read the situation, and Jett will pick them off."

"They'll be easy to pay off. I know Officer Harold will hold them back for a grand a minute."

Daniel considers it and then offers another plan. "The alternative would be using explosives. But the street is a good location and that's a mess that'll bring too much attention."

"Hit them tomorrow night with the automatics. Pay off the cops for four hours and we'll hit the Talvery line up north as a distraction with the RDX, my explosive of choice courtesy of the shit Talvery put us through. Set off the explosives there at the same time as the hit on Carlisle Street. Let them focus on the bombings while we destroy their front line."

Daniel nods in agreement, relaxing into the chair, although his foot doesn't stop tapping on the floor, giving away his anxiety.

"Who all is there?" I ask him as my own qualms creep up on me.

"What do you mean?"

"Of Talvery's men, who…?" I pause to swallow thickly and ask my brother flat out, "Are any of them Aria's family?"

"Her cousin, Brett, comes by the bakery in the morning. It looks like their usual meet-up spot. He's been there every morning for the last three days, according to Jett. But at night, no. None of her blood. What she considers family is debatable though."

"You would think Talvery would be going out full force against Romano," I answer back instead of entertaining his thoughts on who Aria's family is.

"He was until yesterday. He moved the men to Carlisle, to our border the night after the dinner." He clarifies what night he's referring to when I give him a questioning look. "The night she killed Stephan and Romano passed the message to him. Then, yesterday, something else changed."

I close my eyes remembering that night, remembering the feeling of pride and lust I had for her growing that night she ended Stephan's life. "When it was confirmed that we had Aria."

"Yeah, that's when he moved more of his men to our side."

"So, now he's coming after us?" I can't help that I smirk, loving the challenge and the flow of adrenaline in my blood.

"There are equal numbers of men posted on the two borders. But if I were him, I'd be gunning for you."

"He knows we let her kill Stephan."

"Maybe that's why it's equal and why all his men aren't raiding our turf?"

"A man with two enemies, both pointing guns at him, who knows what he's thinking?"

Daniel's tone turns morose. "I have to tell you something you aren't going to like."

"And to think… you're interrupting this pleasant conversation …"

"Look who's making jokes now."

"Maybe I'm learning a thing from you."

"What happened last night that led him to move more men closer to us?"

I ask my brother, "Is that what you have to tell me?" I tap the pen against the desk as I think about everything Romano told me about his plans to decimate them in only four days flat.

Daniel repositions himself and nods, but his eyes are full of worry. "Romano and Talvery know where the girls are." He visibly swallows and adds, "They followed us."

I only nod, not wanting to acknowledge that truth. "Are you sure?" I ask him, feeling the tension build in my shoulders.

"Yeah," he answers with a tired voice, the fidgeting of his foot finally halting as he asks me, "What do we do with the women?"

"If she doesn't come willingly… I want mine back in the cell when this is over with."

Daniel's expression hardens. His disappointment and anger even, are evident. I don't care what I told her, what promises I've made or how fucked a position she's put me in. I don't care about any of it. The possessiveness stirs in my blood and I struggle to contain myself, so I settle on redirecting Daniel. "What you do with yours is up to you."

"You can't do that to her." Daniel dares to tell me what I can do. "You can't lock her up and expect her not to fight back."

"You're just pissed this is affecting you and Addison, and I'm sorry for that, but I'm not letting Aria walk away from me. I won't allow it." The last sentence is barely spoken through clenched teeth as my heart rate quickens and my hands form white-knuckled fists.

"Do you want a prisoner or a partner?" Daniel's question catches me off guard.

"She'll never see me as her partner. I will always be the enemy." I speak the truth that fills me with dread. This war has to happen. I will kill her father. And she will never see me as anything but an enemy once it's done.

"Not if you treat her as a partner."

"I want someone who wants me back," I confess to him. "I want her to want me back, and that will never happen once this week is done."

"You're so blinded by hate that you don't see it," Daniel tells me as if I'm a fool.

"You and Addison are different. Don't look at me like we're in the same situation. And you fucking know that's true." He shakes his head but remains silent.

"I'll put her back in the cell if I have to," I tell him with finality, staring past him and at the closed door. She wanted me once and I'll make it happen again. She'll learn to forgive.

"What are you doing? I've never seen you like this." Daniel's expression is worried, but more than that, sympathetic.

"I loved her," I say, and my answer is harsh; I can feel my control slipping again. It slips so easily with her.

"And?" he questions me as if he doesn't understand. As if it isn't obvious that the woman I love is the enemy. Even when all of them are dead and I've taken her back, I will always be the enemy to her and there's nothing I can do about it. Not a damn thing.

"You still love her, so why would you do that to her?"

"I don't know what love is."

"You're being fucking stupid and this 'woe is me' bullshit doesn't look good on you, Carter."

"Fuck you," I seethe as I tell my brother off. "Addison will run, and you'll follow like a little puppy dog, but she'll come back to you because you didn't do a damn thing to her. Aria..." My throat gets tighter as I speak, threatening to strangle me if I speak the words aloud. "I'm going to kill her family. I've locked her up, I've punished her."

"What you have is different, but it's obvious to her that you love her. You'll see."

"Love isn't enough sometimes. I don't know how you've gotten stuck on some fantasy, Daniel. I live in the real world, where I'm the villain. So, go ahead and tell me she'll love me after this. Keep telling yourself that too. Whatever helps you sleep."

Daniel doesn't answer. A moment passes and then another before he stands up abruptly and leaves me alone.

The second the door slams shut, I turn back to the monitors, focusing on them as my blood simmers and my gut starts to churn.

My body is ringing with anger, contempt, and fear. I haven't felt fear in so long. True fear threatens to consume me at the very real possibility of losing her.

Not if you treat her as a partner. Daniel's words echo in my head, but how can he say that when he knows what that means in this world we inhabit?

Aria's still staring at the phone and without hesitation, I pick up the phone on my desk and call her.

Only yesterday, she lay across my desk while I played with her cunt and her ass, knowing she loved it and thinking she loved me.

A day can change everything.

The line only rings once before she answers, cradling the phone close with both hands.

"Hello?" Just the sound of her voice is soothing. Everything about her is a balm for the burning rage inside of me.

"Do you hate me?" I ask her, needing to know.

"Have you killed them?"

A sad smirk kicks my lips up as I touch the tips of my fingers to the screen. I can see her swallow as the silence stretches, I can see her start to crumble when I don't immediately respond. And I hate it. I hate that this is what will happen to her.

"No." The moment I speak the word, her head falls forward and I hear her take in a deep breath. "But you know it has to happen," I remind her as she sits up straighter, still cross-legged on the bed.

"I know," she answers. I watch as she picks at the comforter and then readjusts but winces as she moves. No doubt the lashes from the belt are causing her pain. They barely left a mark on her. I held back, but even so, I know she's still hurting from it.

I struggle to breathe as she asks me, "So, it's inevitable that I'll hate you then?"

"That's your choice."

"I know some of the men who have died already," she confesses with pain etched in her voice. Her words are so strangled and unwilling to be spoken that I almost don't hear her. It takes me a second and then another, the ticks of the clock marking each of them.

She covers her mouth with her hand, pulling the phone to one side as she gathers her composure, but keeps the other end pressed close to her ear.

"There is always loss in this business," is all I can give her until I think to add, "I'm sorry."

"I'm sorry too," she tells me after a moment.

"This is no different than before when men standing in front of your father were shot, so to speak. They fight for him, and they die for him. It's all happened before."

"I'll tell you something that maybe you don't find obvious, Carter." Aria finds her strength and it gives me hope until she speaks. "I hated the men who killed them before. I just didn't have a face to associate with their deaths."

"Romano."

"What?" she questions and in even a single word, I feel the hope start to rise inside of me again.

"Direct your hate there, not at me." Maybe I'm a coward for hiding behind Romano while I can, but she can't hate me. I don't know what I'll become if she does.

She lies back slowly on the bed, ever so slowly, and stares at the ceiling before she asks, "This, wasn't you?

"I haven't had to do anything yet, but things have changed."

"What's changed?" she immediately asks, but her voice is even, devoid of emotion. I can hear her swallow as she asks me, "What exactly has changed?" She bunches the top sheet in her hand absently, waiting for my answer.

I question telling her for only a moment. But ultimately, I decide to give her what she wants. To treat her like a partner in this.

"The number of your father's men that have moved closer to Carlisle Street."

"Where's Carlisle?" she asks with her hand falling back onto the bed, but still gripping the sheet.

As much as she'd like to know what's going on, she has so much to learn.

"One street up from where our territories are divided, Miss Talvery." My cock hardens as I speak to her like this as if I'm negotiating with the enemy. My little songbird is playing the part of the queen. And what a queen she would make.

"I don't like it when you call me that," she says quietly, but her lips stay parted long after the word is spoken. I watch on the screen as her hand moves to her belly.

"Your father is preparing to invade and conquer and he's making it obvious."

"He's defending his territory." She's quick to reply, and I find her logic appropriate. Which makes me sit back farther in my seat.

"Remember who you are, Aria."

"I'm still figuring out who I am, Carter." The air of dominance wraps around her like a cloak when she talks to me like that, with only a whisper of submission. When she gives herself to me with no pretense, only honesty.

And I take that moment to tell her exactly who she is and will always be. "You're mine."

"Am I?" Her voice is coated in sadness as she closes her eyes.

"Yes," the word is practically hissed as I lean closer to the screen, wishing I were there with her now.

"And if I leave this place; if I leave… to see someone?" she asks me, and I know exactly what she's talking about. "Would I still be yours?" My pulse hammers in my ears and I bite back the initial response and the next.

I give her the only truth I know, "You will always be mine."

"Carter," Aria's voice breaks and she covers her eyes with her hand as she talks. "I'm scared."

"You're brave," I tell her, and she lets out a humorless laugh on the other end of the phone.

"I'm afraid I'm going to fail and we'll both be left with no one," she tells me, wiping under her eyes and repositioning herself on the bed, once again wincing. My gaze flicks to the nightstand where I left the cooling balm, still right where it was last night.

Ignoring her statement and refusing to think of that possibility, I ask her instead, "Are you still hurting from your punishment?"

Again, I'm given that huff of a laugh before she answers, "Yes. You left your mark on me, Mr. Cross."

"It's not the only mark I want to leave on you, songbird."

I hear her breathe in deeply on the other end and I lower my voice, forgetting everything but the two of us when I ask her, "Do you love it when I call you that?"

A second passes before she whispers, "Yes."

Again, I reach up to the screen, wishing I could touch her right now. But I can't. Not when I know the enemy could come at any moment. My men will stay with her and protect her. So long as she's safe, that's all that matters.

"You need to use the balm I gave you," I tell her and watch for her reaction.

She glances at it but doesn't move. The tension rises inside of me at her ignoring the request. A request made to help her.

"What if I want to feel it?" she asks me before I can scold her, and confusion runs through me. "What if I think I deserve to still feel the pain and I don't want the balm?" Her voice cracks slightly, but she holds her ground.

My poor Aria. The weight of two conflicting worlds is resting on her shoulders. And the consequences are heavier than any one person could possibly bear.

"You need to heal, so that if you disobey me again," I tease her, "I'll have a fresh canvas to work with when you do." I feel the ease of a smile grow on my face as the tension subsides with her genuine laughter. It's muted, soft, and just as feminine as Aria is.

"I guess I didn't think of that," she says before climbing to the edge of the bed and kicking off the thin sweatpants she's wearing. She isn't wearing any underwear.

The realization reminds me that I'm hard for her.

My dick throbs as it presses against my zipper and I want to lean back, to readjust, but I find myself leaning in closer to the monitor.

Holding the phone between her ear and her shoulder, she's able to grab the balm. She asks me, "Can you see me right now?"

"Yes."

I'm rewarded with a small smile on her lips as she looks around the room, searching for cameras she won't find.

"Put the balm down, Aria," I command her, feeling my cock twitch with need. I watch as she obeys me, setting it back down and standing in nothing but a thin cotton t-shirt.

"Yes, Carter," she simpers into the phone.

"Put the phone on speaker," I tell her, keeping my voice even so she won't have an inkling of my deep and heavy lust for her. She does as I tell her, and the moment she does I give her another command. "Set it on the bed and get on all fours like how I had you last night."

With the angle of the camera, I can see her pussy easily. I can even see up her shirt as it hangs around her waist and her pale pink nipples are obviously visible. "You're fucking perfect," I groan deep in my throat as I unzip my pants and fist my cock, pumping it once and then again.

Swallowing hard I watch as her fingers move to her sex, and she glistens with arousal.

"Do you like this, Mr. Cross?" she asks me with the sultry voice of a vixen.

"Miss Talvery, I fucking love it." I push my confession through clenched teeth. As I stroke myself, she presses her fingers into her cunt and when she does, her eyes close and her cheek pushes against the pillow.

Her lips part and I can just barely hear the sweet moan of pleasure.

"I wish I could shove my cock down your throat right now," I tell her as precum leaks from my slit. I rub it over the head of my dick and shivers of desire run down my spine and straight through my body, making my toes curl.

Like the good girl she is, she tells me back, "You'd make me choke on it. I love it when you do that." Her dirty words make my cock impossibly hard and I know I'm going to cum.

"Fuck yourself faster," I command her, and she immediately obeys. Pushing her small fingers in and out of her tight cunt. Her back bows and her hips sway with her impending orgasm.

"Hold still and grab your ass where I struck you while you cum for me," I tell her as my balls draw up. And she does. With her head pressed into the pillow, one hand squeezing the marks on her ass and the other fucking herself, she cums violently, falling to her side and screaming out my name.

My name.

I lose myself with her, cumming into my hand like a high school prick and wishing there was nothing that separated us. Wishing we lived in a different world.

CHAPTER 10

Aria

I T'S AN ODD RUSH OF EMOTION THAT FLOWS THROUGH ME. THE fear and anxiety are most easily described, but there are others tangled in a knot in the pit of my stomach.

Carter made it all go away when he told me to touch myself. Submitting to him makes everything go away and the feeling lasts long after he hangs up the phone.

As I walk out of the bedroom, knowing I'm doing something he'd prefer I didn't, the haze and comfort that comes from submitting to him dims. It's a consequence I accept. Before he ended our conversation, he told me what I chose tonight is up to me. He's giving me the choice, and I won't waste it.

I want to be more than I have been all my life.

A touch of shame washes over me as I think, *I want to be a woman who could stand by Carter's side.* It's shameful because this isn't for Carter. This meeting isn't for my father.

This meeting with Nikolai isn't even for him.

It's for me.

My heart pounds in my chest, as does the adrenaline in my blood. Tonight, I'll live up to my name. To be Aria Talvery, daughter of a ruthless crime lord. And a woman standing between two men waging war.

My father would have me stay willingly in my room. My lover would have me stay willingly locked in his house.

I'll stay and stand where I want after tonight until I see my end. No matter if that means I'll lose both men.

Even if the pleasure Carter gave me only an hour ago is still coursing through my veins.

I can hear Addison making something in the kitchen and I

hesitate to go in to see her. I haven't told her a damn thing and it feels like I'm lying to her by keeping these secrets from her.

As I step in to tell her I'm going out, the microwave beeps and the smell of chicken noodle soup fills my lungs. Comfort food, even though there's no comfort here.

The air is easy between us, but I know it won't last when she turns around and sees me. I've been struggling with whether or not I should tell her since I got the note. I want to lean on her, to confide in her, but I also want to save her from this awfulness that rages inside of me.

I don't know what to do. I honestly have no idea what to do, but I know if she asks me, I'll tell her about everything. And I'll never lie to her.

"Dinner?" I ask her as she pulls the door open, not peeking back behind her to answer me. I wish she would. I wish I could get this part over with.

"You want some?" she asks softly, devoid of the cheeriness I anticipate from her. I watch as she sets the bowl down after removing the paper towel covering the top and trashing it. That's when she finally looks up at me.

"Are you okay?" I ask her a question first, but she ignores it, asking her own instead.

"Where are you going?" Addison's voice is thick with sleep. "Are you meeting Carter?" The deep crease in the center of her forehead is evidence enough of her concern, but she quickly fists her hands and places one on each hip as her chest rises. The act actually makes me smile and eases some of the nerves bubbling inside of my chest.

I love her and her protectiveness. I wish I could hide in it.

"I have a meeting with someone else," I tell her and feel that unease rise up higher, into my throat and bringing true fear with it as she asks me, "Does Carter know?"

"Yes," I answer her in a single unsteady breath.

Shifting her weight from one foot to the other, she doesn't respond, and I watch as the fight in her subsides. I can read the questions on her face, but she chooses not to ask any of them. The biggest two being "who?" and "why?" I was so like her once in my life.

"I'll be okay." I can at least give her that to ease her worries, although it feels like I won't be okay. It feels like I'm risking everything, and the consequences will be severe. I know it all already, I've weighed all the risks and thought of each outcome.

But I have to do this. "I have to try something to stop all of this." I give her a little more, hinting at what I'm doing, but she doesn't ask additional questions.

"You surprise me," Addison admits, her lips turned down into a frown although I'm not sure why.

"What's wrong?" I ask, ignoring the obvious and feeling my heart try to climb into my throat. I cautiously step closer, not wanting to hurt her or leave her feeling like she's anything but my friend, my closest friend.

I have to clasp my hands together in front of me to keep from reaching out to her, but it doesn't matter, because she reaches out to me first. Brushing her hand against my forearm, she gives me a hesitant smile.

"You handle it all so much better than I do, and I just..." As she trails off, her tone says it all. *She feels weak.*

I can't stand her reaction and I squash her thoughts as quickly as I can. "I don't handle it well; I barely handle it at all." I try to joke with her, but it doesn't work. She takes in a deep, unsteady breath and then looks back to the bowl of soup.

"Daniel asked me to forgive him yesterday."

The sudden change in topic startles me and I don't know if she's upset with me or not. I ask in a near whisper, "What did you say?"

"I said that I didn't know how I could. That when I fell in love with him, he was a different man."

"I'm sorry," I tell her as I grab her hand.

She's choked up and I find it contagious as she looks up toward the tallest cabinet and speaks to it, rather than me to keep from crying. "He said I'm good at lying to myself but that it's okay and that he still loves me." She sniffles, wiping under her eyes even though the tears haven't fallen yet. "Can you believe the balls he has?" Her lips twitch up into a sad smirk, but it doesn't stay long as she gives in to the tears.

"I miss him," she cries softly into my shoulder and clings to me. I'm quick to hold her tightly, hugging her as she breaks down. It fucking hurts seeing her like this. If I could go back, I'd keep her from learning the truth. I wish she'd never seen what happened. I wish she'd never peeked into this world I can't escape.

She pulls away after only a few seconds, shaking out her hands and walking away, but then comes right back. Her unease shows as she paces like I do but in much smaller circles.

"I feel crazy," she mutters and sniffles again.

"The Cross boys are good at making the women they love go crazy," I answer her in a deadpan tone with a weak smile. It takes a minute for her to look me in the eyes, and when she does, she doesn't accept the humor in my response.

"I swear I didn't know the things they do. But he told me he's always been a bad man and that it never stopped him from loving me. Or me from loving him before."

I rub her arm, feeling like it's all my fault and hating myself for it. I wish I could go back. If only I could. There's so much I would change.

"I want to leave with him, but he won't leave his brothers and I don't think I could ever ask him to do that, but together they will live like this... rule like this."

"He's not a bad man, Addie." I don't know where she's going with this, but I refuse to let her focus on something that will never change. "And what they do... they do because they have to." I swallow down the pain of the words, knowing I've had to choke on that excuse for as long as I've lived.

"How can we live like this, knowing what they do? What they're capable of?"

"We remember why they are the way they are. And we give them the love they need, so long as they give it back to us." I stare into her eyes, meaning every word.

"I know they need love. They desperately need to be loved." Tears prick at my own eyes as she looks away from me, but I see from her expression that she knows it's true. There's nothing in the world that would deny that truth.

Addison wipes under her eyes with the sleeves of her pajama shirt. She's dressed for bed, exhausted and dealing with the weight of loving a man from the world I grew up in. Part of me is jealous of her, a very small part, but it's there. "He loves you, Addie," I whisper to her, squeezing her hand.

She squeezes mine back and then lets her hand drop to her side. "I know, but if I accept it, I'm no better than he is. And I'll never be okay with what Carter did to you. I don't care if you are."

"Carter and Daniel are different men." My answer comes out harsher than I wanted, and I attempt to soften it by adding, "And I know Carter's reason, Addie." I try to tell her more, but the words won't come out. I can't tell her about what my father did and what Carter thinks he heard. If I told her that, the next logical thing to say would be that it wasn't me he heard. The voice he heard that gave him the strength to keep living didn't belong to me.

My heart plummets painfully in my chest at the thought of my secret, making me feel sick once again.

"When are you leaving me?" Addie asks, changing the subject again and moving back to the counter to grab a spoon from the drawer. The metal clinks against the ceramic as she stirs her soup. "A secret meeting in the middle of the night?" She tries to add a sense of playfulness into the chide, but it doesn't come out strong enough.

As I answer her, she lifts the spoon to her lips, blowing on the soup and then swallowing it.

"Not so secret, and I'll be back soon."

"Should I ask what it's about?"

I don't know what to tell her, and I remember all the times I was curious but too afraid to ask. I wish someone had taken my fear away from me and told me more about the world I was living in. That's what fuels me to tell her, "I'm meeting a friend I grew up with who's one of my father's men."

Her face pales as she peeks toward the doorway to the kitchen. Maybe she expects to find Eli there, I don't know, but then she whispers, "Should you be doing that?"

Her eyes plead with me to be truthful and so I answer her honestly, putting a hand on her shoulder and not daring to take my gaze away from hers as I say, "I should have done it sooner."

"What if he tries to take you back?" The raw note of fear in her voice means more to me than I could ever tell her.

I shake my head. "Eli is coming with me, and Carter knows about it. I'm not leaving you, Addison. I promise. He wouldn't let it happen."

"So, you two...?" She doesn't finish the question.

"Are... speaking, but still not okay," I answer slowly.

"Why go then?" she asks, and I know she'll understand my reasoning.

"He's my friend, and he's going to die or he's going to help kill the man I love." Tears brim, but I hold them back. It's the painful truth, and I know I need to change it. "If I don't do something, those are the only two outcomes."

"Are you..." Addie looks anywhere but at me, until she gathers her thoughts and finally asks a question I don't know the answer to. "Whatever you tell him, or ask of him... will he listen to you?"

Cason comes into view from the very doorway she was just looking toward. "I don't know," I answer her with a weak smile, although I stare back at Cason. Something thuds hard within my chest knowing Nikolai has always tried to keep things from me. He thinks it protects me, but I know now that he's wrong.

Addison's gaze follows mine and the clinking of her spoon against the bowl as she places her dishes in the sink marks the finality of our discussion. "Be safe," she tells me quietly as she leaves.

"You too," I tell her and listen to the sound of her retreating down the hall to the bedrooms as Cason steps into the kitchen. His jeans are dirty, covered in mud from the knees down.

He was doing something... and I can only imagine it involved a shovel and shallow grave.

"I heard you might be going out." Cason starts talking the moment Addie's out of the kitchen. I wonder if she stopped in the hall, holding her breath and staying as still as she can so she can listen.

I've done that more times than I can count.

"I am." My answer is hard as I look Cason in the eye. "Right now, actually."

"Are you sure you want to do that?" he questions me. The man's nearly a foot taller than me, with broad shoulders and arms that are a dead giveaway he spends too much time in the gym.

"You're the muscle." I ignore his question and ask him my own. "Aren't you?"

He tilts his head, considering me.

"You guys have a certain look to you," I explain as I walk through the kitchen and head to the living room. It's a modern house with an open concept floor plan, so he has no problem viewing me as he crosses his arms and leans against the wall.

"The scar on your chin, the tattoos across your knuckles, probably where they're scarred too," I speak to him as the vision of men my father referred to as the muscle, invades my memory. They'd come to the house every once in a while, with big envelopes stuffed full of cash they'd leave for him. As polite as they were to me, I knew what they did.

They beat the shit out of men who didn't pay up. My gaze drifts to the mud on Cason's shins... and they buried the men who didn't learn the lesson fast enough.

Slipping on my shoes, leather ballet flats, I peek up at Cason and ask him, "Do you have bullet hole scars too?"

His eyes are still assessing me as the silence drags on. It doesn't even look like he's breathing as I stand tall and make my way back to him. There's a matte black earpiece in his right ear, and I wonder if Carter's listening. I wonder if Carter's asking him to stop me because he doesn't have the balls to do it himself.

Fed up with Cason forcing me to talk to myself, I tell him, "It's three blocks down, and Eli is accompanying me. Thank you for your concern."

As I walk toward the stairway, glancing at the clock on the stove to make sure I'm on schedule, Cason decides to walk in front of me, his large chest becoming as unyielding and firm as a brick wall.

"I urge you to reconsider," he tells me with a voice that comes from deep in his throat. Towering over me, he's a man who creates fear. And it stirs in my blood, warning me to back down and simply survive the encounter. I look him in the eyes and tell him calmly with a hint of a smile and a narrowed glare, "See, I knew you were the muscle." Inwardly, I feel like I'm about to choke on a spiked ball of panic.

I stare into his dark eyes, meeting his gaze and refusing to back down. Not this second, and not the next. Never.

"I'm going," I tell him with finality and strength I don't feel anywhere else.

"As you wish." His answer is accompanied by a look of disappointment. Clenching his jaw, he moves his gaze back to the kitchen.

My body sags and I heave in a breath when Cason turns his back to me to go down the stairs first. The sinking feeling that chills every inch of my skin is something I've felt before and I hate it. It will always come. Those who are bigger, scarier, and hold an air of darkness around them will always bring out my survival instinct to run. But they die just like the rest of us.

I only peek up to Cason's back when I hear him as he grabs his ear. I can hear the bellowing that's coming from it from where I stand.

"Aria," Cason starts speaking before he's fully turned to me. "Please forgive me for trying to intimidate you." He chokes on his words as if terrified of getting them wrong and the look in his eyes couldn't be further from the look that gave me goosebumps only moments ago.

"I forgive you," I answer him slowly, questioning my own response and wanting to know what the fuck just happened. The question lingers in my words as they reach his ear. Or rather, the earpiece that's still filled with the yells of someone on the other end. An enraged Carter, naturally. My lips threaten to tug into a smile as I hear his voice, but I contain it as Cason continues.

"Your decisions are your own and I have absolutely no right to interfere. I'm only here to protect you."

It's as if he's speaking an oath. His gaze is genuinely full of remorse and I wonder what he really thinks of me. I haven't thought of that at all until this moment.

"I'll never turn my back on you again," he tells me with both of his hands clasped in front of him apologetically. He even lowers his head some, hunching his shoulders to meet my gaze at eye level. "Would you like me to take you to Eli?"

"No need." Eli's voice startles me and I'm ashamed I jump backward. Eli's smile is wicked like he's proud he got to me. With my hand on my chest and my back against the wall, he passes me a white jean jacket.

"You scared me," I tell him in the same breath I exhale. My heart still feels like it's about to leap out of my chest.

"I know," he says, grinning like a Cheshire cat before resuming his normal dominating stance.

"Carter wanted me to give this to you, in case you'd be needing it," he tells me, and I snatch it from him. It matches my outfit, which I do and don't like about this situation. I want to ask where the cameras are. I want to question both men and demand they tell me everything Carter tells them, but I don't want to give away how little I know. Not to them.

"Asshole," I mutter as I right myself and steady my breath. Cason lets out a snort of a laugh and the tension between the three of us eases some. But only for a moment.

"I'm sorry, Aria," Cason tells me as I drape the jacket over my forearm. "I have strong opinions and I know I need to keep them to myself and I'm sorry," he rambles slightly, but his tone is genuine, and his green eyes shine with remorse.

"I get it," I tell him. "I know what war means and what this means." I look him in the eyes as I answer and neither of us wavers, not until Eli speaks up.

"Are you ready to meet with the enemy?" Eli asks me, and I can't look at either of them as I answer, "I already have."

From the corner of my eye, I see the smile wane on his face, but Eli nudges me with his shoulder before walking out in front.

"Be smart, Aria," Cason warns as my small footsteps echo in the foyer. My quickened pulse increases even more and I have to walk a little quicker to keep up with Eli.

It didn't feel real until just now.

The crickets are out tonight, and the sky is lit with so many stars. More stars than I've ever seen in Fallbrook.

"How long until we're there?" I ask Eli, breathing in the crisp air of the cool summer night and ignoring the roiling in the pit of my stomach. The anxiety numbs my hands and I clench and unclench them before deciding to shrug on the jacket and slip my hands into my pockets.

Taking a look around to my left and right, this street is nothing but houses. I barely remember that from the drive up. The next street is where the houses are grouped closer together and there's something on the corner, a church or a liquor store, maybe both. I don't remember.

"Not long, he's already waiting," Eli tells me, but the playfulness, the easiness from the stairwell are all but forgotten.

He glances at me as I keep my pace steady with his, taking strides more often since he's taller than me. The sound of a car driving up the next street over makes him pause and he holds his arm out, stopping me from moving out into the street and pushing me closer to the brick fence of the house to my left. A moment passes, and the sound of the car diminishes. The voices from the same earpiece Cason was wearing make me stare at Eli. I can't hear what they're saying, but I know he's getting information about something.

Dread and panic mix together, making my legs feel weak. Eli glances up at the house, to the second floor and waits, then a sound creeps into his ear and he nods.

The nod wasn't for me and as Eli looks down at me and smiles politely, both of us know it.

"It's clear, Miss…" He stops and clears his throat then says, "Aria."

The dread's still there, making my hands clammy and causing my throat to tighten.

"I was hoping you wouldn't do this," Eli tells me and continues to stare straight ahead even as I look up at him, willing him to look me in the eyes.

Since he doesn't look back at me, I stare straight ahead as well. "If you thought I'd lie down and let this go on without trying to stop it, you were wrong."

"There's no way to stop this."

"I stood by before and did nothing while I watched family die," I speak quietly and swallow the knot that forms in my throat as I think of my mother. After taking a moment to compose myself, I tell Eli with finality, "I won't do it again."

CHAPTER 11

Carter

I HATE BEING IN THIS OFFICE. WATCHING CAMERAS AND WAITING. I don't miss the rush of being on the streets, but I hate not being beside the men who are risking their lives for me right now. Without the first move made on this side, the leaks and intel can't be trusted.

I'm waiting. The adrenaline competes inside of me with the hate and pent-up rage. And here I sit. Waiting.

"Carter." Jace's voice carries through the closed door. I haven't left since Daniel slammed it shut earlier and it's only now that I remember our fight. My brothers rotate in and out of my office, I'm used to them coming and going. And seemingly forgetting past conversations in order to handle business.

"Come in," I call out to him, and instantly the door opens.

"The Red Room, the stash in the backroom is gone, and the fucker who broke in last night to take it was found face down in the river this morning." Jace's words come out like an assault as he paces to the chair across from me, gripping the back of it and staring at me waiting for answers.

All day, this is what I do. Accept information and move chess pieces. That's how true empires are built. The bloodshed is nearly the conquering of a knight. Some poor fool dies, so the men with power make a simple move, knowing more are to come and there's more game left to play.

"Do the cops have any idea who did it?" I ask him, bringing my thumb to my chin and running the pad along the stubble there. I need to shave. Jace and I are more alike than I care to admit. The back and forth of the motion keeps me focused on Jase and this shitstorm.

Jace speaks in rapid fire, giving me all the details from his conversation with Officer Harold. No leads on a suspect, no trace of him on any city cameras once he leaves the edge of town and heads down to the woods on the edge of Jersey. Yet, he's found dead at the river next to his house hours later.

"It doesn't add up," I answer Jace, meeting his gaze as he lowers himself to the chair opposite mine on the other side of my desk. His thumb raps on the armrest as he nods.

"Someone's fucking with us. Letting us know that they can steal from us, kill on our turf, and they can get away with it."

"Marcus," I say the name without thinking. "He's the only man who's ever been able to get away with that shit."

"And only because he's a fucking ghost with no face." He takes a calming breath before adding, "Just one look on a tape and we've got his ass."

"How many decades now has he gotten away with it? Any territory, any head he wants severed?"

"Why fuck with us though? Why us?" He leans forward, letting the anger show in his voice and his posture.

"Daniel turned on him first, blaming him for what happened to Addison with no proof." Instead of indulging in the rage of having product stolen from us and the opportunity for justice torn from my hands, I consider everything logically. It's how it needs to be handled. With nothing but cold-hearted control.

"I don't know... If he set up Addison..." Jase's thoughts are left unfinished, but I know what he's thinking. If Marcus is after us, it's only a matter of time before we find out what he truly wants.

And if he went after Addison, he won't stop until he has her.

"The cameras and men have the safe house fully under surveillance?" I question Jase, although it's more of a reminder to myself. He nods with his thumb brushing across his lip.

"Yeah, there's no way he'd get in without us knowing."

"And who knows?" I ask him as the pieces fall one by one into the puzzle of how to handle this.

"Who knows what?" he asks to clarify, a brow lifting.

"Who knows we had someone steal from us and then they turned up dead?"

"Jared and two of his men. The men in our pocket at the station want to know what to do; they haven't asked outright, but they think it was our hit on the fucker."

"Good." My quick response in a hardened voice surprises my brother. He should know better by now. "Tell Jared I handled the prick who broke in. Tell the police that we're grateful for their cooperation and pay them off." Jase's eyes go wide and a look of outrage is there for only a moment. But as soon as it comes, it's gone.

"So, no one thinks we don't have this under control?" he surmises.

"Exactly."

"But we don't."

"It's about perception, Jase. One moment of what could look like weakness and our allies become enemies. The men we have under our thumb think they can wiggle free and take a shot back."

"What do I do about finding out who did this shit?"

"Put Declan on it. He needs to go through home security system footage around the river starting at the dead fuck's house. We can't rely on the city surveillance."

As Jase nods, he settles into the chair. No one steals from us or fucks with us. Even Marcus wouldn't dare. I never thought it was him when it came to Addison. Daniel came up with that shit himself because he had no one else to blame.

"I'll let Declan know," he tells me, still nodding in agreement.

"You're not going to tell me one thing and then turn around and tell our men something else, are you?" I let the words slip out with my disappointment and a trace of animosity evident in my tone.

"Don't do that shit," he bites back, shaking his head. "Tell me I didn't do the right thing, and I'll apologize."

The large clock ticks steadily in the background as my grip tightens on the armrest and a tic in my jaw spasms.

"You were... in a state where I think you would agree I needed to step in." He raises his hands quickly as my gaze narrows and the temperature of my blood rises. "It was a difficult night, and I would have never stepped in if what happened wasn't *exactly* how it happened."

My blunt nails dig into the leather armrests as I try to contain my anger, even as my brother sits there as if we're just having a casual conversation as if he's no threat to me.

"I won't do it again," he tells me easily, and then clears his throat. "I didn't want…" he trails off and looks away over to his left, to the box still on the ground and out of place. "I just," he looks back up at me and I can read the sincerity on his face, "I didn't want her to hate you."

It takes a moment for him to contain the uncertainty and pain in his expression. With each second, every tick of the clock, the truth of what he says chips away at the resentment I feel over what he did. "You've been mad at me before; I know you'll get over it. This isn't the first time I've crossed the line and it won't be the last. But I love you, as my brother and my friend, and I didn't want her to hate you. I know you love her."

I haven't seen Jase like this in years. Not since the last funeral he went to. And the second his confession is over, he starts up a new conversation, never giving me the chance to respond.

"I didn't come in here to bother you with this shit."

My throat is dry, and I reach behind me for two tumblers and whiskey before asking him, "What shit did you come in to bother me with then?"

"About Aria meeting with Nikolai."

"I know she decided to go. I spoke to Eli when they left."

"She already left?" he questions, shaking his head. "What is he going to tell her?"

"It doesn't matter," I say to put an end to his bullshit. "I let her go. She wanted to go to him." I down the whiskey in my glass before pouring myself more and then pouring three fingers into his glass and offering it to him.

He takes it but doesn't drink.

"How many men did he bring?" he asks me.

"Just him," I tell him, and he lets a smirk spread on his face in response.

"He may be young, but even I'm not that stupid."

"I know why he did it." Even though I realize I'm talking to

Jase, I speak absently, knowing why Nikolai came alone and what he bargained away just for her to get the note. "He's desperate."

"He has a death wish," Jase speaks up, and I move my attention from him to the screen.

"I told Eli to let her make the decision. If she wants to go to him, let her... and she did."

"It would be easy to simply lock the door and coming from me..." Jase shakes his head and takes the first sip of his whiskey.

"I want to see what she'll do." Every ounce of me wants to control her. To demand she behave exactly how I want her to. Even as I stared at the monitor a half hour ago on the computer, watching her as she picked up a silk blouse I bought her, intending on wearing it for him, the urge to get to her faster than she could walk into that room raced through my mind. To keep her there if I couldn't convince her otherwise.

"Are you sure that you're sure?" Jase questions me again. I should feel angry that it's becoming a habit for him to question me, but I know he's thinking what I'm thinking, that she'll choose him again.

With a painful thud in my chest that numbs my body, I answer him, "Yes. She's already there, waiting."

"Waiting for what?"

"For me to tell Eli to let her in."

"You aren't going to be there?" he questions me with a look of complete disbelief.

Placing my palms on the desk and leaning forward so he can understand exactly why I'm not there, I ask him, "Do you think it would be helpful if he were in my presence right now?" My jaw hardens, and I can't help it as I tell him, "This is for her." It fucking hurts to admit, "She wouldn't want me there." He's shaking his head, and I shrug.

I tell Jase, "She's not in danger. The only thing that could happen is if she..."

"If she chooses him and tries to run." Jase finishes my thoughts and I nod once, bringing my attention back to the monitors. Jase looks like he's contemplating what to say next, so I remain silent.

"Eli will kill him if he tries?" I nod again at his question and throw back my second glass of whiskey.

"I just have to give Eli the go-ahead to let her in," I admit to him as I stare at the screen knowing I'm giving her what she wants, but not knowing how it will affect us and I can't fucking stand it.

The moment he touches her, I'll see her reaction.

I will never forgive her if she chooses him over me.

CHAPTER 12

Aria

I REMEMBER THE FIRST TIME I SAW NIKOLAI. WE WERE ONLY children. His father worked for my father until he was killed.

The funeral home always had the prettiest flowers, and that's what I looked at whenever we went there, all of the pretty flowers. But that day, I let myself watch the boy next to the casket.

I never liked to look at the people there. They always cried, and it made me want to cry, but I wasn't allowed. We were Talverys and we weren't allowed to cry, no matter how much I wanted to.

The boy was crying. He was taller than me and in a black suit that didn't fit right, because he was too tall for it. His ankles were bare although his black shoes were new.

He looked so angry as he stared at the casket, wiping away his tears like they were nothing but a nuisance.

I never wanted to speak to anyone, not like my mother and father did. I never wanted to give anyone a hug or even be near any of them. Especially, the ones who smiled and laughed at funerals. I didn't understand it and it made me angry to see people laughing when they were supposed to be mourning. I didn't learn until years later that everyone mourns differently. Apparently, my coping mechanism is solitude.

And Nikolai's was anger.

I remember how hesitant I was to touch his shoulder and ask him, "Are you okay?"

He was the first person I'd ever talked to at the many funerals I'd attended by this point. When he looked at me, when he glanced over his shoulder to answer me, he had a look of pure rage, maybe even disgust, but then he saw me, and it softened. Not just softened; his expression crumpled. The boy bared his soul to me and I saw the pain and the loneliness. He didn't speak; he only shook his head. But then I tried to hug him, and he let me.

My father hired him to do collections, even though he was only fourteen. He said the boy needed a distraction and I was happy I got to see him every week.

And then my mother died. And I felt the grief, the solitude that begged me to hide away and isolate myself. But Nikolai refused to let me be alone. He promised me he'd stay with me. He was the first person who said it was okay to cry and he held me while I did.

Ever since that day, we were inseparable.

He was my only friend. My only lover. And the only person I ever trusted in this world other than my mother.

The door to the back room of a candy shop three blocks north of the safe house is all that stands between Nikolai and me. My fingers keep pinching and twisting the cuffs of the jean jacket. Deep inside of me, the fear that they've hurt Nikolai is very real. That he's cuffed to a chair and on death's door is likely. I've seen it before. So many times.

"He's okay, right?" I ask quietly, not hiding my fear as I peek up at Eli. He considers me for a long moment before nodding his head and each fraction of a second that passes ramps up my anxiety.

"Thank you," I whisper my gratitude, although I'm not sure I entirely believe him and look toward the door with my shoulders squared as if it'll open any second.

"You can go in now," Eli tells me from behind and I reach for the knob, but he stops me, gripping my forearm and telling me, "Let me."

Nodding, I wait with bated breath for the door to open. It's on rusted hinges and they screech with the motion of the heavy door opening.

"Aria," Nik breathes my name before I even see him, and his voice is drowned out by the sound of metal chair legs scraping against the concrete floor as he pushes away from a small card table in the center of the barren room. Barely aware that Eli is watching and that there are two other men in the room also watching, I run to him, meeting him halfway and clinging to him.

I don't care in this moment. They can all watch and judge.

All I can see as I hold him is the gun touching the back of his head and I can't get it out of my mind. Burying my face into his hard chest, I feel so much relief, unjustified relief, but it's there.

Nikolai holds me even tighter. Like if he loosens his grip on me, I'll be gone forever.

I inhale a deep, steadying breath as he whispers, "Thank God."

"Nik," I barely breathe his name as try to hold on to my composure. "Nik." I keep saying his name, but I can't help it. *He's okay,* I tell myself over and over as he pulls back slightly to look at me before hugging me back against his chest.

"I've missed you so much," he whispers against my hair, and I can feel his warm breath all the way down to my shoulder.

"How did you find me?" I ask him and pull back to look at him. The sight of his face shreds my composure. Faint bruises and a split lip are evidence left behind from days ago.

It's only then that he releases me, looking between me and Eli and then to the table. "Sit with me?" he asks as if there's any chance at all I would deny him, and it's the first time I can smile. It's a sad smile, the kind that comes with a pain that everyone else can feel.

"Of course," I barely get the words out and I have to clear my throat. Brushing my hair back and breathing in deeply to steady myself, I tell him, "I'm so happy to see you." My next words come out rushed. "I'm happy you're okay."

"Me too," he replies, but his voice is cloaked in sadness and he doesn't stop looking over every inch of me. "Are you okay?" he asks me and then reaches across the table to take my hand. His is large and warm, easily dwarfing my hand. Hands that have held mine for as long as I can remember.

I nod, swallowing the knot in my throat and not wanting to tell him or anyone else everything that's happened. "How did you find me?" I repeat my question and try to remember everything I wanted to tell him.

"I did what I had to do." His answer is short, but he doesn't stop rubbing soothing circles on the palm of my hand. It comforts me like he'll never know. He's done the same thing all my life. Every tragedy, every heartache. It's such a simple thing, but with that gentle touch, I can breathe, feeling as if everything is all right, even when I know it's not.

"Does my father know?"

"Yes, he…" Nik's voice gets tighter as he swallows whatever he was going to say. "He knows."

"What is it?" I ask him, and I don't hide the urgency in my voice when I demand, "Tell me everything."

"We have eyes on Carter. And I know," he struggles to keep a straight face, his fortitude failing him. "I know what he did to you," Nik says with a sickness at the end of words. "I'm so sorry, Aria." He breaks down in front of me, covering his eyes for a moment and apologizing over and over.

"Stop it." My command comes out harsher than I planned and I nearly rip my hand away from him. I won't be a charity case for sympathy.

"I swear I'll kill him." His expression hardens, and his eyes turn sharp. "I'll make him pay for what he did to you." I can see Eli shift his weight out of the corner of my eye and my pulse quickens, pounding at my temples, the adrenaline pumping harder and harder.

"No, you won't," I tell him quietly, grabbing his hand with both of mine. I hope he can read the message in my eyes telling him to shut the fuck up. Nik is hotheaded and reckless, but he can't be so stupid as to say that kind of thing right now. "Stop it," I warn him.

"After what he did to you?" he questions me, his brow furrowed, and forehead creased.

"You don't know what he did." It's all I can tell him, wanting to deny any of the accusations he could throw at me, even if they're true.

I know my expression is a mix of worry and sadness, but I can't help it. I can't control the emotions on my face. Not with Nikolai.

"I know enough. I'm going to kill him for it," Nik repeats his threat, the anger coming in full force and I feel lightheaded with indignation.

"I'll never forgive you," I whisper the words, feeling the ache sit against my ribcage, etching into my bone and eating away at whatever soul I have left.

"What's wrong with you?" Nik raises his voice with incredulity and backs away from me, his hands pushing against the edge of the flimsy table and inching it closer to me. He's breathing heavily as his composure crumbles. "He'll pay for what he did!"

"I didn't come here to talk about that," I say and struggle to look Nik in the eye. Belatedly, I remember what Carter told me about the men on Carlisle and what I'd planned to say.

"We're family," Nik reminds me, his tone wretched, his gaze covering every inch of my face and doesn't stay steady in the least. He's losing it. "I'll protect you!" he declares, and I take this moment to gain control of the conversation.

"Then move the men on Carlisle," I tell him quickly, staring into his eyes, although my words stumble into one another. Moving my hands into my lap, I resist the urge to fidget and straighten my back. "The war is between my father and Romano. Romano's the one who took me."

Nik's expression is pained as he says, "This isn't a negotiation, Aria."

He looks over at Eli, but only for a moment before giving in and spilling the plans my father has set in motion. He barely considers withholding the information and something doesn't feel right about it.

"The men on Romano's turf are decoys. He's letting them die and preparing to rampage Cross's territory."

I worry my bottom lip between my teeth and I struggle to breathe, but somehow manage to tell him, "Change his mind."

"Not after what Cross did to you."

I wish he could understand. I wish he felt like I do. I cannot fail. I won't live to see the men I love kill each other. I won't fucking do it!

"Then create a reason. Have Mika go up to... to..." I'm blanking on the street name that divides the territories. I've heard them all so many times before, but I rarely left the house. When I did, I never wandered far and so the street names mean nothing to me.

Whipping my gaze to Eli, I raise my voice and say, "Help me!" I stare at him as if he's failing me because he is. They're all failing me, and this is a losing cause. "The street where Romano territory meets Talvery territory."

"Bedford." Eli's response comes easily. He's not shaken in the least and I gather my composure, pushing my hair out of my face and staring at the steel table until I'm able to speak calmly.

"Bedford, move them up to Bedford," I plead with Nik, keeping the cadence of my voice soft and even. "Please," I beg him, desperate for him to understand.

"You think that will stop this war between Talvery and Cross?'" he asks me with an air of ridicule. "The men you're dealing with aren't men who have mercy, Aria." Nikolai talks to me as if I don't know them and it pisses me off.

I know firsthand how cruel they are.

"I'm not asking for mercy, Nik. I'm asking for fucking common sense." I practically spit the last few words. I lean back in the chair, keeping one wrist balanced on the edge of the table. "If they die, it's because you failed."

"Failed at what?" he asks me. "Taking charge of an army I don't control?"

"We have control. It's easy to take control," I say words my father once said to me. He said I needed to be harder, that I needed to wield my name and authority. I never imagined I would heed his advice.

"Send Mika to Bedford; he's at the top of the chain like you. No one would be surprised if he dies there, so make sure he does, Nikolai," I harden my voice, remembering my absolute hatred for Mika and all the evil shit he's done. "You know he deserves far less than an honorable death. Take him up there on a false pretense, shoot him in the back of the head and be done with him." I'm nearly shaken by the venom in my tone, by how meticulously I'm planning murder and interfering with war. "Tell my father it was Romano, and that you have to retaliate. Do it tonight."

"Mika's dead." It takes a moment to even comprehend what Nikolai said before he adds, "Your father killed him."

A cocktail of incredulity and anguish mix in my blood. "What? What happened?" My questions leave me in a single breath, a quiet one as I'm too afraid to speak any louder. As if doing so would change the truth of what happened.

Nikolai glances at Eli before leaning forward and speaking in a hushed voice. "Your father thought you ran away or that you were dead. He went through the tapes and Mika was the last person to speak to you."

With a deep breath, his eyes drift from me to Eli again before he turns his attention back to me. "He asked Mika why he was there and what he said that got you so upset."

"And?" I question him, my voice not nearly as low as Nik's, but it doesn't matter. I know Eli can hear. I know they can all hear.

"Mika didn't answer fast enough. Your father shot him in the head in front of everyone."

"Oh, my God." My heart pumps the blood coldly through my veins as I picture the scene and worry about what my father is thinking and everything he's been through.

"I won't lose sleep over Mika, but your father's losing it, Aria."

My chest feels like it's collapsing, and I struggle to grab hold of every bit of anger I've had toward my father since I've been here.

"He didn't come for me." I can barely speak the words.

"As soon as he found out where you were, he did. We did."

A moment passes and then another. I've held so much pain and anger inside of me at the thought that my father didn't care. Fuck. I wish I knew more. I'm losing this game. Each pawn I think I can capture has already been taken before I make my first move.

"He won't move those men or hold back against Cross, Aria. He wants justice." He adds firmly and with a conviction that sends a shiver down my spine, "We all do."

"This isn't justice. It's senseless death." I stare into Nik's eyes, willing him to understand me.

"You deserve justice, Aria."

"I'm fine, Nikolai. Carter didn't do anything to me that I didn't want."

Disbelief mars his handsome features. "You aren't thinking right," he says and slowly a look of sympathy replaces any hint of anger. "Aria, please come with me."

"I can't let that happen." Eli's quick to step closer to us, and I'm equally as quick to shove my hand against his stomach and tell him to back off. Eli takes in my expression before nodding his head and falling back into place. I don't know what he saw on my face at that moment, but he'll never know how much I needed him to side with me.

"I'm not leaving, Nik, and you need to find a way to move the men. Find a way," I implore him, but not a word is getting through to him.

"I won't let you stay here," Nikolai says then puts both fists on the table, breathing heavier and looking at Eli.

"I won't let you do this; I won't let you choose to stay with a man who hurt you."

"It's my choice." I don't defend what Carter's done. But I'll always defend myself and my ability to control my fate, now and until the day I die. "I *finally* have a choice," I tell him with a hardened voice, seeing my friend for the first time as my enemy.

"Is that what you call it?" he questions me.

"I can hide away. I can run. Or, I can know I have enemies and be prepared for what they'll do to me," I tell him staring into his eyes and not backing down. My shoulders shake from the sheer adrenaline and I can barely contain myself. "I don't want you to be an enemy."

"Aria," he breathes my name with agony. "I will never be your enemy."

"Then understand that I will not leave him." I question telling him the whole truth as he stares into my gaze. I don't want to know what he thinks of it, but I need him to know. "I love him, Nikolai."

"You're sick," he tells me with nothing but sadness in his broken gaze. "I won't let you go like this." His voice begs me to understand, but I know there's no reasoning with him. Just as there's no reasoning with me.

"Maybe I am sick," I play along with him and somewhere deep in my soul, I even agree. "But wasn't I sick all along? Hiding away in my room and afraid of everything." The defensiveness in my voice is nothing compared to the anger I feel at remembering how pathetic my life used to be. Life might be too kind a word to describe what I had before Carter took me.

"That's why I tried to save you," Nik tells me and reaches for my hand, but I pull away. His fingers brushing against mine feel like a fire that burns deep into the bone.

The cords in his throat tighten as he watches the space between us grow and he confesses, "I wanted you to be free. You deserve to live a better life than this."

His words ring in my ears and echo over and over. It fills the hollowness in the crevices of my chest. *He tried to save me?*

"You what?" I breathe the question.

Everything slows to a crawl as he answers, a look of shame showing on his face. "This," he motions with his hands, "this is all my fault." He struggles to look me in the eye when he tells me, "I knew you'd think it was Mika. I wanted you out, so you could run, but Cross lied to me."

My heartbeat ticks in slow motion. So slowly, the world tilts on its axis and I feel lightheaded. I have to grip the table to stay upright.

"He said he would get you out. He promised me he'd save you. He fucking lied to me, and I fell for it!" He contains his resentment when I don't respond, and leans forward begging me to understand, "All I ever wanted was for you to be free from this. I won't let this ruin you. You deserve so much better than this."

I can't speak. I can't move. I can't even breathe as I hold onto the table to keep me upright.

"Aria?" Eli calls out my name, but I don't look at him. I don't look at Nikolai when he begs me to forgive him. All I can do is stare at a scratch on the steel card table and try to hold on to my sanity.

"You were my friend," I whisper as tears prick my eyes. This all happened because of him. Because of the one person I had in life. The one person I thought I could fully trust.

"I love you, Aria, and you need to run." The word run makes my lips twitch. *Run.* That's how little he thinks of me. To him, I'm merely a scared girl who needs saving. A girl who should run, not one worthy of staying and fighting.

Letting my gaze find his, I peer into his soft blue eyes and whisper, "You don't know who I am anymore."

"You're innocent in this. You're too innocent for this life."

"Nothing about me is innocent, Nikolai. It's only what you all *think* of me."

"You know that it's not—" Nik tries to backpedal but I cut him off. I'm tired of being the scared little girl. I refuse to be seen as such.

"I never knew I had a choice until it was taken from me. I won't let anyone take it back."

"I can make this right, Aria," Nik reaches for my hand again, leaving his palm up on the table. And I take it willingly because I still love him, even if he's made all the wrong choices and doesn't see it. I still love him. He may not know how I've changed, but the boy inside of him is the same. My friend is staring back at me. I know that much.

I rub soothing strokes on the back of his hand as I look him in the eyes, letting my anger go and knowing he will never agree with me. My voice is hoarse as I whisper, "I'm fine, Nikolai."

"You're not. I can see you clearly, Aria. I always have." His voice begs me to listen, and I am, I just don't agree.

"I wish I was a better man, so I could save you. I tried," he tells me even though he looks past me with disappointment and regret equal in his expression. "I tried."

My heart pains for his. He'll never understand, and I don't know what this means for us, but I know this meeting was useless for this war.

"Try to move the men on Carlisle. I can save myself." My response gets his attention, and he shoots me a halfhearted smile, but one from a friend to a friend. One that warms the chill that runs through me.

"You're not doing a very good job of that, Ria." He uses the same nickname my mother had for me and it breaks the wall of strength I've been holding on to.

"It's been so long since someone's called me that," I tell him with a smile that matches his.

"I'll always love you," he tells me and he grips my hand harder. He whispers, "Always, Ria," before kissing my wrist. A move that makes Eli shift his stance once again.

His smile dies before mine does. "I will never forgive myself if something happens to you," he says, and his voice is choked. "I can't do anything now, but I promise I'll make this right, even if you hate me for it."

"I wish you would just listen to me," I tell him as the door opens behind me. The rusty hinges make it known without turning my head to see.

"I'll make it right," Nikolai says hurriedly as two men walk around the table on either side of me and take him away. I have to grip the edge of my seat to keep from reaching for him. My heart splinters, not knowing when I'll see him again and feeling as if I've failed miserably.

"Don't be stupid, Nikolai," I call after him.

He peeks over his shoulder at me with a smile that I recognize and one that brings tears to prick the back of my eyes. "I'll try not to, Ria."

"You'll let him go?" I ask Eli quickly and with a desperation that's obvious.

He doesn't hesitate to answer, "So long as he doesn't do anything stupid."

I can only nod a response, not trusting myself to speak, knowing full well Nikolai would do foolish things to save me.

The door closes, and Eli tells me we're waiting for a moment, but I hardly hear him as I think about everything that was revealed in the last thirty minutes.

I never thought much of who I wanted to be as I got older. I only knew what I was running from.

I didn't want to marry someone my father approved of, like Mika. I never wanted that, and I thought if I stayed quiet and listened, my father wouldn't marry me off as some of the whispers I'd heard hinted at that possibility.

I didn't want to be the reason the man I fell in love with died. That's the exact reason Nikolai and I ended what we had. When my father started watching me closely, when he asked me if anyone had touched me because he'd kill them if they had, I denied it.

And when he cornered Nikolai and asked him, Nikolai told my father what he wanted to hear, that we were nothing but friends, but he would honor my father's request to leave me alone.

I knew I didn't want to be alone; I didn't want to run away. And so, I sat there in my room, quietly hiding from everything I knew I didn't want, but I never thought of what I wanted. I never chased what I knew deep down could be mine.

Nothing will stop me from chasing it now.

CHAPTER 13

Carter

"WHISKEY?" DANIEL ASKS ME AS I WATCH ARIA'S THROAT tighten as she stares at the table. She did well, but still, watching it was fucking agony.

"Give her a minute," I speak into the microphone to Eli as I nod at Daniel. The amber liquid swirls in the bottle and reflects the pale moonlight filtering into my office.

Sitting back in my chair, I refuse to acknowledge how on edge my body feels. I'm on the edge of breaking down once again. My throat is dry and tight, my fingers and toes numb.

"She loves him," I admit the truth that splinters my chest in a whisper as I stare at the screen. It was clear to see in the way she spoke to him and held him and comforted him. But more than that, it's obvious he loves her as well.

That's something I can't allow.

"I don't want to hear you talk about the woman you love, not in that context. Not about her loving someone else." Daniel's response leaves no room for negotiation and I turn to him as he hands the tumbler to me.

Bringing the glass to my lips, I know what he's referring to and maybe it makes me coldhearted, but the pain that lies in between his words brings me comfort. The whiskey burns my chest as I tilt back the glass and take it all at once.

"Another?" I ask him, holding out the glass for him to refill even though his is still very much full. Three fingers' worth of whiskey is still evident in his glass.

He fills mine higher than before; the bottle that was full only two days ago is nearly empty now. As I take a large swig, I can hear his blunt nails tapping rhythmically against the glass. He leans against the window behind me rather than taking his seat.

"You have all of his files, so you could blackmail him into leaving." Daniel offers me a way to take care of the pesky problem. It's a solution that would work for most people, but not for Nikolai.

"He's irrational," I answer him, knowing all too well Nikolai won't stand down.

"You mean stupid?" he jokes, and I give him a rough chuckle in response, but the smirk that tries to tug at my lips ultimately fails to show itself.

"Do you think she'll hate me now that she knows I set her up all along?" I ask him. The nerves roil in my gut, and I shut them up with another swig. That's what I'm truly worried about. Everything else is meaningless. But that piece of information could hurt us. Romano set it all up, technically, creating the meeting between the two of us. But I'm guilty and won't refute what he told Aria.

"I'm sure she already blamed you." Although there's a hint of humor in his answer, the truth of it causes my blood to turn to ice.

I scoff as I watch as my songbird stand, pushing in the chair and staring long and hard at the empty one across from her before preparing to leave. She doesn't stop staring at where Nikolai was sitting and every second her gaze stays there, the crack in my heart feels like dry lightning splitting the sky into two.

"She loves you," Daniel says from behind me, but it doesn't offer me any comfort.

"Will she when this is over?" The question alone causes the pain to run up my spine and I put the glass to my lips, only to find it empty. With a sigh, I place it on the desk.

The truth is, I don't think she will.

"I'm more concerned with her giving orders and trying to interfere, aren't you?" Daniel questions. Glancing over my shoulder, I watch my brother sip the whiskey although his eyes stay on mine.

"She can do as she wishes," I tell him the same thing I've told Eli. "I want to see what she'll do."

"She's different than I thought."

I feel restless as I watch his gaze flick to the screen, no longer focused on the back room and instead, watching Eli accompany Aria back to the safe house. Men are in multiple homes spread throughout the two blocks and each of them has eyes on her as they move from street to street.

"How's that?" I question him.

Bringing his gaze back to mine, he sets his glass on the windowsill and tells me, "She's… more…" he chooses his words carefully, "*involved* than I thought she'd be." The nervousness that prickles down my fingers intensifies when he adds, "I'm not sure what to make of it."

Cracking my knuckles, I don't look him in the eyes when I respond, "It means she'll be even more disappointed when all of it is over."

My brother considers me for a moment before nodding once and picking up his glass to finish off the drink.

He runs his fingers along the rim of the empty glass, watching as he does so and tells me, "I'm taking Addison out for the night." His lips pull down into a frown and his eyes reflect a well of sadness. "She hasn't been to The Hard Stone." He finally looks up to me and I nod, letting him know I heard him. The Hard Stone is the restaurant next to the Red Room. It's heavily guarded already, as is the club.

"I hope it goes well," I offer him, and it's genuine. I hate what's happened to them. I don't want to see my brother revert back to the man he is without her. There are only two versions of him. And I greatly prefer the one who is loved by Addison and loves her in return.

Running my thumb over the pad of my pointer, I think about Aria being all alone tonight and how she'll be thinking of Nikolai.

"Keep her out late," I tell Daniel, waiting for his eyes to reach mine. "Don't come back to the safe house for a few hours."

He lips are slow to pull into a smile, but they do.

"Do you have plans with your girl as well?" he asks me with a sense of humor that lights his eyes.

"I do now."

CHAPTER 14

Aria

IT'S QUIET. TOO QUIET.

The kind of quiet that makes you feel unsettled deep inside. Staring down at the empty glass of wine, I bite down on my bottom lip knowing full well that it doesn't matter if it's quiet or if I was in a room full of people chattering because I was going to feel like this tonight regardless.

This sick, numbing feeling spreads over every inch of me the second I'm consciously aware and not drifting down a memory I wish I could hide in.

Letting out a deep sigh, I push the glass away from me and wrap the woven blanket tighter around my shoulders as I get off the barstool at the kitchen island.

I finally ate today, but the food's tasteless and I can barely stomach a thing. Not when I feel like this.

Addison left half an hour ago, and I asked Eli to tell the guys to leave me alone tonight. Part of me regrets it. I'd like to pretend I could go downstairs and join them for a drink. Lord knows I need more than just one glass of Cabernet. I need a distraction and something that doesn't feel like my world is falling apart and collapsing on top of me, but that's all I have to accompany me tonight.

My bare feet pad softly on the hardwood floor as I make my way down the hall to the bedroom. All I keep thinking about is the phone on the nightstand. It only allows me to call Carter, or for Carter to call me. There's not even a number in the settings for me to give someone else.

I hate that he limits me like this, but I understand the need for him to control it right now. Because if I could, I'd call my father. I'd tell him I'm sorry I left and was stupidly taken. I'd tell him I'm okay. I'd beg him to stop all this.

And I'd be judged, found lacking, and a failure. I already know it, but I would still try.

Just the thought of it makes me pause outside the bedroom door, my hand on the carved glass knob as a shuddering breath leaves me. I hate this feeling of hopelessness that numbs my skin. I hate this feeling of being confined and pushed to the side.

I hate everything.

When the door creaks open, my feet sink into the plush carpet and I try to flick the light on, but it doesn't work.

My stomach drops even lower and I try it again, hearing the click but not seeing a change. It doesn't stop me from furiously flicking the switch back and forth rapidly.

"I didn't want any light tonight." Carter's voice paralyzes my body. It's a slow drip, like the venom from a snake bite. That's how my body reacts to his deep, rough tone.

It takes a moment for my eyes to adjust, but when they do, I see his broad shoulders from the corner of the room, sitting on a chair that wasn't there this morning.

"Carter," I say his name and then glance at the mess of sheets on the bed, and he follows my gaze to where I was hours ago, pleasuring myself as he ordered me to. "I didn't expect you to be here," I tell him softly and make my way toward him.

It amazes me how drawn I am to him. As if nothing matters but going to him.

Maybe Nikolai was right. Maybe I am sick. Because all that nervousness and anxiety doesn't exist anymore.

"I missed you," he tells me, and it sounds so unlike the man I knew while I was in the cell, and the man who rules with an iron fist but it's my Carter, the man who gives me everything behind closed doors. Flutters in the pit of my stomach travel up higher and lower at the same time, warming every inch of me.

"I need you," I whisper as I reach him, not hesitating to climb into his lap and wrap my legs around his waist. His large hands splay along my lower back and ass. He squeezes just as my lips brush against his and instead of kissing him like I intended, my neck arches back and I moan from the pain.

From the pain.

It's all he gives me at this moment, but sitting like this, being with him and feeling his heat is exactly what I need right now. The pain alone sends ripples of pleasure through my body.

He lowers his lips to the dip in my throat, letting his stubble drag along my skin as he plants open-mouth kisses right there and then trails up my neck.

He nips my earlobe before whispering in a way that creates a shiver down my spine, "I want you on the bed."

I take a kiss from him first. Stealing it quickly, I love that I catch him off guard and he nearly misses the chance to kiss me back.

He takes it though and then sits back as I leave his lap and lie on the bed.

"Strip," he commands, and I obey. I do it slowly, letting my fingers linger over my sensitized skin and reveling in the power I have. He wants me. He loves wanting me. And it's a heady feeling to have such a powerful man give in to the need of wanting you.

The clothes fall carelessly to the floor and the cool air kisses my skin as I writhe on the bed and run the tips of my fingers over my hardened nipples.

Carter stands slowly, and I barely turn my head to watch him stalk around the bed, stripping slowly for me as well. With the only light coming from the windows behind me, the shadows dance around him and it's intoxicating.

I can hear the clink of handcuffs before I see the metal shine in the pale moonlight, and it only makes me hotter for him. Before he commands me to, I raise my arms above my head and to the headboard made of thin planks. He only uses a single pair of cuffs, looping them through the planks and cuffing each of my wrists.

His fingers burn along my wrists and he lets them travel down my arm, tickling me, my breasts, my waist and then he dips a hand between my legs and I spread myself wide for him.

The groan deep in his throat is my reward, as is the spread of pleasure that runs through my body when he trails his thick fingers from my hot entrance up to my clit.

Writhing on the bed sends a mix of pain from the belt marks

rubbing against the sheets and the pleasure from his touch.

He leaves me like that, breathing heavily on edge for him for a moment to grab something from the floor.

A tie, his tie. The silk runs along my cheek and then he tells me to close my eyes as he wraps it around me like a blindfold. My heart races at not being able to see and a new kind of excitement courses through my body.

Without being able to see, I can hear it clearly when he takes out another cuff as his fingers travel down my leg, to my ankle where he cuffs me. He does the same to the other side and I'm blindfolded and restrained for him.

My breathing comes in chaotically when I hear him walk around the bed again and the cold metal heats while the chill in the air makes me beg him to be touched. "Carter," I whimper his name.

"Tell me the truth, songbird." Carter's voice is deep. but laced with something I haven't heard from him in the bedroom for so long. A hard edge I don't like to hear.

Although my heart batters in my chest with the mix of fear slipping into my veins, I whisper, "Anything."

"You hate me, don't you?" he asks me and with his question comes a click and buzzing. My back bows as he touches the cold metal of the vibrator to my clit. The pleasure is immediate and spikes through me.

"I love you," I moan recklessly into the air as I pull at my cuffs, unable to move away from the intense pleasure.

He pushes it harder against me and I let out a strangled cry of ecstasy. I can feel myself clench around nothing as the intense waves of pleasure approach like the tide, creeping up and crashing harder and harder.

I'm so close. So, fucking close.

And then he pulls it away.

A gasp is torn from me and I try to look around. I want to hear where he is and what he's doing over the sound of my own ragged breath. But as I do, my impending orgasm slowly dims, leaving me slick with my own arousal and desperate for him to get me off.

Swallowing down the disappointment and trying not to pull on the cuffs that dig into my wrists and ankles, I wait for him.

"You hated me when you came to the cell."

I breathe in deeply, not wanting to remember how we started. My voice is raspy when I tell him, "I knew I wanted you."

His thick fingers push inside of me and I can feel his knuckles brush against my front wall. My breasts swing, and my shoulder blades dig into the mattress as he finger-fucks me. "Fuck," I moan, feeling the warmth spread through my body like wildfire as the bundle of nerves in my core heat and prepare to ignite.

"Carter," I breathe his name as my neck arches and I feel the pleasure build higher and higher. "Carter," I moan his name just before I cum.

And he pulls away before I can finish. My breathing's chaotic and I try to rip the blindfold away, but my hands are cuffed.

"Carter!" I yell at him and all I get in return is a rough chuckle. He kisses my jaw even as I pull away from him.

"I don't like this," I warn him in a voice that wavers. I can feel a sense of dread flow into my blood.

"All you have to do is answer me." His voice is easy as if this isn't a trap. "Did you hate me?" he asks again, and my voice tightens.

The buzzing gets louder and this time the vibrator hits me at full force. My head pushes back and the pleasure races through my blood. I'm so close. I'm already on the edge with only a few seconds of its touch.

And then it's taken away. Gritting my teeth, I struggle to move, feeling tears prick my eyes. "Carter!" I scream at him with unadulterated anger, but all I get is the vibrator back on my swollen nub.

Again, he takes it away just before the pleasure can consume me, leaving me with dimming fire and I can't fucking take it.

"Yes, I hated you! You hurt me, and I hated you for taking me!"

The pain that sweeps through me is like nothing I've felt before. Admitting what happened and knowing what I felt back then... I hate it. I hate that he's bringing it up. "Is that what you wanted?" I ask him, furious that he's doing this. "I hate this!" I yell at him but as the last word leaves my lips, the vibrator hits my clit and he leaves it there, my body flying higher and higher and then I fall from the sky, sending a tingling sensation to wreck my body all at once.

It lasts and lasts as I lie paralyzed and still at Carter's mercy.

"You loved me afterward though?" he asks me, his lips so close to mine and I push myself up as high as I can and steal his lips with mine. He kisses me back ravenously. I can feel his body close to mine and I wish I could wrap my legs around him and hold on to him, but I'm bound, and he pulls away from me.

I'm still reeling from my orgasm and the kiss I was too starved for to remember what he asked me, so he asks me again.

Breathlessly, I answer him, "Yes, I love you. I love you, Carter."

As his name leaves my lips, he pushes the vibrator back to my sensitized bud and it's nearly too much. I scream his name and he captures my lips with his as I detonate beneath him. The pleasure consumes me as the night sky is consumed with stars. Again and again.

I want to kiss him, but more than anything I want him to know how much I mean it when I say it. I love him, and he's all I want.

"Do you love Nikolai?" he asks me, and the question destroys the moment. I struggle to answer, but I do know the truth and I won't lie to him.

"Yes. But not like you," I answer him, feeling the high fall and my pulse slow. A second passes and another without him making a sound or touching me and fear races through my blood. "Carter?" I call out his name and he asks me another question.

"If I wasn't here, would you be with him?"

The silence stretches as I remember wanting Nikolai but being too afraid to tell my father. That girl, the one who doesn't go after what she wants and simply prays not to be seen, that girl is long dead.

"I don't know," I answer him in a breath and again he denies me, pushing the vibrator to my clit and finger-fucking me until I'm so close to my release I can't breathe.

Gasping for air, I search for some kind of relief, brushing my ass against the silky sheets, but Carter tsks me, holding my hips down.

"Just tell me the truth, songbird. I'll take care of you," he whispers in a voice I don't trust. One that's sinful.

"I don't know Carter. Please," I try to beg him, but he doesn't listen. He presses the vibrator against my clit and pulls away nearly instantaneously. My body bucks and the metal bites into my skin. "Fuck!" I cry out. I'm so close. I'm so fucking close again.

Off and on, off and on, he teases me.

The tides of my pleasure rush to the surface, igniting every nerve ending, but as soon as they're ready to go off, he pulls away and waits for the embers to die before bringing the fire back.

"If I wasn't here, would you be with him?" he asks me softly, calmly, his lips close to the shell of my ear. His breath traveling along my skin is enough to nearly get me off. I don't answer, I only bite down on my lower lip and shake my head, but I can't answer him.

And he does it again. Finger-fucking me ruthlessly, but the second my orgasm approaches, he pulls away. The smell of sex and the feel of my slickness on my inner thighs tease me into thinking there's more. But he leaves me panting and again my orgasm dies before I can get off.

It's the last bit I can take.

"Yes! I would try to be with Nikolai if you were gone." I can hardly believe I've spoken the sin out loud, much less to Carter. I know it hurts him and I hate it. I fucking hate it, but it's the truth. "I would try to be with him," I suck in a deep breath, brushing the tears off my face away with my forearms and wishing I could do the same with my shame, "but I don't know that I could ever have what we have. I wouldn't be the person I am without you." Tears leak down my face as the confession is forced out of me. "I love you, Carter. I don't want him when I have you."

He ruthlessly strokes against my front wall and I cum instantly. He pulls the orgasm from me, drawing it out and my body arches and goes rigid as the silent scream of ecstasy is ripped from me.

He doesn't stop until I'm limp and struggling to breathe.

"Carter, stop please," I beg him in a strangled voice that doesn't sound at all like me. "I hate this. I chose you! I fucking chose you!"

"Shh," he shushes me as I struggle to breathe. The touch of his splayed hand on my belly makes me jump, but he caresses my skin with soothing strokes until my entire body has calmed. With soft kisses on my neck, I beg him to stop again and let me love him. It's all I want to do right now, love him and feel the love he has for me.

"One more question," he tells me, and I stay as still as I can, waiting for it and dreading it. I can't stop crying, knowing what I've already confessed to him and worried that he won't love me because of it.

"Will you still when your family is gone? Will you still love me then?"

I already know the answer, but I don't want to say it.

The buzz from the vibrator makes me cry harder. He runs it along my pubic bone and my hips buck, trying to move away. I can't take any more.

"Tell me the truth," he whispers in a voice coated in hopelessness. He already knows the answer; I've already told him. He doesn't need to torture it out of me.

"No," I cry out. Hating him for what he's doing. I don't want to think about any of this, let alone admit what it would do to us.

"I love you, but if you do it… if you kill them, I will hate you forever," I gasp out as tears stream down my face. Agony tears through me both in the physical sense and emotional. He wrecked me. Carter destroyed whatever guard I had that protected me from this truth.

"I love you, Carter." I hear the cuffs click and then the metal leaves my skin. It's biting into my wrists and the second he unlocks them; I cradle my wrists to my chest.

I'm still crying into the blindfold when I hear the bedroom door open and shut. The hollowness in my chest collapses on itself and I refuse to believe he left me.

But when I finally take the blindfold off and beg him to hold me, he's not there.

Carter left me.

He doesn't love me. Carter Cross doesn't love me.

CHAPTER 15

Carter

I CAN STILL FEEL HER CUNT SPASMING ON MY COCK THE FIRST TIME I took her. I still dream of it.

I can still taste the sweet wine on her lips.

I can still hear her screams of pleasure and her whispers that she loves me.

I know for as long as I live, I'll remember it all. I'll remember what I had with her.

Tonight, I wage war against her family; I'll kill as many of them as I possibly can.

I'll destroy what we have together and risk her hating me forever. She was telling the truth and I can't stand it. Tonight, I will lose the woman I love.

My gaze drops to the phone on the bathroom counter just as Jase knocks on my bedroom door.

"In here," I call out to him and turn on the faucet to wet my razor. The shaving cream is already slathered on my skin. Since leaving her last night, I've fallen back into my old habits and I'm distracting myself by focusing on the war and everything else involved in this business.

He talks as I shave, ridding myself of the stubble and preparing to look the part of a man in control of an empire. "I have a proposition," he starts, and my eyes move to his in the reflection of the mirror before moving back to my jaw.

Each stroke of the blade is precise and smooth, skimming along my skin.

He takes a step forward, filling in the doorway. "I think our problem is that we've been content."

"Our problem?"

"The reason men think they can steal from us, the reason

Romano is creating competition and involved us in this war." I consider him for a moment before going back to shaving, tapping the razor against the sink before bringing the blade down my skin again. I couldn't give two shits about any of it anymore. I'll kill those who defy me or stand in my way. And I'll be fucking content with that regardless of whether or not Jase is.

He tells me with a raised brow, "We aren't expanding."

"We have other ventures. The club. The restaurant." I don't know why I bother reminding him. I can see the look in his eyes. He won't stop until he gets what he wants.

"That money doesn't compare. You know, I know, and everyone else knows it." He speaks hurriedly like he can't wait to make his point, but I drag it out. Just to torture him.

"We're moving into Crescent Hills," I tell him.

"Because you want to take on that place, not because there's money there." His voice is flat, his expression expectant.

I can't argue that truth. "It'll be worth it to be closer to the docks," I tell him, and he shakes his head in disagreement. My patience ebbs as I tap my razor again on the sink and hold it under the running water.

"I think we need to go north. A true expansion," he tells me and waits with bated breath.

"Talvery territory?" I question him, my eyes on his in the mirror and he nods his head. "I already gave it to Romano."

"It hasn't been taken yet, and Romano can go fuck himself." Jase's voice is harsh and his persistence shines through. Jase keeps his gaze on me even though he's breathing harder with excitement. "We were going to give Fallbrook to Romano and he already has the entire upper east. Talvery turf should be ours."

His eyes dart over to mine, waiting for a reaction but I give him none. I didn't sleep for shit and I don't give a fuck about expanding.

"Are you that bored?" I ask him dully. I remember what it was like to take control, what was required to have my name permanently carved into this territory. The sickness of it all and the risk. It's not worth the money it makes.

"Bored?" Jase breathes out forcefully. "It's a lost opportunity." I don't respond. Instead, I finish shaving, careful not to react when Jase adds, "And what about Aria?"

I rip the hand towel from where it hangs at my right and dampen it under the faucet. It's hard to contain what I feel for her. The loss is too real. It's too close.

"What about her?" As I clean off my face, ignoring the screaming pain in my chest, he tells me, "I heard about how she's handling things." I grip the towel tighter, praying my brother doesn't say something that drives me to break his fucking jaw. Last night... I can't even think about how the truth stabbed me in the heart like nothing else has before.

He tells me, "I think she'd want this."

My brow furrows and I focus on breathing and controlling my expressions. "Want what?" Speaking hurts. Even breathing hurts. Everything fucking hurts.

"I think she'd want to still have the territory... maybe for her?" he offers, tilting his head and raising his brow. "Can you imagine how she'd react if we killed her family and gave her land to Romano?"

Using the dry section of the towel, I run it over my jaw, knowing exactly how she's going to react and hating it. I swallow thickly, knowing I can keep her here. Physically, I have the means to keep her here, but that will only add to her hate. And I want her to love me. I need her to love me.

"What if, instead, we do as little damage as possible?" He moves out of the doorway as I toss the towel into the sink and make my way past him to my dresser for my cufflinks. I'm running through the motions, focused on every mundane detail that's led me to this point in life.

"Any damage we do will break her, Jase," I tell him halfheartedly.

"I'm telling you, this is a good idea, Carter."

He stands a few feet from me, leaning against the wall with his arms crossed. "We already told Romano, but I say we hit them back to back. Talvery, then Romano and we take it all."

"With what men?" I ask him, feeling the tingling rage creep up my spine. "Do you remember the cost of it all? How many men have to die for you to be satisfied?" My voice is raised, and my pulse quickens. I swallow back the anger when he doesn't respond.

He flinches at the severity of my tone.

I add, "This isn't a game and every move has consequences."

"It's all a game, brother." He looks me in the eyes as he says, "A well-played and thought-out game."

He stares at me and I him as he tells me, "If Aria was able to convince those men to do what she suggested yesterday, we would have the upper hand. Talvery and Romano would lose men, and we'd be waiting to take out the rest," he talks with an evenness that sounds so reassuring.

"Only Aria doesn't know that," I tell him while taking a step forward and reaching for my jacket, which is draped across the dresser. "She doesn't know how many will die. And she will never be okay with wiping out her family."

The hint of a smile that was on his lips falters. "She has more to learn," is all he can say.

"Tonight, her family legacy starts to fall, and she will never forgive me, let alone rule alongside me." Jase's smile completely vanishes, and he glances at his feet before looking me back in the eyes, ready to say something else, but I don't let him. "Do you think she'll want to rule when her territory is nothing, but a graveyard of old memories and people forgotten?"

It fucking kills me knowing how she'll react. "She's going to fucking hate me," I bite out the words, grinding my back teeth against one another.

My breathing is ragged as he nods his head and runs his thumb over his bottom lip. "So, you're saying it's too late?" he asks.

That's exactly how it all feels. It's too late to keep her.

I let his question sit with me as I shrug on the jacket and button it. "I still think she would want this. Even if the war leaves a path of death to her throne, not everyone will die. She'll have some."

"Like Nikolai?" I reply with spite barely above a murmur, and it only makes Jase smirk at me.

"I have a feeling that fellow isn't going to make it," he jokes but it doesn't do anything to soothe the nerves that won't allow me to relax.

"In thirty minutes, they'll open fire," I tell him as I observe the little hand on my watch marching along steadily. "The next time you have an idea about damage control, maybe come to me sooner?" I suggest, and he huffs a laugh while shaking his head.

"The war has only started," he says, not giving up. "Just tell me you'll consider it."

Screwing over Romano is inevitable; doing it at the right time is crucial.

But the worst mistake Jase is assuming is that Talvery can already be counted as dead. I've made that mistake before, and I won't make it again.

"I consider everything, Jase."

CHAPTER 16

Aria

THREE CANVASES ARE SPREAD OUT ACROSS AN OLD BEDSHEET on the floor of the living room. Three canvases with three profiles on each of them. Two men I love, and my mother, who's long gone make up the three. All the while, my mind focuses on the news that plays on the television in the background.

The list of names goes on and on. I can't look at the faces. I can't look at the scenes as they show them on the screen.

Addison is cuddled up on the sofa, staring blankly at the TV. The names don't mean anything to her, but to me, each name means far too much.

I'm barely holding myself together, knowing I should be at their funerals. Knowing I failed to save them. There's a mix of contempt and dread for Nikolai. I wonder if he even tried to move them. He knew, and what did he do? I remember what he said though, it was an army he didn't control.

It's only a matter of time before his name is spoken, added to the mounting death toll of the senseless murders between rival gangs, or so the reporter tells us on the flat-screen TV. Even the thought, forces me to choke on a dry sob, but I hold it down.

"Does this happen a lot?" Addison asks me, and I can feel her eyes on my back, but I don't trust myself to look at her, so instead, I place the flat brush in the cup and watch the red pigment bleed into the water.

"No, not like this," I answer her with my back to her. I am so used to death that it shouldn't break me like this. But it's the first time I tried to stop it.

And I failed.

"Do you need anything else?" Eli's voice comes from the doorway to the stairwell and I peek up at him, but I don't respond. He got me the paints from the corner store a few blocks down. The other things were in the package from Carter. I need a lot of things, I think. But as my lips pull down into a frown and my throat goes tight, I don't look back at him. Instead, I just shake my head no.

I hate him for standing by and doing nothing while men are dying. I hate myself for hating him, which is even worse.

"I want to go get them myself," I tell him as the thought hits me. I need to get out of here and go for a walk. I need to clear my head. I need something. I squeeze the cheap bristles over the cup before rinsing it again. "It would be nice to get some fresh air." I'm surprised by how even my voice is and how in control I seem. It's only because of Addison. If she weren't here, I have no idea how I would react to tonight.

The metal ferrule that holds the bristles clinks softly on the side of the glass as I tap it and then set it down gently on the paper towel.

I finally look up again and Eli's watching me closely. Addison's looking between the two of us and the air is tense among all three of us. She doesn't ask questions though and tonight, I can feel anger growing inside of me from her not wanting to know any more than whether or not this is normal.

"I want to go for a walk to the corner store, so I can buy a few things… please," I say the last word through clenched teeth.

"Give me an hour," Eli responds and then adds, "please." He mocks me, but in a way I know is meant to ease the tension. It doesn't though.

Giving him a tight smile, I nod once and watch him leave, although I still can't find an even breath. Everything is tense, and nothing is right. I feel like I'm breaking down. I'm losing it every second I sit here, guarded and watching the list of deaths grow.

"Are you okay?" Addie asks me as the sound of Eli's footsteps diminishes.

"No," I answer her honestly.

I wanted to help my family, and Nikolai ignored me.

I told Carter I loved him, I chose to stay with him, and he left me.

I'm a fool. I'm a fucking fool.

I'm helpless, hopeless and I feel like I'm at my limit.

Fallbrook (Calvary)
Bedford
upper east (Romano)
N
W
E
S
Highway
Back Ridge
candy store
corner store
Main St.
1st St.
2nd St.
3rd St.
Abbey Rd
Bishop's Rd
Safe House
Canal Rd
Dorset Rd
crescent hills

The sofa groans as Addie slips off of it and makes her way toward me. She's quiet as she sits cross-legged next to me and leans in to give me a hug.

"I wish I knew what to say or do," she consoles me in a quiet voice and I instantly regret the thoughts I had moments ago. I'm so eager to lash out, I could see her being the misguided target of my frustrations, but I would never forgive myself.

Grabbing on to her forearm and giving her a semblance of a hug back, I tell her, "I wish I knew too."

Time passes slowly until she grabs the remote and turns off the TV. The click of the picture going black is louder than I've ever heard it before. I want it to stay on, so I'll know what happened, but I'm grateful she turned it off because I can't take any more.

"Do you want to talk?" she asks me, and I shake my head. I'm ashamed of how much of myself I give to Carter, only to have him hold back in return. I don't think I could tell her without her hating him even more. And after the night she had with Daniel, I couldn't do that to her.

"You could distract me and tell me what happened last night again," I offer, feeling a swell of jealousy and pain grow in my chest. Last night, I felt used. For the first time, I felt used and foolish for loving him.

"It was just a good night," Addie says, moving her hands to her lap. I know she doesn't want to rub it in, so I just nod and let it go. I stare at the doorway as if Eli will magically appear and let me go outside. The thought makes me roll my eyes. I'm stupid to think I had any sense of control.

Before I can spiral down the path to self-pity that kept me up all last night, Addison asks me, "Do you want to read my tarot cards?"

I watch her chew on the inside of her cheek, waiting for an answer. I'm so grateful for her that I would do anything she asked right now. For the distraction, for the genuine friendship, and so I nod.

"Let's do it," I answer her.

With a deep breath, I scoot backward and turn to her, sitting opposite her and cross-legged too as she reaches behind her on the coffee table for the deck of cards Carter got me however long ago.

"Okay, what do I do?" Addison asks, placing the deck of cards in front of her and staring at them like they'll magically shuffle themselves.

"Knock on them first," I tell her in a deadpan tone, knowing full well she's going to look up at me like I'm crazy.

"I'm serious," I say again and nod to the cards, folding my own hands in my lap. "You have to knock on them to get rid of any previous readings and put your own energy into the cards."

She does what I tell her, lifting the deck and knocking weakly on the back card although she's grinning the entire time. Already I feel a thread better. Only a thread, but it's one more than I had before.

"Now shuffle the deck and think about something you'd like insight to. Or don't." I shrug and stretch from where I'm sitting, feeling the ache from leaning over the canvases for the past few hours. Just glancing at them reminds me about everything and I'm quick to turn back to Addison.

"Is that enough?" she asks me, holding out the cards and I offer her a soft smile and then gesture to the deck. "Split them into three piles, however, you want, and then stack them on top of each other into one pile again."

"Is this how it's always done?" she asks me while doing as I say.

"No," I tell her, feeling a deep ache in my chest. "I learned to read cards from my mother. But she didn't do it like this."

"Oh, how did she do it?" she asks me, and I have to grab the cards and look at them rather than in her eyes when I tell her, "I don't remember. I just had to learn on my own when I decided I wanted to use her deck."

It's quiet for a moment, but she continues the conversation, steering it to a more positive side. "Are these hers?" she asks me as I lay out the cards one by one.

"No, these are ones that Carter got me." Somehow that pulls even more emotion from me as I set the final card down. I don't tell her that I was locked in a cell losing my mind when I was given these cards. And that Jase is the one who actually gave them to me. That day, or night, comes back to me and I nearly get sick.

"This is the horseshoe spread," I tell her as I lay out the cards, refusing to fall backward; I won't go backward. "The significator is in the center, but each place in this spread has a unique meaning and the seven other cards are spread in a horseshoe around it. The significator, this card, is basically you at this moment."

"The four of wands is me?" she asks me although her eyes are on the card I'm currently touching the edges of.

I nod and then add, "There are four suits: the swords, the wands, the pentacles, also known as coins, and the cups. They each represent something different in life and the wands represent creativity. Swords are conflict, pentacles are money, thus also being called coins, and the cups are emotional wellbeing. More or less.

"The four of wands in this deck—"

"I feel like this is a professional reading," Addison exclaims, barely holding in her excitement and I have to give her a small laugh.

"I've read a lot about cards. A few years ago, I thought it would bring me closer to my mother." I wish I hadn't said that last bit, but Addison doesn't focus on the negative. Instead, she says, "Well, this is freaking awesome." She reaches behind her for the glass of wine and then sits up at attention. "Please, continue." She gestures comically and takes a sip of her wine.

I have to let out a snicker that's almost a snort and remember where I left off. "Right," I say out loud, "The four of wands. In this deck, the four of wands is a literal marriage." As I say the last word, I breathe in deep, realizing how emotional Addison's been and watch her reaction, but she only sips her wine and listens. It takes a lot of pressure off of me, so I continue.

Some people take the cards literally, but I have a feeling Addison won't. She just wants a distraction, just as I do.

"The significator is a snapshot of who you are right now and the four of wands is a resting point. There's been a sense of accomplishment, and there's a sense of celebration over it, thus a marriage as the picture on the card. It's a deeply happy card about solidifying some sense of community. Which may not seem at all like where you are in this moment," I pause, feeling a wave of insecurity, but I continue, giving her the reading I think this card points to, "but it can also mean friendship, solidifying a friendship."

"So, it's us?" she asks me, and I try to keep my voice even and devoid of the intense emotion that rises inside of me when I tell her, "Yeah. I think this card is about us."

Addison settles into her position, an elbow on each knee and tells me, "I like that."

With a deep breath, I point to the first card of the seven that makes the horseshoe. "This is your immediate past and this card, the six of pentacles, is a card of generosity and harmony. It's a card depicting someone who was in a good place with the in and outflow of their money, but it doesn't always refer to money. It can also refer to charity and gracefully accepting or giving of money, time or safety." I pause and swallow before adding, "Like how you helped me. That's what this card could mean."

Addison only nods and takes another sip of wine, so I keep going, moving through the motions rather than thanking her again and bringing up that awful night.

"The immediate present, the next card, is the priestess card. She's a figure who has deep intuition."

"What about the suits? What suit is she?" Addison interrupts and it's only then that I really know she gives a fuck about the card reading or at least she's paying attention.

"The suits are in the minor part of the deck; the major part of the deck has figures basically. So, they aren't a part of the suits. There are basically two types of cards, suits, the minor cards, and then figures, the major cards."

"Oh." She nods and then clears her throat before looking at the other cards in the deck to see how many others are major cards and minor, I assume. "Okay, so the immediate present, is the priestess?"

I nod and then smirk as she adds, "I like that too. So far, this is a very likable reading."

My shoulders shake with a huff of laughter as I continue. "The priestess is a person with deep intuition and she's kind of a major arcana echo of the queen of wands. So, not only does she have a deep intuition about herself, but she has it about other people. In other cards, she's pictured holding a mirror that she can point to herself or to others. She's someone who has otherworldly energies and someone who can observe others for who they are. And also see what they need instinctually."

"Like how I knew Daniel was the man he is?" Addison asks me in a flat tone as she pulls the sleeve of her shirt over her wrist and then wipes under her eyes. With my mouth parted, I'm shocked by her response and I struggle to answer her quickly enough. "Ignore me, I'm sorry." She breathes in deeply and shakes out her wrists. "Sorry, I just had a moment."

"It's okay," I barely speak the words and look back down at the card. "It could mean lots of things," I tell her and then shrug. "Or nothing at all."

"I knew," she tells me with a grief that darkens her eyes. A sad smile graces her lips and she says, "Don't stop, please. For the love of God, let's move past that one."

Clearing my throat, I move on to the next card, but then decide to move back to the priestess. "It could also mean that you know what people need and I don't know your story, but knowing you, I would think you knew he needed you." Addison stares at me with glassy eyes but only nods.

My place isn't between them, so I move back the spread, to the third card in the horseshoe and the immediate future. "The king of wands is your immediate future. The kings in the deck are the last of the suits and they have control over the suits. The pages learn, the knights chase, the queen embodies and the king controls. And so, the king of wands is someone who's able to understand and empathize with creativity and life, but he, himself, is not personally creative or spiritual in a really emphatic sense. Instead, he's someone who works closely with creative or spiritual people, but he's distant from them and that's what makes him good at what he does. It's the distance that allows him to be there for others, but it also prevents him from being a part of it."

Struggling to place this card in the current context, I think back on other meanings for the card.

"The king of wands can also be a person who's charismatic but reserved. Still waters run deep in this person, but he's distant."

"So, someone who's controlling is coming?" Addison asks flatly and then snorts into her wine. "I didn't need cards to tell me that one."

I shake my head, knowing she's referring to Carter or Daniel, but this card wouldn't be either of them. It's someone else. "Someone who's distant and uninvolved," I correct her and feel a chill run along my skin. It pricks every nerve and forces each small hair along my skin to stand on edge.

I can hear her swallow the wine and instead of asking who or considering the meaning, I simply keep going to the very bottom of the horseshoe and the fourth card. She doesn't object.

"This card, your path, is the eight of swords. And in my deck at home…" I pause and almost regret saying home, but I don't acknowledge it. Thankfully, Addison doesn't press me. "In my mother's deck, the eight of swords depicts Queen Guinevere, she's tied to the stake and she's going to be executed for infidelity. And the interesting thing about the eight of swords is that often you'll see the woman is holding her own bindings around the pole. Different decks have different art though." I take a moment to look at the deck that Carter got me and it's not obvious in this card. "You can't really see it here, but it looks like this woman is trapped to such a horrible fate in the eight of swords, but actually the only thing that's trapping her is herself. She's the one who has to be able to let go and free herself from her restraints." I look at the card again and realize it doesn't look like that on this deck and it's the only deck I've ever seen where the bonds are truly tied. I continue though, refusing to let her think she's tied inextricably to this fate.

"The woman in this card is not going to be rescued, but she's not doomed to this terrible fate either. The only thing trapping her is herself. The good news is that she's able to save herself; she's not actually tied to the stake."

I take a moment, thinking about everything as Addison finishes off her wine and doesn't say a word. *These cards could be for me.* The idea that they are sends a shiver down my spine. Addison knocked on the cards, I remind myself. Without a word from Addison and not liking where my thoughts are headed, I continue.

"The perceptions of others is the next card, the fifth spot in the horseshoe. The knight of wands is your card in this spot. The knight of wands is all about deep fire and chasing. Do first, think later. They tend to be impulsive."

Addison laughs into her empty glass as she twirls the stem of it between two fingers. "Sounds like that one could be true," she says with a smile on her lips and I can't help but smile too.

"The next card is the challenge to be faced and this is an interesting card to be sitting here." I think out loud, not censoring anything. "The nine of cups is on the cusp of culminating happiness. It's the difference between being engaged and being married. There's anticipation that there's something that's still held back. And then the next card, the ten is complete happiness and marriage, nothing left to come."

Addison nods all the while that I explain the card and I'm not sure how she's perceiving it until she speaks.

"So, there's still more to come? More that would make me happy?"

"Well this is the challenge card, so that's the obstacle you're facing." My answer tugs her lips down and her gaze moves toward the cards. "So, the challenge here is that you're almost there, but not quite and that's where the tension is." I don't stop. I don't want her to think about it right now, but I don't think she'd tell me even if she had ideas of what the cards could mean.

"The final card is the outcome, and for you, it's the queen of wands. She's someone who is safe, confident and she's able to empathize and nurture but she's also powerful and creative in her own right. She's someone who can wield power, but also stands on her own two feet. She's the fiery enchantress."

"That's my final outcome? I get to be a fiery enchantress?" she jokes but I'm so relieved the reading seems to be ending on a happy note.

With a nod, I tell her, "Yes, Addie. You get to be the fiery enchantress." I can't keep my face straight as I tell her that.

"So, when does that happen?" she asks me, and I have to snort a laugh while smiling.

"The priestess in the present position means this person often holds this role. It's also a major arcana card and that typically means it takes time, but it's in the immediate present position. That means there's something otherworldly about her, so she's always carrying this inside of her. Everything else is minor arcana so that would mean days... maybe weeks. But probably days." My gaze falls back to the king of wands and my blood chills. *Someone is coming.*

Addison smiles and bites down on the edge of her wine glass as she glances at the cards one last time.

Again, the king of wands is all I can see, and I'm focused so intently although I don't want to be. He calls to me. The distanced man who's coming and a chill flows down my spine in a way that feels like a nail raking down my back.

"If you're done," Eli's voice breaks through my thoughts and I've never been more grateful.

"Yes," I'm quick to tell him as Addison collects the cards, quickly putting them back on top of the deck. She seems to be just as absorbed with the card as well. I watch as she stacks all the cards neatly in the deck and puts him down last, right at the end of the deck.

"Do you want me to come with you?" Addison asks me as I push up off the floor, shaking out my hands and nerves, and try to shake off the uneasy feeling creeping along my skin. The tiny hairs at the back of my neck refuse to go unnoticed. They don't leave me alone; even as I walk across the room and put the jean jacket on, the chill stays with me.

"I think I'm going to try to sleep then," she tells me although I think she said it more to herself. She covers her face when she says, "I need that stuff, though."

"The stuff?" I ask her to clarify as I stop a few feet from Eli and think back to the vial of sweet lullabies. The drug he gave me to sleep.

"Daniel gave it to me because I wasn't sleeping, and I don't know what I did with it." She looks at the coffee table as if she left it there, but there's nothing there.

"It gave me nightmares. The lullaby stuff."

"That's a shame," she says with true pity. "I slept so well with it. And today has been…" she doesn't finish, she only shakes her head. I can only imagine how she's feeling. I know she wants to go back to Daniel. I could see it in her eyes and hear it in her voice when she told me all about last night at breakfast. I know she loves him. And I think she could forgive him if he wouldn't keep secrets from her anymore once this war has ended.

He's kind to her. He wants her. And I know she wants him too. The only thing that stands in the way are the names the reporter keeps talking about on the television and the fact that Addison now knows Daniel has a hand in that tragedy.

"I was having nightmares before, so maybe that's why?" I surmise and then shrug, pretending like the vision of my mother didn't just take over my mind this second. I glance at Eli, still standing there a few feet away, looking straight ahead and waiting for me. Focusing on him and not on where my thoughts were going.

"Nightmares?" she asks, and I only nod as I swallow down the memory.

"I'm sorry," Addie says, and I wish she didn't. I don't need more sympathy. Sympathy doesn't do shit.

"It's been a while since I've had them." I know I have Carter to thank for that. "Anyway, there's a vial that was in my bag in the drawer of my nightstand. If you want it," I offer her, and she gives me a small smile.

"Thanks," she tells me in a way that I know she's truly grateful as she yawns and then stands graciously.

"Sleep well, Fiery Priestess," I tell her with a small smile and watch as she picks up the cards off the floor and puts them on the coffee table.

"You too, Ria," she tells me and uses the nickname only two other people have used for me all my life. She doesn't see how my face blanches, but I'm able to fix it in time before she looks up at me with a sweet smile. "Ria, the card reader," she adds to the nickname and smiles.

I leave without saying goodbye, but it doesn't escape me that Eli keeps looking at me curiously because he saw how I reacted. Eli sees everything.

Tonight feels darker than the night before. Maybe because there aren't any stars out, or maybe it's just my perception. Either way, it's pitch fucking black.

It's colder too and as I huddle into the jacket, I find myself walking faster to get to the corner store that I saw a few shops down last night.

"You're quiet," Eli comments as the wind blows and my hair whips around my face. His faint accent comes through more now than I've heard before. I almost ask him about it, but my mind is spinning over the king of wands and who it could be. I always look too much into my cards… and that reading wasn't even mine.

"I'm always quiet," I answer him and when he gives me this charming, perfect smile, I nearly smile too. I watch him as he looks up to a house in the middle of the street and I know to wait when he does that, just like last night, so I do. Shoving my hands in my pockets, I breathe out and let the cool air flow over me, calming my anxiety.

"I had a girlfriend once who liked those cards. The reading ones."

"Tarot cards," I tell him as he rocks on his heels, still waiting at the edge of the street.

"Yeah, she liked to read mine, one a day, and tell me how my day was going to go."

A simper pulls at my lips. "Was she right?" I ask him, and he huffs a laugh while shaking his head.

"She was so wrong that I could almost guarantee the opposite of whatever she said was actually going to happen."

"They're really just to get you thinking," I tell him and ask, "Are you still together?"

He shakes his head and says, "She was fucking crazy." A genuine laugh bubbles in my chest at the expression on his face, and for the first time today, I feel warmth flow through me. I feel real for a moment… until the reality of everything going on hits me hard in the center of my chest.

"You're good at distractions," I say while pulling my hair to the side as another breeze comes by. As I do, the sound of a car driving a street or two down catches my attention. "Thank you for that," I add with as much sincerity as I can.

"I'm sorry you're in the middle of this," Eli offers me and all I can do is force a fake smile to my lips.

His earpiece buzzes with someone's voice and I step forward, ready to continue but his large forearm blocks me. "We're going back." His voice is stern and offers no negotiation.

"What's wrong?" I ask him feeling my heart race, and counting how many streets we've walked down. Three. It's right around the corner and the safe house is only three streets away.

I can barely breathe as he tells me, "Now," ignoring my question and wrapping his arm around my waist to quicken my steps.

I can't keep up with his fast pace as my body catches fire with fear.

As the muted voices come through his earpiece again, I peek up at him, trying to listen, wanting to know what's going on.

There was no one on the streets. Not a soul. What the hell happened?

Headlights come from my right. And between it all—the voices, the panic, the lights—I stumble, falling to the ground like a fool.

My knees and palms both hit a lawn hard as Eli tries to pull me along, cutting through the yard to head straight to the house, but I struggle to push him off of me, so I can stand up. I just want to stand up but he's hurting me as he tries to pull me up.

The parked car to my right roars to life, its engine turning and the sound filling the night just as I hear guns firing.

Bang! Bang! Bang! The guns going off make me scream and my heart leaps into my throat.

"Stay down," Eli grunts as he lies on top of me, covering me, but he doesn't stay there for long. The bullets aren't coming this way; they aren't even close.

I can barely see Eli pull out his gun, the cold metal brushing my shoulder before he fires a shot at the car.

There are so many guns going off. Too many to count and I don't know where they're firing, but it's not at me.

Some hit the car. I can hear them crunch into the metal. It pings and some bullets ricochet. Bullets hit the house Eli was looking at, the brick splintering and chips falling past the porch light as if snow is falling on this cold summer night.

Everything happens in slow motion as I peek up, the back of my head slamming into Eli's chest as he fires at the car again, telling me to stay down, but I won't. I need to know what's going on. I keep low, but I refuse to cover my head and not find out what's going on, so I can prepare myself if I have to.

There are four men in the car. I can see them clearly even though they're dressed in all black and hoodies cover their faces. Two are still firing at the building, rapidly pulling the triggers. Men from the building are firing back. Bullet casings hit the ground and the tinkling distracts me as another round of bullets comes closer to us, aimed at another house with men in those windows firing too. We're only separated from the car by a white picket fence that offers no protection and maybe three feet in a yard of grass.

The other two men who were in the car run as I take in the scene. Both of them run down the street to flee although they turn and fire, hiding behind cars and the brick fence. They're running closer to us.

I don't know the car they came from. I don't know the men, but one of them running falls instantly, screaming in agony and grabbing his leg on the sidewalk, the bright red shining brightly as he's bathed in the streetlight.

Bang.

He's silenced and goes still. My heart races, my pulse thrumming so hard I can barely hear the gunshots anymore.

The smacking of shoes carries down the street louder than the gunshots.

"Stay quiet," Eli tells me, intent on hiding as the fucker who's running tries to get away.

He's going to let him get away.

Anger and rage like I've never felt before war inside of me and it burns. It burns too bright. It burns too hot and I can't stand it.

I don't even know it's my own scream as I rip the gun from Eli unexpectedly and run down the street toward the coward who fired at me and the men protecting me. The coward who hid and waited to attack me. I won't fucking let him run.

I won't let him get away. I fucking refuse.

My feet slam so hard on the ground that I feel the pain spike through my thighs. He's only feet away from me and running faster, but he turns to fire at the building again, he slows and turns and that gives me a chance. With a deep intake of the cold air that pains my lungs, I lunge at him, seeing nothing but red.

His head crashes on the cement sidewalk and I hear his gun fall into the street and sounds like it hits metal... maybe a gutter. I didn't recognize him farther away and I don't know him now that I'm close up either. I don't know who he is other than someone who attacked us.

Even as the metal slams into his skull, I don't hear the gunshots stop. Even as the blood splatters onto my face, the heat of it nothing compared to the raging burn that flows through my own blood, I don't hear Eli yelling for me.

I don't stop, I can't make myself stop pummeling his flesh with the butt of the gun. I can't even see what I'm doing with the tears flowing down my face. I try punching him with the gun held in my hand and the metal clashes against the thin skin over my knuckles. It hurts, I know it does, but that only fuels me to do it again.

The footsteps are loud and they're coming closer, but I can still feel the man beneath me shoving me away. His hands pushing against my chest, my face, anywhere until they stop to cover his face.

I pause for only a second and it's a second too much as he reaches for the gun. Panicking, I lean forward, head-butting him and crashing my forehead against his nose. He screams out, but he doesn't stop.

He's still trying to reach for his gun and so I whip the butt of the gun in my hand down hard against his throat and his hot blood bubbles up from his lips as he coughs.

Strong hands grip my shoulders and then my arms, but I kick out, desperate to connect with the fucker who dared to wage war with men protecting me.

My left shoe hits his chin and his head snaps backward, bashing against the cement. Everything in my mind becomes a fog as Eli holds me close to him, telling me to calm down and dragging me away. All I can see is that man running away, getting away without any consequences while they escort me back, through the yards and straight back to where we came from.

It all happened so fast that I'm still breathing chaotically and shaking when Eli and another man, who helped him rip me away, bring me inside.

"Get her inside." I hear Eli's words, but they're slurred as I struggle to breathe.

The air isn't cold anymore. Nothing is cold. It's all hot and I feel like I'm suffocating.

The second the bright light of the foyer hits me, I shove them away. I don't want to be touched, I can't be touched right now.

I refuse to talk to them, to listen to them telling me to stop and calm down.

Calm down? How can I calm down when this is what my life is?

"I'm tired of taking orders!" is all I can yell out, my voice raw from screaming. The memory of what I've done seeps in slowly as I rock on the floor. I was screaming. I didn't realize it then, but I was screaming.

Every time I swallow, it hurts. My shoulders shudder and Eli tries to comfort me but I shove him away. Backing into the corner of the foyer, I'm only seeing the vision of me running after the man and fighting him.

Time passes slowly.

I steady my breathing and slowly calm down, watching my hands and willing them to stop shaking. There's so much blood on them and I wipe them off on my pants, but that just spreads the blood.

I walk myself to my room, gripping on to the railing to keep me upright. Eli follows but stays a good distance behind. Carefully stripping out of the stained clothes, I step into the hot shower to wash the blood away, although my knuckles are raw and cut. It will take time for those to heal.

Maybe an hour passes, and I spend the entire time in the shower. When I'm clean, I walk downstairs and open the front door to the house to see Eli, the other man, and two others standing guard.

All I want to know is his name. I want the name of that man. I don't know why it matters as much as it does, but I need to know his name.

I know I look foolish with wet hair that clings to my face and pajamas on, but still, I speak up.

"Who is it?" I ask Eli as I stand in the light of the foyer, and he stays on the other side of the doorway, bathed in darkness. "What's the man's name?"

"We'll find out soon and I'll tell you immediately," he answers me, and it only makes me angrier. How can he not know? It still hurts when I swallow and hurts, even more, when I clench my hands into fists at my side.

"Where is he?" I ask Eli with my teeth clenched, "I'll beat it out of him myself." The rage I feel is unjustified and I know I'm out of control and crossing a line, but I don't care about boundaries anymore. Not when everyone else crosses them.

The silence is only broken by the chirp of crickets from beyond the yard. There are three men in front of me and no one answers me.

I can hear Eli swallow as the other men stare at me, and still, no one answers.

"Where is he?" I repeat myself, ready to tell them to go fuck themselves if they refuse to tell me. I don't care what Carter ordered. I don't care if I'm their enemy or they think I'm just being babysat. "I need to know his name!"

"He's dead, Aria." Eli's voice is softer than I expected, and I have to take in a shuddering breath. His gaze is assessing, but comforting. "He died."

My eyes flicker over his and then dart to the other men. "Who killed him?" My voice is full of both shock and remorse for speaking to him like that, along with everything else. As time moves forward, I seem to come down, to ground myself again. As if blinking finally removed the red rage that blinded me.

One man steps to the side, another whispers something on the porch, but Eli's voice brings my attention back to him.

He answers me, "You did."

CHAPTER 17

Carter

"Do you think she'll be a problem?" Jase asks me in low tones as he stares across the bar at the brunette. She stands out in the club full of women dressed in tight shirts and short skirts.

Dressed in jeans with rips in the knees and a loose black tank top designed for comfort, she doesn't belong here. More than that, she's slamming her hands against the bar and screaming across the counter at both the men working tonight.

"She's not why we're here," I remind him. "Let the bartender handle it," I tell him and walk past the crowds of people, but Jase stays behind a moment longer, staring at the deranged brunette.

All I care about are the men in the back room right now. Men who lost a family member tonight. Two of our guys were shot in the back while they were out on their runs to collect. The fucked-up part is that they were on the most southern portion of our turf. So, some fucker came into our territory, hid low, and shot them in broad daylight. Some fucker named Charles Banner who's now buried in a shallow grave thanks to Cason.

It doesn't bring the men back though. Death is final.

When I walk up to the back doors, Jared opens them immediately and the hushed voices of the six men inside are silenced. I can hear Jase pick up his pace behind me and come in before the doors close, quieting the music of the club.

Around the table, all six men have drinks in front of them, two of them with shots untouched. Cigarettes are lit and one of the guys takes the last puff before putting out the butt. As he blows out the smoke, the rest of the five greet me and then he follows.

The metal chair legs drag on the floor as Jared pulls out seats for both Jase and me and then goes back to his position to guard the doors.

"James and Logan." I swallow thickly after I look both men in the eyes. The youngest one, James, lost his brother and his eyes are still bloodshot. He can't stop himself from crying as I tell him, "I'm sorry." Logan lost his cousin, his only cousin and he's the one who brought him in. I can see the look of regret on his face and there's nothing I can do to take that back.

The other four men all lost a close friend.

Only two men have died tonight on our side, and we took out nearly thirty of Talvery's crew. It doesn't make the losses any easier to take. Not for the six men sitting here.

"What happened was a tragedy and one that needs to be rectified."

"I thought they said you got him?" A kid with a deep scar down the left side of his face and blonde hair speaks up. His lips stay parted as he stares at me with wide eyes. "They said he's dead."

"The asshole who stole the lives of my men?" I question him, bringing my hand to my chest. "The one who pulled the trigger was shot in the back of the head and buried in the back of the construction site off the highway. Tomorrow cement will cover him, and his name will be forgotten." I pause as the kid nods. His name escapes me, and I look around at the other four. I know three of them and then I come back to the blonde. Matthew. That's right. "Matthew?" I call him out and he nods again, bringing his gaze up from where it was focused on the table.

"You can call me Matty." He brightens for a moment, and it's then that I remember one of the guys who died was his neighbor. They grew up together.

"How old are you?"

"Just turned twenty-two," he tells me, and I turn around and motion for Jared to come closer. "Get him as many drinks as he wants all week. A birthday should be celebrated. Every day alive should be celebrated."

"Thank you, Boss," Matty tells me and I shake my head, not wanting any gratitude.

"The man who's responsible for your brother's death," I look to James and then to Logan as I continue, "and your cousin's death, Nicholas Talvery, will die the second I have a chance to end his life."

I pause as the memories of how he tried to kill me, how sneaky the fucker is, spring to mind. Always preparing and setting up his men to blindside the unsuspecting, like my brothers, when we were only kids. "No one," my voice hardens, "will take from us without having consequences."

My heart races as I look the two men on my right in the eyes. "He killed your family and I'll have his head for it."

"To the end of Talvery," Matty raises the shot glass in his hand and the other men do the same.

Talvery.

I'm numb as they throw back the shots and commiserate together.

"To the end of this war," Jase speaks up, grabbing another shot glass and filling his and then the others.

The guy's spirit picks up, although Logan still looks lost. James pats him on the back as Logan hunches over, shaking his head and crying again.

This war is useless. A fight between two men, Romano and Talvery, who already have enough. Greedy, selfish men who will risk lives to hurt the other.

And I supported it.

And Jase wants more of it.

And Aria lies in the middle of all of it.

"If you need anything, you know who to call," I hear Jase speak quietly to the two men on the right and then he stands, and I do the same. Buttoning my jacket and taking a good look at each of the men sitting there.

None of them blame me and that's the worst part of it. I'm bitter knowing they don't blame me when they should. I brought them into this.

For her.

I agreed to this... for her.

The sound of Jase walking ahead of me is all I can follow as I feel like I'm suffocating. Maybe that's how I'll die. I'll choke on every fucked-up decision I ever made.

I feel my phone vibrate in my pocket. It's been going off since the bar, but I wanted to get in and out and give the men the respect they deserve. That's the least I could do.

Feeling it go off again as we step out into the night air and wait for the car to come around, brings on the restlessness and unease that hasn't left me since I left Aria alone on the bed.

"That brunette's gone," Jase comments, leaning against a post by the curb that details all the drink deals inside.

As I pull out my phone, I glance at his profile and for a moment I see the look of loss in his eyes. He's looking out into the parking lot and past it to the busy street. I know what he's thinking about. I know what that look means.

"You all right?" I ask him, and he clears his throat, coughing into his fist and kicking off the post.

"Yeah," he answers and runs his hand down the back of his neck. "I just can't believe Talvery would waste a man like that. Did he really think he'd get out alive?" he questions, and I wonder if he's telling me the truth about what he was thinking, or if I was right.

The rumble of the engine and the soothing sound of my car pulling up grabs our attention and saves me from asking him and prying.

It's not until I walk around and open the door that I check my phone and see the missed calls and texts. Eli never texts, and he knows not to.

A's safe and sound but shit happened. Call me when you can.

It's the only text I've ever received from him. And I read it over and over, not breathing.

She's safe. Anxiety creeps up and doesn't leave me, forcing me to unbutton my collar as I walk around the other side and tell Jase to get out and drive. My hand slams on the roof when he doesn't move fast enough. "You drive!" I scream at him and feel raw fear at the back of my throat.

She's safe.

"What's wrong?" He doesn't object but stares at me the entire time he moves around to the other side.

With the key in the ignition, he sits there staring at me while Eli's phone rings.

"Come on," I grit out.

"What's wrong?" he asks again.

"Drive to the safe house," I yell at him, irritated by Eli not answering and pissed off that I'm here and not with Aria. But more than anything I'm scared that something happened to her. It's been nearly forty minutes since he called.

The ringing stops and it goes to his voicemail. *Motherfucker.* I lean forward, my palms on the dash and try to calm the fuck down. *She's safe.*

"Tell me again how we should take on more when this shit is out of hand," I mutter to Jase as he pulls up to a stop sign.

"What happened?" he asks again, incredulity in his voice. I stare at my brother, not knowing what to say because I don't fucking know. I need to know.

"She's safe," I say out loud but it's more of a reminder to myself and Jase asks, "Aria?"

As I nod my head, the phone rings in my hand.

"Eli," I answer quickly, feeling my pulse throb harder.

"We have a problem," he tells me as Jase makes a right and then stops at the light. He's staring at me instead of watching the road.

"Four men on First Street took a shot at our crew. They knew where they were and went for the two stations at the end of the security block. Only one of our guys took a shot, he's with the doc now and he'll be fine."

One breath out, a deep, low breath and I swallow the spiked knot of fear. *She's fine*, I remind myself. My eyes close and my head falls against the headrest.

My heart is thudding, rather than beating.

"Whose men?" I ask him, and he answers, "Not Romano or Talvery."

My jaw clenches, as does my fist. Fucking great. That's the last thing I need right now. Another asshole fucking with me.

"Anything else?" I ask him, opening my eyes and staring at the cabin of the car. The red and white lights from outside dance on the ceiling as he speaks. "All four men are dead, but they were known to hang out with the man who tried to take Addison. The one Daniel killed back when he was checking out Iron Heart. Men for hire. And Carter," he pauses and so does the beat in my chest. I know it has to do with Aria. I can feel it. "I was with Aria at the time. She was there."

I can't swallow. I try, but I can't. There's something in the way and I can't breathe.

"She's okay. But she was there, and she fucked up one of the guys."

My gaze shifts to Jase, who's asking me what's going on. I can only stare at him as I question Eli, "What do you mean, she fucked one of them up? You're supposed to protect her!" The rage is minuscule compared to everything else I feel. The shock and fear that she was there, the relief that she's safe and fine. The pride that she fought alongside my men.

I can hear him huff and it sounds like he switches ears to tell me, "She killed a guy. She got away from me, chased him down the street and beat the piss out of him."

My Aria. My songbird.

"I'll remember that the next time she lets me off with a warning," I say softly, imagining it happening but I can't. I can't see it.

"Is she upset?" I ask him, knowing she will be. I yearn for a time when she's happy again. When this is all over and she looks at me the way she did before.

"She's not handling it well, but she honestly wasn't doing that good before it went down."

"Anything else I should know?" I ask him as I see the sign for Hill Road and Jase turns the corner, not slowing down. The tires squeal as Eli tells me that's it.

"I'll be there in a minute. Gather the guys, I want to go over everything and see the footage."

CHAPTER 18

Aria

I'VE KILLED TWO MEN, YET I DON'T FEEL SORRY.

Staring at myself in the mirror as I brush out my hair, I don't feel sorry at all. I'm empty inside, and there's no sense of remorse; I don't even have anger left. Nothing. I feel nothing for the man I killed tonight. I remember his wide eyes full of fear. I can feel his hands on me, pushing me away. I can feel the thud of the gun hitting my skin over and over as it crashed into him.

And yet, I feel nothing.

Even Stephan. Thinking of him makes me feel nothing at all.

The hairbrush tugs as I pull it through a knot, and I take my time to carefully brush it away.

I think I must be sick. It can't be normal to feel nothing at all when hours ago I killed a man. My eyes drift to the mirror and I stare at the woman I've become. I look the same as before. The same eyes, my mother's eyes. The same everything as months ago.

But I'm not that girl anymore. The problem is, I don't know who I am.

Without Carter... suddenly the emotions flood back, and I have to slam the brush down on the vanity. It's an antique piece of furniture and I stare at the weathered wood top wishing it would give me answers and take this pain away.

He told me I would always be his and it gave me a freedom. But that freedom scares me now that he left me. I don't think he'll ever take me back and it leaves me feeling hollow inside. There's nothing remaining but the ache of him not loving me.

I suck in a breath, knowing I need to accept it and think about where I'll go and who I'll be once this week and this war are over.

All I know for certain is that I'll be alone. And that sounds like the worst thing in the world when you're empty inside.

I don't want to be alone.

The knock at the bedroom door startles me and I nearly jump in my seat. "Come in," I call out, opening the drawer to the vanity and placing the hairbrush inside.

My gaze catches the phone still sitting on the vanity. A phone that's been silent all day and all night.

What's the point of giving it to me if he had no intention of using it?

It works both ways. I know I could call him. But I'd rather let the tension sever what's left between Carter and me. It's best to let it slip away so when my time's up here, it'll be easier to walk away.

"You're not in bed yet?" Addison's soft voice carries into the room.

"Can't sleep," I tell her, not looking her in her eyes. I may not feel sorry for what I did, but I still don't want Addison to know. I don't want her to look at me and see the heartless killer I can be.

"I know the feeling," she sighs and makes her way to my bed. Sitting on the end of it, she pulls her knees up and pushes her heels into the mattress. "I wanted to check on you," she tells me hesitantly. Her voice is careful, considerate, but her eyes dart from her painted toenails to where I'm sitting as if she doesn't know if what she has to say should be said.

My pulse flutters. Maybe she already knows.

"What's up?" I ask her, refusing to let the anxiety take over. I am who I am. I've done what I've done. If she doesn't understand that, there's nothing I can do about it. I can't take back what's been done.

"Eli said you needed a little space earlier when I came down." I thought I heard something outside... I decided not to sleep and just shower, but when I got out it sounded like..." She picks at the fresh polish on her nails and peeks at me. "He said you were in the shower but to give you some space because you didn't seem like yourself?" she questions me, not trusting what Eli said to be true.

Swallowing thickly, I nod and then wet my lips. "There was an incident on the way to the corner store, but it's okay." I shrug my shoulders and turn back to the vanity, picking up the phone and holding it up for her to see before dropping it into my lap. "Nothing serious enough for Carter to call and reprimand me," I huff a sarcastic response while rolling my eyes, trying to lighten the truth of what happened.

Glancing at the phone, and then meeting my gaze she asks, "So you're all right?"

"Yeah." My answer is easy and I'm hoping she'll drop it.

"And you and Carter?" she asks and then adds, "If you don't want to talk, that's fine." Her voice is stronger, louder and contains no offense whatsoever. "I know sometimes people like to keep things in."

"I like to talk," I tell her honestly and then feel the tug of a sad smile. "Sometimes." My voice is low and so quiet I'm not sure she heard. "Some things I'd rather not talk about, but even still, I always like to talk about something. And when it comes to Carter..." The emotions swell in my throat, stopping the words from coming easily. "When it comes to Carter, I think maybe the best thing to talk about is how to move on from someone you love when they don't love you."

"I'm sorry." The sympathy in Addison's voice pushes the ache in my chest down to the pit of my stomach.

"It is what it is. He made mistakes, I made mistakes, but none of it matters anyway. We could never be together. Not being the people we are." The words come out easier and clearer than I imagined they would. Addison's expression remains soft as she searches my gaze for something. I'm not sure what.

"What's going to happen then?" she asks me, breathing in deeply and wrapping her arms around her legs while setting her chin on her knees. Sitting feet away from her at the vanity, I wish I had an answer for her, but all I can think is, "Maybe I'll do what my friend, Addison did once, maybe I'll travel the world."

With a hopeful smile and optimism in my voice, I add, "I'd like to be like her."

Addison's smile is less than joyous as she replies, "I heard she did that because she was afraid." Her lips pull down and she bites down on her bottom lip. "I ran away, Aria. I ran because I couldn't face what was left here."

"Do you regret it?"

"No," she answers in a quick breath and seems to struggle to say something else, so I push her to speak her mind. "Whatever you're thinking," I tell her, "you don't have to hide it from me. I won't judge you."

"I don't regret it, because it all brought me back here and brought me back to Daniel." Her voice cracks and she looks away, back to the closed door of the bedroom.

"So, you and Daniel?" I ask her and keep my weak smile in place, no matter how my gut churns. She's going back to him and I'm going to be alone.

"I love him, Ria," she tells me softly, not realizing how she's pulling at every emotion inside of me.

"I know you do," I somehow, some way, speak the truth without letting on how much pain my heart is in. I'll lose Carter because I'm not the woman he needs. And I'll lose Addison because Daniel will never let her go and she'll never let him go either. Even if that means she'll turn a blind eye to the things he does.

As if reading my mind, she tells me, "I don't agree with what he does sometimes, but I know he has his reasons. And I'm so sorry, Aria," she apologizes, and I cut her off, waving my hand in the air recklessly.

"Stop it. Don't apologize. You get it now, don't you?" I ask her, feeling winded by the question. By the idea that with her answer, she still may not understand this complicated mess of pain and love that Carter and I make together.

"I don't agree with it," she tells me with sad eyes, but she doesn't deny that she understands why.

"You don't have to," I tell her and then wipe the sleep from my eyes. "It's weird, but it makes me feel better knowing you understand. Even if it's still not..." Right. Right is the word I nearly say, but it can't be the correct word. Because I don't care how wrong what we had was, it was right for me. It was right for me.

And I refuse to call what we had wrong.

"Does it upset you that I still love Daniel?" she asks me, and I shake my head no.

"If I were you, I'd love him too. He'll fight for you till the day he dies." I almost get choked up, knowing Daniel would do just that. While Carter won't even tell me he loves me. It shouldn't matter to me as much as it does. But not hearing those words from him… it's killed a part of me that I don't think will ever breathe again.

A yawn creeps up and the exhaustion and weight from everything that happened today, every loss, every failure, makes me crave sleep.

I could sleep forever if sleep would take away this pain.

"I didn't mean to get into all that," Addie tells me, moving off the bed and brushing her hair to the side. She runs her fingers through her hair as she tells me, "I didn't sleep earlier, and I was wondering if you had that vial?"

Getting up from the vanity, I leave the phone on the worn wood top and make my way to the dresser. It's so quiet tonight, it's only as I open up the dresser drawer and hear the pull that I realize I can't hear the crickets. There have been crickets the last two nights, so loud that I had to pretend they were singing me a lullaby in order to sleep.

With the vial in my one hand, I shut the drawer with a hard thud and peek out of the window.

"It's so dark tonight, isn't it?" I ask Addison, the thin curtain grazing my fingers before I pull it back and face her.

"It is. Maybe tomorrow we'll see the stars," she says with a hint of a smile on her lips.

"Sweet dreams." The words slip from me as I pass the vial to her and she tells me goodnight.

As she leaves me alone in the quiet, dark room, I can't help but feel like it's the last night I'll tell her goodnight. Something inside of me, something that chills every inch of me is certain of it.

The covers rustle as I pull them back and climb into bed. I pull them closer to me, all the way up to my neck and stare at the glass knob on the door praying sleep will take me, but the nerves inside of me crawl in my stomach, in a slinking way that makes me feel sick and no matter how tightly I hold the covers, I'm freezing cold. My toes especially.

I almost get up to put socks on, almost. But I can't. A childish fear and feeling deep in my soul wants me to stay right where I am and I listen to that fear, I obey it.

Until my tired eyes burn and the darkness slips in.

Just as I close my eyes, feeling the respite of sleep flow over every inch of me, I think I hear the door open, but when I open my eyes, it's closed. There's no one here.

It's only the darkness and quietness… the signs of loneliness that lie with me tonight.

The screams from Addison rip me from my dreamless sleep. My heart pounds against my ribcage as I hear her scream again.

The clock on the dresser blinks at me; hours have passed, and I must have fallen asleep.

My legs feel heavy as I fight with the covers to move fast enough, to get out and go to Addie.

Heaving in a breath I make it halfway to the door before it bursts open. Addie's eyes are wide, her face pale and her hair a messy halo around her head.

"Aria," she cries out my name, pulling me hard into her, so hard it knocks what little breath is in my lungs out of me, but the way she trembles, the way her nails dig into me, I know something's wrong.

"He was here," she whispers in a voice drenched in terror. "I felt him," she whimpers, pulling away from me to close my bedroom door.

As she backs away from me, she almost bumps into me and startles when I carefully take her hand.

Her fear is contagious, and I struggle to remain calm but without any idea of what she's talking about, I have to ask her, "Who? Who was here?"

"Tyler," she tells me and then tears leak from her eyes. She doesn't blink, she stares at me, willing me to believe her as the tears freefall and cradle her cheeks. "Tyler… it felt so real. He was there, Aria. I felt him."

Goosebumps travel over every inch of me and the same coldness that pricked the back of my neck when I saw the king of wands lingers there once again.

"Tyler?" I question her, knowing Tyler's the fifth Cross brother. The youngest. The one who died.

"It was so real," she tells me as she grabs my wrists hard. Too hard. Although it hurts, I don't pull away; I can't. "He's angry," she says, and her words are hoarse and hushed. The intense look in her eyes refuses to let me feel anything but the sincerity and desperation in her words.

Rushing her words, she tells me, "At first, he only held me and I swear I felt him. I could feel him holding me so tightly." She releases me to cover her eyes as she falls to her knees crying harder and harder, but she doesn't stop telling me what happened.

"He held me and told me he still loves me. He said it's okay to love Daniel. He still loves me, and he'll stay with me. But Aria," she finally looks back up to me, with red-rimmed eyes, "he's angry we left. He was never mad. Tyler never got angry and he said we need to go back. He grabbed my arms. He made me promise." She gasps for breath as she grips her own arms, still on her knees and shaking with fear.

My own legs are weak as I lower myself to her eye level. My knees hit the cold hardwood floor. Gripping her shoulders softly, I wait for her to look me in the eyes.

"It was a dream," I tell her, and she shakes her head.

"It was so real."

"The drug," I try to tell her, but she shakes her head harder, her hair viciously flailing around her shoulders.

"He told me to tell you something." Blinking away the tears, she sniffles and tells me, "He said to hold him as tight as you can, or he'll die." My blood turns to ice as I stare into her eyes.

I remember the terror I had. It was only a dream.

It's only a dream. But I don't know how to convince her.

"He told me to leave and I have to," she tells me in a whisper of a breath. "I have to go back." The remorse in the air between us is palpable. And my heart sinks lower.

I don't say a word, I only grip her close to me, squeezing her until the sound of the bedroom door flinging open startles both of us.

My stomach's still in my throat when I see Eli in the doorway, his figure black and silhouetted by the light from the hall.

"I heard screaming and came up to your room," he breathes heavily and then steps in, a look of relief settling over his face. "When I got there, it was empty. You scared the shit out of me, Addison," Eli's accent is thick as he runs his hand over his face, sleep and worry both evident in his bloodshot eyes.

Addison doesn't let go of me, she doesn't move. All she does is look up at him in silence.

"Are you all right?" he asks her, and she shakes her head no.

Her voice croaks when she starts to tell him but then looks at me, "I want to go…"

She holds my gaze and I offer her a small smile, squeezing her hand and sitting back on my heels to tell her, "Go."

"What's going on?" Eli asks and Addison hugs me tight. The tears don't stop when she whispers, "Come with me please."

The idea of going back to Carter…

"He doesn't love me," is all I can tell her, feeling the last petal wither and die inside of me. "There's nothing for me there."

Her gaze doesn't leave mine. Even as Eli walks closer to us, towering over us and waiting for an answer.

"Tomorrow," she whispers and then hugs me one last time. I can feel her tears on my shoulder and I promise myself to remember this. We'll share a friendship forever, even if we never see each other again.

She breaks the hug before I'm ready to let go, standing and smoothing her nightgown out before wiping the tears under her eyes.

Rubbing her arm and looking sheepish, she tells Eli, "I don't want to sleep."

She walks past him before he can say anything else, slipping into the yellow light pouring from the doorway and going right rather than left, heading to the kitchen, away from her bedroom.

"Is she okay?" Eli asks me in a tone suggesting he truly needs to know; he's genuinely concerned for her.

I feel the ache deep in my body as I stand up on shaky legs, still cold, still tired, and in the depths of my bones, scared. I don't like what terrors that drug brings.

Hold him as tight as you can, or he'll die.

A chill flows over my skin and I look Eli in the eyes to tell him, "She just had a nightmare. It was only a nightmare."

He doesn't speak for a moment and I peek over my shoulder to check the time, it's past three and I just want a few hours of sleep.

"You should stay with her," I offer him, wanting to be alone and his forehead pinches with a question he doesn't voice.

He stands there a second longer than I'd like, so I look to the door pointedly and then back to him.

"I can never get a good read on you," Eli says and almost turns from me to leave, but I stop him.

"What does that mean?"

"I don't know where you stand and that makes you…"

"It makes me what?" I press him to continue, although there's a threat in the way I say it. The days of him protecting me are few. I know where I'll stand when my father's dead. He's not my friend. I'm smart enough to know that.

"It makes you dangerous. It makes me not trust you because I don't know who you stand for or against."

"I stand for a lot of people. The only ones I stand against are the ones who get in my way." Walking him to the door, I look him in the eyes and tell him, "Remember that," before closing the door and trying to shake off the sick, empty feeling that grows inside of me.

CHAPTER 19

Carter

L EANING AGAINST THE RAILING AT THE BOTTOM OF THE STAIRS, I keep hearing her say the lie.

He doesn't love me.

It's a lie to me, but maybe she truly believes it.

"She certainly has a way about her," Eli mutters as he pinches the bridge of his nose and slowly sits at the bottom of the stairs.

"That's one way to put it." My expression is unmoving, and I can't control the scowl. Swallowing the knot in my throat is painful.

"I'm fucking tired," he mutters, and I tell him to go to bed then.

"You staying here?" he asks and I nod. I can't fucking move after hearing her say that. Addison's scream woke me up, but she was faster than I was. I couldn't hear everything, but I got the gist of it: Addison wants to go back, and Aria doesn't.

My heart feels like it's been stomped on, driven over by a tank, and then left for scraps in the dirty gutter.

"I don't know what to do with her," I speak out loud, not liking where my thoughts are going. I want her back in the cell. The core of my soul is screaming at me to put her there. She'll be safe, and she'll forgive me with time. She has to.

"You don't trust her?" he asks and peers up at me and waits for my response.

"I trust that I know what she'll do at this point." I focus on keeping my breathing steady as I listen to Addison upstairs, turning on the faucet in the kitchen. Our voices won't carry well, but if she wanted to, she could hear us.

Eli sighs as he nods his head and runs a hand over his knee.

I hated her father when I was a kid. I hated him for what he did to me. I hated him for letting me go alive. I hated him for what he did to my home and what he tried to do to my brothers.

But I've never hated him more now. Knowing when I put a bullet in his skull, it will kill her. I can already see how she'll look at me. I can feel her nails dig into my skin as she claws at me. I can hear her screaming.

I can already feel his death tearing her away from me. We're hanging on by a single thread and it's because of him. My jaw clenches and I breathe out low and steady, gazing at the molding that lines the stairwell even though I feel Eli's eyes on me.

The silence stretches until I ask him, "What do you think of her?"

"Of Aria?"

With a single nod, I appraise his expression, his body language, his tone. Everything. I can't explain how whenever one of my men is by her or mentions her or her name, I can't explain how anxiety races through me. She's my weakness and I want her to receive nothing but respect for her. Respect and fear.

But given everything that's happened, I don't think anyone knows what to think of her, or what to think of us.

"I think she has the heart of a lover and the temper of a fighter."

"You sound like a true Irishman," I tell him as I huff a response to his answer.

With his asymmetric smirk, he adds, "I wouldn't want to be her enemy and I think the two of you... together, is something that will be feared."

"I wouldn't want to be her enemy either," I say flatly as my stomach knots and my throat gets tighter. But I am. And I always will be.

It's not her that makes it impossible to be together.

It's not me either.

We never had a chance. My gaze falls as I control the numbness that pricks along my skin. I wanted her so badly, I didn't dare look past the desire for her and see the challenges rooted in our very souls.

She may try to love me, but she will always hate me.

"You think you know what she'll do after tomorrow? When they're all dead?" he whispers his question and I nod, feeling the unbearable knot twist even tighter. With the media in an uproar, the cops aren't holding off for much longer. We promised them tomorrow would be the last day we needed them to stay on the west side while we invade from the east. A single bullet to Talvery's head and his factions will fall.

Tomorrow, I'm going to murder her father.

"I think she'll kill me. And I think she'll hate herself for it but feel it was what she needed to do." Eli's gaze falls and my stomach sinks with it. My fingers are so numb I have to clench and relax my hand repeatedly, but it doesn't work to bring life back to it.

"That's ... a..." he fails to respond.

"I'm choosing to be her enemy and to take everything from her. It doesn't matter if she thinks she loves me." The coldness spreads through my chest like ice crackling. "Hate is stronger." I'm surprised by how strong and unforgiving my words are. "She'll want revenge for what I'm going to do. I would want it too."

Eli looks over his shoulder and down the hall, toward Aria's bedroom. "Is that why you haven't gone to her?"

Not trusting myself to speak, I only nod. I can't look her in the eyes and confess how much she means to me, knowing how badly I'm going to hurt her tomorrow.

I won't do that to her. I'm not that cruel.

Bang, bang, bang, bang!

Adrenaline spikes from my toes straight up through my core, freezing my body, then heating it all at once at the sound of guns going off in the distance. My grip on the railing is white-knuckled as Eli stands and speaks clearly into the device on his wrist.

"Where'd they come from?" he asks, and I bring up the surveillance on my phone, all the while listening. It sounded like it came from blocks away and within seconds I can see two cars blocking the road and men leaning out of the windows.

"East," Eli answers but I already know. My heart pumps harder and the blood is fueled by the need to react. To grip the hard metal of a gun in my hand and feel the recoil again my palm after I've pulled the trigger.

I can hear the men screaming from down the street and the bullets firing as my blood heats. Three blocks at most.

A sick smirk begs to pull at my lips. I should have known Talvery would respond recklessly. Sending what's left of his men to their funerals.

The voices ring clear from Eli's earpiece:
Shots fired on Main Street.
Four men on Abbey Road.
Two cars coming up Dorset.

"Block off Fourth Street; make them come in on foot and don't hold back fire." I give Eli the command and he repeats what I said word for word.

The guns sound off like fireworks and Addison's hard paces carry through the hall. She's soon pounding on Aria's door.

Taking the stairs two by two, I grip the railing and get to her as quickly as I can. My lungs heave as I get to her door. "Stay in there and lock the door. Don't open it for anyone but Eli." All the words stumble out in a single breath and she looks at me for a moment, breathless and hesitant before nodding.

My heart pounds so hard, harder than it has in a long time. It takes me a moment to realize it's due to fear. The very real fear of losing Aria.

"I won't let anything happen to either of you," I say and stare into Addison's eyes and wish they were Aria's. She's just behind the door and I'm drawn to her. My body aches knowing she's so close, but I refuse to go in there.

If I do, I don't know how I'll leave her.

"Stay in her room." I barely get the command out, but Addison hears me. For a moment, I wonder if Aria heard me from behind the door. *My songbird.* The spiked ball grows in my throat as Addison opens the door before retreating behind it. She didn't say a word to me.

Not a single word.

Every muscle in my body is tight and at odds with what I need to do.

The muted sounds of a man screaming, and the continued gunfire is accompanied by Eli yelling out demands on the floor below us.

I try to calm myself and summon the ruthless side of me that will end this as quickly as it started.

The bullets ring out clearly. Automatic weapons that tear through the brick of houses and metal cars. Windows shatter and men yell out.

So, I move.

Quickly and with determination down the stairs.

My stomach clenches and it's the first time I can remember where so much was at stake. Where my thoughts are torn between tactics and emotion.

Between fighting to steal the woman I love and running as fast as I can.

"Bring up all the cars and block off every street," I command Eli while bringing out my phone to text Daniel and tell him where Addison is. The last I heard from him, he was trying to get in touch with Marcus and find out anything he can about the fucker he killed back in Iron Heart.

My heart pounds, and my muscles coil as I listen closely to every word that comes in from the earpiece as I switch to the surveillance screens and watch everything unfold.

I need to move. Standing here is fucking killing me but I have to remind myself that this is war and decoys are common. I won't be fooled like Talvery was.

Three streets on two sides are under attack, two on top of each other to the east and one furthest to the west of this house.

"They hit three streets at once."

"Do we have a count on how many men are firing?" I need numbers. Talvery can't have more than fifty men left.

Eli's earpiece buzzes and it takes everything in me not to rip it out and take it for myself. "It looks to be about thirty."

"They may be distractions, hitting the two sides and leaving the south side untouched. Don't move the men on the south side."

"Yes, sir," Eli answers, speaking into the device.

"Count of our men," Eli barks out the order before relaying what I said. I have fifty men to his thirty. Fifty well-armed and guarded but spread out.

Two men down.
One man down.
We're holding.

I stare at my phone, waiting for Daniel to reply, but I get nothing. Where the fuck is he?

"Three total, Boss," Eli's voice is tight as I grip the phone tighter and scream internally for him to tell me where the fuck he is. The cords in his throat tense as he rips the Velcro of his holster, moving it to the side and checking his ammo.

Three men dead.

Three more men dead.

"Kill them all," I grit out, feeling the rage turn incandescent. My head feels light as I take in a deep breath.

"You and Cason stay with the women," I give the command while my phone pings and Jase tells me he's close and coming up the south side and he already told the guards there.

His jaw is hard and clenched, and I know he wants to be out there, but I need him here.

"You two stay here." I harden my voice and look him in the eyes until he nods.

Shoving my phone in my back pocket, I reach for my gun and then move past Eli to the back room where the other weapons are stored as he tells me, "Yes, Boss."

I need men with them who know when to leave.

The back room has shelves of guns and I choose from the racks of metal shining back at me, picking up one and shoving it and the ammunition into the waist of my pants before picking up another.

Talvery's on the outer edge. There's no way he'll get in and this entire ground is a safe house. But every safe house can be broken into. I've done it before. Sebastian knew that when he built this place.

With time ticking, and the bullets still firing every minute, I turn my back on the arsenal and prepare to join my men. I only stop to tell Eli one thing, "The basement has an underground exit. The code is six, fourteen, eight, eight. Repeat it to me."

"Six, fourteen, eight, eight." He's quick to answer, but I can see the defiance in his eyes.

"Don't forget it, and if I—"

"We have enough men," Eli cuts me off and I struggle to hold back the anger. "There's no way—"

"If I tell you to," I say looking him in the eyes as my nostrils flare and my body heats with the need to strike back, "take them and lock the door behind you."

I don't wait for him to answer, although as I turn my back to him and head down the stairs, I hear him say he'll do it. The buzzing in my ears is like white noise as I climb down the stairs. I'm ready with a gun in my right hand as I stare at the front door.

I pray Talvery's here in the flesh and blood, ready to finally pay for all his sins.

"Carter," Eli calls out to me as I reach the front door.

"What?" I snap at him, feeling the rage, the immediacy, the fear even of losing men and protection for Aria and Addison.

"Your estate… He sent men there." Eli visibly swallows as my blood chills.

"My brothers?" I ask him quickly, my breathing coming in short pants. The gun in my hand slips and I grip it tighter, praying and swallowing down my fear.

"Jase said he's coming," I speak as I remember the text and Eli confirms with a brief nod.

"Jase and Declan are together, they're on their way and missed it."

Daniel. My heart beats slow, so slow it's painful. "Three bombs hit the east wing. And another four to the south wing and the garage."

"How many men are dead?" The question comes out without conscious consent, all I can think of is Daniel and the last time I saw him when he told me he had plans with Addison.

"Six currently."

"Where's Daniel?" I ask him, feeling the threat of a pain that can never be soothed brimming inside of me.

"We don't know."

CHAPTER 20

Aria

"F UCK, FUCK," ADDISON'S ROCKING BACK AND FORTH ON the bed, her legs tucked up under her as the guns continue to fire.

Men shout from the floor below us and farther down the streets outside.

"I've never heard it last for so long," I whisper as I peek out into the black night. I watch as each of the streetlights is hit, one by one, spraying shards of white light before fading into the darkness.

Addison's voice is strained and coated in worry as she asks, "Why would they do that?"

"So they can't see," I tell her.

"But then no one can see."

"It's a risk they decided was worth taking." I feel the numbness flow through my blood.

"Who did it? Who shot them?" she asks me as if I'd know.

Tires squeal in the distance and metal crashes against metal. She cries harder, falling apart and then checks her phone again. She buries her face in her knees, rocking harder.

"We can hide in the closet," she offers although her words are panicked, and I don't know if she means it or not. "We'll put the clothes on top of us," she gasps for breath and rocks again, "they'll open it but not see us. I used to do it when I was younger. They won't see us. They won't see us."

She's losing it. The way she rocks, the rapid rate with which she's talking and the look of terror in her eyes are clear signs. She's fucking losing it.

"We should have left," she croaks with tears in her eyes and the numbness turns to a freezing cold along my skin.

"He told us to leave."

"It was intuition, Addie," I breathe an excuse even as the gun-shots sound louder, closer, the violence making its way to the finish line.

"Where's Daniel?" She covers her mouth as she cries again and struggles to breathe.

I don't know what comes over me as I watch her wither away and dissolve into nothing but fear and sorrow, but my hand whips across Addison's face and she stares up at me in shock before slowly moving her hand to cover the bright red mark.

My hand stings and my heart lurches with the fear of hurting her and losing a friend, but I move closer to her, gripping her shoulders and staring into her eyes to tell her, "We will not die like this."

Her chest rises and falls with heavy breathing as she waits for me to tell her more.

"Come on," I say and pull her wrist. "We're leaving," I tell her, but she pulls away.

"He told us to stay here," she breathes and lets her gaze dart between the door and me.

"I don't care what Eli said." The frustration, the anger, the terror, and lack of sleep, it all makes my body feel as if it's on fire and like I'm losing control, but I raise my voice to yell at her, "Come with me!" My dry throat screams in pain as I swallow and tell her, "We need to run."

The gunshots get louder from outside and steal our attention. They're getting closer. My heart pounds in my chest and the sound of the door opening behind me makes both of us scream. Addison's is shrill and so sharp it nearly punctures my eardrum.

Cason's out of breath as he makes his way toward us and says, "We're going to the basement." Addison shakes her head violently, and asks the only question she's been praying to have an answer to, "Where's Daniel?"

The pang in my chest strikes hard and I feel like I'm suffocating as I pray to know the same, but about Carter.

The phone is silent. My text to him unanswered.

Are you okay?

It's all I wanted to know. And he didn't answer.

"Basement. Now!" Cason yells just as bullets fly past us. The windows shatter, the small pieces raining over Addison, who covers her head with her arms and drops as far as she can forward onto the bed. I fall instantly, lying flat on the floor as I hold my breath, too afraid to move at all. Her shrill scream fills the room again as bullets ricochet and leave a trail of marks from left to right over the wall and bedroom door.

My eyes reach Cason as he stands up straight. He didn't move. He never had the chance to move. The bullet holes in his chest slowly bleed out, the bright red diffusing and spreading like watercolor paints on canvas.

"No," I breathe, tears pricking my eyes as his hand moves to one of the punctures at the same time as he falls to his knees. "Cason!" I scream out his name and reach for him, but it's useless.

The gunshots have stopped; it was a single string of bullets that clattered across the house. But they return again within seconds. Hitting him again in his neck and head, eyes closed before he falls to the floor.

Addison doesn't scream this time although I can hear her sobs from where I am. Reaching up for her, I pull her down and together we crawl on our stomachs under the bed.

"Daniel," Addison cries his name over and over, her hands clasped as she prays for him to be all right.

I can't breathe. It's so hot and the bullets rain down with no signs of letting up for minutes. More time passes with nothing. No signs of anything and that's when I see the gun on the floor. Cason's gun. As I crawl out, Addison grabs me and yells for me not to leave her. My heart lurches at the sound of a door being kicked in downstairs.

"Shh," I hush her, putting my finger over my lips and then nodding to the gun. With wide eyes, she watches me as I crawl out to get it. The cold beating in my veins picks up as the sound of a man coming up the steps gets louder and louder. The open bedroom door shows his shadow in the hall just as I reach the gun with my fingertips.

The cold metal slips in my grasp and the sound of it sliding across the floor rips my gaze up to the doorway. Without looking, I snatch the gun and Addison pulls me back under the bed.

The gun is heavy, so heavy in my hand. Addison's hands are covering her mouth as a shadow steps into the room. The floor creaks with the man's weight and his black boots are splattered with blood.

I grip the gun with both hands as he takes three agonizingly slow steps closer to Cason's body, right before kicking his shoulder over with his boot to see his face.

Bending down, I get a partial glimpse of the man as he steals Cason's phone from his pocket. The fear is paralyzing. I can't breathe. I can't do anything.

My gaze moves to the vanity and I can see my reflection, but I can see the man's too as he scowls down at Cason's dead body and lifts his gun to his head.

Bang, bang!

The gun goes off and Addison jolts each time, her eyes closed tight and her hands pressing harder against her mouth.

My heart hammers, praying he didn't hear her, but it doesn't matter if he did or not, because the man's eyes reach mine in the mirror. Cold and dark, with wrinkles that show his age. He's in the same black hoodie as the man I killed earlier, and I know this man is not one of my father's men.

The attacks out there, I think they're from my father. But the men who have made it to the safe house... they're not.

He's quicker than me, taking a large stride and grabbing me from under the bed. His grip on my left forearm is paralyzing and I nearly drop the gun. My back scratches against the underside of the wire bedframe and the pain forces a scream from me.

My finger is on the trigger and I can't get it to go off. I pull it again and again.

"The safety." Addison's voice is hoarse, and the words pushed through clenched teeth.

He reaches down with his other hand, grabbing my other wrist and that's when Addison rips the gun from me and fires. The heat from the barrel of the gun singes my skin and I scream from the pain.

Bang! Bang!

She pulls the trigger again and again as my left side falls to the floor with the man's grip nonexistent.

I can hear Addison's gasp and the clunk of the gun as the man's dead white eyes stare back at me.

My hollow chest is gutted as I stare at him and then to the doorway. My heart beats too loudly to hear anything and I have to swallow and blink away the fear to grab the gun Addison dropped and point it at the door.

I lie half under the bed, half out, with a burn scorching my forearm and wait. Time passes quickly, as quickly as my blood races through my veins.

"He's dead," Addison whispers a painful truth. "I killed him," she whispers.

"Shh," I hush her, "Quiet!"

The pounding of my heart slows as I realize the man almost got me and she saved me.

"You saved me," I whisper with tears in my eyes although I stare straight ahead.

"I killed him," she says back in a harsh whisper.

It's only then that I realize it's silent once again. No gunshots. Not from outside and not a sound inside the house.

I listen closely and hear cars outside a few blocks down, but they aren't rushed and the tires don't squeal. Rising slowly, I nearly scream when Addison grabs my ankle.

"Fuck," I barely get out the word over the harsh beat of fear in my chest.

"Is it safe?" Addison asks, and I tell her the truth, "I don't know."

It's hard to contain terror, even when there's no present danger. My gaze doesn't leave the doorway as I crawl to the window. Even as I rise up slowly and pull the curtain ever so softly, I don't dare take my eyes from the doorway for a few minutes longer.

No more gunshots and lights are on inside the houses that were black now. A car passes with its headlights and I see some men I recognize a street down.

"I think it's over," I whisper to her but still crawl to reach her. "Take the gun," I put it in her hand and when she objects I tell her I'm taking the dead man's gun.

"I'm going downstairs." With my words, Addison's eyes go wide and she grips my wrist with a bruising force. My breathing is still unsteady, and my heart doesn't find a normal cadence either.

"I have to make sure it's okay. I'm going to find Eli," I tell her, and the mention of Eli seems to calm her down. Her cheeks are red, and tears still linger in her eyes.

"Stay here," I whisper and put my hand over hers. I squeeze it once before leaving her, crawling past the dead man, and taking his gun with me. I don't stand up until I'm past the door. Blood coats my pajama pants from where I crawled through it. Standing outside the door and staring at the stairwell, I breathe in deeply over and over, trying to calm myself.

Small shards of glass pierce my forearms and I pick them out, wincing as I do. The pain is nothing with all the adrenaline running through me, but still, I'm mesmerized by the bright red and the evidence of what we've just been through.

The moment I close my eyes, a phone rings behind me.

Ring, ring and my heart shudders in my chest. A shuddering as if being brought back to life. "Daniel," Addison's voice rings out clear, the moment I think Carter's name.

My throat goes dry as I swallow and hear her tell him how worried she was.

Carter didn't call.

It's not Carter.

It takes everything in me to step forward. The feeling of loss runs deep in my blood and I struggle to keep it together. One heavy step after another, with the gun in my right hand and my left hand gripping the railing, I walk down the steps quietly, hearing the faint sounds of Addison from the bedroom and nothing else in the house.

I may not have felt anything for the man I killed upstairs, nothing but hate, and less than that for the other man in the same black hoodie who died earlier today, but as I stand over Eli's dead body in the foyer, I cry.

Heavy sobs that bring me to my knees and steal the warmth from my body.

I can't breathe as my trembling fingers touch his throat, searching for a pulse, but finding none.

My feet kick out and I crawl backward, away from his body until my back hits the wall.

Covering my face in the crook of my arm, I can't stop crying.

His life was wasted on mine. Cason's life wasted on mine.

How much death can I be responsible for, before I lose any love I could possibly have for myself?

The opening of the back door, the slamming of the knob into the wall forces me to go silent. I hold my breath and crawl to the other corner as the footsteps quicken.

"Fuck, no," Daniel's voice carries into the foyer as he reaches Eli. "Shit," he breathes the word with true mourning before his heavy footsteps hit the stairs.

"Addison!" he cries out her name as my head hits the wall and my breath comes in staggered, sharp pulls.

The back door is still open, the wind carries through the house and the cool air calls to me like a siren.

I'm numb as I stand and make my way to the door, with trees lining the back of the yard, it's pitch black, but I can see there's no one here.

There's nothing here.

Nothing but the dark and the quiet as I take a single step out. And then another as the cold flows over my skin. And another.

The thoughts of how life has spiraled downward ever since I laid eyes on Carter Cross run through my mind. Or maybe ever since he laid eyes on me. It's hard to know which, really.

The thoughts consume me as I breathe in the cold air.

The thoughts... and then the hard chest that slams my back into it and the large hand that covers my mouth as I scream.

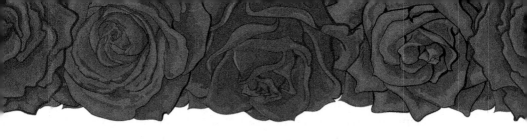

CHAPTER 21

Carter

I RECOGNIZE SOME OF THESE FACES. MEN WHO HAVE STARED AT me from a distance with hate but didn't have the balls to pull the trigger. I've passed so many of them on street corners as I drove past Carlisle and sometimes into Talvery territory over the years.

Bang!

I've imagined the bullet holes in their foreheads for years.

My blood is ringing with anger as I point the trigger at a man hunched behind the car and waiting with his back to me for one of my men to come into his view. He won't even see it coming. *Bang!*

Declan's iPad shows each of the streets, lined with dead bodies and riddled with bullet holes, broken glass and the shells of bullets that have stolen dozens of lives tonight.

War comes with a hefty cost and it's sickening but it fuels my need for vengeance.

"Four more on Second Street," Declan speaks into his mic.

Jase and I watch him carefully and keep an eye out on each side of the building we're stationed behind. Declan cheats at war, using surveillance that doesn't let a soul hide.

"Straight down from the street sign, head up the right side of the street and get them from the back. They're behind the—"

Shots ring out and I glance at the screen to see each of the four turning around too late. Their guns held in the air, aiming, but too slow to do anything before their bodies drop.

The night air is quiet.

It hasn't been more than thirty minutes since I've left, but the realization of how much time has passed since I've heard a word about Aria sends a tremor of terror rocking through me like a slow wave.

"We still have the two," Jase reminds me and tugs my arm to follow him.

Only two of Talvery's men are left. But he wasn't among them and neither was Nikolai.

The thought reminds me of Aria, crying on the bed as she confessed how she'll never forgive me if I killed them. How easy it would have been for the two of them to have died tonight at the hands of other men.

Swallowing the regret, I check my phone and see Cason's text that they're secured and safe. He sent it only ten minutes ago. *She's safe.* And at this moment, she's still in my grasp. That's all that matters.

I didn't realize I'd been holding my breath until I read that message and then the next, a text from Daniel saying that he was almost to the safe house.

Go straight to them, I text him and then add, *It's over. There's just a message left to send.*

Jase is peeking over my shoulder and his lip twitches as he mutters, "message to send," and then kicks in the back door, a door scarred with bullet holes. It reveals two men on their knees with a row of my men behind them.

"What are your names?" My voice bellows in the small room that looks like it was once used for entertainment. A busted bookshelf stands in the back left corner, board games spilling out over the floor and the projector screen straight ahead is littered with small holes.

Nearly every house on this block and the next will be just like this. The people were cleared out two days ago, bribed or threatened to leave, whichever method was more effective.

Jase crouches down in front of one of the two men and says, "If I were you, I'd answer my brother." The man behind him, the one pointing a gun at our captive lets out a single rough laugh and the man next to him follows.

"Fuck you," the old man says. He's on his knees and bent like that makes his stomach look even larger. He's got to be in his forties and as he spits at Jase's feet, the wrinkles on his face tighten. He nearly topples over without being able to put his hands out in front of him; they're cuffed behind his back, just like his friend to the right of him.

Jase stands up and moves to the next man, but when he does, my heart drops and a sick feeling spreads through my veins. "Where'd you get that hoodie?" I ask him and come closer to him, close enough to grab his collar and pull him up to look at his face.

He's younger with beady eyes and thin lips. He doesn't say anything at all, but there's a hint of a smile on his lips like he knows a secret I don't.

"You," my voice comes out harsh as I drop the asshole in the black hoodie and let him fall hard on the ground. He coughs up a laugh and I grab the old man's shirt, fisting it and the back of his head with my other hand.

"What's his name," I grit out the question and shake the old man, repeating myself in a scream that rips up my throat when he doesn't answer. "What's his name!"

"Fuck, I don't know!" The old man looks back at me like I've gone mad as I breathe heavily, my lungs heaving air.

"This one is Talvery," I drop the old man and move to the one in the hoodie, the one whose eyes are nothing but a well of blackness.

"This one is hired," I speak as I crouch in front of him, feeling my heart race.

"Talvery doesn't need to hire anyone." The old man speaks up until his executioner chambers a round and the click shuts him up.

"Where did you find this one?" I ask the man standing behind him. When I peer up, I see it's Logan.

He looks to his left and then to his right, stuttering to answer.

"Logan," I stand slowly, "Where did this one come from?"

"He was inside the line, shooting at the target, sir," another man speaks up.

"The target?" My heart pounds, but I remind myself that Daniel should be there.

"The safe house," the soldier clarifies.

A cold numbness runs through me as the man in the black hoodie, barely on his knees says, "My partner went in and finished what I started."

I turn to my brother, who's already on his phone. "Where's Daniel?" I ask him as my chest heaves for air. I squeeze the gun harder and when the fucker laughs at me, a deep laugh that chills the very marrow in my bones and fills the room, I whip it across his face, feeling the force of it splinter up my hand.

"Confirmed man dead in the safe house, wearing a black hoodie," Jase's response soothes the fear, bringing my rage down to a simmer.

"He's dead?" I ask Jase to tell me again as relief teases me.

"Addison said Aria shot him."

"She never fails to amaze me." As much as the pride fills me, there's nothing but rage that shows. Anger that they got close to her. To my songbird. They came close enough to hurt her. My fists clench tightly, spreading the thin skin across my knuckles as I breathe in slowly, deeply, seeing nothing but red.

"Daniel came up the south side, where there was less action and he's with Addison now."

I hear Jase's words, I know I do, but they don't register.

This man with the sick smile on his knees in front me, he conspired to hurt her. My stomach churns at the thought of how narrowly Addison and Aria escaped being hurt, or worse.

The first punch to his jaw, I don't even realize came from me. Not even as the skin across my knuckles splitting sends a pain up my arm. Again and again, I land punches across his face, listening to the cracking of bone in the deafening silence that fills the room.

The pulse of my racing blood is all I can hear. That and the sound of the man spitting blood across the floor as I grab him by the collar and roll him on his back to crouch on top of him. With his hands cuffed behind him, his back arches and he tries to roll back to his side, clenching and giving me daggers through his narrowed eyes.

"Who hired you?" I grit out the question and a beat passes, then another. He huffs a breath through his nose and the corners of his lips pick up in an asymmetric grin, displaying a ring of crimson blood around his teeth.

The fingers of my right hand crush his throat, forcing it to the ground and feeling his blood rush beneath my grip as I slam my fist into his face again. His eye is swollen and when I punch him again, I hear his nose crack and watch blood seep around his eyes, making them black although not nearly as black as the depth of his irises.

"How did you get past my men?" I scream the question, bringing my face close to his. The words tear up my throat, grating as they go and leaving a searing pain. All I can see is Aria, surrounded by men in black hoodies and before he can even answer, I slam my head into his, hearing the sickening crunch of his broken bones grinding against one another from the impact.

I have to release him, to get up and walk around him, staring at the man on the ground and picturing Aria standing over another just like him.

They got too close. Too fucking close.

"That one… that one I'd love to answer." I barely make out the words, they're spoken so softly. He coughs up blood, but then rests his head down on the floor, staring up at the ceiling. The man sways, barely coherent, but the smile still wishes to stay on his lips. It falters as he blinks slowly, his consciousness failing him.

Licking my lower lip, I steady my breath and bend down to get closer to him, gripping the back of his head. I grip onto his skull as I tug at his hair and force him to look at me.

"Tell me," I utter the demand gravely and his eyes flash with something. A look of delicious contentment. It's only then I realize how much I've shown him. How much I've shown everyone.

Aria is my everything. She alone has the will to turn me into a madman.

"Tell me," I push out the words through clenched teeth and feel my muscles coil, ready to assault him again, but he answers quickly this time.

"Every exit is an entrance."

My eyes search his, trying to register the meaning of his words. "I don't have time for—"

"Your little underground escape route… it was our way in. My job was easy, get outside and cause a ruckus, so my partner could do his job." He answers my unspoken question and seems to settle, so I grip his hair tighter, not giving him a moment of comfort.

"And what was his job?"

My heart beats faster, knowing they wanted Addison, but unsure of where Aria stands.

"Wouldn't you like to know," he mutters under his breath as his eyes roll into the back of his skull. I shake the fucker, waking him and stare into his cold gaze.

"Tell me." My command comes out low and vicious, my face getting closer to his as the life slips from him.

"I'll tell you one thing. It was only one girl a month ago, but then he upped it to two."

Bastards! My throat closes, and I struggle to stay where I am, my muscles burning to go to her. To Aria and to keep everyone away from her forever. No one will ever get to her. Never!

"Who did?" I don't know how I'm able to ask the question or to stay still as I wait for his answer.

"I'll die before I tell you," he replies, but then his head falls back. He's close to death already. Close, but not quite there yet.

"Logan," I say and raise my voice, but I don't look away from the man in my grasp. He'll soon be dead.

"Sir?" he asks hesitantly from somewhere to my right. I can hear his feet drag again the floor as he comes closer. "Brass knuckles?" I question him and then the sound of other men moving about registers.

"Someone," I say as I stare straight into my victim's icy gaze, "give me brass knuckles."

"Carter!" Jase shouts my name and rips my attention away. The warmth of blood splatters on my forearm and the man coughs in my grasp.

"What?" My question is sneered, pissed off that he would dare interrupt this. "He came after Aria!" I scream so loud; her name reverberates off the walls as I stare at Jase.

My chest rises and falls, my breathing coming in ragged and faster.

"Carter," Jase's voice is low but accompanied by the sound of the man in my grasp speaking at the same time.

"I couldn't wait to get them," he mutters beneath his breath.

"Carter!" My brother screams at me as I slam my fist into his jaw, hearing it crack as it dislocates. It dangles from his face and the sight only fuels me to take out more of my rage on him.

My shoulders are wound tight, needing more of a release as the asshole falls forward and Jase screams my name again. "Carter!"

"I'm not done with him," I grind out the words as I push Jase away from me, refusing to look at him and not the man who dared threaten my Aria. The man rocks on his shoulder, his face deformed and covered in blood. He has to roll forward to keep from choking on it or drowning in his own blood as he struggles to cough it up, but his movements are weak and slow. He's close. Too fucking close. I want him to live to see what true pain really is.

"Sir," Logan's voice is heard as a metal block is placed in my periphery. I've never smiled as sadistic of a smile as I do now.

"Should I do him the favor of killing him?" I ask no one in particular as I crouch in front of him and slip the thumb of my right hand over the brass that covers the knuckles on my left hand.

"Carter!" My gaze narrows as I peer up at my brother who's reaching out for me, reaching his hand out with a look that begs me to listen to him.

I don't take his hand, but I search his expression. He's worried, his eyes a pit of loss and despair. All the heat in my body suddenly feels doused with ice. A chill runs through me as I ask him with the last breath I have, "What?"

I barely register the painful groan the man, still barely alive, utters at my feet.

"What about Aria?" Jase asks me with a look of desperation and I finally hear the other men in the room. The war isn't over, and this place isn't safe now that it's been breached.

"I'm taking her home." I give him the only answer I can. It doesn't matter what she wants; a man got to her and that's unacceptable. Fuck! I grind my teeth and throw the brass knuckles into the torn projector screen when I remember the house was hit.

My body is shaking, vibrating with the need to protect her yet having my options limited. *I will protect her.* The very thought soothes me. She is mine and no one will hurt her. I'll never let anyone close to her again.

"I'll take her wherever I go." I give him my answer in a tone that brooks no further discussion, hiding the agony of what's devouring my every thought, but that doesn't change the look on his face. It doesn't remove an ounce of the fear in his expression.

"Where is she?" Jase asks, and my pulse slows, the adrenaline leaving me at the very thought of being with Aria tonight. Even if she hates me tomorrow.

"Daniel has her." I feel my brow furrow when I look at him, and everything slows. It slows and the world around us turns to a faded, blurred image. My heart beats once. He was just talking to Daniel. My heart beats again. "He has her," I repeat when Jase does nothing but visibly swallow and the already quiet room goes completely silent.

"No, he doesn't." I see nothing but red and everything turns to white noise as Jase tells me, "Aria's gone."

To Be Continued...

ENDLESS

BOOK 4

He holds a power over me like no one else ever could.

Maybe it's because my heart begs to beat in time with his.
Maybe it's because my body bows to his and his alone.
Maybe it's because he thought he loved me before he even laid eyes on me.

He thought wrong, and nothing has made me suffer like keeping that secret from him. He thought I belonged to him, but he was wrong. It was never supposed to be me.

Our memories are deceiving, but my heart is not.
I know exactly what I want.
What I need more than anything.
I won't rest until he's as much mine, as I am his.
It's always been him.

PROLOGUE

Aria

I ONLY KNOW WHAT TYLER LOOKS LIKE BECAUSE OF PICTURES. BUT even before then, when I first had the dream, I knew the boy was someone related to Carter. The Cross brothers all look so alike. He stared at me in the dream, his dark eyes piercing me even from across the field of blues and whites.

I should have been scared because I knew I didn't belong in this make-believe land conjured by my dream, but a soft smile lingered on his lips. Welcoming and endearing. He was kind. A kind soul among the flowers, although his words were anything but.

"She lied to you," he said casually. Words that etched confusion onto my face, but sent a prick of fear to chill my blood like ice.

It's only then that I heard my mother. I knew it was her instantly from her voice; we sounded so alike. A rustling noise came from somewhere on my right as she walked through the thick field. Her name begged to spill from my lips, rasping up from deep in my throat, but my voice was silent. And my body longed to move to her side, closer to where she was as she walked away slowly from me. But my limbs were still.

I was caught in place as they moved nearer one another, yet continued speaking to me, looking at me. As if they knew I was there even though I was held prisoner by whatever kept me immobile and quiet.

Tears leaked from the corners of my eyes and heated my skin as they rolled down my cheeks.

My father always spoke of my mother's beauty, and I knew it to be true, but she was older in the dreams than I remembered her to be. Age was more than kind to her though.

I tried to call out to her again, ignoring the boy, the Cross brother who had long since passed.

"I never lied," my mother spoke to me, but all I could feel was the way her words soothed my soul. It's been so long since I heard her voice. Too long. My fingers itched to move, to reach out to her and feel her embrace once more. I needed to be held so badly and my breath halted, imagining that she would come to me since I couldn't go to her, but she didn't.

Her hazel eyes were drenched in sorrow as she whispered, "I never lied to her." The biting wind carried her voice over the field.

As if her words were a cue, the sky darkened and dry lightning cracked it in two.

"Did you even love her?" the boy asked, looking up at her. "In all of this... did you even love her?" he asked my mother and the anger I felt was immediate, pushing the words up my throat although they still hung silent in the air. Of course she loved me. A mother always loves her children.

Even though the words had gone unvoiced, they both heard me and peered at me, judging my silent comment, but neither answered me. What I silently say to them changes each time the dream comes back, but the lack of an answer never does.

"Of course I did... I still do," she said and my mother's voice dragged with regret. "I died for her." She spoke clearly although pain riddled her words, and Tyler's expression only showed more agony as he shook his head.

With her head hung low, my mother pushed the hair from her face and delicately wiped the tears from under her eyes. The glossiness of her tears made her eyes more vivid and they called to me to ease her pain.

I've cried a thousand wretched screams, praying she could make out my words that I love her. That I miss her. But it doesn't change what happens next.

With the dark gray sky opening up and hard hail raining down on us mercilessly, pieces of the vision fall like a painting soaked in water. The colors smear and run together before fading to a blank canvas, and I'm left with nothing. Nothing but the sound of them arguing over her hate versus her love and what all really mattered the night she died. And another night... the night she changed the course of fate. She screams out that she died for me. Her confession is filled with a note of anger that burns through my veins.

But the last thing I always hear before I wake screaming, is her muttering, "We do stupid things for the ones we love."

No matter how many years pass, the nightmare never leaves me.

The first time it happened, I was in the cell. All those years ago when Carter, my love, first took me. But the visions have clung to me over the years, stained into my soul.

CHAPTER 1

Aria

"**D**ON'T SCREAM."
With my breath caught in my throat, my body paralyzed from the rush of fear forced into every inch of my body, I hear the voice, but I don't obey.

My scream is muffled by his large hand and he holds me tighter, pulling me closer into his hard chest, his strong fingers digging into my skin.

The sound of his voice shushing me as I kick out, butting my head uselessly against the wall of muscle I'm pressed to—that sound is what calms me. I've heard it before.

Daniel.

My body relaxes slowly, barely held up by my weak legs. Adrenaline still courses through my veins, but consciously I'm aware that it's him. The man who grabbed me and held me tight, *it's only Daniel.*

"Don't scream," he repeats, his lips close to the shell of my ear. So close that his warm breath tickles my neck and sends goosebumps down my shoulder. Too fucking close. He didn't just startle me; he scared the shit out of me.

I'm slow to remove my fingers from his forearm, one by one, knowing my sharp nails are digging into his arms. Blood is everywhere and so many stabs of pain race through my body, I'd rather be numb. Numb after everything that just happened.

It's only then that he loosens his grip and slowly moves in front of me, a hand still gripping my wrist.

"What are you doing?" The words rush from me in a single breath, but Daniel doesn't answer. As my heart pounds harder, he only observes me closely, noting my expression. The night air feels colder, and it's so much darker now that he's here than it was just a moment ago.

He looks behind me before meeting my gaze to ask, "Were you going to run?"

Of everything that he could have asked me just now, this question brings me more guilt than I'll ever admit. With Eli lying dead on the ground behind us, Addison upstairs somewhere, hiding from everything that's just happened, the fact I even thought about running makes me sick to my stomach. I could have. I could have run and left all of this behind like a horrid nightmare.

And I seriously considered it too.

"No," I whisper the word, not knowing if it's the truth or a lie. The nip of the evening air licks along my exposed skin as I stand in the open doorway of the safe house. The night is dark and unforgiving, much like Daniel's gaze. I can't hold it, knowing the emotions I'm feeling are written on my face.

Taking half a step back, I feel the pain of a small cut on my heel shoot up my leg, but it's nothing. Nothing compared to the pain of knowing what happened. All the small scrapes I got from the broken window, shattered from bullets, mean nothing.

War is here. The deafening sounds of gunshots have come and gone. But death has only just begun.

"What happened?" I voice the question with raw pain present in every whispered word. "Carter?" I ask him and open my eyes to meet his as they soften, then add, "My father?"

"Your father didn't come. Neither did Nikolai." His answer is clearly spoken and holds no pretense into what his thoughts are as his eyes roam over my face.

Before I can speak Carter's name again, feeling the familiar pain of loss already numbing my heart, he says, "Carter's fine. The Talvery men took a hit coming here. They should have known better."

Talvery men.

Men I'm supposed to be loyal to, and allies with. I don't know what to feel or who the real enemy is anymore. I just want it all to stop.

The breath I didn't know I was holding finally escapes, slipping through my parted lips as I lean against the doorway, letting the cool air drift along my heated face. But my throat is tight, the words and emotions tangled together and trying to escape me all at once.

"How many…?" I start to ask, but can't finish my question with the knot in my throat. *How many died tonight?*

"A lot," Daniel answers me and my eyes whip to his, demanding more. "Dozens, Aria."

I grip the top of my pajama shirt, balling the fabric together right at my chest, twisting it and wishing I could steal the pain away but it stays, growing with every beat.

I won't cry, even though a part of me wishes for nothing but to mourn. I've failed. And the very notion leads to a sarcastic response in the form of a hiss from the back of my mind. *As if you ever had the power to stop this.*

"Do you want to leave?" Daniel asks me, and the question is one I hold on to, craving the thought of running to take my mind elsewhere. Somewhere away from the thoughts of betrayal and mourning.

My lips part, but no words come out. Not at first. Daniel looks behind me once again, down the hall and to the front door of the large estate. He's waiting for someone to come, and I know deep in my gut this conversation needs to be finished before that person arrives. "I don't know," I answer him honestly and his gaze returns to me.

"You can go home. I'll make sure you get there safe. Or you can come back with us." He gives me the choice that's haunted me for weeks now. "There is no other way I leave you, Aria."

"Carter… he'll know you-"

"He thinks you're missing. He thinks your family took you back… or worse."

"They aren't my father's men." My head shakes vigorously, knowing he's speaking of the man upstairs and wanting to deny any ties to him. "That man was coming for us, both Addison and me, but I don't know him. I don't know who he is or what's going on, but he's not someone my father sent." Reaching out to him, I grab Daniel's jacket and he lets me, returning the gesture and shushing me once again.

"It doesn't matter. That's not the point." His words are more blunt and drenched with impatience I haven't seen from him before. Lowering my hand, I take a half step back as he tells me, "Right now, Carter thinks you've been taken by someone. But I can get you out of here, away from all this if it's what you want." My gaze falls to his throat as he swallows. The noises of the night are drowned out by the sound of my blood rushing in my ears at the thought of leaving Carter.

"You're offering me a way out?" *Thump.* My heart slams against my ribcage and I can't pinpoint which reason it's chosen in this moment to remind me it still exists. Either from the hope, or the fear of leaving.

Daniel only nods once before telling me, "Away from here and to your family, or wherever you want. You can go, Aria. I..." He struggles to complete his thought and turns away to cover his face with his hand before looking back at me. "I know you and Carter are on bad terms, and I..." He trails off again and swallows thickly before lowering his hand and looking me in the eyes.

He sees my pain, my agony; they're reflected in his dark gaze. "You can go. Or you can stay."

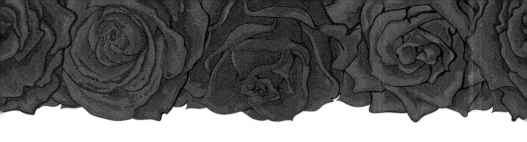

CHAPTER 2

Carter

TIME MOVES TOO FUCKING SLOW. THE DRIVE BACK TO Sebastian's place… every fucking roll of the tire is too goddamn slow.

If it weren't for the knowledge that I can pull the video feed from the security cameras on the property, evidence that will lead me to her, I wouldn't own a shred of sanity any longer. The phone in my hand is closer and closer to breaking as I bound up the steps and the anxiety grows. It's been in danger of breaking since the moment I first heard that Aria was missing. In danger of being splintered and thrown however far I could just to release the tension and pain still rippling inside of me at the thought of losing her.

"Where are the monitors?" I don't hide the anger in my tone the second the door is ripped open wide, Jase beside me, his footsteps barely keeping up with mine.

Before I can even scream at whoever's in here to get me the fucking tapes, I nearly trip over something on the floor. Stumbling forward, I barely catch myself. Eli. Fuck!

My throat closes and a sickness shoots through me. I can't help but reach to his throat and press my fingers against his icy skin. Even though he's cold, I still hope for a pulse. One second passes, and it hurts. Another second with nothing, and I can't fucking stand the cost of waging war. A war I choose to fight. All for her.

He's gone.

His eyes are closed and his blood is pooled around him. Jase has to step in a bit of blood to get around me and the bright red is smeared across the floor. We share a look as a few of our men come in behind us.

"Get him home." I give the command evenly, not revealing a shred of the emotions I'm feeling.

Control.

Eli dying is a reminder that I need control now more than anything. He will be missed and he will be mourned, but even he would tell me to focus on revenge right now.

"She's outside," Jase says and at first I don't understand what he's talking about until I turn to look over my shoulder. With the wind sweeping her locks off her shoulders and showing more of her skin, Aria glances at me.

She's here. She's safe. Relief is all-consuming for the briefest of moments.

I have her.

Those beautiful hazel-green eyes of hers swirl with a mix of pain and regret. Not the relief I've been envisioning since I was told she was gone.

"She's here." The words leave me without consent, buried under my breath as I slowly stand.

"Carter." Daniel's voice carries across the hall as I make my way to them. He steps in front of her, but I still see her face, not daring to break her gaze as my pace picks up.

"Where were you?" I'm only half aware of how hard my voice comes out and that it echoes in the hall. My heart thuds painfully in my chest as I brush Daniel aside to get to her, gripping Aria by her shoulder to pull her inside and slam the door closed.

Her feet don't move fast enough, but I couldn't care less. *What the fuck is she thinking?* Having the door open is welcoming danger.

"What the fuck were you thinking?" I say, and the words come out with a vengeance. Hating that she'd put herself in danger and be so fucking stupid.

"Get off," she says as she pushes me away. In front of everyone, she looks back at me wild eyed and as if I'm the enemy. Like I'm the one who's to blame for every ounce of turmoil that wreaks havoc inside of me.

A numbness flows through me as I regard her, all while she regards everyone else.

She wraps her arms around her shoulders and glances at my men behind me. It's then that I see what's captured her attention. The blood. It's everywhere. Soaked into the knees of their pants where they crouched on the floor and waited for more men to kill. Splattered on their shirts. My gaze falls to my own hands, stained with the blood of her family.

"I wasn't running…" Aria barely gets the words out before she stops and audibly swallows.

She doesn't run to me. She doesn't try to hold me. She glances at Eli and then pales.

As I look to my brother, the men behind me, and then to Addison slowly climbing down the stairs, the reality hits me.

She's still the enemy. She's not on my side. No matter how much I wish she were. *This war will break us.*

Aria's gaze travels the length of my suit, inventorying every bit of blood that's sprayed and spattered across it. Blood from men I've just killed.

I wish I knew what she was thinking. I wish I knew what to do.

Wrapping her arms tighter around herself, she looks at me with the silence surrounding us, suffocating us.

The only noise is the creaking of the stairs as Addison sneaks closer to Daniel.

"I wasn't running," she repeats. It sounds as if she regrets her words.

I don't know whether or not to believe her, but I know the feeling that seeps into my veins. Betrayal. And it comes from the woman I love, in the heart of war, in front of my brothers and army.

She left me once, and she'd do it again.

I imagined when I saw her, that she would run to me. That she would cling to me the same way I wish to cling to her.

The cold actuality is harsh and indisputable.

She's still a mistake—a drug I'm addicted to that's fucking up everything I've worked so hard for almost my entire life. I've never seen it more clearly than I do now.

If I didn't feel all of this for her, for a woman who chooses her family over mine, it would be all too easy. But why would she ever choose my family over hers? I don't know how I fell in love with her. It was nothing but a mistake.

It's in this moment I remember who I am.

A ruthless man with plans on tearing everything away from Aria's life, all because of who her father is and what destroying him does to her.

This isn't what I expected. I wanted to be her savior, her knight. But all I am is the fucking villain.

I'm as dead inside as I ever have been. And it's because of her. All of this bullshit is because of her. No, it's because I wanted her so badly I was willing to wage war, consequences be damned. Eli died, because of me.

"Whoever tried to take them knew her father was hitting us tonight." I speak loud enough for everyone to hear and leave Aria standing where she is.

A slow tide of agony fills my gut and rises higher until I taste bile in my throat. "I want to see the security feed, now." Two men run off, heading for the stairwell that leads down to the basement.

"Is the house secure?" I ask Daniel and he hesitates to answer me, his eyes narrowing as he glances between Aria and me.

His gaze speaks a thousand words, most of them begging for me not to be the man I was forced to become, but I'm the one who had to bear that burden, not him. He has Addison.

I have no one. Not until Aria has no one left but me. And even then…

Finally, he nods. "It's secure to return but it'll take weeks to repair, or longer."

"All men back there," I tell him and then look Jase and the other men in the eyes. "Fix the mess her father caused."

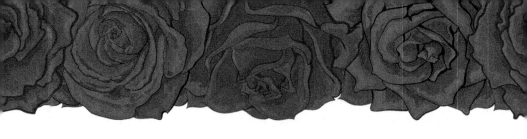

CHAPTER 3

Aria

"**Y**OU OKAY?" JASE ASKS ME AS WE STAND IN THE FOYER OF the Cross estate. Everyone was silent on the ride over here. Cars escorted ours in front and back, even on the sides when the road was wide enough. The security detail was hovering close around me, but it seemed more like guarding a prisoner than protecting an ally. Every minute that passed made me feel more and more like I didn't belong.

It made me feel like I'd made a mistake not leaving when I could have.

"Hey, you okay?" Jase asks me again as the men filter out of the foyer.

"You sure you should be talking to me?" I ask him in return and his huff of a laugh soothes a small part of my broken spirit. Without a doubt, I've fallen for Carter, but it wasn't until today that I realized how much I love his family too. Even while coated in the blood of my own family.

"It's tense, but everything will be all right."

"I don't know how you can think that," I answer him and my voice cracks. I know the men departing must hear how weak I am, and I hate it. This isn't the woman I want to be. Clearing my throat and focusing on the one thing I can confide in Jase about, I tell him, "He's angry with me."

"He was worried, Aria. We all were. We thought those men took you." It takes me a moment to realize what he's saying, to realize what Carter must've felt and guilt and insecurity weigh heavily against my chest.

So guilty. What have I done to bear all this guilt that has seeped into my gut?

"Besides, Carter's always angry." Jase tries to joke, to lighten the pain of what happened tonight. It doesn't help me though. There's nothing in this world that can help me now.

"I thought things were different," I whisper. But I didn't know this would happen. Deep down I knew it was coming, although I wanted to deny it. It's all coming to a head and I know I'm going to hate the outcome either way. There was never a thing that could have helped me. Not a damn thing that would have saved me. I'm a woman born to breed pain and misery. My last name demands it.

"We're still at war. A single battle was fought and men on both sides died. It's going to cause tension."

"Tension," I scoff, although it's not meant to come out in an offensive way. It's just that tension isn't a strong enough word to describe the animosity and uncertainty stretching the space between us. The pure agony stifling both of us.

"Aren't you the one who called us the enemy?" Jase asks, reminding me of the words I told Eli only hours before his death. The memory sends a trickle of regret down my spine.

"Is that not what we are?" I ask him back in a low breath, peering into his eyes and wishing he would tell me otherwise. Even if it is a lie.

A beat passes, and there's nothing but silence. I wonder vaguely if the other men can hear. Or if Carter is maybe listening. If he even cares to listen at this point. He didn't speak a word to me in the car. He sat in the front, not in the back with me.

Jase only nods solemnly but squeezes my hand, then adds, "Falling in love with the enemy is torture." With a sad smile that doesn't reach his eyes, he lets go. I'm forced to watch him leave me, walking down the foyer, his footsteps echoing in the empty hall until my gaze lands on the photograph at the very end. The black-and-white shot of a house that feels as if it's lingered in the back of my mind. The importance of it, my thoughts long to remember.

If I had a choice, I'd go there now, just to see why the image haunts me. It has to do with Carter, I know it does. And I need to know anything and everything that has to do with Carter.

Our families and pride may be at war, but not my heart. My

heart belongs to him. I know it with everything in me. It's why I could never leave him, even if the option was handed to me so easily.

But in this moment, it feels as if he's ripped it from my chest and thrown it out in the cold, leaving it there to die. Covered in my family's blood and ripping me from the doorway, slamming it shut and screaming at me as if I'm a fool wasn't at all what I expected.

Whatever point he wanted to make in front of his men, I'm sure they heard it loud and clear.

He doesn't love me.

How many times have I said, "I love you," to him and I was given nothing in return?

A parched sensation blankets my throat, so dry it's futile to try to swallow.

The sound of heavy footsteps coming closer to me from the doorway at the end of the long hall, makes my body flinch with each step. They're brutal and dominating. They belong to Carter, no doubt.

Confirming my thought, the brooding beast enters the hall, a bottle of whiskey in his left hand and a tumbler with ice in his right. He doesn't bother to hide how pissed he still is. Pissed at me, judging from his acrimonious glare. Again I find myself unable to swallow, but I can't help confronting him.

"What did I do to deserve this?" I bite out the words as he starts to walk past me, down to the hall leading to his wing and presumably his bedroom or office. "What the fuck did I do but merely exist in the painful life I didn't choose?"

My heart batters against my chest while I wish to either run with fear, or beat him with pent-up rage. I'm not sure which.

Even though my own legs feel weak and numb from everything that's happened tonight, keeping me planted where I am, Carter's move forward as he ignores my question.

How fucking dare he ignore me.

With my ragged voice raised, I scream at him until my face is hot. "What did I do to deserve this?"

It only takes three strides before Carter's powerful presence is towering over me, and I nearly stumble backward. Nearly, but I keep my ground. I'm breathing chaotically and waiting for him to give me something. Anything is better than being ignored, made to feel like I don't even exist.

"Where do I start, *Miss Talvery*?" His voice is low as he moves down until his face is eye level with mine. He practically sneers my name and it shreds me from the inside. "You pointed a gun at me. You stand with your ex-lover and your father who have tried to kill me, not once, not twice, but every chance they get. Including the time one week ago, by said, fucking, ex, in which you knew what was happening but said nothing." The last word is sneered. He inhales deeply, pausing as pain rips through me.

I worry my bottom lip between my teeth before I bite down on it hard. The physical pain is vastly preferable to the emotional pain that boils inside of me at his aggressive attitude.

Carter already knew all of that when he fucked me the other night. When he held me like he loved me. Nothing has changed for me, and I don't deserve this. I love him. I've chosen him time and time again. The fact I'm still here after everything is proof of that.

"And then you tried to run," he adds and I whip my hand across his face. It's purely out of instinct, generated by his arrogance and the way I feel used and defiled by him. My palm smacks hard against his chiseled cheek and my fingers follow.

His face is like fucking stone. My hand throbs with a stinging, burning pain and as I wince, my eyes stay on Carter's unmoving expression. It didn't affect him in the least. All of the sickness and hurt that ache inside of me, I feel it all and he feels nothing.

Nothing.

"I didn't," I tell him, knowing I didn't try to run. It was only a passing thought and I won't be accused of anything more than that. Not when everything is stacked against us and I'm doing everything I can to stay by him. Even when he stands firmly against me.

Time passes and he merely stares at me, judging me, but I let him see the pain. I want to hide myself in this lonesome tower he's put me in, but I stand in front of him with my hands in fists by my side and beg him to feel what I feel. And to take it away.

"I don't deserve this, Carter," I say and my voice is strangled.

Please just take it all away. I wish he could do that for me. However it entails, I don't want to feel this way for a second longer.

"I thought they'd taken you," he continues to talk with a look of disgust on his face, even though pain is etched into his words. "But you were just sneaking out to run away. What a fucking fool I was," he sneers.

"You are a fucking fool." I mimic his mocking tone, refusing to give him all of me when he chooses to believe otherwise. Holding my hand, which has started to go numb, I back away from him, knowing this battle is over and both of us have lost. "I wasn't running," I tell him the truth and then add, "And I won't say it again." The strength in my voice comes from some part of me deep inside. The part of me that knows I could stand beside this man. The part desperate to do exactly that.

His gaze assesses me, scrutinizing my expression.

"I'm not lying, Carter. I have no reason to lie to you." I let my voice soften, to show him the vulnerability. "I love you. Even through all this, I can't stop loving you. Yes, I had a chance to run, and I didn't take it. I wanted to stay with you."

My heart flickers in my chest, barely holding on to life as Carter's expression doesn't change, then another second passes and another.

"You don't believe me?" I say weakly with disbelief.

"You've hurt me once. Right there," he says then gestures with his hand behind me, to the hall that leads to the room where I held a gun to his head. "How can I believe you?"

"If you didn't think you could believe me," I say to try to numb the pain growing inside of me, like a ball of bile that drops in my stomach, "then why bring me back here?" All I can think is that he doesn't love me. He doesn't anymore.

Silence.

It's unbearably silent as my stomach churns while Carter walks off, leaving me without an answer. Without telling me that he loves me, even though I'm the fool who spoke those words to him.

Carter

My phone is constantly ringing, pinging, vibrating. Constantly distracting me from life itself and reminding me that I'm in control. It never lets up. Even now, the instant I turn notifications back on I'm flooded with alerts.

Every second the car moved and she said nothing—my Aria said nothing at all, not one fucking word to me or anyone else—every second of silence that passed only made the hate for what she'd done grow. She may not have been with her father or his men. But she sided with him nonetheless.

My phone goes off again, vibrating in my hand and it rattles against the cut crystal tumbler. With the adrenaline and anxiousness still ringing in my blood, my grip tightens, feeling the hard metal of the phone digging into my flesh as I open my bedroom door.

I need a fucking minute. One goddamn minute to take control again.

The incessant buzzing in my hand mocks me and I slam the door shut behind me, feeling my muscles tighten and the air thin as I struggle to keep my breathing steady.

Setting down the tumbler and bottle of whiskey on the dresser, I glance at my phone, unable to simply shut the fucking thing off.

It's Sebastian.

The intensity dims, the heat subsides. He always has a way of showing up when I need him most.

I heard what happened, his message reads and as I stare at his text, another comes in. *I know you'll probably say the same as always, that you don't need me to come back, but I have to ask. Do you want my help?*

I stare at the last line, taking in the word "want." When Sebastian left, it was a while before we talked again, given everything that changed the very next day. The day I had my unfortunate introduction to Aria's father.

I thought you were busy with Chloe and work? I write back then press send, still staring at the word "want."

He's asked a few times, when shit got rough over the years, if I needed him to come back.

"Need" being the operative word. And back then, knowing what happened between him and Romano, I never would have allowed him to come back and risk a damn thing. Not with a girl by his side. The girl who is now his wife, not to mention very much pregnant.

The guard job is over; it was just a summer gig.

He never stopped traveling. They moved from place to place when they ran from our hometown. He had enough money to keep them afloat until they found a bed and breakfast to hide away in, located on a huge cattle farm. He's been there for a while and it took him a long time, not until last year, nearly ten years after leaving this place to come back. The farm's shut down, the land's sold, and Chloe's pregnant. He has no reason to come back, not with the money he still has and the extra he makes doing security detail work. But I know he longs to come home, especially given Romano has no control here anymore. Even if he doesn't want to admit the one thing that's really held him back is Chloe.

I thought you said you and this city just don't mix. I can't help asking, pushing him away further and knowing full well what I'm doing.

Do I want him back? Yes. I need him now more than ever. Every piece of what I've built is crumbling and a part of me, the part that's very much alive, wishes desperately that I could do what he did. That I could take Aria and simply run. To leave this shit behind, and make it just Aria and me. No one else, no problems, nothing but what we pack in a car before taking off. If I could trade places with him, I would.

But I have my brothers to look after, and consequences to suffer.

At one point, Sebastian was like the older brother I never had. And when he came here to see the safe house last year, I thought he'd stay. I should have known better. The world changed when he left, becoming darker, colder, and he didn't want it for Chloe.

I knew I was descending deeper and deeper into the pits of hell, a misery of my own making, when I watched them drive away. He said he'd be back, but it's been roughly a year. A year of messaging off and on. And a year that's changed everything.

I don't care what I said before. I want to come back, Carter. You need my help.

Aria

It takes a long time for me to move from where Carter's left me. Daniel comes to check on me, to tell me Addison's in the study if I want company. He's not nearly as soft toward me as he was back at the safe house. I appreciate it either way though.

The thought of facing Addison though, knowing how she has Daniel and I don't have Carter… I can't take it right now.

Jase comes by again, although he doesn't speak. He only squeezes my shoulders and offers me a weak smile that I return with a shake of my head.

Even Declan comes by and tells me he'll make me something to eat if I want, but I know I would throw it up if I could even manage to take a bite of anything at all.

It takes me a long, long time before I start walking down to Carter's wing. The idea of staying in the hideaway room offers a small bit of comfort. I could be alone and break down where the only person who would see is Carter, if he bothered to check on me.

But I don't want to hide—even if I do want to be alone. Time is precious and I don't want to live like this.

I'm halfway to Carter's bedroom when my pace picks up. His door is closed, and I'm scared it will be locked when I grip the carved glass knob, but it turns easily for me.

Too easily, even.

The savage man I love is standing at his dresser, the whiskey bottle still sealed in front of him. But shattered glass scatters moonlight around the room as the curtains sway from the air blowing through the vents, letting in glimpses of the light.

It looks as if he must've slammed the glass down too hard and with another step into the room, my eyes assessing his hand as I close the door behind me, I can see the cuts that line his skin.

From the glass, or from earlier today, I'm not sure. Maybe the mixture of wounds is from both. The reminder he's killed men today, men who may have protected me in the past, men who I've had dinner with, men who have fought for my father for years, settles an eerie chill in my bones as the door clicks shut and Carter's dark eyes peer back at me from over his shoulder.

There's a slam of fear in my chest, but it's gone quickly as Carter turns his head forward again toward the bottle, not even bothering to look at me for more than that split second.

And then I'm given more silence.

In that moment, I almost turn and walk away. I almost run out of the room. Almost… but I don't. I have a voice, and I'm going to use it.

"I'm not going to stay here as a prisoner. If you don't want me, I'm leaving." I don't know how I manage to say the words so clearly, but I do. I hold on to that small accomplishment as Carter answers me.

"I have a right to be angry." There's no menace in his voice at all. Merely truth.

"You don't have a right to treat me like I'm nothing," I dare to respond with a harshly spoken whisper.

"Did it even cross your mind that maybe I was dead?" he asks, slowly turning to face me. His eyes are tired and his voice wretched.

"Yes," I answer him quickly as my breathing catches in my chest, remembering all the worry the gunshots crying out in the night brought me.

"And what did that do to you?"

"It made me angry… angry that you didn't call." I swallow thickly, remembering how I held the phone. "I messaged you and you didn't bother to give me any sign at all that you were all right or that you cared." I confess a raw truth, baring more of myself to him, "And it hurt in every way possible. Every piece of me went numb thinking you were out there… that you were gone like Eli was." It feels wrong even speaking of Eli right now. His memory should be honored and not brought up like this.

"Daniel had already told me you were all right." I hope that truth eases something in him as I realize at least one of the reasons why I'm angry. "I knew you were all right and even if I was mad that you were ignoring me, I promise you I couldn't have felt more relief at finding out that you were okay." Every time I turn soft for him, I lose that hard edge that makes me his equal. I know it, yet I do it every time.

Carter's quiet for what seems like an eternity, as if registering what I may have been feeling for the first time. Please, I pray he'll understand. With so much against us, we need to understand each other if nothing else.

"I thought you were dead and I was ready to kill anyone who stood in my path to find you, Aria. And yet, when I got there, you didn't..."

"I didn't what?" I question him with a raised voice, begging him to tell me everything. With a hesitant step forward, I stop when he answers.

"You didn't react to seeing me."

"What did you want from me?" I ask him, honestly not knowing what he wanted. "You grabbed me like I was a child acting up." Instinctively, my hand moves to my forearm where he ripped me from the doorway and yanked me inside of the house.

"You didn't even ask if I was all right," he spits at me, condemning me for not comforting him when I'd just witnessed more death firsthand than I ever have in my life.

"There was death everywhere around me, and I knew my family was out there but-"

"It's your family you care about!"

I'm taken aback by the venom in his words. "You already knew I loved them and that I didn't want this-"

"I would do anything for you. I would kill for you. I feel like I would die without you. Yet when I got to you... all you wanted was for me to let you go."

"Carter, you don't understand."

"No, I don't." His answer is hard and unmoving.

"I'm sorry," I say, giving him an apology I truly mean. "I didn't want to upset you; I'm just not okay right now... and I was even worse earlier."

Carter's expression softens slightly, but I can tell he's holding on to his reservations. I know he doesn't trust me. I've lost his trust completely and it makes me feel trapped and desperate, needing him to give me a chance.

"I'm sorry. Do you believe me?" My question is pleading as I take the few small steps needed to stand in front of him. I swear he can hear my heart pounding as I dare to tell him, "If I could go back, I would. I would make sure I gave you what you needed, even as I dealt with all of this... this agony inside of me."

I'm careful as I raise a hand and cup his jaw. His five o'clock shadow is rough against my fingertips. The anger wanes from him as I rub my thumb up and down his cheek.

"I'm sorry. I didn't want any of this to happen, but I don't want to lose you." My words slip from me easily, raw, transparent and true. I mean every word of it.

Carter takes a step to his left, closer to the bed and says under his breath, "There's no room to be sorry in this life."

Crying is something I'm done with. I swallow down the spiked pain and embrace it rather than succumb to weakness. A second passes as Carter strips out of his shirt, unbuttoning it and then tossing it onto the floor.

He may have grabbed me earlier as if I was a defiant child walking out recklessly into a busy street, but right now, he's the one acting like a child.

"You just want to be angry with me, don't you?" I pause my thoughts as he removes his cotton undershirt, stained with blood too. "There's nothing I could say or do to change your mind. You want to be pissed at me."

He looks at me from over his shoulder, a derisive glance. "Why would I want that, little songbird?"

"Because if you aren't angry, you'll have to deal with everything else that's brewing inside of you. If you aren't a beast, then you have to be a mere mortal and deal with what you're feeling." I spew the words, not even conscious of them until they've left me.

"Ever the artist, aren't you?" He makes light of the truth, not willing to admit how accurate my words are as he turns to me and stalks closer, wearing nothing but his pants. His hardened muscles ripple in the dim light and his dark eyes seem bright with a challenge.

"Make light of it all you want. You simply want to be angry with me." He takes a large step forward and I take a small one back, not letting him get close enough to touch me. "And I'm fine with it, so long as you know it's bullshit and that I'm very aware of what bullshit it is." I spit out the last words, hating him for what he's doing. He's using his rage as a buffer to maintain his veneer of control. And it's not fair. "I love you, Carter Cross. I chose you." I have to add in the last statements, if for no other reason than to be honest with myself. Even now, I still love him. He's ruthless; an uncaring and brutal asshole. And I'm the fool who loves him and wants him to give up a piece of his armor, knowing I'll protect that part of him with everything I have.

"You didn't choose me," he insists and I start to respond, but he continues. "Choose me now, and kneel."

My pulse quickens at the look in his eyes. I've seen it before, so many times. And I'm grateful for the change. Hopeful to reach the man I love through this veil of hate.

I look him in the eyes as I obey him. The blood that rushes through my veins heats with desire. There wasn't a single part of me that hesitated.

He crouches in front of me, bringing him to eye level, and my gaze stays pinned to his. The depths of his dark irises ignite with power, with a primal need.

Take from me, Carter. Take what you need and what's left of me will still love you.

Spearing his fingers through my hair, he makes a fist and forces my head to tilt. My breath hitches with the sudden grip, and my body bows to his. There's barely a hint of pain; it's merely him taking control as he crashes his lips to mine. My hands reach up instinctively, bracing either side of his jaw as he ravages me.

The kiss is everything. It's warmth. It's home. It's a touch that awakens the pieces of me that have been silent and waiting for him to come back. I moan into his kiss, wishing I wasn't in this position so I could lean into his hold, so I could take more of him and show him how desperate I am for us to go back to what we were.

But there's no way we could ever go back.

You can never go back.

My lips feel swollen and bruised by the time he releases me, slowly loosening his grip. My chest heaves for air, and I love it. When I peek up at him, my vision hazy with lust, I see his eyes closed and his own lips parted as he takes in a steadying breath, then opens his eyes to pin me in place.

The gaze of a hunter, a predator even, stills my beating heart.

In the pale light of the early morning trickling through his curtains, the soft shadows line his jaw and make him look even more domineering.

He stands slowly, leaving me where I am and I can see his thick length as he does, pressing against his pants.

He paces in front of me, deliberating on what to do next, and I'm eager to find out.

"You'll pay for what you did."

"What I did?" The question is spoken with confusion. I have to blink away the desire as fear creeps in.

"Raising a gun to me. Standing in opposition to me." He doesn't hold any anger in his words. Only truth and certainty.

"I thought I already did." My voice is choked as I gasp out the words.

"You lost my trust."

I can only nod, not trusting myself to speak. I think about everything he's done to me since the first night I laid eyes on him. How he's deprived me, lied to me, locked me away and punished me with both pleasure and pain.

"Holding grudges hardens the heart," I murmur to myself, but my words are for him as well.

"I don't have a heart, songbird." His response is quick, but so is mine.

"I don't like it when you lie to me."

It's quiet for a moment. Carter's mind is made up for tonight. But we have time. I don't know how much, but there's always hope. And I know my soul speaks to his. My soul is desperate to stay with his. It's the only truth that matters. *I need him.*

"If you're staying in my bed tonight, you're going to have to satisfy me." As Carter speaks, my gaze is drawn to his strong jaw and then to his throat. I watch as his chest rises and falls and he stands in front of me, unbuckling his belt. The sound of the leather hissing in the air as it's pulled through the loops makes my pussy heat and clench.

"I'm staying with you," I tell him with a mix of defiance and the greedy need to be taken by him. I can't help but think he just needs to be touched. To be loved. To be given free rein over me and to *feel* how much I need him. *This* is what we need.

He doesn't speak as he unzips his pants and then lets them fall to the floor with a soft thud.

His cock bobs in front of me, swollen and each vein protruding. I can practically feel his thickness pulsing inside of me already. He may need this, but I know I need it too. I need to be loved. Loved for the person I am, by this man and this man alone.

"Lie on the bed on your belly," he commands me and I'm eager to move.

I want to make this right between us however I can.

And if this is how he chooses, to command me, defile me, degrade me in his bed, I'll obey him without objection. Because I fucking love it too.

As I crawl up the bed, stripping as I go and tossing the clothes on the floor, I hear Carter open a bedside drawer. I'm not sure what it is he's getting, but I don't care. I just want him. However I can get him.

With a cheek pressed to the pillow, I lie still on the bed, naked and waiting for him to do as he pleases. I know he won't hurt me. Not like this. His words are venomous, and his deprivation of affection is torturous, but here, like this, he won't hurt me. I know he won't. Whether he says it or not, a piece of him loves me more than his entirety could ever hate me.

The bed dips in time with my heart at the thought, and Carter climbs on top of me, his hard erection digging into my thigh as he leans over me. His fingers trail up my side and make my whole body shiver. He gently pulls back the hair over my ear to kiss my neck, giving me goosebumps that cause my nipples to harden and a shudder to run down my shoulders.

"You think you love me, Aria," he whispers in a threatening tone that turns my blood to ice. "Let me show you exactly what kind of a beast I can be."

Letting my hair fall back into place, he sits up straighter and the air around me suddenly feels colder without him there any longer.

My heartbeat quickens, but I ignore the lingering threat and welcome whatever he wants to do to me. He is mine, and I am his.

A click sounds in the air at the same time a sudden coldness hits my ass. It's wet and slick, and it takes me a moment to realize what it is.

Carter drizzles lube over my ass and then runs his finger down to my forbidden entrance. Heat rolls through my body and I struggle to stay still, knowing what he's going to do.

He takes his time, teasing me, stretching me, pushing himself in and out for what feels like too long. I can't take it. I can't stand waiting any longer, knowing what he wants and what he's going to take from me.

"Carter," I say and his name is a plea on my lips. My head moves from side to side as he shushes me.

He presses his head inside of me and it's already too much. I jump away from him, my teeth clenching.

"Push back," he commands me and then adds as he slips inside of me, "Push back right now."

My hips tilt up slightly, although only because of his grip on them and I do what he says, but it's so much. Too much. My body blazes with the forbidden touch.

I'm so hot. So full already. Every inch of my skin tingles as I try not to writhe underneath him. With one of his hands on my hip and the other gripping my shoulder with a bruising force, he slams all of himself inside of me in a swift, unforgiving thrust.

The pain of being stretched this way for the first time forces me to bite down on the pillow as tears flood and sting my eyes. I can feel him pulse inside of me, growing harder and larger and it's too much. It's all too much.

My body's on fire, alternated with freezing cold as he moves behind me at a slow, but relentless pace.

"Carter," I whimper his name as the overwhelming sensation begs me to move away but then, with just as much need, to push back and take more of him this way.

My clit rubs against the comforter beneath me and I moan. A single moan of utter pleasure, my body choosing it over the pain. Carter takes it as his cue to pick up his pace, ruthlessly fucking my ass and shoving my body down into the bed with each hard pump.

"Fuck," I moan out and he responds with a low groan from deep in his chest.

My fingers dig into the comforter, my nails scratching along the threads as my head thrashes and I struggle to breathe. Pleasure and pain mix in a cocktail I'm already drunk on.

He whispers at the shell of my ear, "You're such a dirty whore for me." At the same time, he shoves his fingers inside of my pussy and presses his thumb to my clit.

Holy fuck!

My mouth hangs open with a silent scream of ecstasy. The pleasure ripples through my body and paralyzes me as he thrusts behind me, pistoning his hips and filling me to the point where it's nearly too much with both his fingers and his cock. I've never felt like this. So full, so hot, so consumed by bliss.

He fucks me harder once my orgasm begins to wane. He doesn't stop, not even when he sinks inside of me so deep that I feel like he'll split me in two. I try to spin around out of instinct and push him away.

Instantly, Carter stops. Barely keeping himself inside of me, he tells me with a cold gaze, "Keep your hands down." There's no desire in his voice, no sense of mercy or love. Nothing but anger that I've dared to push him away.

It's a shock to my system. Seeing him like that while I feel nothing but desire and love is sobering. An icy gust sweeps through me even as he changes his expression, softening it and gently pushing my shoulders back to the bed.

"It's too much," I whisper and although the pain is gone, the intensity of what we had has vanished.

"Lie back down," he commands me in a way that leaves a deep fracture in my heart. I can hear it splinter as I return my cheek to the pillow.

He doesn't touch me again; he doesn't resume fucking me. He doesn't allow himself to cum.

Instead, he gets up and moves away from me. I try to keep from crying as the pleasure from my orgasm withers to nothing while he enters the bathroom and flicks on the light.

I feel alone in this moment, broken and used. Utterly alone. It reminds me of the last time we were together, of him tying me up and not fucking me. Instead he left me after torturing the truth out of me.

Is that all this was? More torture?

I stay still as he wipes me down and returns to the bathroom. My chest feels hollow and it's hard to swallow. Maybe I didn't lose him tonight. Maybe I lost him that night when I told him I would never forgive him. Maybe I lost him the moment I picked up the gun and I've only just now seen it.

All I know right now is that I feel like I've lost him.

Refusing to cry, I bite the inside of my cheek and listen to him walk back to the bed after turning off the light. The bed creaks as he gets in beside me. He doesn't crawl under the sheets he laid on top of me, and I don't move from where I am. I'll wait for him.

He loves me. I know he loves me, but why does it feel like he doesn't at all? *Why do I feel like I'm lying to myself?*

"I love you," I whisper and chance a look at him. The sun has risen and he can't hide in the darkness. His eyes are tired and his face looks older than it ever has before.

I watch his throat bob as he lies back in the bed and says nothing. He says nothing.

More silence. And that's the last bit I can take.

Licking my dry lips, I realize his intention was simply to hurt me, at least in that moment I turned around, the moment where it was too much. I'm quick to get up and move away from him, pushing the sheets aside.

His grip is hot, burning into me as he wraps a strong hand around my hip and pulls me into his hard, chiseled chest.

"You know I care for you." He says the words sternly, but he doesn't look at me. Not at first. The pounding in my chest rises to my throat until his eyes find mine, swirling with pain.

The chaos warps and twists inside of me. I'm hurting for him, a man who feels betrayed and doesn't know what to do because every time life has given him a challenger, he's simply murdered them, yet here I stand.

But I'm also in pain. For falling for a man so merciless and heartless as Carter.

"Don't ever do that again," I say, barely keeping my voice from breaking. "Don't ever treat me like I'm nothing to you."

"Is that a threat?" he asks, still not looking at me.

"No. Not a threat, a promise. Carter, look at me." My voice sharpens and his eyes find mine. "If you ever do that again, I'll leave you." It takes everything in me to tell him that, because I know it's true. And I'm worried it will happen. It feels so close to being inevitable.

"Do what exactly?" he asks me, daring to play as if he doesn't know. As if he doesn't realize how much he's hurt me tonight.

"Fuck me just to prove how willing I am for you to have me. Walk by me as if I'm meaningless in your life." I nearly choke on my last words, remembering how I felt in the foyer. "Treat me like I'm not worth sparing a glance."

"First, I wanted you. I fucked you because I wanted you." His tone is sharp until he adds, "But something… changed."

"Something?" I ask him, but he doesn't answer me. He keeps on speaking as if I hadn't voiced the question at all.

"What was it like to hold a gun to my head?" he asks, and his voice is thick with emotion. "Did you think it made me feel like I meant something to you?" He doesn't hide the pain behind a mask of cold indifference. I can hear him swallow and for the first time, he shows me everything in his expression. I've hurt him so deeply and I didn't even know.

"Carter, don't…" I start to say, inching closer to him although he stays perfectly still. "I was just trying to survive," I say, begging him to understand. "If I could take it back-"

"You wouldn't," he cuts me off, and I know he's right. Under that circumstance, I wouldn't allow him to murder my friends and family. It's fucked up how much that very knowledge guts me. There's no way for me to make it out of this alive.

"You were just surviving. Maybe pretending that you mean nothing to me is a way for me to just survive."

I'm struck by his confession, and I hate it. I hate the lives we have, and how fate has put us in each other's path.

"Please don't do this, Carter." My throat is tight as despair claws its way up. "I know we're broken, but stop this. Don't do this again. Don't make it worse."

"I can't make it better," he rebuts.

"Tell me you care for me again," I whisper, getting closer to him and ignoring the pain that still lingers. When I walked back into Carter's grasp, easily letting him take me back here, I had no idea that we were so broken. How could I have been so fucking foolish to think that loving him was going to fix it all? As if it could put a stop to the war, rewrite the past, and make us invincible for whatever lies ahead.

He tells me he cares about me after a moment, but then he tells me a truth I hadn't dared to admit I already knew until he spoke the words. "I wish I didn't. It would all be easier if I didn't."

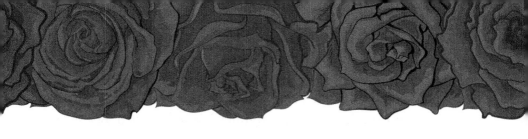

CHAPTER 4

Carter

E very time I thrust inside of her, I remembered the confessions she made the other night. How she told me she'd be with Nikolai if I wasn't in the picture, and how she'll never forgive me. She meant them. She still does.

Being inside of her is heaven, but last night, it was hell. There was no way I could have taken any pleasure in her. Not when all I can think is how she's going to hate me when this is over. There's no way I'm going to be able to keep her. It's fucking impossible.

A numbness spreads through my hand as I form a fist, letting the cuts split open and feeling the pain rip through my knuckles. Leaning back in my office chair, I clench and unclench my hand again and again, just to feel something else.

I've never wanted to forget so much. To erase the mess I've gotten us into. To run away with her and start over.

It's a pain I've never felt and a position I never considered I'd be in. Because I've never felt this way about anyone else. No one else has meant so much to me before. Not even my brothers.

I don't know how we're going to make it out of this together. And I've never wanted anything more.

The long strand of pearls that starts out with small spheres growing in size until they reach the center, stares back at me from its velvet box on the desk. The iridescence shines off the polished pearls, stealing my gaze. They mesmerized me, as did my Aria. Anything that can keep my attention should belong to her.

I needed to replace her previous necklace with one she could wear forever. This necklace is timeless and even if she leaves me, I pray she'll keep it forever. I pray that what we had will be endless, even if us being together is only a dream I could dare to return to in my sleep.

As I hear Aria's footsteps patter closer to my office right before the door creaks open, I shut the velvet box. Aria's eyes are still puffy and red from lack of sleep, and her lips are swollen. She grips her sleepshirt with one hand and playfully knocks on the door even though it's open and our eyes have already met.

She attempts a smile, but it disappears as quickly as it came. Fuck, it hurts. I want nothing more than for her to be happy. Truly happy with me, with the man I am and will always be.

"I wasn't sure if you wanted me to dress," she barely speaks before adding, "since there weren't any clothes laid out."

I watch her throat as she swallows, and again she balls the thin cotton of her sleepshirt in her hand. She doesn't wear it in bed, only when she leaves the bedroom. The tension in the air is thick, and it makes my fingers go numb again and prick with anguish.

"You still want me to?" I ask her and she nods swiftly and without hesitation. I love this submissive side of her, this trusting side. I love that she wants this side of me. Even more, I love that I can so easily give her what she wants.

"I like it when you do things like that," she answers.

With a single nod, I stand up and make my way to the other side of the desk, swallowing down the lump and remembering that I need to be in control at all times. For her, and for the sake of my family and everyone else relying on me. Aria stands where she is, looking lost and insecure.

I hate it, even though I know I'm the reason for it all. I could easily bring her back into my arms and love her. But it would only end in her hating me, in her breaking me and destroying the last bit of my sanity.

If it ends this way, slowly, and with a growing chasm between us, it'll be easier to accept. For both of us.

"For you," I say and hold out the black box for her to take, and only then does she step forward. As the box creaks open, I move the chair to face her and take a seat, explaining as my back hits the smooth leather, "It's your birthday gift."

She forces a small smile to her lips, but the sadness lingers there. "It's beautiful," she says, although she doesn't look at me. "What happened to my other... necklace?" Instinctively, her hand reaches for her collar, to the place where the diamonds and pearls used to lay.

"It's where you left it," I tell her and then glance at the box, still pushed against the wall but not lined up exactly with where it normally goes. I don't want it to go back to where it was. I want to remember. I *have* to remember. My gut churns at the memory of how I felt, sitting in this very chair, while she locked herself in that box. I'm sickened by all the hate and anger I had, but more than that, the realization that what I wanted would never be.

"Are we okay?" Aria's gentle question, laced with both want and fear, brings my attention to her gorgeous face.

"I don't know that we'll ever be okay." My answer is instant and calmly spoken as if it's a certainty. "But that doesn't make you any less mine."

"I don't know what I can do, Carter." Aria's voice is wretched as she stares at the pearls, her fingertips barely skimming along each one. "I want to make this right."

"This was never going to be right, Aria. It wasn't right what I did, and what I'm going to do... it's not right to you." I don't like the way my words come out. As if I'm letting her go, because I'm not. I won't be the one to break things off, but I know she'll leave me.

It's inevitable.

"You don't get to decide what's right for me." Her answer is sharp, that defiance I love slicing through the painful truth even she can't deny: We were never meant to be.

"You're still angry at me, aren't you? For grabbing the gun." Her voice wavers as she adds, "I'm sorry, Carter." Her words are rushed and she barely breathes as she takes a single step toward me, closing the space until I reach out to take her waist in my hands. I could pull her into my lap, but I don't. I keep her right where she is, at arm's length.

"I know you are," I tell her solemnly.

"Does this mean you don't forgive me?" The pain isn't hidden in the least. Not in her words, or the way her hands hold on to mine, not in the shades of amber and jade in her eyes.

"It's not about forgiveness, Aria. I understand why. I respect it, even. But it would happen again. You would do it again." I speak to her without reservations. She'll come to the same realization I have. She will, even if it hurts her with the same pain it does me.

"You're the one who put me here. Who put me right in the middle, Carter. You could lock me in the cell, and then I wouldn't be in the way." She pleads with me, wanting me to take away her freedom and the woman she was always meant to be just so I can have her.

"You're the one who wanted out of your cage to fly away. Isn't that right?" I know it doesn't change anything. Giving her freedom only to be disappointed with what she does with it, doesn't change a damn thing between us.

"You're the one who didn't clip my wings," she says and the hazel concoction in her eyes begs me to fall for her. To give in and simply love her. They don't know it, just as she doesn't. I already do. I love her with everything in me. But this is all I can offer her. I'm already giving her everything I have. "You let me find you. You gave me that choice… I know you must've," she tells me and I don't deny it.

"To clip your wings… to keep you out of it all… that would have been the greatest of crimes, my songbird."

To clip your wings...
to keep you out of it all
that would have been
the greatest of
crimes, my songbird.

Hales Powers

CHAPTER 5

Aria

I HAVEN'T LEFT THE HIDEAWAY ROOM IN ... I DON'T KNOW HOW long.

The pearls are still on my pillow, where I left them. Both the strand of pearls Carter gave me this morning, and the loose pearls and diamonds I retrieved from the box in his office. He left me standing there, knowing we were broken beyond repair. And I did my best to clean it up. Picking up the evidence of my broken collar all while hot tears slid down my cheeks and fell into the box where I lay only a week ago.

I know the pain of a love being over. It's an undeniable feeling that stretches out slowly through each limb and finger. It's numbing, yet unforgivingly sharp.

My chest heaved with each sob until I fell to the floor.

Love isn't enough, and that's the worst thing in the whole world. Love is supposed to conquer all. It's supposed to persevere. Instead all it's done is caused us both unbearable pain. A pain I would do anything not to feel ever again.

I've lain in the makeshift bed, a pile of pillows on top of the plush rug, warring with myself. I've thought every possible situation through. Ranging from walking into the cell willingly and locking it behind me until it's all over, to telling Carter I'd kill my father and Nikolai with my own two hands.

And I hate the woman in each scenario. I despise her. And I also know I would never be able to live with myself. I would simply be waiting until the day I died. Living each moment with a resentment toward Carter that I don't think I could hide.

Fate is cruel, and this world is colder than I ever imagined.

My body is sore and it takes a moment when I stand up to begin to move. I haven't had anything to drink or eat in … I don't know how long. I'm dizzy and there's a pounding in my temple that won't quit.

I move slowly to the kitchen, listening to my bare feet pad softly on the floor and breathing in and out as deeply as I can. A cup of coffee is what I'm after, a piping hot cup that's mostly sugar and cream. I only need the coffee for the caffeine. But what I get are the sounds of Addison and Daniel carrying from the kitchen to the hallway.

I stop just outside the doorway, listening to Addison tell Daniel how she'll never leave him again.

"You promise?" Daniel's voice is soothing and there's a smile that's hidden in his voice; I can see in my mind the exact smile that would play at his lips.

"I don't want to run away anymore." Addison's voice is nothing but sincere. "Nothing will come between us, Daniel. If we can make it through that…"

My cheek rests on the outside of the doorway as I listen to them, feeling the love between them that's always been there.

I can't help but feel a pang of jealousy and to wish it were that easy for Carter and me.

"Then marry me." Daniel's response makes my eyes widen and suddenly I feel like an intruder. Not at all like a friend or family. I'm only an eavesdropper who needs to go away and not stain their memory, even if they don't realize it.

Her voice is soft as she tells him yes between quick kisses I can hear even as I push away from the doorway. Turning around, I feel nothing and everything all at once. Jealousy and happiness. Emptiness from knowing I'll never have what they share, and a sense of completion for accepting it.

Is this what it feels like to completely break down?

With a single deep breath, my eyes closed and my muscles tight, I take a step forward only to be hit by the heat of a hard body as I walk forward.

My pulse quickens when I open my eyes.

"Lost?" Carter's voice isn't muted like my footsteps were, and I can hear Addison and Daniel come out from the kitchen and into the doorway to the hall.

My body's stiff, and it takes a moment for me to even gather the courage to look over my shoulder at them.

I don't belong here. It's never been more apparent to me. I shouldn't be here.

"Aria," Addison's quick to call out for me, but I can't even stand to look at her knowing we couldn't be any further apart in what we're feeling right now. She doesn't need me dragging her down, ruining this special moment for her, and there's nothing she can give me in this moment that I would accept.

"I'm good," I say and barely turn to look over my shoulder at the only friend I have in here. With my hand raised, she stops where she is. "Please." The single word is a plea for her to leave me alone, and she listens.

Stepping around Carter, I leave them as quick as I can. I only glance back once to see Daniel holding Addison's wrist as she stares at me with tears in her eyes. Carter's gone; where to? I don't know, and I don't care.

I've never felt so torn in my life.

I knew life would never be easy for me. Not with the man my father is. But I never imagined I'd fall in love with the enemy. So much so that I would be here with him, willingly, while my family mourns deaths committed by his hand. Or that I would be mourning the loss of a love that never should have been.

So what does that make me?

Who does that make me?

CHAPTER 6

Carter

WAR STOPS FOR NO ONE.

Death never waits.

"Each wing is secure and the repairs are underway, sir," Aden tells me with a nod of his head as he stands outside of Jase's office in his wing. Most of the damage was done to Declan's wing, but everything is salvageable.

"What's the timeline?" I ask Aden. He's a new guard, one of a dozen. When the death toll came in, we lost more men than I thought originally. Right now we're keeping everyone close, but it's only temporary; it's just until we get eyes on both Romano's men and Talvery's. Jett's taking care of that with a small crew. Everything's waiting on him. But I fucking hate waiting.

"Two weeks tops until everything is replaced," he answers and I give him a nod, effectively dismissing him before walking into Jase's open door and closing it behind me.

Jase's office is nothing like mine. There's not a single book. There's no desk either. I only refer to it as an office because he does. The fireplace is almost always lit though, and flames reflect off of the mirrored coffee table in front of it. The mirrored surface has a thick patina that's developed over time. I guess Jase prefers it that way, or he'd polish it.

The shelves that line the wall to the right hold the rare antique weapons he collects. Mostly swords and knives. The ancient feel they have and their crude primitive backgrounds are at odds with the clean lines of the rest of the room. Overall, the aesthetic is modern and barren.

"How is she?" Jase asks me. His gaze stays on the fire until I take the seat next to him on the sleek, black leather sofa. It's only then that he looks up at me.

I don't answer him, the words fighting with my emotions in the back of my throat.

"That bad?" he asks, and I only nod.

The fire crackles in front of us while I sit with my brother, remembering how we got here nearly a decade ago. When I was only a kid, left at death's doorstep and wishing for it to come quickly. Jase is the one who made the first move. He killed each of the men who grabbed me from the street corner. He was fueled by anger alone, but when I recovered and learned what he'd done, I knew there would be far more death before that anger would be allowed to leave him.

One by one, we killed, we stole, we ruled with a fear we once had for others.

But fear has a way of changing you. And I would be a liar to say I wasn't motivated by it now.

I'm afraid I'm going to lose the only woman worth fighting for. The only woman I'm capable of loving.

The thick leather groans as Jase leans back, rubbing his thumb over his jaw and tells me, "It'll be all right when this is over. She'll be all right in time."

"Or she'll be consumed by anger," I say and give him a knowing look, but the expression on his face doesn't waver.

"She loves you," is his only response.

I break his gaze to stare at the fire, wondering how long it'll take for a flame so high and hot to burn down to nothing but ash and smolder.

"I didn't come to talk about her."

"It's all about her, isn't it?" he questions and my chest tightens. If I could go back to that moment and tell him not to fight for revenge, if I could go back and instead take my brothers and leave that horrid place, I would. I'm not proud of who we've become and I know it's because of me.

"You know what I mean," I tell him rather than lying to him and pretending I didn't get us into this shit because of a sick need to have Aria to myself.

"What did you come to talk about then?" Jase asks and then lays his head back. He picks up a knife from the table and plays with the blade between his fingers.

"What do you want to do from here?" I ask him. The fight in me is subdued and he can see it. I'm certain everyone can. I've never felt so weak in my life.

"I say we wait," he offers, staring into the roaring fire. The flames dance in the darkness of his eyes.

"We could hit them now... Let the streets run with blood," I suggest to him, knowing the day is coming soon. That's how this works. The winner takes the final blow.

"Two reasons. The first is that Sebastian is coming back."

Sebastian. My initial reaction to hearing that he's coming back is nothing I expected. I feel as if I've failed him. I'm ashamed for him to come back and see me like this. Ever since Aria came here, I've messaged him to keep him apprised. He's been my confidant ever since he had the safe house built. He's anchored me more than once. And he knows about Aria, and how badly we've fallen.

"When?" I ask and have to clear my throat after.

"He'll be here tonight, although he's going to his estate and the safe house first to see the damage."

A grunt leaves me before I ask, "He hasn't seen the extent of the damage yet, has he?"

I didn't want to believe it hurt as much as it did when he left. Over time the pain eased. But I can't deny that the memory of him leaving and then not coming back for so long fucking kills me. He was family. He still is.

"Not yet," Jase answers evenly and then adds, "Chloe isn't coming for a while."

"That's understandable," I say absently. Deep in the back of my mind, I always knew he stayed away because of three reasons:

Chloe never wanted to be here.

Romano would have him killed if he still had the power to do so.

Marcus.

When Marcus approaches people, they tend to do his bidding and then move far, far away. My brothers and I are the only ones who seem to have defied that pattern.

It's quiet as the wood splits in the roaring fire and specks of ash fly in the heated air.

"You said there were two reasons?" I remind Jase, waiting on the other reason we shouldn't destroy what's left of Talvery.

"Her father retreated," he tells me, still running his fingers along the blade as he leans back in the chair. He's simply waiting for war. I'm the reason my brothers were pulled into this life, and I fucking hate myself for it.

I hate that he refers to Talvery as "her father" just as much.

"He has to leave eventually. He can't hide forever."

"Until he does, we wait?" Jase asks and I can only nod. Every day this war lasts is a day longer that I have Aria so close, yet unreachable.

"You don't often come to me for advice," Jase comments and I don't respond for a moment.

"I'm tired," I tell him honestly, but I don't tell him everything else. How all I can think about is what I'll be when she leaves me. I'll be the shell of a man waiting to die, the way Jase is waiting for this war.

His gaze burns into me, but he doesn't press me for more. Maybe he already knows.

"Talvery called as well."

My head whips to his and my brows pinch together in both shock and anger at his admission. "When? Why didn't-"

"Just now, before you came in." I try to interrupt him, pissed off that I wasn't told, but Jase continues, "He only wanted to know one thing and then he hung up."

"And you told him what he wanted to know?" My blunt fingernails dig into the soft leather of the armrest.

"He wanted to know if Aria was still alive. If she was okay." He speaks evenly, staring into the fire before looking at me when I ask, "What did you tell him?"

"The truth."

I have to bite my tongue when I nearly ask him what truth he told Talvery. Because I know she's not okay. There's nothing about either of us that's okay.

CHAPTER 7

Aria

I'LL NEVER FORGET THE FIRST FIGHT I HAD WITH NIKOLAI. AS I SIT in my hideaway room, staring at the beautiful wallpaper in front of me with a blank canvas at my feet and a stick of unused chalk in my hand, I remember how I screamed at him and how he screamed back at me.

It was a quarrel of young love. But it was also the beginning of the end and we both knew it.

He'd taught me to shoot that day, letting me fire his gun. He was only seventeen and I was sixteen. I'd begged him to let me fire it. I wanted to know what it felt like and he told me he shouldn't, and that I would never need to know anyway.

I can't explain how angry it made me, but it didn't matter, because he moved behind me as we stood in front of the forest behind my home. His chest pressed against my back and his hands held mine as he taught me how to fire it.

The gun kicked back, but he held it steady in my hands. I remember the heat that spread through me when he asked me how it felt, whispering the question in my ear. We'd been seeing each other late at night, nearly every night for a while.

I knew he cared for me, but he hadn't said those three words to me that I'd confessed to him.

I peeked over my shoulder, and his lips were right there, so close to mine. I stared at them for a moment and thank God I did, because that's the moment my father stormed out of the house.

I tore myself away from Nikolai before he even saw my father.

That night we didn't fight over the gun, or whether or not I should learn how to fire one. We fought because he wanted to end what we had. He said my father would never allow it.

We fought because I wanted to run away with him, but Nikolai refused. Deciding it was better to stay where we were and to stop seeing each other, rather than to take the risk to leave and keep what we had.

He didn't want to be seen with me again, and that's why I screamed. He was all I had, and he knew it. It hurt me deeply, although I understood why he didn't want my father to find out. The second I showed him my pain, he took it away.

Nikolai kissed it away and said he would make it better. That he was doing it all for me, and one day I'd see. It took time for me to get used to not having him. And every time I cried, every time I needed him, if only for a moment, he came to me.

He never told me he loved me until after I'd gotten over what we had and only considered him a friend. But I knew he did before he told me. Because when you love someone, you can't stand to see them in pain.

Carter's not like that, though. He's not a man to soothe or be soothed. He's the type who puts his thumb inside of a raw gunshot wound and pushes harder. That's the kind of man Carter is.

There's no kissing away my pain with Carter. He wants me to live in it, because he lives in his. To stand by his side means to revel in the agony, and more so, to rule in it.

The knock at my door startles me. It's soft and although I wish it were Carter on the other side, I already know it's not.

Carter's not the type to knock so gently, either.

"Yes?" I call out from behind the closed door.

"It's me." Addison's voice carries through the door and I have to take a steadying breath before I can answer her.

My eyes are tired and burn from lack of sleep as she walks in.

"How did you know I was here?" I ask her and only then do I hear how hoarse my voice is.

As I sit up on my pile of pillows and look around, I realize how pathetic this looks. How pathetic *I* look.

"Daniel told me," she says softly, with a smile that doesn't quite reach her eyes. She looks around awkwardly for only a brief second before coming to sit with me on my makeshift bed.

I want to tell her that I'm happy for her, for what I overheard. I want to hug her and confide in her that I already know the good news, although it was an accident. I want to do many things, but Addison came with a purpose and she doesn't give me a chance to speak first.

I'm grateful for that because seeing her makes me anxious and awkward, given the circumstances.

"When I first moved here... well," she pauses and clears her throat, then continues, "close to here, when I moved to Crescent Hills, I had no one."

I pull my legs into my chest and lean my back against the wall as I watch her sit cross-legged. There's a small pile of plush throw blankets folded next to me and she takes the palest pink one, a soft chenille, and pulls the blanket up around her.

"I know what that's like," I tell her and she shakes her head no.

"I was an orphan," she tells me with her voice cracking and I'm taken aback.

"I had no idea."

"I don't look like an orphan?" she raises her brow and jokes, but the accompanying small laugh is sad. "I don't talk much about it, you know?" I nod as she talks, and I try to imagine what that was like.

"Anyway, I moved between a few different families and the one here was okay; it wasn't any better than the others in a lot of ways. They didn't care about me, they just got paid to keep me alive, you know?" Addison chews on her bottom lip for a moment and I can't help but wonder why she's telling me all this. She takes in a heavy breath and looks me dead in the eye. "I stayed because of Tyler."

"Tyler?" A freezing sensation sweeps across my skin at hearing his name. It feels as if I know the Cross brother who died. I've dreamed of him, and the words he gave Addison in her dream haven't left me.

"All of us grew up poor, and so he didn't judge me, not like the other kids at school. His father was an alcoholic, and his brothers were... well, they did what they had to in order to survive. And it scared me sometimes. But he loved me, and I loved him in a lot of ways. I also realized I loved his brother—I loved Daniel more, even if we were nothing back then. I hardly spoke to Daniel at the time." Tears cloud her vision and she brushes them away. "The Cross boys, they protected me, they looked out for me in a way no one had. Including

Carter." She lets the tears fall and sniffles before telling me, "I swear to you, there's so much good in there."

She licks her lower lip, gathering the tear that lingers there and it's then I realize she thinks I'm not okay because I want to leave. Because I don't love Carter.

"I know there is," I tell her and she waits for more. For the "but" that isn't going to come from me. "I love him and I love this family." Emotions spill from me, emotions I wish I could bury deep down inside until I can't feel them anymore. "I want to be a part of this family more than you could ever know."

She tilts her head and gives me a look, and I actually crack a smile. "Well, maybe you do know." I sniff and look at the ceiling to keep from tearing up at the thought of being a part of this family, a family who has protected me and has loved me. Even if they are ... the men they are.

"So you do love him?" she asks and reaches out to me, laying a hand on my knee. "You forgive him?"

I nod my head, knowing it's true. Both statements are so true.

"He doesn't forgive me." I tell her the truth that burns a hole in my chest. I have to reach into the pocket of the sleepshirt so I can pull out a few of the loose pearls from the necklace I used to wear. The beads click together softly in my hand as I tell her, "He doesn't trust me and he's not going to show any mercy, not to me or to anyone."

"I wanted to come in here and tell you something. Something that's scaring me, Aria." Addison's voice drops and her eyes darken with an intensity I haven't seen from her before.

"Go ahead," I tell her in a whisper, feeling the temperature of my blood drop. She rubs her palms on her jeans as she breathes out slowly.

"I went to Tyler's grave." Tears gather in her eyes the same way clouds do as a storm threatens, slowly and with an impending necessity. "There were so many forget-me-nots." She looks past me, to the window that's covered in beautiful linens, yet locked and will never open. I doubt she knows that little fact though. Her gaze stays there as she tells me, "I brought two packets of seeds with me before I left, and I scattered them all around his grave." Her eyes drift to mine. "It's nothing but a field of blue and white now," she tells me and a chill flows down my spine. An odd sense of déjà vu pricks its way deeper into my bones.

She lets out a steadying breath and shakes her head gently. "I've been dreaming of him since we came back. It's the same dream, Aria."

I remember a dream that's come and gone since I first got here. Since the first week I was locked in the cell in this place, but it's not what she describes.

"Tyler keeps telling me to remind you. Hold him tight. Don't let go… or else he'll die."

In the depths of my being, I know Carter needs someone to love him and someone he can love in return. He's a man in pain, a beast trapped in a castle of his own making. I'm just not convinced that I can be that woman.

Or that he'll let me close enough to be that woman.

"I know," I tell her truthfully. "But it's not all up to me."

"Try," she begs me. "Please, just try to hold on to him."

I swallow my heart, which has traveled all the way up to my throat, and only nod. She has no idea how much I wish I could.

CHAPTER 8

Carter

LAST NIGHT SHE STAYED IN HER ROOM. THE ONE I'M NOT supposed to go in. I sat by the door and listened to her cry softly. I don't know how much more of this I can take.

My thumb taps on the desk as I stare at the box. She fixed it. She did it. Not me. She didn't ask, and she doesn't know what it does to me. Part of me wants to rip it out. The other part is hoping it means something. Something beyond what I'm capable of controlling.

Knock, knock. The gentle rap at the door disturbs my thoughts. It's early. I've already met with Aden and Jase. We know where every enemy and ally is, and what they're planning. There's nothing to do but wait for Romano to lay Talvery to rest. He'll lose men doing it, but my side has lost enough. And I informed him of exactly that. His options are limited.

Knock, knock. She knocks again and I have to clear my throat, feeling the roughness at the back as I straighten in my chair and call for her to come in.

The door opens slowly, revealing Aria to me with sleep still in her eyes. Her hair flows down her bare back in waves, and the only thing she's wearing is a thin, black silk nightie with the white pearls draped down her breasts. My cock instantly hardens as she takes a single careful step in, quietly walking on the balls of her feet until she turns and shuts the door with her back to me.

"You look… breathtaking," I say, the words falling from my lips.

Her head turns first, bringing with it the sway of her hips, the gentle swing of her hair around her shoulders and those beautiful eyes that toy with my emotions. Her lips tip up, pulling into a feminine smile as a blush rises up her chest and climbs all the way to her temple. With her head tilted down, she peeks up at me through her lashes, brushing a stray lock from her face and murmurs, "That seems fitting ... since you leave me breathless."

She takes deliberate but slow steps, so I know right where she's headed as she rounds the desk. I don't know why I turn off the monitors, shut my laptop and scoot the chair back, spreading my legs so she can easily climb into my lap. As she adjusts, her small hand slips to my groin and a muffled groan escapes my throat, rumbling my chest. Aria's eyes light with a playfulness, but also so much more. Her eyes always give me more than I deserve.

"I miss you," she whispers as her ass presses against my cock and she lies heavily against my chest. Her hair tickles my neck until she rests her cheek on my shoulder, and lazily presses a small kiss to my throat.

I have a small moment, a split second where I wonder if this is real or a dream. The tension is gone; the thoughts of what will come don't exist in this moment. She simply wants me, and I her. As her nails gently run down my throat, playing among the overgrown stubble, she swallows thickly and I have to wonder if the same thought has hit her as I see pain grow in her expression in the reflection on the black monitor in front of me.

"I didn't think you would come to me," I tell her quietly, and pluck at one of the pearls of her necklace, rolling it between my thumb and forefinger. She nuzzles against my shoulder and whispers in a sultry voice, "I thought you knew me better than that, Mr. Cross." The rough chuckle I give her in return shakes my chest, and along with it, her. Her breasts press against my chest, and I feel her nipples harden from the slight movement.

"I love you," she whispers and kisses my neck again, softer this time, leaving a touch of wetness behind. "There's nothing that could stop me from loving you. I tried. I can't stop," she tells me softly, lifting her head to look me in the eyes.

Instead of answering her, I cup her pussy in my lap, pressing my fingers against the thin silk that separates my hand from her hot entrance. She's damp immediately. Wet and hot for me.

As she reaches up to hold on to my shoulders instinctively, I maneuver my fingers around the fabric and press them inside of her. Her back arches and her breasts come closer to my face. I bend down just enough to gently nip the hardened peak of one nipple through the thin fabric, leaving a mark on her nightie.

She squeals in my embrace, jolting slightly, but she doesn't let go of me, she only clings tighter, her nails pressing deeper into my skin through the dress shirt.

"I want you," I breathe against her slender neck as I thrust my fingers in and out of her, moving some of the wetness up and down her cunt and then to her backside, around her tight hole. I need to make the other night right and fuck her there the way she needs.

"I love you," she tells me again in a strangled moan as I unzip my pants and reposition her to straddle me.

Again I don't say it back, and instead I crash my lips to hers, pressing them as deeply as I can as I shove my dick inside of her as swiftly as possible. With both of my hands on her shoulders, my forearms supporting her back, I slam her down, forcing her to scream into my kiss with an ecstasy I love to give her.

This I can give her. As much as she needs.

She's so fucking tight. Feeling her squeeze my cock with every thrust is something I don't deserve.

Her nails dig into my shoulders and she moans with each upward thrust. The soft sounds are short and come in muted gasps, urging me to push her higher and higher.

The air is hot but my skin is hotter as I feel her tighten around me. I'm close, but I don't want to get off. I don't want to take from her any more than I already have.

I can't breathe as I pound into her with a primal need to force the pleasure to rip through her, but she doesn't let go. She isn't breathing either as her head lolls back, her teeth digging into her bottom lip.

She's watching me as I watch her. With each slam of my hips I want to see her light up with unrelenting pleasure, but she shakes her head gently, barely able to speak as she whispers, "Not without you."

My grip on the flesh of her hip tightens, the threat of her holding back enraging a side of me. A part of my soul buried deep inside that wants nothing more than to give her everything.

With the back of my arm sweeping across the desk, I clear a spot for her, letting everything else crash to the floor so I can move her to lay flat on the desk. The laptop stays to one side, but the phone, the papers and journal with all the numbers, my cell—all that shit clatters to the floor. Her ass is hanging off the desk and my cock is still buried deep inside of her.

I'll make her cum. She won't refuse me.

I take a second, only a single fucking second to wrap her leg higher around my hip so I have the perfect angle to slam myself deep inside of her until she can't hold on any longer. So she'll shatter beneath me like I need her to. But in that second, her eyes widen and she reaches for me, her hand grabbing my shirt and fisting it as she leans up, her shoulders lifting off the desk. As she swallows, I see the plea in her eyes, and how tense her neck becomes.

"Please," she begs me as I hammer myself inside of her, forcing her head to be thrown back as her neck and back both threaten to arch. Even with my ruthless pace, she screams out for me to cum with her, to fall from the highest high and get lost in pieces beneath the world and the reality that plagues us.

"Carter," she moans my name and I cave. I pick up my pace and feel the tingle at the base of my spine. My toes curl and I let them.

As much as I know this won't last, I can't deny her. I won't do it. I love her too much, and that will be my downfall.

CHAPTER 9

Aria

I T'S A MIX OF HIM NOT SAYING HE LOVES ME, EVEN THOUGH I KNOW he does, and the way he leaves me after sex.

He left me panting and reeling on his desk, my nightgown torn and the pearls wrapped around me so tightly, I felt like they were holding me down. I was a mess, destroyed by him. And he left to clean up, taking his time without me to gather up his own pieces. Every second felt raw. Every moment another bit of reality intruded on the moment.

It reminds me of the time we had in his bathroom when I realized I'd missed my birthday and never went to see my mother. It feels like so long ago when we fought and fucked on the tiled floor. And when he stood, with his back to me and the look of regret clearly written on his face… I'll never forget the way it felt. And that's exactly what it feels like now.

Hold on to him, a voice whispers as the emotions try to strangle my throat. *Hold on to him.*

"I'm trying," I whisper.

"What?" Carter asks and I swallow the dry words, propping myself up on his desk even though I can feel moisture between my legs. I have to wad up the bottom of the nightgown, the bit that should cover my legs, and press it against myself to keep from making a mess. Carter only comes to help me down then. And only to help me down. The moment the balls of my feet hit the hardwood floors, he lets go of me.

I need someone to hold me too. My voice is weak as I answer him, "Nothing." The moment is broken and I feel it inside of me. The sharp edges of it dig into my chest and let the real world find its way back into my head.

Carter's gaze is like fire, burning into the side of my face as I turn away from him, the way he did to me just a moment ago.

"I need to go change." I offer up the excuse and then hate myself for it. I hate that I can pretend in the least that I'm all right.

My hair tickles my upper back as I turn to stare back at the man I love, the man whose love will kill me. With a shiver running down my shoulders and the coolness of his office replacing the much-needed heat I felt a minute ago, I tell him the truth. "It feels like you regret it almost every time you touch me now."

I have to swallow thickly after letting the words out. It is almost every time, isn't it? Each time since the safe house... he never came, not until now.

It's a slow change in his expression, as the slight concern morphs to indifference. To the mask he always wears. "Do you regret this?" I ask him. Before he can even answer, I push out more of the raw truth, saying, "I don't want to feel like this afterward. I don't want to feel..." I trail off as my hand reaches up to my chest and my fingers tangle around the strand of pearls, not knowing what the words are that accurately portray what I feel.

I feel like I lose him more and more when he does this after. But when I'm with him, truly with him, I'm whole. "I want you back." I whisper the words in a ragged voice drenched in despair.

"This isn't going to last." Those are the only words Carter gives me, but his expression says more. His steady gaze belies the hollow depths of his pain. Looking closer, the softness around his eyes shows just how tired he is, how vulnerable, even.

It's only then that tears prick, but still, I hold them back. Sorrow will do nothing for us. It only eats at the precious time we have left.

"Stop." I can only give him a single word before I have to take a steadying breath. I can feel myself breaking, but I won't. He must see it, but he doesn't come to me. He doesn't try to comfort me and I have to reach behind me, gripping the edge of the desk to brace myself.

"You said it yourself." Carter starts to give my own words back to me, and I have to look away from him, staring at the massive windows although I don't see anything at all. "You said you'd never forgive me, and we both know it's the truth and what I deserve."

With my fingers wrapping tight around the pearls, I speak calmly and aimlessly, "Such a reasonable gesture then, to pull away from me and not fight for me." On the last word, I turn to look at him. "Just end it then, send me back?"

Although it's a false threat, a cold chill creeps up my body. It slows everything—my breath, my pulse.

A tic in Carter's jaw starts to spasm as he turns away from me, leaning his hips against the desk and bracing himself on it as I am to look out toward the windows with me.

"The moment I heard your voice, I knew once I had you, I'd never let you go." His voice is low and full of solace. Inside I'm reeling with the ticking time bomb of the truth he doesn't know.

"Which moment?" I ask him.

I can't look at him, knowing what's about to spill from my lips. The revelation that could change everything. If ever there was a time to confess what I've been hiding, it's now, when there's nothing left to hold us together.

"When your father let me go. He let me live, and it's only because you called out."

"It wasn't me," I blurt out, and the words are dead on my lips, completely at odds with the emotion in his. I have to clear my throat and repeat my words when he says nothing at all. "I never knocked at the door. It wasn't me."

"I heard your voice," Carter starts to speak and even takes a half step closer to me, but I cut him off, and stare into his eyes as I confess.

"It wasn't me. I never went to that side of the house." My head shakes as my voice goes hoarse and I have to pause and swallow. My mother died on the floor directly above where my father worked. I never wanted to go back to that side of the house ever again after it happened. "I would have never told my father I needed him. I would have never interrupted his work." My heart clenches with unbearable pain at the look in Carter's eyes. "More than that, my father wouldn't have stopped what he was doing for me," I tell him a truth that causes the small part of me that still craves more love from my father to twist in pain. "It wasn't me you heard."

"You're lying," Carter speaks but there's no conviction.

"You know I don't need to lie to you." With a deep breath in and then a desperate one out, I tell him, "I love you, but if you only want me here because you wanted the girl who saved your life," bastard tears gather in my eyes but I refuse to let them fall as I swallow and continue, "if you only wanted some girl you've dreamed about…"

I can't continue as Carter's eyes narrow at me and his grip tightens on the desk behind him.

"I didn't want to tell you because I thought if you knew, you wouldn't want me anymore." A single tear falls, and I ignore it. "If you only wanted me because of that night, because you thought it was me, then let me leave." When I lick my dry lips, I taste the salt of more tears. Tears I refuse to acknowledge.

"It was never supposed to be me," I whisper as I wipe under my burning eyes and gaze at the bookshelf behind him. His own gaze is unreadable and unforgiving; the mask has slipped back into place.

"I don't believe you," he says and Carter's voice is low and threatening. With the cold air settling against my bare skin, I feel more exposed in this moment than I have in so long. "I know your voice. It was you."

My heart flickers as Carter moves a half step closer, his gaze sizing me up like when I was first in the cell.

"I'm not lying, Carter. It was never supposed to be me."

"I just don't know why you're lying." Carter continues as if I haven't exposed a truth that ruins everything he thought about me, every piece he both hated and loved before he even saw me.

"Stop calling me a liar." A small flame ignites inside of me as he stalks closer, invading my space and towering over me. My voice is firm, bordering on hard.

I can feel my eyes narrowing on his as he approaches so close I can feel the heat from his skin. The flames lick between us as he smirks at me, letting his gaze roam up and down my body.

"What did you think telling me that would accomplish?" he questions me. It's a fucking interrogation.

Rage burns in my blood. I have to quickly take in a deep breath to keep from snapping.

"I wanted to share something with you that would change things.

Something that would sway the position you hold on how we've always been enemies and-"

He cuts me off and rebuts in a casual tone, "But our families have always been enemies."

His gaze is ever assessing. I'm the enemy in this moment. I'm a liar in his eyes.

"You're a fool to think I'd lie to you." My response comes with more pain than I imagined it would.

The smile that graces his lips doesn't hide his hurt. "Am I?"

"I'm not a liar." My hands clench at my sides and the emotions that crept up before crash into me suddenly, like rough waves at the shore. "And this was a mistake." I don't know if I mean telling him he's mistaken, not running when I could... or falling in love with him to begin with. Maybe all of it.

"It was all a mistake," I whisper to myself before looking back at Carter. At a version of him that's guarded and impenetrable while all I am is vulnerable to him. "I know that now." The realization is sobering.

I meet his gaze as I tell him, "I'm not who you think I am. I'm Aria Talvery and this was never supposed to happen."

With one of his palms braced on the desk, he lowers his gaze until we're eye to eye and his lips are close to mine. So close, and that side of me that wants nothing more than his affection begs me to take them with my own and silence whatever words he dares to speak. But I don't.

"You may be a Talvery, but you're on the wrong territory, little songbird." Backing away slightly, he searches for something in my expression before adding, "And even if you hate me, I won't be letting you go."

CHAPTER 10

Carter

*I*T WASN'T HER?

The fuck it wasn't her.

It's all I can think about as I lead her back to the bedroom. The sounds of our footsteps are heavy, but not as heavy as the beating of my pulse.

I know that night, I know her voice. That night, that moment even, changed my life forever. I know every detail. The cadence of her words. I've dreamed of them and been consumed by that moment for years.

The bedroom door closes with a resounding click as I walk to the dresser, where a new glass and bottle of whiskey wait for me.

I go through the motions, barely listening to her undressing and moving through drawers as I try to calm down.

It's an impossible task. Every second, the anger rises.

How dare she lie to me. How dare she look me in the eyes and deny something that led me down a path of violence and self-hate. How fucking dare she do that, yet claim to love me.

I've never hated how capable she is of affecting me more than I do in this moment.

I'll never tell her how much it hurts to hear her deny it. I refuse to let her know. I'll be damned if I ever give her that truth and that power.

As I breathe, the amber liquid flows between the cubes of ice. My grip on the tumbler is loose as I swirl it, but it's no use. I have no appetite for liquor tonight.

I want to punish her. It's all I can think about.

I've handled everything wrong because I've underestimated her, but now that she's shown her cards and revealed what lows she's willing to go to, I won't make that mistake again.

She was right. I should have clipped her wings.

"I don't know why you can't believe me," Aria speaks softly, so softly the rustling of the covers almost drowns out her words as she climbs into bed. Glancing over my shoulder, I watch as she pulls them up closer to her throat and looks back at me the way she always should have, as if I'm the enemy.

I bite down on my tongue to keep from replying as I breathe in through my nose heavily. I don't know why she'd lie about it. What motive is behind her lies?

My shoulders tense as I lean down to grab what's inside the top drawer of my dresser. The sound of it opening is ominous. The metal is cold in my hand as the cuffs clink together. While I walk to her, I think about how to cuff her, but the thought of touching her right now is dangerous. So fucking dangerous.

She casts a spell over me each and every time my skin touches her. I can't risk it.

I toss them on the bed as the thought hits me. "Cuff your left hand to the bedpost," I command her as I drag the chair in the corner of the room toward the bed, closer to her.

With my back to her, I wonder if she'll even obey me until the telltale snap of the closure echoes in the bedroom.

Only then do I breathe and sink down into the chair. I have her, and she's not going anywhere.

The light from the moon shines down on her soft skin in a way that makes my chest ache. She's so fucking beautiful. She brushes her chestnut locks away from her face and stares expectantly at me before resting back against the headboard.

"Are you just going to keep me here until the war is over and I hate you forever?" she asks when I don't say anything. Her voice is flat, but she can't hide the pain in her eyes. She can't hide that from me. Not when I've seen the raw agony the cell brought her, the torment killing Stephan gave her, and the sorrow loving me has stained into those gorgeous hazel eyes.

"That's not a bad idea," I remark, not hiding the exhaustion from my voice.

The huff that leaves her lips is humorless. She tries to get comfortable, but she's cuffed herself too high on the post. The cuff is between the middle and top rung, instead of at the bottom. She can reach the nightstand, where a bottle of wine and a glass from earlier lay, along with her cell phone. At least she can reach those, but nothing else is at her disposal.

Agitation quickly shows in her pursed lips as she props a pillow under her arm. Letting out a sigh, I lean forward, resting my elbows on my knees and stare her down. I wait for her to look at me to ask her, "Why lie?"

Fire smolders in her gaze as she pushes out the words, "It wasn't me."

Tick, tick. It's not the clock, it's the steady beat of my heart, on edge and wanting to know why she'd try to hurt me like she is.

"I have all the time in the world," I tell her and lean back. As I swallow, I realize how much it kills me, the very idea that it was someone else. "It was you," I say, hardening my voice, refusing to entertain the thought the voice that saved me belonged to another. I know it was Aria. Deep in my bones, I know it was her.

"I'm sorry, Carter." Aria's whisper is pained. She scoots closer to me on the bed and I watch as the cuff keeps her away from me. Fuck, I'm a goddamn wreck and she can see.

She could always see me though. Something about her simply knows who I am. Her soul knows mine.

"I didn't want to tell you," she whispers and I'm taken back to that night, to the pain, to the desperation to die.

"I wanted to die and you saved me," I tell her, knowing how true it is. It was her voice that called out to me as I felt the cold hand of death pull me closer to the ground. Not to a white light and salvation, but down to the dirty concrete floor. And I prayed for it to happen. I coveted nothing less than death to come to me and take the pain away. The torture I endured had destroyed any chance of peace and happiness a boy like me could ever have.

"I'm sorry," is again all she can say as emotion wells in my chest and then higher, up my throat.

"You're not," I speak through clenched teeth and hold on to the fact that she's lying. I know the voice that saved me. "You're a liar."

As Aria tries to wipe away her tears that have slid down her flushed cheeks, she brings her left hand up, only to have it held back by the cuff.

"And you'll stay right there until I'm done doing what I have to do." Standing abruptly, I watch her eyes widen. "You can stay there. Right there where you belong." My words are hollow, but the threat is real. I won't give her up so easily. If she thought lying to me would give her freedom from me, she thought wrong.

"Carter," Aria calls out and moves on the bed, the sheets falling around her body in a messy puddle, but her left arm is restrained behind her. Frustration joins the desperation in her eyes.

Her right hand moves to her left as if she could pry it free as I stalk to the door. "Carter!" She yells out my name to get me to stop as I stand in the doorway. I stare back at my songbird, naked on her knees in my bed, and chained to it willingly. A dull pink mark still shows on her breast from where I touched her earlier, right beneath the pearls that sway slightly down her front. She's a beautiful fucking vision. Beautiful, but wretched with sadness.

"Don't leave me here," she demands, as if she could, and then swallows visibly.

"You're not in a position to give the commands," is all I give her. I'm only able to take half a step out of the room before the shattering sound of glass at my right is accompanied by wetness along the right side of my cheek, my jaw, my neck and down my shirt. The dark red liquid seeps into my white dress shirt and I stare at the blotches, watching them spread over the fabric before looking back at Aria. The cracked bottle is in pieces at my feet, and there's a small dent in the drywall. It's surrounded by streaks of burgundy that are dripping down to the floor.

My heart races in my chest from shock, but also anger.

"Now you can't hide at the bottom of it." My words are spit with venom as control slips from me.

"Fuck you! I hate you!"

She screams it like she truly means it. Like her hate is the only thing keeping her alive, and I know that's what it is. I've been there. I hated her before she even knew my name.

"I knew you did. I know you hate me. It doesn't change that you're mine." I can't hide the lack of control, the unraveling of composure as I stare her down, watching her chest rise and fall with chaotic breathing.

"I won't let you do this to me," she speaks with conviction and the dry laugh that erupts from my lips is dark and genuine as I grip the doorknob to keep from approaching her.

"Fuck you!" she sneers as she rips her arm away from the bedpost. Not tugging, but yanking her wrist against the cuff. Pain echoes in her face and in the shriek that tears up her throat. My heart slams in my chest as I watch her do it again. And again. My body temperature drops and for a second I don't believe it. She wrenches her body away until a horrid scream comes from her lips. Tears stream down her face as her arm lays limp, and her wrist, still cuffed, is red and raw with cuts from the metal.

"Fuck you," she cries, her words low and full of suffering. She rips her arm away again, although this time she can only use the weight of her body and the action is done without conviction.

Fuck.

I'm too fucking weak for her. Her agony destroys any rational thought I have. I can't get to her quick enough, although I'm not thinking logically and I don't have the key. In an attempt to help, I grip her as gently as I can to push her back against the headboard to loosen the tension of the cuff, but Aria's hate is stronger than her reason.

Even with a dislocated shoulder, she shoves me with her uninjured hand. "Stay away," she screams at me with tears still falling freely. "Get away!" It's only when she tries to push me again that her body refuses to obey and she clutches at her shoulder.

"Aria," I start to say, ready to plead with her to be reasonable and let me help.

"I meant it, I hate you!" Her confession is sobering. Her face is red as she swallows down the pain and stares me straight in the eye. "You wanted me to be like this? To chain me up and make me pay? You can't go back. That's your thing, right?" She pauses for a moment to breathe and then backs up against the headboard, holding on to her shoulder and sniffling. "Well, you can't go back." Her breathing's unsteady and she speaks softer. "You did this. You made me hate you." Her face crumples with the last confessions. "This is what you wanted, and now you can have it."

The pain is numbing. It takes a minute and then another for me to even retrieve the key to uncuff her. She doesn't look at me at all while I put her shoulder back into place.

And when she sobs, I want nothing more than to hold her, but she pushes me away and lies on her side, her back to me and her injured shoulder in the air.

I've never hurt so much in my life.

I remember everything from that night years ago. And even that pain doesn't compare to this.

The whiskey is more than tempting this time and it goes down easy.

Each glass is easier than the last, and each brings the picture of our past to me like the way Aria paints. Each moment seems made up of beautiful strokes on her canvas. She could paint a painful past, yet make you desire to touch it with the masterful way her brush moves when she's creating art.

For the longest time, all I see are the moments we've had together.

The next glass brings out my jealousy. And the thought of sending Nikolai a video of me fucking Aria and showing him how much she loves it.

She brings out a possessive side of me I've never known. She makes me lose my control. She ruins everything, but she's the reason for it all.

She's mine.

That's the only thing that matters.

I would never do it; I'd never let a man like Nikolai see her cum. He had a chance with her, and he lost it. I fucking refuse to lose her like he did. I won't let it happen.

At the thought, the tumbler slams down on the desk. For a moment, I think I've broken it.

I haven't, but the whiskey is humming in my veins and knowing that, I push the glass away from me.

I get down on my knees, feeling lightheaded as I pick up all the shit I threw down from my desk earlier so I could have her. Placing the last few items where they belong, I let my hand rest where her lower back rested only hours ago. The hard chestnut is bitter cold and nothing like her warmth.

My gaze falls to the polaroid pictures laying haphazardly on top of a stack of papers. Pictures I brought out days and days ago to show Aria. Pictures of the house she says is so familiar. And one of them has my father and mother on the porch.

He loved her. Anyone who looked at them could see it. My father loved her with everything he had.

When she died a slow, slow death, he died with her.

I never learned how to love, only how to survive.

Maybe that's what Aria's been doing. Thinking on the past makes me reach for the tumbler again. The liquid burns as I swallow more down in large gulps and remember how she lay on the sofa in the corner of my office that first time.

She was so tired, but well fed and well fucked. The effects of what I'd done to her were still evident. Her skin lacked color and her ribs still poked through her flesh.

I did this to her. I put her in this position to simply survive.

That day she lay on the sofa, she slept off and on. Each time she woke startled and terrified until I went to her. I calmed her. I took her nightmares away.

Tears prick in the back of my eyes as I struggle to breathe. Yes, I hurt her, but I took it all away. All the pain, all the fear.

I thought it counted for more than it did.

As she slept that first day, I couldn't do a damn thing but watch her and every small movement of her body. I remember every inch of her frame. I've never felt so sickened by who I am like back then.

But I tried to take it all away.

My elbows slam down harder than I wanted on the desk as I rest my forehead in my hands and let out a heavy sigh, burdened by all the sins I've committed against Aria Talvery.

It's too much. Tonight has been too much.

I search the top right drawer for the small vial of sweets, but I don't find it. The papers are scattered by the time I'm done, but I don't care. When I slam it shut, the one below opens and I pull it ajar to find what I'm looking for right on top.

I know the liquor will numb me enough to sleep, but I never sleep long and tonight I need it. With a full vial, I swallow it all and when a moment passes and sleep doesn't come, I grab another vial and take more of the drug.

My legs are heavy as I move to the sofa she slept in and lie in her place.

I don't know if I would take it all back. I don't know how I can ever have her. All I wanted was her, and I still do. I can't help it. All I want is for Aria to be mine.

I hear her shuddering breath first. And when I lift my gaze from the floor beneath the desk to her flushed cheeks and then those gorgeous eyes, I feel a weight lifted from me.

Like the pain doesn't exist anymore. Because she's crawling to me. She's coming to me. My songbird.

"Are you still angry?" I ask and my voice feels rough, as if it's been unused for a long time. I can feel my brow pinch in confusion at the thought, and it's then that I realize I feel cold. So cold.

None of it matters when Aria shakes her head. The messy hair around her face lets me know she's been sleeping here in this room. She was waiting for me to wake up.

"I'm not angry." Her voice is soft as she reaches me, but the tears don't stop. My fingers splay in her hair as I cup my hand behind her head and pull her closer to me. I don't even remember what the fight was about when I touch her. Nothing else matters when I touch her. She clings to me, her hands on my thighs as she lifts up her lips and kisses me.

With her lips to mine, everything feels right again and the pain doesn't exist. Not until I feel the wetness from her tears on my face and she shudders in my grasp, pulling away to whisper, "Please forgive me."

It takes me a moment, the haze of the whiskey dulling my thoughts as I struggle to remember tonight. How she lied, how she said it wasn't her.

"Why did you lie?" I ask her, but she doesn't answer. She only pleads for me to forgive me.

Her voice is wretched as she says, "You never told me that you did and after so long ... please, Carter. Please forgive me."

My head pounds with a pain that comes from drinking too much and it takes me a minute to register what she's said. I ask her, "What do you mean 'after so long?'"

She feels so right in my arms, and neither of us are willing to let go, but I feel so dizzy. So cold and confused. The room tilts suddenly. "Fuck," I say, the word stretched in the air and the room tilts again, as if it's trying to make me fall.

"It's been so long since I've seen you," Aria tells me as she touches her fingertips to my face ever so gently. She sniffles and adds, "Since I've gotten to talk to you."

"I just saw you." It's all I can manage to say, but Aria doesn't seem to hear me.

"I love you so much," she says, and her bottom lip wobbles when her eyes find mine. "Please tell me you forgive me. I need it, Carter." She pulls at my hand, holding it in both of hers and cradling my hand to her chest.

"Stop crying," I tell her, trying to breathe but feeling the air become thinner. It's like I'm suffocating. Something's wrong.

I don't want to take my hand away from her, but I need to reach for my collar. I can't fucking breathe. It's then, when I think about moving my hand, that I feel how cold she is against my knuckles. And how still her chest is. And how pale she is.

"Aria." Her name is whispered, but I don't know if I've said it. The chill seeps into my blood. She's not breathing.

"Carter, no. No," she tells me as if she knows what I'm thinking. "It was supposed to end like this. I could never be in the middle of war. I was always going to be the one to die."

What is she saying? No! I scream but there's no sound that escapes from my mouth. The room is silent, save her plea to me. "It's okay. When it happens... I'm okay dying for you. I just need you to forgive me, please. Forgive me and love me, as I love you. I'll always love you."

The prick at the back of my neck flows down every inch of my skin. The room darkens and I still can't breathe. I can't think. She can't be dead. Aria! I scream again, but it's silent.

"We don't have much time. Please, please, Carter. Forgive me." Her eyes search mine as I scream and it's then she sees my mouth moving but there's no sound.

She yells something at me as the distance between us stretches, but her voice is gone.

Aria! I scream her name, reaching for her and holding on to her cold hands with every ounce of strength I have. Don't leave me! I forgive you! I pray she hears me but all she does is cry as the darkness invades every sense I have.

The gasp that fills my chest sends a pain spiking down my back and I fall off the sofa and onto the hard floor of the office. I'm sweating and my heart is beating wildly in my chest.

My elbow scrapes against the floor as I struggle to get up fast enough.

"Aria!" I scream out, even though there's no way for her to hear me. "Aria!" It's all I can say as I run to her, to my bedroom and throw the door open to find her small form in bed. It's not enough. I can't swallow, I can't breathe, I can't do anything until I yank the covers back and see her chest rise and fall. She moans a small protest in her sleep from the cold, but even still, I lay my hand against her chest, right where it was moments ago, but there's warmth and the steady beat of her heart.

There's a suffocating lump in my throat at the sight of her. Still alive and still here with me. I fall to my knees beside her before covering her with the sheets again.

She doesn't stir from her sleep, and a glance at the nightstand reveals a bottle of painkillers she must have found in the bathroom. It makes sense, given her arm. She's passed out after taking the last two pills I had. But she's here, and she's alive.

It was only a dream. But it felt so fucking real. I struggle to breathe on the floor beside her and even worse, I struggle to get the vision of her out of my head.

I won't sleep until this is over.

I've never hated myself more. I don't care if she lied. I don't care if those words didn't come from her. I've never loved anything or anyone in this life like I do her, the Aria I know, the woman who I know loves me in return. The girl I took and broke, then placed the splintered pieces back together as best I could.

I won't let her die.

Aria Talvery, my songbird, can't die.

CHAPTER 11

Aria

THERE'S SO MUCH PAIN WHEN I WAKE UP, I FEEL SICK. LITERALLY sick to my stomach as I roll onto the wrong side, my left side, and a screaming pain shoots down my back and then travels up the front of me.

Seething through my clenched teeth, my eyes open wide as I bolt awake in the late morning and I struggle not to vomit.

I wish I could say I was drunk when I lost my shit last night. That's exactly what I did. I have lost all composure when it comes to this man.

It takes me a long time, longer than it should, to realize I'm alone in the bedroom. I expected to see him on the chair watching me, or in bed. I'm not sure why I expected it. I shouldn't have. He's never here in the morning. But we've never been like this before. So broken and each of us hurting the other.

We aren't throwing stones; we're tipping boulders over a steep cliff while the other lies helplessly in the dirt below.

I chose him. I wanted to be with him, and he's choosing to make me feel so fucking alone. The thin top sheet gathers in my hands as fists form and I struggle to hold back the pain from everything.

Waking up alone hurts more than it ever has before. I don't want to be alone anymore. I don't want to be hurting. I don't want to be the cause of Carter's pain either. And I think that's all I'll ever be. After last night, I don't know how I could ever be anything but a painful reminder to him.

Cradling my sore shoulder, I sit up on the bed and let my legs hang off the side as I test out my arm. It hurts like a bitch, but it's my own damn fault. The deep gouges in my wrist are worse though.

The floor's cold under my bare feet as I make my way to the bathroom in search of more painkillers and something I can use to clean the cuts. I don't find either, but I get ready, thinking about the bathroom located off the foyer. I bet there's some in there.

All the while I brush my teeth, I stare at myself in the mirror. As I brush my hair, my reflection does the same, watching the woman I am. There's not an ounce of happiness. There's nothing but darkness.

I read in some article a while back, that pets start to look like their owners because they learn to mimic their facial expressions. It's the same with adopted children resembling parents who aren't biological. The more time spent with someone, the more you inherit their features.

And as I stare at myself, all I see is the darkness that is Carter. The brewing pain deep inside. It inhabits me in a way I hadn't seen before.

The room is silent as I turn off the water and carefully set my brush on the granite counter.

None of this belongs to me. None of it is mine.

Every piece was a gift, comfort items meant to placate me. With a step back, it's hard to swallow. With a peek up in the mirror, it's hard to withstand the sight.

It's never been more clear to me that I need to leave than in this moment. Carter Cross is a drug I'll never kick. A drug that's seeped into my veins and wrapped its way around every small piece of me.

I'm addicted to what he does to me and he'll just continue to hurt me. He knows how much he hurts me, as do I, and yet here I am.

When I turn my back, it feels like someone else is there, someone behind me. The girl in the mirror maybe. She's watching me and it sends pricks down my neck as I slowly leave the bathroom, too cold and disturbed to dare shut the door.

Even as I dress, slowly and with a searing burn every time I have to move my left shoulder, I stare at the bathroom as if somewhere deep inside, a part of me is waiting for a person to leave it.

I can't shake this feeling. Not until I leave the bedroom. At least for a moment.

It feels too empty as I walk alone to the foyer bathroom. I'm hollow inside with the wretched truth so clear in my mind.

Leaving someone who hurts you shouldn't feel like this. Like you're losing a part of your soul. As if inside, there's a fissure that's expanding, and as it does, it's damaging whatever it is that makes a person alive. Whatever makes me feel is being scarred with every step I take.

Because the closer I get to the front door, the more I want to leave and never look back.

I could never, even for a second, look behind. I can already imagine his face and the way he'd look at me if I left him.

I can *feel* his pain.

As I round the corner, I'm careful to contain my emotions so I don't break down again.

With a quick intake of air, I stiffen the moment I look ahead of me, straight at the open bathroom door.

Even my heart stills, not wanting me to be heard or seen.

Addison doesn't see me as she pulls her hair into a ponytail. She's in her head, I know she is. I can practically see the wheels spinning as she walks down the right hall, past the bathroom.

It's only when she's out of sight that I even dare breathe.

I still don't move though. My limbs don't allow it.

How did I let my life come to this? Where I'm afraid to see the only friend I'm able to interact with because … because why? Because I'm ashamed, and scared, and miserable with who I am and the choices I've made, and I can't tell her any of that… because she's on the side of the enemy.

That fissure deep inside of me, the one destroying everything in its path, rips me wide fucking open as I walk as quietly as I can to the small half bath and close the door.

The click sounds like the loudest thing I've ever heard as I sit down on the toilet and cover my face with my hands.

I feel hot and immediately I have the urge again to vomit as I reach up and my shoulder sends a bolt of pain down my back. *Fuck!*

I bite down on the inside of my cheek so hard, I can taste the metallic tang of blood. It was worth it not to scream though. Still, I want to scream so badly. I want to get all of this out of me.

I'm stronger than this, but it feels like there's something inside of me that's falling apart in a way where I know it will never be whole again.

There's a line in one of my favorite stories from *Alice in Wonderland*, that goes something to the effect of, there's no use to going back to yesterday, you're a different person than you were then.

I hate that line now. I used to love it. I could have lived by that sentiment, feeling purposeful and fulfilled. Right now? The very idea of that quote forces me to jump off the toilet seat so I can hurl what little I have inside of me into the bowl.

It's fucking disgusting. The taste, the smell, the burning feeling. And when I'm done, while I'm washing my mouth out with the running water, I don't feel any better at all.

Deep breaths get me through cleaning it all up. It's when I'm searching under the sink for a new hand towel to replace the one I used to wipe my mouth that I see the box of pregnancy tests.

Addison.

"Oh my god." The words leave me in a whisper and for the first time this morning I smile. It's only a hint of one, but now I have a light that's growing, if dim. She's pregnant. I fall down on my ass and lean against the wall as I hold the box of pregnancy tests and wonder what she's feeling and thinking. She's going to have a baby. And what a wonderful mother she'll be. I know she will.

The light inside of me is quick to fade though as I realize she didn't tell me. But maybe there's nothing to tell. The thick wrapper on the test I pull out crinkles in my hand and I think back to my last period… before all of this started.

The days have faded and with the shot Carter gave me, I never considered any other reason for not getting my period.

I'm constantly tired, irritated and emotional, and now sick. Sick to my stomach. But sick and tired would also describe anyone in my situation. Still, a heated wave of anxiousness rolls through me until I move to take the test.

Tick.

Tick.

Time passes and my thoughts run wild.

Tick.

Tick.

Time passes as the turmoil and sickness subside, leaving a dust to settle and a clear picture to form.

Tick.

Tick.

I don't know how long I sit there holding the box.

Or how long I wonder if it's worthless. If all of this is worthless.

I don't need a friend. I don't need someone to love me either.

I need to get the fuck out of here.

CHAPTER 12

Carter

I CAN'T GET THE SOUND OF HER PLEADING FOR ME TO FORGIVE HER out of my head. The words are etched inside of me, ricocheting around the walls of every room I enter.

Exactly how her words years ago followed me, but these pleas are haunting in a way I've never felt.

It was too real.

Even though I'm in my desk chair, waiting on my brothers, I can't stop staring at where she was last night. I'm still staring at the spot when the door opens and that's when I glance at the monitor, expecting to see Aria sleeping, but she's already up and getting dressed.

I don't know who's come in, but I start talking anyway. "We need to call the doctor." I let the air in my lungs leave me before seeing Jase and Declan walk in and each take a seat. Jase sits easily in the chair in front of the desk on the right. Declan leaves the one on the left, presumably for Sebastian or Daniel.

Sebastian got in late last night to his place, where he slept, going against what I recommended, and he's on his way here now. I need him here. I need my friend to help me figure out what's wrong with me.

Declan leans against the bookshelf, slipping his phone into his pocket and letting his head fall back against the wooden slat to ask me, "The doctor?"

His brow is pinched and I take a moment to really look at him. He's aged so much in the last few years.

I can hear Daniel's heavy steps sounding down the hall as I nod at Declan, feeling my throat getting tighter even though I attempt to relax and lean back into my chair. "Aria hurt her shoulder last night."

The pain in my chest radiates. "Last night was difficult." I can't look my brothers in the eyes, and Daniel walks in just then. The door closes quietly as I peek back to the sofa I slept on last night and then to Daniel, who asks for the time.

"We have six minutes," Jase answers him and quickly gets back to me and my lost thoughts. "What'd she do?" he asks me.

Shame is bitter. It tastes so fucking bitter.

"Is she all right?" Declan asks, and Daniel is quick to ask what's wrong as he takes the left seat across from my desk.

"Aria hurt her shoulder last night is all. She's fine," I say. It's a lie and with how silent the room is, my brothers know it too. I can't tell them what happened though. I can barely stand to look at myself, knowing what happened last night.

"Five minutes." Jase breaks the silence, lifting his arm to check his watch. The light glints off the shiny metal and I welcome the distraction. I wish I hadn't brought it up at all, but I'm not used to hiding anything from my brothers.

"When we're done, I'll handle that, but this call will hopefully give us something."

"Just so you know, we gave the last case of guns to Romano and pulled everyone."

"So they have everything they wanted?" Daniel clarifies with Jase at the news, and Jase nods.

We've been involved enough, and Talvery doesn't have the men to threaten us anymore.

"Good," Declan remarks, "Let the two of them kill each other."

My grip tightens on the smooth leather of the armrest as I stare at Jase and tell him, "All I want is to keep them all away from here." He nods easily at first, in complete agreement but when he looks back at me, his expression becomes more serious. "No one gets close," I say, and my voice hardens, thinking about keeping Aria safe. I won't let her die.

"Of course," Jase tells me, his gaze searching my face for what's changed since I last spoke to him yesterday about pulling everyone. I know I'm still shaken and out of everyone, I know Jase can tell something's off.

I'm saved from his inquisition as the door opens, and Sebastian comes in. His hair is longer, his scruff now a short and neatly trimmed beard. His eyes have aged, but the man I once knew like a brother, walks into the office and I can feel the tension start to leave my body almost immediately.

"Sorry I'm late."

"Welcome home," I tell him, meeting his gaze, but my own words are drowned out by those of my brothers. When we were younger, Sebastian was all we had to guide us.

My body's stiff as I make my way around to greet him. Seeing him is bittersweet. Time has passed, and both of us have changed. But in this cruel world we live in where you have to fight to survive, there's nothing like a friend who's been there every time you've needed them.

In Sebastian's case, every time but one, but there's no time to dwell on the past. Again my gaze shifts to the empty sofa as I head back toward my seat.

I'm still so fucking cold, and for a moment I feel like I can't breathe again.

"It's good to see you guys again," Sebastian says and then takes us in one by one.

"I wish things were different," I tell him and no words could speak more truth.

"It's only a little bloodshed," Sebastian offers, smirking and leaning back against the wall.

"You all right?" he asks me, and he doesn't hide the concern in his question. He never has, and with those words I'm taken back to when I was only a child and all the times he asked me the exact same thing.

"I'm ready for this to be over," I answer him and we share a knowing look.

"I guess it's good that I came then." His answer is firm, but comes out in a way that makes me feel slightly relieved.

I give him as much of a genuine smile as I can as he walks over the spot Aria was in last night and then back to the door. *It was only a dream.* I have to remind myself.

Sebastian asks Declan as he leans against the closed door, "Are you all set?" My brother gives him a nod, and an arrogant smirk in return.

Declan stalks from the bookshelf and walks closer to the desk, his eyes on the telephone seated in the left corner as he says, "Tracers are on and these are new. Even if he's bouncing his signal off multiple towers, or the call cuts off in seconds, I can find him."

My back is stiff with tension… but also the creeping feeling of danger. We're going to hunt down the grim reaper, one of the names Marcus goes by.

"Are you sure?" He nods at Daniel's question and then all of us stare at the phone, preparing to get answers we've waited far too long for as it rings, as if daring Declan to be right.

Ring.

I can feel the desk vibrate and the small shaking movements of the phone as I reach for it.

Lifting the handset up and putting it on speaker, I let Marcus know we're all here.

"The Cross brothers," he speaks. Marcus, the grim reaper, the ghost… whatever name he goes by, he's finally gracing us with a call. My teeth clench when I hear his voice, and my blood goes cold.

His voice has always reminded me of a snake. Not a snake you can easily kill by cutting off its head, but the kind of snake that myths make immortal.

It's the way his words linger in the air and settle into your bones.

"It's been a while," Marcus comments and Daniel's quick to reply, "Not because of our doing."

My left hand raises silently in the air, quieting Daniel although I can see the anger rising inside of him as he's barely grounded in the chair. He knows Marcus has answers, and he's refusing to give them to us.

"I believe our desired outcomes may no longer be aligned, Marcus." My heartbeat quickens, but I keep my voice even and remain calm and in control. "Is that why you've been quietly avoiding us?" I question him.

Silence. For one beat, and then another.

I can feel my brothers watching me, their eyes boring into me, but I stare at the phone, willing Marcus to answer.

And finally, I'm given a response. "Not necessarily," he answers me and then adds, "You made a change that I didn't necessarily agree with, Cross."

"You'll have to be more clear on which of us you're referring to," I tell him as I rest my elbow on the table and my chin on my fist. My thumb runs along my stubble as I glance at Declan, who's watching the tablet in his hand with an unyielding stare.

"I suppose you're right…" Marcus says and then pauses before adding, "Two of you have in fact, gone off course."

Daniel's eyes meet mine at the same time I look at him.

"What exactly changed that you decided we were no longer allies?" I ask Marcus, feeling hotter and growing irritated. Marcus is an unparalleled force, but he aggravates the fuck out of me with how cautious he is. When I can use him to my advantage, which I have in the past, I think highly of the man. I've both feared and admired him.

But to be on the other side of his temper is … enraging.

"I needed to make a deal with Nicholas Talvery." Marcus surprises me with a straight answer.

I surmise, "And my interfering was…"

"Unappreciated." Marcus finishes my sentence and I merely nod, my mouth set in a grim, straight line.

"What happened with Addison?" Daniel asks, and Marcus ignores him.

"I want Aria Talvery." Marcus's demand gets a reaction from me that he can't see. My brow raises and a smile wavers against my lips.

"No." I'm surprisingly calm as I answer, "That's not going to happen."

The ever-present ticking of the clock passes in the silence until Marcus responds, "I didn't anticipate your response to be so…. shortsighted."

"Daniel asked you a question," I remind Marcus and watch my brother. "Why was she involved?" I'm not positive that Marcus is behind what happened, but I know that he knows the answer.

"Why did you try to take her?" Daniel's question comes with a raised voice behind clenched teeth and barely contained anger. His inability to keep calm is understandable, but ineffective.

"I didn't. You already know who did."

I barely contain my irritation, watching Daniel come unhinged as Marcus continues to skirt around the one thing he needs to know.

"If we knew, we wouldn't be asking you," I tell Marcus pointedly.

"Who tried to take Addison?" Daniel speaks up with the only question he wants answered. I have so many I could drown in them, but he only has one.

I expect a single name. Or the denial of information entirely. Instead, Marcus continues to evade the answer, but he also surprises me.

I don't like to be surprised, because it means I'm lacking in information, which means I'm lacking in control.

"The same man who hurt you years ago and started all this." *Years ago?* His words repeat in my head. In the decade since we've taken power, no one has dared to hurt us until recently.

Marcus continues and this time, he places a small clue in his response. "She wouldn't be yours if it hadn't happened."

"If what hadn't happened?" Jase asks, speaking for the first time. And now I'm left wondering if Marcus is referring to Addison or Aria.

"The first hit your family took," Marcus says, giving more information to solve a riddle rather than providing an answer that would be so easy to give.

"You talk in circles and riddles," Daniel sneers and then slams his fist down before raising his voice to tell him, "I just want a name."

"And I just want Aria," Marcus answers, ever calm in a way that makes my blood turn to ice.

My brother looks at me, desperate for information, but before I can respond, Daniel narrows his eyes at the phone and tells Marcus, "If all you're after is Aria, this conversation is useless. We will never give her to you."

The line clicks dead and the moment it does, I stare at Daniel, who won't take his gaze from the silent phone. With his jaw clenched and every emotion written on his face, I feel nothing but sorrow for him. Maybe shame as well. I'm ashamed I brought my brothers into this, and I don't have a way to fix it.

"Years ago?" Sebastian repeats Marcus's words and opens the door as Declan moves to leave, looking pissed off.

"Did it-"

Before Sebastian can even finish his question, Declan's fist slams against the doorframe, splintering it with his rage.

He doesn't speak; he doesn't even slow his pace. Declan's the first to leave and Daniel follows.

"Can I have a minute with Sebastian?" I ask Jase, letting go of my thoughts of figuring out what Marcus was hinting at. With a nod, Jase is gone, leaving only Sebastian and myself.

"Don't let anyone close to this place and only trust us," I tell Sebastian, not wasting a second as he stalks to where Jase was just sitting. With both hands wrapped around the back of the chair, he looks at me closely.

"Are you all right?" he asks me again and the sad smirk comes faster this time.

"No."

"What has to happen?" he asks, and I'm grateful for that question rather than the obvious, *why?*

"She needs to be kept safe. Aria Talvery."

"Because he wants her?" he guesses and I keep my expression still and unwavering, but after a short moment, I shake my head. "It has nothing to do with Marcus. She simply needs to be kept safe."

His eyes search mine, and I hate his hesitation.

"You know what she means to me," I speak with desperation and hate that I have to say it at all. It was his idea to give Stephan to Aria. Between my brothers and Sebastian, they know all my secrets. Loving Aria isn't a secret anymore, and Sebastian knows it.

"I don't care what happens, as long as you keep her safe. She can't be hurt. In any way."

"So you want me to … be her guard?" he offers and I hadn't thought of it like that, but I nod, knowing I need someone to watch over Aria.

Sebastian nods and tells me we'll talk more in detail soon before turning and leaving. And that's the end of this very short meeting.

After he leaves, I wish he hadn't. I'm alone in the room with the memories of last night, and riddles I don't know how to begin to solve. The world feels like it's closing in on me, and years of sin are mere seconds from destroying what's left of me.

"I had a thought," Jase speaks and I open my eyes, realizing that I didn't even hear him come back in.

"I need to check on Aria," I tell him, not wanting to deal with more shit. She has to meet Sebastian, and a strange sensation curdles the bit of bile in the pit of my stomach at the thought of what she'll tell him about me.

"Just listen for a minute."

"One minute," I say. I focus on the phone, on the conversation that keeps repeating itself in the back of my mind as Jase tells me we should meet with Nikolai and let Aria see it all. Let her watch as Nikolai shows himself to be the man he is in front of her.

"What if she saw him the way we do?" he suggests and stares at me expectantly.

"I can't even begin to understand why you would think that's a good idea."

"Let Aria see. Let her see you give him the chance to walk away, and show her the side of him she doesn't know about."

"Why-" I almost question my brother's sanity until I realize he thinks I'm fucked up today because of Nikolai. He has no idea what weight I'm carrying today, but his first guess is that it has to do with Aria and Nikolai.

"You think that she'd be all right with him dying then? You're wrong." I don't give him a moment to respond.

"I don't give a fuck about Nikolai, and I've resigned myself to the fact that Aria is going to hate me for what I'm about to do. What she knows and doesn't know is irrelevant."

Defeat crosses Jase's expression when I tell him a truth I wish didn't exist.

"She loved him first, I know that. And she loves me now." I swallow thickly and then tell him, "A part of her will always love him, but a part will always love me too."

"I'm struggling here," Jase says and runs a hand through his hair. "Something's wrong."

How could he not see? How could anyone not understand?

"I don't know how this is supposed to end any other way but with us apart."

There's no way for this to end other than for her to hate me, or for me to die.

"She understands-"

"And I understand she'll hate me when it's over," I cut him off with my rushed words. "What everyone needs to understand is that even if…" I have to pause and take a deep breath, staring past my brother at the closed door as I continue, "Even if she leaves… Even if she decides she can't live with…" I've thought of this ending so many times, but I've never fully accepted it until this moment.

"Even if she doesn't want me anymore when this is all over, I want her protected. I want her safe. Even if she can't live with being my wife, my lover, my … everything. Even still, I need everyone to know that she's protected and that she'll always be mine."

CHAPTER 13

Aria

CARTER NEVER CHANGED THE LOCK.
It's funny how regret sweeps through me as I open the front door. My hand is heavy with it and as I look over my shoulder, back down the hall, so are my legs. When I put my hand to the scanner, I didn't expect for it to work. I didn't think it would be so effortless.

Saying goodbye is never easy. Especially the kind of goodbye that's final. The kind that hurts to say out loud, but it hurts even more when buried deep down inside.

I only stand in the doorway for a moment before I feel the breeze in the early evening air. I'm surprised no one's running down the hall when I close the door behind me.

Even more surprised when I wrap my arms around myself, careful with my left shoulder, although it's feeling better now with the pain pills I found in the half bath's medicine cabinet.

The wind brushes my hair from my shoulder, exposing my skin to the cold. Goosebumps flow over my skin as I take each step down, each step farther away from Carter.

Part of me wonders if he's watching. Another part knows that he is.

He won't let me get far. I already know that, but I need to know how far he'll allow before someone will come and scoop me up to take me back to him.

Whether it happens today, or tomorrow, or a week from now, I'll never stop trying to leave. I repeat those words in my head as I take another step.

I don't think of the reasons. There are too many at this point, and only the outcome matters.

I can't stay here any longer. This isn't the life I want. It's never been more clear than it is now.

My pace doesn't slow until I get to a metal gate at the end of the drive. I hadn't seen it before through all the trees, and I guess it was open last time the cars drove through.

I can't imagine they keep anything out but vehicles, because the gaps in the intricate metal are plenty wide enough for a person to pass through.

And I do.

My fingers grip the cold iron and I duck my head as I turn to slip through the bars.

Peering back at the house, I know he's watching and when I turn back to the remaining driveway that carries on for at least a quarter mile and then weaves through a thick forest, I know he's going to stop me soon. The cameras at the top of the gate swivel, following me.

My heart flickers weakly. The stupid thing doesn't understand. It's still filled with hope.

There's no hope though. There never was.

CHAPTER 14

Carter

MAYBE IF SHE'S NOT WITH ME, SHE WON'T DIE FOR ME.
The thought comes and goes quickly, but as I watched her walk down the porch steps, it was there for a moment. That I could let her go to save her.

She can't die for me, if I'm not with her.

The thought is only a small blip in my consciousness, but it keeps coming back. Even as Sebastian runs into the room to tell me she's out front. I don't have time to question fate and what I've done. I can't leave her unprotected. That's not an option. I won't allow it.

"I know." The words come out even but low, with a threatening menace I can't hide.

"We've got an eye on her." He's catching his breath, his chest rising and falling with heavy pants, but his demeanor is calm. His words though, are prying. "Does she normally walk out past the gate?" He's careful not to ask outright if she's trying to escape, which is something I'm not used to from him. I can see the change in the way he looks at me. Time's changed many things since the last time we've done something like this together.

It takes a moment, another moment before I can even breathe at the realization. A decade has passed, and I hate what I've become.

I didn't want to be this man. I didn't ask for this life.

As much as I wish I could, I can't go back. My gaze centers on Sebastian, holding the authority I've fucking earned. "Lock her up." Every syllable comes out hard, and each word is accompanied with a slamming in my chest.

She can't die then. She's safe here.

"Everything is barricaded, guarded and armed. No one is getting close and no one is going to hurt her." The words echo in the room and Sebastian is silent. He already knows I'm merely reassuring myself.

"Just snatch her up?" Sebastian asks easily, as if there's nothing at all wrong with what I'm doing. I nod, feeling a knot wind tighter in my stomach, twisting unforgivingly at the fact that she's trying to leave me. Willing to leave me.

"I know she's angry." I try to justify the fact that she's leaving, but I swallow my words. "I'll make it right with her," I say as I turn away from Sebastian and move to the window to see how much farther she's gone. "Don't let her get much farther than the gate."

"You think she'll go all the way down the drive?" Jase questions from behind me. There are men lining the estate, past the drive although it's still not safe. I don't bother to turn to him as the sun sets beyond the trees, where it's least protected. The light blue in the sky instantly darkens as the auburn leaves weave patterns with the remaining light.

"Just get her." The knot climbs up my stomach and twists and turns inside of me. It's a pain I haven't felt before.

Last night plays out as I look at myself in the reflection of the window. I love her. I love her completely and without hesitation. But the man I am is one who destroys.

The fact that some part of her loves me, only means she's setting herself up to be ruined. Every piece of her broken… by me.

As I swallow down the thought, my hands move to my pockets and I vow to fix this between us. I don't have another option. I won't let her go.

"You all right?" Jase's voice brings me back to the present and as I turn to him, I look back to the sofa. Empty. Just as the floor is in front of my desk. The visions of last night pass like another blip.

Sebastian's gone, and Jase has taken his place. Time is moving like the flickering images of an old movie reel with some of the frames missing. I don't know how long Sebastian's been gone or when Jase came into my office.

"No," I answer my brother honestly and my next words come out ragged. "I've never been like this. I've never," I pause to pull my hands from my pockets and run them over my face. Staring at the drawer to my desk, I remember taking the sleep aid last night. It's only a drug and it's never affected me like this. It has to be the drug. *The sweets.* The last time I took it was years ago.

"She's just angry," Jase says then looks over his shoulder before shutting the office door and coming to take his seat opposite me.

"I don't want to sit," I tell him with agitation before he can sink into the chair.

I watch his knuckles tighten as he grips the back of the seat. "I want this over. We need to end it." My words come out harder and faster as the desperation to move past this with Aria takes over.

"We're letting Romano-"

"Fuck Romano!" I slam the back of my clenched hand against my chair, needing to feel something other than this pain that's creeping inside of me. Needing to do something other than wait.

"We can't do both, Carter." Jase's voice is calm, but full of reason. He doesn't move from where he is, but his eyes watch me with increased interest. "We can't guard the estate and also attack Talvery's." He finally moves, backing away from the chair although his hands still grip it. "You can't have it both ways."

Time marches on as I consider my brother. The one thing he's always had is an opinion. Constant fucking ideas. Constant pushing. Yet as I lean forward, breathing in to steady myself, he's quiet. He's not pushing either way.

"What would you do?" I ask him, not looking at him, but instead staring at the closed door behind him.

"I can't answer that," he tells me and I fucking hate him for leaving me with nothing. The back of my jaw clenches as I peer down at the screen. She's at the gate.

She's leaving me.

It was never supposed to be me.

Her words from last night, words that wrecked me and caused all of this shit. Those words come back and as I watch her, I believe her.

"She told me," I swallow before finishing my thought, questioning telling Jase any of this but deciding I need to tell someone, "She told me it wasn't her all those years ago."

It takes Jase a moment before his expression registers what I'm talking about. He knows about that night. As well as Declan and Daniel, Sebastian too. That night changed everything. For her to deny being a part of it... I can't fucking stand it.

"Who else could it have been?"

"No one." My answer is immediate and unforgiving, joined with a similar pain in my throat as it tightens. My eyes close as I think to myself, *how would I know? How could I possibly know if another woman was there?*

"Carter," Jase's voice cuts off the memory of that night. "What happened to her shoulder?"

"I cuffed her to the bed. Well, she did, because I told her to." Jase doesn't waver as I lick my lower lip, hiding the shame. "I told her she could stay there until it was over." My eyes lift and I find his as I explain, "And then she ripped her arm away until it dislocated and I uncuffed her, but she..." I can't even finish.

"She did it to herself?"

"Physically... yes." It feels like a lie on my tongue. I'm the reason it happened. It's my fault.

Jase's nod of understanding is short and then he peers past me to the window. "Well, that explains why she ran."

"She'll always run," I tell him as the knowing defeat gets the better of me.

"Stop lying to yourself." Jase's calm voice catches me off guard. "You love her. I know it. And she loves you. Don't let anything come between you."

Love isn't always enough, I think, but I don't say it out loud. Instead my gaze turns to the floor in front of my desk, last night still reeling in my mind. The image of her lying there comes and goes with the blinking of my eyes. "You need to help me keep her safe." I don't know how I even speak. My body is stiff and my limbs are frozen.

"You're scaring me with the way you've been today." Again Jase's feet and posture shift, but his grip remains stiff, keeping him where he is.

I look back to the sofa while I tell him the one thing that's responsible for how I've been today, "I don't want her to die."

"It's not going to happen." Jase's answer is nothing but confident. I wish last night hadn't stolen that same certainty from me. I almost tell him about the nightmare. About how real it was, and how it's fucking with me.

"Whatever's gotten into your head," he starts to say, the concern etched in Jase's words making me look back to him as he finishes his thought, "get it out."

"I just didn't sleep well." I give him a half truth.

"Well tell Aria you love her, fuck her until she forgets why she's angry and sleep. Both of you need to sleep."

"Is that all I need to do?" I question him to lighten the tension, but it does just the opposite.

"You can start with showing her more respect than you have in the past. More love. Tell her you love her."

"She's not leaving because I don't say it back to her." I scoff at his suggestion.

"I think that's exactly why she's leaving. That, and the fact that you told her what to do." His words register one by one. "I think she would let you destroy everything in her world but you, so long as you showed her how much you loved her and told her often."

I don't know when my brother became the voice of reason, but everything he's saying sinks in deep and slow, numbing the anger, the need to fight. Numbing the guilt and the worries. It all seems to fade at the very thought that I can keep her. That it's possible.

"If she felt the love you have for her, she wouldn't leave. No one would give that up." His dark eyes shine with a memory of something else. Something I know has nothing to do with me, but his next words are exactly what I need to hear at this moment. "She doesn't feel loved, and I know you can make her feel it."

How can she not feel everything I feel for her? How can she not feel *this*?

Just as the question consumes me, the phone rings and it's the same number as before.

Marcus.

CHAPTER 15

Aria

MAYBE A QUARTER MILE.

The driveway to the estate is miles long. Miles. The cast iron streetlights that line it cast a pale yellow glow down the paved road that winds through the woods, and I got maybe a quarter mile from the gate before I heard the gravel kick up as tires moved behind me. Gazing to place where the woods begin, I think maybe they're another quarter mile away.

The car heading toward me isn't driving fast and I merely walk to the side of the road and stand there crossing my arms when I hear it approach. I imagine I look like a petulant child, but it's only because I'm cold. The evening air in the shade is bitter and unforgiving.

My shoulder is numb, and so is all the pain. I'm ready for it to end. However it comes, I'm prepared for what's next.

The thought makes my throat tighten and that's when the window rolls down. It's Sebastian, not Carter. It takes me a moment to even recognize that it's him. Addison told me about him when we were at his safe house. She showed me a few pictures of Carter and his brothers with Sebastian in them. I know it's him, but that doesn't dampen the disappointment that Carter didn't come himself.

"Carter sent you?" I ask beneath my breath. Hating that I even expected Carter to bother with acquiring me. Of course he wouldn't. With the car idling, I wait for the man to speak.

He's obviously older, but his features are classically handsome. He's the type of man who could get away with whatever he wanted; he could charm you into anything. Even if there is an air of danger that surrounds him.

"Will you do me a favor and get in easy?" he asks me and a handsome smirk shows off his perfect teeth. "I'll do you a favor in return," he offers.

Kicking at the driveway, I let my gaze fall and then feel the chill in the breeze before I ask him, "What's that?"

"I'll drive; we can drive a bit until you calm down?" he offers. "You can tell me why you're upset."

Although he's seemingly kind, I loathe what he just said. "Upset?" I swallow thickly after speaking and Sebastian puts both of his hands up in defense.

"I don't want to make anything worse or step on anyone's toes, Aria." His voice pleads with me as he adds, "Just help me make this better if I can."

The sky darkens as I wait a moment. Watching this man and finding myself envious of him. He knew Carter. The boy before he turned into what he is now. Curiosity overwhelms any anger with that thought.

My legs move on their own and I find myself climbing into the car. The door shuts with a dull thud, silencing the faint sounds of the forest.

"I'm Aria," I offer him even though he already knows. "I'm sorry we had to meet this way." My manners seem to come back to me as he lets off the brakes and we move forward.

The locks in the car are automatic and they slam down, sounding far louder than they should and reminding me what all of this is for me, a prison.

"I've met people under worse circumstances," he tells me. He keeps his word, driving slowly on the long path. So slow I could walk faster than this, but I'm simply grateful to be heading away from Carter's castle of heartlessness.

"I don't want to go back," I say absently. I don't expect it to make any bit of difference. As the confession leaves me, I stare at the lock on the door, so easily lifted if only I were to reach out.

"You know I have to give you back to him, right?"

My pulse races and then seems to frost over as I remember Daniel offering me an out only days ago. I could have run, I could have accepted Daniel's offer, although who knows if he truly meant it or not.

"I've never seen him like this." Sebastian starts to say something else, but then he shakes his head and waves off the thought. "I don't want to get in between you two," he tells me.

"Everyone else is," I answer flatly and then really look at him until his eyes dart to mine. "Everyone has always been between us." That's the sad truth. If it were only us, there's no question I'd be by his side.

Parts of Sebastian remind me of Eli, or maybe I simply long for someone to confide in, someone who understands and respects the situation the way Eli did. The thought brings a swell of emotion up my chest and I stare out of the window, at the dark green leaves strewn in between the dried-up amber ones.

"Hey." Sebastian's voice brings my focus back to him.

"Have you talked to him today?" The concern on his face seems out of place as he waits for me to answer.

"I just got up, and..." I trail off to swallow the sickness rising up my throat, remembering what happened when I made it to the bathroom. "I haven't." There's nothing left to say. That's the truth of the situation, but I don't bother to voice it.

The silence in the car is awkward. Sebastian asks questions I don't want to answer.

"What's wrong?"

I don't bother to even give him a response to that one.

"Do you like the quiet too?" he asks me after a moment passes with neither of us talking.

"You like the quiet?" I ask him to clarify and he shakes his head no.

"Carter always did."

Again I turn to the window. It's not shocking that the brooding man prefers silence. And the way that little fact tugs at me makes me wish I hadn't climbed into the car.

"Although some days he'd turn up the radio just to numb it all out." He clears his throat and turns the car around. As he's making the three-point turn to head back to the estate he tells me, "When he'd stay with me, back when his mom was sick, he always wanted it to be quiet. He used to say the quiet was his safe place, but then again, he grew up with four brothers and the only time it was quiet was when he wasn't home... so..." He shrugs.

"What was he like back then?"

Sebastian regards me for a second and slows down as we near the estate.

"Stubborn, ambitious," he answers me and then says, "loyal to a fault."

He stops in front of the gate and I ask him to go around just one more time. My hands feel clammy as my gaze flicks to the lock and then back to him. I don't think he saw though.

"So he's always been like this?" It comes out as more of a statement than a question, but Sebastian refutes it.

"Carter wasn't ever like this. He wasn't brutal, he was fair. He didn't…" Sebastian stops his thoughts again and this time a darker set of emotions plays on his face. "I should have never left," he confides in me and I give him a weak smile.

"If I could go back," he starts to say, but I cut him off, stating, "You can never go back."

The moment ends with silence as the car continues to move farther away. Closer and closer to the point in the road where I've chosen. The place where he turned around last time. Where he slowed down the most, and the farthest down the drive that he'll go.

"Why did you leave?" I ask Sebastian, more to distract him than anything else.

Sebastian doesn't even spare me a look as I reach for the lock. He's too busy pinching the bridge of his nose to keep whatever emotions are haunting him at bay.

Click. I shouldn't have turned to look at him, wasting the split second but also feeling guilty from the look of surprise and hurt on his face when he sees me rip the handle back and push the door outward.

He hears the lock click up though and his fingers wrap around my wrist, my left one with the deep gouges from the cuff last night. Fuck! The pain travels quickly and in a single electric motion. I hiss from the sudden jolt of pain as I rip my arm from his grasp, nearly falling out of the car until I have both feet on the ground and run as fast as I can. I don't stop. Not for a moment. Not when he cusses and puts the car in park. Not when I nearly trip moving from asphalt to dirt as I enter the woods. Every breath hurts my lungs as I heave in air.

A few men's voices are carried into the woods. I know there are more men who guard the estate, but I don't know where they are. Somewhere they saw, which means they're close.

My legs are far too weak, and I can hear Sebastian's car door open and then his hard steps on the pavement as I whip past branches. More men shout and the tree limbs lash out at me as if to punish me, and I take it. I take every bite of the thin boughs and when I get to a sudden edge, I fling myself over, eager to get away. To fall hard, and that's exactly what I do. Landing on my back, I hit the cold dirt and roll.

My palm braces against something at the same time my legs bash into the rough trunk of a tree. The bark tears at my legs and I bite down to keep from screaming in agony. It hurts to stand up, but I do. Feeling lightheaded and weak, I stumble at first but keep moving. The voices sound farther away now. I hope they are.

I don't know which way is which, but I run as fast and hard as I can. I can't outrun Sebastian; he's far too big, and I've never been a runner. But I'll hear him when he comes, and I can at least hide.

"Fuck!" Sebastian's voice reverberates in the forest and it sends birds flying out of the treetops. Their sudden movement makes my heart lurch, and I'm staring up at them as I run into something hard.

Something with hands.

Something that grabs me.

The scream in my throat is held back by a large hand over my mouth.

My heart thumps and my anxiety spikes wildly until he shushes me, holding my small body close to his and hiding behind a thick tree.

"Shh, be calm, Ria." Nikolai's voice is the most comforting thing I could have asked for in this moment. Tiny cuts on my arms and face sting as I cling to Nikolai. Tears burn in the back of my eyes.

"I've got you now."

CHAPTER 16

Carter

"I THOUGHT THERE WAS NOTHING TO TALK ABOUT?" I ANSWER the phone with Jase across from me. He's slow to take his seat in the chair but quiet as he does it. There's not a sound in the room other than my own heart beating until Marcus answers.

"I forgot I wanted to mention something," he tells me over the phone. "Are your brothers with you?" he asks me and then adds, "They may be interested to hear this as well."

"I've just messaged them," Jase answers and sets his phone down on the table. It vibrates with a response and then another.

"I'm glad you're here, Jase," Marcus says and I can hear the smile that must be plastered on his face. His voice carries through the space and over to the door as it opens, bringing Daniel into the office. He's still catching his breath and slowing his pace after taking quick steps into the room.

"And which one is that?" Marcus asks as Declan comes in next, his tablet in hand. "Is it the one attempting to track me?" Marcus asks and instinctively I move my gaze to Declan. He merely stares at the phone on my desk, not answering.

"Of course we're trying to track you," I answer Marcus, slowly taking my seat and ignoring my own phone going off. "It's only fair, and you know it." He gives a low chuckle, but says nothing.

"What is it you want to tell us?" I ask him and glance at the monitor to see Sebastian's car parked in the street. I know he was talking to her. The nagging voice in my head is only concerned with Aria, but she's not even back yet. This call is going to be quick. First I'll handle this, and then I'll deal with Aria.

Soon. Soon I'll have her back, and I'll take Jase's advice.

"I have more information regarding the first time the lines were drawn in the sand," Marcus says. "Lines you failed to see."

"No more riddles." I cut Marcus off and grit my teeth before telling him, "I'm tired of games. Tell us who tried to take Addison and Aria." I harden my voice as I add, "I want names."

It's quiet for a second and then another, but Marcus eventually speaks.

"Jase, do you remember the articles I sent you?" Marcus asks and Jase's gaze narrows as he stares at the phone, not with anger, but with recollection. And we all look to him.

"About Tyler?" Jase asks and instantly my blood turns to ice. "The articles about the woman who hit him?" Jase clarifies and my mind races.

Lines drawn in the sand.

The first hit our family took.

"Tyler's death was an accident," Daniel speaks up and then visibly swallows, walking closer to the edge of the desk and daring the voice on the phone to deny that truth.

It was five years ago. Almost six now.

Tyler's death was before all this. Years ago. After I went against Talvery, once I started making a name for myself, yes. But I was no one. It's only in the last few years that my name has become synonymous with fear. Jase and I had barely gained ground, let alone anything worth the attention of hurting Tyler.

"His death was an accident," I say steadily, repeating Daniel's words.

Still, the coldness doesn't leave me. Slowly the memories come back of my youngest brother. He was the only good soul of the five of us. If ever a death was cruel, cutting his life short was just that.

"What were the articles?" I ask Jase, but Marcus answers instead.

"About her addictions…" Marcus's voice drawls until he says, "About her sudden death while waiting for her sentencing."

Daniel's face is pale and his eyes are glazed over. He saw it happen. He was there when Tyler was struck by her vehicle.

"What are you getting at?" I question Marcus, keeping my voice even and not letting the emotion get to me.

"She died in her sleep," Jase speaks over me and Marcus responds without hesitation, to say, "She was murdered."

"A name, Marcus," I remind him. "You wanted to tell us something, so tell us all of it. A woman being murdered in jail means nothing."

"No, but the name of the contract hit she was given, does. A hit I denied. The name was Jase Cross." Overwhelming nausea rises inside of me as Marcus weaves a tale and paints the picture of my past differently than I've ever seen it. "A small-town thug from Crescent Hills. A boy who was getting in the way and needed to be taken care of before he and his brothers gained too much ground. But she knew too much and had to die once she did her bidding."

"What?" Jase's voice carries disbelief as a growing numbness covers my skin with goosebumps.

"A hit?" Declan questions. Incredulity is written on his face.

I can't move. There's so much tension in every part of my body.

"Tony Romano came to me first." Hearing Romano's name sparks the need for vengeance, but I won't act quickly. I'll listen first, and assess. But imagining my youngest brother, only sixteen years old and dead in the street, proves that task to be futile. "He said either of the two would do, but settled on Jase." Marcus continues to tell his story while I wonder if it's possible. If it's true.

If Tyler was murdered all those years ago. If he took the place of Jase.

"The article I sent to Jase in particular was the biggest clue of all. His picture was there. What was he wearing, Jase?" Marcus leads Jase with the question, and it's only then that Jase's face crumples with torment. "Your hoodie." Marcus answers his own question, and I can hear Jase swallow.

"It was meant to be Jase, and she saw a boy who looked like him, on a rainy night in the same sweatshirt she was looking for. She wasn't a drunk driver, she was an alcoholic and drug addict hired by Romano because I refused."

"That's why you were there?" Daniel speaks up, his voice loud enough for Marcus to hear over the speaker. "You knew it was going to happen?"

"I thought it was going to be you. I wanted to save you. I had other plans for you." My throat's tight as I listen to Marcus, finding it harder and harder to disagree with his version of what happened. No matter how much I want to deny these revelations coming to light, years later.

"He wanted to end you, but instead he delivered a death that fueled both of you to conquer without remorse."

"Romano?" Declan questions, and we share a knowing look.

"Romano," Marcus confirms.

He's dead. He's fucking dead.

"Why now?" Daniel asks, not hiding the emotion in his voice. "You were there. You knew all this time and you didn't tell me back then, you didn't warn me... but now?"

"Why tell us this now?" Declan repeats Daniel's question.

"For one, you asked who tried to take Addison and Aria. I'm giving you an answer. But the other reason, the much bigger reason, is because I knew Carter would listen. I knew I'd have his attention." Marcus's voice lacks the same depth it had during his tale. Like he's snapped back to the present and he's no longer interested.

"You would've had my attention whenever you wanted it, Marcus," I tell him honestly.

"Yes," he answers, "but I didn't want it back then. I wanted it now." And with that, the line goes dead.

None of my brothers speak after the click fills the room.

He didn't want it back then?

Another riddle. I let the words sink in, but they hardly mean anything. Marcus has never lied. Romano had my brother killed. Romano has taken his last free breath.

"He's a dead man," I speak out loud although none of my brothers react.

Jase hasn't moved. He's as still as he can be, and Declan keeps looking between him and Daniel.

"It wasn't your fault," Daniel offers Jase, but Jase only shakes his head.

Mourning the loss of a loved one is the worst feeling in the world. There's no drug that can take that pain away, because there's no drug that can bring them back. They're simply gone forever.

But to learn the truth of a tragedy, to learn that there was more to the story, more than what you were told before and to still have no control, it adds salt to the wound.

And for Jase… he's in fucking agony, knowing it was supposed to be him.

The vibrations from my phone are a muted distraction. I don't even know how long it's been going off—Jase's is going off too—and I'm eager to pick it up, only to realize what Marcus meant.

He didn't want my attention back then. He wanted it now, because he didn't want my attention elsewhere.

Anger ignites inside me like never before as I read the message out loud. "Aria's gone."

I'll kill them all.

CHAPTER 17

Aria

MY HEART WON'T STOP RACING. IT'S ALL MOVING SO FAST. One decision could change the course of everything. I didn't know when I walked through that gate that it would happen like this, moving easily from one side to the other. I was foolish to think I could just run away from this life. The thought echoes in the chambers of my mind as my left foot crunches the twigs on the ground and my right side leans heavier into Nikolai. He's walking so fast, pulling me in closer to him. It's all moving too fast.

There are small scratches everywhere. My jeans are torn and covered in dirt and my arms are smeared with blood. What's worse is that I can't stop shaking. I think it's just the adrenaline, or maybe it's due to anxiety. I don't know which, but I can't stop shaking and it makes Nikolai hold me that much tighter.

The branches crack beneath our feet with every step and I keep looking back. They must hear us. It's darker with every passing moment, and I don't know where we're going but it doesn't matter; Nikolai leads me away. *Nikolai will be the one Carter blames.*

Every small sound behind us makes me jump, but even then, I'm not given a moment to stop; Nikolai doesn't let up. I can hear his heart pounding, and I know he knows he's dead if Carter's men catch us before we get out of here.

I don't think he'd hurt me, but he'll kill Nikolai.

"He can't find us together." The words rush from me as I reach up and grab Nikolai's shirt, forcing him to stop and think. "He can't think you took me; he'll kill you. He can't—" the words don't stop tumbling out of me, but Nik hushes me.

"I have you, and I don't care if he knows it." He's surprisingly calm, and justified in his response. "I've waited too long to get close enough to save you." My thoughts race, wondering how he even got through Carter's security, where they are and how long Nikolai has waited out here for this moment.

"How did you know?" I ask him, my eyes searching his for all of the answers.

"Someone told me to come. He told me I'd be able to save you." As he speaks, Nik's voice is full of so many emotions. "I'm sorry it took so long, Ria," he says, his voice cracking as he grips my waist and urges me forward. I stumble, refusing to move and waiting for him to look back at me. I need him to realize how serious this is.

"He's going to kill you," I say and stare deep into his light blue eyes, knowing it's true. Before I can urge him to run, he tells me, "Not if I kill him first."

"Don't talk like that." The words are torn from my throat, immediate and raw, just as instincts are. Betrayal flashes in Nikolai's eyes and I wish I could take the words back, if only to ease his pain, but I can't. He's stunned and pained, crushed from my words, but it doesn't last long.

The sound of heavy footsteps behind us forces me to crush myself into Nik's embrace. Gripping onto his shirt, I beg him in a whisper, "Run."

I can feel his large hand splayed along my shoulder, pulling me closer to him as he whispers against my hair, "Never. Never again."

My face is buried in his chest when I hear my name called out behind me. For a moment I imagine any way that I can barter my life for Nikolai's, but I don't believe for one second that Carter would negotiate with me. Not when I have no control and nothing left to offer.

The moment is short lived, because I hear the voice again. So familiar, yet it feels as if it's been forever since I last heard my cousin Brett.

Shock forces me to pull away from Nik, but again everything happens so fast. Even as he grabs me in a bear hug, Brett drags me along the edge of the woods to a dirt road where an old, beat-up truck is idling. There are two other men with us, but I don't remember their names and with Brett clinging to my side, I don't have time to ask.

"I'm so sorry, Ria," my cousin keeps saying as we move to the truck. "I'm a bastard and a coward, and I'm sorry."

"It's okay," I tell him repeatedly, not knowing what else to say or how to comfort him. Or where the fuck he came from. "I told you to run," is all I can settle on, but he shakes his head, remorse flooding his eyes.

"Two in the back, armed and ready." Nik gives the command as the truck door swings open with a creak that carries through the woods.

"Ria." Brett says my name reverently before hugging me one last time and helping me up into the truck. The dried leather seats are cracked. I've never seen this car in my entire life.

"Don't worry, it's sound, just made to look like it's something to be ignored," Nik says, as if reading my mind. My gaze finds his as the truck sways with Brett and one of the other guys climbing into the back and under a tarp, guns slipped through inconspicuous holes. This truck was made for getaways. The quiet hum of the engine is all I hear for a moment.

It's only then that I feel like it's real. Like I'm actually leaving Carter and going home.

Going back to my father and his men.

The two other men I can't place, although their faces are so familiar, but their names still elude me in this moment. I can feel their eyes on me as they climb into the back, assessing, judging, and questioning. Wanting to know what happened and more importantly, whose side I'm on, I'm sure.

He let me get away. It's all I can think. Carter let them take me. That's the only way it could be this easy.

The thought brings a swell of emotion up my throat and I feel like I'm going to be sick again. The dry heave forces me to open the door and lean out of it. The air is cold against the sudden heat spreading through my body and traveling up to my face.

Everything is quiet as the sickness leaves me. It's disgusting and leaves an acidic burn in its wake. But even when it's over, I can't bring myself back into the car fully. I lean out of it, feeling the cool air and wishing I could leave as easily as the wind can.

It's all too much. It's all too fast and I hold my belly, not knowing what to think or what to do.

It's only when Nik gently rubs my back and whispers that we have to leave that I resign myself to the fate I chose.

"I didn't plan for this," I confess to Nikolai as he pulls me back into the truck and gives me a napkin to wipe my mouth.

I didn't plan to leave the man I love. I didn't plan on him allowing it.

I didn't plan to run back to my family, to his enemy.

And I didn't plan for the small life I wanted to protect from all of this.

I needed to run to get away. Not to fall back into the same game, only to find the color of my pieces have changed.

"He's going to hate me," I cry out softly and once again, Nikolai pulls me into him. The truck is still idle and I know time is ticking. Precious time.

Nik calls out for one of the guys to come drive and scoots to the middle so he can comfort me, even as I cry over Carter.

As the other man gets into the driver's seat, giving me a look of sympathy, Nik reaches behind the seat and pulls out a thick, wool blanket.

"It's all right," Nik tells me, not taking the moment to curse Carter or question my sanity. "We're going home."

For the first ten minutes, I kept expecting bullets to fly out of nowhere. I was ready for the ping of steel to slam against the truck. And then I thought maybe Carter would just appear in front of the truck. Standing in the middle of the road like a madman.

It took too long for me to swallow the jagged pill. I've truly left Carter. He's not coming to take me back.

"You don't have to tell me now." Nik's voice slices through my thoughts. The man at the wheel, a man named Connor, glances at me. I know he's curious. I can't imagine what everyone thinks of me, knowing I chose to stay with Carter when they came to rescue me.

Shamefully, I consider making up a lie, just so they won't know how I've fallen for him and how I betrayed them by doing so. The idea comes and goes with the rumble of the truck being carried into the fall air.

"You don't have to tell me right now," he repeats and I gaze into Nik's eyes as he continues, "but I need to know everything you remember." He nods slightly, as if wanting me to agree to such a thing.

"You don't want to know, Nik," I answer him, feeling the painful fissure again in my chest. My cheeks heat as I stare down at my hands and pull away from him. I start to tell him that I love Carter and that I only ran because he doesn't love me in a way that's healthy. I only ran because I can't bear to think of a child growing up in this world we inhabit. I wanted to run away from it all, but as the truck jostles over a bump, I know I only ran into another hell.

"You're safe now," Connor says calmly from his seat. It takes me a long second to remember who he is. To place his face and his voice. Turning around in my seat, I remember the other man from when we were younger. The memories pooling together and reminding me who I am.

"How about I tell you a secret?" Nik offers. He sets his hand on my thigh and rubs a soothing circle with the pad of his thumb. He's so much taller than me, I have to crane my neck to look up at him after watching him swallow.

The air changes instantly, tensing and becoming thick. Too thick as Nik starts, "Do you remember the day we met? At my father's funeral when we were just kids?"

My pulse feels weak as I answer him, knowing deep inside of me that Nikolai will never hurt me, but also feeling that whatever he's about to tell me, whatever it is, is going to cause me pain. It's the look in his eyes. I recognize it too well.

"You have to wait for me to finish," Nik presages his confession, and I nod. "Tell me you will. Promise me, Ria," he commands me, his voice hardening.

I glance at Connor, who cautiously looks back to us before I tell Nikolai, "I promise." With a quick breath I add, "I'll let you finish."

Butterflies flutter in the pit of my stomach as Nikolai says, "I was working for Romano at the funeral. When my father died, I was working for Romano."

The words hit me over and over. *Working for Romano.* A revolting wave of nausea spreads through me as Nikolai swallows and peers down at me, waiting for a response. I can't breathe.

Romano. The man who took me and traded me for a war. The man who would have seen me dead that night I killed Stephan rather than to have his ally murdered.

My body stiffens and I can't control it. I've never feared Nikolai, not until this moment.

"Romano told me your father had my father killed. That's why I was so angry when you touched me. When you came over to me as if you had any right to."

I can't swallow and I struggle to breathe.

"I don't know what my father—" I battle the need to explain, to defend, to do whatever I have to do to survive with the anger that slowly rises. Lies. My life has been built on so many lies and with so many men I can't trust.

Nikolai cuts me off. "It doesn't matter. None of it matters, Ria."

I have to bite down on my lip to keep from screaming at him not to call me by the name my mother called me. The betrayal and rage stir inside of me, brewing a cocktail I'm not sure I can control.

My best friend. My only friend. Deceived me for years. He was a rat. A fucking rat!

"Your father told me that it was Romano who'd done it. That Romano had my father killed. And I didn't know who to believe. I had no one, yet both of them had hired me. I was only a kid; I was angry and more than that, I was scared and so fucking lonely."

The truck moves steadily along until we're out of the brush and dirt road entirely, headed down a back road of thin asphalt.

The day at the funeral comes back to me slowly with the quiet rumble, the picture painted in a different hue than I've seen it before.

"I'm still the same, Ria. You have to understand. I was a kid, and you don't say no to men like your father… or to men like Romano."

"Did my father know?" I manage to ask him as the anger wanes and the boy in my memory looks back at me. I remember his face. I remember the anger and I remember how he held me in return. How I needed someone just like he did. He was my someone. But the lies... I'm so sick of the sins and secrets.

"No." His answer is solemn. "Romano wanted me to keep eyes on Talvery, and Talvery hired me to do shit work. I figured one day, one of them would kill me." Nik's voice is resigned and flat, with no motive revealed in his words other than survival. "Romano would kill me for not telling him everything. Or your father, for being a rat. I didn't want this. I was only a boy."

Through my lashes, I peek at Connor, who doesn't respond. That's when it hits me that Connor knew too.

Adrenaline spikes through me, numbing me as Connor's gaze catches mine.

"I don't work for Romano," Connor tells me before I have to ask. "But I've known what Nik has—all of us have—for years."

My gut churns. My throat's tight as I look up at Nik. "You didn't tell me?" The words are merely whispers.

Nik doesn't speak, he only looks down at me with regret, but Connor answers in his place. "Your father will kill us if he finds out we know, Aria." I can barely tear my gaze from Nik to look back at Connor. "You didn't deserve to be put in the middle."

The irony of his words aren't lost on me.

"I had to stay and as everything happened, I did what I had to do to survive."

"You didn't have to stay," I argue.

"Yes, I did."

"Why did you stay? You could have left any time and just run." I push the words out, containing my anger that's dimming, and remembering all the times we've been together. At one time in my life, he was my everything, and yet, he held onto secrets that could have destroyed me.

It's quiet for so long, I start to think I didn't ask the question, until I look up at him.

He stares back at me with such pain in the depths of his haunted eyes. Pain that I don't already know, yet somewhere deep in my soul I did know. I've always known.

"I could never leave you, Ria," he tells me and then rips his gaze away to look straight ahead as his eyes gloss over.

"Then why let them take me?" I ask him and swallow the hard lump growing in my throat. "You gave me to Romano!" My voice raises and I can't help it, but as it does, Nik grips me tighter and peers at me with a fierceness that's undeniable.

He told me that he's the reason I was taken. It's Nikolai's fault all of this started. If he loved me so much, why would he dare risk it?

"No, I didn't. He fucked me over, and he'll pay for that." Nik's jaw is hard and his eyes dark with anger. The kind of anger that I've seen before. Anger that comes with revenge.

"I wanted you away from this life," he confesses to me, his shoulders relaxing as he stares out the window behind me. "Your father is getting older. Everyone knows his time is coming to an end. What do you think would have happened to you?"

I don't answer Nik's question.

"He promised he'd save you. I lured you out, taking your notebook, and I knew you'd try to retrieve it. I knew you'd think it was Mika. And Romano lied to me. I'm sorry, Ria. Your father doesn't have long, and I needed to protect you. I needed you away from all of this."

"It wasn't your decision to make," is all I can say to him. My notebook. It's an odd feeling to have an object mean so much in a life where nothing is meaningful anymore.

"I can't believe it was all you."

"I had to save you," he tells me and settles back into his seat, apparently done with the conversation.

It's hard not to blame it all on him. Everything I've gone through. I struggle with all the emotions running through my blood.

"You love him, don't you?" he asks me with a hint of disgust in his tone. "He's brainwashed you." He gives himself an explanation without waiting for my response.

"I do," I say, staring Nikolai right in the eye. "I love Carter Cross..." I have to swallow before finishing. "But I'm not dumb enough to think we'd last... Because he doesn't love me. Not how I need."

My heart does this awful thing just then. It pumps, but it's life-less. It beats, but there's no sound. It gives up on me in this moment, and I can feel it as it happens.

It's a lie on my lips. I hear a whisper in the back of my head.

I have to remember why I left. I have to remember this life and what it does to people.

"I need to get out of here," I murmur beneath my breath, not to Nikolai or Connor, but to myself.

"I can help you," Nik is quick to tell me, pulling me close to him although I'm still in his grasp. "I'll make it right. I'll get you out of here, Ria. I just have to do one thing first."

CHAPTER 18

Carter

"**O**F COURSE HE'D BRING HER BACK TO HIM." THE WORDS are accompanied by silence as we watch Nikolai and his crew pull up and wait for the gates of the Talvery estate to open.

She didn't run to Nikolai—or even to her father. I fucking know she didn't. She ran, and she had good reason with the way I treated her, but she didn't run to him.

I saw the footage.

"I'm sorry," Sebastian says from the back of the Grand Cherokee SRT. The black SUV sits in the shadows. With tinted windows and an engine that can hit sixty miles per hour in four point eight seconds, it's our go-to vehicle, armed and equipped for anything coming our way.

We got it years ago so we could haul ass after making hits.

As we sit idle along the forest two miles away from the Talvery estate, I don't give a fuck about speeding away from anything. Not without Aria.

"She was going to run however she could," I mutter under my breath at the driver's seat, excusing Sebastian.

"Still…" he mumbles, running his hand through his hair. He can barely look at me and I hate it. It's not his fault she ran. It's not his fault she got away. It's mine.

The wheel is hot under my grip and everything inside of me is pushing me to get out and storm the front doors of her father's estate.

Which would leave me dead on the polished marble front steps.

She's so fucking close, but out of my reach as the neatly trimmed bushes that line the path to the door sway with the wind on the screen. I've only been closer to this property once in my life.

At the mercy of her father when I was just a boy.

I swallow down the memory as the car door opens and several men with machine guns approach Nik's beat-up truck.

That fucking prick.

My heart slams in my chest when I see her. Her brunette locks tumble around her shoulders. Her shirt's torn and there's still dirt covering half of her ass all the way down her leg.

She doesn't carry herself like the girl she used to be. Her head is held high and her shoulders are straight, but the fear is still there, dancing in her doe eyes.

As much as she can't hide that she's a woman meant for this life, she can't hide the fear it brings her to be caught in the middle of a war either.

Aria doesn't stop looking all around her as Nikolai ushers her into the front door, looking over his shoulder in the direction of the camera we've hacked into. As if he knows we're here.

It's only when the men surround her, that I realize how quiet it is in the SUV.

The shame and regret hardly register anymore. Shame from the way I've treated her. And regret for it all.

"I'll do better by her," I tell them and still not a damn man speaks up. I see Sebastian nod in my periphery and I have to close my eyes and take in a steadying breath before opening them to see Nikolai's hand on the small of Aria's back. And then the large front door closes.

"It'll be different when the war is over," Jase offers and Sebastian agrees. As if any of it is because of the war.

"It'll be less complicated." Daniel chimes in.

"Less need to fight," Declan adds.

It was never the war though. It's my fault.

Knowing Nik's with her eases some of the strain coursing through me. The jealousy is present as always, but I don't have time for that. He'll protect her, and that's the only saving grace I have right now. Nikolai won't let a damn thing happen to her, and I owe him for that. I know more about Nikolai than any other Talvery man for one reason. He's the one who was always with Aria. He's the one I wanted every detail on. And he does love her, I know he does. I owe him more than I'll ever let him know.

He can be her hero for the moment. He can protect her.

I don't give a fuck if I'm nothing but the villain who captures her. The villain who holds her against her will until her will changes.

The villain who will put an end to this war and to the empire her last name gives power to.

The villain who will stop at nothing to have her completely.

And the rest of me, whatever is left, the rest of me will belong to her. Always.

I don't have a choice; that is all I'll accept.

And she'll learn to accept it too.

"We already know the place, and we have the count on the men." Jase is the first to get to business. Tonight, Talvery will finally fall.

There are eight men at the front entrance. Another four towers along the tall brick walls that surround the property. Each of them with a handful of men armed and ready.

There will be even more men inside. They'll have to die as well.

"Wherever we hit will be a distraction," Declan says as if he's thinking out loud, "but they'll also send Talvery into the safe room."

"We need to contain him and Aria too if we can," Jase responds to Declan's statement, leaning forward in his seat to stare at the blueprints on the tablet.

"The safe room is large, but if we get rid of it as an option, they'll have nowhere to go, they're outnumbered… it's just the matter of the safe room and if there's anything at all that we don't see."

"Hit the safe room first then," I answer without thinking twice, but then add, turning to face Jase, "Unless they take Aria there."

Her locked away in a room, refusing to let me in even though she knows I'll be waiting for her and only time is keeping her away from me, is exactly what our relationship has been. I can see it reversed though just as easily.

Tonight I take that option away. Tonight I change the course of our fate. I choose us. Forever. No more fighting; I've fought enough in this life already. I only want to love her.

"Is everyone in place?" I ask Jase and he nods solemnly. We left our home and every piece of property we own unguarded. Every single man is here. Every man ready for blood. The only exception is a small crew guarding Addison right now, far away from all of this.

"I've got the security feeds." As Declan speaks, my eyes open and I wait for the screen to flick to a new video stream, one that shows the hacked footage inside each and every one of Talvery's rooms until it lands on a picture of Aria.

The images flick by on the screen, moving as she moves, and focused on her expression.

My poor Aria. Fuck, I've never known pain like this before.

"You're good for something, Declan," Daniel tells him, with his hand on the loaded gun in his lap.

"Fuck you too," Declan replies with a smirk.

"Feels like old times," Jase says and I turn to look at him, looking at each of my brothers and Sebastian. It does.

"It's been a while, hasn't it?" I tell him, feeling each pulse in my veins. The tension, the buildup. But something else too.

"Since it's felt like everything is riding on this one moment?"

"Yeah," I answer him.

"Too long," Sebastian says lowly, checking his gun and then slamming the magazine into place with the butt of his hand.

"It used to be thrilling, though," Jase says quietly, glancing at the screen showing the men outside the door to where Aria's been taken. A few men wait outside, but Nikolai goes in with her. "This is different."

"There's too much riding on this one," I tell them all and their nods are instant.

"We'll get her and bring her home," Jase tells me and Sebastian looks between the two of us.

"When this is over," Sebastian says, "I'm not leaving. I'll bring Chloe home; she'll come with me." I don't have time to answer him.

"First Talvery, then Romano. Your ass isn't going anywhere." Jase's answer pulls Sebastian's lips into an asymmetric smirk.

It's hard to let the words go, but I tell my brothers something I often don't. "Thank you." I swallow thickly and then turn to each of them, the leather seats groaning as I do. "Thank you for being here. For helping me and for helping her."

"Of course," Jase says, his eyes searching mine and the sad smile showing. "We survived together. Fought together... Loved together."

"I wouldn't be anywhere else. You need me," Sebastian tells me and looks me in the eyes. "Mostly because I fucked up, but still, you need me."

His joke lightens the mood a touch, enough to let the other emotions in just slightly. The emotions that remind me she left me. The ones that prove to me it's because of me.

With his hand gripping my shoulder, Sebastian tells me, "We'll get her back."

"And I'll keep her," I tell them, meaning every word. I'll keep all of her every way I know how.

"All right, enough with this shit," Declan says, and Daniel huffs a short laugh. It's been a long time since I've had a conversation like this one. One that's real, and touches a piece of me that remains dormant. A piece Aria holds hostage.

"I've got it all covered now," Declan speaks up from the back of the SUV. "The safe room is empty, but it's not close enough to the outside rooms to be hit easily."

"Does Aden have vision anywhere near the safe room?"

"He can hit the west side through the hall window, send in the smoke bombs and ambush that side of the house. We'll be in and out with the bombs within a few minutes, but they'll react. The odds of coming out are not the best." Jase answers for Declan, and I can see the plan already formulating in his head.

Aden is already waiting on the other side. They're waiting for Jase's cue.

"We need to hit them all at once," I tell Jase. The adrenaline in my blood is nearly suffocating me. Only because I'm sitting here. I need to move, to get this shit over with and have her back. "Tell them all to hit on my command."

As I say the words, the vision on the screen changes and it turns back to Aria. Her arms are crossed tight, and she stands by herself awkwardly in the center room. Facing Nikolai, neither of them moving, but both of them the picture of regret.

There's no fucking way I won't do everything I can to hold on to her.

"Hit the towers, the front entrance, and the safe room all at once.

We have more men than they do." The words leave me the second the screen changes again.

"What about Romano?" Declan asks.

"What about him?" The anger and hate in Daniel's tone reflects the same in every single one of us.

"He could try to make a move on us while our backs are turned," Declan says and then cuts to a feed showing his men lining the territory. They're ready to strike, waiting for Talvery to weaken. If we bring them down first, Romano will have us surrounded and if he desired, he could strike.

"He doesn't know we know, not yet," Jase answers him and then Sebastian states, "We'll keep the north side the strongest for Talvery, pushing his men toward the heaviest side Romano has armed. We don't have to kill them all, just enough to outnumber them. Enough to make them realize Talvery, the name, the empire, is no more."

"It's just like before, no one willingly dies for a dead man." Jase's eyes shine with the memories of all the challengers we've taken down in the past. The name Talvery may be old, it may hold power, but when the man is dead, the name will mean nothing.

"What's the plan?" Jase asks me and then adds, "Step by step."

"We need to get in close first," I tell him. "She's in the east wing, so we can cut the feeds, take out the east tower discreetly with no bombs, make our approach through that way and once we're in, hit the other towers and the safe room."

"They'll be looking everywhere but at us," Jase responds, nodding his head and breathing in deep. "You go in and get her, Bastian and I will come with and take out whoever comes running."

"Kill the feeds as soon as we get close to the east tower. We'll walk along the tree line," I tell Declan and he's quick to answer, "The cameras rotate every ninety seconds. You're going to need the feeds handled before you get past this road. Or else they'll see you coming."

"There are men on the ground," Jase pipes up. "Cut the feeds, we'll get in there, kill those two fuckers outside the east tower and use them to get in."

Sebastian looks at Declan and asks, "It's fingerprints right?" With a nod from Declan, Jase adds, "Dead fuckers still have prints. It'll work."

With my brother and my friend behind me, my men surrounding the enemy and ready to wage war, it's time. My heart pounds as I run through the forest and raise my gun, hearing the startled shouts from the towers regarding the security feeds going down. I can hear their fear; I can fucking feel it as I raise my gun in the shadows. The three of us shoot, the bullets muffled with the silencers, before the two men, men just like me, even see us. The first two men to die tonight. Their bodies are still warm, heavy and limp as we drag them to the security pad, wipe the blood from their fingers on our pants to gain entrance, and begin to end this war.

CHAPTER 19

Aria

"I CAN'T SEE YOU WITH HIM." NIKOLAI'S VOICE IS CALM, somehow sounding forgiving as he watches me pace in my father's office.

I stare past him at the pictures on my father's wall. There's a picture of my mother and father, with my uncle between them. I never met him. In the photo he's holding them close, his arms wrapped around their shoulders. It's a black-and-white snapshot, taken just before my uncle was murdered. It's only one of nearly a dozen pictures on the wall to the right of my father's desk. But only that photo, and one other hold any of my attention.

I breathe in and out slowly as I stare at the second picture, trying to stand upright and not let on that anything's wrong.

It's Carter's house. The Cross brothers' home. The same photograph that's in Carter's foyer. An icy prick spreads over my skin and all I can hear are my shallow breaths.

I swear it's the same. I knew when I first saw it that the picture was familiar. I thought maybe I'd been there before, but this is why it was so familiar.

My father has a picture of Carter's old house, the house he destroyed, hung up in his office. Is it a fucking trophy? A reminder of something? My stomach roils as I cross my arms tighter, feeling more and more like a trapped animal. I wish my father were here so I could ask him. So I could face him after everything that's happened. If he were though… I can't even imagine where we'd begin. A lifetime has come and gone. I'm not the same person I was when I last stepped foot in this home.

It doesn't matter though. He's not here, and I doubt he'll come for me until he has the time. Business has always come first.

"What did he do to you, Ria?" Nik asks me and I turn to him. Seated in the whiskey-colored leather wingback chair in the corner of the room, I see Nikolai in a different light than I ever have before.

Not as my friend or former lover, not as the boy who needed me. But as a man in pain and on edge, reckless and wanting change, needing it and ready to take it.

I see him as a danger.

"Nikolai, you're scaring me," I whisper with a quietness that begs for them to stay silent, but somehow the words find him. The corner of his lips drag down as his eyes flick with a light of recognition.

"I don't mean to, I just don't think you realize what has to happen," he tells me and then swallows with a look of anguish in his features.

"What has to happen?" I ask him, feeling my hands go cold as I stand aimlessly in the room. Knowing I'm once again at the mercy of men who find me lacking.

"Today men will die."

"Men die every day," I'm quick to respond and he gives me a sad smirk with his huff, leaning forward with his elbows on his knees. He stares at the floor and not at me. His eyes close as I whip around to the door of the office, hearing shouts echo down the halls. The feeds are down. Nik's cell phone goes off, but only for a second before he silences it and his gaze moves from it to me.

"It's all right. You had to know he'd come for you," he tells me, his eyes begging me to deny it, but he already knows the truth.

The pounding in my chest intensifies, and a warmth spreads through me but not nearly enough to stop frigidness that clings to me.

"Will you hate me if I made it easier?" Nik asks me, shifting his weight and reaching behind him for the gun tucked in the back of his pants. "If I killed him, would you hate me?" he asks me but shakes his head before I can even answer. My lips are parted and the words are there, *yes, I'll hate you forever if you kill him*. The pleas not to are the same I've heard before, spoken from my own mouth.

"You know that I love you," he tells me and then he adds, "And you know he's no good for you." I watch the muscles in his neck tense as he swallows. He stands and pulls a drawer open in my father's desk, taking another gun, checking that it's loaded and placing it on the desk before closing the door.

"You ran from him… But still, you want him to live."

"I can't explain it," I tell Nikolai, watching every small movement.

He peeks up at me, hearing the trace of fear in my words and lowers his head. "I'd never hurt you, Ria. Stop looking at me like I would."

"There are different kinds of pain. And I've recently come to accept that some people, some men very close to me, can't help but to cause me the worst kinds of pain."

"Don't compare me to him," he retorts, and the menace in his voice is as chilling as the sharpness in his eyes when he looks at me.

The sarcastic and flat response comes from a place of pain deep inside of me. "How dare I do such a thing."

"You're just sick." Nikolai speaks more to himself than to me. "You'll see. When this is all over, you'll see."

"I've thought long and hard about that. About whether or not I was sick," I tell him as he rounds the desk and leans against the front of it. "I think maybe for a moment I was. Maybe when I wasn't well, and I know I wasn't well because of him. But I can see clearly now. And I'm thinking more about myself these days." My fingers itch to touch my lower belly, but I don't. I don't want him to know or anyone else. I'll bide my time and then I'll run far, far away. I'll be someone else. And leave all traces of Aria Talvery and this world behind.

"Don't you think if you were sick, you wouldn't know it?"

I nod once, feeling a strength rise inside of me. "You're not wrong, but the thing is, even if I am sick, I like who I am more now than I did before. I see the world for what it is, and I'm stronger for it." I don't tell Nikolai, but deep inside I know I can be whoever I choose. I can do whatever I choose to do.

At this moment, running is what I choose, because I want this child to live a life surrounded by love. And I don't know if it's possible to have that with Carter. No matter how much I love him or how much he thinks he loves me. He doesn't know how to love. And I won't allow that life for my child.

At that thought, it feels as if a jagged nail runs down the length of my chest from the inside. Tearing at me. It's not right and it's not fair, but nothing about this tale has been.

"You're strong, Aria, but I can give you a world where you don't have to be," Nikolai tells me. His voice caresses the pain that cascades over me. Three scenarios play in my mind, warring within.

One where Nikolai holds me like he used to. Where I look at him with the love and desire that used to be, and then I look down to a small child in my arms, one who doesn't belong to him. A baby who will forever remind me that I don't love Nikolai nearly as much as I once loved another. Nikolai would take care of me, he'd love me and provide for not just me, but also this baby. And I would use him; I know deep in my heart that's all it would ever be.

Another version of the fucked-up fairytale has me back on Carter's bed, cross-legged with an infant nestled and bundled in my lap while I peek up at the man I love, sitting across the room in a chair, watching me from a distance he chooses.

The father of my child.

The beast of a man.

If things were different, I'd never leave his side. But wishes and hopes do nothing. Things aren't different, and I won't raise a child with the venom and tension that comes with standing by Carter's side.

And in the third vision, the one I choose, I'm alone on a quiet porch, rocking an infant in my arms. I see the small home set back in the distance off a dirt road. Away from it all. Maybe a boy or maybe a girl, but either way, there will be no hate, no vengeance that lingers around us. The wind will whisper lullabies and although this baby won't have a father, I'll give him or her everything I have and protect them from what I once was and this vicious world I came from.

One day I'll tell him a story so raw and so true that he won't believe it. It will only be a fairytale gone wrong. More importantly, that child will be stronger and better than I ever will be. I can't choose a better life for myself. But I can give one to this little life.

"I love you, Nikolai," I whisper as I open my eyes and then I make sure he sees me, really sees me before I tell him, "but it's not the love you have for me. And I love another more than you."

"You left him," Nikolai reminds me and I nod my head, feeling the rawness scratch up my throat.

"If he would have shown me the love I needed, I would still be with him." I let my hand travel to my stomach, where I know Nikolai sees as I tell him, "Right now I can't risk anything."

The door to the office swings open without notice, bringing with it the sound of my father's voice. "Still be with who?" The words sound cautious. My heart races as he slowly closes the door behind him and the lights go out, darkness taking over until the backup power comes on.

My father stares behind me, sharing a look with Nikolai before looking back at me. My breaths come in quick pants.

"Father," I breathe out, and I don't know what to think. I don't know what to do. In many ways I feel like his enemy. Simply because I've fallen into bed, but also in love with the man who longs to see my father take his last breath.

"Still be with Carter?" my father questions, walking closer to me, each step feeling intimidating.

I can only swallow until he lets out a deep breath and looks down at me with sympathy. "I didn't hear everything," he says, his eyes flicking to Nikolai before finding my gaze again and continuing, "but child, this isn't your fault, and I'm sorry." A sudden wave of relief flows through me. My lungs are still and refuse to move, even with the reassurance. "It's all right, Aria." My father's voice is calm and gives nothing but comfort. I can't help but to move to him and as I do, he opens his arms.

To be loved unconditionally is something so rare. But from a parent to a child, there is forgiveness in every moment. The guarded walls crumble even though I'm so aware of Nikolai behind me and my father in front of me, coming forward to pull me in close. He whispers it isn't my fault. His words are apologetic.

He holds me close to him, he holds me like he has before, but back when I was a child. Back when I let him.

"I'm so sorry, Aria," he says and holds me tight, although his voice is tense.

"It's not your fault," I tell him, because it's true. This is the life we lead and breed. No one is to blame for the hate and havoc it brings. It simply exists.

"I'm scared," I confess against his chest. The smell of soft leather and spiced cologne wraps around me just as his arms do.

"You think you love him, and considering what he did, I understand." It's almost shocking to hear his words, but then he whispers, "I'm not sorry that I have to kill him."

My body stiffens in his embrace but if my father realizes that, he doesn't let on. A single breath leaves me and my eyes open, staring at the wall across from my father's desk where the pictures stare back at me. "I should have done it long ago," he says as I pull back slightly, wanting nothing more than to run once again. *Run far, far away*, I think as my fingers drift past my belly and I back away from my father. Pulling back from my father, I see his eyes are as cold and dark as they ever were.

One step, then two.

The second step comes with the shaking of the ground. A rumble at first, but then a movement so sharp, I nearly lose my step.

Bombs. One after another and seemingly all around us. Harsh intakes of air. A spike of fear and adrenaline.

We're under attack. And I don't know if it's Romano…. or if it's Carter coming for me.

Men scream, but not the two I'm with though. They're silent as I fall to the ground on my ass and move to the edge of the room. To hide in the corner and brace myself there. The explosions are close, but not close enough to hit us. Still, they keep coming. Each one sounding closer than the last.

Nikolai and my father don't seek cover like I do. They act like they expected it as they simply brace against the wall of the room, letting each rocking blow hit without a difference in their expression.

The ground shakes and the sounds of explosions reverberate through the room. The bombs must be close, because the shelves jostle and with it, books fall. I watch the gun as it rattles on the desk, the metal skimming along the edge as it finds its way closer to falling, but somehow manages to hang on, even as the monitor crashes to the floor, cracking the frame and forcing a scream from me with the next loud explosion.

That makes seven.

The lamp's shifted to the edge of the desk, where it topples in slow motion at the last blast. It hits the gun Nikolai left there on the corner, and my father's gaze lingers on the steel.

"Boss." Nik's voice is stern, direct, almost a statement rather than a question and the hard gaze between two men verifies my father recognizes that too.

"What can I do to help?" Nik's question is casual, at ease this time.

"Seven," I whisper the word, daring to go against the wishes of my frozen body. The only thing I can feel is the numbing tingle of fear. But I counted seven. "Seven explosions." My father's eyes stay on mine and only when he turns his attention to Nikolai am I able to breathe again. He doesn't answer me, he doesn't say a damn word to me as I stay where I am, hunkered down and counting each second from now until another bomb will hit. But the next one never comes.

The heavy footsteps carry through the room and in time with my quickened pulse as my father walks around his desk, kicking his fallen computer as he does. My shoulders hunch forward and my eyes slam shut at the cracking sound of the screen.

I shudder again when Nikolai lays a hand on my back, splayed and meant to comfort. I can't help but to let out a short cry and back away until I see it's him.

"Fuck," I gasp out and try to calm my racing heart. It's too much. This world is too much.

"You're all right here," Nik tells me and the moment he does, my father commands him away.

"Get down to the west wing. Get Connor and the rest of them. Block anyone who comes in." I've never seen my father look the way he does now. With both of his hands lightly placed on his desk as he stands at its head, everything on top of the sleek black surface is in disarray and even the paintings behind him are crooked.

The room reflects nothing of the controlled, powerful man who's ruled from that very spot for years. And neither does the look in his eyes. There's a sadness wrapped around the dark swirls of his gaze. And a sense of acceptance, plus a tiredness I've never seen.

"Dad?" I dare to speak up, and he dares to ignore me.

"Block off the hall and kill anyone who enters." He doesn't speak to me. Only to Nikolai.

A crease lines the center of Nik's forehead as he gestures to the phone in his hand, the screen of it brightening with notifications every few seconds. "There's no sign of anyone-"

"I know! You don't think I saw the messages?" my father screams at him with hurried words. Anger and fear lace his expression, but this time, Nik doesn't object. All I see is his back as his determined stride leads him away from me and out of the room.

Leaving me alone with my father.

I'm still on the ground, waiting for another sign of what's to come when my father tosses something across the room. It lands hard in front of me, maybe a foot away and again, I'm scared shitless. My stupid heart won't quit trying to escape my chest.

This is what war is, but I don't know how much more of it I can take.

"Your journal," my father says. "You should take it while you still can." I can hardly make out his words, let alone what the item is with the adrenaline and fear spiking through me. My sketch notebook I've long lost, the notebook that started all of this.

I'm still struck with betrayal at the knowledge that it was Nikolai. That all this shit started with him luring me out and letting me believe it was someone I loathed, someone who would have damaged it just to get a rise out of me, or worse, burned it or thrown it away, simply because he could. Knowing it wasn't Mika, and that it was Nikolai makes me hold the sketchbook tighter. I believe in fate and that everything happens for a reason.

The front cover is nothing special. Merely an array of wildflowers painted in watercolors. It came that way. But inside its pages are sketches of the world I used to live in. The one kept safe in the confines of my bedroom on the other side of the estate. Fantasies I dared to dream. And lives I've never lived.

As I stare at the journal, I realize how much has changed so quickly. But one thing never has. It will never change.

"I thought there would be clues as to where you'd gone," my father tells me, explaining why he has it. Nikolai stole it from me. As I crawl closer to it, clutching it close, I'm still reeling from his confession.

"Is Mom's picture still inside?" I somehow get the courage to ask him.

My father only stares at me, a hard gaze that I can't place. It's almost shame, almost hate that comes from him and I don't know why. He doesn't answer me, forcing me to swallow with a dry mouth and throat as I scoot closer to the notebook and let the pages flick by my fingers until they land on the same spot I'd last seen. The one where I drew her, but the picture isn't there.

Just as the sharp gouge in my chest seems to deepen, the edges of the pages fall from the pad of my thumb until they stop, revealing the picture tucked tightly just behind the front cover.

The kind eyes of my mother gaze at me, in black and white, and the memories of her dance in the back of my mind. When the days were not as long and filled with the terror they bear today.

Back when I knew I was safe and loved and nothing bad would happen, and yet it was all a lie.

With a small, sad smile, I swallow the dryness in my throat and pick up the picture to show my father, while whispering a ragged, "Thank you."

A cold prick sweeps over my shoulders, causing a shudder to run down my spine until I tuck the photo back away. It's an odd feeling. One that reminds me of how I felt in the bathroom this morning in Carter's room. A feeling like someone else is here.

"She was always so beautiful." My father's statement is hard. Not an ounce of emotion given to the words. Again my eyes find her photo on the wall, a younger version of my mother, hung beside the photo of Carter's home.

"She was," I speak without consent and then nod my chin toward the wall, and as I do, someone yells from down the hall. It sounds more like a command than anything else, somewhere off in the distance, but it's all I've heard since the ground stopped shaking.

I wait a moment, my body still, wanting to know more of what's going on, but my father doesn't hesitate. He doesn't seem to react at all to what's going on outside of this room, and I don't understand why.

"That's not the photo you keep looking at," he says and the chill comes back to me, like the edge of an ice cube running down the back of my neck. "Did he show you a picture too? The picture of his house?"

My stomach churns as I nod once, forcing my gaze to meet my father's. "Yes," I breathe the word, drawing strength from the truth and feeling an edge of defiance I didn't know I had. "Why do you have it?" I ask him evenly, slowly standing, and gripping the notebook tightly in my right hand.

"The same reason I've hung all these photos here. They're the failures that led to my demise," he tells me, turning to look at the pictures and ignoring me. "Each one of them, my mistakes."

I can feel the agony rip through me as I look back to my mother. To the picture of her with my uncle and my father. Swallowing thickly, I try to speak but I can't.

His finger taps on the glass of the picture frame, the one of Carter's house that was destroyed. "I should have made sure they'd all died that night. When I hung this, I thought they'd be the ones to kill me. They still may be. Maybe tonight even."

A part of me wishes to console my father, to assure him that it's going to be all right. But it would only be lies, and he knows better than that.

"Are they the ones who are here?" I manage to ask him, hiding my desperation to know and why I want to know. Anxiety whispers along every inch of my skin.

My father's smirk makes his eyes wrinkle and the rough chuckle is accompanied with the telltale cough that comes from a smoker's lungs. While I was away, praying he'd come save me, I forgot how old my father's become in the past few years.

"Yes, of course they are." His answer is what I'd hoped, although I know I shouldn't. My heart hammers and my pulse quickens, but I don't show my father anything. I give him no indication of how that knowledge makes me feel.

At my lack of shock, my lack of emotion, not knowing how to react as thoughts race through my mind, my father offers me a small smile and then points to the photo of my mother, tapping his finger once again, but this time on the very edge of it. Almost like he's afraid to touch it.

"You know that I love you," my father says and it's then that his voice cracks and his expression crumples. "I was never a good father, but I chose you and I thought it counted for something."

"You are a good father," I say, pushing out the words in a shallow breath, trying to contain the guilt and fear of what's to come. I could drown in my emotions as I take a shaky step closer to him, needing to hold him as he's held me before. "I know you were hard on me, but this life is hard and I needed it." I get it now, why he always made me stand on my own. Maybe he knew this day would come sooner than I did. The day someone would take it all away from him.

"No, no, Aria," my father says as he shakes his head. His eyes search mine, not giving away any secrets but hiding every one of them.

Another yell is heard, this time farther away and it takes my attention but only for a split second until I hear my father say, "Your mother didn't belong to me. She was supposed to marry my brother."

One beat of my heart, ragged and jagged.

"She loved him and his money… his power. He was supposed to inherit everything. He was the one meant to rule."

Another beat of my heart and my father takes down the photo, the frame making an awful cracking noise as he does, the frame splintering, from being so old perhaps. I know my uncle was supposed to be the don, the head of the family. He was older than my father, but he was killed before he could take charge.

What I didn't know, is that my mother was involved with my uncle. I've never been told such a thing.

"She fell in love with you after he died?" I assume out loud.

"She was pregnant and afraid," my father says, not looking at me at all, or the slow realization that comes to form on my face. "She needed someone to protect her after her quick affair with him, and I loved her. I wanted her."

I can't breathe, I swear to it. An unseen hand seems to strangle me as my father slowly raises his gaze to mine.

"What?" The disbelief cloaks the whisper.

"They were only together for a short time and most people had no idea. But when he was murdered, she was pregnant, alone, and with a price on her head."

"Mom?" I don't know how her name escapes me, my breath strangling me as it refuses to leave.

"I told her no one would ever know, and she accepted." The thumb of his left hand runs along the place a wedding ring would hug his ring finger. "I always wanted you. I always loved you as my own."

My head shakes on its own and my eyes go wide. Wide with shock, wide with fear in the way my father's speaking.

"I tried to love you and show you how much you were loved. Yes, I was hard on you. I was hard on you because this life is hard, but also … you look just like your mother."

I reach behind me for something to steady me, but there's nothing.

"She never loved me." As he speaks, the soft reminiscence is instantly replaced by hate. "Until she decided she wanted more. She wanted someone else and would do anything to get away from me. She was a rat. I'm not sure how many mistakes I truly made because of your mother. Taking her in, not killing her sooner, or having her murdered."

Everything in my body is cold, the numbing kind that makes me feel like I can't be here. Like this can't be real. He didn't. He didn't have Mom killed.

"No." The word comes unbidden as fear settles deep into my bones.

"You were never a mistake, Aria. Even when I'm gone, I want you to know that. I know I was hard and cold, but it wasn't because of you. I loved you."

I can see it in his eyes, he's telling me the truth. Every bit of it. Dark and callous.

"You couldn't have," I say, but my words are weak and desperate.

The sad smile carved into his expression is riddled with agony. "She was going to have me killed, Ria. It was either her or me."

"No." My memory is warped and twisted. My reality even more so.

"I do know she was a mistake, your mother was. One that's stayed with me and still lingers in this house."

I almost call him Dad; I almost beg him to stop. To tell me everything he just said was a lie. But I can't speak a damn word. I can't even move.

"I always had to see you, though. You were a constant reminder."

CHAPTER 20

Carter

"ONE MORE HALL," I HEAR DECLAN TELL ME SOFTLY FROM my earpiece. "Two men on the right at the corner."

The eerie calmness that comes at times like these surrounds me. With four large steps I make it to the end of the hall, stop right at the corner and wait. Listening to every sound.

Sebastian and Jase are quiet behind me, but they're there, both armed and ready with the silencers. Only Jase is marked with a splatter of blood, but each of us has killed since we slipped in through a window, shattering it during an explosion and sneaking into the dark halls of this forbidden castle.

We're moving too slow. The thought keeps my pace fast. Every second away from her is another moment something could happen to her. A moment someone could take her away from me.

It doesn't escape my attention that I almost died here nearly a decade ago. Every quiet step reminds me of what may have been had my life been cut short.

Turning back to my brother, I nod and all at once, the three of us step out into the hall. Holding my breath and then letting it out, my grip on the gun tightens, the metal kicks back, and the bullet whips through the air, hitting the back of some fucker's skull. There's a sharp crack, a mist of blood sprayed against the pristine wall to my right. The bang of another bullet and then another are followed by the thumps of limp, heavy bodies falling to the ground.

"Four men coming, from behind you and another to your left. They know something's wrong," Declan says in the earpiece as the adrenaline spikes and Jase and I share a glance.

"Get her, we'll take care of them," Jase tells me, reaching up and squeezing my shoulder with his left hand. Sebastian nods, holding his gun with both hands and keeping his back against the wall as the sound of footsteps and a yell for someone to answer echoes up the long corridor.

"I'll have her soon," I tell them both, "and then I'll come back here." I don't know why, but it feels like a lie. Like I'm not coming back.

Jase gives me a smirk and quickly turns around, the faint sounds of him reloading his weapon carrying over to me.

Sebastian looks over his shoulder one last time to look at me before he follows Jase back down the way we came.

Without them it feels different. It's not about revenge or murder. It's not about a war or a power play for territory. It's only about *her*. About Aria.

I won't fail her. I won't let her die.

Fueled by the memory of my nightmare, I move forward. Each step feels heavier, louder than before, even though I'm still silently moving through.

I'm vaguely aware of Declan telling me something, but I ignore him. He doesn't need to say a damn thing as I come up to the corner and hear voices.

Two voices.

Light filters under the closed door in the dark hall. And with it are the sounds of Aria pleading with her father. Begging him for something.

My heart twists into a wretched knot. That sound shouldn't exist. The pain in her cadence. It shouldn't be allowed.

My vision tricks me, giving me flashes of weeks ago. Of Aria on her knees and at my mercy. I wish I could take it back. As my hand settles on the cold steel knob of the door that mutes her cries, I wish I could take everything back.

Every piece of it. Even the moment I clung to life at the sound of her voice carrying through a closed door.

It only takes a half second for me to push the door open, the gun raised and ready to fire, but it's useless. The barrel of one already stares back at me.

"Did you really think I wouldn't be ready for you?" Talvery hisses as Aria sucks in a breath, wide eyed and backed in a corner. Tears stream down her face and I could kill the fucker now.

"Dad, please," she begs him and I can't stop looking at her, even as the sweat in my hand makes me hold the gun tighter.

"Drop your gun," he demands and the gun slips slightly in my grasp as I hear Aria whisper my name. Not in fear, not in anger. I can hear how she needs me. It won't be denied from her voice.

In my periphery, she takes a step toward me and her father cocks his gun in response. The click is resounding and foreboding. Aria stills instantly.

It's only now, in the face of actually having to make the decision, that I question if I can kill him in front of her. If I could steal her father from her.

"Don't," she begs him in a breathless whisper. She still loves me. I can feel it in the way she speaks. A piece of her still cares for me.

I tighten my grip on the gun, not knowing if she'll still love me after.

If she weren't here, he'd be dead. I could do it if she weren't here. But with her watching, still begging and hoping for the inevitable fate to change before her eyes... I'm hesitating. I've spent a decade waiting to kill this man. Waiting to make him suffer for what he did to me.

But if she hates me after... then I may as well be the one that died.

In any other situation, I wouldn't have hesitated. Talvery would be dead simply because he took time to speak. I need Aria to love me though. A life without love is no life at all.

I don't want to die, either. I don't want her to see me die.

For the first time in years, I don't want to die. I need to protect her. I need to make it right.

"Aria." I say her name simply because I need to see her one more time. I need to know she loves me still. I need her to know it's okay. But as she looks at me, her father speaks.

"Did you think I couldn't see you?" Talvery sneers, but I don't listen to him.

"Please, Dad," Aria begs, her chest rising higher and falling deeper.

"That I didn't have backup cameras?"

All I can think, is that I need to save her. In the back of my mind, although I'm looking between Aria and Talvery, all I can see is her on the floor of my office. On her knees between my legs, cold and not breathing.

I won't let it happen.

"I'm tired and growing old. But I'm not done fighting yet. And I'm not that fucking stupid," he says lowly and I know he's going to pull the trigger. "I won't lie down and die."

"No!" Aria's scream rings through the air at the same time that he speaks his last word.

Talvery's statement again means nothing, but Aria hurling herself forward, reaching for the gun tempting her on the corner of the desk, is everything.

Her lunge distracts both of us. But when he turns to her, I can't do anything but throw myself between the gun he points at her and the woman I need to protect. The only reason I've ever had to live.

My gun fires at him the same time his goes off, barely skimming the arm he holds the gun with as he cusses.

I don't feel the first shot. I don't even feel the second, but I see it. I see the barrel of the gun and even as the bullet flies toward me, I swear I see it. The sound of the shot is like white noise and it means nothing compared to the sound of Aria screaming. Her voice fills the room and it seems to drag across time as my heart beats slowly. Only a single beat to her long scream as she wraps her arms around me.

Her voice turns to a song, a lowly sung hum of words; I can't make out what she's saying as I stare at my chest, the bright red soaking through the crisp white shirt as I fall to the floor.

My arm doesn't brace me, it merely hits the ground hard, followed by my back and it's then that I feel the sharp twinges of pain.

I try to swallow, but blood comes up instead. A mouth full of it that spills from me as I try to say her name.

Somewhere in the back of my mind I think that I should have shot him when I first came in. I shouldn't have concerned myself with Aria. I should have killed him without thinking twice.

A dizzy sensation comes over me as my head drops back but I force my neck up, I force myself to look at Aria, to command her to get behind me, but she's not looking at me and I can't speak. Every time

I try, hot blood fills my mouth. It's all I can taste; it's all I can smell. I struggle to breathe, to move even and it's not the pain. The pain is nothing. Something else is holding me down.

"No!" I hear Aria scream, but it sounds so far away.

"I'm sorry," I try to tell her, but the words are muffled as I choke on my own blood. Hate fuels me to keep my eyes open as Aria yells something I can't hear to her father. She's right here, so close to me, but I can't move my arms to hold her anymore. My body's so numb, so heavy.

I'm sorry I put her in the middle of this. I'm sorry I put her in danger. I'm sorry I made her want to run again. I'm sorry I can't protect her. That's my worst sin.

As I see the darkness settle in, the sounds fade to nothing, and her touch wanes, I'm most sorry that I can't protect her.

Fuck, no. I need to protect her still.

I don't want to leave her. I don't want to die.

"Aria," I try to say her name, but I can't.

I try to fight the heavy weight that's holding me down. "I love you," I say, but the words fail to be heard. Did I say them?

She must know them. She must.

"You can't die, Carter," I hear Aria whisper and she sounds so close but I can't see her, I can't feel her.

For the first time in so long, I'm scared. I'm terrified.

I couldn't care less about life and death. But I don't want to be without her. I need Aria. I need to protect her. And as the darkness takes over, I'm truly terrified that I'll never see her again.

The last thought I have, is that if I die, she can't die for me. Suddenly, the cold feels peaceful.

She didn't die for me. If the price to change the course of fate was that I must die for her… so be it.

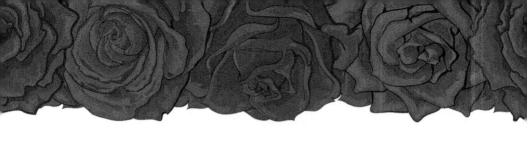

CHAPTER 21

Aria

THE BLOOD IS EVERYWHERE. MY HANDS ARE STAINED WITH IT as I apply pressure to the bullet wound and scream at Carter to answer me.

"Look at you." My father hasn't stopped talking, hasn't stopped shaming me for staying at Carter's side. Hasn't stopped shaming me for reaching for the gun.

I had to try. With a man on either side of me, both wanting to kill the other, I couldn't stand by helplessly, doing nothing.

The blood isn't nearly as hot as the tears that won't stop. He's not answering me; he isn't responding to me no matter how loud I scream. His name tears up my throat as I scream his name. As I do, the pressure lifts just slightly on the wound nearly in the center of his chest and more blood pools around him.

Hold him tight, or else he'll die.

Words from a man I've never met come back to me, and I shove my body down, clutching Carter and putting all of my weight on both of my hands, still compressing the wounds. "Don't leave me," I cry as my hair sticks to my wet face and the hot tears mix with his blood as I lay my cheek in the crook of his neck.

I can feel his heart.

It beats as the door to the office creaks open and my father yells at me to get up. To be a Talvery and to prove he made the right choice all those years ago. That I'm truly his daughter. His words mean nothing to me. They hang in the air. All I listen to is the faint beat of Carter's heart and how slow it is. It's slowing.

I only turn my head to look at my father when I hear him cock the gun again.

My throat is tight with emotion as I look from the barrel of the gun up to him. The pressure I have on Carter's gunshot wounds doesn't waver though.

"I love him," I plead with my father and as I do, I belatedly notice a gun laying only a foot from where I am, so close I could reach it. What a useless thing to come to me now. If I let go, Carter will die. I know it deep in my soul.

If I were to reach it, to manage to grab it and kill my father to end all of this, what point would there be in living?

I'd rather die like this, doing everything I can to save the one I love, than live knowing I let him die.

My eyes move from the gun to the portrait of his family home and I close my eyes, pressing my cheek to Carter's chest as I hold him tighter. I can't feel his chest moving anymore though. I don't hear him breathing either.

"Choose your family, Aria. Step aside and let me finish him. I forgive you," my father stresses the last sentence. Slowly, I look to him. His eyes glass over as he grips the gun tighter. "It doesn't matter what happened before, but now you need to listen to me. You need to act like the woman you were raised to be," my father tells me and instead of hearing him I only hear Tyler's words.

I can't look at my father, or the gun.

"I'm sorry," I whisper. Not to my father, but to the version of me that could have done better. To the hopes of what could have been and then I remember, I remember the small life inside of me and I cry harder. I mourn all of us and what we may have been had fate treated us better.

"Forgive me," I cry into the crook of Carter's neck and then I hear that voice again, the one I've only heard in my terrors. *Hold him tight, or else he'll die.*

"I am," I whisper to no one.

And with that I hear my father whisper how his own daughter betrayed him and then he tells me goodbye with a gunshot following close behind. The bullet is loud and it makes my shoulders jump, but I stay close to Carter, clinging to him with everything I have.

I know I heard it. I swear I did, but I felt nothing. Nothing at all.

My eyes open slowly, and I'm too afraid to breathe. I know I heard him shoot, but it didn't hit me. A long moment passes before I hear a body fall. First a thud and then a louder thump. I have to turn around, to face the desk to see my father, laying on his belly on the floor, his eyes staring ahead of him but looking at nothing as blood pools around him, spilling from the hole in his cheek.

A second passes, *tick*.

I can't do anything. The scream is silent.

Another second passes, *tock*.

And that's when I notice movement from behind the desk.

My eyes travel up the suit pants, to the fitted shirt covered in blood.

Nikolai's expression isn't cold, it isn't angry. He's heartbroken as he lowers his gun and I watch him swallow.

"Do you want to tell them it was you? Or should we tell them I did it?" he asks me and his last word is strangled. He looks between Carter and myself and I can't even answer him. I can't think about anything but how long it's been since I've felt Carter's heartbeat.

A weak pulse is the only response I get at that thought.

"Help me," I plead with him.

CHAPTER 22

Aria

THEY TOOK HIM AWAY. THEY TOOK HIM AWAY FROM ME. JASE pried my fingers back and Sebastian pulled me away as I screamed. The memory loops over and over again, but it's not me. I'm merely watching it happen like the scenes of a movie.

"It hurts so much," I struggle to say out loud and I don't know who can hear me because I don't even know who's around me.

"You need to change, Aria." I hear Jase's voice, and the tremors rocking through my body only pick up.

"Is he okay?" I cry the words and he lets me fall into his embrace. When I look forward, Nikolai is watching. He saved me. He saved Carter.

"They're doing what they can," is all Jase tells me in hushed words, as if we shouldn't be talking and the tears fall, but I don't cry any longer. Instead I take in the room. I take in everyone. How did I even get down the stairs? How did I get here, and why are Nikolai and my father's men in the same room with Jase and Sebastian? There are other men here too. Men from both sides.

My face is hot; my pulse runs fast. Before I can beg him to take me to Carter, and bring him back to see me, I hear another voice.

"This truce isn't going to last long." Brett's voice carries through the room along with the sound of several guns.

The sound of guns raised quickly behind me, and seeing guns on all sides, heats my blood.

"Put them down." The words are torn from me and I'm quick to push Jase away. I'm walking on shaky legs, but with purpose until I rip the gun from his hand.

This war is over.

The bloodshed is over.

I'm fucking done with it.

A look of shock is written on Brett's face, but I have no mercy for him. There is no mercy for anyone, not anymore.

"There's been more than enough death today."

Carter. My heart rips in half at the thought of him dying. He's barely hanging on and I'm not by his side. I can't stop seeing his face. Or hearing the way he said my name.

The gun is hot in my hands and I turn to my left. Standing in front of the staircase, I slam the gun down on the table, shaking the precious vase my mother used to fill with flowers when I was a child. I declare, "I won't allow any more to happen." The darkly spoken words leave me even though I turn to no one.

In my periphery, I barely see the men lower their guns. Their eyes burn into me, wondering if I have any authority, and I wonder the same.

This needs to end, and I need to go to Carter. It's all I can think as the emotions well up in my throat.

"We want Romano dead," Jase speaks and his voice carries through the large space and all the way up to the tall ceilings.

"Fight with me," I tell him, hardening my words and feeling the anxiety stretch in every limb I have. Every inch of my body is hot. Every pulse seems loud and hard.

"Someone needs to pay for all this. And that man is Romano," I whisper to Jase, although it's loud enough for all in this room to hear.

"My father is dead, but I won't let anyone else die, not on your side," my voice tightens as I tell him, looking Jase in the eyes, "and not on mine. Is that understood?"

Jase's lip quirks. "It is," he says, and then turns to Nikolai.

"What about your father?" Brett asks me.

"He betrayed my mother and his loyalty," I speak up although my words are choked. I don't know what to think or believe; all I know is that he's dead and my mother is never coming back. I don't have any answers, I'll never have a way to acquire them. "My father's reign is over, and that's all that matters."

"Who reigns now?" someone to my right asks and the room resonates with the sound of shifting feet.

"We reign together." I don't hesitate to speak up. My voice is clear and carries strong conviction. "Until Romano is ten feet under, that's the top priority for all of us." I feel lightheaded with the tense air and the lack of a clear answer. "Right?" I push out the word, daring either Nikolai or Jase to disagree.

"Cross." The word is practically spit from Nik's mouth and the air thickens and practically suffocates me as I watch the men meet face to face.

"What's the status of your war, Hale?" It's been a while since I've heard anyone call Nikolai by his last name.

"My war?" he asks with a crease in his forehead, stepping up to Jase.

"I don't want to fight," Jase tells him easily, letting his tense shoulders fall and moving his hand away from his gun. My heart pitter-patters and Nik steps back slightly. "I agree with Aria," Jase says and swallows thickly, looking Nikolai in the eyes. "I side with her on this. We all fight together."

"You were on his side before," Nikolai comments as whispers spread through the room like wildfire. The hissing of the words doesn't stop when Jase speaks up along with Sebastian, explaining that Romano is now an enemy and they would rather side with me and my family than with Romano any longer.

"I have to admit, I'm surprised to still see you here," Brett says after a moment of quiet to Sebastian. "It's been a long time since you've come around." The air between the two of them is easy. They must know each other. Maybe from a time before this, I'm not sure.

"I chose my side."

"And what side is that?"

"The one with Aria."

My cousin's lips kick up into a half smirk. "I like that side," he tells Sebastian.

"You need men?" Jase asks and Nikolai answers, "We need guns."

"We have guns," Sebastian says easily as he leans against the wall.

"We can come to an agreement," I say to break up the conversation, ready for it to end. "There will be no more death between us." My voice carries a note of finality with it and no one disagrees as I walk to the end of the staircase, staring up its vacant space as I grip the railing.

The side of the house it leads to gives me an eerie feeling. A sickness in my gut. A fear that doesn't come from logic or truth.

The type of fear that lingers and creeps up on you. A fear of what has passed and is no longer. Death is stained in these halls. And with death, darkness.

"Where is Carter?" I ask and turn quickly, facing each man who was in that room, each man who pried me away from Carter as he lay on the floor, bleeding out with no sign of stopping.

Nikolai doesn't answer, and neither does Sebastian. The men on my father's side are quiet, but they watch me. I don't care if they do.

They should all know. I love him. I chose him.

"We didn't have time for the doctor to come to us. He's in the hospital," Jase answers me.

"And?" I ask, the word barely spoken.

"And we're waiting."

I won't cry in front of these men. I won't cry with an army watching my every move, an army who need strength and decisiveness. So I only nod.

"Aria, I'll handle this," Sebastian tells me and my cousin nods at him.

"What do we do with the house?" Connor asks. I've just learned he's Nik's second-in-command. "The cops may stay back, but reporters are going to come soon."

The men start to talk. A few at once, and I cut them all off.

"Burn it down." The words come from a place of hurt. A place of pain. "Burn this house to the ground," I give each word the hate they've earned before turning calmly to the men, still gripping the railing and telling them, "It was a house fire… and nothing more."

Silence and shock greet me. The house is eerily quiet, and from this day on, that's all it will ever be.

I don't know if these men will stick to the quick truce we've made or what will happen once I leave, but I'm done with all of it. The useless killing and the constant threats especially.

Before a single man can respond, I hold Jase's gaze and demand,

"Take me to him." Finally releasing the railing, I step forward, my pace confident even as I fall apart, and head to the door. My stride doesn't slow and it doesn't wait for anyone.

I need Carter.

The war has changed; the players have transitioned, and pawns have been taken.

None of it matters if he dies though.

I need Carter.

Are you okay?

I stare at the message on my phone for the longest time. The hospital's waiting room is vacant with the only exceptions being Addison and myself. I only left Carter's side because the nurse said I had to. Only four people are allowed to be in the room at one time. Sebastian and Carter's three brothers wanted to see him and I'd been in there since the moment we got here. It's been ten hours now.

I slept by his side, my hand in his and my cheek on the edge of his bed. I was only in and out of sleep though and each time I fell to the depths of a dream, he was there, waiting for me.

He holds me in my dream and tells me it's okay. But it's not. It's not okay. And I tell him that over and over again. He needs to come back to me. I need him here. I can't live without him.

With tears clouding my vision, I look at the message again and instead of answering Nikolai, I ask him the same.

Are you?

It took me a while to message him back, but his reply is immediate: *My answer depends on yours.*

"You okay?" Addison asks, breaking the silence in the room. The only sound is a clock at the far end of the waiting room clicking each time the numbers change. It mocks us.

Swallowing down the ragged lump in my throat, I grab her hand when she reaches for mine and I squeeze tight, but then I let her go, moving it back to my phone. "Just a message," I answer her weakly. Everyone asks if I'm okay, as if that's even a possibility right now.

Wiping under my eyes gently with the sleeve of the baggy black hoodie Sebastian gave me, I shake my head.

"I'm right here," Addison says with a weak smile that doesn't last. It merely flickers on her face.

"And I'm here for you," I tell her back and she leans into me, resting her head on my shoulder for just a moment before bringing her knees into her chest and wrapping herself in the blanket Daniel gave her. The waiting room is so cold. But I suppose it's better that way.

I didn't expect for this to happen. I finally answer Nik.

For what? he asks.

I want to tell him—all of it. To be taken, to fall in love, to learn who I am and what I want. I haven't told Addison or anyone about the baby. Only a nurse, who I confided in because I was scared with everything that had happened. I was scared the baby would be gone. She said she wouldn't be able to tell me unless I was at least six weeks pregnant. So now, it's a matter of waiting.

It's all a matter of waiting.

Talk to me. Where are you? Nik messages me.

Hospital. He's not okay. As I write the last word and press send, that sick feeling of loss weighs me down.

You really love him? Nik answers me with the question and I don't wait to tell him that I do. To admit it.

I want to stay with him, Nikolai. I need him to be okay.

I wait and wait this time as he types but doesn't send anything. All I'm given is a bubble of dots, letting me know he's there, but the words don't come.

I don't want to lose you, I write to him before he can answer. I can feel him slipping away in my heart. As if him realizing I truly love Carter and Carter loves me, is the last string breaking that once held us together.

He'll never let us be friends. If I was him, I wouldn't.

I know he's right, but it hurts. Saying goodbye is never easy.

I won't work under him, Aria. I have to leave.

I don't even know if he'll be all right, I message him back. It's selfish of me to want for him to be there for me, even knowing this is good-bye, but Nikolai has always let me be selfish. He's always loved me. And I'll forever love him. Just not the way I love Carter, and he deserves for someone to love him that way. Everyone needs someone to love like this. With your whole body and soul. To be consumed by it.

He'll be okay. Carter knows how to fight. And there's no way he'd let me have you. He'll come back just to keep me from you.

Nik's words break me. I know this will be the end of us and whatever we had. All he'll ever be anymore is a memory.

I'll always be here for you, but you have to reach out to me. I won't be something that comes between the two of you. I'm here for you, but when he comes back to you, you know I can't be there anymore.

I love you, is all I can tell him. My last words to him.

Always, he messages back. His last words to me.

He's right. I already know Nikolai is right. Whether he's just a friend or more, doesn't matter. It's either Nikolai or Carter and between the two, there's no decision to be made. It was always Carter.

But he needs to come back to me.

"I need you," I whisper the words, gripping my phone in both of my hands as I lean forward, praying to anyone who will listen.

The last time the doctor came out, they said the surgery was done. It's only a matter of whether or not he'll wake up. And they don't know that he will.

He can't leave me like this. It's all I keep thinking. How selfish am I in this moment, but I am. I need him. Carter can't leave me. He can't leave me alone. Not when it's finally over. My hand slips to my belly. Not when I didn't even tell him he has another life to care for.

My bottom lip wobbles as I let my head fall back against the hard wall and stare up at the stark white ceiling of the waiting area outside Carter's room.

"I need you," I whimper the words and I don't know if I'm speaking to Carter, the man I love who can do nothing but try to survive, or my mother. Praying to her to do something. To save him and to keep me from being left alone in this cold world.

"I need you," the whispered plea that comes from me is ragged as I close my eyes.

The last time I spoke these words like this was when I held my mother's dead body as she lay on the floor. In the room above where my father used to work.

My eyes slowly open as Carter's story comes back to me.

He said I knocked on the door.

He said I told my father I needed him.

He claims it was my voice.

And all the while I thought he was wrong because I never went to that side of the house. Not since I last spoke those very words and my mother died. All because I swear I used to feel her there. I never roamed to that side; it scared me to even think of going, because I felt her and I know she was angry. Bitter and waiting for something I couldn't give her.

Slowly the twine unravels in my mind. The truth pricks chills down my spine.

I don't know who knocked on the door. I don't know if that's why my father stopped and let Carter go or not.

But I know where those words came from.

How could my words, spoken on the floor above Carter when my father nearly beat him to death, be echoed years later? How could he have heard my pleas and think they were meant for him?

I never knocked on the door, that wasn't me, but I did cry out, "I need you." Only it was years before Carter would ever be brought into the room beneath the bedroom where my mother was murdered.

Those words were given to my mother. I spoke them, I know I did.

But they weren't for Carter. They were never meant for him or my father.

Years later, I think my mother gave them to him. She gave them to a vulnerable boy on the brink of death, so close to the edge of a place she lingered. She gave them to him, a helpless boy caught in a horrid place, who would turn into a ruthless, merciless man. And he would one day, give her revenge in return.

The story is there, tickling the edge of my mind, and it keeps me frozen in my seat, gripping the edge of the chair.

The last few months play out in my head, slow motion for some moments, and only glimpses for other scenes.

The only reason I fell into Romano's trap was because Nikolai took my drawing pad… the one that had my mother's picture in it.

I only fought for it because of the picture.

Swallowing is futile; my pulse quickens and an anxiety I haven't felt since I ventured into the east wing of my father's house returns. The wing where my mother died.

I remember the way I felt when I stabbed Stephan. My skin felt like ice. And there was a hand, a hand over mine that wouldn't stop. I couldn't stop stabbing him. The thought is sobering to my tired mind. The exhaustion that weighs my eyelids down seems to vanish as I try to swallow, each of the events that have led me to this point falling into place in my mind like puzzle pieces.

A chill spreads over my skin as I hold on to the armrest of the chair with a white-knuckled grip. My blood runs even colder, and I can't shake it. I can't shake the freezing fear that flows through me. It's something unnatural and my thoughts make no sense. It's not truth. It's not real. It's only a coincidence.

Still, I turn slowly, ever so slowly to Addison and ask her, barely breathing the words, "Do you think the ones we lost stay with us forever in some way?"

"Ria," Addison breathes out as she takes my hand in both of hers, freeing it from gripping the armrest and pats the top of it soothingly. "He's going to make it," she says and her voice is hoarse with emotion.

I shake my head, rubbing under my eyes with the hand she doesn't have and telling her, "No, not him. Not Carter." A second passes, one painful beat in my chest before I look into her soft gaze and ask, "Do you think others, others we loved but who have passed stay with us?"

She searches my gaze for only a moment before nodding her head.

"They must." Her answer is final with no room for doubt.

At the same time as the doctor walks through the doorway, heading straight to us, Addison adds, "Even death can't sever love."

CHAPTER 23

Carter

S HE WAS HERE. I KNOW IT. I CAN STILL SMELL THE SOFT CITRUS scent of her shampoo. As death threatened to drag me to hell where I belong, I swear I heard her sing for me. The cadence of her sweet, feminine voice, carried past the damnation I knew was sure to come and I clung to it.

I will forever cling to her.

I could hear her, even feel her, but I couldn't open my eyes. I couldn't speak either. All I wanted to do was to tell her I love her. But I couldn't.

I would rather her pull a gun out on me any day than to lose her.

Knock, knock. The door creaks open as the knocks filter into the room.

A trot in my chest proves I'm still waiting on Aria, but it's not her. My brothers come in, but Aria's not here. For a split second, I think maybe it was all in my mind. That she wasn't here at all.

Maybe it was only a dream.

Fear consumes every piece of me. She didn't die in my place. Aria can't die. No!

"Aria," I breathe her name and Sebastian tells me she's okay. She's in the hall waiting.

A sharp pain shoots through my chest, a pain I've never felt before and I can hear the beeping of a machine over and over as I grimace.

"You don't have to sit up," Daniel tells me, moving to my side and trying to keep me from moving. I want to go to her. To see her. "Don't overdo it," I hear Jase tell me. As my head starts to feel lighter, I focus only on breathing.

"Fuck off," I say and shove him away, ignoring the heat of an agonizing pain rip up my right side. I seethe inwardly and in that moment, at this weak moment in my life, the door opens and Aria's there.

It's all like a dream. My body slumps back, my focus entirely on her and the way her eyes lift to mine, brightening at the sight of me looking at her.

"Just relax," Jase tells me as he drags a chair across the room, cutting off my path to Aria for a split second and again I try to get up and go to her, but it fucking hurts.

Daniel tries to push me back down, a gentle push, but he can fuck off.

He doesn't need to do a damn thing anyway; the pain is enough to keep me from moving. It's such a sharp pain, I can feel it everywhere. It heightens the slight twinge from the needles in my arm. The pressure on my chest feels like too much.

All of this pain is negligible though. She's here. We survived.

"I'm fine," I grit through my teeth, refusing to take my eyes away from her.

"Have it your way," Daniel says then raises his hands and backs up to lean against the wall in front of me. His head rests against the cream walls, next to a painting of some church. Seeing it reminds me where I am. The doctor came in a moment ago. Saint Francis Hospital is small and off a back road. They're also now equipped with two dozen men outside this room, this hall, and this building.

The doctor said I need at least a week in bed. I'll give it two days.

I want to be home. With Aria.

I won't stay here for long.

"How are you doing?" Jase asks me and I give him a side-eye.

"Fucking peachy," I answer him. My heart tightens as I watch Aria take a half step closer. Her fingers wring around one another nervously. She's still quiet and hasn't said a word.

I remember those last moments, but I also remember that she ran away.

And the last time we were alone… I remember that too. How she cuffed herself to the bed at my command. At my arrogance.

Never again. I'll never let it happen again.

"What happened?" I hate that I have to ask and the knot in my throat nearly suffocates me knowing that regardless of what happened when I blacked out, my songbird went through it alone. I wasn't strong enough for her.

I failed her.

My throat constricts when Jase tells me Nikolai killed her father. He shot him and now we have a truce. One built on the condition that we join forces to eliminate Romano.

Nikolai was her knight in shining armor. I knew I'd owe him, but I never imagined I'd owe him for my own life.

"Romano is the new target then," I tell Jase with a tight voice, letting go of the jealousy and the hate I have for the first love Aria ever had. I force the semblance of a smirk to my lips as I shift on the bed. Every movement exacerbates the pain of the needles digging into my arms.

I needed a blood transfusion. Three ice cold bags of the shit. I may not have been able to speak or even open my eyes. But I felt it. I felt everything as I hovered the edge of death, fighting to get back to Aria, moving toward the sound of her mournful hums.

"It's the right move to go after Romano. We can let Talvery's men choose what position they take afterward, but for now, Romano is the only enemy," Jase says and Daniel agrees.

"I know." I swallow gravely and watch Aria in my periphery. My brothers may be in front of me, but I couldn't give two shits about them. I don't care about the war. The territories. I don't care about anything other than never putting Aria in the line of fire again.

"He knows we fucked him." Jase's voice is even as he slips his hands into his pockets. I can see through his jeans how he balls them into fists before releasing them and then does it all over again as he speaks.

My heartbeat is faint and the voices around me are nothing but muted white noise as I stare at him. The soft beeps of the monitor continue all the while I have to force myself to focus on what they're saying.

All I want to do is make sure we're all right. I need to know that Aria and I are all right and that she forgives me. For everything.

I'm so fucking weak for her.

She has me in every way she can. Forever more.

"With Aria being seen and involved, the Talvery men won't turn on us." He peeks over his shoulder and pauses, seemingly biting his tongue before adding, "For now."

I gauge Aria's response, but she gives away nothing. Nothing at all. Her small frame doesn't even sway as she keeps her focus on me. On the tubes that connect to the needle in my veins and the monitors on my chest. I wish I could rip the fuckers out right now. I don't want her to see me like this.

I may be weak for Aria, but I won't be like this, confined to this bed, for long.

"Nikolai won't betray us so long as he thinks Aria is safe," Jase says.

"Nikolai won't betray us," Aria speaks for the first time, her voice hard as she gives her full attention to Jase, daring him to deny what she's saying is true. "He'll keep his word."

"The war between our families is over. We'll act as one." Aria's strength and determination are barely offset by the raw emotion in her voice. The reluctance to accept anything else will be her downfall. But I'll catch her. And I will bend to her volition as best I can.

"For now," Daniel speaks up. "Someone from your ranks may want to go their own way, to take men and rally against you, Aria. But for now, Nikolai is on our side. And even if they split off, we can let them. We don't need to fight for their territory."

Aria assesses him, her chest not moving as she refuses to breathe. With a single nod, she gives way to what may happen. I've seen it before, small factions separating. Generally, it ends with bloodshed, but we'll handle that when the time comes.

Jase holds her stare for only a moment before nodding once. "Either way," he speaks to me, "Romano is a dead man. He can hide in his safe house all he wants. I'll find him. I'll kill him."

"Another day and the enemies change," Daniel comments.

"We can talk about it once you're feeling better," Jase says.

"You and Sebastian handle this, plan the attack, but keep me informed." The ease with which I give up control shocks Jase, if his raised eyebrow is any indication.

"I have other things to attend to." As I speak, my hand grips the edge of the bed and I wish it was Aria's hand. I need her close to me. I need to know every piece of us fits back together how it should, how it was meant to all along.

I need her to love me.

That's all I need.

"One more thing," Jase tells me, rocking on his heels just as Daniel kicks off the wall, ready to leave us alone. Jase can't get the fucking hint.

"What?" I don't hide my annoyance in the curt response. But it only makes both of my brothers smile.

"Do you remember that woman in the Red Room?" Jase asks me and I feel the pinch in my forehead as I shake my head no.

He lets out an exasperated sigh but says it doesn't matter. "Her sister is the girl we met in the Red Room. Jennifer something. She died and her sister is causing a scene. She's making threats and calling the cops."

"Who is she?" I ask him, wondering why the fuck we should care. Plenty of assholes call the cops on us when they don't know any better. We pay the cops to tell us exactly who and why. And we pay them well.

"The sister of the girl who wound up dead. The one we questioned about the SL stash bought in bulk."

I peek at Aria, who squirms where she stands, her gaze shifting from me to Jase.

"And?" My heart races, wondering what she's thinking.

"I figured I'd stop by and see what she knows."

"And how are you going to get that information?" Aria asks, again speaking up but only to make her presence known as well as her new-found authority.

"Don't worry, Miss Talvery," Jase rolls her name off her tongue, "I'll be a gentleman."

"I don't believe you," she tells him but the hint of a smile graces her lips.

"Do you need someone to come with you?" Daniel asks and it's only then that I realize how tired he is. How tired they all are.

"I can go on my own—I just wanted you to know," he tells Daniel and then looks back at me.

It's quiet in the room for a moment and every second that passes, I wonder if he's all right. Ever since Marcus told us the truth about Tyler's death, sadness and despair have clouded Jase's eyes.

"Are you okay?"

Agony ripples through his dark blue eyes, but he plays it off. He's always handled hardship that way. "You're asking me when you're the one strapped to a fucking bed?"

"I'll only be here for a day or two." I keep my voice low and warning. "Remember that."

Daniel's chuckle is genuine, but Jase's smile doesn't reach his eyes. "Yeah, I'm fine. Why?"

Shaking my head, I say, "Nothing."

"Is that all?" Daniel asks Jase and he responds by holding up a finger. He goes on to tell me about the money coming in and how the last week's been fucked. How another shipment of sweets was stolen. I don't fucking care anymore. I just don't care. He can take on the problems now.

All the while Jase speaks, Aria's eyes don't leave me. I can feel her gaze burning into me. My flesh. My very soul.

"Could you guys give us a minute?" I ask my brother as a spike of pain ricochets up my right side, from my toes to my hip and up the back of my shoulder and down the front. My entire body is in agony.

But it's my chest that hurts the most. The pain that fills the vacant hollowness of my chest where there should be warmth. I finally look at Aria, letting my gaze roam down her small body. Her thin cotton shirt is wrinkled, presumably from waiting in the chairs all this time for me to wake up.

Please God, let her have waited for me. It must mean something for her to be here. I don't remember everything that happened, but I'm sure I told her I loved her. I'm certain if ever there were words I would utter as death came to take me away, they would be only those that spoke of what she meant to me. *Everything.*

"I need to speak with Aria."

CHAPTER 24

Aria

"**P**LEASE FORGIVE ME." I'VE ASKED HIM SO MANY TIMES tonight. This time it's to his face while he's conscious, not while his eyes are closed and he's far away from me, close to death's door and never able to hold me again.

The second the door closed, I couldn't help but to plead once more for him to forgive me. "I shouldn't have left." I let the words fall from my lips as I make my way closer to him.

He has the darkest eyes I've ever seen, but the specks of silver pierce into me... always. The way he looks at me, as if I only exist to be consumed by him, will haunt me until the day I die. And I wouldn't have it any other way.

I'm dying inside being this far away from him. I need to touch him, to hold him and make sure he's really here. My heart doesn't believe he's all right. And it hurts inside of me like no other pain I've ever felt.

"As long as you forgive me, I'll forgive you of any and every sin you've ever dared commit. Just love me. All I want is you, Aria. I can't lose you." His last words are strained, the pain of his wounds showing even with the steady drip of the IV forcing painkillers into his veins.

I can't even think about forgiving him, knowing it didn't have to end like this. I didn't have to run. It seems childish now, standing in front of him, seeing the consequences of my fear and my rash decision to hide the truth from him and flee from it all.

"Carter," I say, and his name is a tortured word on my tongue. "I'm so sorry," I utter painfully as I reach for him, getting closer to the hospital bed and letting my hand fall onto his forearm. My legs are weak; I'm barely able to stand seeing him like this.

My beast, hooked up to a machine and riddled with pain. All because of me and my foolishness.

"Forgive me," I can barely get the words out, letting everything between us fall. Every pretense, every wall. There's no room for any of it between us. "I shouldn't have run from you."

"I forgive you." His deep voice is raw. "I already told you I have. All I want is you."

All the words I wanted to tell him are strangled in the back of my throat, refusing to come out at the sight of him.

"We aren't perfect. And if I could, I'd go back and change the way we came to be, but I'll be damned if I'd let you go."

He's saying everything I dreamed he'd say, but I still have to tell him and I can't.

I can't bear to tell him why I left.

"It's okay, songbird," Carter tells me, soothing me and luring me to come even closer. "I love you," he whispers and that breaks me. Finally, and completely, I break for him. Every piece of me shatters.

And I've never felt more complete in my life. Thoroughly ruined for the man I love.

There's one secret left. One small truth that could change everything. And it won't be kept hidden any longer.

"Do you want to know something?" I ask him, feeling the tension in my body increased with anxiety. The secret I've been holding is going to swallow me whole unless I give it the freedom to be spoken.

With his gaze tired, the exhaustion of everything weighing down the strength Carter possesses, he brushes my cheek with his knuckles, and I take his hand in both of mine.

"Anything and everything," he tells me and lets out a deep exhalation.

With a small smile wavering on my lips, I let out the secret just beneath my breath, "I think I'm pregnant. That's why I ran." The secret punctures my chest, creating a crater so deep it will never be filled if Carter's reaction doesn't mend the wound. "I didn't know what to do."

He may forgive me for keeping it from him. But I never will. In this moment, seeing and feeling with every piece of me how much he loves me, I can't believe for a moment I ever dared to not tell him. To hide this from him.

A second passes and a thump in my chest feels raw and painful as pain and betrayal flash in his eyes.

"Pregnant?" he questions and I can only nod.

In the seconds that tick by without a response from him, without knowing what he's thinking, the pain trickles into my veins and I creep closer to Carter, needing him to give me something.

"I'm sorry," I whisper the words, feeling the remorse consume me. I was going to run away, and take his child with me. Tears fall freely down my cheeks. If he hated me, I would understand; there's no way I would ever forgive him had he dared to do the same to me.

There's a moment when someone looks directly into your soul, and you feel what they feel. The loss, the insignificance, the agony of being alone. I can feel it from him as he looks up at me and I can't stand seeing it. My hand finds his and I squeeze it with both of mine, needing him to know I'm here now. "I don't want to leave, and I regret it. I regret ever walking out that door," I plead with him. And he squeezes my hand back before bringing my wrist to his lips and leaving a slow, tender kiss there. A kiss that feels like goodbye.

Finally, he speaks and it's nothing that I ever expected. "I promise I'll be a good father. I swear to you I will."

I can't speak.

"Give me a chance. Just one chance," he begs me, as if I'd ever leave his side again. "I'll be good to you, I'll be a good father, I promise." He swallows thickly.

"I'm ashamed at what I did and who I was. Please, Aria, we don't have to tell him."

"What?" I question him as I struggle to keep up with whatever he's thinking. I know he's not well now, he's still in pain and on meds. He's only just woken up. "Tell who?" I ask him, my heart racing.

"Our baby," he says as he looks up at me and brings his hand to my cheek, his thumb running under my eye to brush away the tears gathered there. "We don't have to tell them what a monster I was," he whispers the strained words and I lose all composure, covering my mouth with my hand and falling into him. I'm mindful of my weight and make sure to keep it off of him, but my God do I need him to hold me. And I need to hold him.

In this moment and forever.

"I love you, Carter," is all I can manage when I finally look up to him.

My breath and words leave me as a heat flows over me, taking every bit of the bitter cold and banishing it from me. I crash my lips to Carter's and he's quick to cradle my head with his hand, pinning me to him and deepening the kiss. His tongue slips between my lips and I grant him entry. Our tongues mingle and he massages mine with swift, possessive strokes.

I don't breathe until he breaks away.

"I would do anything for you." He says the words as if they're a confession. "I swear, you are the only thing that matters to me. Nothing else matters. Only you and our baby." As he speaks, his hand slips to my waist. He gazes at my midsection as if he can already see me swollen with our child. The very vision is what caused me to run in the first place.

"I'm scared." The wretched confession makes me feel that much weaker.

"Don't be." Carter's words are simple, but impossible.

"I don't know what's going to happen," I tell him, feeling the raw truth of fear lingering in the statement.

Carter's eyes search mine as I climb into the small bed with him, needing to be closer to him and not giving a shit if there's barely any room. I need my body pressed to his. I need to feel him breathing. The second he embraces me, my worries slip away, lost in the haze of knowing I'm where I'm supposed to be. Beside Carter Cross. Our present and our future tied together.

"We will rule. That's what's going to happen, my songbird."

I can feel my heart twist in my chest, praying I'll be the woman he wants me to be. Praying our lives can't pull us apart anymore. And as my mind whirls with every possible outcome of what could be, I realize there's not a damn thing that could tear me away from him. Not one fucking thing.

"Marry me. You belong with me, Aria." Carter's dark eyes pin me in place, taking my breath and refusing to give it back. "Marry me," he repeats lowly, a barely spoken yet desperate whisper. His warm breath cradles my cheek as he lowers his lips to mine and gently kisses me before I can answer. With his forehead leaning against mine and his hand gripping my hip in place, he whispers his plea again. "Marry me."

I cling to him, burying my head in his chest and breathing in the scent of a man I'm madly in love with as I nod my head and let the ragged whisper leave me with the desperation for all of this to be real, "Yes." He's alive. He's with me. And he wants me as his partner, his wife, his love.

He lifts my head with both of his hands on my face and presses a soft kiss to my lips. It's only then that I taste the salt of tears I hadn't known I was shedding.

"You're everything to me," he whispers against my lips as he brushes away the tears with his thumb.

"Tell me everything is going to be all right," I beg him. My words beg him. My body caves to his in the way it's always willed me to. The moment I saw him, I knew deep in the marrow of my bones that I belonged to this man. The other half to my soul. Holding his life to mine is the worst thing I've ever felt in this world. Every second that passed, I was afraid to move, knowing he was bleeding out beneath me. He lost so much blood, he barely made it and I can't help but to think that if I'd made the wrong move, if I hadn't held him as tightly as I could for as long as I did, he wouldn't be here anymore. I would have lost him.

"I never want you to leave me again. Never," I whisper the last word, pushing myself closer to him; every inch of me that can be pressed against him is. And Carter does what he's best at. He keeps me close, holding me to him as if I'll fly away if only he loosened his grip. But I'll never do that again. Never.

"As long as you love me, it will." His words are whispered along my skin, sending a trail of goosebumps down my body as he plants a small kiss on my shoulder. "Because I love you." His rough stubble grazes my shoulder, and I hope it scars me. I hope I can feel him, see him, have evidence of his love forever.

"I love you, Carter." The truth is the easiest thing to speak in this moment. A raw confession that will save us from whatever is to come.

"I love you, songbird." His rough voice is deep, the depths of sincerity so true, it numbs every pain inside of me. Every pain that's ever existed.

Days have passed since we came home.

It's odd to think of this place as home, but that's all it is to me now. It's more of a home to me than my father's place ever was. Simply because of the people in it.

"You need to take it easy." I try to keep my voice from sounding like I'm nagging Carter, but every time he leans to his side on the bed to grab something from the bedside table, I see him grimace. "You're still healing."

I'm quick to reach over, careful not to put my weight on him and grab his phone for him. The vibrating of notifications is a constant, but even still, the moment I hand it to him, he silences it.

Jase and Sebastian have taken the lead while Carter's been on bedrest at home. It'll take time for the wounds to heal, even if my beast still thinks he's untouchable.

I still can't breathe around him. The fear of losing him won't leave me.

"You keep saying that," he remarks with the same evenness I give him, but the smile on his lips, the genuine happiness in his eyes, haven't left him since I told him about the baby. Every time I look into his eyes, I see it and it's so raw, so much so, that I can barely stand to hold his gaze.

"I'm serious, Carter," I reprimand him although my actions are anything but. Moving to straddle him on the bed, the sheet slips around me, puddling behind us as I settle gently in his lap and take his stubbled jaw in my hands. "I need you," I whisper.

The corners of his lips kick up, and his large hands wrap around my waist, gentle and comforting. I rest my forehead on his with my lips so close to his as he tells me, "I need you too."

He gives me a quick kiss. And then another.

"Did you take another test?" he asks me and I can hear the playfulness in his voice. He thinks I'm odd for taking a pregnancy test every day, but I have my reasons. The line is supposed to stay strong and dark, because then it means the baby is still there and until the six-week mark is here, I need the tests for my sanity.

"Yes," I tell him. I almost mention how Addison's the one who told me. She said the line gets weaker if you lose the baby. She's waiting like I am.

Instead, I'm distracted by a kiss on my neck. A languid one that makes my nipples pebble. His rough stubble runs along my skin, instantly making me wanton.

"You need to heal." I practically hiss the words with longing as his lips move to the dip just below my collar and his right hand reaches up to my breast. Plucking my nipple between his fingers, he finally raises his gaze to my eyes and tells me, "All I need is you."

He's wrong though. There's so much more he needs. Much more than I could ever give him.

He's a wounded man, with scars so deep he can't help but to be weighed down by them.

I'm still waiting on edge for something to come between us, but Carter seems hellbent on keeping us together. And so am I. I won't allow for love not to be enough.

Carter's fingertips glide easily up my neck, leaving goosebumps in their wake until he wraps his hands around my throat. His thumb runs down the underside of my chin and then lower, down to the center of my throat. His lips are parted just slightly, his breathing ragged as he hardens under me, his thick length pressing against me.

"I will do anything for you." He utters the words with such an intensity before slowly raising his gaze to meet mine.

My damn heart belongs to him. It only starts beating when he looks at me like that. I swear it's true. Whatever else it does when he's not around isn't what it's doing now.

"You're so intense," I whisper, not knowing what else to say, but my words are lost in the haze of lust that lingers between us.

I don't know if it's the fact that I'm obviously hot for him or some other reason, but Carter gives me a lazy smirk before moving the back of his fingers up my silk shirt and gently pinching my nipple.

My natural instinct is to playfully smack him away, but he's too quick, grabbing my wrist and pinning it behind me.

Even while I straddle him, he commands me.

"You make me this way," he tells me with a deep voice and leans forward to kiss me at the same time as he pinches my hardened peak. I have to gasp as he does, breaking the kiss and arching my neck. He takes the moment to lightly run his teeth along my sensitized skin, and I know I'm done for. Any authority I had over him is gone.

Carter is an untamable beast. But I'll be damned if I'd have him any other way.

"It all feels better when I'm with you," he murmurs against my skin and his tone sounds raw and hints at the pain that will forever scar who we are. With both hands on his jaw, I stare deep into his eyes, bright with sincerity. "All of it," he tells me.

"It's going to be okay." I offer him words I pray are true. I'd do anything for this man and without anything between us, nothing will keep us apart.

"Better than okay," he says before kissing me sweetly, only breaking away to add, "I promise."

CHAPTER 26

Jase

*I*T WAS SUPPOSED TO BE ME.

The car moves over a speed bump a little too fast, and my hard body sways in the sedan. My grip tightens on the wheel, and I try to swallow the hard lump that's been suffocating me since I learned the truth about Tyler's death.

It was a hit… on me. A fucking hoodie is the reason he's ten feet in the ground and I'm still here, taking every day for granted.

Slowing at the stop sign, I let a deep breath calm the anxiety running through me. With a war raging and an unknown enemy taking pieces of us as he pleases, I don't have time to get lost in the unfortunate past. No matter how much I long to go back. If only we could go back.

The hum of the engine as I roll over another speed bump keeps me in the present.

I shouldn't have come out right now. Spending the afternoon in the burbs isn't exactly on my normal to-do list.

But I had to get out of the house and away from my brothers. The regret and guilt and mourning that lingers in their eyes haunts me day and night. It was supposed to be me. It wasn't.

There's nothing I can do to change it. But I can pay Beth a visit and quiet her.

My keys jingle as the ignition turns off and the soft rumble of the engine is silenced.

Wiping a hand over my face, I get out of the car, not caring that the door slams as my shoes hit the pavement. The neighborhood is quiet and each row of streets is littered with picture-perfect homes, nothing like the home I grew up in. Little townhouses of raised ranches, complete with paved driveways and perfectly trimmed bushes. A few houses have fences, white picket of course, but not 34 Holley, the home of Bethany Fawn, also known as the woman who keeps raising hell at the Red Room. More recently she's been calling the cops and demanding answers. She's the woman who blames Carter for her sister's untimely death. Her sister Jennifer, a girl we met in the Red Room weeks ago. A girl in a mess she couldn't get out of, with a drug addiction she couldn't kick.

I know all about wanting someone to blame and looking for answers to questions that don't make any difference once you have them. Bethany's hurt and angry, but she won't find any answers from us. A simple warning should scare her off.

The skin over my knuckles tightens and the cuts from a few nights before crack open, sending a pain shooting up my arm. I welcome the seething reminder that I'm alive.

Knock, knock, knock. She's in there, I can hear her. Time passes without anything but the sound of scuttling behind the door, but just as I'm about to knock again, the door opens a few inches. Only enough to reveal a peek of her.

Her chestnut hair falls in wavy locks around her face. She brushes the fallen strands out of her face to peek up at me.

"Yes?" she questions and my lips threaten to twitch into a smirk.

"Bethany?" Her weight shifts behind the door as her gaze travels down the length of my body and then back up to meet mine before she answers me.

The amber in her hazel eyes swirls with distrust as she tells me, "My friends call me Beth."

"We haven't met before... but I'll happily call you Beth." The flirtatious words slip from me easily, and slowly her guard falls although what's left behind is a mix of worry and agony. She doesn't answer or respond in any way other than to tighten her grip on the door.

"Mind if I have a minute?"

She purses her her full lips slightly as the cracked door opens an inch more to cautiously reply, "Depends on what you're here for."

My heartbeat gallops, trotting faster in my chest as the anxiety rises. I'm here to give her a warning. To stay the hell away from the Red Room and to get over whatever ill wishes she has for my brothers and me.

It's a shame really; she's fucking gorgeous. There's an innocence, yet a fight in her that's just as evident and even more alluring. Had I met her on other terms, I would do just about anything to get her under me and screaming my name.

The swirling colors in her eyes darken as her gaze dances over mine. As if she can read my thoughts and knows the wicked things I'd do to her that no one else ever could. But that's not why I'm here, and my sick perversions will have to wait for someone else.

I lean my shoulder against her hard walnut front door and slip my shoe between the gap in the doorway, making sure she can't slam it shut. Instead of the slight fear I thought may flash in her eyes as my expression hardens, her eyes narrow with hate and I see the beautiful hue of pink in her pale skin brighten to red, but it's not with a blush, it's with anger.

"You need to stay out of the Cross business, Beth." I lean in closer, my voice low and even. My hard gaze meets her narrowed one, but she doesn't flinch. Instead she clenches her teeth so hard I think they'll crack.

With the palm of my hand carefully placed on the doorjamb and the other splayed against her door, I lean in to tell her that there are no answers for her in the Red Room. I want to tell her my brother isn't the man she's after, but before I can say a word she hisses at me, "I know all about Marcus and the drug and why you assholes had her killed."

My pulse hammers in my ears but even over it, I hear the strained pain etched in her voice. Her breathing shudders as she adds, "You will all pay for what you did to my sister." Her voice cracks as her eyes gloss over and tears gather in the corners of her eyes.

"You don't know what you're talking about," I tell her as the anger rises inside of me. Marcus. Just the name makes every muscle inside of my body tighten and coil.

The drug.

Marcus.

Before I can even tie what she's said together, I hear the click of a gun and she lets the door swing open, throwing me off-balance.

Shock makes my stomach churn as the barrel of a gun flashes in front of my eyes. She leans back, moving to hold the heavy metal piece with both hands. Lunging forward, still off-balance as fear stirs in my blood, I grip the barrel and raise it above her head, shoving her small body back until it hits the wall in her foyer.

Bang!

The gun goes off and the flash of heat makes the skin of my hand holding the barrel burn and singe with a raw pain. Her lower back crashes into a narrow table, a row of books toppling over and mail falls onto the floor as I stumble into her and finally pin her to the wall.

Her small shriek of fear is muted when I bring my right hand to her delicate throat. My left still grips the gun. She struggles beneath me but with a foot on her height and muscle she couldn't match no matter how hard she tried, it's pointless. Her heart pounds so hard, I feel it matching mine.

She yelps as I lift the gun higher, ripping it from her grasp. Both of her hands fly to the one I have tightening on her throat.

She tried to kill me. I can't fucking believe it.

Barely catching my breath, I don't let anything show except for the absolute control I have over her. The door is wide open and I'm certain someone would have heard. A faint breeze carries in from behind me and I take a step back, pulling her with me just enough so I can kick the door shut and then press her back to it. Her pulse slows beneath my grip and her eyes beg me for mercy as her sharp nails dig into my fingers. A second passes before I loosen my grip just enough so she can breathe freely.

Through her frantic intake, I lean forward, crushing my body against hers until she's still. Until her eyes are wide and staring straight into mine. The sight of her, the fear, the desperation, the eagerness to live … it thrills a dark side of me that's been begging to be brought to the surface.

"You're going to tell me everything you know about Marcus." I lower my lips to the shell of her ear, letting my rough stubble rub along her cheek. "And everything you know about the drug."

With a steadying breath, my lungs fill with the sweet smell of her soft hair that brushes against my nose.

I comb my fingers through her hair and let my thumb run along her slender neck before I lean into her, letting her feel how hard I am just to be alive. Just to have her at my mercy.

"But first, you're coming with me."

Irresistible Attraction, Jase Cross' story, is available now.

This is not the end of Carter and Aria. I'm obsessed with their story, and there is much more to come. Their love story will show in the background of the next books in the Merciless World. I hope you fall madly in love with these characters just as I have. You have no idea what's coming…
Happy reading, xx.

ABOUT THE AUTHOR

Thank you so much for reading my romances. I'm just a stay at home mom and avid reader turned author and I couldn't be happier.

I hope you love my books as much as I do!

More by Willow Winters
www.willowwinterswrites.com/books

Printed in Great Britain
by Amazon

36535283R00421